GLAMORAMA

'His best work to date . . . He remains a
laser-precise satirist, but the wit now dominates'
Esquire

'Ellis invents a fresh hell on every page . . . Through
all this mayhem the style remains mysteriously elegant'
New Yorker

'*Glamorama* is a moral satire from first to last. It has plot,
suspense and all sorts of old-fashioned literary devices
to give its hologram of an image-addicted society
permanence and depth'
Laura Cumming, *Waterstones Magazine*

'You really should try and read *Glamorama*,
because sooner or later someone *is* going
to ask you for an opinion on it'
Sam Richards, *Arcade*

'The author of *American Psycho* has produced a
masterful, mature work which constantly turns in
on itself and keeps the reader wondering'
Robert Colbeck, *Yorkshire Evening Post*

'Read this book, unless you happen to be in it'
Paul Oswell, *Footloose Magazine*

'[Bret Easton Ellis's] cold eye, cast on Nineties
foibles and vacuity, makes for seductive satire . . .
the most thrilling book I've read in years'
Sharon Barnes, *Image*

Also by Bret Easton Ellis in Picador

Less Than Zero

The Rules of Attraction

American Psycho

The Informers

Lunar Park

BRET EASTON ELLIS

GLAMORAMA

PICADOR

First published 1998 as a Borzoi Book by Alfred A. Knopf Inc., New York

First published in Great Britain 1998 by Picador

First published in paperback 2000 by Picador

This edition published 2011 by Picador
an imprint of Pan Macmillan, a division of Macmillan Publishers Limited
Pan Macmillan, 20 New Wharf Road, London N1 9RR
Basingstoke and Oxford
Associated companies throughout the world
www.panmacmillan.com

ISBN 978-0-330-54454-2

9 8 7 6 5 4 3 2 1

A CIP catalogue record for this book is available from
the British Library.

Typeset by SetSystems Ltd, Saffron Walden, Essex
Printed and bound in the UK by
CPI Mackays, Chatham ME5 8TD

Visit **www.picador.com** to read more about all our books and to buy
them. You will also find features, author interviews and news of any author
events, and you can sign up for e-newsletters so that you're always first to hear
about our new releases.

For Jim Severt

My thanks

Gary Fisketjon

Amanda Urban

Julie Grau

Heather Schroder

Sonny Mehta

There was no time when you nor I nor these kings did not exist.

— Krishna

You make a mistake if you see what we do as merely political.

— Hitler

GLAMORAMA

1

33 "Specks—specks all over the third panel, see?—no, *that* one—the second one up from the floor and I wanted to point this out to someone yesterday but a photo shoot intervened and Yaki Nakamari or whatever the hell the designer's name is—a master craftsman *not*—mistook me for someone else so I couldn't register the complaint, but, gentlemen—and ladies—there they are: *specks*, annoying, tiny specks, and they *don't* look accidental but like they were somehow done by a machine—so I don't want a lot of description, just the story, streamlined, no frills, the lowdown: who, what, where, when and don't leave out why, though I'm getting the distinct impression by the looks on your sorry faces that *why* won't get answered—now, come on, goddamnit, what's the *story?*"

Nobody around here has to wait long for someone to say something.

"Baby, George Nakashima designed this bar area," JD quietly corrects me. "Not, um, Yaki Nakamashi, I mean Yuki Nakamorti, I mean—oh shit, Peyton, get me out of this."

"*Yoki* Naka*muri* was approved for this floor," Peyton says.

"Oh yeah?" I ask. "Approved by *who?*"

"Approved by, well, moi," Peyton says.

A pause. Glares targeted at Peyton and JD.

"Who the fuck is Moi?" I ask. "I have no fucking idea who this Moi is, baby."

"Victor, please," Peyton says. "I'm sure Damien went over this with you."

"Damien *did*, JD. Damien *did*, Peyton. But just tell me who Moi is, baby," I exclaim. "Because I'm, like, shvitzing."

"Moi is Peyton, Victor," JD says quietly.

"I'm Moi," Peyton says, nodding. "Moi is, um, French."

"Are you sure these specks *aren't* supposed to be here?" JD tentatively touches the panel. "I mean, maybe it's supposed to be, oh, I don't know, *in* or something?"

"Wait." I raise a hand. "You're saying these specks are *in?*"

"Victor—we've got a long list of things to check, baby." JD holds up the long list of things to check. "The specks will be taken care of. Someone will escort the specks out of here. There's a magician waiting downstairs."

"By tomorrow night?" I roar. "*By to-mor-row night*, JD?"

"It can be handled by tomorrow, no?" JD looks at Peyton, who nods.

"Around here, 'tomorrow night' means anywhere from five days to a month. Jesus, does anybody notice I'm seething?"

"None of us have been exactly sedentary, Victor."

"I think the situation is simple enough: *those*—I point—"are specks. Do you need someone to decipher that sentence for you, JD, or are you, y'know, *okay* with it?"

The "reporter" from *Details* stands with us. Assignment: follow me around for a week. Headline: THE MAKING OF A CLUB. Girl: push-up bra, scads of eyeliner, a Soviet sailor's cap, plastic flower jewelry, rolled-up copy of W tucked under a pale, worked-out arm. Uma Thurman if Uma Thurman was five feet two and asleep. Behind her, some guy wearing a Velcro vest over a rugby shirt and a leather windjammer follows us, camcording the scene.

"Hey baby." I inhale on a Marlboro someone's handed me. "What do you think about the specks?"

Girl reporter lowers her sunglasses. "I'm really not sure." She thinks about what position she should take.

"East Coast girls are hip," I shrug. "I really dig those styles they wear."

"I don't think I'm really part of the story," she says.

"You think any of these bozos are?" I snort. "Spare me."

From the top floor, Beau leans over the railing and calls down, "Victor—Chloe's on line ten."

Girl reporter immediately lifts the W, revealing a notepad, on which she doodles something, predictably animated for a moment.

I call up, staring intently at the specks: "Tell her I'm busy. I'm in a meeting. It's an emergency. Tell her I'm in a meeting *and* it's an emergency. I'll call her back after I put the fire out."

"Victor," Beau calls down. "This is the *sixth* time she's called today. This is the *third* time she's called in the last *hour*."

"Tell her I'll see her at Doppelganger's at ten." I kneel down, along with Peyton and JD, and run my hand along the panel, pointing out where the specks begin and end and then start up again. "Specks, man, look at these fuckers. They glow. They're *glowing*, JD," I whisper. "Jesus, they're everywhere." Suddenly I notice an entire new patch and yelp, gaping, "And I think they're *spreading*. I don't think that patch was here before!" I swallow, then croak in a rush, "My mouth is incredibly dry because of this—could someone get me an Arizona diet iced tea in a bottle, *not* a can?"

"Didn't Damien discuss the design with you, Victor?" JD asks. "Didn't you know the existence of these specks?"

"I don't know anything, JD. Nothing, nada. Remember that. I . . . know . . . nothing. Never assume I know anything. Nada. Nothing. I know nothing, not a thing. Never—"

"I get it, I get it," JD says wearily, standing up.

"I really can't see anything, baby," Peyton says, still on the floor.

JD sighs. "Even Peyton can't see them, Victor."

"Ask the vampire to take off his fucking sunglasses," I snarl. "Spare me, man."

"I will not tolerate being called a vampire, Victor." Peyton pouts.

"What? You tolerate being sodomized but *not* being called Dracula in *jest*? Am I on the same planet? Let's move on." I wave my arm, gesturing at something invisible.

As the entire group follows me downstairs toward the third floor, the chef—Bongo from Venezuela via Vunderbahr, Moonclub, Paddy-O and MasaMasa—lights a cigarette and lowers his sunglasses while trying to keep up with me. "Victor, we must talk." He coughs, waves smoke away. "Please, my feet are killing me."

The group stops. "Uno momento, Bongo," I say, noticing the worried glances he's throwing Kenny Kenny, who's connected in some weird way to Glorious Foods and has yet to be informed he has nothing to do with catering tomorrow night's dinner. Peyton, JD, Bongo, Kenny Kenny, camcorder guy and *Details* girl wait for me to do something, and since I'm at a loss I peer over the third-floor railing. "Come on, guys. Shit, I mean I've got three more floors and five more bars to check. Please, give me some space. This is all very hard. Those specks almost made me literally sick."

"Victor, no one would deny the existence of the specks," Peyton says carefully. "But you have to place the specks within a, um, certain, well, context."

On one of the monitors lining the walls on the third floor, MTV, a commercial, Helena Christensen, "Rock the Vote."

"Beau!" I yell up. "Beau!"

Beau leans over the top railing. "Chloe says she'll be at Metro CC at eleven-thirty."

"Wait, Beau—Ingrid Chavez? Has Ingrid Chavez RSVP'd?" I yell up.

"I'm checking—wait, for the dinner?"

"Yes, and I'm gritting my teeth, Beau. Check the Cs for dinner."

"Oh my god I have got to speak to you, Victor," Bongo says in an accent so thick I'm unsure of its origin, grabbing my arm. "You *must* let me have my time with you."

"Bongo, why don't you just get get the the hell out of here," Kenny Kenny says, his face twisted. "Here, Victor, try a crouton."

I snatch one out of his hands. "Mmm, rosemary. Delish, dude."

"It is sage, Victor. *Sage*."

"You you sh-sh-should go to hell," Bongo sputters. "And take that sickening crouton with you."

"Will both of you mos take a Xanax and shut the fuck up? Go bake some pastries or something. Beau—goddamnit! Speak to me!"

"Naomi Campbell, Helena Christensen, Cindy Crawford, Sheryl Crow, David Charvet, Courteney Cox, Harry Connick, Jr., Francisco Clemente, Nick Constantine, Zoe Cassavetes, Nicolas Cage, Thomas Calabro, Cristi Conway, Bob Collacello, Whitfield Crane, John Cusack, Dean Cain, Jim Courier, Roger Clemens, Russell Crowe, Tia Carrere and Helena Bonham Carter—but I'm not sure if she should be under *B* or *C*."

"Ingrid Chavez! Ingrid Chavez!" I shout up. "Has Ingrid Chavez fucking RSVP'd *or not*?"

"Victor, celebs and their overly attentive PR reps are complaining that your answering machine isn't working," Beau calls down. "They say it's playing thirty seconds of 'Love Shack' and then only five seconds to leave a message."

"It's a simple question. Yes or No is the answer. What else could these people possibly have to say to me? It's not a difficult question: Are you coming to the dinner and the club opening or are you not? Is that hard to grasp? And you look just like Uma Thurman, baby."

"Victor, Cindy is not 'these people,' Veronica Webb is not 'these people,' Elaine Irwin is not 'these people'—"

"Beau! How are the As shaping up? Kenny Kenny, don't pinch Bongo like that."

"All nine of them?" Beau calls down. "Carol Alt, Pedro Almodóvar, Dana Ashbrook, Kevyn Aucoin, Patricia, Rosanna, David and Alexis Arquette and Andre Agassi, but no Giorgio Armani or Pamela Anderson."

"Shit." I light another cigarette, then look over at the *Details* girl. "Um, I mean that in a good way."

"So it's like . . . a good shit?" she asks.

"Uh-huh. Hey Beau!" I call up. "Make sure all the monitors are either on that virtual-reality videotape or for god's sake MTV or something. I passed a screen that had VH1 on it, and some fat hick in a ten-gallon hat was weeping—"

"Will you meet Chloe at Flowers—sorry, Metro CC?" Beau yells down. "Because I'm not gonna lie anymore."

"Oh, you'll lie," I scream up. "That's all you ever do." Then, after glancing casually at the *Details* girl: "Ask Chloe if she's bringing Beatrice and Julie."

Silence from upstairs makes me cringe, then Beau asks, thoroughly annoyed, "Do you mean Beatrice *Arthur* and Julie *Hagerty*?"

"No," I shout, gritting my teeth. "Julie *Delpy* and Beatrice *Dalle*. Spare me. Just do it, Beau."

"Beatrice Dalle's shooting that Ridley Scott—"

"The speck thing has really gotten to me. You know why?" I ask the *Details* girl.

"Because there were . . . a lot?"

"Nope. Because I'm a perfectionist, baby. And you can write that down. In fact I'll wait a minute while you do so." Suddenly I rush back to the panel beneath the bar, everyone rushing back with me up the stairs, and I'm wailing, "Specks! Holy Christ! Help me, somebody, *please*? I mean everyone's acting like there's a question as to whether these specks are an illusion or a reality. I think they're pretty goddamn real."

"Reality *is* an illusion, baby," JD says soothingly. "Reality *is* an illusion, Victor."

No one says anything until I'm handed an ashtray, in which I stub out the cigarette I just lit.

"That's, uh, pretty heavy," I say, looking at the girl reporter. "That's pretty heavy, huh?"

She shrugs, rotates her shoulders, doodles again.

"My reaction exactly," I mutter.

"Oh, before I forget," JD says. "Jann Wenner can't make it, but he wants to send a"—JD glances at his notepad—"check anyway."

"A check? A check for *what*?"

"Just a"—JD glances at his pad again—"a, um, check?"

"Oh god. Beau! *Beau!*" I call up.

"I think people are wondering why we don't have a whatchamacallit," Peyton says. Then, after much finger snapping, "Oh yeah, a *cause*!"

"A cause?" I moan. "Oh god, I can only imagine what kind of cause *you'd* want. Scholarship fund for Keanu. Find Marky Mark a gay brain. Send Linda Evangelista to the rain forest so we can pounce on Kyle MacLachlan. No thank you."

"Victor, shouldn't we have a cause?" JD says. "What about global warming or the Amazon? Something. Anything."

"Passé. Passé. Passé." I stop. "Wait—Beau! Is Suzanne DePasse coming?"

"What about AIDS?"

"Passé. Passé."

"Breast cancer?"

"Oh groovy, far out," I gasp before slapping him lightly on the face. "Get serious. For who? David Barton? He's the only one with tits anymore."

"You know what I'm trying to say, Victor," JD says. "Something like Don't Bungle the Jungle or—"

"Hey, don't bungle *my* jungle, you little mo." I consider this. "A cause, hmm? Because we can"—I mindlessly light another cigarette—"make more money?"

"*And* let people have some fun," JD reminds me, scratching at a tattoo of a little muscle man on his bicep.

"Yeah, and let people have some fun." I take a drag. "I'm considering this, you know, even though the opening is in, oh, less than twenty-four hours."

"You know what, Victor?" Peyton asks slyly. "I'm getting the, ah, perverse temptation, baby, to, ah—now don't get scared, promise?"

"Only if you don't tell me who you've slept with in the last week."

Wide-eyed, Peyton claps his hands together and gushes, "Keep the specks." Then, after seeing my face contort, more timidly offers, "Save . . . the specks?"

"Save the specks?" JD gasps.

"Yes, save the specks," Peyton says. "Damien wants techno, and those little fellas can definitely be construed as techno."

"We *all* want techno, but we want techno *without* specks," JD moans.

The camcorder guy zooms in on the specks, and it's very quiet until he says, yawning, "Far out."

"People people people." I lift my hands up. "Is it possible to open this club without humiliating ourselves in the process?" I start to walk away. "Because I'm beginning to think it's *not* possible. Comprende?"

"Victor, oh my god, please," Bongo says as I walk away.

"Victor, wait up." Kenny Kenny follows, holding out a bag of croutons.

"It's just that this is all so . . . so . . . '89?" I blurt out.

"A fine year, Victor," Peyton says, trying to keep up with me. "A triumphant year!"

I stop, pause, then turn slowly to face him. Peyton stands there looking hopefully up at me, quivering.

"Uh, Peyton, you're really whacked out, aren't you?" I ask quietly.

Shamefully, Peyton nods as if coaxed. He looks away.

"You've had a pretty tough life, right?" I ask gently.

"Victor, please." JD steps in. "Peyton was joking about the specks. We're not saving the specks. I'm with you. They're just not worth it. They *die*."

While lighting a gargantuan joint, camcorder guy shoots out the huge expanse of French windows, the lens staring at a view of a leafless Union Square Park, at a truck with a massive Snapple logo driving by, limousines parked at a curb. We are moving down another set of stairs, heading toward the bottom.

"Will someone please just give me one spontaneous act of goodness? Remove the specks. Bongo, go back to the kitchen. Kenny Kenny, you get a consolation prize. Peyton, make sure Kenny Kenny gets a couple of colanders and a nice flat spatula." I wave them off, glaring. We leave Kenny Kenny behind, on the verge of tears, rubbing a shaky hand over the tattoo of Casper the Friendly Ghost on his bicep. "Ciao."

"Come on, Victor. The average life span of a club is what—four weeks? By the time we close, no one's gonna notice them."

"If that's your attitude, JD, there's the door."

"Oh Victor, let's be realistic—or at least fake it. This isn't 1987 anymore."

"I'm not in a realistic mood, JD, so spare me."

Passing a pool table, I grab the 8 ball and slam-roll it into the corner pocket. The group is moving farther down into the club. We're now at the first floor and it's getting darker and Peyton introduces me to a huge black guy with wraparound sunglasses standing by the front entrance eating take-out sushi.

"Victor, this is Abdullah, but we shall call him Rocko, and he's handling all the security and he was in that TLC video directed by Matthew Ralston. That toro looks good."

"My middle name is Grand Master B."

"His middle name is Grand Master B," JD says.

"We shook hands last week in South Beach," Abdullah tells me.

"That's nice, Abdullah, but I wasn't in South Beach last week even though I'm semi-famous there." I glance over at the *Details* girl. "You can write that down."

"Yeah man, you were in the lobby of the Flying Dolphin, getting your photo taken," Rocko tells me. "You were surrounded by clams."

But I'm not looking at Rocko. Instead my eyes have focused on the three metal detectors that line the foyer, a giant white chandelier hanging above them, dimly twinkling.

"You did, um, know about these, right?" JD asks. A meek pause. "Damien . . . wants them."

"Damien wants *what*?"

"Um." Peyton gestures with his arms as if the metal detectors were prizes. "These."

"Well, why don't we just throw in a baggage check-in, a couple of stewardesses and a DC-10? I mean, what in the hell *are* these?"

"This is security, man," Abdullah says.

"Security? Why don't you just spend the night frisking the celebrities as well?" I ask. "What? You think this is a party for *felons*?"

"Mickey Rourke and Johnny Depp both RSVP'd yes for dinner," Peyton whispers in my ear.

"If you'd like us to frisk the guests—" Rocko starts.

"What? I'm gonna have Donna Karan frisked? I'm gonna have Marky Mark frisked? I'm gonna have fucking Diane Von Furstenberg frisked?" I shout. "I don't think so."

"No, baby," Peyton says. "You're going to have the metal detectors so Diane Von Furstenberg and Marky Mark *aren't* frisked."

"Chuck Pfeiffer has a metal plate in his goddamned head! Princess Cuddles has a steel rod in her leg!" I shout.

JD tells the girl reporter, "Skiing accident in Gstaad, and don't ask me how to spell that."

"What's gonna happen when Princess Cuddles walks in through one of these things and alarms go off and buzzers and lights and— Jesus, she'll have a fucking heart attack. Does anybody really want to see Princess Cuddles have a coronary?"

"On the guest list we'll mark down that Chuck Pfeiffer has a metal plate in his head and that Princess Cuddles has a steel cod in her leg," Peyton says, mindlessly writing it down on a notepad.

"Listen, Abdullah. I just want to make sure that no one is gonna get in who we don't want in. I don't want *anyone* passing out invites to other clubs. I don't want some little waif mo handing Barry Diller an invite to Spermbar during dinner—got it? I don't want *anyone* passing out invites to other clubs."

"*What* other clubs?" Peyton and JD wail. "There *aren't* any other clubs!"

"Oh spare me," I wail back, moving across the first floor. "Jesus—you think Christian Laetner is gonna fit under one of those things?" It gets darker as we move into the back of the first floor, toward the staircase that leads to one of the dance floors located in the basement.

From the top floor, Beau calls down, "Alison Poole on line fourteen. She wants to speak to you *now*, Victor."

Everyone looks away as the *Details* girl writes something down on her little notepad. Camcorder guy whispers something and she nods, still writing. Somewhere old C + C Music Factory is playing.

"Tell her I'm out. Tell her I'm on line seven."

"She says it's very important," Beau drones on in monotone.

I pause to look at the rest of the group, everyone looking anywhere but at me. Peyton whispers something to JD, who nods curtly. "Hey, watch that!" I snap. I follow Camcorder's lens to a row of sconces he's filming and wait for Beau, who finally leans over the top-floor railing and says, "A miracle: she relented. She'll see you at six."

"Okay, folks." I suddenly turn around to face the group. "I'm calling a sidebar. Bongo, you are excused. Do not discuss your testimony with any-one. Go. JD, come over here. I need to whisper something to you. The rest of you may stand by that bar and look for specks. Camcorder man—turn that away from us. We're taking five."

I pull JD over to me and immediately he starts babbling.

"Victor, if this is about Mica not being around and us being unable to get ahold of her, please for the love of god don't bring it up now, because we can find another DJ—"

"Shut up. It's not about Mica." I pause. "But wait, where *is* Mica?"

"Oh god, I don't know. She DJ'd at Jackie 60 on Tuesday, then did Edward Furlong's birthday party, and now poof."

"What does that mean? What does *poof* mean?"

"She's disappeared. No one can find her."

"Well, shit, JD. What are we—no, no—*you* are gonna fix this," I tell him. "I have something else I want to talk about."

"If Kenny Kenny's going to sue us?"

"No."

"The seating chart for dinner?"

"No."

"The awfully cute magician downstairs?"

"Jesus, *no*." I lower my voice. "This is a more, um, personal problem. I need your advice."

"Oh, don't drag me into anything sick, Victor," JD pleads. "I just can't take being dragged into anything too sick."

"Listen . . ." I glance over at the *Details* girl et al., slouching against the bar. "Have you heard anything about a . . . photograph?"

"A photograph of who?" he exclaims.

"Shhh, shut up. Jesus." I look around. "Okay, even though you think Era-sure is a good band, I think I can still trust you."

"They *are*, Victor, and—"

"Someone's got a, let's just say, incriminating photo of me and a certain young"—I cough—"young lady, and I need you to find out if it's, um, going to be printed sometime in the near future and maybe even tomorrow in one of the city's least respectable but still most widely read dailies or if by some miracle it will not and that's about it."

"I suppose you could be more vague, Victor, but I'm used to it," JD says. "Just give me twenty seconds to decode this and I'll get back to you."

"I don't have twenty seconds."

"The young lady I'm supposing—no, I'm hoping—*is* Chloe Byrnes, your girlfriend?"

"On second thought, take thirty seconds."

"Is this a That's Me in the Corner / That's Me in the Spotlight moment?"

"Okay, okay, let me clarify: a compromising photo of a certain happening guy with a girl who . . . and it's not like that bad or anything. Let's just say this girl attacked him at a premiere last week in Central Park and someone unbeknownst to them got a, um, photo of this and it would look . . . strange since I am the subject of this photograph . . . I have a feeling that if I make the inquiry it will be—ahem—misunderstood. . . . Need I go on?"

Suddenly Beau screams down: "Chloe will see you at nine-thirty at Doppelganger's!"

"What happened to Flowers? I mean eleven-thirty at Metro CC?" I yell back up. "What happened to ten o'clock at Café Tabac?"

A longish pause. "She now says nine-thirty at Bowery Bar. That's the end of it, Victor." Then silence.

"What horrible thing do you want me to do?" JD pauses. "Victor, would this photo—if published—screw up this guy's relationship with a certain young model named Chloe Byrnes and a certain volatile club owner of . . . oh, let's just say, hypothetically, this club, whose name is Damien Nutchs Ross?"

"But that isn't the problem." I pull JD closer and, surprised, he winks and bats his eyes and I have to tell him, "Don't get any ideas." I sigh, breathe in. "The problem is that a photo exists. A certain cretinous gossip columnist is going to run this photo, and if we think Princess Cuddles having a heart attack is bad . . . that's nothing." I keep looking over my shoulder, finally telling everyone, "We have to go downstairs to check the magician. Excuse us."

"But what about Matthew Broderick?" Peyton asks. "What about the salads?"

"He can have two!" I shout as I whisk JD down the long steep ramp of stairs heading into the basement, the light getting dimmer, both of us moving carefully.

JD keeps babbling. "You know I'm here for you, Victor. You know I put the stud back in star-studded. You know I've helped pack this party to the rafters with desirable celebs. You know I'll do anything, but I can't help you on this because of—"

"JD. Tomorrow in no particular order I've got a photo shoot, a runway show, an MTV interview with 'House of Style,' lunch with my father, band practice. I even have to pick up my fucking tux. I'm booked. Plus this dump is opening. I—have—no—time."

"Victor, as usual I'll see what I can do." JD maneuvers down the stairs hesitantly. "Now about the magician—"

"Fuck it. Why don't we just hire some clowns on stilts and bus in an elephant or two?"

"He does card tricks. He just did Brad Pitt's birthday at Jones in L.A."

"He did?" I ask, suspicious. "Who was there?"

"Ed Limato. Mike Ovitz. Julia Ormond. Madonna. Models. A lot of lawyers and 'fun' people."

It gets even colder as we near the bottom of the staircase.

"I mean," JD continues, "I think comparatively it's pretty in."

"But in is out," I explain, squinting to see where we're heading. It's so cold our breath steams, and when I touch the banister it feels like ice.

"What are you saying, Victor?"

"Out is in. Got it?"

"In is . . . *not* in anymore?" JD asks. "Is that it?"

I glance at him as we descend the next flight of stairs. "No, in is out. Out is in. Simple, non?"

JD blinks twice, shivering, both of us moving farther down into the darkness.

"See, out is in, JD."

"Victor, I'm really nervous as it is," he says. "Don't start with me today."

"You don't even have to think about it. Out is in. In is out."

"Wait, okay. In is out? Do I have that down so far?"

At the bottom, it is so cold that I've noticed candles don't even stay lit, they keep going out as we pass, and the TV monitors show only static. At the foot of the stairs by the bar, a magician who looks like a young German version of Antonio Banderas with a buzz cut idly shuffles a deck of cards, slump-shouldered, smoking a small joint, drinking a Diet Coke, wearing ripped jeans and a pocket T, the back-to-basics look, exaggeratedly sloppy, the rows of empty champagne glasses behind him reflecting what little light exists down here.

"Right. Out is in."

"But then what exactly *is* in?" JD asks, his breath steaming.

"*Out* is, JD."

"So . . . *in* is *not* in?"

"That's the whole p-p-point." It's so cold my biceps are covered with goose bumps.

"But then what's *out*? It's *always* in? What about specifics?"

"If you need this defined for you, maybe you're in the wrong world," I murmur.

The magician gives us the peace sign in a vague way.

"You did Brad Pitt's party?" I ask.

The magician makes a deck of cards, the stool he's sitting on, one of my slippers and a large bottle of Absolut Currant disappear, then says "Abracadabra."

"You did Brad Pitt's party?" I sigh.

JD nudges me and points up. I notice the massive red swastika painted onto the domed ceiling above us.

"I suppose we should probably get rid of that."

32

Zigzagging toward Chemical Bank by the new Gap it's a Wednesday but outside feels Mondayish and the city looks vaguely unreal, there's a sky like from October 1973 or something hanging over it and right now at 5:30 this is Manhattan as Loud Place: jackhammers, horns, sirens, breaking glass, recycling trucks, whistles, booming bass from the new Ice Cube, unwanted sound trailing behind me as I wheel my Vespa into the bank, joining the line at the automated teller, most of it made up of Orientals glaring at me as they move aside, a couple of them leaning forward, whispering to each other.

"What's the story with the moped?" some jerk asks.

"Hey, what's the story with those pants? Listen, the bike doesn't have a card, it's not taking out any cash, so chill out. Jesus."

Only one out of ten cash machines seems to have any cash in it, so while waiting I have to look up at my reflection in the panel of steel mirrors lining the columns above the automated tellers: high cheekbones, ivory skin, jet-black hair, semi-Asian eyes, a perfect nose, huge lips, defined jawline, ripped knees in jeans, T-shirt under a long-collar shirt, red vest, velvet jacket, and I'm slouching, Rollerblades slung over my shoulder, suddenly remembering I forgot where I'm supposed to meet Chloe tonight, and that's when the beeper goes off. It's Beau. I snap open the Panasonic EBH 70 and call him back at the club.

"I hope Bongo's not having a fit."

"It's the RSVPs, Victor. *Damien's* having a fit. He just called, furious—"

"Did you tell him where I was?"

"How could I do that when *I* don't even know where you are?" Pause. "Where are you? Damien was in a helicopter. Actually stepping out of a helicopter."

"*I* don't even know where I am, Beau. How's that for an answer?" The line moves up slowly. "Is he in the city?"

"No. I said he was in a helicopter. I said that he—was—in—a—heli-cop-ter."

"But where *was* the heli-cop-ter?"

"Damien thinks things are getting totally fucked up. We have about forty for dinner who have *not* RSVP'd, so our seating list might be interpreted as meaningless."

"Beau, that depends on how you define meaningless."

A long pause. "Don't tell me it means a bunch of different things, Victor. For example, here's how the *O* situation is shaping up: Tatum O'Neal, Chris O'Donnell, Sinead O'Connor and Conan O'Brien all yes but nothing from Todd Oldham, who I hear is being stalked and really freaking out, or Carrie Otis or Oribe—"

"Relax," I whisper. "That's because they're all doing the shows. I'll talk to Todd tomorrow—I'll see him at the show—but I mean *what is going on*, Beau? Conan O'Brien *is* coming but Todd Oldham and Carrie Otis *might not*? That just isn't an acceptable scenario, baby, but I'm in an automated teller right now with my Vespa and I can't really speak—hey, what are *you* looking at?—but I don't want Chris O'Donnell anywhere at my table for dinner. Chloe thinks he's too fucking cute and I just don't need that kind of awful shit tomorrow night."

"Uh-huh. Right, no Chris O'Donnell, okay, got that. Now, Victor, first thing tomorrow we've got to go over the big ones, the *M*s and the *S*s—"

"We can pull it together. Don't weep, Beau. You sound sad. It is now my turn to get some cash. I must go and—"

"Wait! Rande Gerber's in town—"

"Put him under *G* but *not* for the dinner unless he's coming with Cindy Crawford then he *is* invited to the dinner and you then know which consonant, baby."

"Victor, you try dealing with Cindy's publicist. You try getting an honest answer out of Antonio Sabato, Jr.'s publicist—"

I click off, finally push in my card, punch in the code (COOLGUY) and wait, thinking about the seating arrangements at tables 1 and 3, and then green words on a black screen tell me that there is no cash left in this account (a balance of minus $143) and so therefore it won't give me any money and I blew my last cash on a glass-door refrigerator because *Elle Decor* did a piece on my place that never ran so I slam my fist against the machine, moan "Spare me" and since it's totally useless to try this again I rustle through my pockets for a Xanax until someone pushes me away and I roll the moped back outside, bummed.

Cruising up Madison, stopping at a light in front of Barneys, and Bill Cunningham snaps my picture, yelling out, "Is that a Vespa?" and I give him thumbs-up and he's standing next to Holly, a curvy blonde who looks like Patsy Kensit, and when we smoked heroin together last week she told me she might be a lesbian, which in some circles is pretty good news, and she waves me over wearing velvet hot pants, red-and-white-striped platform boots, a silver peace symbol and she's ultrathin, on the cover of *Mademoiselle* this month, and after a day of doing shows at Bryant Park she's looking kind of frantic but in a cool way.

"Hey Victor!" She keeps motioning even when I've pulled the Vespa up to the curb.

"Hey Holly."

"It's Anjanette, Victor."

"Hey Anjanette, what's up pussycat? You're looking very Uma-ish. Love the outfit."

"It's retro-gone-wacko. I did six shows today. I'm exhausted," she says, signing an autograph. "I saw you at the Calvin Klein show giving Chloe moral support. Which was so cool of you."

"Baby, I wasn't at the Calvin Klein show but you're still looking very Uma-ish."

"Victor, I'm positive you were at the Calvin Klein show. I saw you in the second row next to Stephen Dorff and David Salle and Roy Liebenthal. I saw you pose for a photo on 42nd Street, then get into a black scary car."

Pause, while I consider this scenario, then: "The *second* fucking row? No way, baby. You haven't started your ignition yet. Will I see you tomorrow night, baby?"

"I'm coming with Jason Priestley."

"Why aren't you coming with me? Am I the only one who thinks Jason Priestley looks like a little caterpillar?"

"Victor, that's not nice," she pouts. "What would Chloe think?"

"She thinks Jason Priestley looks like a little caterpillar too," I murmur, lost in thought. "The fucking *second* row?"

"That's not what I meant," Anjanette says. "What would Chloe think of—"

"Spare me, baby, but you're supergreat." I start the Vespa up again. "Take your passion and make it happen."

"I've heard you've been naughty anyway, so I'm not surprised," she says, tiredly wagging her finger at me, which Scooter, the bodyguard who looks like Marcellus from *Pulp Fiction*, interprets as "move closer."

"What do you mean by that, pussycat?" I ask. "What have you heard?"

Scooter whispers something, pointing at his watch, while Anjanette lights a cigarette. "There's always a car waiting. There's always a Steven Meisel photo shoot. Jesus, how do we do it, Victor? How do we survive this mess?" A gleaming black sedan rolls forward and Scooter opens the door.

"See you, baby." I hand her a French tulip I just happen to be holding and start pulling away from the curb.

"Oh Victor," she calls out, handing Scooter the French tulip. "I got the job! I got the contract."

"Great, baby. I gotta run. What job, you crazy chick?"

"Guess?."

"Matsuda? Gap?" I grin, limousines honking behind me. "Baby, listen, see you tomorrow night."

"No. *Guess?*."

"Baby, I already did. You're mind-tripping me."

"*Guess?*, Victor," she's shouting as I pull away.

"Baby, you're great," I shout back. "Call me. Leave a message. But only at the club. Peace."

"*Guess?*, Victor!" she calls out.

"Baby, you're a face to watch," I say, already putting a Walkman on, already on 61st. "A star of tomorrow," I call out, waving. "Let's have drinks at Monkey Bar after the shows are over on Sunday!" I'm speaking to myself now and moving toward Alison's place. Passing a newsstand by the new Gap, I notice I'm still on the cover of the current issue of *YouthQuake*, looking pretty cool—the headline 27 AND HIP in bold purple letters above my smiling, expressionless face, and I've just got to buy another copy, but since I don't have any cash there's no way.

31 From 72nd and Madison I called Alison's doorman, who has verified that outside her place on 80th and Park Damien's goons are *not* waiting in a black Jeep, so when I get there I can pull up to the entrance and roll my Vespa into the lobby, where Juan—who's a pretty decent-looking guy, about twenty-four—is hanging out in uniform. As I give him the peace sign, wheeling the moped into the elevator, Juan comes out from behind the front desk.

"Hey Victor, did you talk to Joel Wilkenfeld yet?" Juan's asking, following me. "I mean, last week you said you would and—"

"Hey baby, it's cool, Juan, it's cool," I say, inserting the key, unlocking the elevator, pressing the button for the top floor.

Juan presses another button, to keep the door open. "But man, you said he'd see me and also set up a meeting with—"

"I'm setting it up, buddy, it's cool," I stress, pressing again for the top floor. "You're the next Markus Schenkenberg. You're the white Tyson." I reach over and push his hand away.

"Hey man, I'm Hispanic—" He keeps pressing the Door Open button.

"You're the next Hispanic Markus Schenkenberg. You're the, um, Hispanic Tyson." I reach over and push his hand away again. "You're a star, man. Any day of the week."

"I just don't want this to be like an afterthought—"

"Hey man, spare me." I grin. "'Afterthought' isn't in this guy's vocabulary," I say, pointing at myself.

"Okay, man," Juan says, letting go of the Door Open button and offering a shaky thumbs-up. "I, like, trust you."

The elevator zips up to the top floor, where it opens into Alison's penthouse. I peer down the front hallway, don't see or hear the dogs, then quietly wheel the Vespa inside and lean it against a wall in the foyer next to a Vivienne Tam sofa bed.

I tiptoe silently toward the kitchen but stop when I hear the hoarse breathing of the two chows, who have been intently watching me from the other end of the hallway, quietly growling, audible only now. I turn around and offer them a weak smile.

I can barely say "Oh shit" before they both break out into major scampering and rush at their target: me.

The two chows—one chocolate, one cinnamon—leap up, baring their teeth, nipping at my knees, pawing at my calves, barking furiously.

"Alison! Alison!" I call out, trying desperately to bat them away.

Hearing her name, they both stop barking. Then they glance down the hallway to see if she's coming. After a pause, when they hear no sign of her—we're frozen in position, red chow standing on back legs, its paws in my groin, black chow down on its front paws with Gucci boot in mouth—they immediately go to work on me again, growling and basically freaking out like they always do.

"Alison!" I scream. "Jesus Christ!"

Gauging the distance from where I'm at to the kitchen door, I decide to make a run for it, and when I bolt, the chows scamper after me, yelping, biting at my ankles.

I finally make it into the kitchen and slam the door, hear both of them skidding across the marble floor into the door with two large *thumps*, hear them fall over, then scamper up and attack the door. Shaken, I open a Snapple, down half of it, then light a cigarette, check for bites. I hear Alison clapping her hands, and then she walks into the kitchen, naked beneath an open Aerosmith tour robe, a cell phone cradled in her neck, an unlit joint in her mouth. "Mr. Chow, Mrs. Chow, down, down, goddamnit, *down.*"

She hurls the dogs into the pantry, pulls a handful of colored biscuits from the robe and throws them at the dogs before slamming the pantry door shut, the sounds of the dogs fighting over the biscuits cut mercifully short.

"Okay, uh-huh, right, Malcolm McLaren . . . Yeah, no, Frederic Fekkai. Yeah. *Every*body's hung over, babe." She scrunches up her face. "Andrew Shue and Leonardo DiCaprio? . . . What? . . . Oh baby, no-o-o way." Alison winks at me. "You're not at a window table at Mortimer's right now. Wake up! Oh boy . . . Ciao, ciao." She clicks off the cellular and carefully places the joint on the counter and says, "That was a three-way with Dr. Dre, Yasmine Bleeth and Jared Leto."

"Alison, those two little shits tried to kill me," I point out as she jumps up and wraps her legs around my waist.

"Mr. and Mrs. Chow *aren't* little shits, baby." She clamps her mouth onto mine as I stumble with her toward the bedroom. Once there she falls to her knees, rips open my jeans and proceeds to expertly give me head, deep-throating in an unfortunately practiced way, grabbing my ass so hard I have to pry one of her hands loose. I take a last drag off the cigarette that I'm still holding, look around for a place to stub it out, find a half-empty Snapple bottle, drop in what's left of the Marlboro, hear it hiss.

"Slow down, Alison, you're moving too fast," I'm mumbling.

She pulls my dick out of her mouth and, looking up at me, says in a low, "sexy" voice, "Urgency is my specialty, baby."

She suddenly gets up, drops the robe and lies back on the bed, spreading her legs, pushing me down onto a floor littered with random issues of WWDs, my right knee crumpling a back-page photo of Alison and Damien and Chloe and me at Naomi Campbell's birthday party, sitting in a cramped booth at Doppelganger's, and then I'm nibbling at a small tattoo on the inside of a muscular thigh and the moment my tongue touches her she starts coming—once, twice, three times. Knowing where this will not end up, I jerk off a little until I'm almost coming and then I think, Oh screw it, I don't really have time for this, so I just fake it, moaning loudly, my head between her legs, movement from my right arm giving the impression from where she lies that I'm actually doing something. The music in the background is mid-period Duran Duran. Our rendezvous spots have included the atrium at Remi, room 101 at the Paramount, the Cooper-Hewitt Museum.

I climb onto the bed and lie there, pretending to pant. "Baby, where did you learn to give head like that? Sotheby's? Oh man." I reach over for a cigarette.

"So wait. That's it?" She lights a joint, sucks in on it so deeply that half of it turns to ash. "What about you?"

"I'm happy." I yawn. "Just as long as you don't bring out that, um, leather harness and Sparky the giant butt plug."

I get off the bed and pull my jeans and Calvins up and move over to the window, where I lift a venetian blind. Down on Park, between 79th and 80th, is a black Jeep with two of Damien's goons sitting in it, reading the new issue of what looks like *Interview* with Drew Barrymore on the cover, and one looks like a black Woody Harrelson and the other like a white Damon Wayans.

Alison knows what I'm seeing and from the bed says, "Don't worry, I have to meet Grant Hill for a drink at Mad.61. They'll follow and then *you* can escape."

I flop onto the bed, flip on Nintendo, reach for the controls and start to play Super Mario Bros.

"Damien says that Julia Roberts *is* coming and so is Sandra Bullock," Alison says vacantly. "Laura Leighton and Halle Berry and Dalton James." She takes another hit off the joint and hands it to me. "I saw Elle Macpherson at the Anna Sui show and she says she'll be there for the dinner." She's flipping through a copy of *Detour* with Robert Downey, Jr., on the cover, legs spread, major crotch shot. "Oh, and so is Scott Wolf."

"Shhh, I'm playing," I tell her. "Yoshi's eaten four gold coins and he's trying to find the fifth. I need to concentrate."

"Oh my god, who gives a shit," Alison sighs. "We're dealing with a fat midget who rides a dinosaur and saves his girlfriend from a pissed-off gorilla? Victor, get serious."

"It's *not* his girlfriend. It's Princess Toadstool. And it's *not* a gorilla," I stress. "It's Lemmy Koopa of the evil Koopa clan. And baby, as usual, you're missing the point."

"Please enlighten me."

"The whole point of Super Mario Bros. is that it mirrors life."

"I'm following." She checks her nails. "God knows why."

"Kill or be killed."

"Uh-huh."

"Time is running out."

"Gotcha."

"And in the end, baby, you . . . are . . . alone."

"Right." She stands up. "Well, Victor, that really captures the spirit of our relationship, honey." She disappears into a closet bigger than the bedroom. "If you had to be interviewed by *Worth* magazine on the topic of Damien's Nintendo stock, you'd want to kill Yoshi too."

"I guess this is all just beyond the realm of your experience," I murmur.
"Huh?"

"What are you doing tonight for dinner?" she calls out from the closet.
"Why? Where's Damien?"

"In Atlantic City. So the two of us can go out since I'm sure Chloe is très exhausted from all dat wittle modeling she had to do today."

"I can't," I call back. "I've got to get to bed early. I'm skipping dinner. I've got to go over—oh shit—seating arrangements."

"Oh, but baby, I want to go to Nobu tonight," she whines from the closet. "I want a baby shrimp tempura roll."

"You *are* a baby shrimp tempura roll," I whine back.

The phone rings, the machine picks up, just new Portishead, then a beep.

"Hi, Alison, it's Chloe calling back." I roll my eyes. "Amber and Shalom and I have to do something for Fashion TV at the Royalton and then I'm having dinner with Victor at Bowery Bar at nine-thirty. I'm so so tired . . . did shows all day. Okay, I guess you're not there. Talk to you soon—oh yeah, you have a pass backstage for Todd's show tomorrow. Bye-bye." The machine clicks off.

Silence from the closet, then, low and laced with fury, "*Seating* arrangements? You—have—to—go—to—bed—*early*?"

"You can't keep me in your penthouse," I say. "I'm going back to my plow."

"You're having dinner with *her*?" she screams.

"Honey, I had no idea."

Alison walks out of the closet holding a Todd Oldham wraparound dress in front of her and waits for my reaction, showing it off: not-so-basic black-slash-beige, strapless, Navajo-inspired and neon quilted.

"That's a Todd Oldham, baby," I finally say.

"I'm wearing it tomorrow night." Pause. "It's an *original*," she whispers seductively, eyes glittering. "I'm gonna make your little girlfriend *look like shit!*"

Alison reaches over and slaps the controls out of my hand and turns on a Green Day video and dances over to the Vivienne Tam–designed mirror, studying herself holding the dress in it, and then completes a halfhearted swirl, looking very happy but also very stressed.

I check my nails. It's so cold in this apartment that frost accumulates on the windows. "Is it just me or am I getting chilly in here?"

Alison holds the dress up one more time, squeals maniacally and rushes back into the closet. "What did you say, baby?"

"Did you know vitamins strengthen your nails?"

"Who told you that, baby?" she calls out.

"Chloe did," I mutter, biting at a hangnail.

"That poor baby. Oh my god, she's so stupid."

"She just got back from the MTV awards. She had a nervous breakdown before it, y'know, so be *reasonable*."

"Ma-jor," Alison calls out. "Her smack days are behind her, I take it."

"Just be patient. She's very unstable," I say. "And yes, her smack days *are* behind her."

"No help from you, I'm sure."

"Hey, she got a huge amount of help from me," I say, sitting up, paying more attention now. "If it wasn't for me she might be dead, Alison."

"If it wasn't for you, pea brain, she might not have shot up the junk in the first fucking place."

"She didn't 'shoot' anything," I stress. "It was a purely nasal habit." Pause, check my fingernails again. "She's just very unstable right now."

"What? She gets a blackhead and wants to kill herself?"

"Hey, who wouldn't?" I sit up a little more.

"No Vacancy. No Vacancy. No Vac—"

"Axl Rose and Prince both wrote songs about her, may I remind you."

"Yeah, 'Welcome to the Jungle' and 'Let's Go Crazy.'" Alison walks out of the closet wrapped in a black towel and waves me off. "I know, I know, Chloe was born to model."

"Do you think your jealousy's giving me a hard-on?"

"No, only my boyfriend does that."

"Hey, no way do I want to get it on with Damien."

"Jesus. As usual, you're so literal-minded."

"Oh god, your boyfriend's a total crook. A blowhard."

"My boyfriend is the only reason, my little himbo, that *you* are in business."

"That's bullshit," I shout. "I'm on the cover of *YouthQuake* magazine this month."

"Exactly." Alison suddenly relents and moves over to the bed and sits down next to me, gently taking my hand. "Victor, you auditioned for all three 'Real World's, and MTV rejected you *all three times*." She pauses sincerely. "What does that tell you?"

"Yeah, but I'm one fucking phone call away from Lorne Michaels."

Alison studies my face, my hand still in hers, and smiling, she says, "Poor Victor, you should see just how handsome and dissatisfied you look right now."

"A hip combo," I mutter sullenly.

"It's nice that you think so," she says vacantly.

"Looking like some deformed schmuck and suicidal's better?" I tell her. "Christ, Alison, get your fucking priorities straightened out."

"*My* priorities straightened out?" she asks, stunned, letting go of my hand and placing her own to her chest. "*My* priorities straightened out?" She laughs like a teenager.

"Don't you understand?" I get up from the bed, lighting a cigarette, pacing. "Shit."

"Victor, tell me what you're so worried about."

"You really want to know?"

"Not really but yes." She walks over to the armoire and pulls out a coconut, which I totally take in stride.

"My fucking DJ's disappeared. That's what." I inhale so hard on the Marlboro I have to put it out. "No one knows where the hell my DJ is."

"Mica's gone?" Alison asks. "Are you sure she's not in rehab?"

"I'm not sure of anything," I mutter.

"That's for sure, baby," she says faux-soothingly, falling onto the bed, looking for something, then her voice changes and she yells, "And you *lie*! Why didn't you tell me you were in South Beach last weekend?"

"I wasn't in South Beach last weekend, and I wasn't at the fucking Calvin Klein show either." Finally the time has come: "Alison, we've got to talk about something—"

"*Don't* say it." She drops the coconut into her lap and holds up both hands, then notices the joint on her nightstand and grabs it. "I know, I know," she intones dramatically. "There *is* a compromising photo of you with a girl"—she bats her eyes cartoonishly—"supposedly moi, yada yada yada, that's going to fuck up your relationship with that dunce you date, but it will also"—and now, mock-sadly, lighting the joint—"fuck up the relationship with the dunce *I* date too. So"—she claps her hands—"rumor is it's running in either the *Post,* the *Trib* or the *News* tomorrow. I'm working on it. I have people all over it. This is my A-number-one priority. So don't worry"—she inhales, exhales—"that beautiful excuse for a head of yours about it." She spots what she was looking for, lost in the comforter, and grabs it: a screwdriver.

"Why, Alison? Why did you have to attack me at a *movie premiere?*" I wail.

"It takes two, you naughty boy."

"Not when you've knocked me unconscious and are sitting on my face."

"If I was sitting on your face no one will ever know it was you." She shrugs, gets up, grabs the coconut. "And then we'll all be saved—la la la la."

"That's not when the picture was taken, baby." I follow her into the bathroom, where she punches four holes in the coconut with the screwdriver and then leans over the Vivienne Tam–designed sink and pours the milk from the shell over her head.

"I know, I agree." She tosses the husk into a wastebasket and massages the milk into her scalp. "Damien finds out and you'll be working in a White Castle."

"And you'll be paying for your own abortions, so spare me." I raise my arms helplessly. "Why do I always have to remind you that we shouldn't be seeing each other? If this photo gets printed it'll be time for us to *wake up*."

"If this picture gets printed we'll just say it was a weak moment." She whips her head back and wraps her hair in a towel. "Doesn't that sound good?"

"Jesus, baby, you've got people out there watching your apartment."

"I know." She beams into the mirror. "Isn't it cute?"

"Why do I always need to remind you that I'm basically still with, y'know, *Chloe* and *you're* still with Damien?"

She turns away from the mirror and leans against the sink. "If you dump me, baby, you'll be in a *lot* more trouble." She heads toward the closet.

"Why is that?" I ask, following her. "What do you mean, Alison?"

"Oh, let's just say rumor has it that you're looking at a new space." She pauses, holds up a pair of shoes. "And we both know that if Damien knew that you were even *contemplating* your own pathetic club-slash-eatery while you're currently being paid to run Damien's own pathetic club-slash-eatery, therefore insulting Damien's warped sense of loyalty, the term 'you're fucked' comes vaguely to mind." She drops the shoes, leaves the closet.

"I'm not," I insist, following her. "I swear I'm not. Oh my god, who told you that?"

"Are you denying it?"

"N-no. I mean, I *am* denying it. I mean . . ." I stand there.

"Oh never mind." Alison drops the robe and puts on some panties. "Three o'clock tomorrow?"

"I'm swamped tomorrow, baby, so spare me," I stammer. "Now, who told you I'm looking at a new space?"

"Okay—three o'clock on Monday."

"Why three o'clock? Why Monday?"

"Damien's having his unit cleaned." She tosses on a blouse.

"His unit?"

"His"—she whispers—"extensions."

"Damien has—extensions?" I ask. "He's the grossest guy, baby. He is so evil."

She strides over to the armoire, sifts through a giant box of earrings. "Oh baby, I saw Tina Brown at 44 today at lunch and she's coming tomorrow sans Harry and so is Nick Scotti, who—I know, I know—is a has-been but just looks *great*."

I move slowly back toward the frost-covered window, peer past the venetian blinds at the Jeep on Park.

"I talked to Winona too. She *is* coming. Wait." Alison pushes two earrings into one ear, three into another, and is now pulling them out. "Is Johnny coming?"

"What?" I murmur. "Who?"

"Johnny Depp," she shouts, throwing a shoe at me.

"I guess," I say vaguely. "Yeah."

"Goody," I hear her say. "Rumor has it that Davey's very friendly with heroin—ooh, don't let Chloe get too close to Davey— *and* I also hear that Winona might go back to Johnny if Kate Moss disappears into thin air or a smallish tornado hurls her back to Auschwitz, which we're *all* hoping for." She notices the half-smoked cigarette floating in the Snapple bottle, then turns around, holding the bottle out to me accusingly, mentioning something about how Mrs. Chow *loves* kiwi-flavored Snapple. I'm slouching in a giant Vivienne Tam armchair.

"God, Victor," Alison says, hushed. "In this light"—she stops, genuinely moved—"you look gorgeous."

Gaining the strength to squint at her, I say, finally, "The better you look, the more you see."

30

Back at my place downtown getting dressed to meet Chloe at Bowery Bar by 10 I'm moving around my apartment cell phone in hand on hold to my agent at CAA. I'm lighting citrus-scented votive candles to help mellow the room out, ease the tension, plus it's so freezing in my apartment it's like an igloo. Black turtleneck, white jeans, Matsuda jacket, slippers, simple and cool. Music playing is low-volume Weezer. TV's on—no sound—with highlights from the shows today at Bryant Park, Chloe everywhere. Finally a click, a sigh, muffled voices in the background, Bill sighing again.

"Bill? Hello?" I'm saying. "Bill? What are you doing? Getting fawned over on Melrose? Sitting there with a headset on, looking like you belong in an air traffic controllers' room at LAX?"

"Do I need to remind you that I am more powerful than you?" Bill asks tiredly. "Do I need to remind you that a headset is mandatory?"

"You're my broker of opportunity, baby."

"Hopefully I will benefit from you."

"So baby, what's going on with *Flatliners II*? The script is like almost brill. What's the story?"

"The story?" Bill asks quietly. "The story is: I was at a screening this morning and the product had some exceptional qualities. It was accessible, well-structured and not particularly sad, but it proved strangely unsatisfying. It might have something to do with the fact that the product would have been better acted by hand puppets."

"What movie was this?"

"It doesn't have a title yet," Bill murmurs. "It's kind of like *Caligula* meets *The Breakfast Club*."

"I think I've seen this movie. Twice, in fact. Now listen, Bill —"

"I spent a good deal of lunch at Barney Greengrass today staring at the Hollywood Hills, listening to someone trying to sell me a pitch about a giant pasta maker that goes on some kind of sick rampage."

I turn the TV off, search the apartment for my watch. "And . . . your thoughts?"

"'How near death am I?'" Bill pauses. "I don't think I should be thinking things like that at twenty-eight. I don't think I should be thinking things like that at Barney Greengrass."

"Well, Bill, you *are* twenty-eight."

"Touching a seltzer bottle that sat in a champagne bucket brought me back to what passes for reality, and drinking half an egg cream solidified that process. The pitcher finally tried to make jokes and I tried to laugh." A pause. "Having dinner at the Viper Room started to seem vaguely plausible, like, i.e., not a bad evening."

I open the glass-door refrigerator, grab a blood orange and roll my eyes, muttering "Spare me" to myself while peeling it.

"At that lunch," Bill continues, "someone from a rival agency came up behind me and superglued a large starfish to the back of my head for reasons I'm still not sure of." Pause. "Two junior agents are, at this moment, trying to remove it."

"Whoa, baby," I cough. "You're making too much noise right now."

"As we speak I am also having my photo taken for *Buzz* magazine by Fahoorzi Zaheedi. . . ." Pause, not to me: "That's not how *you* pronounce it? Do you think just because it's *your* name that *you* know?"

"Billy? Bill — hey, what is this?" I'm asking. "*Buzz*, man? That's a magazine for flies, baby. Come on, Bill, what's going on with *Flatliners II*? I read the script and though I found structural problems and made some notes I still think it's brill and *you* know and *I* know that I'm perfect for the part of Ohman." I pop another slice of blood orange into my mouth and, while chewing, tell Bill, "And I think Alicia Silverstone would be perfect for the part of Julia Roberts' troubled sister, Froufrou."

"I had a date with Alicia Silverstone last night," Bill says vacantly. "Tomorrow, Drew Barrymore." Pause. "She's between marriages."

"What did you and Alicia do?"

"We sat around and watched *The Lion King* on video while eating a cantaloupe I found in my backyard, which is not a bad evening, depending on how you define 'bad evening.' I made her watch me smoke a cigar and she gave me dieting tips, such as 'Eschew hors d'oeuvres.'" Pause. "I plan to do the same exact thing with Kurt Cobain's widow next week."

"That's really, uh, y'know, cutting edge, Bill."

"Right now while *Buzz* is taking my photograph I'm prepping the big new politically correct horror movie. We've just been discussing how many rapes should be in it. My partners say two. I say half a dozen." Pause. "We also need to glamorize the heroine's disability more."

"What's wrong with her?"

"She doesn't have a head."

"Cool, cool, that's cool."

"Add to this the fact that my dog just killed himself. He drank a bucket of paint."

"Hey, Bill, *Flatliners II* or not? Just tell me. *Flatliners II* or no *Flatliners II*. Huh, Bill?"

"Do you know what happens to a dog when he drinks a bucket of paint?" Bill asks, sounding vague.

"Is Shumacher involved or not? Is Kiefer on board?"

"My dog was a sex maniac and very, very depressed. His name was Max the Jew and he was very, very depressed."

"Well, I guess that's why, y'know, he drank the paint, right?"

"Could be. It could also be the fact that ABC canceled 'My So-Called Life.'" He pauses. "It's all sort of up in the air."

"Have you ever heard the phrase 'earn your ten percent'?" I'm asking, washing my hands. "Have you seen your mother, baby, standing in the shadows?"

"The center cannot hold, my friend," Bill drones on.

"Hey Bill—what if there's *no* center? Huh?" I ask, thoroughly pissed off.

"I'll pursue that." Pause. "But right now I am quietly seething that Firhoozi thinks the starfish is hip, so I must go. We will speak as soon as it's feasibly possible."

"Bill, I've gotta run too, but listen, can we talk tomorrow?" I flip frantically through my daybook. "Um, like at either three-twenty-five or, um, like . . . four or four-fifteen . . . or , maybe even at, oh shit, six-ten?"

"Between lunch and midnight I'm collecting art with the cast of 'Friends.'"

"That's pretty ultra-arrogant, Bill."

"Dagby, I must go. Firhoozi wants a profile shot sans starfish."

"Hey Bill, wait a minute. I just want to know if you're pushing me for *Flatliners II*. And my name's not Dagby."

"If you are not Dagby, then who is this?" he asks vacantly. "Who am I now speaking with if not Dagby?"

"It's *me*. Victor Ward. I'm opening like the biggest club in New York tomorrow night."

Pause, then, "No . . ."

"I modeled for Paul Smith. I did a Calvin Klein ad."

Pause, then, "No . . ." I can hear him slouching, repositioning himself.

"I'm the guy who everyone thought David Geffen was dating but wasn't."

"That's really not enough."

"I date Chloe Byrnes," I'm shouting. "Chloe Byrnes, like, the supermodel?"

"I've heard of *her* but not *you*, Dagby."

"Jesus, Bill, I'm on the cover of *YouthQuake* magazine this month. Your Halcion dosage needs trimming, bud."

"I'm not even thinking about you at this exact moment."

"Hey," I shout. "To save my life I dumped ICM for you guys."

"Listen, Dagby, or whoever this is, I can't really hear you since I'm on Mulholland now and I'm under a . . . big long tunnel." Pause. "Can't you hear the static?"

"But I just called you, Bill, at your *office*. You told me Firhoozi Zahidi was shooting you in your office. Let me talk to Firhoozi."

A long pause, then disdainfully Bill says, "You think you're so clever."

29

It's so diabolically crowded outside Bowery Bar that I have to climb over a stalled limo parked crookedly at the curb to even start pushing through the crowd while paparazzi who couldn't get in try desperately to snap my photo, calling out my name as I follow Liam Neeson, Carol Alt and Spike Lee up to Chad and Anton, who help pull us inside, where the opening riffs of Matthew Sweet's "Sick of Myself" starts booming. The bar is mobbed, white boys with dreadlocks, black girls wearing Nirvana T-shirts, grungy homeboys, gym queens with buzz cuts, mohair, neon, Janice Dickerson, bodyguards and their models from the shows today looking hot but exhausted, fleece and neoprene and pigtails and silicone and Brent Fraser as well as Brendan Fraser and pom-poms and chenille sleeves and falconer gloves and everyone's smoochy. I wave over at Pell and Vivien, who are drinking Cosmopolitans with Marcus—who's wearing an English barrister's wig—and this really cool lesbian, Egg, who's wearing an Imperial margarine crown, and she's sitting next to two people dressed like two of the Banana Splits, which two I couldn't possibly tell. It's a kitsch-is-cool kind of night and there are tons of chic admirers.

While scanning the dining room for Chloe (which I realize a little too slowly is totally useless since she's always in one of the three big A booths), I notice Richard Johnson from "Page Six" next to me, also scanning the room, along with Mick and Anne Jones, and I sidle up to him and offer a high five.

"Hey Dick," I shout over the din. "I need to ask you about something, por favor."

"Sure, Victor," Richard says. "But I'm looking for Jenny Shimuzu and Scott Bakula."

"Hey, Jenny lives in my building and she's supercool and very fond of Häagen-Dazs frozen yogurt bars, preferably piña colada, not to mention a good friend. But hey, man, have you heard about a photograph that's gonna run in like the *News* tomorrow?"

"A photograph?" he asks. "A *photo*graph?"

"B-b-baby," I stammer. "That sounds kind of sinister when you ask it twice. But it's, um, do you know Alison Poole?"

"Sure, she's Damien Nutchs Ross's squeeze," he says, spotting someone, giving thumbs-up, thumbs-down, then thumbs-up again. "How are things with the club? Everything nice and tidy for tomorrow night?"

"Cool, cool, cool. But it's like an, um, embarrassing photo like maybe of me?"

Richard has turned his attention to a journalist standing by us who's interviewing a very good-looking busboy.

"Victor, this is Byron from *Time* magazine." Richard motions with a hand.

"Love your work, man. Peace," I tell Byron. "Richard, about—"

"Byron's doing an article on very good-looking busboys for *Time*," Richard says dispassionately.

"Well, *finally*," I tell Byron. "Wait, Richard—"

"If it's an odious photograph the *Post* won't run an odious photograph, blah blah blah," Richard says, moving away.

"Hey, who said anything about *odious*?" I shout. "I said *embarrassing*."

Candy Bushnell suddenly pushes through the crowd screaming "Richard," and then when she sees me her voice goes up eighty octaves and she screams *"Pony!"* and places an enormous kiss on my face while slipping me a half and Richard finds Jenny Shimuzu but not Scott Bakula and Chloe is surrounded by Roy Liebenthal, Eric Goode, Quentin Tarantino, Kato Kaelin and Baxter Priestly, who is sitting way too close to her in the giant aquamarine booth and I have to put a stop to this or else deal with an unbelievably painful headache. Waving over at John Cusack, who's sharing calamari with Julien Temple, I move through the crowd toward the booth where Chloe, pretending to be engaged, is nervously smoking a Marlboro Light.

Chloe was born in 1970, a Pisces and a CAA client. Full lips, bone-thin, big breasts (implants), long muscular legs, high cheekbones, large blue eyes, flawless skin, straight nose, waistline of twenty-three inches, a smile that never becomes a smirk, a cellular-phone bill that runs $1,200 a month, hates herself but probably shouldn't. She was discovered dancing on the beach in Miami and has been half-naked in an Aerosmith video, in *Playboy* and twice on the cover of the *Sports Illustrated* swimwear issue as well as on the cover of four hundred magazines. A calendar she shot in St. Bart's has sold two million copies. A book called *The Real Me*, ghostwritten with Bill Zehme, was on the *New York Times* best-seller list for something like twelve weeks. She is always on the phone listening to managers renegotiating deals and has an agent who takes fifteen percent, three publicists (though PMK basically handles *everything*), two lawyers, numerous business managers. Right now Chloe's on the verge of signing a multimillion-dollar contract with Lancôme, but a great many others are also in pursuit, especially after the "rumors" of a "slight" drug problem were quickly "brushed aside": Banana Republic (no), Benetton (no), Chanel (yes), Gap (maybe), Christian Dior (hmm), French Connection (a joke), Guess? (nope), Ralph Lauren (problematic), Pepe Jeans (are we kidding?), Calvin Klein (done that), Pepsi (sinister but a possibility), et cetera. Chocolates, the only food Chloe even remotely likes, are severely rationed. No rice, potatoes, oils or bread. Only steamed vegetables, certain fruits, plain fish, boiled chicken. We haven't had dinner together in a long time because last week she had wardrobe fittings for the fifteen shows she's doing this week, which means each designer had about one hundred twenty outfits for her to try on, and besides the two shows tomorrow she has to shoot part of a Japanese TV commercial and meet with a video director to go over storyboards that Chloe doesn't understand anyway. Asking price for ten days of work: $1.7 million. A contract somewhere stipulates this.

Right now she's wearing a black Prada halter gown with black patent-leather sandals and metallic-green wraparound sunglasses she takes off as soon as she sees me approaching.

"Sorry, baby, I got lost," I say, sliding into the booth.

"My savior," Chloe says, smiling tightly.

Roy, Quentin, Kato and Eric split, all severely disappointed, muttering *hey mans* to me and that they'll be at the opening tomorrow night, but Baxter Priestly stays seated—one collar point sticking in, the other sticking out, from under a Pepto-Bismol-pink vest—sucking on a peppermint. NYU film grad, rich and twenty-five, part-time model (so far only group shots in Guess?, Banana Republic and Tommy Hilfiger ads), blond with a pageboy haircut, dated Elizabeth Saltzman like I did, wow.

"Hey man," I sigh while reaching over the table to kiss Chloe on the mouth, dreading the upcoming exchange of pleasantries.

"Hey Victor." Baxter shakes my hand. "How's the club going? Ready for tomorrow?"

"Do you have the time to listen to me whine?"

We sit there sort of looking out over the rest of the room, my eyes fixed on the big table in the center, beneath a chandelier made of toilet floats and recycled refrigerator wire, where Eric Bogosian, Jim Jarmusch, Larry Gagosian, Harvey Keitel, Tim Roth, and oddly enough, Ricki Lake are all having salads, which touches something in me, a reminder to deal with the crouton situation before it gets totally out of hand.

Finally sensing my vibe, Baxter gets up, pockets his Audiovox MVX cell phone, which is sitting next to Chloe's Ericsson DF, and clumsily shakes my hand again.

"I'll see you guys tomorrow." He lingers, removes the peppermint from full pink lips. "Until then, um, I guess."

"Bye, Baxter," Chloe says, tired but sweet, as usual.

"Yeah, bye, man," I mutter, a well-practiced dismissal, and once he's barely out of earshot I delicately ask, "What's the story, baby? Who was that?"

She doesn't answer, just glares at me.

Pause. "Hey, honey, you're looking at me like I'm at a Hootie and the Blowfish concert. Chill."

"Baxter Priestly?" she says-asks morosely, picking at a plate of cilantro.

"Who's Baxter Priestly?" I pull out some excellent weed and a package of rolling papers. "Who the fuck is Baxter Priestly?"

"He's in the new Darren Star show and plays bass in the band Hey That's My Shoe," she says, lighting another cigarette.

"Baxter Priestly? What the fuck kind of name is that?" I mutter, spotting seeds that cry out for removal.

"*You're* complaining about someone's name? *You* hang out with Plez and Fetish and a person whose parents actually named him Tomato—"

"They conceded it might have been a mistake."

"—and you do business with people named Benny Benny and Damien Nutchs Ross? And you haven't apologized for being an hour late? I had to wait upstairs in Eric's office."

"Oh god, I bet he loved that," I moan, concentrating on the pot. "Hell, baby, I thought I'd let you entertain the paparazzi." Pause. "And that's Kenny Kenny, honey."

"I did that all day," she sighs.

"Baxter Priestly? Why am I drawing a blank?" I ask earnestly, waving down Cliff the maître d' for a drink but it's too late: Eric has already sent over a complimentary bottle of Cristal 1985.

"I guess I'm used to your oblivion, Victor," she says.

"Chloe. *You* do fur ads *and* donate money to Greenpeace. *You're* what's known as a bundle of contradictions, baby, not this guy."

"Baxter used to date Lauren Hynde." She stubs her cigarette out, smiles thankfully at the very good-looking busboy pouring the champagne into flutes.

"Baxter used to date Lauren Hynde?"

"Right."

"Who's Lauren Hynde?"

"Lauren Hynde, Victor," she stresses as if the name means something. "You *dated* her."

"I did? I *did*? Yeah? Hmm."

"Good night, Victor."

"I just don't remember Lauren Hynde, baby. Solly Cholly."

"Lauren Hynde?" she asks in disbelief. "You don't remember dating her? My god, what are you going to say about *me*?"

"Nothing, baby," I tell her, finally done deseeding. "We're gonna get married and grow old together. How did the shows go? Look—there's Scott Bakula. Hey, peace, man. Richard's looking for you, bud."

"Lauren Hynde, Victor."

"That's so cool. Hey Alfonse—great tattoo, guy." I turn back to Chloe. "Did you know Damien wears a hairpiece? He's some kind of demented wig addict."

"Who told you this?"

"One of the guys at the club," I say without pausing.

"Lauren Hynde, Victor. Lauren Hynde."

"Who's *dat*?" I say, making a crazy face, leaning over, kissing her neck noisily. Suddenly Patrick McMullan glides by, politely asks for a photo, complimenting Chloe on the shows today. We move in close together, look up, smile, the flash goes off. "Hey, crop the pot," I warn as he spots Patrick Kelly and scampers off.

"Do you think he heard me?"

"Lauren Hynde's one of my best friends, Victor."

"I don't know her, but hey, if she's a friend of yours, well, need I say anything but *automatically*?" I start rolling the joint.

"Victor, you went to school with her."

"I didn't go to school with her, baby," I murmur, waving over at Ross Bleckner and his new boyfriend, Mrs. Ross Bleckner, a guy who used to work at a club in Amagansett called Salamanders and was recently profiled in *Bikini*.

"Forgive me if I'm mistaken, but you went to Camden with Lauren Hynde." She lights another cigarette, finally sips the champagne.

"Of course. I did," I say, trying to calm her. "Oh. Yeah."

"Did you go to college, Victor?"

"Literally or figuratively?"

"Is there a difference with you?" she asks. "How can you be so dense?"

"I don't know, baby. It's some kind of gene displacement."

"I can't listen to this. You complain about Baxter Priestly's *name* and yet you know people named Huggy and Pidgeon and Na Na."

"Hey," I finally snap, "and you slept with Charlie Sheen. We all have our little faults."

"I should've just had dinner with Baxter," she mutters.

"Baby, come on, a little champagne, a little sorbet. I'm rolling a joint so we can calm down. Now, who is this Baxter?"

"You met him at a Knicks game."

"Oh my god that's right—the new male waif, underfed, wild-haired, major rehab victim." I immediately shut up, glance nervously over at Chloe, then segue beautifully into: "The whole grunge aesthetic has ruined the look of the American male, baby. It makes you *long* for the '80s."

"Only *you* would say that, Victor."

"Anyway, I'm always watching you flirt with John-John at Knicks games."

"Like you wouldn't dump me for Daryl Hannah."

"Baby, *I'd* dump you for John-John if I really wanted the publicity." Pause, mid-lick, looking up. "That's not, um, a possibility . . . is it?"

She just stares at me.

I grab her. "Come here, baby." I kiss her again, my cheek now damp because Chloe's hair is always wet and slicked back with coconut oil. "Baby? Why isn't your hair ever dry?"

Video cameras from Fashion TV sweep the room and I have to get Cliff to tell Eric to make sure they come nowhere near Chloe. M People turns into mid-period Elvis Costello which turns into new Better Than Ezra. I order a bowl of raspberry sorbet and try to cheer Chloe up by turning it into a Prince song: "*She ate a raspberry sorbet . . . The kind you find at the Bowery Bar . . .*"

Chloe just stares glumly at her plate.

"Honey, that's a plate of cilantro. What's the story?"

"I've been up since five and I want to cry."

"Hey, how was the big lunch at Fashion Café?"

"I had to sit there and watch James Truman eat a giant truffle and it really really bothered me."

"Because . . . you wanted a truffle too?"

"No, Victor. Oh god, you don't get anything."

"Jesus, baby, spare me. What do you want me to do? Hang around Florence for a year studying Renaissance pottery? You get your legs waxed at Elizabeth Arden ten times a month."

"You sit around plotting seating arrangements."

"Baby baby baby." I light up the joint, whining. "Come on, my DJ's missing, the club's opening tomorrow, I have a photo shoot, a fucking show *and* lunch with my father tomorrow." Pause. "Oh shit—band practice."

"How is your father?" she asks disinterestedly.

"A contrivance," I mutter. "A plot device."

Peggy Siegal walks by in taffeta and I duck under the table with my head in Chloe's lap, looking up into her face, grinning, while taking a deep toke. "Peggy wanted to handle the publicity," I explain, sitting up.

Chloe just stares at me.

"So-o-o anyway," I continue. "James Truman eating a giant truffle? The lunch? 'Entertainment Tonight,' yes—go on."

"It was so hip I ate," I hear her say.

"What did you eat?" I murmur indifferently, waving over at Frederique, who pouts her lips, eyes squinty, like she was cooing to a baby or a very large puppy.

"I ached, *ached*, Victor. Oh god, you never listen to me."

"Joking, baby. I'm joking. I really see what you're saying."

She stares at me, waiting.

"Um, your hip ached and—have I got it?"

She just stares at me.

"Okay, okay, reality just zapped me. . . ." I take another toke, glance nervously at her. "So-o-o the video shoot tomorrow, um, what is it exactly?" Pause. "Are you, like, naked in it or anything?" Pause, another toke, then I cock my head to exhale smoke so it won't hit her in the face. "Er . . . what's the story?"

She continues to stare.

"You're not naked . . . or . . . you are, um, naked?"

"Why?" she asks curtly. "Do you care?"

"Baby baby baby. Last time you did a video you were dancing on the hood of a car in your *bra*. Baby baby baby . . ." I'm shaking my head woefully. "Concern is causing me to like pant and sweat."

"Victor, you did how many bathing suit ads? You were photographed for Madonna's sex book. Jesus, you were in that Versace ad where—am I mistaken?—we did or did not see your pubic hair?"

"Yeah, but Madonna dropped those photos and let's just say *thank you* to that and there's a major difference between my pubic hair—which was *lightened*—and your tits, baby. Oh Christ, spare me, forget it, I don't know what you call—"

"It's called a double standard, Victor."

"Double standard?" I take another hit without trying and say, feeling particularly mellow, "Well, I didn't do *Playgirl*."

"Congratulations. But that wasn't for me. That was because of your father. Don't pretend."

"I like to pretend." I offer an amazingly casual shrug.

"It's fine when you're seven, Victor, but add twenty years to that and you're just retarded."

"Honey, I'm just bummed. Mica the DJ has vanished, tomorrow is hell day and the *Flatliners* II thing is all blurry and watery—who knows what the fuck is happening there. Bill thinks I'm someone named Dagby and jeez, you know how much time I put into those notes to shape that script up and—"

"What about the potato chip commercial you were up for?"

"Baby baby baby. Jumping around a beach, putting a Pringle in my mouth and looking surprised because—why?—it's *spicy*? Oh baby," I groan, slouching into the booth. "Do you have any Visine?"

"It's a job, Victor," she says. "It's money."

"I think CAA's a mistake. I mean, when I was talking to Bill I started remembering that really scary story you told me about Mike Ovitz."

"What scary story?"

"Remember—you were invited to meet with all those CAA guys like Bob Bookman and Jay Mahoney at a screening on Wilshire and you went and the movie was a brand-new print of *Tora! Tora! Tora!* and during the entire movie *they all laughed*? You don't remember telling me this?"

"Victor," Chloe sighs, not listening. "I was in SoHo the other day with Lauren and we were having lunch at Zoë and somebody came up to me and said, 'Oh, you look just like Chloe Byrnes.'"

"And you said, er, 'How dare you!'?" I ask, glancing sideways at her.

"And I said, 'Oh? Really?'"

"It sounds like you had a somewhat leisurely, um, afternoon," I cough, downing smoke with a gulp of champagne. "Lauren *who*?"

"You're not listening to me, Victor."

"Oh come on, baby, when you were young and your heart was an open book you used to say live and let live." I pause, take another hit on the joint. "You know you did. You know you did. *You know you did.*" I cough again, sputtering out smoke.

"You're not talking to me," Chloe says sternly, with too much emotion. "You're looking at me but you're *not* talking to me."

"Baby, I'm your biggest fan," I say. "And I'm admitting this only somewhat groggily."

"Oh, how grown-up of you."

The new It Girls flutter by our booth, nervously eyeing Chloe—one of them eating a stick of purple cotton candy—on their way to dance by the bathroom. I notice Chloe's troubled glare, as if she just drank something black or ate a piece of bad sashimi.

"Oh come on, baby. You wanna end up living on a sheep farm in Australia milking fucking dingoes? You wanna spend the rest of your life on the Internet answering E-mail? Spare me. Lighten up."

A long pause and then, "Milking . . . *dingoes*?"

"Most of those girls have an eighth-grade education."

"You went to Camden College—same thing. Go talk to them."

People keep stopping by, begging for invites to the opening, which I dole out accordingly, telling me they spotted my visage last week at the Marlin in Miami, at the Elite offices on the hotel's first floor, then at the Strand, and by the time Michael Bergen tells me we shared an iced latte at the Bruce Weber/Ralph Lauren photo shoot in Key Biscayne I'm too tired to even deny I was in Miami last weekend and so I ask Michael if it was a good latte and he says so-so and it gets noticeably colder in the room. Chloe looks on, oblivious, meekly sips champagne. Patrick Bateman, who's with a bunch of publicists and the three sons of a well-known movie producer, walks over, shakes my hand, eyes Chloe, asks how the club's coming along, if tomorrow night's happening, says Damien invited him, hands me a cigar, weird stains on the lapel of his Armani suit that costs as much as a car.

"The proverbial show is on the proverbial road, dude," I assure him.

"I just like to keep—abreast," he says, winking at Chloe.

After he leaves I finish the joint, then look at my watch but I'm not wearing one so I inspect my wrist instead.

"He's strange," Chloe says. "And I need some soup."

"He's a nice guy, babe."

Chloe slouches in the booth, looks at me disgustedly.

"What? Hey, he has his own coat of arms."

"Who told you that?"

"He did. He told me he has his own coat of arms."

"Spare *me*," Chloe says.

Chloe picks up the check and in order to downplay the situation I lean in to kiss her, the swarming paparazzi causing the kind of disturbance we're used to.

28

Stills from Chloe's loft in a space that looks like it was designed by Dan Flavin: two Toshiyuki Kita hop sofas, an expanse of white-maple floor, six Baccarat Tastevin wineglasses—a gift from Bruce and Nan Weber—dozens of white French tulips, a StairMaster and a free-weight set, photography books—Matthew Rolston, Annie Leibovitz, Herb Ritts—all signed, a Fabergé Imperial egg— a gift from Bruce Willis (pre-Demi)—a large plain portrait of Chloe by Richard Avedon, sunglasses scattered all over the place, a Helmut Newton photo of Chloe walking seminude through the lobby of the Malperisa in Milan while nobody notices, a large William Wegman and giant posters for the movies *Butterfield 8*, *The Bachelor Party* with Carolyn Jones, Audrey Hepburn in *Breakfast at Tiffany's*. A giant fax sheet taped above Chloe's makeup table lists Monday 9am Byron Lars, 11am Mark Eisen, 2pm Nicole Miller, 6pm Ghost, Tuesday 10am Ralph Lauren, Wednesday 11am Anna Sui, 2pm Calvin Klein, 4pm Bill Blass, 7pm Isaac Mizrahi, Thursday 9am Donna Karan, 5pm Todd Oldham and on and on until Sunday. Piles of foreign currency and empty Glacier bottles litter tables and countertops everywhere. In her refrigerator the breakfast Luna has already prepared: ruby-red grapefruit, Evian, iced herbal tea, nonfat plain yogurt with blackberries, a quarter of a poppyseed bagel, sometimes toasted, sometimes not, Beluga if it's a "special day." Gilles Bensimon, Juliette Lewis, Patrick Demarchelier, Ron Galotti, Peter Lindbergh and Baxter Priestly have all left messages.

I take a shower, rub some Preparation H and Clinique Eye Fitness under my eyes and check my answering machine: Ellen Von Unwerth, Eric Stoltz, Alison Poole, Nicolas Cage, Nicollette Sheridan, Stephen Dorff and somebody ominous from TriStar. When I come out of the bathroom with a

Ralph Lauren fluffy towel wrapped around my waist, Chloe is sitting on the bed looking doomed, hugging her knees to her chest. Tears fill her eyes, she shudders, takes a Xanax, wards off another anxiety attack. On the large-screen TV is a documentary about the dangers of breast implants.

"It's just silicone, baby," I say, trying to soothe her. "I take Halcion, okay? I had half a bacon sandwich the other day. We smoke."

"Oh god, Victor." She keeps shuddering.

"Remember that period you chopped off all your hair and kept dyeing it different colors and all you did was cry?"

"Victor, I was suicidal," she sobs. "I almost overdosed."

"Baby, the point is you never lost a booking."

"Victor, I'm twenty-six. That's a hundred and five in model years."

"Baby, this insecurity you've got has to, like, split." I rub her shoulders. "You're an icon, baby," I whisper into her ear. "*You* are the guideline." I kiss her neck lightly. "You personify the physical ideal of your day," and then, "Baby, you're not just a model. You're a star." Finally, cupping her face in my hands, I tell her, "Beauty is in the soul."

"But *my soul* doesn't do twenty runway shows," she cries out. "My soul isn't on the cover of fucking *Harper's* next month. My soul's not negotiating a Lancôme contract." Heaving sobs, gasps, the whole bit, the end of the world, the end of everything.

"Baby . . ." I pull back. "I don't want to wake up and find you've freaked out about your implants again and you're hiding out in Hollywood at the Chateau Marmont, hanging with Kiefer and Dermot and Sly. So y'know, um, chill out, baby."

After ten minutes of silence or maybe two the Xanax kicks in and she concedes, "I'm feeling a little better."

"Baby, Andy once said that beauty *is* a sign of intelligence."

She turns slowly to look at me. "Who, Victor? *Who?* Andy who?" She coughs, blowing her nose. "Andy Kaufman? Andy Griffith? Who in the hell told you this? Andy Rooney?"

"Warhol," I say softly, hurt. "Baby . . ."

She gets up off the bed and moves into the bathroom, splashes water on her face, then rubs Preparation H under her eyes. "The fashion world is dying anyway," Chloe yawns, stretching, walking over to one of her walk-in closets, opening it. "I mean, what else can I say?"

"Not necessarily a bad thing, baby," I say vaguely, moving over to the television.

"Victor—whose mortgage is *this*?" she cries out, waving her arms around.

I'm looking for a copy of the *Flatliners* tape I left over here last week but can only find an old Arsenio that Chloe was on, two movies she was in,

Party Mountain with Emery Roberts and *Teen Town* with Hurley Thompson, another documentary about breast-implant safety and last week's "Melrose Place." On the screen now, a commercial, grainy fuzz, a reproduction of a reproduction. When I turn around, Chloe is holding up a dress in front of a full-length mirror, winking at herself.

The dress is an original Todd Oldham wraparound: not-so-basic black-slash-beige dress, strapless, Navajo-inspired and neon quilted.

My first reaction: she stole it from Alison.

"Um, baby . . ." I clear my throat. "What's that?"

"I'm practicing my wink for the video," she says, winking again. "Rupert says I wasn't doing it right."

"Uh-huh. Okay, I'll take some time off and we'll practice." I pause, then carefully ask, "But the dress?"

"You like it?" she asks, brightening up, turning around. "I'm wearing it tomorrow night."

"Um . . . baby?"

"What? What is it?" She puts the dress back in the closet.

"Oh honey," I say, shaking my head. "I don't know about that dress."

"You don't have to wear it, Victor."

"But then neither do you, right?"

"Stop. I can't deal with—"

"Baby, you're gonna look like Pocahontas in that thing."

"Todd gave me this dress especially for the opening—"

"How about something simpler, less multicult? Less p.c., perhaps? Something closer to Armani-ish?" I move toward the closet. "Here, let me choose something for you."

"Victor." She blocks the closet door. "I'm wearing *that*." She suddenly looks down at my ankles. "Are those scratches?"

"Where?" I look down too.

"On your ankles." She pushes me onto the bed and inspects my ankles, then the red marks on my calves. "Those look like dogs did this. Were you around any dogs today?"

"Oh baby, *all* day," I groan, staring at the ceiling. "You don't even know."

"Those are dog scratches, Victor."

"Oh, *those*?" I say, sitting up, pretending to notice them too. "Beau and JD groveling, mauling at me . . . Do you have any, um, Bactine?"

"When were you around dogs?" she asks again.

"Baby, you've made your point."

She stares at the scratches once more, passively, then silently gets into her side of the bed and reaches for a script sent to her by CAA, a miniseries set on another tropical island, which she thinks is dreadful even though "miniseries" is not a dirty word. I'm thinking of saying something along the lines of *Baby, there might be something in tomorrow's paper that might, like, upset you.* On MTV one uninterrupted traveling Steadicam shot races through an underfurnished house.

I scoot over, position myself next to her.

"It looks like we've got the new space," I say. "I'm meeting with Waverly tomorrow."

Chloe doesn't say anything.

"I could open the new place, according to Burl, within three months." I look over at her. "You're looking vaguely concerned, baby."

"I don't know how good an idea that really is."

"What? Opening up my own place?"

"It might destroy certain relationships."

"Not ours, I hope," I say, reaching for her hand.

She stares at the script.

"What's wrong?" I sit up. "The only thing I really want right now at this point in my life—besides *Flatliners II*—is my own club, my own place."

Chloe sighs, flips over a page she didn't read. Finally she puts the script down. "Victor—"

"Don't say it, baby. I mean, is it so unreasonable to want that? Is it really asking anyone too much? Does the fact that I want to do something with my life bore the shit out of you?"

"Victor—"

"Baby, all my life—"

Then, out of the blue: "Have you ever cheated on me?"

Not too much silence before "Oh baby." I lean over her, squeezing the fingers lying on top of the CAA logo. "Why are you asking me this?" And then I ask, but also know, "Have *you?*"

"I just want to know if you've always been . . . faithful to me." She looks back at the script and then at the TV, showcasing a lovely pink fog, whole minutes of it. "I care about that, Victor."

"Oh baby, always, *always.* Don't underestimate me."

"Make love to me, Victor," she whispers.

I kiss her gently on the lips. She responds by pushing into me too hard and I have to pull back and whisper, "Oh baby, I'm so wiped out." I lift my head because the new Soul Asylum video is on MTV and I want Chloe to watch it too but she has already turned over, away from me. A photo of myself, a pretty good one, taken by Herb Ritts, sits on Chloe's nightstand, the only one I let her frame.

"Is Herb coming tomorrow?" I ask softly.

"I don't think so," she says, her voice muffled.

"Do you know where he is?" I ask her hair, her neck.

"Maybe it doesn't matter."

Arousal for Chloe: Sinead O'Connor CD, beeswax candles, my cologne, a lie. Beneath the scent of coconut her hair smells like juniper, even willow. Chloe sleeps across from me, dreaming of photographers flashing light meters inches from her face, of running naked down a freezing beach pretending it's summer, of sitting under a palm tree full of spiders in Borneo, of getting off an overnight flight, gliding across another red carpet, paparazzi waiting, Miramax keeps calling, a dream within the dream of six hundred interview sessions melding into nightmares involving white-sand beaches in the South Pacific, a sunset over the Mediterranean, the French Alps, Milan, Paris, Tokyo, the icy waves, the pink newspapers from foreign countries, stacks of magazines with her unblemished face airbrushed to death and cropped close on the covers, and it's hard to sleep when a sentence from a *Vanity Fair* profile of Chloe by Kevin Sessums refuses to leave me: "Even though we've never met she looks eerily familiar, as if we've known her forever."

27

Vespa toward the club to have breakfast with Damien at 7:30, with stops at three newsstands to check the papers (nothing, no photo, small-time relief, maybe something more), and in the main dining room, which this morning looks stark and nondescript, all white walls and black velvet banquettes, my line of vision is interrupted frequently by flashes from a photographer sent by *Vanity Fair* wearing a Thai-rice-field-worker hat, a video of *Casino Royale* on some of the monitors, *Downhill Racer* on others, while upstairs Beau and Peyton (ahem) *man* the phones. At our table Damien and me and JD (sitting by my side taking notes) and the two goons from the black Jeep, both wearing black Polo shirts, finish up breakfast, today's papers spread out everywhere with major items about tonight's opening: Richard Johnson in the *Post*, George Rush in the *News* (a big photo of me, with the caption "It Boy of the Moment"), Michael Fleming in *Variety*, Michael Musto plugging it in the *Voice*, notices in Cindy Adams, Liz Smith, Buddy Seagull, Billy Norwich, Jeanne Williams and A. J. Benza. I finish leaving a message under the name Dagby on my agent Bill's voice mail. Damien's sipping a vanilla hazelnut decaf iced latte, holding a Monte Cristo cigar he keeps threatening to light but doesn't, looking very studly in a Comme des Garçons black T-shirt under a black double-breasted jacket, a Cartier Panthere watch wrapped around a semi-hairy wrist, Giorgio Armani prescription sunglasses locked on a pretty decent head, a Motorola Stortac cell phone next to the semi-hairy wrist. Damien bought a 600SEL last week, and he and the goons just dropped Linda Evangelista off at the Cynthia Rowley show and it's cold in the room and we're all eating muesli and have sideburns and everything would be flat and bright and pop if it wasn't so early.

"So Dolph and I walk backstage at the Calvin Klein show yesterday—just two guys passing a bottle of Dewar's between them—and Kate Moss is there, no shirt on, arms folded across her tits, and I'm thinking, Why bother? Then I drank one too many lethal martinis at Match Uptown last night. Dolph has a master's in chemical engineering, he's married and we're talking *wife* in italics, baby, so there wasn't a bimbo in sight even though the VIP room was filled with eurowolves but no heroin, no lesbians, no Japanese influences, no *British Esquire*. We hung out with Irina, the emerging Siberian-Eskimo supermodel. After my fifth lethal martini I asked Irina what it was like growing up in an igloo." A pause. "The evening, er, ended sometime after that." Damien lifts off the sunglasses, rubs his eyes, adjusts them for the first time this morning to light, and glances at the headlines splashed over the various papers. "Helena Christensen splitting up with Michael Hutchence? Prince dating Veronica Webb? God, the world's a mess."

Suddenly Beau leans over me with the new revised guest list, whispers something unintelligible about the Gap into my ear, hands over a sample of the invitations, which Damien never bothered to look at but wants to see now, along with certain 8 × 10s and Polaroids of tonight's various waitresses, stealing his two favorites—Rebecca and Pumpkin, both from Doppelganger's.

"Shalom Harlow sneezed on me," Damien's saying.

"I've got chills," I admit. "They're multiplying."

I'm looking over the menu that Bongo and Bobby Flay have come up with: jalapeño-cured gravlax on dark bread, spicy arugula and mesclun greens, southwestern artichoke hearts with focaccia, porcini mushrooms and herb-roasted chicken breasts and/or grilled tuna with black peppercorns, chocolate-dipped strawberries, assorted classy granitas.

"Did anyone read the Marky Mark interview in the *Times*?" Damien asks. "The underwear thing is 'semi-haunting' him."

"It's semi-haunting me too, Damien," I tell him. "Listen, here's the seating arrangements."

Damien studies Beau suspiciously for a reaction.

Beau notices this, points out certain elements about the menu, then carefully says, "I'm semi-haunted . . . too."

"Yesterday I wanted to fuck about twenty different strangers. Just girls, just people on the street. This one girl—the only one who *hadn't* seen the 600SEL, who *couldn't* tell Versace from the Gap, who didn't even *glance* at the Patek Philippe—" He turns to the goons, one who keeps eyeing me in a fucked-up way. "That's a watch *you* might never own. Anyway, *she's* the only one who would talk to me, just some dumpy chick who came on to me in Chemical Bank, and I motioned sadly to her that I was *mute*, you know, *tongue*less, that I simply couldn't *speak*, what have you. But get this—she knew sign language."

After Damien stares at me, I say, "Ah."

"I tell you, Victor," Damien continues, "the world is full of surprises. Most of them not that interesting but surprising nonetheless. Needless to say, it was a mildly scary, humiliating moment. It actually bordered on the horrific, but I moved through it." He sips his latte. "Could I actually not be in vogue? I panicked, man. I felt . . . *old*."

"Oh man, you're only twenty-eight." I nod to Beau, letting him know that he can slink back upstairs.

"Twenty-eight, yeah." Damien takes this in, but instead of dealing he just waves at the stacks of papers on the table. "Everything going as planned? Or are there any imminent disasters I should be apprised of?"

"Here are the invites." I hand him one. "I don't think you ever had the time to see these."

"Nice, or as my friend Diane Von Furstenberg likes to say—*nass*."

"Yeah, they were printed on recycled paper with boy-based—I mean *soy*-based ink." I close my eyes, shake my head, clear it. "Sorry, those little mos upstairs are getting to me."

"Opening this club, Victor, is tantamount to making a political statement," Damien says. "I hope you know that."

I'm thinking, Spare me, but say, "Yeah, man?"

"We're selling myths."

"Mitts?"

"No, *myths*. M-y-t-h-s. Like if a fag was gonna introduce you to Miss America, what would he say?"

"*Myth* . . . America?"

"Right on, babe." Damien stretches, then slouches back into the booth. "I can't help it, Victor," he says blankly. "I sense sex when I walk around the club. I feel . . . *compelled*."

"Man, I'm so with you."

"It's not a club, Victor. It's an aphrodisiac."

"Here is the, um, seating arrangements for the dinner and then the list of press invited to the cocktail party beforehand." I hand him a sheaf of papers, which Damien hands to one of his goons, who stares at it, like duh.

"I just want to know who's at my table," Damien says vacantly.

"Um, here . . ." I reach over to grab the papers back, and for an instant the goon glares at me suspiciously before gradually releasing his grip. "Um, table one is you and Alison and Alec Baldwin and Kim Basinger and Tim Hutton and Uma Thurman and Jimmy and Jane Buffett and Ted Field and Christy Turlington and David Geffen and Calvin and Kelly Klein and Julian Schnabel and Ian Schrager and Russell Simmons, along with assorted dates and wives."

"I'm between Uma Thurman and Christy Turlington, right?"

"Well, Alison and Kelly—"

"No no no no. I'm between Christy and Uma," Damien says, pointing a finger at me.

"I don't know how that is going to"—I clear my throat—"fly with Alison."

"What's she gonna do? *Pinch* me?"

"Cool cool cool." I nod. "JD, you know what to do."

"After tonight no one should get in for free. Oh yeah—except very good-looking lesbians. Anyone dressed like Garth Brooks is purged. We want a clientele that will *up* the class quotient."

"Up the class quotient. Yeah, yeah." Suddenly I cannot tear my eyes off Damien's head.

"Ground Control to Major Tom," Damien says, snapping his fingers.

"Huh?"

"What in the fuck are you looking at?" I hear him ask.

"Nothing. Go ahead."

"What are you looking at?"

"Nothing. Just spacing. Go ahead."

After a brief, scary pause Damien continues icily. "If I see anyone and I mean *anyone* un*hip* wandering around this party tonight I will kill you."

"My mouth suddenly is so dry I can't even like gulp, man."

Damien starts laughing and joking around, so I try to laugh and joke around too.

"Listen, bud," he says. "I just don't want the city's most bizarre bohemians or anyone who uses the term 'fagulous' near me or my friends."

"Could you write that down, JD?" I ask.

"No one who uses the term 'fagulous.'" JD nods, makes a note.

"And what's with the fucking DJ situation?" Damien asks disinterestedly. "Alison tells me someone named Misha's missing?"

"Damien, we're checking all the hotels in South Beach, Prague, Seattle," I tell him. "We're checking every rehab clinic in the Northeast."

"It's a little late, hmm?" Damien asks. "It's a little late for Misha, hmm?"

"Victor and I will be interviewing available DJs all day," JD assures him.

"We've got calls in to everyone from Anita Sarko to Sister Bliss to Smokin Jo. It's happening."

"It's also almost eight o'clock, dudes," Damien says. "The worst thing in the world, guys, is a shitty DJ. I'd rather be *dead* than hire a shitty DJ."

"Man, I am so with you it's unbelievable," I tell him. "We have a hundred backups, so it's happening." I'm sweating for some reason, dreading the rest of this breakfast. "Damien, where can we find you if we need to get ahold of you today?"

"I'm in the Presidential Suite at the Mark while they finish doing something to my apartment. Whatever." He shrugs, chews some muesli. "You still living downtown?"

"Yeah, yeah."

"When are you gonna move uptown with everyone else—hey, leave the foot-shaking outside," he says, staring at a black lace-up from Agnès b. my foot happens to be in. "Are you okay?"

"Fine. Damien, we've got—"

"What is it?" He stops chewing and is now carefully studying me.

"I was just gonna ask—" I breathe in.

"What are you hiding, Victor?"

"Nothing, man."

"Let me guess. You're secretly applying to Harvard?" Damien laughs, looking around the room, encouraging everyone else to laugh with him.

"Yeah, *right*." I laugh too.

"I just keep hearing these vague rumors, man, that you're fucking my girlfriend, but there's like no proof." Damien keeps laughing. "So, you know, I'm *concerned*."

The goons are not laughing.

JD keeps studying his clipboard.

I'm inadvertently doing Kegels. "Oh man, that's so not true. I wouldn't touch her, I swear to God."

"Yeah." You can see him thinking things out. "You've got Chloe Byrnes. Why would you do Alison?" Damien sighs. "Chloe fucking Byrnes." Pause. "How do you do it, man?"

"Do . . . what?"

"Hey, Madonna once asked this guy for a date," Damien tells the bodyguards, who don't show it but in fact are impressed.

I smile sheepishly. "Well, dude, *you* dated Tatjana Patitz."

"Who?"

"The girl who got fucked to death on the table in *Rising Sun*."

"Ri-i-ight. But you're dating Chloe fucking Byrnes," Damien says, in awe. "How do you do it, man? What's your secret?"

"About . . . hey, um, I don't have any secrets."

"No, moron." Damien tosses a raisin at me. "Your secret with women."

"Um . . . never compliment them?" I squeak out.

"What?" Damien leans in closer.

"Not disinterested, exactly. If they ask tell them, y'know, their hair looks bleached. . . . Or if they ask tell them their nose is too wide. . . ." I'm sweating. "But, y'know, be careful about it. . . ." I pause faux-wistfully. "Then they're yours."

"Jesus Christ," Damien says admiringly, nudging one of the goons. "Did you hear that?"

"How's Alison?" I ask.

"Hell, you probably see her more than I do."

"Not really."

"I mean, don't you, Vic?"

"Oh, y'know, me and Chloe and, um, probably not, but whatever, never mind."

After a long and chilly silence, Damien points out, "You're not eating your muesli."

"Now I am," I say, lifting my spoon. "JD, some milk, please."

"Alison, oh shit," Damien groans. "I don't know whether she's a sexpot or a crackpot."

A flash: Alison sneering at me while letting Mr. Chow lick her feet, punching open a coconut, listing her favorite male movie stars under twenty-four, including the ones she's slept with, slugging down Snapple after Snapple after Snapple.

"Both?" I venture.

"Ah hell, I love her. She's like a rainbow. She's like a flower. Oh god," he moans. "She's got that damn navel ring, and the tattoos need serious laser sessions."

"I . . . didn't know Alison had a, um, navel ring."

"How *would* you know that?" he asks.

"Anywa-a-a-ay—" JD starts.

"I also hear you're looking at your own space." Damien sighs, staring right at me. "Please say I'm hearing abstract, unfortunate rumors."

"A *vicious* rumor, my friend. I'm *not* into even *con*templating another club, Damien. I'm looking at scripts now."

"Well, yeah, Victor, I know. It's just that we're getting a lot of press for this and I cannot deny that your name helps—"

"Thanks, man."

"—but I also cannot deny the fact that if you use this as—oh, what's a good phrase? oh yeah—a *stepping-stone* and will then dump all of us the minute this place is SRO and then with that *cachet* open up your own place—"

"Damien, wait a minute, this is a complex question, wait a minute—"

"—leaving me and several investors along with various orthodontists from Brentwood—one who happens to be part vegetable—who have placed big bucks into this—"

"Damien, man, where would I get the money to do this?"

"Japs?" He shrugs. "Some movie star you've boned? Some rich faggot who's after your ass?"

"This is what's known as *big news* to me, Damien, and I will ponder who leaked this rumor profusely."

"My heartfelt thanks."

"I just wanna put a smile back on clubland's face."

"I've gotta play golf," Damien says vacantly, checking his watch. "Then I'm having lunch at Fashion Café with Christy Turlington, who was just voted 'least likely to sell out' in the new issue of *Top Model*. There's a virtual-reality Christy at Fashion Café—you should check it out. It's called a spokesmannequin. It looks exactly like Christy. She says things like 'I look forward to seeing you here again soon, perhaps in person,' and she also quotes Somerset Maugham and discusses Salvadorian politics as well as her Kellogg cereal contract. I know what you're thinking, but she brings class to it."

Damien finally stands up, and the goons follow suit.

"Are you going to any of the shows today?" I ask. "Or is another Gotti on trial?"

"What? There's another one?" Damien realizes something. "Oh, you're kind of funny. But not really so much."

"Thank you."

"I'm going to shows. It's Fashion Week, what else does one do in this world?" Damien sighs. "You're in one, right?"

"Yeah. Todd Oldham. It's just guys who date models escorting them down the runway. Y'know, it's like a theme: Behind every woman—"

"There's a weasel? Ha!" Damien stretches. "Sounds fan-fucking-tastic. So you're ready for tonight?"

"Hey man, I am a rock. I am an island."

"Who's gonna dispute that?"

"That's me, Damien. All dos, and no don'ts."

"Are you down with OPP?"

"Hey, you know me."

"Crazy kid," he chuckles.

"Lucidity. Total lucidity, baby."

"I wish I knew what that meant, Victor."

"Three words, my friend: Prada, Prada, Prada."

26

On a small soon-to-be-hip block in TriBeCa and up a flight of not-too-steep stairs and through a dark corridor: a long bar made of granite, walls lined with distressed-metal sconces, a medium-sized dance floor, a dozen video monitors, a small alcove that can easily convert into a DJ booth, a room off to the side cries out for VIPs, mirror balls hang from a high ceiling. In other words: The Fundamentals. You see a flashing light and you think you are that flashing light.

"Ah," I sigh, looking around the room. "The club scene."

"Yes." JD nervously follows me around, both of us guzzling bottles of Diet Melonberry Snapple he bought us.

"There's something beautiful about it, JD," I say. "Admit it, you little mo. Admit it."

"Victor, I—"

"I know just inhaling my manly scent must make you want to faint."

"Victor, don't get too attached," JD warns. "I don't need to tell you that this club's going to have a short life span, that this is *all* a short-term business."

"*You're* a short-term business." I run my hands along the smooth granite bar: chills.

"And you put a lot of energy into it, and all the people who made it beautiful and interesting—hey, don't snicker—in the first place go somewhere else."

I yawn. "That sounds like a homosexual relationship."

"Sorry, darling, we got lost." Waverly Spear—our interior designer, dead ringer for Parker Posey—sweeps in wearing sunglasses, a clingy catsuit, a wool beret, followed by a hip-hop slut from hell and this dreadfully gorgeous mope-rocker wearing an I AM THE GOD OF FUCK T-shirt.

"Why so late, baby?"

"I got lost in the lobby of the Paramount," Waverly says. "I went *up* the stairs instead of going *down* the stairs."

"Ooh."

"Plus, well . . ." She rummages through her black-bowed rhinestone-dotted Todd Oldham purse. "Hurley Thompson's in town."

"Continue."

"Hurley Thompson is in town."

"But isn't Hurley Thompson supposed to be shooting the sequel to *Sun City 2*? *Sun City 3*?" I ask, vaguely outraged. "In *Phoenix*?"

Waverly moves away from her zombies and motions me toward her, pulling me from JD.

"Hurley Thompson, Victor, is in the Celine Dion Suite at the Paramount trying to persuade someone not to use a rubber as we speak."

"Hurley Thompson is *not* in Phoenix?"

"Certain people *know* this information." She lowers her voice gravely. "They just don't know the *why* of it."

"Does someone in this room? And don't tell me one of the idiots you brought."

"Let's just put it this way: Sherry Gibson can't shoot any more 'Baywatch Nights' for a while." Waverly puffs greedily on her cigarette.

"Sherry Gibson, Hurley Thompson—I dig the connection. Friends, lovahs, great PR."

"He's been freebasing so much that he had to leave the set of *SC3* after he beat Sherry Gibson up—yes, in the face—and Hurley is now registered under the assumed name Carrie Fisher at the Paramount."

"So he *is* quitting *Sun City*?"

"And Sherry Gibson resembles a weepy raccoon."

"Nobody knows this?"

"Nobody knows but moi."

"Who's Moi?"

"That means me, Victor."

"Our lips are sealed." I move away, clap my hands, startling the other people in the space, and walk toward the middle of the floor.

"Waverly, I want a minimal generic look. Sort of industrial-preppie."

"But with a touch of internationalism?" she asks, following, out of breath, lighting another Benson & Hedges Menthol 100.

"The '90s are honest, straightforward. Let's reflect that," I say, moving around. "I want something unconsciously classic. I want no distinctions between exterior and interior, formal and casual, wet and dry, black and white, full and empty—oh my god, get me a cold compress."

"You want simplicity, baby."

"I want a no-nonsense approach to nightlife." I light a Marlboro.

"Keep talking like that, baby, and we're on our way."

"To stay afloat, Waverly, you need to develop a reputation for being a good businessman *and* an all-around cool guy." I pause. "And I'm an all-around cool guy."

"And, ahem, a businessman?" JD asks.

"I'm too cool to answer that, baby," I say, inhaling. "Hey, did you see me on the cover of *YouthQuake?*"

"No, ah . . ." Waverly says, then realizes something and adds, "Oh, that was *you? You* looked great."

"Uh-huh," I say, somewhat dubiously.

"But I saw you at the Calvin Klein show, baby, and—"

"I wasn't at the Calvin Klein show, baby, and have you noticed that whole wall is the color of pesto, which is, like, a no-no, baby?"

"De rigueur," says the impeccably-put-together young thing behind her.

"Victor," Waverly says. "This is Ruby. She's a bowl designer. She makes bowls out of things like rice."

"A bowl designer? Wow."

"She makes bowls out of things like rice," Waverly says again, staring.

"Bowls made from rice? Wow." I stare back. "Did you hear me say 'wow'?"

Mope-rocker wanders over to the dance floor and looks up at the dozen or so disco balls, trancing out.

"What's the story with goblin boy?"

"Felix used to work at the Gap," Waverly says, inhaling, exhaling. "Then he designed sets for 'The Real World' in Bali."

"Don't mention that show to me," I say, gritting my teeth.

"Sorry, darling, it's so *early.* But please be nice to Felix—he's just out of rehab."

"What—he OD'd on stucco?"

"He's friends with Blowpop and Pickle and he just designed Connie Chung's, Jeff Zucker's, Isabella Rossellini's and Sarah Jessica Parker's, er, closets."

"Cool, cool." I nod approvingly.

"Last month he went and fucked his ex-boyfriend—Jackson—in the Bonneville salt flats and just three days ago they found Jackson's skull in a swamp, so, you know, let's be careful."

"Uh-huh. My god it's freezing in here."

"I see orange flowers, I see bamboo, I see Spanish doormen, I hear Steely Dan, I see Fellini." Waverly suddenly gasps, exhaling again, tapping her cigarette. "I see the '70s, baby, and I am wet."

"Baby, you're ashing on my club," I say, very upset.

"Now what about Felix's idea for a juice bar?"

"Felix is thinking about where he's going to score his next animal tranquilizer." I drop my cigarette carefully into the half-empty Snapple bottle

JD holds out. "Plus—oh god, baby, I don't want to have to fret over a juice bar that serves only—what—oh god—*juice*? Do you know how many things I have to worry about? Spare me."

"So *nix* the juice bar?" Waverly asks, taking notes.

"Oh please," I moan. "Let's sell submarine sandwiches, let's sell pizza, let's sell fucking *nachos*," I sigh. "You and Felix are being muy muy drippy."

"Baby, you are so right," Waverly says, mock-wiping sweat from her forehead. "We need to get our shit together."

"Waverly, listen to me. The new trend is no trend."

"No trend's a new trend?" she asks.

"No, *no* trend is *the* new trend," I say impatiently.

"In is out?" Waverly asks.

I smack JD on the shoulder. "See, *she* gets it."

"Look—goose bumps," JD says, holding out an arm.

"Lemons, lemons everywhere, Victor," Waverly says, twirling around.

"And Uncle Heshy is *not* invited, right, baby?"

"Sweet dreams are made of this, huh, Victor?" JD says, watching vacantly as Waverly twirls around the room.

"Do you think we were followed here?" I ask, lighting another cigarette, watching Waverly.

"If you have to ask that question, don't you think that opening this behind Damien's back is not, like, such a good idea?"

"Nonresponsive answer. I move to strike," I say, glaring at him. "Your idea of hip is missing the boat, buddy."

"I just don't think it's hip to have your legs broken," JD says warily. "Over a *club*? Have you ever heard the phrase 'Resist the impulse'?"

"Damien Nutchs Ross is a nonhuman primate," I sigh. "And your POV should be: sleeping person zzzzz."

"Why do you even *want* to open another club?"

"My *own* club."

"Let me guess. Bingo! Instant friends?" JD shivers, his breath steaming.

"Oh spare me. I see all this and think money-in-the-bank, you little mo."

"A guy needs a hobby, huh?"

"And you need some more Prozac to curb your homo-ness."

"And you need a major injection of reality."

"And you need coolin', baby, I'm not foolin'."

"Victor. We're not playing games here," JD asks, "are we?"

"No," I say. "We're going to the gym."

25 At a gym in the Flatiron District, in what last week became the most fashionable stretch of lower Fifth Avenue, my trainer, Reed, is being filmed for a segment on "Entertainment Tonight" about trainers for celebrities who are more famous than the celebrities they train, and in the gym now—which has no name, just a symbol and below that the motto "Weakness Is a Crime, Don't Be a Criminal"—beneath the row of video monitors showing episodes of "The Flintstones" and the low lighting from a crystal chandelier Matt Dillon, Toni Braxton, the sultan of Brunei's wife, Tim Jeffries, Ralph Fiennes—*all* in agony. A couple of male models, Craig Palmer and Scott Benoit, pissed off over something I said about Matt Nye's luck, semi-avoid me as they towel off in the Philippe Starck–designed changing room. Danny Errico from Equinox set the place up for Reed when the issue of *Playgirl* Reed appeared in sold something like ten million copies and he subsequently was dropped from the Gap's new ad campaign. Now Reed's costarring in a movie about a detective whose new partner is a pair of gibbons. Reed: $175 an hour and worth every goddamn penny (I stressed to Chloe), long blond hair *never* in a ponytail, light 'n' sexy stubble, naturally tan, silver stud in right ear, designer weight-belt, a body with muscles so well defined he looks skinned, license plate on his black BMW reads VARMINT, all the prerequisites. It's so freezing in the gym that steam rises from the lights the "ET" camera crew has set up.

The *Details* reporter arrives late. "Sorry, I got lost," she says vacantly, wearing a black cashmere sweater, white cotton shirt, white silk pants and, in true girl-reporter-from-*Details* fashion, tube-sock elbow pads and a bicycle-reflector armband. "I had to interview President Omar Bongo of Gabon and his cute nephew, um . . ." She checks her notepad. "Spencer."

"Ladies and gentlemen." Reed spreads his hands out, introducing me. "Victor Ward, the It Boy of the moment."

Mumbled "hey"s and a few "yeah"s come from the crew, who remain darkened behind the steaming lights set up in front of the StairMaster, and finally someone tiredly says, "We're rolling."

"Take those sunglasses off," Reed whispers to me.

"Not with those lights on, uh-uhn, spare me."

"I smell Marlboros," Reed says, pushing me toward the StairMaster. "You shouldn't smoke, baby, it takes years off your life."

"Yeah, my sixties, great. Don't wanna miss those."

"Ooh, you're tough. Come on—hop up here," Reed says, patting the side of the machine.

"I want calves and thighs and *definitely* abs today," I stress. "But no biceps," I warn. "They're getting too big."

"What? They're thirteen inches, baby." Reed sets the StairMaster to Blind Random, level 10.

"Isn't your T-shirt, uh, a little tight?" I ask, taunting.

"Arms are the new breasts," Reed intones.

"Oh, and look," I say, noticing a tiny blackhead. "You have a nipple."

"Cut," the segment director sighs.

"Victor," Reed warns. "Pretty soon I'm gonna bring up that bounced check of yours—"

"Hey, Chloe took care of the bill."

"This is a business, baby," Reed says, trying to smile. "*Not* a charity."

"Listen, if you need more work, I need bouncers."

"This *is* work, man."

"What? Being familiar with fitness equipment? Spare me."

"I already supplement my income, Victor."

"Listen, as long as the sex is safe I personally think being a male whore is cool—*if* it pays the bills."

Reed smacks me upside the head and growls, "We're doing squats today."

"And *abs*," I stress. "I have a photo shoot, baby."

"Okay," the director calls out. "We're running."

Automatically, without trying, Reed starts clapping his hands and shouts, "I want some strain, some pressure, some *sweat*, Victor. You're too tense, buddy. Out with that tension. In with some love."

"I've sworn off caffeine, Reed. I'm teaching myself how to relax by deep-sea visualization. I'm avoiding the urge to check my voice mail on a half-hourly basis. I'm hugging people left and right. And look." I reach under my CK T-shirt. "My new tranquillity beads."

"Far out, baby," Reed wails, clapping his hands together.

Looking into the camera, I say, "I've been to Radu and Pasquale Manocchia—that's Madonna's personal trainer, by the way, baby—and Reed is definitely the first name in celebrity training."

"I have an obsession with biceps, with triceps, with forearm flexors," Reed admits sheepishly. "I have a major sinewy-arm fetish."

"I have the endurance of a horse but my blood sugar's low and I need a Jolly Rancher badly."

"After the next song," Reed says, clapping endlessly. "PowerBar time, I promise."

Suddenly Primal Scream's "Come Together" blares out over the sound system. "Oh god," I moan. "This song is eight minutes and four seconds long."

"How do you know things like that?" the *Details* girl asks.

"The better you look, baby, the more you see," I pant. "Dat's my motto, homegirl." My beeper goes off and I check it: JD at the club.

"Reed, baby, hand me your cellular." I let go of the rails and dial, smiling into the camera. "Hey Leeza! Look, no hands!"

This causes Reed to push up the speed, which I thought was impossible because I didn't know StairMasters could go past level 10.

"Hey, am I invited to the dinner tonight?" Reed asks. "I didn't see my name mentioned in any of the columns."

"Yeah, you're at table 78 with the Lorax and Pauly Shore," I snap. "JD— talk to me."

"Now don't get too excited, Victor," JD says breathlessly. "But we've— myself, Beau and Peyton—set up an interview with DJ X."

"With who?"

"DJ X. You have a meeting with him at Fashion Café at five today," JD says. "He's willing to do the party tonight."

"I'm on a StairMaster now, baby." I'm trying not to pant. "What? Fashion Café?"

"Victor, DJ X is the hottest DJ in town," JD says. "Imagine the publicity and then come all over yourself. Go ahead—shoot that load."

"I know, I know. Just hire him," I say. "Tell him we'll pay anything he wants."

"He wants to meet with you first."

"Oh dear god."

"He needs some kind of reassurance."

"Send him a bag of candy corn. Send him some cute, extrasuckable pacifiers. Tell him you give excellent head . . . do you?"

"Victor," JD says, exasperated. "He won't do it without meeting you first. We need him here tonight. Do it."

"I'm taking commands from someone who uses the word 'dish' as a verb?" I yell. "Shut up."

"Fashion Café," JD says. "Five o'clock. I've checked your schedule. You can make it."

"JD, I'm in the middle of becoming some kind of brooding god," I groan. "I mean, is it too fucking much to ask—"

"Fashion Café at five. Bye, Victor." JD clicks off.

"JD—don't click off on me, don't you *dare* click off on me." I click off myself and blindly announce, "I'm suddenly seized by the need to climb."

"I think you've been doing that your whole life, buddy," Reed says sadly.

"You turned down a Reebok ad and that makes you tough?"

After "ET" films me doing a thousand crunches and I've moved over to the Treadwall, an indoor rock-climbing simulator where you stay in one place while climbing, I notice *Details* girl slouching against a wall, holding her pad under the debut issue of a new magazine called *Bubble*. It's so cold in the gym that it feels like I'm climbing a glacier.

"Jesus," I moan, noticing the magazine's cover. "Yeah, that's just great. Luke Perry's opinion of Kurt fucking Russell. We need more of that."

"So what's the story?" she asks vacantly. "Excited about tonight?"

"Remember what the dormouse said," I say cryptically, watching Dillon walk by slurping a powershake. "Hey Matt, rock on."

"You're really into this," *Details* girl says.

"What's wrong with looking good?"

She ponders this semi-thoughtfully. "Well, what if it's at the expense of something else? I'm not implying anything. It's just a hypothetical. Don't be insulted."

"I forgot the question."

"What if it's at the expense of something else?"

"What's . . . something else?"

"I see." She attempts to complete a facial expression I'd hoped she wouldn't.

"Hey baby, we're all in this together," I grunt, my hands dusted with chalk. "Yeah, I wanna give this all up and feed the homeless. I wanna give this all up and teach orangutans sign language. I'm gonna bike around the countryside with my *sketchbook*. I'm gonna—what? Help improve race relations in this country? Run for fucking President? Read my lips: Spare me."

24 By the time I arrive at Industria for today's photo shoot I'm getting that certain feeling of being followed, but whenever I look behind me it's only bicycle messengers carrying models' portfolios for Click, Next, Elite, so to stamp out the paranoia I duck into Braque to grab a not-too-foamy decaf latte with skim milk and Alison keeps beeping me as I move through an enormous series of white empty spaces. The guys—nine of us, some already in bathing suits—are just hanging: Nikitas, David Boals, Rick Dean, newcomer Scooter, a couple of guys I'm not really sure about, including a waiter from Jour et Nuit, hunky with dreadlocks, who's being followed around by a camera crew from "Fashion File," a pair of twins who work at Twins on the Upper East Side, plus some European guy who has arguably the best body here but a face like a donkey. All the guys basically look the same: cute head (one exception), great body, high hair, chiseled lips, cutting edge, naughty or however you want us.

While waiting my turn for eyebrow tweezing I browse through the CD library and make time with this girl eating rice and broccoli while getting a pedicure and the only word she knows is "Blimey!" and all over the place I'm sensing a distinct laissez-faire attitude, no more so than when I'm handed a stick of Wrigley's Doublemint gum by Stanford Blatch. The Caesar haircut has made another comeback and cowlicks are in which infuriates Bingo and Velveteen and the photographer Didier, so a lot of PhytoPlage gel is brought out while opera plays and to endure all this some of the guys drink champagne, check their horoscopes in the *Post*, play cat's cradle with dental floss. Madonna's ex–party planner Ronnie Davis, someone from Dolce & Gabbana, Garren (who did the hair at Marc Jacobs' and Anna Sui's last shows) and Sandy Gallin are hanging out, staring at us impassively, like we're for sale or something, and let's just face it—*as if.*

Three setups: Bermudas, Madras shorts and Speedos. The guys will be positioned in front of a huge blue drape and later a beach will be superimposed by Japanese technicians to make it look like we were actually on a beach, "maybe even one in Miami," Didier promises. Fake tattoos are applied on biceps, pectorals, on three thighs. It's freezing.

Bingo slaps gel on my scalp, wetting my hair, runs it through to the ends as Didier paces nearby, inspecting my abs, twenty-two and sucking on a pacifier. Dazed-looking Scooter—studying for his SATs—sits next to me on a high stool, both of us facing giant oval mirrors.

"I want sideburns," Bingo moans. "I need elongation."

"Forget about natural, Bingo," Didier says. "Just go for the edge."

"Doesn't anyone shampoo anymore?" Velveteen shudders. "My god."

"I want a rough style, Bingo. I want a bit of meanness. A hidden anger. There has to be a hidden anger. I want the aggressive side to this boy."

"Aggressive?" Bingo asks. "He's a pastry chef at Dean & Deluca."

"I want the aggressive-pastry-chef look."

"Didier, this boy is about as aggressive as a baby manatee."

"Oh god, Bingo—you're such a fussbudget," Velveteen sighs.

"Am I being challenged?" Didier asks, pacing. "I think not, because I'm getting bored very quickly."

"Velveteen," Bingo shouts. "You're mushing Scooter's do."

"Bingo, you're being a wee bit off."

"I want extreme," Didier says. "I want Red Hot Chili Peppers. I want energy."

"I want a big fat spleef," Scooter mutters.

"I want garish *and* sexy," Didier says.

"Let's usher that combo in, baby."

"I'm fizzy with excitement," Didier murmurs thoughtfully. "But where are these boys' sideburns? I requested sideburns. Bingo? Bingo, where are you?"

"*I* have sideburns?" I offer, raising my hand. "Uh, dude, that's facial moisturizer," I have to point out to Bingo.

"Not *too* in-your-face. Right, Didier?" Velveteen asks sourly. "Not *too* much of that hot Mambo King look."

We're all in front of the big blue drape, some of us doing bicep curls with free weights, a couple of us on the floor crunching, and Didier wants cigars and passes them out and Didier wants glycerin because the guys in Bermuda shorts should be crying while smoking cigars because we are sad and smoking cigars in front of the big blue drape which will be the beach.

"Sad *because* we are smoking cigars?" I ask. "Or sad because this is just too 'Baywatch'?"

"Sad because you are all idiots and just now on this beach you have realized it," Didier says vaguely, ready to Polaroid.

Scooter looks at his cigar wonderingly.

"Do to that what you did to get this job," I tell him. "Suck on it."

Scooter goes pale. "How . . . did you know?"

"David—remove the nicotine patch," Didier calls out from behind the camera.

"My girlfriend sees this," Scooter moans, "and she's gonna think I'm gay."

"You still with Felicia?" Rick asks him.

"No, this is some girl I met in the bathroom in the lobby of the Principe di Savoia," Scooter says blankly. "I was lost and she looked like Sandra Bullock. Or so they say."

"What's her name?" David asks.

"Shoo Shoo."

"Shoo Shoo what?"

"No apparent last name."

"How did you lose the CK job, man?" Nikitas asks him.

"Calvin got pissed," Scooter says. "I cut my hair, but it's considerably more, er, complex than that."

Silence, a considerable pause, heavy nodding, the camera crew from "Fashion File" still circling.

"Believe me," I say, holding up my hands, "Calvin and I have tussled many a time." I do a few more bicep curls. "*Many a time.*"

"He gave you pretty good seats for the show, though," David says, stretching his calf muscles.

"That's because Chloe was in it," Rick says.

"I wasn't at the Calvin Klein show," I say calmly, then shout, "I *wasn't* at the fucking Calvin Klein show."

"There's a picture of you at the show in WWD, baby," Rick says. "You're with David and Stephen. In the second row."

"Someone find me that photo and you shall be proven wrong," I intone, rubbing my biceps, freezing. "Second row my ass."

One of the twins is reading today's WWD and cautiously hands it to me. I grab it and find the photos taken at yesterday's shows. It's not a clear photograph: Stephen Dorff, David Salle and myself, all wearing '50s knit shirts and sunglasses, slouching in our seats, stone-faced. Our names are in bold type beneath the photo, and after mine, as if an explanation was necessary, the words "It Boy." A bottle of champagne topples from a table, someone calls out for a shawalla.

"So what's the story, Victor?" David asks. "Let me get this straight. You *weren't* at the show? You're *not* in that photo? Let me guess—that's Jason Gedrick."

"Isn't anybody going to ask how the club's going?" I finally ask, thrusting the paper back at the twin, suddenly indignant over this fact.

"Um, how's the club going, Victor?" the other twin asks.

"I want to rock 'n' roll all night and party every day."

"Why wasn't I invited to the opening?" Rick asks.

"I—want—to—rock-'n'-roll—all—night—and—party—every—day." I grab the WWD back from the twin and study the photo again. "This must be a mistake. This must be from another show. In fact, that *must* be Jason Gedrick."

"What other shows have you been to this week?" someone asks.

"None," I finally murmur.

"When you stop orbiting around Jupiter, let us know, okay?" David says, patting me on the back. "And Jason Gedrick's in Rome shooting *Summer Lovers II*, baby."

"I'm in the here *and* the now, baby."

"That's not what I hear," Nikitas says, crunching.

"I'm not really interested in what information you're able to process," I tell him.

"Everything cool with you and Baxter and Chloe?" David asks this casually and Nikitas and Rick manage sly grins, which of course I notice.

"It's so cool it's icy, baby." I pause. "Er . . . what do you mean, O Wise One?"

The three of them seem confused and their expressions lead me to believe that they expected an admission of some kind.

"Um, well . . . ," Rick stammers. "It's, well, y'know . . ."

"Please," I groan. "If you're going to hand out shitty gossip about me, at least make it fast."

"Did you ever see the movie *Threesome?*" David ventures.

"Uh-huh, uh-huh, uh-huh."

"Story is that Chloe, Baxter and Victor are intrigued by that premise."

"We are not speaking of Baxter Priestly, are we, gentlemen?" I ask. "Surely we are not speaking of that little mo waif."

"*He's* the mo?"

"I mean, I know you're a hip guy, Victor," David says. "I think it's like cool, really cool."

"Wait a minute, wait a minute." I hold my hands up in front of me. "If you think for one *second* I'd *share* Chloe—Chloe *Byrnes*—with that pipsqueak . . . oh baby, spare me."

"Who said *you're* sharing anybody, Victor?" someone asks.

"What does that mean?"

"Who said it was your idea?" David asks. "Who said you were happy about it?"

"How can I not be happy about something that's not happening?" I glare.

"We're just telling you what's out on the street."

"*What* street? What street do you live on, David?"

"Uh . . . Ludlow."

"Uh . . . Ludlow," I mimic without trying.

"Victor, how can we believe you about anything?" Rick asks. "You say you weren't at the CK show, but there you were. Now you say you're not involved in a heavy ménage with Baxter and Chloe, yet word around town—"

"What else have you fucking heard?" I snap, waving a light meter out of my face. "I dare you, come on, I dare you."

"That you're fucking Alison Poole?" David shrugs.

I just stare for a couple seconds. "Enough, enough. I'm *not* seeing Alison Poole."

"The straight face is impressive, dude."

"I'm gonna ignore that because I don't fight with girls," I tell David. "Besides, that's a dangerous rumor for you to spread. Dangerous for her. Dangerous for me. Dangerous for —"

"Just go with it, Victor," David sighs. "Like I really even care."

"You'll be folding twenty-dollar sweaters at the Gap soon enough anyway," I mutter.

"My little minnows," Didier calls out. "It's time."

"Say, shouldn't David have like some beach moss or some kind of sand covering his face?" I ask.

"Okay, Victor," Didier calls out from behind the camera. "I'm looking at you like you're naked, baby."

"Didier?" one of the twins says. "I *am* naked."

"I'm looking at you like you're naked, Victor, and *you love it*." A longish pause while Didier studies the twin, then he decides something. "Make me chase you."

"Uh, Didier?" I call out. "*I'm* Victor."

"Dance around and yell 'pussy.'"

"Pussy," we all mumble.

"Louder!" Didier shouts.

"Pussy!"

"Louder!"

"*Pussy!*"

"Fantastic yet not so good."

Speedos after Bermudas, baseball caps are positioned backward, lollipops are handed out, Urge Overkill is played, Didier hides the Polaroid, then sells it to the highest bidder lurking in the shadows, who writes a check for it with a quill pen. One of the boys has an anxiety attack and another drinks too much Taittinger and admits he's from Appalachia, which causes someone to call out for a Klonopin. Didier insists we cup our balls and finally incorporates the camera crew from "Fashion File" into the photo shoot and then everyone except me and the guy who fainted go off for an early lunch at a new spot in SoHo called Regulation.

23 Moving fast through autumn light up the stairs toward the offices at the top of the club, Rollerblades slung over my shoulder, a camera crew on the third floor from (unfortunately) VH1 interviewing power-florist Robert Isabell and the way everyone dresses makes you realize that lime and Campbell's-soup orange are *the* most conspicuous new colors of the season and ultra–lounge music from the band I, Swinger floats around through the air like confetti saying "it's spring" and "time to come dancing" and violets and tulips and dandelions are everywhere and the whole enterprise is shaping up into everything one wants: cool without trying. In the office photos of pecs and tanned abs and thighs and bone-white butts are plastered over an entire wall along with an occasional face—everyone from Joel West to Hurley Thompson to Marky Mark to Justin Lazard to Kirk Cameron (for god's sake) to Freedom Williams to body parts that could or could not be mine—here in JD and Beau's inner sanctum, and though it seems like I'm tearing down Joey Lawrence 8 × 10s on a daily basis, they're always replaced, all the guys so similar-looking it's getting tougher and tougher to tell them apart. Eleven publicists will work this party tonight. I bitch to Beau about croutons for seven minutes. Finally JD walks in with E-mail printouts, hundreds of faxes, nineteen requests for interviews.

"Has my agent called?" I ask.

"What do you think?" JD snorts, and then, "Agent for *what*?"

"Loved that piece you wrote for *Young Homo*, JD," I tell him, going over the newly revised 10:45 guest list.

"Which one was that, Victor?" JD sighs, flipping through faxes.

"The one called 'Help! I'm Addicted to Guys!'"

"Point being?" Beau asks.

"Just that you are both very *un*heterosexual," I say, stretching.

"I might be a homo, Victor." JD yawns. "But I'm still a man—a man with feelings."

"You are a homo, JD, and I don't want to hear another word about it." I'm shaking my head at the new pinups—of Keanu, Tom Cruise, various Bruce Weber shots, Andrea Boccaletti, Emery Roberts, Jason Priestley,

Johnny Depp, my nemesis Chris O'Donnell—covering the wall above their desk. "Jesus, it takes nothing to get you little mos turned on. A good bod, a nice face—Christ."

"Victor," Beau says, handing me a fax. "I know for a fact that you've slept with guys in the past."

I move into my office, looking for some Snapple or a joint. "I dealt with that whole hip bi thing for about three hours back in college." I shrug. "Big deal. But now it's strictly the furburger era for me."

"Like that plastic vagina Alison Poole's a big improvement over—who?—Keanu Reeves?" JD says, following me.

"Dude, Keanu and I have *never* gotten it on," I say, moving over to the stereo. "We're just 'good friends.'" I'm scanning my CD rack: Elastica, Garbage, Filter, Coolio, Pulp. I slip Blur in. "Did you know that Keanu in Hawaiian means 'cool ocean breeze' and he won the Japanese Oscar for his role as the FBI agent turned surfer in *Point Break*?" I preprogram tracks 2, 3 and 10. "Jesus—and we're *afraid* of the Japanese?"

"You have got to stop having sex with Damien's girlfriend, Victor," Beau blurts out, whimpering. "It makes us nerv—"

"Oh shit," I groan, throwing a CD case at him.

"If Damien finds out he will *kill* us, Victor."

"He'll kill *you* if he finds out I'm really opening up my own club," I say carefully. "*You* will be implicated *no matter what.* Just, um, slide into it."

"Oh Victor, your nonchalance is so cool."

"First of all I don't understand why you little mos think I'd be fucking Damien's girlfriend in the first—"

"And you lie so well too."

"Hey—who the hell's been listening to *ABBA Gold*? Oh wait—let me guess."

"Victor, we don't trust Damien," Beau says. "Or Digby or Duke."

"Shhh," I say, holding a finger up to my lips. "This place could be bugged."

"That's not funny, Victor," JD says grimly. "It could be."

"How many times do I have to tell you guys that this town is filled with horrible human beings?" I groan. "Get—used—to—it."

"Digby and Duke are cute, Victor, but so wasted on steroids that it would make them quite happy to beat the living shit out of you," Beau says, then adds, "As if you didn't need it."

I check my watch. "My father's gonna do that to me in about fifteen minutes, so spare me," I sigh, flopping onto the couch. "Listen, Digby and Duke are just Damien's, er, friends. They're like bouncers— What?"

"Mob, baby," JD says.

"Oh Jesus," I moan. "The mob? For who? Banana Republic?"

"Mob, Victor." Beau nods in agreement.

"Oh hell, they're bouncers, guys." I sit up. "Feel sorry for them. Imagine dealing with cokeheads and tourists for a living. Pity them."

Beau loses it. "Pity *you*, Victor, once Damien sees that goddamn photo of you—ouch!"

"I saw you step on Beau's foot," I say to JD very carefully, staring over at them.

"Who are you protecting, JD?" Beau gasps. "He *should* know. It's true. It's gonna happen."

I'm up off the couch. "I thought this was all taken care of, JD."

"Victor, Victor—" JD holds his hands up.

"Tell me *now*. What, where, when, who?"

"Did anyone catch that he didn't ask the most important question: why?"

"Who told you there's a photo? Richard? Khoi? Reba?"

"Reba?" JD asks. "Who in the fuck is *Reba*?"

"Who was it, JD?" I slap at one of his hands.

"It was Buddy. Get away from me."

"At the *News*?"

Beau nods solemnly. "Buddy at the *News*."

"And Buddy says . . ."

I motion for him to go on.

"Um, your fears about a certain photo are, um, 'intact' and the, um . . ." JD squints at Beau.

"Probability rate," Beau says.

"Right. The probability rate is that it will, um . . ." JD squints over at Beau again.

"Be published," Beau whispers.

"Be published are, um . . ." JD pauses. "Oh yeah, 'up there.'"

Silence, until I clear my throat and open my eyes. "How long were you going to wait until you fed me this tidbit of info?"

"I paged you the minute this rumor was verified."

"Verified by who?"

"I don't divulge my sources."

"When?" I'm groaning. "Okay? How about *when*?"

"There really is no when, Victor." JD swallows nervously. "I just confirmed what you wanted me to. The photo exists. Of what? I can only guess by your, um, description yesterday," JD says. "And here's Buddy's number."

A long pause, during which Blur plays and I'm glancing around the office, finally touching a plant.

"And, um, Chloe called and said she wants to see you before Todd's show," JD says.

"What did you tell her?" I sigh, looking at the phone number JD handed me.

"'Your poorly dressed bitter half is having lunch with his father at Nobu.'"

"I'm being reminded of a bad lunch I haven't even had yet?" I cringe. "Jesus, what a day."

"And she says thanks for the flowers."

"What flowers?" I ask. "And will you puh-leeze stop staring at my bulge?"

"Twelve white French tulips delivered backstage at the Donna Karan show."

"Well, thank you for sending them for me, JD," I mutter, moving back to the couch. "There *is* a reason I'm paying you two dollars an hour."

Pause. "I didn't . . . send the flowers, Victor."

Pause. My turn. "Well, *I* didn't send the flowers."

Pause. "There was a card, Victor. It said, 'Ain't no woman like the one I've got' and 'Baby, I'm-a want you, Baby, I'm-a need you.'" JD looks at the floor, then back at me. "That sounds like you."

"I can't deal with this right now." I wave my arms around but then realize who might have sent the flowers. "Listen, do you know this kid named Baxter Priestly?"

"He's the next Michael Bergin."

"Who's the last Michael Bergin?"

"Baxter Priestly's in the new Darren Star show and in the band Hey That's My Shoe. He's dated Daisy Fuentes, Martha Plimpton, Liv Tyler and Glenda Jackson, though not necessarily in that order."

"Beau, I'm on a lot of Klonopin right now, okay, so nothing you're saying is really registering with me."

"Cool, that's cool, Victor."

"What do I do about Baxter Priestly?" I moan. "He of the faggy cheekbones."

"You jealous fuck," Beau hisses.

"What do you mean, what do *you* do about him?" JD asks. "I mean, I know what *I'd* do."

"Amazing cheekbones," Beau says sternly.

"Yeah, but what a lunkhead. *And* I don't want to suck him off," I mutter. "Hand me that fax."

"What does Baxter Priestly have to do with anything?"

"Enrolling him in a total-immersion English course wouldn't hurt. Oh shit—I've got to get going. Let's get down to business." I squint at the fax. "Does Adam Horowitz go under Ad-Rock or Adam Horowitz?"

"Adam Horowitz."

"Okay, what's this? New RSVPs?"

"People requesting to be invited."

"Shoot. Run through 'em."

"Frank De Caro?"

"No. Yes. No. Oh god, I can't do this now."

"Slash and Lars Ulrich are coming together," JD says.

"And from MTV, Eric Nies and Duff McKagan," Beau adds.

"Okay, okay."

"Chris Isaak is a yes, right?" JD asks.

"The perfect cutie," Beau says.

"He's got ears like Dumbo, but whatever. I guess I'd do him if I was a fag," I sigh. "Is Flea under *F* or does he have like a real name?"

"It doesn't matter," JD says. "Flea's coming with Slash and Lars Ulrich."

"Wait a minute," I say. "Isn't Axl coming with Anthony?"

"I don't think so." Beau and JD look at each other uncertainly.

"*Don't* tell me Anthony Kiedes isn't coming," I groan.

"He's coming, Victor, he's coming," Beau says. "Just not with Axl."

"Queen Latifah? Under *Q* or *L*?" JD asks.

"Wait," I exclaim, while going over the *L*s. "Lypsinka's coming? What did I tell you guys: we don't want *any* drag queens."

"Why not?"

"They're like the new mimes, that's why."

"Lypsinka is *not* a drag queen, Victor," Beau scolds me. "Lypsinka is a gender illusionist."

"And you're a little mo," I snarl, ripping down a photo of Tyson in a Ralph Lauren ad. "Did I ever tell you that?"

"And you're a fucking racist," Beau shouts, grabbing the crumpled page from me.

I immediately pull out a Malcolm X cap I got at the premiere—signed by Spike Lee—and shove it in JD's face. "See? Malcolm X cap. Don't accuse *me* of not being multicultural, you little mo."

"Paul Verhoeven said *God* is bisexual, Victor."

"Paul Verhoeven is a Nazi and *not* invited."

"You're a Nazi, Victor," Beau sneers. "*You're* the Nazi."

"I'm a pussy Nazi, you little mo, and you invited Jean-Claude Van Damme *behind my back*?!?"

"Kato Kaelin's publicist, David Crowley, keeps calling."

"Invite David Crowley."

"Oh, people like Kato, Victor."

"Have they seen his last movie, *Dr. Skull*?"

"It doesn't matter: people totally lock on to the hair."

"Speaking of: George Stephanopoulos."

"Who? Snuffleupagus?"

"No. George—"

"I heard you, I heard you," I groan dismissively. "*Only* if he's coming with someone recognizable."

"But Victor—"

"Only if"—I check my watch—"between now and nine he gets back together with Jennifer Jason Leigh or Lisa Kudrow or Ashley Judd or someone more famous."

"Um—"

"Damien will have a fit, JD, if he shows up solo."

"Damien keeps reminding me, Victor, that he wants a little politics, a little class."

"Damien wanted to hire MTV dancers and I talked him out of *that*," I shout. "How long do you think it'll take me to make him eighty-six that little Greek?"

JD looks at Beau. "Is this cool or useless? I'm not sure."

I clap my hands together. "Let's just finish the late RSVPs."

"Lisa Loeb?"

"Oh, this will certainly be a glittering success. Next."

"James Iha—guitarist from Smashing Pumpkins."

"Billy Corgan would've been better, but okay."

"George Clooney."

"Oh, he's so alive and wild. Next."

"Jennifer Aniston and David Schwimmer?"

"Blah blah blah."

"Okay, Victor—we need to go over the Bs, and Ds, and the Ss."

"Feed me."

"Stanford Blatch."

"Oh dear god."

"Grow up, Victor," JD says. "He owns like half of Savoy."

"Invite whoever owns the other half."

"Victor, the Weinstein brothers love him."

"That guy is so gross he'd work in a pet store just so he could eat free rabbit shit."

"Andre Balazs?"

"With Katie Ford, yes."

"Drew Barrymore?"

"Yes—and dinner too."

"Gabriel Byrne?"

"Without Ellen Barkin, yes."

"David Bosom?"

"Okay, but party only."

"Scott Benoit?"

"Party only."

"Leilani Bishop."

"Party."

"Eric Bogosian."

"Has a show. Can't make dinner. Will come to the party."

"Brandy."

"Jesus, Beau, she's sixteen."

"'Moesha' is a hit and the record's gone platinum."

"She's in."

"Sandra Bernhard."

"Party only."

"Billy, Stephen and/or Alec Baldwin."

"Dinner, party only, dinner."

"Boris Becker."

"Uh-huh. Oh my god, this is sounding more and more like a Planet Hollywood opening you'd never want to eat at," I sigh. "Am I reading this fax right? *Lisa Bonet?*"

"If Lenny Kravitz comes, she won't."

"Is Lenny Kravitz coming?"

"Yes."

"Cross her off."

"Tim Burton."

"Oh god I'm hot!"

"Halle Berry."

"Check."

"Hamish Bowles."

"Uh-huh."

"Toni Braxton."

"Yes."

"Ethan Brown?"

"Oh, I don't care what's real anymore," I moan, and then, "Party only."

"Matthew Broderick."

"Dinner if he's with Sarah Jessica Parker."

"Yes. Antonio Banderas."

"Do you know what Antonio said to Melanie Griffith when they first met?"

"'My *deeck* is *beeger* than Don's'?"

"'So you are Melanie. I am Antonio. How are you doing?'"

"He's got to stop telling interviewers that he's 'not silly.'"

"Ross Bleckner."

"Check."

"Michael Bergin."

"Check it out—right, guys?"

"David Barton?"

"Oh, I do hope he comes with Suzanne wearing something cute by Raymond Dragon," I squeal. "Party only."

"Matthew Barney."

"Yes."

"Candace Bushnell."

"Yes."

"Scott Bakula."

"Yes."

"Rebecca Brochman."

"Who's that?"

"The Kahlúa heiress."

"Fine."

"Tyra Banks."

"It's all I can do to just hold myself until I calm down."

"Yasmine Bleeth."

"I am *shuddering* with pleasure."

"Christian Bale."

"Uh-huh."

"Gil Bellows."

"Who?"

"He's famous in a, um, certain universe."

"You mean area code."

"You mean zip code. Proceed."

"Kevin Bacon."

"Fine, fine. But please, where's Sandra Bullock?" I ask.

"Her publicist said . . ." Beau pauses.

"Yes, go on."

"She doesn't know," JD finishes.

"Oh Jesus."

"Victor, don't scrunch your face up," Beau says. "You've gotta learn that it's more important to these people to be invited than to actually show up."

"No," I snap, pointing a finger. "People just really need to learn how to embrace their celebrity status."

"Victor—"

"Alison Poole *said* Sandra Bullock *was* coming, *is* coming—"

"When did you talk to Alison?" JD asks. "Or should I even be asking?"

"Don't ask why, JD," Beau says.

"Oh shit." JD shrugs. "What could be cooler than cheating on Chloe Byrnes?"

"Hey, watch it, you little mo."

"Is it because Camille Paglia once wrote eight thousand words on Chloe and not *once* mentioned you?"

"That bitch," I mutter, shuddering. "Okay, let's do the Ds."

"Beatrice Dalle."

"She's shooting that Ridley Scott movie in Prussia with Jean-Marc Barr."

"Barry Diller."

"Yes."

"Matt Dillon."

"Yes."

"Cliff Dorfman."

"Who?"

"Friend of Leonardo's."

"DiCaprio?"

"He will be wearing Richard Tyler and red velvet slippers and bringing Cliff Dorfman."

"Robert Downey, Jr."

"Only if he does his Chaplin! Oh please please get Downey to do his Chaplin!"

"Willem Dafoe."

"Party."

"Michael Douglas."

"Not coming. But Diandra is."

"I have assiduously followed the shattered path of their marriage. Check."

"Zelma Davis."

"I do not think I can control myself much longer."

"Johnny Depp."

"With Kate Moss. Dinner, yes."

"Stephen Dorff."

"Stephen"—I start, hesitantly—"Dorff. I mean, *why* are these people *stars*?"

"DNA? Dumb luck?"

"Proceed."

"Pilar and Nesya Demann."

"Of course."

"Laura Dern."

"Yikes!"

"Griffin Dunne."

"No party is complete."

"Meghan Douglas."

"Somebody needs to hose—me—down."

"Patrick Demarchelier."

"Yes."

"Jim Deutsch."

"Who?"

"A.k.a. Skipper Johnson?"

"Oh right, right."

"Shannen Doherty is coming with Rob Weiss."

"A special couple." I'm nodding like a baby.

"Cameron Diaz."

"What about Michael DeLuca?"

"Yes."

"Great. Let's move on to the Ss."

"Alicia Silverstone is a yes."

"Fan-fucking-tastic."

"Sharon Stone is a maybe, though it 'looks likely.'"

"On and on and on—"

"Greta Scacchi, Elizabeth Saltzman, Susan Sarandon—"

"Tim Robbins too?"

"Let me cross-reference—um, wait, wait—yes."

"Faster."

"Ethan Steifel, Brooke Shields, John Stamos, Stephanie Seymour, Jenny Shimuzu—"

"Okay, okay—"

"David Salle, Nick Scotti—"

"More, more, more—"

"Sage Stallone."

"Why don't we just invite the fucking Energizer bunny? Go on."

"Markus Schenkenberg, Jon Stuart, Adam Sandler—"

"But *not* David Spade."

"Wesley Snipes and Lisa Stansfield."

"Okay, my man."

"Antonio Sabato, Jr., Ione Skye—"

"She's bringing the ghost of River Phoenix with her," Beau adds. "I'm serious. She demanded that it be put on the list."

"That's so fucking hip I want it faxed to the *News* immediately."

"Michael Stipe—"

"Only if he doesn't keep flashing that damn hernia scar."

"Oliver Stone, Don Simpson, Tabitha Soren—"

"Oh boy, we're in the hot zone now."

"G. E. Smith, Anna Sui, Tanya Sarna, Andrew Shue—"

"*And* Elisabeth Shue?"

"And Elisabeth Shue."

"Great. Okay, what are we playing during cocktails?" Beau asks as I start walking out the door.

"Start with something mellow. An Ennio Morricone soundtrack or Stereolab or even something ambient. Get the idea? Burt Bacharach. Then let's move on to something more aggressive but unobtrusive, though *not* elevator music."

"Space-age bachelor-pad Muzak?"

"Mood sounds?" I'm flying down to the fourth floor.

"Some Polynesia tiki-tiki or crime jazz." JD flies after me.

"Basically an ultralounge cocktail mix."

"Remember, you have a meeting with DJ X at Fashion Café," Beau calls down. "At five!"

"Any news from Mica?" I call up from the third floor, where it's freezing and a couple of flies merrily buzz past.

"No. But Fashion Café at five o'clock, Victor!" Beau shouts out.

"Why hasn't anyone found Mica yet?" I shout, moving farther down into the club.

"Victor," JD shouts from behind me. "Can you tell the difference between a platitude and a platypus?"

"One's a . . . beaver?"

"Which *one*?"

"Oh god, this is hard," I moan. "Where's my publicist?"

22 My father sent a car to "insure my presence" at lunch, so I'm now in the backseat of a Lincoln Town Car trying to get Buddy at the *News* on my cell phone, the driver traversing noontime traffic on Broadway, sometimes stuck in place, heading down to Nobu, passing another poster of Chloe in a bus shelter, an ad for some kind of Estée Lauder light-diffusing makeup, and the sun glints so hard off the trunk of a limousine in front of us that it traumatizes my eyes with a hollow pink burn and even through the tinted windows I have to slip on a pair of Matsuda sunglasses, passing the new Gap on Houston, adults playing hopscotch, somewhere Alanis Morissette sings sweetly, two girls drifting along the sidewalk wave at the Town Car in slow motion and I'm offering the peace sign, too afraid to turn around to see if Duke and Digby are following. I light a cigarette, then adjust a microphone that's hidden beneath the collar of my shirt.

"Hey, no smoking," the driver says.

"What are you gonna do? Just keep driving. Jesus."

He sighs, keeps driving.

Finally Buddy clicks on, sounds like accidentally.

"Buddy—Victor. What's the story?"

"Confirm this rumor for me: Are you dating Stephen Dorff?"

"Spare me, Buddy," I groan. "Let's make a deal."

"Shoot," he sighs.

I pause. "Wait. I just, um, hope I'm still not on your guys-I-wanna-fuck list."

"No, you already have a boyfriend."

"Stephen Dorff is *not* my goddamn boyfriend," I shout.

The driver eyes me in the rearview mirror. I lean forward and bang on the back of his seat. "Is there like a divider or partition or something that separates *me* from *you*?"

The driver shakes his head.

"What have you got, Victor?" Buddy sighs.

"Baby, rumor has it that in your possession is a picture of, um, well, me."

"Victor, I've got about a million."

"No. A specific picture."

"Specific? A *specific* picture? I don't think so, pookie."

"It's of me and a, um, certain girl."

"Who? Gwyneth Paltrow? Irina? Kristin Herold? Cheri Oteri?"

"No," I shout. "Goddamnit—it's of me and Alison Poole."

"*You* and Alison *Poole*? Doing—ahem—*what*?"

"Having a little iced latte while playing footsie on the Internet, you raging fuckhead."

"Alison Poole—as in Damien Nutchs Ross's girlfriend? *That* Alison Poole?"

"She's also fucking like half the Knicks, so I'm not alone."

"A naughty boy. Living on the edge. Not so nice."

"What is that—Bon Jovi's greatest hits? Listen to—"

"I assume this photo was taken with Mr. Ross's and Miss Byrne's permission and approval, you nonethical little bastard."

"*Me* nonethical?" I choke. "Whoa—wait a minute. *You* peddled Robert Maxwell's autopsy photos, you scumbag. *You* had fucking Polaroids of Kurt Cobain's blown-apart skull. *You* had shots of River Phoenix convulsing on Sunset. *You*—"

"*I* also gave you your first break in the media, you ungrateful little shit."

"And you're totally, totally right. Listen, I wasn't putting you down. I meant to say I was impressed."

"Victor, you get written about, mainly by me, for doing nothing."

"No, man, I mean it, take it to the limit, that's *my* motto, so y'know—"

"Successful sucking up requires talent. Or at least a species of charm that you simply do not possess."

"Bottom line: what can I give you in exchange for the photo?"

"What have you got? And let's make this fast. I'm about to be interviewed by 'A Current Affair.'"

"Well, um, what do you want to, like, know?"

"Is Chloe dating Baxter Priestly and are you all involved in some kind of hot sicko threesome?"

"Oh shit, man—*no*. For the last time—*no*," I groan. And then, after Buddy's suspicious pause, "And I'm *not* dating Stephen Dorff."

"Why is Chloe doing so much runway work this season?"

"Oh, that's easy: it's her last year as a runway model. It's her big farewell, so to speak," I sigh, relieved.

"Why is Baxter Priestly at all her shows?"

I suddenly sit up and shout into the phone, "Who *is* this little shit?" Trying to relax, I shift modes. "Hey Buddy—what about, um, Winona?"

"What about Winona?"

"She's, um, y'know, coming to the opening tonight."

"Well, that's an auspicious start, Victor. Oh sorry, my ass just yawned. Who's she with?" he sighs.

"Dave Pirner and the Wrigley's Doublemint gum heiress and the bassist from Falafel Mafia."

"Doing what? Where?"

"At the Four Seasons, discussing why *Reality Bites* didn't open bigger."

"My ass is yawning again."

I pause, staring hard out the window. "Hurley Thompson," I finally say, hoping he'll let it pass.

"Now I'm vaguely enthralled."

"Um, oh shit, Buddy . . ." I stop. "This is *totally* not from me."

"I never reveal my sources, so please just tell your master what's going on."

"Just that, y'know, Hurley's, like, in town."

Pause. "I'm getting a little hot." The sound of computer keys clicking, and then, "Where?"

Pause. "Paramount."

"You're stroking my boner," Buddy says. "Why isn't he in Phoenix shooting *Sun City* 3 with the rest of the cast?"

Pause. "Um, Sherry Gibson . . ."

"I'm getting hot. You're getting me very very hot, Victor."

"She . . . dumped him . . ."

"I'm rock hard. Continue."

"Because of . . . a freebasing problem. His."

"You're gonna make me come."

"And he, um, beat . . . Sherry up."

"I'm coming, Victor—"

"And so Sherry had to drop out of 'Baywatch Nights'—"

"I'm shooting my load—"

"Because her face is all messed up—"

"I'm coming I'm coming I'm—"

"And he is now looking for a rehab clinic in the Poconos—"

"Oh god, I've shot my load—"

"And Sherry resembles a, um, oh yeah, 'weepy raccoon.'"

"I've shot my load. Can you hear me panting?"

"You motherfucker," I whisper.

"This is cosmic."

"Buddy, I feel like we've become very close."

"Where's Hurley's brother? Curley?"

"He hung himself."

"Who was at the funeral?"

"Julia Roberts, Erica Kane, Melissa Etheridge, Lauren Holly and, um, Salma Hayek."

"Didn't she date his dad?"

"Yeah."

"So he was in and out of the picture?"

"So no photo, Buddy?"

"The photo of you and Alison Poole has vanished."

"For the record, what was it of?"

"For the record? You don't want to know."

"You know, Buddy, Alison just lost the role in the film version of *The Real Thing*," I add, "for what it's worth."

"Which is nada. Thank you, Victor. 'A Current Affair' has arrived."

"No—thank *you*, Buddy. And please, this was *not* from me." I pause, then realize something and shout, "Don't say it, don't—"

"Trust me." Buddy clicks off.

21 Nobu before noon and I'm biting off half a Xanax while passing what's got to be Dad's limo parked out front, and inside: various executives from MTV, a new maître d' being interviewed by "The CBS Morning News," Helena Christensen, Milla Jovovich and the French shoe designer Christian Louboutin at one table, and at another Tracee Ross, Samantha Kluge, Robbie Kravitz and Cosima Von Bulow, and Dad is the thin Waspish dude wearing the navy-blue Ralph Lauren suit sitting in the second booth from the front doodling notes on a yellow legal pad, a folder lying thick and suspicious next to a bowl of sunomono. Two of his aides have the front booth. He should look middle-aged but with the not-too-recent face-lift and since according to my sister he's been on Prozac since April (a secret), everything is vaguely cool. For relaxation: hunting deer, an astrologer to deal with those planetary vibes, squash. And his nutritionist has stressed raw fish, brown rice, *no* tempura but hijiki is okay and I'm basically here for some toro sashimi, some jokey conversation and a charming inquiry about some cash. He smiles, bright caps.

"Sorry, Dad, I got lost."

"You look thin."

"It's all those drugs, Dad," I sigh, sliding into the booth.

"That's not funny, Victor," he says wearily.

"Dad, I don't do drugs. I'm in great shape."

"No, really. How are you, Victor?"

"I'm a knockout, Dad. A total knockout. I'm rippin'. Things are happening. I'm in control of all the elements. You are laughing somewhat jaggedly, Dad, but I am in continuous flux."

"Is that right?"

"I'm staking out new territory, Dad."

"Which is?"

I stare straight ahead. "The future."

Dad stares glumly back, gives up, looks around, smiles awkwardly. "You've become much more skillful, Victor, at expressing, um, your ambitions."

"You bet, Dad. I'm streamlined and direct."

"Thass wonderful." He motions to Evett, the waiter, for more iced tea. "So where are you coming from?"

"I had a photo shoot."

"I hope you're not doing any more of those naked Webster shots or whatever. Jesus."

"*Near* naked. Bruce *Weber*. I'm not trying to freak you out, Dad."

"Wagging your ass around like—"

"It was an Obsession ad, Dad. You're acting like it was some kind of porno movie."

"What's your point, Victor?"

"Dad, the point is: the—column—blocked—my—crotch."

He's already flipping through his menu. "Before I forget, thank you for the, um, Patti Lupone CD you sent me for my birthday, Victor. It was a thoughtful gift."

I scan the menu too. "No sweat, dude."

Dad keeps glancing uneasily over at the MTV table, some of the executives probably making wisecracks. I resist waving.

Dad asks, "Why are they staring over here like that?"

"Maybe because you have 'lost white guy' written all over you?" I ask. "Christ, I need a glass of bottled water. Or a dry beer."

Evett comes over with the iced tea and silently takes our order, then moves uncertainly toward the back of the restaurant.

"Nice-looking girl," my dad says, admiringly.

"Dad," I start.

"What?"

I can't really look at him. "That's a guy, but whatever."

"You're kidding me."

"No, that is a guy. He has that whole, y'know, boy-girl thing going."

"You've forgotten to take off your sunglasses."

"I haven't forgotten." I take them off, blinking a couple of times. "So what's the story, morning glory?"

"Well, I've been keeping tabs on you." He taps the folder ominously. "And whenever I think about my only son, my thoughts drift back to that conversation we had last summer about perhaps returning to school?"

"Oh shit, Dad," I groan. "I went to *Camden*. I barely graduated from Camden. I don't even know what I majored in."

"Experimental Orchestra, as I recall," Dad says dryly.

"Hey, don't forget Design Analysis."

My father's gritting his teeth, dying for a drink, his eyes roaming the room. "Victor, I have contacts at Georgetown, at Columbia, at NYU for Christ sakes. It's not as difficult as you might think."

"Oh shit, Dad, have I *ever* used you?"

"I'm concerned about your career and—"

"You know, Dad," I interrupt, "the question that I always dreaded most at Horace Mann was whenever my counselor would ask me about my career plans."

"Why? Because you didn't have any?"

"No. Because I knew if I answered him he'd laugh."

"I just remember hearing about you being sent home for refusing to remove your sunglasses in algebra class."

"Dad, I'm opening this club. I'm doing some modeling." I sit up a little for emphasis. "Hey—and I'm waiting to hear if I have a part in *Flat-liners II*."

"This is a movie?" he asks dubiously.

"No—it's a sandwich," I say, stunned.

"I mean, my god," he sighs. "Victor, you're twenty-seven and you're only a model?"

"*Only* a model?" I say, still stunned. "*Only* a *model*? I'd rethink the way you phrased that, Dad."

"I'm *think*ing about you working hard at something that—"

"Yeah, Dad, I've really grown up in an environment where hard work is the way people get rich. Right."

"Just don't tell me you're looking for, um, artistic and personal growth through—let me get this straight—modeling?"

"Dad, a top male model can get eleven thousand dollars a day."

"Are you a top male model?"

"No, I'm not a top male model, but that's not my point."

"I lose a lot of sleep, Victor, trying to figure just what your point is."

"I'm a loser, baby," I sigh, slumping back into the booth. "So why don't you kill me?"

"You're not a loser, Victor," Dad sighs back. "You just need to, er, find yourself." He sighs again. "Find—I don't know—a new you?"

"'A new you'?" I gasp. "Oh my god, Dad, you do a great job of making me feel useless."

"And opening this club tonight makes you feel what?"

"Dad, I know, I know—"

"Victor, I just want—"

"*I* just want to do something where it's all mine," I stress. "Where I'm not . . . replaceable."

"So do I." Dad flinches. "I want that for you too."

"A model . . . modeling is . . . I'm replaceable," I sigh. "There are a thousand guys who've got pouty lips and nice symmetry. But opening something, a club, it's . . ." My voice trails off.

After a longish silence Dad says, "A photo of you in *People* magazine last week was brought to my attention."

"What issue? I didn't see this. Who was on the cover?"

"I don't know," he says, glaring. "Someone on my staff brought it to my attention."

"Goddamnit!" I slam my hand down on the table. "*This* is why I need a publicist."

"The point being, Victor, that you were at a fairly lavish hotel some-where—"

"A fairly lavish hotel somewhere?"

"Yes. In Miami."

"I was at a hotel? Somewhere in Miami?"

"Yes. A hotel. In Miami. Wearing—*barely*—a bathing suit made of white linen and very, very wet—"

"Did I look good?"

"Sunglasses. Smoking what I can only hope was a cigarette, your arms around two nubile well-oiled *Penthouse* Playmates—"

"I really need to see this, Dad."

"When were you in Miami?"

"I haven't been to Miami in *months*," I stress. "This is so sad—mistaking your own flesh and blood, your own *son*, a—"

"Victor," my father says calmly, "your name was in the caption below the photo."

"I don't think that was me, dude."

"Well," he starts lightly, "if it wasn't you, Victor, then who was it?"

"I will have to check this out, baby."

"And what's with your last name?" he asks. "You're still sticking with Ward?"

"I thought changing my last name was *your* idea, bro."

"It seemed like a good idea at the time," he murmurs, delicately opening a folder containing press clippings, faxes of press clippings, photos of me.

"This is a quote from"—my father turns a blurry fax over—"from the *New York Times* Styles section, actually. A smallish article about you, and this pull quote: 'In the uterus of love we are all blind cave fish.' Is this true, Victor? Could you please explain the term 'uterus' in the context of that sentence? And also if blind cave fish actually exist?"

"Oh boy—a two-parter. Dude, this is so bogus," I sigh. "The press *always* distorts what I say."

"Well, what are you saying?"

"Why are you so literal-minded?"

"A CK One ad. Here it looks as if there are two guys—though what the hell do I know, it could be two gals—and yes, they're kissing each other and you're looking on with your hands down the front of your pants. Why are your hands down the front of your pants? Is this gesture supposed to tell us that CK One is a reliable product?"

"Sex sells, dude."

"I see."

"The better you look, the more you see."

"Here's an interview from, um, *YouthQuake*—and by the way, congratulations on making the cover, wearing an eye shadow that's a lovely shade of brown—"

"It's terra-cotta," I sigh. "But whatever."

"—and they ask you who you would most like to have lunch with, and your answers are: the Foo Fighters, astrologist Patric Walker—who is dead, incidentally—and (this isn't a misprint, right?) the Unabomber?"

I stare back at him. "So?"

"You want to have lunch with . . . the Unabomber?" he asks. "Is this valuable information? Do we really need to know this about you?"

"What about my fans?"

"Another quote attributed to you, unless this is another distortion: 'Washington, D.C., is the stupidest city in the world, with the, like, dumbest people in it.'"

"Oh Dad—"

"I work and live in Washington, D.C., Victor. What you say and do actually affects my life, and because of what my life is like, it can be acutely embarrassing for me."

"Dad—"

"I just wanted to point this out."

"Spare me, please."

"It also says here that you're in a band called Pussy Beat, which used to be called"—he gulps—"Kitchen Bitch."

"We've changed the name. We're the Impersonators now."

"Oh Jesus, Victor. It's just that whole crowd—"

"Dad, I freaked out when Charlie and Monique tattooed their baby. Jeez—what? You think I'm some kind of delinquent?"

"Add to this that your sister says outtakes of you from that Madonna book are showing up on the Internet—"

"Dad, it's all under control."

"How can you say that?" he asks. "It's just tacky, Victor. Very tacky."

"Dad, life is tacky."

"But you don't need to win first prize."

"So what you're saying, basically, is that I'm a mixed bag."

"No," he says. "Not exactly."

"So I guess more cash is out of the question?"

"Victor, don't do this. We've been over that many, many times."
I pause. "So I guess more cash is out of the question."
"I think the trust should suffice."
"Hey, New York's expensive—"
"Then move."
"Oh my god, get real."
"What are you trying to tell me, Victor?"
"Dad." I breathe in. "Let's face it. I'm broke."
"You have a check coming in a couple of days."
"It's gone."
"How can the check be gone if you haven't even received it yet?"
"Believe me, I find it a total mystery too."
"Your monthly check is *it*, Victor," Dad stresses. "No more. No less. Understood?"
"Well, I guess I'll just have to max out my Visa."
"Really smart idea, son."
Amanda deCadenet stops by the table and kisses me hard on the mouth and says she'll see me tonight and leaves without being introduced to Dad.
"How's Chloe?" he asks.

20 Lunch was mercifully short and now it's only 1:10 and I tell the driver to drop me off at Broadway and Fourth so I can stop by Tower Records before band practice to pick up some badly needed new CDs, and inside, the pop group Sheep— *the* new alternative rock band, whose single "Diet Coke at the Gap" is the buzz clip on MTV this month—is milling around the front of the store blinking into various video cameras as Michael Levine—the Annie Leibovitz of alternative rock—snaps pictures and "Aeon Flux" is on all the monitors and I scan the magazine rack for the new issue of *YouthQuake* to see if there are any letters about the article on me. In my basket: Trey Lewd, Rancid, Cece Pensiton, Yo La Tengo, Alex Chilton, Machines of Loving Grace, Jellyfish, the 6th's, Teenage Fanclub. I've also snuck my modeling portfolio in and I spot this cute Oriental girl wearing white jeans with a silver chain-link belt, a V-neck jersey tunic and flat black sandals looking at the back of an ELO CD and I "accidentally" drop the portfolio, bathing suit shots scattering around her feet. I pause before I bend down to pick them up, pretending to be mortified, hoping that she'll check it out, but she just gives me a why-bother? look and walks away and then this cute-as-a-button little gay guy starts helping me. "It's okay, it's okay," I keep saying, pulling a thong shot out of his hand, and then I see the hottest-looking girl in Tower Records.

She's standing by a listening station, headphones on, pressing buttons, swaying, wearing a pair of tight melon-colored Capri pants that meld into small black boots and an opened violet-beige Todd Oldham overcoat, and as I move closer I can see she's holding Blur, Suede, Oasis, Sleeper CDs. I'm right behind her as she pulls the headphones off.

"That's the coolest record," I say, pointing at the Oasis CD. "Tracks three, four, five and ten are all excellent."

She turns around, startled, sees my face, and what can only be described as a strange expression—one-third worried, one-third smiling, maybe one-third something else—creases her features and then she asks, "Do you know me?" but it's in this teasing way that I'm accustomed to and so I'm able to answer confidently, "Yeah—L.A. or Miami, right?"

"No," she says, her eyes hardening.

"Did you"—I have a small flash—"go to Camden?"

"You're getting less cold," she says simply.

"Wait—are you a model?"

"No," she sighs. "I'm not."

"But Camden is near the target?" I ask hopefully.

"Yes, it is." She sighs again.

"Yeah, yeah, foliage is definitely coming my way."

"That's good." She crosses her arms.

"So you *did* go to Camden?" I ask and then, to make sure, "The one in New Hampshire?"

"Is there another one?" she says impatiently.

"Hey baby, whoa."

"Well," she says, tapping the Oasis CD, "thanks for the record review, Victor."

"Oh man, you know me?"

She slings a red suede zip-top circular purse over her shoulder and lowers Matsuda sunglasses—blue eyes—and pouts, "Victor Johnson? I mean, that's if you *are* Victor Johnson."

"Well, yeah," I admit sheepishly. "Actually it's Victor Ward now but, um, it's still the same me."

"Oh, that's just great," she says. "So you got married? Who's the lucky guy?"

"The little pinhead over there with the strawberry strudel on his head." I point to the gay guy who I'm just noticing has kept one of the bathing suit shots. He smiles, then scampers away. "He's, uh, shy."

Finally I realize that I actually know this girl. "Oh man, I'm so bad with names," I apologize. "I'm sorry."

"Go ahead," she says, holding something in, "be a big boy—take a guess."

"Okay, I'm gonna have a psychic moment." I bring my hands to my temples and close my eyes. "Karen . . . Nancy . . . Jojo . . . You have a brother named Joe? . . . I'm seeing a lot of, er, Js. . . . I'm seeing, I'm seeing a . . . a . . . a kitten . . . a kitten named Cootie?" I open my eyes.

"It's Lauren." She looks at me dully.

"Lauren, ri-i-ight."

"Yeah," she says in a hard way. "Lauren Hynde? Remember now?"

I pause, freaked. "Gosh. Lauren Hynde. Whoa . . ."

"Do you know who I am now?" she asks.

"Oh baby, I'm really . . ." Stumped, I admit, "You know, they say Klonopin causes short-term memory loss, so—"

"Why don't we start with this: I'm Chloe's friend."

"Yeah, yeah," I say, trying to get comfortable. "We were just talking about you."

"Mmm." She starts moving down an aisle, running her hand along the rim of the CD racks, moving away from me.

I follow. "Yeah, it was a totally nice, um, *chat*, y'know?"

"What about?"

"Just, y'know, positive things."

She keeps walking and I hang back, taking my sunglasses off to check out the body beneath the open coat: thin with full breasts, long and shapely legs, short blond hair, everything else—eyes, teeth, lips, whatever—equally nice. I catch up, keep moving with her, casually swinging the basket of CDs at my side.

"So you remember *me* from Camden?" I ask.

"Oh yeah," she says half-scornfully. "I remember you."

"Well, did you act this way at college or am *I* acting different?"

She stops moving and turns to face me. "You really don't remember who I am, do you, Victor?"

"Yes I do. You're Lauren Hynde." I pause. "But y'know, I was away a lot and Klonopin causes long-term memory loss."

"I thought it caused short-term memory loss."

"See—I already can't remember."

"Oh god, forget it."

She's about to turn away when I ask, "Am I the same?"

She looks me over carefully. "Pretty much, I guess." She focuses on my head, scanning my face. "Well, I don't think you had those sideburns."

An opening that I leap into. "Learn to love the sideburns, baby. They're your best friends. Pet the sideburns." I lean in, offer my profile, purring.

She just looks at me like I've lost it.

"What? What is it?" I ask. "Pet the sideburns, baby."

"*Pet* the sideburns?"

"People worship the sideburns, baby."

"You know people who worship hair?" she asks, semi-appalled. "You know people who want to look twenty forever?"

I wave a fly away. I move into another mode.

"So what's going on, Lauren Hynde? God you look great. What's the story? Where've you been?" Maybe I ask this with the wrong tone, because she segues into the inevitable.

"I ran into Chloe at Patricia Field's last week," she says.

"Patricia Field's apartment?" I ask, impressed.

"No," she says, looking at me strangely. "Her store, dummy."

"Oh. That's cool."

A long pause, during which various girls pass by. A couple of them say hi to me but I casually ignore them. Lauren eyes them skeptically, troubled, which is a good sign.

"Um, I'm unsure of what we were talking about—"

My beeper goes off. I check the number: Alison.

"Who's that?" Lauren asks.

"Oh, y'know, probably just another call about unionizing male models." I shrug, then add, after a pause, "I'm a model."

"Unionizing male models?" She starts walking away again, which only makes me want to follow her more.

"You say that like it's a joke."

"I think you need committed people to form a union, Victor."

"Hey, no dark sarcasm in the classroom."

"This is ridiculous," she says. "I've gotta go."

"Why?"

"I'm having lunch with someone." Her hand is actually trembling as she runs it through her hair.

"Who?" I ask.

"Why?" she asks back.

"A guy?"

"Victor."

"Aw, come on."

"Baxter Priestly, actually, if you must know."

"Oh great," I groan. "Who is this little shit? I mean, spare me, baby."

"Victor, Chloe and I are friends. I assume you know this," she says, staring straight at me. "At least you're supposed to know this."

"Why am I supposed to know this?" I smile.

"Because she's your girlfriend?" she asks, her mouth hanging open.

"That's an excuse?"

"No, Victor. A reason. *You're* making it an excuse."

"You're losing me, baby. This is getting kinda trippy."

"Well, steady yourself."

"Hey, what about a cappuccino?"

"Don't you know who your girlfriend's acquaintances are? Don't you talk to her?" Lauren is losing it. "What's with you—oh god, why am I asking? I know, I *know*. I've gotta go."

"Wait, wait—I want to get these." I gesture toward the basket of CDs I'm holding. "Come with me and I'll walk you out. I've got band practice but I can squeeze in a latte."

She hesitates, then moves with me toward the registers. Once there, my AmEx card doesn't go through. I moan "Spare me" but Lauren actually smiles—a smile that causes a major déjà vu—and puts it on her card when she pays for her CDs and she doesn't even say anything about paying her back.

It's so cold in Tower that everything—the air, the sounds revolving around us, the racks of CDs—feels white, snowed in. People pass by, moving on to the next register, and the high-set fluorescent lighting that renders everyone flat and pale and washed out doesn't affect Lauren's skin, which looks like ivory that's tan, and her presence—just the mere gesture of her signing the receipt—touches me in a way I can't shrug off, and the music rising above us—"Wonderwall"—makes me feel doped and far away from my life. Lust is something I really haven't come across in a long time and I follow it now in Tower Records and it's getting hard to shake off the thought that Lauren Hynde is part of my future. Outside, I put my hand on the small of her back, guiding her through the sidewalk crowd to the curb on Broadway. She turns around and looks at me for a long time and I let her.

"Victor," she starts, responding to my vibe. "Look—I just want to make something clear. I'm seeing someone."

"Who?"

"That doesn't matter," she says. "I'm involved."

"Well, why don't you tell me who it is?" I ask. "And if it's that twerp Baxter Priestly I'll actually give you a thousand bucks."

"I don't think you have a thousand bucks."

"I have a big change bowl at home."

"It was"—she stops, stuck—"interesting to see you."

"Come on, let's go get a café au lait at Dean & Deluca. Sounds hip, huh?"

friend in a medical-drama pilot that ultimately was never produced but it didn't really matter since I was so out of it I even had to reread things Paula Abdul said in interviews. Chloe was always "dying of thirst," there were always tickets for some lame-o screening, our conversations were always garbled, the streets were always—inexplicably—covered with confetti, we were always at barbecues at Herb Ritts', which were always attended by either Madonna or Josh Brolin or Amy Locane or Veronica Webb or Stephen Dorff or Ed Limato or Richard Gere or Lela Rochon or Ace of Base, where turkeyburgers were always served, which we always washed down with pink-grapefruit iced tea, and bonfires were always lit throughout the city along with the giant cones of klieg lights announcing premieres.

When we went to an AIDS fund-raiser thrown by Lily Tartikoff at Barneys, cameras flashed and Chloe's dry hand clutched my limp hand and she squeezed it only once—a warning—when a reporter from E! television asked me what I was doing there and I said, "I needed an excuse to wear my new Versace tuxedo." I could barely make it up the series of steep staircases to the top floor but once I was there Christian Slater gave me a high five and we hung out with Dennis Leary, Helen Hunt, Billy Zane, Joely Fisher, Claudia Schiffer, Matthew Fox. Someone pointed someone else out to me and whispered "The piercing didn't take" before melting back into the crowd. People talked about cutting off their hair and burning their fingernails.

Most people were mellow and healthy, tan and buff and drifting around. Others were so hysterical—sometimes covered with lumps and bruises—that I couldn't understand what they were saying to me, so I tried to stay close to Chloe to totally make sure she didn't fall back into any destructive habits and she wore Capri pants and Kamali makeup, canceled aromatherapy appointments that I was unaware she had made, her diet dominated by grape- and lemongrass- and root-beer-flavored granitas. Chloe didn't return phone calls from Evan Dando, Robert Towne, Don Simpson, Victor Drai, Frank Mancuso, Jr., Shane Black. She was bawling constantly and bought a print by Frank Gehry for something like thirty grand and an Ed Ruscha fog painting for considerably more. Chloe bought Lucien Gau shogun table lamps and a lot of iron baskets and had it all shipped back to Manhattan. Rejecting people was the hot pastime. We had a lot of sex. Everyone talked about the year 2018. One day we pretended to be ghosts.

Dani Jansen wanted to take us to mysterious places and I was asked by four separate people what my favorite land animal was and since I didn't know what these were I couldn't even fake an answer. Hanging out with two of the Beastie Boys at a house in Silver Lake, we met a lot of crew-cut blondes and Tamra Davis and Greg Kinnear and David Fincher and Perry Farrell. "Yum—ice" was a constant refrain while we drank lukewarm

Bacardi-and-Cokes and bitched about taxes. In the backyard a pool that had been drained was filled with rubble and the chaise longues had empty syringes scattered all over them. The only question I asked during dinner was "Why don't you just grow your own?" From where I stood I watched someone take ten minutes to cut a slice of cheese. There was a topiary in the shape of Elton John in the backyard, next to the rubble-strewn pool. We were eating Vicodin and listening to Nico-era Velvet Underground tapes.

"The petty ugliness of our problems seems so ridiculous in the face of all this natural beauty," I said.

"Baby, that's an Elton John topiary behind you," Chloe said.

Back at the Chateau, CDs were scattered all over the suite and empty Federal Express packages littered the floor. The word "miscellany" seemed to sum up everything we felt about each other or so Chloe said. We had fights at Chaya Brasserie, three in the Beverly Center, one later in Le Colonial at a dinner for Nick Cage, another at House of Blues. We kept telling each other it didn't matter, that we didn't care, fuck it, which was actually pretty easy to do. During one of our fights Chloe called me a "peon" who had about as much ambition as a "parking lot attendant." She wasn't right, she wasn't wrong. If we were stuck in the suite at the Chateau after a fight there was really no place left to go, either the kitchen or the balcony, where two parrots, named Blinky and Scrubby the Gibbering Idiot, hung out. She lay in bed in her underwear, light from the TV flooding the darkened suite, the Cocteau Twins droning from the stereo, and during these lulls I would wander out by the pool and chew gum and drink Fruitopia while reading an old issue of *Film Threat* or the book *Final Exit*, rereading a chapter titled "Self-Deliverance via the Plastic Bag." We were in a nonzone.

Ten or eleven producers were found dead in various Bel Air mansions. I autographed the back of a Jones matchbook in my "nearly indecipherable scrawl" for some young thing. I mused about publishing my journal entries in *Details*. There was a sale at Maxfields but we had no patience. We ate tamales in empty skyscrapers and ordered bizarre handrolls in sushi bars done up in industrial-chic decor, in restaurants with names like Muse, Fusion, Buffalo Club, with people like Jack Nicholson, Ann Magnuson, Los Lobos, Sean MacPherson, a fourteen-year-old male model named Dragonfly who Jimmy Rip really dug. We spent too much time at the Four Seasons bar and not enough at the beach. A friend of Chloe's gave birth to a dead baby. I left ICM. People told us that they either were vampires or knew someone who was a vampire. Drinks with Depeche Mode. So many people we vaguely knew died or disappeared the weeks we were there—car accidents, AIDS, murders, overdoses, run over by a truck, fell into vats of acid or maybe were pushed—that the amount for funeral wreaths on Chloe's Visa was almost five thousand dollars. I looked really great.

18

At Conrad's loft on Bond Street it's 1:30 which is really the only time to practice since everyone else in the building is at work or at Time Café acting like an idiot without trying over lunch, and from where I slouch in the doorway leading into the loft I can see all the members of the Impersonators lying around in various positions, each next to his own amp: Aztec's wearing a Hang-10 T-shirt, scratching at a Kenny Scharf tattoo on his bicep, Fender in lap; Conrad, our lead singer, has a kind of damp appeal and dated Jenny McCarthy and has wilted hair the color of lemonade and dresses in rumpled linens; Fergy's wrapped in an elongated cardigan and playing with a Magic 8 Ball, sunglasses lowered; and Fitzgerald was in a gothic rock band, OD'd, was resuscitated, OD'd again, was resuscitated again, campaigned mindlessly for Clinton, modeled for Versace, dated Jennifer Capriati, and he's wearing pajamas and sleeping in a giant hot-pink-and-yucca-striped beanbag chair. And they're all existing in this freezing, screwy-looking loft where DAT tapes and CDs are scattered everywhere, MTV's on, Presidents of the United States merging into a Mentos commercial merging into an ad for the new Jackie Chan movie, empty Zen Palate take-out boxes are strewn all over the place, white roses dying in an empty Stoli bottle, a giant sad ragdoll photo by Mike Kelly dominates one wall, the collected works of Philip K. Dick fill an entire row in the room's only bookcase, Lava lamps, cans of Play-Doh.

I take a deep breath, enter the room casually, brush some confetti off my jacket.

Except Fitz, they all look up, and Aztec immediately starts strumming something from *Tommy* on his Fender.

"He seems to be completely unreceptive," Aztec sings-talks. "The tests I gave him show no sense at all."

"His eyes react to light—the dials detect it," Conrad chimes in. "He hears but cannot answer to your call."

"Shut up," I yawn, grabbing an ice beer out of the fridge.

"His eyes can see, his ears can hear, his lips speak," Aztec continues.

"All the time the needles flick and rock," Conrad admits.

"No machine can give the kind of stimulation," Fergy points out, "needed to remove his inner block."

"What is happening in his head?" the three of them sing out.

"Ooh I wish I knew," Fitzgerald calls from the beanbag chair for one lucid moment. "I wish I kneeeeew." He immediately rolls over into a fetal position.

"You're late," Conrad snaps.

"*I'm* late? It takes you guys an hour just to tune up," I yawn, flopping onto a pile of Indian pillows. "I'm *not* late," I yawn again, sipping the ice beer, notice them all glaring at me. "What? I had to cancel a hair appointment at Oribe to make it here." I toss a copy of *Spin* that's lying next to an antique hookah pipe at Fitz, who doesn't even flinch when it hits him.

"'Magic Touch,'" Aztec shouts out.

I answer without trying. "Plimsouls, *Everywhere at Once*, 3:19, Geffen."

"'Walking Down Madison,'" he tosses out.

"Kirsty MacColl, *Electric Landlady*, 6:34, Virgin."

"'Real World.'"

"Jesus Jones, *Liquidizer*, 3:03, SBK."

"'Jazz Police.'"

"Leonard Cohen, *I'm Your Man*, 3:51, CBS."

"'You Get What You Deserve.'"

"Big Star, *Radio City*, 3:05, Stax." I yawn. "Oh, this is too easy."

"'Ode to Boy.'"

"Yaz, *You and Me Both*, 3:35, Sire."

"'Top of the Pops.'" Aztec's losing interest.

"The Smithereens, *Blow Up*, 4:32, Capitol."

"If only you gave the band that much attention, Victor," Conrad says in Conrad's hey-I'm-hostile-here mode.

"Who came in here last week with a list of songs we should cover?" I retort.

"I'm *not* gonna sing an acid-house version of 'We Built This City,' Victor," Conrad fumes.

"You're throwing money out the window, dude." I shrug.

"Covers are nowhere, Victor," Fergy pipes in. "There's no money in covers."

"That's what Chloe always tells me," I say. "And if I don't believe *her*, how am I gonna believe *you*?"

"What's the point, Victor?" someone sighs.

"You, babe"—I'm pointing at Aztec—"have the ability to take a song that people have heard a million times and play it in a way that no one has ever heard it played before."

"And *you're* too fucking lazy to write your own material," Conrad says, pointing back, full of indie-rock venom.

"I personally think a cocktail-mix version of 'Shiny Happy People' is hopping—"

"REM is classic rock, Victor," Conrad says patiently. "We do not *do* classic-rock covers."

"Oh god, I want to kill myself," Fergy moans.

"Hey—but the good news, everyone, is that Courtney Love's over thirty," I say happily.

"Okay. I feel better."

"What kind of royalties is Courtney getting from Nirvana sales?" Aztec asks Fergy.

"Was there a prenup?" Fergy wonders.

Shrugs all around.

"So," Fergy concludes, "since Kurt's demise maybe nothing."

"Hey, come on—Kurt Cobain didn't die," I say. "His music lives on in all of us."

"We really need to focus on new material, guys," Conrad says.

"Well, can we at least write one song without a shitty reggae beat that starts off with the line 'I was a trippin in da crack house late last night'?" I ask. "Or 'Dere's a rat in da kitchen—what I gonna do?'"

Aztec pops open a Zima and restrums his Fender contemplatively.

"When's the last time you guys made a demo?" I ask, noticing Chloe on the cover of the new *Manhattan File* next to the latest *Wired* and the copy of *YouthQuake* with me on the front, totally defaced with purple ink.

"Last week, Victor," I hear Conrad say through gritted teeth.

"That's a million years ago," I murmur, flipping around for the article about her. It's all blah blah blah—the last year of doing runway shows, the Lancôme contract, her diet, movie roles, denying the rumors about heroin addiction, Chloe talking about wanting to have kids ("A big playpen, the whole thing," she's quoted), a photo of us at the VH1 Fashion and Music Awards, with me staring vacantly into the camera, a photo of Chloe at the Doppelganger party celebrating the Fifty Most Fabulous People in the World, Baxter Priestly trailing behind her—and I'm trying to remember what my relationship with Lauren Hynde was like back at Camden or if there even was one, as if, right now, in the loft on Bond Street, it matters.

"Victor," Conrad's saying, hands on hips, "a lot of bands are in the music biz for the totally wrong reasons: to make money, to get laid—"

"Whoa, wait a minute, Conrad." I hold my hands out, sitting up. "*These* are the *wrong* reasons? Really? Let me just get this straight."

"All you do here, Victor, is drink beer and reread magazines that you or your girlfriend happen to be in this month," Conrad says, looming over me.

"And you're all so lost in the past, man," I say wearily. "Captain Beefheart records? *Yogurt?* What the fuck is like going on here, *huh?*" I exclaim. "And Jesus, Aztec—cut your toenails! Where are your fucking morals? What do you even *do* besides going to fucking poetry readings at Fez? Why don't you go to a fucking gym or something?"

"I get enough exercise," Aztec says dubiously.

"Rolling a joint isn't exercise, guy," I say. "And shave off that goddamn facial hair. You look like a fucking billy goat."

"I think it's time you calm down, Victor," Aztec says, "and take your place with the glitterati."

"I'm just offering you an escape from that whole stale hippie vibe."

Fergy looks over at me and shivers vaguely.

"You're jeopardizing our friendship, dude," I say, though it emerges from my mouth without a lot of concern.

"You're never here long enough, Victor, to jeopardize anything!" Conrad shouts.

"Oh spare me," I mutter, getting up to leave.

"Just go, Victor," Conrad sighs. "No one wants you here. Go open your big tacky club."

I grab my portfolio and bag of CDs and head toward the door.

"You all feel this way?" I'm asking, standing over Fitz, who wipes his nose on the ice-hockey jersey he's using as a pillow, eyes closed, sleeping serenely, dreaming about cartons of methadone. "I bet Fitz wants me to stay. Don't you, Fitz?" I ask, leaning down, trying to shake him awake. "Hey Fitz, wake up."

"Don't even try, Victor," Fergy yawns.

"What's wrong with the Synthman?" I ask. "Besides spending his teen years in Goa."

"He went on a Jägermeister binge last night," Conrad sighs. "He's on ibogaine now."

"And so?" I ask, still prodding Fitz.

"And for breakfast Ecstasy cut with too much heroin."

"*Too* much?"

"Too much heroin."

"Instead of like . . ."

"The right amount of heroin, Victor."

"Christ," I mutter.

"Oh boy, Victor." Conrad smirks. "Farm living's the life for you."

"I'd rather be a farmer than hang out with people who drink their own blood, you fucking hippie vampires."

"Fitz is also suffering from binocular dysphoria and carpal tunnel syndrome."

"Shine on, you crazy diamond." I rummage in my coat pocket and start handing out free drink tickets. "Well, I guess I'm here to tell you I'm quitting the band and these are only good between 11:46 and 12:01 tonight."

"So that's it?" Conrad asks. "You're just quitting?"

"I give you my blessing to continue," I say, placing two free-drink tickets on Fitz's leg.

"Like you even care, Victor," Conrad says.

"I think this is good news, Conrad," Fergy says, shaking the Magic 8 Ball. "I think, Far out. In fact Magic 8 Ball says 'Far Out' too." He holds the ball up for us to see.

"It's just this whole indie-rock scene equals *yuck*," I say. "Y'know what I'm saying?"

Conrad just stares at Fitz.

"Conrad, hey, maybe we should go bungee jumping with Duane and Kitty this weekend," Aztec says. "How about it, Conrad? Conrad?" Pause. "Conrad?"

Conrad continues to stare at Fitz, and as I'm leaving he says, "Has anybody realized that our drummer is the most lucid person in this band?"

17 Walking up Lafayette unable to shake off the feeling of being followed and stopping on the corner of East Fourth I catch my reflection superimposed in the glass covering of an Armani Exchange ad and it's merging with the sepia-toned photo of a male model until both of us are melded together and it's hard to turn away but except for the sound of my beeper going off the city suddenly goes quiet, the dry air crackling not with static but with something else, something less. Cabs lumber by silently, someone dressed exactly like me crosses the street, three beautiful girls pass by, each maybe sixteen and eyeing me, trailed by a thug with a camcorder, the muted, dissonant strains of Moby floats from the open doors of the Crunch gym across the street where on the building above it a giant billboard advertises in huge black block letters the word TEMPURA. But someone's calling "Cut!" and the noise from

the construction site of the new Gap behind me and the beeper going off—
for some freaky reason it's the number of Indochine—moves me toward a
phone booth where before dialing I imagine a naked Lauren Hynde striding toward me in a suite at the Delano with a deeper sense of purpose than I
can muster. Alison picks up.

"I need to make a reservation," I say, trying to disguise my voice.

"I've got something I want to tell you," she says.

"What?" I gulp. "Y-you used to be a man?"

Alison knocks the phone on a hard surface. "Oh sorry, that's my call-
waiting. I've gotta go."

"That didn't sound like, uh, call-waiting, baby."

"It's a new kind of call-waiting. It simulates the sound of someone who's
dating a useless asshole angrily knocking their phone against a wall."

"Essential, baby, you're essential."

"I want you here at Indochine within two minutes."

"I'm inundated, baby, totally inundated."

"What is this? Big-word day?" she snaps. "Just get that ass over here."

"That ass has got to . . . see someone."

"Jesus, Victor, the pregnant pause combined with 'someone' can only
mean one person: that idiot you date."

"Baby, I'll see you tonight," I fake-purr.

"Listen, I have Chloe's number right in front of me, baby, and—"

"She's not at home, Medusa."

"You're right. She's at Spy Bar shooting a Japanese TV commercial
and—"

"Damnit, Alison, you—"

"—I'm in a mood to screw things up. I need to be distracted from that
mood, Victor," Alison warns. "I need to be distracted from screwing
things up."

"You're so phony, baby, it stings," I sigh. "*Ouch,*" I add. "That was for,
um, emphasis."

"Oh Chloe, I'm so sorry. He came on to *me.* He was *un animale.* He told
me he doesn't even wuv you."

"What's your sick little point, baby?"

"I just don't want to share you anymore, Victor," Alison says, sighing as if
she could care less. "I'm pretty sure I came to that conclusion at the Alfaro
show."

"You're not sharing me," I say, which is useless.

"You *sleep* with her, Victor."

"Baby, if I didn't some HIV-positive scumbag would and then—"

"Oh god!"

"—we'd all be in a whole helluva lotta trouble."

"End it!" Alison wails. "Just end it!"

"And you're gonna dump Damien?"

"Damien Nutchs Ross and I are—"

"Baby, don't use the full moniker. It's a bummer."

"Victor, I keep explaining something to you and you act like you haven't heard me."

"What?" I ask, gulping again. "You u-used to be a man?"

"Without me, and by extension without Damien, you would *have no club*. Now, how many times do we need to go over this?" Pause, exhale. "Nor would you have a chance to open that other club you're planning to—"

"Whoa!"

"—open behind all our backs."

We're both silent. I can envision a slow, triumphant smile pulling Alison's lips upward.

"I don't know why you think these things, Alison."

"Shut up. I will only continue this conversation at Indochine." A pause that I let happen. Because of it, Alison calls out, "Ted—could you ring up Spy Bar for me?" She clicks off, daring me.

Past the limousine parked out front next to a giant pile of black and white confetti and up the stairs into Indochine, where Ted the maître d' is being interviewed by "Meet the Press" wearing a giant top hat, and I ask him, "What's the story?" Never breaking eye contact with the camera crew, I follow his finger as it points to a booth in the rear of the empty, freezing restaurant, noise from the latest PJ Harvey CD in the dank background. Alison spots me, stubs out a joint and gets up from a table where she's on her Nokia 232 cell phone to Nan Kempner and eating cake with Peter Gabriel, David LaChapelle, Janeane Garofalo and David Koresh, all of them discussing lacrosse and the new monkey virus, a copy of this month's *Mademoiselle* next to each plate.

Alison pulls me into the back of the restaurant, pushes me into the men's room and slams the door.

"Let's make this quick," she growls.

"As if there's any other way with you," I sigh, spitting out a piece of bubble gum.

She lunges at me, clamping her mouth onto mine. In a matter of seconds she pulls back and frantically tears open a zebra-print waistcoat.

"You were so cold to me earlier," she pants. "As much as I hate to admit it, I got wet."

"I haven't seen you all day, baby." I'm pulling her tits out of a beige push-up bra.

"At the Alfaro show, baby." She pulls an electro-cut miniskirt with charred seams up over tan thighs, pushing down a white pair of panties.

"Baby, how many times do we need to go through this?" I'm unbuttoning my jeans. "I wasn't at the Alfaro show."

"Oh my god, you're such an absolute dick," she groans. "You spoke to me at the Alfaro show, baby." She glares cross-eyed while thrusting her tongue in and out of my mouth. "Barely, but you spoke."

I'm at her neck and in mid-lick I straighten up, my pants falling to the floor, and just stare into her sex-crazed face. "You're smoking wa-a-a-ay too much weed, baby."

"Victor . . ." She's delirious, my hand in her crotch, two now three fingers inside her, lolling her head back, licking her own lips, grinding down on my hand, her pussy tightening around my fingers. "I'm just about through with this—"

"With *what*?"

"Just come here." She grabs my dick, squeezes it hard and pulls it condomless toward her, rubbing its head along the lips of her pussy. "Feel this? Is this real?"

"Against my better instincts, yes," I say, slamming into her, just how Alison likes it. "But baby, I sense someone is causing major mischief."

"Baby, just fuck me harder," she groans. "And lift up your shirt. Let's see that bod work."

Afterwards, walking slowly back through the deserted restaurant, I grab a half-drunk Greyhound off a table and swish some around in my mouth before spitting it back into the highball glass. While I'm wiping my lips with the sleeve of my jacket, Alison turns to me, sated, and admits, "I've been followed all day."

I stop moving. "What?"

"Just so you know, I've been followed all day." She lights a cigarette while moving past me, drifting by busboys setting up tables for tonight.

"Alison—are you telling me that those goons are outside right now?" I slam my hand against a table. "Oww—oh shit, Alison."

She turns around. "I lost those goons in a Starbucks an hour ago." She exhales, offers me the Marlboro. "If you can believe anyone's stupid enough to lose someone in a Starbucks."

"Starbucks can get pretty crowded, baby," I say, taking the cigarette from her, dazed yet relieved.

"I'm not worried about them," she says lightly.

"I think the fact that you can only have sex in the bathroom at Indochine should like give you major pause, baby."

"I wanted to celebrate the fact that our worries about a certain photograph are over."

"I talked to Buddy," I say. "I know."

"What horrible string did you pull?" she asks admiringly. "Confirm Chloe's nasty ex-habit?"

"You don't want to know."

She considers this. "You're right," she sighs. "I don't."

"Did you make Damien buy that new 600SEL?"

"Actually he leased it," Alison mutters. "Asshole."

"Damien's not an asshole."

"I wasn't referring to him, but yes he is."

"Hey, tell me what you know about Baxter Priestly."

"Someone with amazing cheekbones." She shrugs. "In the band Hey That's My Shoe. He's a model-slash-actor. Unlike you, who's a model-slash-loser."

"Isn't he like a fag or something?"

"I think Baxter has a major crush on Chloe Byrnes," she says, eyes flickering gleefully over my face for a reaction, then, after thinking about something, she shrugs. "She could do worse."

"Oh boy, Alison."

She's laughing, relaxed. "Victor—just keep an eye out."

"What are you saying?" I ask, stretching.

"What is it you always say?" she asks. "The better you look, the more you see. Is that it?"

"Are you saying that Baxter Priestly and Chloe are—what, Alison?" I ask, arms still spread out. "*Hump*ing?!?"

"Why are you even worried?" She hands me back the cigarette. "What do you see in that poor little girl besides a staggering intellect?"

"What about Lauren Hynde?" I ask casually.

Alison stiffens up noticeably, plucks the cigarette from my lips, finishes it, starts moving toward the front of the restaurant.

"Barely anything. Two Atom Egoyan movies, two Hal Hartley movies, the latest Todd Haynes. Oh, and a small part in the new Woody Allen. That's about it. Why?"

"Whoa," I say, impressed.

"She's so out of your league, Victor, it's not even funny." Alison takes her coat and purse from a stool at the bar.

"What's that supposed to mean?"

"It means I don't think you have to worry about being taken seriously by her," Alison says. "You're not gonna be."

"I'm just having a fly time, bay-bee." I shrug.

"She apparently had that whole hair-pulling madness disease. It disappeared entirely under Prozac therapy. Or so they say."

"So you're basically saying we're caught in a trap and we can't back out? Is that it?" I'm asking.

"Well, *you're* going to have to take the back way out." She kisses me on the nose.

"There *is* no back way out, Alison."

"Then just give me five." She yawns, buttoning up.

"Where are you going?" I ask sheepishly. "I suppose a ride is out of the question considering the circumstances, huh?"

"I have an extremely vital hair appointment at Stephen Knoll," Alison says, squeezing my cheek. "Kiss-kiss, bye-bye."

"See you tonight," I say, waving wanly.

"Big time," she mutters, walking down the stairs, outside, away from me.

16

Umberto guards the door at Spy Bar on Greene Street waving flies away with a hand holding a walkie-talkie and wishes me luck tonight and lets me in and I head up the stairs smelling my fingers then duck into the men's room where I wash my hands and stare at myself in the mirror above the sink before I remember time is fleeting, madness takes its toll and all that and in the main room the director, assistant director, lighting cameraman, gaffer, chief electrician, two more assistants, Scott Benoit, Jason Vorhees' sister, Bruce Hulce, Gerlinda Kostiff, scenic ops and a Steadicam operator stand around a very large white egg, mute, video cameras circling, filming a video of the making of the commercial, photographers taking pictures of the video team.

Chloe sits away from them at a large booth in the back of the room. A group of makeup artists holding gels and brushes surround her and she's wearing rhinestone-studded hot pants, a minidress with a flippy skirt and she looks unnaturally happy in this twilight zone but after catching my gaze she just shrugs helplessly. Someone named, I think, Dario, who used to date Nicole Miller, wearing sunglasses and a Brooks Brothers coconut hat with a madras band and a telescope crown and sandals, is lying on a tatami mat nearby, with a Mighty Morphin Power Rangers tattoo on his bicep. I use the phone at the bar to check my messages: Balthazar Getty, a check for my tai chi instructor bounced, Elaine Irwin, a publicist from my gym, Val Kilmer, Reese Witherspoon. Someone hands me a café au lait and I hang out with this model named Andre and share a too tightly rolled joint by a long buffet table covered with really trendy sushi and Kenny Scharf–designed ice buckets and Andre's life is basically made up of lots of water, grilled fish and all the sports he can do and he has a look that's young, grungy, somewhat destitute but in a hip way.

"I just want people to smile a little more," Andre's saying. "And I'm also concerned with the planet's ecological problem."

"That's so cool," I say, gazing at thin sheets of light-blue ice that cover an entire wall, lie in patches on the bar and on the mirrors behind the bar. Someone walks by in a parka.

"And I'd like to open a restaurant in the shape of a giant scarab."

We both stand there staring at the egg and then I slowly walk away, explaining, "My café au lait's a little too foamy, guy."

The makeup team has finished and they leave Chloe alone and I move over to where she's staring at us in a giant portable mirror that sits in the middle of the table, magazines scattered everywhere around her, some with Chloe's face on the cover.

"What's with the glasses?" she asks.

"Reef says it's fashionable to look like an intellectual this season." It's so cold our breath frosts, comes out in puffs.

"If someone asked you to eat your own weight in Silly Putty, would you do that too?" she asks quietly.

"I'm a-buggin', I'm a-jumpin', baby."

"Victor, I'm so glad you know what's important and what's not."

"Thanks, babe." I lean in to kiss her neck but she flinches and whispers something about disturbing powder, so I end up placing my lips on top of her scalp.

"What am I smelling?" I ask.

"I've been using vodka to lighten my hair," she says sadly. "Bongo got a whiff at the Donna Karan show and started muttering the Serenity Prayer."

"Don't sweat it, baby. Remember that all you have to do is say cheese about two hundred times a day. That's it!"

"Being photographed six hours straight is sheer torture."

"Who's the dude in the corner, baby?" I gesture toward the guy on the tatami mat.

"That's La Tosh. We go way back. I've known him for weeks. We met over a spring roll at Kin Khao."

"Très jolie." I shrug.

"Supposedly he's one of Rome's best-connected psychos," she sighs. "Do you have any cigarettes?"

"Hey, what happened to the nicotine patch you were gonna wear today?" I ask, concerned.

"It was making me all wobbly on the runway." She takes my hand and looks up into my face. "I missed you today. Whenever I'm really tired I miss you."

I lean in, hug her a little, whisper into her ear. "Hey—who's my favorite little supermodel?"

"Take those glasses off," she says sourly. "You look like somebody who's trying too hard. You look like Dean Cain."

"So what's the story?" I remove the frames, slip them back into their case.

"Alison Poole has called about ten times today," Chloe says, looking around the table for cigarettes. "I haven't called her back. Do you have any idea what she wants?"

"No, baby. Why?"

"Well, didn't you see her at the Alfaro show?"

"Baby, I wasn't *at* the Alfaro show." I pull a small piece of confetti from her hair.

"Shalom said she saw you there."

"Shalom needs new contacts, then, baby."

"So why are you visiting me?" she asks. "Are you sure you don't have a cigarette?"

I check all my pockets. "I don't think so, baby." I find a pack of Mentos, offer her one. "Um, I just wanted to stop in, say hello, the usual. I've gotta be back at the club, meet this DJ we desperately need for the party tonight and then I'll see you at Todd's show."

"I've got to be out of here in forty minutes if I'm going to make it for hair." She takes a sip from a Fruitopia bottle.

"God, it's freezing in here," I say, shivering.

"This week has been hell, Victor," Chloe says blankly. "Maybe the most hellish week of my life."

"I'm here for you, baby."

"I know I should be comforted by that," she says. "But thank you anyway."

"I've just been so swamped today, baby, it's totally scary," I say. "I've just been so totally *swamped*."

"We really need to treat ourselves to a vacation," Chloe says.

"So what's the story, baby?" I try again. "What's this thing about?" I ask, gesturing toward the crew, the egg, the guy on the tatami mat.

"I'm not sure, but Scott is supposed to be some kind of phantom-android obsessed with curry—the spice—and we have a fight about whatever people who look like us have fights about and I throw a cube, some kind of—oh, I don't know—a *cube* at him and then, according to the script, he 'flees.'"

"Yeah, that's right," I say. "I remember the script."

"And then the *bad* phantom-android—"

"Baby," I interrupt gently. "The synopsis can wait."

"*We're* waiting," Chloe says. "Scott forgot his dialogue."

"Baby, I read the shooting script," I say. "He only has one line. Singular."

The seventeen-year-old director moves over to the booth holding a walkie-talkie and he's wearing DKNY silver jeans and sunglasses and it's all kind of a glam combo. "Chloe, we've decided to shoot the first shot last."

"Taylor, I'm desperately needed somewhere in less than an hour," Chloe pleads. "It's a matter of life or death. Taylor, this is Victor."

"Hey," Taylor says. "We met at Pravda last week."

"I wasn't at Pravda last week but oh what the hell, forget it—how's it going?"

"The extras are cool kids but we want to portray a lifestyle that people can relate to," Taylor explains. I'm nodding deeply. "My vision is to create the opposite of whatever smuggling Pervitin back from Prague in a rented Toyota means." An interruption, static from the walkie-talkie, garbled screams from across the room. "That's just Lars, the runner." Taylor winks.

"Taylor—" Chloe starts.

"Baby, you will be whisked out of this room in less than thirty, I promise." Taylor moves back to the group surrounding the egg.

"God, my nerves are fraught," she says.

"What does that mean?"

"It means it has taken a week to shoot this and we're three weeks behind schedule."

Pause. "No, what does 'fraught' mean?"

"It means I'm tense. It means I'm very tense."

Finally: "Baby, we gotta talk about something."

"Victor, I've told you that if you need any money—"

"No, no." Pause. "Well, actually that too, but . . ."

"What?" She looks up at me, waiting. "What is it, Victor?"

"Baby, it's just that I'm getting really, um, I'm getting really nervous opening up magazines and reading about who your ideal man is."

"Why is that, Victor?" She turns back to the mirror.

"Well, I guess the main reason is that"—I glance over at La Tosh and lower my voice—"it's like the total opposite of me?"

"Oh, so what?" She shrugs. "I said I liked blonds."

"But baby, I'm really a brunette."

"Victor, you read this in a magazine, for god's sake."

"Jesus, and all this shit about having kids." I'm moving around now. "Spare me, baby. What's the story? What's the megillah?"

"You'll forgive me, Victor, if I have no idea what 'megillah' means."

"Baby, I'm your best friend, so why don't—"

"A mirror's your best friend, Victor."

"Baby, it's just that . . ." I trail off hopelessly. "I . . . care about us and . . ."

"Victor, what's wrong? What is it? Why are you doing this now?"

I recover slightly. "Nothing, nothing. It's nothing." I'm shaking my head, clearing it.

"I've been holding an ice cube all day," Chloe says.

"Your fingers are turning blue and you've been rolling around with Scott Benoit all day. Is that what you're saying?"

Music from a boom box, something British, Radiohead maybe, a ballad, lush and sad, plays over the scene.

"Victor, all I want to do, in the following order, is Todd's show, your opening and then collapse into bed, and I don't even wanna do two of those."

"Who's Baxter Priestly?" I blurt out.

"He's a friend, Victor. A friend. *My* friend," she says. "You should get to know some of them."

I'm about to take her hand but think better of it. "I ran into one today. Lauren Hynde." I wait for a reaction but there isn't one. "Yeah, I saw her before band practice when I was buying CDs at Tower Records. She seemed like really hostile."

"Buying CDs at Tower? Band practice? These are the essentials? You were *swamped*? What else did you do today? Visit a petting zoo? Take glass-blowing lessons?"

"Hey baby, chill out. I met a friend of yours. That should soothe you—"

"I'm dating an imbecile and I should be *soothed* by this?"

A long pause, then, "Baby, I'm not an imbecile. You're very cool."

She turns away from the mirror. "Victor, you don't know how many times in a day I come within *inches* of slapping you. You just don't know."

"Whoa, baby. I don't think I want to. Makes me nervous." I smile, shivering.

The runner comes by the booth. "Chloe, your limo's here and Taylor needs you in about five minutes."

Chloe just nods. When it becomes clear that I've got nothing else to say she fills the silence by murmuring, "I just want to finish this thing," and since I don't know what *thing* she's really talking about I start to babble. "Baby, why are you even doing this? I thought it was strictly features for Chloe Byrnes. You turned down that MTV thing."

"*You* didn't want me to do that MTV thing, Victor."

"Yeah, but only when I found out what your per diem was."

"No. You said no when you found out that *you* didn't have one."

"Might as well face it," I say. "You're addicted to love."

"Chloe," Taylor calls from the egg. "We're ready. And please hurry. Mr. Benoit might forget his line again."

"I'll see you later, Victor." She slides out of the booth.

"Okay," I say simply. "Bye, baby."

"Oh Victor, before I forget."

"Yeah?"

"Thanks for the flowers."

She kisses me lightly, moves on.

"Yeah. Sure. Forget about it."

15

4:00. From my third-floor vantage the club hasn't been this bustling since its inception and tables are being set by handpicked busboys who just skateboarded in, waiters brandishing glasses and tablecloths and candles also set chairs around the tables and the carpets are being vacuumed by guys with shag haircuts and a couple of waitresses who arrived early are being photographed by shadowy clumps of people while dancers rehearse amid technicians and security teams and guest-list people and three gorgeous coat-check girls chew gum and flaunt their midriffs and pierced belly buttons and bars are being stocked and giant flower displays are in the process of being strategically lit and Matthew Sweet's "We're the Same" is blaring and the metal detectors sit in place at the entrance waiting to be entered and I'm taking it all in blankly, considering fleetingly what it all means and also that being semi-famous is in itself difficult but since it's so cold in the club it's hard to stay still so I rush up two flights to the offices more relieved than I should be that everything's finally falling into place.

"Where was Beau? I called him four times today," I ask JD the second I enter.

"Acting class, then an audition for the new big vampire movie," JD says.

"What's it called?" I throw a clump of invites on my desk. *"Fagula?"*

"Now he's interviewing DJs in the VIP room in case we don't get DJ X tonight," JD says, a fey warning.

"You know, JD, that outfit would look really good on a girl."

"Here, Victor," JD says, grimly handing me a fax.

I KNOW WHO YOU ARE AND I KNOW WHAT YOU'RE DOING is scrawled on the fax addressed to me that JD basically stuffs into my hands, looking vaguely panicked.

"What is this?" I ask, staring at the words.

"Seven of them have arrived since you left for lunch."

"Seven of them?" I ask. "What the fuck does it mean?"

"I think they're coming from the Paramount Hotel," JD says, finding another one. "Someone has made sure that the logo was erased on top of the fax sheets but Beau and I caught half the number on the second one and it matched."

"The Paramount?" I ask. "What does this mean?"

"Victor, I don't want to know what it means," JD says, shivering. "Just make the bad man go away."

"Jesus, it could apply to anything," I mutter. "So ultimately it's like meaningless." I crumple it up. "Would you please eat this? Chew carefully."

"Victor, you need to make an appearance in front of the DJs upstairs," JD says carefully.

"Do you think I'm actually being stalked?" I ask. "Wait—how cool."

"And the *Details* reporter is hanging out with the DJs and—"

I start to move out of the office, JD trailing behind.

"—here are more late RSVPs." JD hands me another fax as we head toward the VIP room.

"Dan Cortese?" I'm asking. "A brave man. He bungee jumps, he sky surfs, he's a Burger King spokesperson, but he needs a nose job and I want Dan Cortese *un*plugged."

"Richard Gere *is* coming, Victor," JD says, keeping up. "And Ethan Hawke, Bill Gates, Tupac Shakur, Billy Idol's brother Dilly, Ben Stiller and Martin Davis are also coming."

"Martin Davis?" I groan. "Jesus, let's just invite George the Pee Drinker and his good friend Woody the Dancing Amputee."

"So is Will Smith, Kevin Smith and, um, Sir Mix-a-Lot," JD says, ignoring me.

"Just apprise me of the crouton situation." I stop in front of the velvet curtains leading into the VIP room.

"The croutons are in excellent shape and we're all incredibly relieved," JD says, bowing.

"Don't mock me, JD," I warn. "I will not be mocked."

"Now wait—before you go in," JD says. "It's pretty much a catastrophe, so just, y'know, give your usual winning spiel and get the fuck out of there. They just want to know that you, er, exist." JD thinks about it. "On second thought—" He's about to hold me back.

"You've got to be sensitive to their needs, JD," I tell him. "They're not just DJs. They're *music designers*."

"Before you go in, Jackie Christie and Kris Spirit are also available."

"Lesbian DJs, man? I don't know. Is it happening? Is it cool?" I slap on a pair of wraparound green-tinted sunglasses before I slip into the VIP room, where a mix of seven guys and girls hang out in two booths, Beau sitting on a chair in front of them with a clipboard. The loony *Details* girl reporter, hovering dangerously nearby, waves and JD says "Hey, Beau" in a very professional way and then glumly introduces me. "Hey everybody—here's Victor Ward."

"My nom de guerre in clubland," I faux-gush.

"Victor," Beau says, standing. "This is Dollfish, Boomerang, Joopy, CC Fenton, Na Na and, um"—he checks his clipboard—"Senator Claiborne Pell."

"So-o-o," I ask, pointing at the guy with blond dreadlocks. "What do *you* play?"

"I play Ninjaman but also a lot of Chic and Thompson Twins, and man, this is all kind of borderline bogus."

"Beau, take note of that," I instruct. "How about you?" I ask, pointing at a girl wearing a harlequin outfit and dozens of love beads.

"Anita Sarko taught me everything I know and I also lived with Jonathan Peters," she says.

"You're warming this place up, bay-bee," I say.

"Victor," JD says, pointing at another DJ, hanging back in the dark. "This is Funkmeister Flex."

"Hey Funky." I lower my sunglasses for a wink. "Okay, guys, you got three turntables, a tape deck, a DAT player, two CD players and a reel-to-reel for delay effects to spin your respective magic. How does that sound?"

Muffled cool noises, mindless looks, more cigarettes lit.

"While you're spinning," I continue, pacing, "I want you all to sulk. I don't want to see anyone enjoying themselves. Got it?" I pause to light a cigarette. "There is techno, there is house, there is hard house, there's Belgian house, there's gabba house." I pause again, unsure of where I'm going with this, then decide to segue into "I don't want to be sweating in an actual warehouse. I want that sweating-in-a-warehouse feeling in a three-million-dollar nightclub with two VIP rooms and four full bars."

"It should be very chill," JD adds. "And don't forget ambient dub—we should have that too."

"I want instantaneous buzz," I say, pacing. "It's not a lot to ask. I just want you to make these people dance." I pause before adding, "And abortion-clinic violence does not interest me."

"Um . . ." Dollfish tentatively raises a hand.

"Dollfish," I say. "Please speak."

"Um, Victor, it's already four-fifteen," Dollfish says.

"Your point, sistah?" I ask.

"What time do you need one of us?" she asks.

"Beau—please take care of these questions," I say, bowing, before sweeping out of the room.

JD follows me as I head back up toward Damien's office.

"Really nice, Victor," JD says. "You inspired people, as usual."

"That's my job," I say. "Where's Damien?"

"Damien has instructed me not to have anyone interrupt him right now," JD says.

"I have got to complain to him about inviting Martin Davis," I say, heading back up the stairs. "Things are getting horrific."

"That's not a good idea, Victor." JD runs ahead of me. "He was very insistent that there be no interruptions."

"Turn the beat around, JD."

"Um . . . why?"

"Because I love to hear percussion."

"Don't do this now, Victor," JD pleads. "Damien wants to be left alone."

"But that's the way, uh-huh uh-huh, I like it, uh-huh uh-huh."

"Okay, okay," JD pants. "Just get that fabulous ass over to Fashion Café, nab DJ X and do not sing 'Muskrat Love.'"

"'Muskrat Suzy, Muskrat Sa-a-am . . .'"

"Victor, I'll do whatever you want."

"London, Paris, New York, Munich, everybody talk about—pop music." I tweak his nose and march toward Damien's chamber.

"Please, Victor, let's go the other way," JD says. "The *better* way."

"But that's the way, uh-huh uh-huh, I like it."

"He doesn't want to be bothered, Victor."

"Hey, I don't either, so get away from me, you little mo."

"Victor, he told me to hold all calls and—"

"Hey—" I stop, turning toward him, pulling my arm out of his grasp. "I'm Victor Ward and I'm opening this club and I am sure that I am—what's the word? oh yeah—*exempt* from Mr. Ross's rules."

"Victor—"

I don't even knock, just stride in and begin bitching.

"Damien, I know you didn't want to be bothered but have you checked the guest list for this thing? We have people like Martin Davis supposedly stopping in and I just think that we have to be careful about who the paparazzi are going to see and who they're not. . . ."

Damien's standing by the windows of his office, a large expanse of glass that overlooks Union Square Park, and he's wearing a polka-dot shirt and Havana-style jacket and he's pressed up against a girl wearing an Azzedine Alaïa wrap coat and a pair of Manolo Blahnik high heels, all covered in pink and turquoise, who immediately disengages from him and flops onto a green hop sofa.

Lauren Hynde has changed since I saw her outside Tower Records earlier this afternoon.

"And, um, I, um . . ." I trail off, then recover and say, "Damien—I love that moneyed beachcomber look on you, baby."

Damien looks down at himself, then back at me, smiles tightly as if nothing's really wrong, and in the overall context of things maybe it isn't, then he says, "Hey, I like that unconstructed boxy look you got going."

Stunned, I look down at my hip-hugger pants, the tight satin shirt, the long leather coat, forcing myself not to glance over at the green hop sofa and the girl lounging on it. A long, chilly silence none of us are able to fill floats around, acts cool, *lives*.

JD suddenly sticks his head in, the *Details* girl looking over his shoulder, both of them still stuck in the doorway, as if there's a dangerous invisible line existing that they are not allowed to cross. "Damien, I'm sorry about the interruption," he says.

"It's cool, JD," Damien says, moving over to the door and closing it in their faces.

Damien moves past me and I'm concentrating on staring out the window at people in the park, squinting to make some of them come into focus, but they're too far off and anyway Damien enters my view, dominating it, and picks up a cigar on his desk and a book of matches from the Delano. The new issue of *Vanity Fair* sits by an Hermès lamp, along with various glossy Japanese magazines, CDs, a PowerBook, a bottle of Dom Pérignon 1983 in an ice bucket, two half-empty flutes, a dozen roses, which Lauren will not carry out of this room.

"Jesus fucking Christ," Damien snaps. I flinch. "Why in the fuck is Geena Davis on the cover of goddamn *Vanity Fair*? Does she have a movie out? No. Is she doing anything new? *No*. Jesus Christ, the world's falling apart and no one cares. How do these things happen?"

Not looking over at Lauren Hynde, I just shrug amiably. "Oh, you know how it happens: a shoe ad here, a VJ spot there, a bit part in 'Baywatch,' a bad indie film, then boom: Val Kilmer."

"Maybe she has cancer." Lauren shrugs. "Maybe she went on a big shopping expedition."

"Do you guys know each other?" Damien asks. "Lauren Hynde, Victor Ward."

"Hey, Lauren." I manage a ghastly little wave, which turns into a peace sign, then back into a ghastly little wave.

"Hi." She tries to smile without looking at me, concentrating on her fingernails.

"You two know each other?" Damien asks again, pressing.

"Oh yeah, sure," I say. "You're friends with Chloe."

"Yes," she says. "And you're . . ."

"I'm her . . . yeah, well . . ."

"You two knew each other at college, right?" Damien asks, still staring at us.

"But we haven't seen each other since then," Lauren says, and I'm wondering if Damien catches the harshness of her tone, which gratifies me.

"So this is like a little reunion?" Damien jokes. "Right?"

"Sort of," I say blankly.

Damien has now decided just to continue staring at me.

"Well, Damien, um, you know . . ." I stop, start again. "The DJ situation is—"

"I called Junior Vasquez today," Damien says, lighting the cigar. "But he has another party tonight."

"*Another* party?" I gasp. "Oh man, that is so low."

Lauren rolls her eyes, continues studying her nails.

Damien breaks the silence by asking, "Don't you have a meeting soon?"

"Right, right, I gotta get outta here," I say, moving back toward the door.

"Yeah, and I have a how-to-relax-in-cyberspace seminar in ten minutes," Damien says. "Ricki Lake told me about it."

JD buzzes on the intercom. "Sorry, Damien—Alison on line three."

"In a minute, JD," Damien says.

"It's hard to tell her that," JD says before getting cut off.

"Victor," Damien says. "You wanna walk Lauren out?"

Lauren gives Damien an almost imperceptible glare and gets up too quickly from the sofa. In front of me she kisses Damien lightly on the lips and he touches the side of her face, each of them silently acknowledging the other, and I can't look away until Damien glances over at me.

I can't say anything until we're outside the club. I picked up my Vespa from the coat-check room and am now wheeling it across Union Square, Lauren listlessly moving next to me, the sound of the vacuums inside the club fading behind us. Klieg lights are being rolled across patches of lawn and a film crew is shooting something and extras seem to be wandering aimlessly all around the park. Guillaume Griffin and Jean Paul Gaultier and Patrick Robinson stroll past us. Hordes of Japanese schoolchildren

Rollerblade toward the new Gap on Park Avenue and beautiful girls drift by wearing suede hats and ribbed cardigans and Irish jockey caps and there's confetti strewn all over the benches and I'm still looking down as my feet move slowly along the concrete, walking across large patches of ice so thick that the wheels on the Vespa can't even crack them and the bike still smells of the patchouli oil I rubbed into it last week, an impulsive move that seemed hip at the moment. I keep my eyes on the guys who pass Lauren by and a couple even seem to recognize her and squirrels skate over the patches of ice in the dim light and it's almost dark out but not yet.

"What's the story?" I finally ask.

"Where are you going?" Lauren hugs her wrap coat tighter around herself.

"Todd Oldham show," I sigh. "I'm in it."

"Modeling," she says. "A man's job."

"It's not as easy as it may look."

"Yeah, modeling's tough, Victor," she says. "The only thing you need to be is on time. Hard work."

"It *is*," I whine.

"It's a job where you need to know how to wear clothes?" she's asking. "It's a job where you need to know how to—now let me get this straight—*walk*?"

"Hey, all I did was learn how to make the most of my looks."

"What about your mind?"

"Right," I snicker. "Like in this world"—I'm gesturing—"my mind matters more than my abs. Oh boy, raise your hand if you believe that." Pause. "And I don't remember you majoring in Brain Surgery at Camden."

"You don't even remember me at Camden," she says. "I'd be surprised if you even remember what happened Monday."

Stuck, trying to catch her eyes, I say, "I modeled . . . and had a . . . sandwich." I sigh.

Silently we keep moving through the park.

"He looks like a goddamn schmuck," I finally mutter. "He gets his shorts tailored. Jesus, baby." I keep wheeling the Vespa along.

"Chloe deserves better than you, Victor," she says.

"What does that mean?"

"When's the last time it was just you and her?" she asks.

"Oh man—"

"No, seriously, Victor," she says. "Just you and her for a day without any of this bullshit around you?"

"We went to the MTV Movie Awards," I sigh. "Together."

"Oh god," she moans. "Why?"

"Hey, it's the twentysomething Oscars."

"Exactly."

A giant billboard of Chloe that went up last week above the Toys 'Я' Us on Park suddenly comes into sharp focus through the dead trees, her eyes glaring down at us, and Lauren sees it too and then I'm looking back at the building the club is in and the windows appear blackened in the cold light of late afternoon.

"I hate this angle," I mutter, pulling us out of the shot and steering Lauren across Park so we have some privacy on a street behind the Zeckendorf Towers. She lights a cigarette. I light one too.

"He was probably watching us," I say.

"So act natural," she says. "You don't know me anyway."

"I want to know you," I tell her. "Can we see each other tomorrow?"

"Aren't you going to be too busy basking in the glow of your success?"

"Yeah, but I want to share it with you," I say. "Lunch?"

"I can't," she says, taking another drag. "I have a luncheon at Chanel."

"What do you want, Lauren?" I'm asking. "Some yuppie guy to take you out to Le Cirque every night?"

"What's better?" she asks back. "Unable to pay your rent and depressed and trembling in the local Kentucky Fried Chicken?"

"Oh please. That's the only alternative?"

"*You'd* marry him if you could, Victor."

"Damien's totally not my type, baby."

"That's probably not true," she says softly.

"You want him to give you—what? *Things*? You want to discover the true meaning of suburban life? You think that goombah's even in the Social Register?"

"Damien *is* in the Social Register."

"Well, yeah, right, sure."

"There was a time, Victor, when I wanted you," she says, taking a drag on the cigarette. "There was actually a moment, Victor, when all I ever wanted was you." Pause. "I find it hard to believe myself, but well, there it is."

"Baby, you're cool," I say very softly. "Please—you're very cool."

"Oh stop it, Victor," she says. "You're so full of shit."

"What? You're still not into me?"

"I need a commitment, Victor," she says. "You're the last person on earth I'd ever ask for one from."

"Like you're gonna get it from Damien Nutchs Ross? Spare me, baby. Just spare me."

She finishes the cigarette and starts to move slowly up Park.

"How long have you been doing it with Alison Poole?"

"Hey, watch it." Almost instinctively I look for Duke or Digby, but they're not around. "Why do you think that shit's true?"

"Is it true?"

"If it is: how do you know?"

"Oh god, Victor, who doesn't?"

"What does *that* mean?"

"The only two books she owns are the Bible and *The Andy Warhol Diaries*, and the Bible was a gift," Lauren mutters. "Queen of the fucking pig people."

"I guess I'm not following."

"That doesn't sound like you, Victor." She smiles at me and then says, "It's nice to have someone responsible around—"

"You mean loaded. You mean rich. You mean moola."

"Maybe."

"What? You don't like me because maybe I'm hustling a little? You don't like me because I'm like affected by the recession?"

"Victor," she says, "if only you cared this much when you first met me."

I lean in, kiss her on the mouth hard, and I'm surprised that she lets me and after I pull away she presses her face up into mine, wanting the kiss to continue, her hand clutching mine, her fingers grasping my fingers. Finally I break it off and mumble that I've got to get uptown and in a very casual, hip way, without even really trying, I hop on the Vespa, kick it into gear and speed up Park without looking back, though if I had been I would've seen Lauren yawning while she waved for a cab.

14 A black Jeep, its top up, its windows tinted, wheels in behind me on 23rd Street and as I zoom through the Park Avenue tunnel whoever's driving flips on his brights and closes in, the Jeep's fender grazing the back of the Vespa's wheel guard.

I swerve onto the dividing line, oncoming traffic racing toward me while I bypass the row of cabs on my side, heading toward the wraparound at Grand Central. I accelerate up the ramp, zoom around the curve, swerving to miss a limo idling in front of the Grand Hyatt, and then I'm back on Park without any hassles until I hit 48th Street, where I look over my shoulder and spot the Jeep a block behind me.

The instant the light on 47th turns green the Jeep bounds out of its lane and charges forward.

When my light turns I race up to 51st, where the oncoming traffic forces me to wait to turn left.

I look over my shoulder down Park but I can't see the Jeep anywhere.

When I turn back around, it's idling next to me.

I shout out and immediately slam into an oncoming cab moving slowly down Park, almost falling off the bike, and noise is a blur, all I can really hear is my own panting, and when I lift the bike up I veer onto 51st ahead of the Jeep.

Fifty-first is backed up with major gridlock and I maneuver the Vespa onto the sidewalk but the Jeep doesn't care and careens right behind me, halfway on the street, its two right wheels riding the curb, and I'm yelling at people to get out of the way, the bike's wheels kicking up bursts of the confetti that litters the sidewalk in layers, businessmen lashing out at me with briefcases, cabdrivers shouting obscenities, blaring their horns at me, a domino effect.

The next light, at Fifth, is yellow. I rev up the Vespa and fly off the curb just as the traffic barreling down the avenue is about to slam into me, the sky dark and rolling behind it, the black Jeep stuck on the far side of the light.

Fashion Café is one block away and at Rockefeller and 51st I hop off the bike and run with it behind the mostly useless vinyl ropes that stand outside the doors keeping away no one because there's no one to keep away.

I'm gasping at Byana, the doorman this afternoon, to let me in.

"Did you see that?" I'm shouting. "Those assholes tried to kill me."

"What else is new?" Byana shrugs. "So now you know."

"Listen, I'm just gonna wheel this in." I motion toward the bike. "Just let me leave it right inside here for ten minutes."

"Victor," Byana says, "what about that interview you promised me with Brian McNally?"

"Just give me ten minutes, Byana," I pant, wheeling the bike inside.

The black Jeep idles at the corner and I duck down to peer through the glass doors of Fashion Café, watching as it slowly makes the turn and disappears.

Jasmine, the hostess, sighs when she sees me move through the giant lens that doubles as a hallway and enter the main room of the restaurant.

"Jasmine," I say, holding my hands up. "Just ten, baby."

"Oh Victor, come on," Jasmine says, standing behind the hostess podium, cell phone in hand.

"I'm just gonna leave the bike there." I point back at the Vespa leaning against a wall near coat check.

"We're empty," she relents. "Go on in."

The whole place is totally deserted. Someone hollowly whistles "The Sunny Side of the Street" behind me and when I turn around nobody's there and I realize it could be the last notes of the new Pearl Jam song over the sound system but as I'm waiting for a new song to start it becomes apparent that it sounded too clear, the whistling was too human and I shrug it off and move deeper inside Fashion Café, past someone vacuuming confetti off the floor and a couple of bartenders changing shifts and a waitress adding up tips at the *Mademoiselle* booth.

The only person at any of the tables is a youngish guy with a Caesar haircut looking like a thirtyish Ben Arnold, wearing sunglasses and what looks like a black three-button Agnès b. suit, sitting in the *Vogue* booth behind the fake Arc de Triomphe that hogs the middle of the main dining room. DJ X is looking a little too sharp this afternoon, though pretty sleek nonetheless.

He looks up questioningly, lowering the sunglasses, and then I take a semi-arrogant turn around the room before moving over to the booth.

He takes the sunglasses off and says, "Hello." He offers his hand.

"Hey, where's the baggy pants?" I sigh, slipping into the booth, lightly slapping the hand around. "Where's the oversized zigzag-print T-shirt? Where's the new issue of *Urb*? Where's that groovy mop of bleached chopped hair?"

"I'm sorry." He cocks his head. "I'm sorry, but *what*?"

"So here I *am*," I say, spreading my arms wide. "I exist. So will you do it or not?"

"Do . . . what?" He puts down a purple menu in the shape of a Hasselblad camera.

"One of the DJs we interviewed today actually wanted to play 'Do the Bartman,'" I moan. "He said it was 'unavoidable.' He said it was his 'signature' song. Can you believe how fucked up the world is at this moment?"

The guy slowly reaches into his jacket and pulls out a card and hands it to me. I look at it, vaguely catch a name, F. Fred Palakon, and below that a phone number.

"Okay, baby," I say, breathing in. "Top fee for a DJ on a Thursday night in Manhattan is five hundred but since we're in a bind and according to all my gay friends you're the hippest thing since Astrolube and we need you badly we'll up it to five-forty."

"Thank you, Mr. Johnson—excuse me, Mr. *Ward*—but I'm not a DJ."

"I know, I know. I meant *music designer*."

"No, I'm afraid I'm not that either, Mr. Ward."

"Well, uh, like who are you then and why am I sitting across from you in a booth in Fashion Café?"

"I've been trying to get ahold of you for weeks," he says.

"You've been trying to get ahold of me?" I ask. "*You've* been trying to get ahold of *me*? My answering machine's not really happening this week, I guess." I pause. "Do you have any pot?"

Palakon scans the room, then looks slowly back at me. "No. I do not."

"So what's the story, morning glory?" I'm staring at the remake of *La Femme Nikita* on one of the video monitors hanging near the Arc de Triomphe. "You know, Palakon, you really got that whole very well dressed educated rich junkie thing going on, man. If you don't have it"—I shrug helplessly—"well, my man, you might as well be sucking up a soft-serve cone in an Idaho Dairy Queen in between painting barn silos, huh?"

Palakon just stares across the table at me. I offer him a cinnamon toothpick.

"Did you attend Camden College in New Hampshire during the years 1982 to, ah, 1988?" Palakon asks gently.

Staring back at him, I blankly answer, "I took half a year off." Pause. "Actually four of them."

"Was the first one in the fall of 1985?" Palakon asks.

"Could've been." I shrug.

"Did you know a Jamie Fields while attending Camden College?"

I sigh, slap my hands on the table. "Listen, unless you have a photo—no dice, my man."

"Yes, Mr. Ward," Palakon says, reaching for a folder sitting next to him. "I happen to have photos."

Palakon offers me the folder. I don't take it. He coughs politely and sets it on the table in front of me. I open the folder.

The first set of shots are of a girl who looks like a cross between Patricia Hartman and Leilani Bishop and she's walking down a runway, the letters DKNY vaguely legible in the background, photos of her with Naomi Campbell, one with Niki Taylor, another of her drinking martinis with Liz Tilberis, various shots of her lounging on a couch in what looks like a studio at Industria, two of her walking a small dog in the West Village and one, which looks as if it was taken with a telephoto lens, of her moving along the commons at Camden, heading toward the rim of that lawn before it drops off into the valley below, nicknamed End of the World by students suffering from vertigo.

The second set of shots abruptly place her in front of the Burlington Arcade in London, on Greek Street in Soho, in front of the American Airlines terminal at Heathrow. The third set I come across is a pictorial I'm in with her and Michael Bergin and Markus Schenkenberg, where we're modeling '60's-inspired swimwear. I'm about to jump into a pool wearing white trousers and a Nautica tank top and she's looking at me darkly in the background; the three of us are fooling around with hula hoops; another has us dancing on a patio; in one I'm on a raft in the pool, spitting out an arc of water while she bends down at water's edge motioning for me to come closer. Since I do not remember this shoot at all, I start to close the folder, unable to look at any more photos. My first reaction is: that's not me.

"Does this help your memory?" Palakon asks.

"Whoa, pre-tattoo," I sigh, noticing my bicep curled around Michael's neck before I close the folder. "Jesus, that must've been the year everyone wore Levi's with ripped knees."

"It, um, may have been," Palakon says, sounding confused.

"Is this the girl who signed me up for Feminists for Animal Rights?" I ask. "FAR?"

"Um . . . um . . ." Palakon flips through his file. "She was a"—he squints at a sheet of paper—"a pot activist. Does that help?"

"Not enough, baby." I open the folder again. "Is this the girl I met at Spiros Niarchos's fortieth-birthday party?"

"No."

"How do you know?"

"We—I—know that you did not meet Jamie Fields at Spiros Niarchos's fortieth-birthday party." Palakon closes his eyes, squeezing the bridge of his nose. "Please, Mr. Ward."

I just stare at him. I decide to try another tactic. I lean in to Palakon, which causes him to lean toward me hopefully.

"I want techno techno techno," I stress, suddenly noticing a half-eaten Oriental chicken salad on a plate with Anna Wintour's face on it at the end of the table.

"I . . . didn't order that," Palakon says, startled, and then, looking at the plate, asks, "Who is that?"

"That's Anna Wintour."

"No." He cranes his neck. "It isn't."

I push some of the rice noodles and a tiny slice of mandarin away, revealing the entire face, sans sunglasses.

"Oh. You're right."

"Really happening place," I yawn.

A waitress walks by. I whistle for her to stop.

"Hey baby, I'll have an ice beer."

She nods. I watch her move away, thinking two words: not bad.

"Don't you have a runway show at six?" Palakon asks.

"I'm a model. I'm a lush. But it's cool. I'm cool." I suddenly realize something. "Wait—is this like an intervention or something?" I ask. "Because I've laid off the blow for—jeez, it must be weeks now."

"Mr. Ward," Palakon starts, his patience snapping. "Supposedly you *dated* this girl."

"I dated Ashley Fields?" I ask.

"Her name is *Jamie* Fields and at one point somewhere in your past yes, you did."

"I'm not interested in any of this, man," I point out. "I thought you were a DJ, man."

"Jamie Fields disappeared three weeks ago from the set of an independently financed movie that was being shot in London. The last sightings of Jamie Fields were at the Armani store on Sloane Street and L'Odeon on Regent Street." Palakon sighs, flips through his file. "She has not been heard from since she left the set."

"Maybe she didn't like the script." I shrug. "Maybe she felt they didn't develop her character well enough. It happens, man."

"How"—Palakon looks down at his file, confused—"would *you* know?"

"Proceed, O Cool One," I say casually.

"There are certain individuals who would be pleased if she was found," Palakon says. "There are certain individuals who would like her brought back to America."

"Like her agent and stuff?"

Palakon, at the instant I say this, immediately relaxes, almost as if he suddenly realizes something, and it makes him smile widely for the first time since I sat down and he says, "Yes. Her agent. Yes."

"Cool."

"There have been unconfirmed sightings in Bristol, but that was ten days ago," Palakon says. "Basically we have not been able to locate her."

"Baby?" I lean in again.

"Er, yes?" He leans in too.

"You're pitching a concept nobody gets," I say quietly.

"I see."

"So she's an MTA?"

"Excuse me?"

"Model-turned-actress?"

"I suppose so."

Models are sashaying endlessly down runways on the giant screen above the Arc de Triomphe, even Chloe a couple of times.

"Did you ever see me on the cover of *YouthQuake* magazine?" I ask suspiciously.

"Er . . . yes." Palakon has trouble admitting this, for some reason.

"Cool." I pause. "Can I borrow two hundred dollars from you?"

"No."

"Cool. That's cool."

"This is superfluous," he mutters. "Totally superfluous."

"What does that mean? That I'm a jerk? That I'm some kind of asshole? That I'm a bakehead?"

"No, Mr. Ward," Palakon sighs. "It doesn't mean any of those things."

"Listen—you've got the wrong guy," I say. "I'm outta here." I stand up. "Spare me."

Palakon looks up at me and with a dreamy gaze says, "We're offering you three hundred thousand dollars if you find her."

There's no hesitation. I sit back down.

"Plus all traveling expenses," he adds.

"Why . . . me, dude?" I'm asking.

"She was in love with you, Mr. Ward," Palakon says loudly, startling me. "At least according to her journal entries for the year 1986."

"How . . . did you get those?" I ask.

"Her parents showed them to us."

"Oh man," I groan. "Why don't *they* come to me, then? What are you— their flunky? That was last decade, man."

"Basically," he says, reddening, "I'm simply here, Mr. Ward, to make an offer. Three hundred thousand dollars to find Jamie Fields and bring her back to the States. That's it. You seem to have meant a lot to this girl, whether you remember her or not. We think you might be able to . . . sway her."

After a while I ask, "How did you find me?"

Without pausing, Palakon says, "Your brother told me where to find you."

"I don't have a brother, man."

"I know," Palakon says. "Just testing. I trust you already."

I'm studying Palakon's nails—pink and smooth and clean. A busboy rolls a barrel of avocados into the kitchen. Loops of the fall shows repeat themselves endlessly.

"Hey," I say. "I still need a DJ."

"I can arrange that."

"How?"

"Actually I already have." He pulls out a cell phone and hands it to me. I just stare at it. "Why don't you call your associates at the club?"

"Uh . . . why?"

"Just do it, Mr. Ward. Please," Palakon says. "You don't have much time."

I flip the cell phone open, punch in my number at the club. JD answers.

"It's . . . me," I say, scared for some reason.

"Victor," JD says breathlessly. "Where are you?"

"Fashion Café."

"Get out of there."

"Why?"

"We've got Junior Vasquez tonight," he squeals.

"How?" I'm staring right into Palakon's face. "How . . . did that happen?"

"Junior's manager called Damien and said Junior *wants* to do it. We're set."

I hang up the phone and place it slowly, deliberately, on the table. I study Palakon's face very carefully, thinking a lot of things through, and then I ask him, "Can you do anything about getting me into *Flatliners II*?"

"We can talk about that later, Mr. Johnson."

"Also any role where I could play a callow American Eurail traveler."

"Will you consider this proposal?" Palakon asks.

"You haven't sent me any faxes, have you?"

"What faxes?" he asks, placing the folder of photos in a thin black brief-case. "What did they say?"

"'I know who you are and I know what you're doing.'"

"I already know who you are, Mr. Johnson, and I already know what you're doing," he says, snapping the briefcase shut.

"Whoa—what are you?" I ask, vaguely impressed. "A fucking watch-dog?"

"You might say so," he sighs.

"Listen." I check my watch. "We'll, um, talk later, I guess. That's just too much moola to ignore, baby."

"I was hoping that you could give me an answer now."

I stare at him, lost. "You want me to go to London and find some girl I don't even remember dating?"

"So you've understood me," Palakon says, visibly relieved. "For a moment there I was worried that nothing was registering."

Suddenly contemplative, I stare into Palakon's face. "You look like the kind of guy who eats his own scabs," I murmur. "Did you know that? That you look like that kind of guy?"

"I've been called many things, Mr. Ward, but a scab-eater has not been among them."

"Hell, there's a first time for everything, buddy," I sigh, pushing myself away from the table, standing up. Palakon keeps staring at me, which makes me nervous and all tingly, creeps me out in a way I've never been creeped out before.

"Hey, look—it's Ricki Lake hugging a street urchin." I point at a video monitor behind Palakon's head.

Palakon turns his head to look.

"Ha-ha—made you look." I start walking away.

Palakon stands up. "Mr. Ward—"

"Hey," I call from across the room. "I've got your card."

"Mr. Ward, I—"

"I'll talk to you later, man. Peace."

The restaurant is still totally deserted. I can't even see Byana or Jasmine or the waitress I ordered the ice beer from anywhere. When I reach my bike someone's stuck a giant fax on one of the handlebars: I KNOW WHAT YOU'RE DOING AND I KNOW WHAT YOU SAID. I grab it and run back into the soft light of the main room to show Palakon, but that room, too, is empty.

13 The show's at Bryant Park even though it was supposed to be in an abandoned synagogue on Norfolk Street but Todd freaked when he heard it was haunted by the ghosts of two feuding rabbis and a giant floating knish and as I roll up to the back entrance—42nd Street jammed with TV vans and satellite dishes and limousines and black sedans—photographers have already lined up, calling out my name as I flash my pass at the security guards. Behind barricades groups of teenagers shout out for Madonna even though she's not expected to show because she's too busy facing down her latest stalker in court but Guy from Maverick Records promised to appear and Elsa Klensch and a CNN camera crew's interviewing FIT students about their favorite designers and just an hour ago the runway was shortened because of the supposed overflow of five hundred and there was a desperate need to add room for the three hundred standees. Video monitors have been set up outside for the overflow's overflow. The show cost $350,000 to put on so everyone needs to see it.

Backstage preshow is a blur of clothes racks and taped instruction sheets and Polaroids of outfits and tables of wigs along with a lot of fierce airkissing and hundreds of cigarettes being lit and naked girls running around and basically no one really paying attention. A huge poster overlooking the scene screams WORK IT in giant black letters, the sound track from *Kids* plays at an excruciating decibel level. Rumors abound that two models are missing, either running late from another show or being abused by their scummy new boyfriends in a limo stalled in traffic somewhere on Lexington but no one really knows.

"The buzzword today is *tardy*, no?" Paull, the director of the show, bitches direly at me. "I don't think so."

"As *if*," I Alicia-Silverstone-in-*Clueless* back at him.

"Okay—five minutes to first looks," calls out Kevin, the producer from Hastings, Minnesota.

Todd runs around frantically, managing to somehow calm shaking, frightened, wiped-out models with just a kiss. I'm kissing a heavily eye-shadowed Chloe, who is surrounded by clothes hanging from racks and looking exactly like someone should look who has been shooting a Japanese soda-pop commercial for most of the day, but I tell her she looks like a "total doll" and she does. She complains about blisters and the brown paper pedicure sandals on her feet while Kevyn Aucoin, wearing a clear plastic tool belt and an orange ruffled Gaultier body shirt, powders her cleavage and glosses her lips. Orlando Pita has done the girls' hair and we're all definitely opting for semi-understatement here and pearly cream pink eye shadow, upper lids done, lower rims just about. Someone rubs a fake tattoo of Snappy the Shark on my left pectoral while I smoke a cigarette then eat a couple of Twizzlers that I wash down with a Snapple an assistant hands me while someone inspects my belly button, vaguely impressed, and someone else camcords the event—another modern moment completed.

Modeling Todd's new '70s-influenced punk/New Wave/Asia-meets-East-Village line are Kate Moss paired with Marky Mark, David Boals with Bernadette Peters, Jason Priestley with Anjanette, Adam Clayton with Naomi Campbell, Kyle MacLachlan with Linda Evangelista, Christian Slater with Christy Turlington, a recently slimmed-down Simon Le Bon with Yasmin Le Bon, Kirsty Hume with Donovan Leitch, plus a mix of new models—Shalom Harlow (paired with Baxter fucking Priestly), Stella Tennant, Amber Valletta—and some older ones including Chloe, Kristen McMenamy, Beverly Peele, Patricia Hartman, Eva Herzigova, along with the prerequisite male models: Scott Benoit, Rick Dean, Craig Palmer, Markus Schenkenberg, Nikitas, Tyson. There will be one hundred eighty costume changes. My first walk: black swimsuit and black T-shirt. Second walk: bare-chested. Third walk: pair of slacks and a tank top. Fourth walk: bikini briefs and a tank top. But everyone will probably be gazing at Chloe, so in a way it's all kind of mooty. Todd recites his preshow instructions: "Big smiles and be proud of who you are."

On the first walk Chloe and I head toward a multitude of long zoom lenses that go nuts when we approach. Under the TV floodlights models glide by each other, each foot swinging effortlessly around the other. Chloe's hips are swaying, her ass is twisting, a perfect pirouette at the runway's end, both our stares unflinching, full of just the right kind of attitude. In the audience I'm able to spot Anna Wintour, Carrie Donovan, Holly Brubach, Catherine Deneuve, Faye Dunaway, Barry Diller, David Geffen, Ian Schrager, Peter Gallagher, Wim Wenders, Andre Leon Talley, Brad Pitt, Polly Mellon, Kal Ruttenstein, Katia Sassoon, Carrie Otis, RuPaul, Fran

Lebowitz, Winona Ryder (who doesn't applaud as we walk by), René Russo, Sylvester Stallone, Patrick McCarthy, Sharon Stone, James Truman, Fern Mallis. Music selections include Sonic Youth, Cypress Hill, Go-Go's, Stone Temple Pilots, Swing Out Sister, Dionne Warwick, Psychic TV and Wu-Tang Clan. After the final walk with Chloe I back off slightly and Todd grabs her by the waist and they both bow and then she pulls away and applauds him and I have to resist the impulse to stand back next to her and then everyone jumps onto the runway and follows everyone else backstage to Will Regan's after-show party.

Backstage: Entertainment Tonight, MTV News, AJ Hammer from VH1, "The McLaughlin Group," "Fashion File" and dozens of other TV crews push through the tents, which are so clogged no one can really move, overhead microphones towering over the crowd on long poles. It's freezing backstage even with all the lights from the video crews, and huge clouds of secondhand smoke are billowing over the crowd. A long table is covered with white roses and Skyy martinis and bottles of Moët and shrimp and cheese straws and hot dogs and bowls of jumbo strawberries. Old B-52 records blare, followed by Happy Mondays and then Pet Shop Boys, and Boris Beynet and Mickey Hardt are dancing. Hairstylists, makeup artists, mid-level transvestites, department store presidents, florists, buyers from London or Asia or Europe, are all running around, being chased by Susan Sarandon's kids. Spike Lee shows up along with Julian Schnabel, Yasmeen Ghauri Nadege, LL Cool J, Isabella Rossellini and Richard Tyler.

I'm trying to meet the vice president of casting and talent at Sony but too many retailers and armies of associates and various editors with what seems like hundreds of cameras and microphones hunched over them keep pushing through the tents, relegating me to the boyfriends-and-male-models-sitting-around-slack-jawed corner, some of them already lacing up their Rollerblades, but then I'm introduced to Blaine Trump's cook, Deke Haylon, by David Arquette and Billy Baldwin. A small enclave consisting of Michael Gross, Linda Wachner, Douglas Keeve, Oribe and Jeanne Beker is talking about wanting to go to the club's opening tonight but everyone's weighing the consequences of skipping the *Vogue* dinner. I bum a Marlboro from Drew Barrymore.

Then Jason Kanner and David, the owner of Boss Model, both tell me they had a wild time hanging with me at Pravda the other night and I just shrug "whatever" and struggle over to Chloe's makeup table, passing Damien, who has a cigar in one hand and Alison Poole in the other, her sunglasses still on, angling for photo ops. I open Chloe's bag while she's being interviewed by Mike Wallace and search her datebook for Lauren Hynde's address, which I find and then take $150 and when Tabitha Soren asks me what I think about the upcoming elections I just offer the peace sign and say "Every day my confusion grows" and head for Chloe, who looks really sweaty, holding a champagne flute to her forehead, and I kiss her on the cheek and tell her I'll swing by her place at eight. I head for the exit where all the bodyguards are hanging out and pass someone's bichon frise sluggishly lifting its head and even though there are hundreds of photo ops to take advantage of it's just too jammed to make any of them. Someone mentions that Mica might be at Canyon Ranch, Todd's engulfed by groovy well-wishers and my feelings are basically: see, people aren't so bad.

12

I pull up to Lauren's apartment at the Silk Building right above Tower Records where I saw her earlier this afternoon and as I roll the Vespa up to the lobby the teenage doorman with the cool shirt picks up a phone hesitantly, nodding as Russell Simmons walks past me and out onto Fourth Street.

"Hey." I wave. "Damien to see Lauren Hynde."

"Er . . . Damien who?"

"Damien . . . Hirst."

Pause. "Damien Hirst?"

"But actually it's just Damien." Pause. "Lauren knows me as just Damien."

The doorman stares at me blankly.

"Damien," I say, urging him on a little. "Just . . . Damien."

The doorman buzzes Lauren's apartment. "Damien's here?"

I reach out to feel the collar of his shirt, wondering where he got it. "What is this?" I'm asking. "Geek chic?"

He waves my hand away, taking a karate stance. A pause, during which I just stare at him.

"Okay," the doorman says, hanging up the phone. "She says the door's open. Go on up."

"Can I leave the moped here, man?"

"It might not be here when you get back."

I pause. "Whoa, dude." I wheel the bike into an elevator. "Hakuna matata."

I check my nails, thinking about the *Details* reporter, the crouton situation, a conversation I had on a chairlift in a ski resort somewhere that was so inane I can't even remember what was said. The elevator doors slide open and I lean the bike in the hallway just outside Lauren's apartment. Inside: all white, an Eames folding screen, an Eames surfboard table, the roses I saw in Damien's office lie on a giant Saarinen pedestal surrounded by six tulip chairs. MTV with the sound off on a giant screen in the living room: replays of today's shows, Chloe on a runway, Chandra North, other models, ABBA's "Knowing Me, Knowing You" coming from somewhere.

Lauren walks out of her bedroom wearing a long white robe, a towel wrapped around her hair, and when she looks up to see me standing in the middle of the room asking "What's the story, baby?" she lets out a little yelp and falls back a few steps but then composes herself and just glares, eyes frozen, arms crossed, mouth set hard—a woman's stance I'm familiar with.

"Aren't you going to bother to hide your annoyance?" I finally ask. "Aren't you gonna like offer me a Snapple?"

"What are you doing here?"

"Don't freak."

She moves over to a desk piled high with fashion magazines, flicks on a crystal chandelier, rummages through a Prada handbag and lights a Marlboro Medium. "You've got to get out of here."

"Hey, can't we just talk for a minute, baby?"

"Victor, *leave*," she warns impatiently and then scrunches her face up. "*Talk?*"

"I'll vacate only after we chat."

She considers this and, grimacing, forces herself to ask quickly, "Okay—how was the Oldham show?"

"Very major," I say, slouching around the room. "Chatted with Elsa Klensch. The usual."

"How *is* Elsa?" she asks, still glaring.

"Elsa and I are both Capricorns so we get along very nicely," I say. "Is it cold in here or is it just me?"

"And otherwise?" she asks, waiting.

"It was, er, very, very—oh yeah—important."

"Important?" Lauren asks semi-dubiously.

"Clothes are important, baby."

"They eventually clean furniture, Victor."

"Hey," I exclaim. "Lighten up, baby."

"Victor, you've *got* to get out of here."

"What were you doing?" I ask, moving around the room, taking the whole apartment in. "Why weren't you at the show?"

"I had a photo shoot promoting a terrible movie I'm in with Ben Chaplin and Rufus Sewell," she hisses, barely able to contain herself. "Then I took a bubble bath and read an article on the impossibility of real emotion on the Upper East Side in *New York* magazine." She stubs out the cigarette. "This was a draining conversation, yet one I'm glad we had. The door's over there in case you've forgotten."

She walks past me, down a hallway covered with a Berber-style woven carpet and Moroccan embroidered pillows stacked against the walls and then I'm in her bedroom, where I flop on the bed, leaning back on my elbows, my feet barely touching the floor, watching as Lauren stalks into the bathroom and begins toweling her hair dry. Behind her a poster for some indie film starring Steve Buscemi hangs above the toilet. She's so annoyed—but maybe in a fake way—that I have to say, "Oh come off it, I'm not so bad. I bet you hang out with guys who say things like 'But what if I want a new Maserati' all the time. I bet your life is filled with that." I stop, then add, "Too."

She picks up a half-empty glass of champagne by the sink, downs it.

"Hey," I say, pointing at the framed poster. "You were in that movie?"

"Unfortunately," she mutters. "Notice where it's hanging?"

She closes her eyes, touches her forehead.

"You just finished a new movie?" I ask softly.

"Yes." Suddenly she searches through an array of Estée Lauder jars, Lancôme products, picks up a L'Occitane butter massage balm that Chloe also uses, reads the ingredients, puts it down, finally gives up and just looks at herself in the mirror.

"What's it about?" I ask as if it matters.

"It's kind of like *Footloose*," she says, then pauses and delicately whispers, "But set on Mars." She waits for my reaction.

I just stare at her from the bed. A longish silence. "That's so cool, baby."

"I wept on the set every day."

"Did you just break up with someone?"

"You—are—a—dunce."

"I'm waiting to see if I'm getting a role in *Flatliners II*," I mention casually, stretching.

"So we're in the same boat?" she asks. "Is that it?"

"Alison Poole told me you were doing pretty well."

She swigs from a nearby bottle of Evian. "Let's just say it's been lucratively tedious."

"Baby, I'm sensing that you're a star."

"Have you seen any of my movies?"

Pause. "Alison Poole told me you were doing—"

"Don't mention that cunt's name in this apartment," she screams, throwing a brush at me.

"Hey baby," I say, ducking. "Come here, baby, chill out."

"What?" she asks, irritably. "Come where?"

"Come *here*," I murmur, staring straight at her. "Come here," I say, patting the comforter.

She just stares at me lying on the bed, my shirt pulled up a little, showing off my lower abs, my legs slightly spread. Sometime during all of this my jacket came off.

"Victor?"

"Yeah?" I whisper.

"What does Chloe mean to you?"

"Come here," I whisper.

"Just because you're a gorgeous guy doesn't give you any more rights than . . . ," she falters, picks up: ". . . anyone else."

"I know, baby. It's cool." I sit up, gazing at her, never breaking eye contact. She moves toward me.

"Come on," I say. "That's it."

"What do you want, Victor?"

"I want you to come over here."

"What are you?" she asks, suddenly pulling back. "One of the fringe benefits of being a pretty girl?"

"Hey, I'm a stud muffin." I shrug. "Take a bite."

A flicker of a smile that tells you she will probably do anything. It's time to relax and play it differently. I reach into my jeans, lifting up my shirt a little more so that she can see the rest of my stomach and spreading my legs even wider so she can spot the bulge in my jeans. I offer her a Mentos.

"You really look like you work out," I say. "How do you keep in such buff shape, doll?"

"Not eating helps," she mutters.

"So you're refusing the Mentos?"

She smiles, barely, and nods.

"Are you coming to the club tonight?" I ask.

"To the Copa? The Copacabana? The hottest spot north of Havana?" she asks, clapping her hands together, eyes wide with fake delight.

"Hey, don't be dissing me, sistah."

"Where's Chloe now, Victor?" she asks, moving closer.

"Who was *your* last significant other, baby?"

"An ex–rogue trader I met at a screenplay-writing seminar, then Gavin Rossdale," she says. "Oh, and Adam Sandler for three days."

"Oh shit." I smack my forehead. "*Now* I know who you are. *Now* I remember."

She smiles a little, warming up. "Who are you dating now, Victor?" She pauses. "Besides Alison Poole?"

"Hey, I thought that name wasn't allowed in this apartment."

"Only someone who owns a voodoo doll of her with five hundred pins stuck in its head and an extra-large Snickers bar strapped to its ass can," she says. "Now, who are you dating, Victor? Just say it. Just let me hear you say a name."

"Four that wanna own me, two that wanna stone me, one that says she's a friend of mine."

She smiles now, standing over the bed.

"Can I ask you something?" I ask.

"Can you?"

"You won't freak out?"

"It depends."

"Okay. Just promise me you'll take this within a certain context."

"What?"

"It's just that . . ." I stop, breathe in, laugh a little.

"It's just what?"

Now, playing it very seriously, I say, "It's just that I really want to stick my tongue up your pussy right now." I'm squeezing my dick through my jeans, staring straight at her. "I promise I won't do anything else. I just have this urge to lick your pussy right now." I pause, shyly. "Can I?"

She breathes in but doesn't move away.

"Are you going to complain about my behavior?" I ask.

"No," she says.

"Come here," I say.

Her eyes move over my body.

"Come here," I say again.

She just stands there, deciding what to do, unmoving.

"Is there a . . . dilemma?" I'm asking.

"Victor," she sighs. "I can't."

"Why?" I ask. "Come here."

"Because it's like you're back from . . . outer space or something," she says. "And I don't know you."

"You're a little hard to unwrap too, baby."

She lets her robe drop.

"I think we should maybe end the conversation here," I say.

She kneels over me, pushing me back down on the bed, straddling my waist. I work one finger into her pussy, finally just easing it in, then two fingers, and her own fingers are rubbing her clit and I sit up and start licking and sucking on her breasts. I take my fingers out of her pussy and put them in my mouth, telling her how much I want to eat her pussy, and then I easily flip her onto her back and spread her legs wide apart and push them back so her whole pussy is spread out, available, and I start fingerfucking her while licking and sucking on her clit. I stick another finger in my mouth and slip it in between her legs, lower, until it touches her asshole, pressing lightly against it. I'm rock hard and I've pulled my pants down to my knees, my ass sticking up in the air, stroking myself off, my tongue way up her cunt, but then she pulls me up to her breasts, urging me to suck her nipples, and still stroking my prick I immediately move up and we start eating each other's mouths, sucking hungrily, and she's gripping my cock and rubbing it against her lower lips and then my cock's sliding up into her without any effort and she starts humping hard on it and I start meeting her thrusts and she's coming and then the intercom buzzes and the doorman's voice announces, "Lauren—Damien Ross is on his way up," and we both freeze.

"Oh shit." She stumbles up and grabs her robe off the floor and then she's running down the hallway, calling out, "Get dressed—Damien's here."

"Oh shit, baby." Panicked, I sit up, misjudge my place on the bed and fall off. I immediately pull my pants up and tuck my boner, aching and still stiff and wet, back into my Calvins.

"He's early," she groans, racing back into the room. "*Shit!*"

"Early for *what*?" I ask.

When I turn around she's at the closet, tearing through dresses and stacks of sweaters until finally she finds a black ladies' hat—cool-looking, with a tiny red flower embroidered on its side—and she studies it for a nanosecond before shoving it at me. "Here."

"What?" I'm asking. "*This* is your idea of a disguise?"

"Tell him you came by to pick it up for Chloe," she says. "And wipe your face off."

"Lauren, baby," I say. "Chill out."

"You shouldn't have come over." She starts moving down the hallway. "I'm an idiot for not throwing you out."

"I thought we were having a pretty good time," I say, following her.

"Well, that's not what we should've been doing," she yells. "That's not what we should've been doing," she whispers.

"Hey, don't say that."

"Let's just find a place to stand and call it a weak moment," she says. "You shouldn't have come over."

"Baby, you've established that—I get it, okay?" I follow her into the living room and find a casual place to position myself.

"No, stand *here*," Lauren says, tying the sash on her robe. "As if we're— oh god—talking."

"Okay, what do you want to talk about?" I ask, calming down. "How hard you make my dick?"

"Just give me that damn hat back."

"Chloe would more likely wear a rotting log around her neck."

"She dates you, so what do *you* know?"

Damien walks in, holds up the cigar in his hand and says, "Hey baby, don't worry, it's not lit." They don't bother to kiss and in a really serene way Damien nods at me, gives a cute little wave and says, "Hey Victor."

"Hey Damien." I give a cute little wave back.

"You're everywhere today, huh?"

"Everywhere at once—that's me."

"Victor," Lauren says. "Tell Chloe she can return this to me anytime, okay, Victor?" She hands me back the hat.

"Yeah, sure, Lauren. Um, thanks." I look at the hat, turning it around in my hands, inspecting it. "Nice . . . hat."

"What's that?" Damien asks.

"A hat," Lauren says.

"For who?" he asks.

"Chloe," Lauren and I say at the same time.

"Victor came by to pick it up for her," she finishes.

"When's she gonna wear that?" Damien asks. "What's the urgency?"

"Tonight," I say. "She's going to wear it tonight."

The three of us look at each other and something weird, something a little too intimate, passes between us, so we all look back at the hat.

"I can't look at this hat anymore," Lauren says. "I have to take a shower."

"Baby, wait," Damien says. "I'm in a real rush. We have to talk about something."

"I thought we already discussed what you want to discuss," she says tightly.

"Victor," Damien says, ushering Lauren out of the room. "We'll be right back."

"No problemo, guys."

I check my messages: Gavin Palone, Emmanuelle Béart, someone from Brillstein-Grey, someone else who I've decided looks good with his new goatee. It's freezing in the apartment. Everything suddenly seems slightly exhausting, vaguely demanding: the lifting of a spoon, the draining of a champagne flute, the glance that means you should go, even pretending to sleep. There's a room somewhere and in that room all the tables are empty but all of them are reserved. I check the time. Next to my watch is a stray piece of confetti I'm too tired to brush off and I could really use some chips and salsa since I'm famished. I know who you are and I know what you said.

At the bar Damien pours himself a shot of Patrón tequila and stares forlornly at his cigar. "She won't let me smoke in here." He pauses. "Well, not cigars." I'm aware for the first time that Damien's actually sort of really good-looking and in this light I can't even tell he has extensions; his hair looks thick and black and strong, and I'm touching my jaw, limply, to see if it feels as hollowed out as Damien's looks.

"It's cool," I say.

"Victor, what are you doing here?"

I hold up the hat.

"Yeah?" he asks. "Really?"

"Hey, I heard about Junior Vasquez DJ'ing tonight," I say, elegantly changing the subject.

Damien sighs tiredly. "Great. Isn't it?"

"How did that happen?"

"On the record?"

I nod.

"Some special-events impresario called," Damien says. "And—voilà."

"Can I ask you a question?" I start, feeling daring.

"What is it?"

"Where did you guys meet?" I ask. "I mean, you and Lauren."

He downs the tequila, gently places the glass back on the bar and frowns. "I met her while we were both having dinner with the world's richest people."

"Who?"

"We're not allowed to give out those names."

"Oh."

"But you'd know them," Damien says. "You wouldn't be surprised."

"Cool."

"Hint: they had just spent the weekend at Neverland Ranch."

"Would you like a Mentos?" I ask.

"I need a favor, Victor."

"I'd do anything for you, man."

"Please don't grovel."

"Sorry."

"Will you take Lauren with you to the opening tonight?" Damien asks. "She won't come otherwise. Or if she does she's threatening to come with fucking Skeet Ulrich or Olivier Martinez or Mickey Hardt or Daniel Day-fucking-Lewis."

"That would be cool," I consider. "I mean if we could get Daniel Day-Lewis—"

"Hey," he snaps. "Watch it."

"Oh yeah. My apologies."

Damien still has traces of this morning's mud mask next to his right ear. I reach out and flick a speck gently away.

"What's that?" he asks, flinching.

"Mud?" I guess.

He sighs. "It's shit, Victor. It's all shit."

I pause. "You had . . . *shit* on your face?" I ask. "Whoa, dude. Don't go there."

"No. My *life*, Victor. My whole fucking life. It's all shit."

"Why, guy?" I ask. "When did this massive dumping occur?"

"I have a girlfriend, Victor," Damien says, staring straight at me.

"Yeah—" I stop, confused. "Alison?"

"No. Alison's my *fiancée*. Lauren's the girlfriend."

"You guys are engaged?" I gasp involuntarily and when I try to hide the gasp, I gasp again. "Oh, I knew that, dude. Um, I knew that."

Damien's face hardens. "How did you know that?" he asks. "Nobody knows that."

Pause, then semi-effortlessly, in a tight voice while holding my breath, out comes: "Man oh man this town, guy."

Damien seems too depressed to not accept this. A long pause.

"You mean," I start, "like getting-married *engaged*?"

"That's usually what it means."

"So I've heard," I murmur.

"When did *you* and Lauren get so close?" he asks suddenly.

"I really don't know her at all, Damien," I say, squeezing the hat. "She's a friend of Chloe's."

"She said she went to school with you," he mutters. "She said you were— and don't take this the wrong way—a total asshole."

"I won't take that the wrong way."

"I can see that your self-esteem is pretty high today, huh?"

"It's funny—I thought she went to school with *you*, man." I chuckle lamely to myself, bowing a little, eyes half-closed. "Didn't you guys go to school together, m-man?"

"Victor, I've got a fucking migraine. Just, y'know, *don't*." He closes his eyes, reaches for the Patrón, stops himself. "So—will you do it? Will you take her?"

"I'm . . . taking Chloe."

"Just take Lauren with you guys." His beeper goes off. He checks it. "Shit. It's Alison. I've gotta go. Tell Lauren goodbye. And I'll see you at the club."

"Tonight's the night," I say.

"I think it'll work," he says. "I think it won't be a disaster."

"We'll see, man."

Damien reaches out his hand. Instinctively I shake it. Then he's gone.

I'm standing in the living room, taking a long time to notice Lauren leaning in the doorway.

"I heard everything," she murmurs.

"That's probably more than I heard," I murmur back.

"Did you know they were engaged?"

"No," I say. "I didn't."

"I guess I'm coming with you guys tonight."

"I want you to," I say.

"I know you do."

"Lauren—"

"I really wouldn't worry about it," she says, brushing past me. "Damien thinks you're a fag anyway."

"An . . . important fag or an unimportant fag?"

"I don't think Damien bothers to differentiate."

"If I *was* a fag I think I'd probably be an important one."

"If we continue this conversation I think I'd probably be entering the Land of the Nitwits."

She turns off the TV and holds her face in her hands, looking like she doesn't know what to do. I don't know what to do either, so I check my watch again.

"Do you know when the last time I saw you was, Victor?" she asks, her back to me.

"At . . . Tower Records?"

"No. Before that."

"Where?" I ask. "For god's sake, don't say the Calvin Klein show or in Miami."

"It was in 'The Sexiest Men in the Galaxy' issue of some crappy magazine," she says. "You were lying on top of an American flag and didn't have a shirt on and basically looked like an idiot."

I move toward her.

"How about before that?"

"In 1985," she says. "Years ago."

"Jesus, baby."

"When you told me you'd come pick me up. At Camden."

"Pick you up from where?"

"My dorm," she says. "It was December and there was snow and you were supposed to drive me back to New York."

"What happened?" I ask. "Did I?"

A long pause, during which the phone rings. Fabien Baron leaves a message. The phone rings again. George Wayne from London. Lauren just stares at my face, totally lost. I think about saying something but then don't bother.

"You should go."

"I am."

"Where?"

"Pick up my tux."
"Be careful."
"It's okay," I say. "I'm a sample size."

11

The last time Chloe and I were in L.A.: a rehab stint in a famously undisclosed location that only me and one of Chloe's publicists knew about. The various strings had been pulled and Chloe bypassed waiting lists, landing in a fairly posh cell: she had her own deluxe adobe-inspired bungalow with a daiquiri-blue-colored sunken living room, a patio with faux-'70s lounge chairs, a giant marble bathtub decorated with pink eels and dozens of mini-Jacuzzi jets, and there was an indoor pool and a fully equipped gym and an arts-and-crafts center but there wasn't a television set so I had to tape "All My Children" on the VCR in the hotel room I was staying at in a nearby desert town, which was really the least I could do. Chloe had her own horse, named Raisin.

At first, whenever I visited, Chloe said that it was "all useless." She bitched about the "too hypernutritious" food served on trays in the cafeteria (even though the chef was from a chic Seattle hotel) and she bitched about emptying her own ashtrays and there had been four suicide attempts that week and someone who was in for Valium dependency had climbed out a window and escaped for three days before anyone on staff noticed until a nurse read about it in the *Star* on Monday. Chloe bitched about the constant rambling and the shoving matches between patients—various self-destructive moguls, kids who copped to sniffing butane in group therapy sessions, heads of studios who had been smoking half an ounce of freebase daily, people who hadn't been in touch with the real world since 1987. Steven Tyler hit on her at a vending machine, Gary Oldman invited her out to Malibu, Kelsey Grammer rolled on top of her "accidentally" in a stretching class, a biofeedback technician commented favorably on her legs.

"But baby, you have full phone privileges," I told her. "Cheer up."

"Kurt Cobain stayed here, Victor," she whispered, dazed, bleached out.

And then, as it always does, time began to run out. The tabloids were casting a shadow, her publicist warned, and "Hard Copy" was getting closer and Chloe's private phone number was being changed daily and I had to remind Pat Kingsley that Chloe's monthly retainer at PMK was $5,000 and couldn't they do better?

And so Chloe finally surrendered. We were left with Chloe's counselor telling us from behind a black granite desk, "Hey, we try to do everything we can—but we're not always successful," and then I was guiding Chloe out to a waiting gold Lexus I had rented and she was carrying a gift bag filled with mugs, T-shirts, key rings, all stamped with the words "One Day at a Time," and someone sitting cross-legged on a lawn was strumming "I Can See Clearly Now" on his guitar while the palm trees swayed ominously above us and Mexican children danced in a semicircle next to a giant blue fountain. That month cost $50,000, not including my suite in the nearby desert town.

10

The movies being shot all over SoHo tonight are backing up traffic everywhere and it's damp and cold as I exit Lauren's place and wheel the Vespa down the sidewalk on Fourth Street to the intersection at Broadway and the red light waiting for me there.

I don't spot the black Jeep until the light turns green (nothing moves, horns blare), and I pretend not to notice as I merge into the traffic heading downtown. In the handlebar mirror I watch the Jeep finally turn slowly behind me, making a right off Fourth, and I casually begin moving across lanes to the far side of Broadway, wheeling past dozens of cars, their headlights momentarily blinding me as I push between them, my breath coming in short, jagged gasps, the Jeep trapped in traffic behind me.

Passing Third Street, I'm keeping my eyes on Bleecker, where I immediately jam a right, zooming around oncoming cars, bumping over the curb onto the sidewalk, almost hitting a group of kids hanging under the awning of the Bleecker Court apartments, and then I make a hard left onto Mercer and take it down to Houston, where I make a wide right, and just when I think I'm clear I almost collide with the black Jeep waiting at the corner. But it's not the same black Jeep, because this one idling at Wooster and Houston has a license plate that reads SI-CO 2 and the one still stuck on Broadway has a license plate that reads SI-CO 1.

As I pass this new Jeep, it pulls away from the curb and surges after me.

At West Broadway I swing a wide left but with construction everywhere and all the movies being shot the street is virtually impassable.

Inching toward Prince Street, I notice vacantly that the first Jeep has somehow gotten in front of me and is now waiting at the end of the block.

In the mirror I notice that the second Jeep is three cars back.

I wheel the bike between two limousines parked at the curb, Space Hog blaring out of one of the sunroofs, and I hop off, take the keys and begin walking very slowly down West Broadway.

On the sidewalk, lights from the stores lining the street throw shadows of someone following me. Stopping suddenly, I whirl around, but no one's there, just this sort of semi-electric feeling that I'm unable to focus in on, and now someone, an extra, really passes by and says something unintelligible.

Behind me someone gets out of the black Jeep.

I spot Skeet Ulrich hanging out in front of the new martini bar, Babyland, and Skeet's signing autographs and wearing suede Pumas and just taped the Conan O'Brien show and finished an on-line press conference and maybe or maybe not has the lead in the new Sam Raimi movie and we compare tattoos and Skeet tells me he has never been more hungover than when we got wasted together at the Wilhelmina party in Telluride and I'm kicking at the confetti that surrounds us on the sidewalk and waving a fly away with a Guatemalan crucifix Simon Rex gave me for my twenty-fifth birthday.

"Yeah," Skeet's saying, lighting a cigar. "We were hanging with the new Thai-boxing champ."

"I am so lost, man."

"Caucasian dreadlocks?" Skeet says. "He had an Ecstasy factory hidden in his basement?"

"Rings a bell, man, but man I'm so wiped out," I say, looking over my shoulder. "Hey, what were we — I mean, what were you doing in Telluride?"

Skeet mentions a movie he was in, while I offer him a Mentos.

"Who were you in that movie, man?"

"I played the 'witty' corpse."

"The one who lived in the crypt?"

"No. The one who fucked the coven of witches."

"And taught them slang in the cauldron? Whoa."

"I'm a strict professional."

Someone walks by and takes our photo, calls Skeet "Johnny Depp," and then Kate Spade says hi and I still have Lauren's folded-up hat hanging out of my pocket and I touch it to remind myself of something. When I casually glance over my shoulder, the guy who got out of the Jeep on West Broadway is standing three doors down, staring into the windows of a new tanning salon/piercing parlor, and I can't help giggling.

"Johnny *Depp*, man?" Skeet mutters. "That's cold."

"You look so much like Johnny Depp it's eerie, man."

"I was relieved to hear that Johnny Depp has won a hard-earned reputation for monogamy."

"He's slightly more famous than you, man," I have to point out. "So you should probably watch what you say."

"Famous for what?" Skeet bristles. "Turning down commercial scripts?"

"Man, I'm so wiped out."

"Still modeling, bro?" Skeet asks glumly.

"Sometimes I wonder how I keep from going under." I'm staring past Skeet at a guy who gets out of the Jeep on Prince and slowly, vaguely, starts walking my way.

"Hey man, you've got it made," Skeet says, relighting the cigar. "You've got it made. You're a pretty good model."

"Yeah? How come, Skeet?"

"Because you've got that semi-long thick hair thing going and those full lips and like a great physique."

The guy keeps moving up the block.

Behind me, the other guy is now two stores away.

"Hey, thanks, man," I say, looking both ways. "Far out."

"It's cool," Skeet says. "Hey man, stop breathing so hard."

I urge Skeet to move with me over to the window of the Rizzoli bookstore. "Let's pretend we're browsing."

I look over my shoulder.

"What, man?" Skeet asks, confused. "Browsing for . . . books?"

The guy walking up from Prince is moving toward me faster.

The other guy's maybe two yards away.

I keep my eyes glued to the window at Rizzoli and I can barely hear Skeet say, "Hey man—what're you doing?" Pause. "Is that browsing?"

Suddenly, just as Skeet starts to pose another question, I bolt across West Broadway and in that instant both guys start after me and when I hit Broome another guy dressed in black runs up the street toward me.

I cut back across West Broadway, almost getting hit by a limo, to the other side of the street, all three guys behind me. A fourth suddenly lunges out of the new Harry Cipriani restaurant and I cross West Broadway again and run up the stairs into Portico, a furniture store.

The four guys—young and good-looking, all wearing black—converge below me on the stairs of Portico, discussing something while I'm hiding behind a white-stained concrete armoire. Someone asks if I work here and I wave her away, hissing. One of the guys on the stairs lifts a walkie-talkie out of his black leather jacket, revealing a gun strapped in a holster, and then mumbles something into the walkie-talkie. He listens, turns to the other three guys, says something that causes them to nod and then casually opens the door and strides into Portico.

I race through the store toward the back exit, which leads onto Wooster Street.

All I hear is someone shouting "Hey!"

I stumble out, grabbing the railing as I leap onto the sidewalk.

I duck in and out of the traffic moving down Wooster and then walk-run up to Comme des Garçons to pick up my tuxedo.

I slam the door behind me and rush downstairs, where Carter's waiting.

"What the fuck's going on?" I shout. "Jesus Christ!"

"Victor, the alterations are done," Carter says. "Calm down. The tux is fabulous. Chloe took care of the bill this—"

"No—some assholes just chased me down West Broadway," I pant.

He pauses. "Are you bragging or complaining?"

"Spare me," I shout.

"Well, you're here, so I'm just saying your ninja skills are reaching their peak, dear Donatello."

Still panting, I throw the tux on and have Carter call CLS for a BMW. JD pages me while Carter circles, mincing and wincing, making sure— along with Missy, the seamstress—that the fit is perfect, both of them grabbing me in totally inappropriate places, and when I call JD back on my cell phone Beau answers and asks why I'm not at my place for the MTV "House of Style" interview, which I've totally forgotten about. Supposedly people are outside my apartment "throwing fits," and the chills I get hearing that phrase relax me somewhat.

Wearing the tux, I stuff my other clothes into a Comme des Garçons bag, and as I'm heading out of the store, peering up Wooster, then down Wooster—totally serpenting to the BMW waiting at the curb—Carter calls out, "Wait—you forgot this!" and shoves the black hat with the red rose back into my sweaty hands.

9

At my place the *Details* reporter leans against a column just hanging out, eyeing my every move while sucking on a raspberry-flavored narcotic lollipop, and there's also a ton of assistants milling around, including this really muscular girl with a clip-on nose ring who places gels the colors of kiwi and lavender and pomegranate over lights, and the cameraman says "Hey Victor" in a Jamaican patois and he's wearing a detachable ponytail because he didn't have one earlier when I saw him on Bond Street this afternoon and he's part Chippewa and the director of the segment, Mutt, is conferring with a VJ from MTV News and Mutt just kind of smiles at me and rubs the scars on his bicep caused from bust-ups on his Harley when I say, "Sorry I'm late—I got lost."

"In your own . . . neighborhood?" he asks.

"The neighborhood is going through what is known as gent-rah-fah-cay-shun, so it's getting, um, complicated."

Mutt just kind of smiles at me and it's freezing in the apartment and I'm slouching in a big pile of white satin pillows that the crew brought and some Japanese guy is filming the interview that MTV will be filming and another Japanese guy is taking photographs of the video crew and I start throwing out names of bands they should play over the segment when it airs: Supergrass, Menswear, Offspring, Phish, Liz Phair ("Supernova"), maybe Pearl Jam or Rage Against the Machine or even Imperial Teen. I'm so lost that I don't even notice Mutt standing over me until he snaps his fingers twice right under my nose and I purse my lips and wink at him and wonder how cool I look in other people's eyes.

"I'm going to smoke a big Cohiba during the interview," I tell Mutt.

"You're going to look like a big asshole during the interview."

"Hey, don't forget who you're talking to."

"MTV policy. No smoking. Advertisers don't like it."

"Yet you sell Trent Reznor's hate to millions of unsuspecting youth. Tch-tch-tch."

"I want to get out of here, so let's start this thing."

"I was chased through SoHo earlier tonight."

"You're not *that* popular, Victor."

I buzz JD on my cell phone. "JD—find out who just chased me through SoHo." I click off and since I'm in my element I'm all smiles so I call out to the really muscular girl with the clip-on nose ring, "Hey pussycat, you could hail a cab with that ass."

"My name's David," he says. "Not Pussycat."

"Whoa—you got that whole boy/girl thing going down," I say, shivering.

"Who is this clown?" David asks the room.

"The same old story," Mutt sighs. "Nobody, up-and-comer, star, has-been. Not necessarily in that order."

"Hey, keep the vibe alive," I say halfheartedly to nobody and then the makeup girl brushes my sideburns teasingly and I snarl "Don't touch those" and then, in a more vacant mode, "Can somebody get me a Snapple?" It's at this precise moment I finally notice the thing that's totally lacking in my apartment: Cindy.

"Wait, wait a minute—where's Cindy?"

"Cindy's not conducting the interview," Mutt says. "She's just introduc-ing it, in her own faux-inimitable style."

"That sucks pretty majorly if you ask me," I say, stunned.

"Does it?"

"I wouldn't be sitting here now if I knew this earlier."

"I doubt that."

"Where the fuck is she?"

"In Beirut, at the opening of a new Planet Hollywood."

"This is seriously demeaning."

"Tough shit, you big baby."

"That—gosh, Mutt—that really shocks me," I say, tears welling up. "That really shocks me that you would talk that way to me."

"Uh-huh." Mutt closes his eyes, holds a viewfinder up to his ear. "Okay."

"Wait a minute, so wait. . . ." I look over at the VJ on his cell phone underneath a giant Nan Goldin that Chloe gave me for a Christmas pres-ent. "That pederast over there's going to do it?" I'm asking, appalled. "That fag pederast?"

"Hey, what's your life? A G-rated movie?"

"I don't want to be interviewed by someone who is known in this busi-ness as a big fag pederast."

"You ever sleep with a guy, Victor?"

Remembering MTV's new all-consuming the-entire-world-is-full-of-homos mentality, I smirk and semi-nod and choke out "Maybe" and then compose myself to add, "But now I am a strict heterosexual." Long pause. "Devout, in fact."

"I'll alert the media."

"You *are* the media, Mutt," I exclaim. "You and the fag pederast VJ *are* the media."

"Ever sleep with a fifteen-year-old?" Mutt asks tiredly.

"Girl?" Pause. "Maybe."

"So?"

Trying to decipher what Mutt's getting at, I pause, squinting, then yelp out, "What the fuck does *that* mean, bozo? Are you trying to make a point? Because it's like, um, eluding me."

The VJ comes over, all boyish smiles and Versace.

"He dates Chloe Byrnes," Mutt says. "That's all you really need to know."

"Super," the VJ says. "Can we work it in?"

"You *will* work it in," I answer for Mutt. "And no questions about my father."

"You're shooting from the hip," the VJ says. "And I like it."

"And *I'm* camera ready."

MTV: "So how does it feel to be the It Boy of the moment?"

ME: "Fame has a price tag but reality's still a friend of mine."

MTV: "How do you think other people perceive you?"

ME: "I'm a bad boy. I'm a legend. But in reality everything's a big world party and there are no VIP rooms."

MTV (pause, confusion): "But aren't there three VIP rooms at your new club?"

ME: "Um . . . cut. Cut. *Cut.*"

Everyone huddles together and I explain the game plan—that I want to discuss my personal relationships with Robert Downey, Jr., Jennifer Aniston, Matt Dillon, Madonna, Latouse LaTrek and Dodi Fayed—and people finally nod, satisfied. Life moves on with a few soft-lob inquiries and a chance to be fashionably rude, which I grab.

MTV: "How was it guest-starring on 'Beverly Hills 90210'?"

ME: "A classic cliché. Luke Perry looks like a little Nosferatu and Jason Priestley *is* a caterpillar."

MTV: "Do you see yourself as a symbol of a new generation in America?"

ME: "Well, I represent a pretty big pie-wedge of the new generation. I'm maybe a symbol." Pause. "An icon? No." Longer pause. "Not yet." Long pause. "Have I mentioned that I'm a Capricorn? Oh yeah, and I'm also for regaining the incentive to get this generation more involved in environmental issues."

MTV: "That's so cool."

ME: "No, *you're* so cool, dude."

MTV: "But what do you picture when you envision your generation?"

ME: "At its worst? Two hundred dead-ass kids dressed like extras from *The Crow* dancing to C+C Music Factory."

MTV: "And what do you think about this?"

ME (genuinely moved to be asked): "It stresses me out."

MTV: "But aren't the 1980s over? Don't you think opening a club like this is a throwback to an era most people want to forget? Don't kids want *less* opulence?"

ME: "Hey, this is a personal vision, man." Pause. "No matter how commercial it, y'know, *feels*. And" — finally realizing something — "I just want to give something back to the community." Pause. "I do it for the people." Pause. "Man."

MTV: "What are your thoughts on fashion?"

ME: "Fashion may be about insecurity but fashion is a good way to relieve tension."

MTV (pause): "Really?"

ME: "I'm completely absorbed by fashion. I seek it. I *crave* it. Seven days a week, twenty-eight hours a day. Did I mention that I'm a Capricorn? Oh, and yeah — being the best at only one thing is counterproductive."

MTV (long pause, mild confusion): "You and Chloe Byrnes have been together how long now?"

ME: "Time is meaningless when it comes down to Chloe. She defies time, man. I hope she has a long-term career as an actress-slash-model. She's gorgeous and, er, is my . . . best friend."

(Sounds of *Details* reporter laughing.)

MTV: "There have been rumors that —"

ME: "Hey, maintaining a relationship is one of the difficulties of my job, babe."

MTV: "Where did you meet?"

ME: "At a pre-Grammy dinner."

MTV: "What did you say when you met?"

ME: "I said 'Hey pussycat' and then that I was — and still am — an aspiring male model of the year."

MTV (after longish pause): "I can tell that you were in a, um, reflective mood that evening."

ME: "Hey, success is loving yourself, and anyone who doesn't think so can fuck off."

MTV: "How old are you?"

ME: "Twentysomething."

MTV: "No, really. Exact."

ME: "Twen-ty-something."

MTV: "What really pisses Victor Ward off?"

ME: "The fact that David Byrne named his new album after a 'tea from Sri Lanka that's sold in Britain.' I swear to God I heard that somewhere and it drove me nuts."

MTV (after polite laughter): "No. What *really* makes you mad? What really gets you angry?"

ME (long pause, thinking): "Well, recently, missing DJs, badly behaved bartenders, certain gossipy male models, the media's treatment of celebs . . . um . . ."

MTV: "We were thinking more along the lines of the war in Bosnia or the AIDS epidemic or domestic terrorism. How about the current political situation?"

ME (long pause, tiny voice): "Sloppy Rollerbladers? . . . The words 'dot com'? . . ."

MTV (long pause): "Anything else?"

ME (realizing something, relieved): "A mulatto, an albino, a mosquito, my libido."

MTV (long pause): "Did you . . . understand the question?"

ME: "What do you mean by that?"

MTV: "Aren't there things going on —"

ME (pissed): "Maybe you've misunderstood my answers."

MTV: "Okay, forget it, um —"

ME: "Just move to the next question."

MTV: "Oh, okay —"

ME: "Shoot."

MTV (really long pause, then): "Have you ever wished that you could disappear from all this?"

8 Having no idea where my keys are I rush up to Chloe's realizing we're running late (also thinking, That's cool) and Lauren Hynde opens the door and we stare at each other blankly until I say "You look . . . wonderful tonight" and she suddenly looks like she's shot through with something like pain or maybe something else like maybe something by Versace and she opens the door wider so I can enter Chloe's apartment where grunged-out Baxter Priestly's sitting on the island in the kitchen with a mullet haircut and Oakley eyewear and he's rolling a joint laced with Xanax and the Sci-Fi Channel is on in the background with the sound turned down and swanky dreampop coming from two ten-thousand-dollar speakers plays over it and Chloe's standing next to Baxter eating a peppermint patty in the Todd Oldham dress and listening to Baxter say things like "I saw a bum with really great abs today" and thirteen bottles of mineral water are in various stages of emptiness on a marble countertop next to faxes sent that say I KNOW WHO YOU ARE AND I KNOW WHAT YOU'RE DOING and the dozen French white tulips that I supposedly sent Chloe are in a giant crystal vase that someone named Susan Sontag gave her.

"You possess repartee in abundance, my friend," I mutter, slapping Baxter's shoulder, startling him out of his inanity, leaning in to kiss Chloe in the same movement, waiting for someone to comment on how chic I look. Behind me Lauren Hynde lingers by the door and Chloe says something like "The limo's waiting on the street" and I nod okay and move sullenly into our bedroom, making sure Chloe catches the scowl I hurl at Baxter while he continues deseeding.

In my closet: white jeans, leather belts, leather bomber jacket, black cowboy boots, a couple of black wool crepe suits, a dozen white shirts, a black turtleneck, crumpled silk pajamas, a high-class porno movie I've watched hundreds of times starring people who look just like us. I'm pretending to go through stuff until Chloe walks in seconds after I've crouched down inspecting a pair of sandals I bought in Barcelona at a Banana Republic.

"What's the story?" I finally ask. "Where's my three-snap blazer?"

"About what?" she asks back, tightly.

"Wasn't he a head in a Mr. Jenkins ad, baby?"

"I told you he was coming."

"What do you think that antifashion look costs?" I ask. "Two thousand bucks? Three thousand bucks?"

"Forget about it, Victor." She's searching for a pair of sunglasses to wear. "Far out."

"Victor," she starts. "What are you looking for?"

"My hair gel." I walk away from the closet and brush by her into the bathroom where I start gelling my hair, slicking it back. My beeper goes off and I ignore it. When it goes off again I wash my hands and find out it's Alison and I'm wondering how everything got so fucked up, but checking out my profile calms me down and I take a few deep breaths, complete a couple of seconds of some deep-sea visualization and then: ready to go.

"The tux looks nice," Chloe says, standing in the bathroom door, watching me. "Who was that?" Pause. "On the beeper?"

"Someone at the club." I just stand there and then I look at my watch and then move back to the bed where I rummage through the Comme des

Garçons bag so the clothes can go to Chloe's dry cleaners. Absently I find the hat Lauren gave me, all scrunched up.

"What's that?" I hear Chloe ask.

"Oops, wrong hat," I say, tossing it back in the bag, a Bullwinkle impression that used to make her laugh but now she doesn't get and she's not really looking at the hat but thinking other thoughts.

"I really want things to work out," Chloe says hesitantly. "Between us," she clarifies.

"I'm mad about you." I shrug. "You're mad about me." I shrug again.

"Don't do this, Victor."

"Do what?"

"I'm happy for you, Victor," she says, strained, just standing there in front of me, exhausted. "I'm really happy for you about tonight."

"You look faux-orgasmic, baby, and nibbling on that giant mint doesn't really help matters much." I brush past her again.

"Is this about Baxter?" she asks.

"That twerp? Spare me. It's freezing in this apartment."

"Hey Victor, look at me."

I stop, sigh, turn around.

"I don't want to apologize about how good my boyfriend is at irritating people, okay?"

I'm just staring at nothing or what I imagine is nothing until I'm finally moved to say, "As a general rule you shouldn't expect too much from people, darling," and then I kiss her on the cheek.

"I just had my makeup done, so you can't make me cry."

7

We'll slide down the surface of things . . . Old U2 on the stereo and gridlock jams the streets two blocks from the club and I'm not really hearing the things that are being said in the back of the limousine, just words—technobeat, slamming, moonscape, Semtex, nirvana, photogenic—and names of people I know—Jade Jagger, Iman, Andy Garcia, Patsy Kensit, the Goo-Goo Dolls, Galliano—and fleeting pieces of subjects I'm usually interested in—Doc Martens, Chapel Hill, the Kids in the Hall, alien abduction, trampolines—because right now I'm fidgeting with an unlit joint, looking up through the limo's sunroof, spacing on the sweeping patterns spotlights are making on the black buildings above and around us. Baxter and Lauren are sitting across from Chloe and me and I'm undergoing a slow-motion hidden freak-out, focusing on our excruciating progress toward the club while Chloe keeps trying to touch my hand, which I let her do for seconds at a time before I pull away to light one of Baxter's cigarettes or to rewind the U2 tape or to simply touch my forehead, specifically not looking in the direction of Lauren Hynde or how her legs are slightly spread or the way she's staring sadly back at her own reflection in the tinted windows. "We all live in a yellow limousine," Baxter sing-laughs. "A yellow limousine," Chloe sings too, giggling nervously, looking over at me for approval. I give it by nodding at Baxter, who's nodding back, and I'm shuddering. *We'll slide down the surface of things* . . .

Finally we're at the curb in front of the club and the first thing I hear is someone yelling "Action!" and U2's "Even Better Than the Real Thing" starts playing somewhere out of the sky as the driver opens the door and Baxter's checking his hair in Chloe's compact and I toss him my cummerbund. "Just wrap this around your head and look dreamy," I mutter. "You'll be okay."

"Victor," Chloe starts.

A wave of cold wind sweeps over the crowd standing behind the barricades in front of the club and causes the confetti strewn over the plush purple-and-green carpet leading up to the entrance to dance and swirl around the legs of cops guarding the place and behind the velvet ropes stand three cool Irish guys Damien hired, each of them holding a walkie-talkie and a separate guest list, and on either side of the velvet ropes are huge gangs of photographers and then the head publicist—smiling warmly until she sees Chloe's dress—asks us to wait where we are because Alison, wearing the same Todd Oldham dress Chloe has on, and Damien in a Gucci tuxedo are making their entrance and posing for the paparazzi, but people in the crowd have already noticed Chloe and shout out her name in high, garbled voices. Damien appears unusually tense, his jaw clenching and unclenching itself, and Lauren suddenly grabs my hand and I'm also holding Chloe's and when I look over at Chloe I notice she's holding Baxter's.

Damien turns around when he hears people shouting out Chloe's name and he nods at me, then smiles sadly at Lauren, who just mutters something indifferent, and when he sees Chloe's dress he does a hideous double take and tries valiantly to smile back a humongous gag and then he hurriedly ushers Alison into the club even though she's in the middle of taking major advantage of the photo ops, obviously pissed at the interruption, and thankfully Chloe's already too blinded by the flashing cameras to have noticed Alison's dress and I'm making a significant mental note about what should happen once inside: dim all the lights, sweet darling, or the night will be over with.

The photographers start shouting out all our names as we move toward the stairs leading up into the club and we linger for the appropriate amount of time—our faces masks, Chloe smiling wanly, Baxter smiling sullenly, Lauren genuinely smiling for the first time tonight, me sufficiently dazed—and above the door in giant '70s lettering is a warning from MTV ("This Event Is Being Videotaped. By Entering You Consent to the Cablecast and Other Exhibition of Your Name, Voice and Likeness") and then we're inside moving through the metal detectors and Chloe whispers something into my ear that I can't hear. *We'll slide down the surface of things* . . .

And U2's "Even Better Than the Real Thing" bursts out as we enter the main room of the club and someone calls out "Action!" again and there are already hundreds of people here and immediately Chloe is pounced on by a new group of photographers and then the camera crews are pushing their way toward her and I let go of her hand, allowing myself to be repositioned by the crowd over to one of the bars, actively ignoring celebs and fans, Lauren following close behind, and I nab the bartender's attention and order a glass of Veuve Clicquot for Lauren and a Glenlivet for myself and we just stand there while I'm admiring Patrick Woodroffe's lighting design and how it plays off all the floor-to-ceiling black velvet and Lauren's thinking I-don't-even-know-what as she downs the champagne and motions for another one and glancing over at her I finally have to say "Baby . . ." and then I lean in and nuzzle her cheek with my lips so briefly it wouldn't register to anyone except someone standing right behind me and I breathe in and close my eyes and when I open them I look to her for a reaction.

She's gripping the champagne flute so tightly her knuckles are white and I'm afraid it will shatter and she's glaring past me at someone behind my back and when I turn around I almost drop my glass but with my other hand hold the bottom to keep it steady.

Alison finishes a Stoli martini and asks the bartender for another without looking at him, waiting for a kiss from me.

I grin boyishly while composing myself and kiss her lightly on the cheek but she's staring back at Lauren when I do this as if I were invisible, which tonight, for maybe the first time in my life, I sort of wish I was. Harry Connick, Jr., Bruce Hulce and Patrick Kelly jostle by. I look away, then down.

"So-o-o . . . *another* Stoli?" I ask Alison.

"I am now entering the stolar system," Alison says, staring at Lauren. Casually, to block her view, I lean into the bar.

"Welcome to the state of relaxation," I say "jovially." "Er, enjoy your, um, stay."

"You asshole," Alison mutters, rolling her eyes, then grabs the drink from the bartender and downs it in one gulp. Coughing lightly, she lifts my arm and uses my jacket sleeve to wipe her mouth.

"Um . . . baby?" I start uncertainly.

"Thank you, Victor," she says, too politely.

"Um . . . you're welcome."

A tap on the shoulder and I turn from Alison and lean in toward Lauren, who very sweetly asks, "What do you two see in that bitch?"

"Let's redirect our conversation elsewhere, 'kay?"

"Spare *me*, you loser," Lauren giggles.

Luckily Ione Skye and Adam Horowitz push through the crowd toward me—an opening I seize upon.

"Hey! What's new, pussycat?" I smile, arms outstretched.

"Meow," Ione purrs, offering her cheek.

"Excuse me while I kiss the Skye," I say, taking it.

"Yuck," I hear Alison mutter behind me.

Camera flashes explode from the middle of the room like short bursts from a damaged strobe light and Ione and Adam slip away into the churning crowd and I've lit a cigarette and am generally just fumbling around looking for an ashtray while Lauren and Alison stare at each other with mutual loathing. Damien spots me and extracts himself from Penelope Ann Miller and as he moves closer and sees who I'm standing between he stops, almost tripping over this really cool midget somebody brought. Shocked, I mouth *Come here.*

He glances at Lauren mournfully but keeps blinking because of all the cameras flashing and then he's pushed forward by the crowd and now he's shaking my hand too formally, careful not to touch either girl, neither one responding to his presence anyway. Behind him Chloe and Baxter are answering questions in front of camera crews and Christy Turlington, John Woo, Sara Gilbert and Charles Barkley slide by.

"We need to talk," Damien says, leaning in toward me. "It's crucial."

"I, um, don't think that's such a good idea right . . . now, um, dude," I say with careful, deliberate phrasing.

"For once you may have a point." He tries to smile through a scowl while nodding at Lauren and Alison.

"I think I'm going to take Lauren over to the 'Entertainment Tonight' camera crew, okay?" I say.

"I have got to talk to you *now*, Victor," Damien growls.

Suddenly he reaches through the crowd and grabs Baxter, yanking him away from Chloe and the MTV camera crew, and then whispers something in Baxter's ear and U2 turns into the Dream Warriors' "My Definition of a Boombastic Jazz Style." Lauren and Alison have both lit cigarettes and are blowing smoke directly into each other's faces. Baxter's nodding intently and lets Damien sandwich him at the bar—in a style I wish was slightly more subtle—between Alison and Lauren, filling the empty space where I used to stand.

"Who's this?" Alison asks Damien dully.

"This is Baxter Priestly, baby," Damien says. "He wants to say hi and, um, wish you well."

"Yeah, yeah, you look really familiar," Alison says, totally bored, waving down the bartender, mouthing *Another*.

"He's in the new Darren Star show," I say. "*And* he's in the band Hey That's My Shoe."

"Who are you in the Darren Star show?" Alison asks, perking up.

"He's the Wacky Guy," Lauren says, staring at the bartender.

"Right, he's the Wacky Guy," I tell Alison as Damien pulls me away and uses my body as a barrier to push through the crowd and up the first flight of stairs to the deserted second floor, where he guides me toward a railing overlooking the party. We immediately light cigarettes. On this floor twenty tables have been set up for the dinner and really handsome busboys are lighting candles. On all the TV monitors: fashionable static.

"What in the fuck?" Damien inhales deeply on the cigarette.

"They're just, um, lighting the candles for dinner," I say, gesturing innocently at the busboys.

Damien smacks me lightly on the side of the head.

"Why in the fuck is Chloe's dress exactly like Alison's?"

"Damien, I know they *look* alike but in actuality—"

He pushes me toward the railing and points down. "What are you telling me, Victor?"

"It's a—it's supposedly a, um, very popular dress this . . . y'know . . ." I trail off.

Damien waits, wide-eyed. "*Yes?*"

". . . season?" I squeak out.

Damien runs a hand over his face and stares over the railing to make sure Alison and Chloe haven't seen each other yet, but Alison's flirting with Baxter and Chloe's answering questions about how high the fabulous factor is tonight while a line of TV crews jostle for the perfect angle and Damien's muttering "Why isn't she wearing that hat you picked up?" and I'm making excuses ("Oribe said it was a no-no") and he keeps asking "Why isn't she wearing the goddamn hat you picked up?" and Lauren's talking to fucking Chris O'Donnell and Damien guzzles down a large glass of Scotch then sets it on the railing with a shaky hand and I'm kind of like infused with panic and so tired.

"Damien, let's just try to have a cool—"

"I don't think I care anymore about that," he says.

"About what? About having a cool time?" I'm asking. "Don't say that." And then after a long patch of silence: "I really don't know how to respond to that." And then after a longer patch of silence: "You look really great tonight."

"About her," he says. "About Alison. I don't think I care about *that*."

I'm staring out over the crowd, my eyes involuntarily refocusing on the expressions Lauren's making while Chris O'Donnell chats her up, swigging from a bottle of Grolsch, Lauren seductively playing with the damp label, models everywhere. "Why . . . did you ever?" I hear myself ask, thinking, At least the press will be good.

Damien turns to me and I look away but meet his gaze when he says, "Whose money do you think this all is?"

"Pardon?" I ask, leaning away, my neck and forehead soaked with sweat.

"Who do you think is bankrolling all of this?" he sighs.

A long pause. "Various . . . orthodontists . . . from, um, Brentwood?" I ask, squinting, wiping my forehead. "Um, *you*. Aren't you like responsible for all of, um, *this*?"

"It's *hers*," he shouts. "It's all Alison's."

"But . . ." I stop, swaying.

Damien waits, looking at me.

"But . . . I don't know how to respond to . . . that."

"Haven't you been paying attention?" he snaps.

We'll slide down the surface of things . . .

"They found Mica," Damien's saying.

"Who?" I ask numbly, staring off.

"The police, Victor," he says. "They found Mica."

"Well, it's a little too late," I'm saying, trying to recover. "Right? Do not pass Go? Do not collect two million bucks, right? Junior's doing a great job and personally I always felt Mica was sort of—"

"Victor, she's dead," Damien says tiredly. "She was found in a Dumpster in Hell's Kitchen. She was beaten with a hammer and . . . Jesus Christ"—he breathes in, waves down into the crowd at Elizabeth Berkley and Craig Bierko, then brings his hand to his mouth—"eviscerated."

I'm taking this in with a large amount of extreme calm. "She OD'd?"

"No," Damien says very carefully. "She was eviscerated, Victor."

"Oh my god," I gasp, holding my head, and then, "What does eviscerated mean?"

"It means she didn't die a peaceful death."

"Well, yeah, but how do we know that?"

"She was strangled with her own intestines."

"Right, right."

"I hope you realize this conversation is off the record."

Below us I'm just looking down at Debi Mazar and Sophie B. Hawkins, who's with Ethan Hawke and Matthew Barney. Below us a photographer spots me and Damien standing by the railing and snaps three, four, eight shots in rapid succession before I can straighten my tie.

"No one knows this yet," Damien sighs, lighting another cigarette. "Let's keep it this way. Let's just keep everyone smiling until tomorrow."

"Yeah man, cool," I say, nodding. "I think I'm capable."

"And please try to keep Alison and Lauren away from each other," he says, walking away. "Let's make a concerted effort to try and pull that off, okay?"

"I think I'm capable, dude."

We'll slide down the surface of things . . .

Someone calls up to me and I move away from the railing and head downstairs back into the party and then Carmen, this Brazilian heiress, grabs my arm. Chris O'Donnell has moved away from Lauren, who spots me from across the room and just stares, and Baxter's still desperately keeping Alison occupied, even though it looks like she's losing interest, because she's rolling her eyes and making yapping gestures with her hands.

"Victor! I just see the film *Beauty and the Beast* and I love it! I—*love*—*it*!" Carmen's shrieking, eyes wide, flailing her arms around.

"Baby, you're cool," I say worriedly. "But it would be somewhat profitable if you chilled out a bit."

Alison pats Baxter on the side of his face and starts to move away from the bar toward the center of the room, where the camera flashes are most intense, and Chloe, predictably, is now standing with Chris O'Donnell.

"But Victor, you hear me?" Carmen's blocking my way. "I love it. I adore both the Beauty *and* the Beast. I love it. 'Be My Guest'—*Oh my god!*"

"Baby, be *my* guest. *You* need a drink." Distressed, I snap at Beau while pointing at Carmen. "Beau—get this chick a Caipirinha."

I push Carmen out of the way but it's too late. Tarsem and Vivienne Westwood grabbing each of my arms, I can only watch helplessly as Alison glides gaily, drunkenly toward Chloe, who's being interviewed with Chris O'Donnell for MTV, her expression becoming more confused the nearer she gets. Once she's behind Chloe, Alison sees the dress, immediately grabs a lighter out of Sean Penn's hand and, horror-struck, waves the flame so she can see Chloe better. Bijoux from MTV isn't looking at Chloe now and has lowered her microphone, and Chloe turns around, sees Alison, smiles, and in the middle of a tiny wave notices Alison's dress, grimaces, squints desperately, tries to take a closer look—Chris O'Donnell is pretending not to notice, which makes things better—and Bijoux leans in to ask a question and Chloe, dazed, turns hesitantly back to the camera to try and answer it, succeeds with a shrug.

Lauren is standing next to me holding a giant glass filled with what I can only hope is not vodka and without saying a word clamps her free hand onto my ass. Alison starts heading toward us, purposefully grabbing a martini off a passing tray and getting about half of it in her mouth.

"How did you get off the Xanax?" I'm murmuring to somebody quasi-famous.

"You mean *get* the Xanax."

"Yeah, yeah, *get* the Xanax, cool."

"I was withdrawing from marijuana addiction and so I went to my mom's doctor and — hey Victor, you're not listening to me —"

"Hey, don't freak, you're cool."

Alison walks up to me, licks my cheek and, standing incredibly close, places her mouth on mine, desperately trying to push her tongue in, but my teeth are clenched and I'm nodding to the guy who's talking about Xanax and shrugging my shoulders, trying to casually carry on my part of the conversation, when Alison finally gives up, pulls back, leaving my mouth and chin slathered with a combo of saliva and vodka, smiles meanly and then stands next to me so that I'm flanked by her and Lauren. I'm watching Chloe, her interview over, squinting into the crowd trying to find me, Chris O'Donnell still nursing his Grolsch. I look away.

Alison leans in and touches my ass, which I tense uselessly, causing her hand to creep across until it touches the back of Lauren's hand and freezes.

I'm asking Juliette Lewis how her new dalmatian, Seymour, is doing and Juliette says "So-so" and moves on.

I can feel Alison trying to push Lauren's hand off but Lauren's hand has clutched the left cheek and will not let go and I look at her nervously, spilling my drink on the cuff of the Comme des Garçons tuxedo, but she's talking to someone from the Nation of Islam and Traci Lords, her jaw set tightly, smiling and nodding, though Traci Lords senses something's wrong and tells me I looked great slouching in the seat next to Dennis Rodman at the Donna Karan show and leaves it at that.

A curvy blonde staggers over with a girl in an African headdress and this Indian dude, and the curvy blonde kisses me on the mouth and stares dreamily into my face until I have to clear my throat and nod at her friends.

"This is Yanni," the curvy blonde says, gesturing at the girl. "And this is Mudpie."

"Hey Mudpie. Yanni?" I ask the black girl. "Really? What does Yanni mean?"

"It means 'vagina,'" Yanni says in a very high voice, bowing.

"Hey honey," I say to Alison, nudging her. "This is Mudpie and Yanni. Yanni means 'vagina.'"

"Great," Alison says, touching her hair, really drunk. "That's really, really great." She hooks her arm through mine and starts pulling me away from Lauren, and Lauren, seeing Chloe approaching, lets go of my ass and finishes whatever she's drinking and Alison's tugging me away and I try to keep my footing to talk to Chloe, who grabs my other arm.

"Victor, what's Alison doing?" Chloe calls out. "Why is she wearing that dress?"

"I'm going to find that out now—"

"Victor, why didn't you want me to wear this dress tonight?" Chloe's asking me. "Where are you going, goddamnit?"

"Honey, I'm checking for specks," I tell her, shrugging helplessly, Alison pulling my shoulder out of its socket. "I've seen none and am gratefully, er, relieved but there might be some upstairs—"

"Victor, wait—" Chloe says, holding on to my other arm.

" 'Allo, my leetle fashion plate." Andre Leon Talley and the massive-titted Glorinda greet Chloe with impossibly wettish airkisses, causing Chloe to let go of my arm, which causes me to collide with Alison, who, unfazed, just drags me up the stairs.

We'll slide down the surface of things . . .

Alison slams the bathroom door, locks it, then moves over to the toilet and lifts up her skirt, pulls her stockings down and falls onto the white porcelain seat, muttering to herself.

"Baby, this is *not* a good idea," I'm saying, pacing back and forth in front of her. "Baby, this is *definitely* not a good idea."

"Oh my god," she's moaning. "That tuna has been giving me total shark-eye all night. Did she actually come with you, Victor? How in the fuck did she weasel in here? Did you see the fucking look she gave me when I first made eye contact?" Alison wipes herself and, still sitting there, immediately begins to rummage through a Prada handbag. "That bitch actually told Chris O'Donnell that I run a quote-unquote highly profitable fat-substitute emporium."

"I think your meeting could definitely be construed as an uh-oh moment."

"And if you keep ignoring me you're gonna have a whole night chock-full of them." In the Prada handbag Alison finds two vials and stands up, her voice brimming with acid. "Oh, but I forgot, you don't want to *see me any-more*. You want to *break up*. You need *your space*. You, Victor, are a *major loser*." She tries to compose herself, fails. "I think I'm gonna be sick. I'm gonna be sick all over *you*. How could you *do* this to me? And *of all nights!*" She's hissing to herself, unscrewing the top of one vial, doing two, three, six huge bumps of coke, then suddenly she stops, inspects the vial, then says "Wrong vial" and unscrews the other one and does four bumps from that. "You're *not* going to get away with this. You're not. Oh my god." She grabs her head. "I think I have sickle-cell anemia." Then, snapping her head up, she shrieks, "And why in the hell is your girlfriend—sorry, *ex*-girlfriend—wearing the same fucking dress I am?"

"Why?" I shout out. "Does it bother you?"

"Let's just say—" Alison starts coughing, her face crumples up and between huge sobs she wails, "it was mildly horrifying?" She immediately recovers, slaps my face, grabs my shoulders and screams, "You're not getting away with this!"

"With what?" I shout, grabbing a vial away from her, scooping out two huge capfuls for myself. "What am I not getting away with?"

Alison grabs the vial away from me and says, "No, that's, er, something else." She hands me the other vial.

Already wired, I'm not capable of stopping myself from kissing her on the nose, an involuntary reaction to whatever I just snorted.

"Oh hot," she sneers miserably. "How hot."

Unable to move my mouth, I gurgle, "I'm speechless too."

"That little conversation we had, Victor, upset me very much," Alison groans, fixing her hair, wiping her nose with Kleenex. She looks at my innocent face in the mirror, while I stand behind her doing a few more hits. "Oh please, Victor, don't do this—do not do this."

"When?" I'm shouting out. "What in the hell—"

"About ninety minutes ago? Stop acting like such an idiot. I know you're a guy who's not exactly on the ball, but please—even *this* could not get past you."

I hand back the vial, wiping my nose, and then say very quietly, hoping to reassure her, "Baby, I don't know what you're talking about."

"That's the problem, Victor," she screams. "You never know."

"Baby, baby—"

"Shut up, shut up, *shut up*," she screams, whirling away from her reflection. "You stand in front of me just ninety minutes ago outside my apartment and tell me it's all over—that you're in love with Lauren Hynde? That you're dumping Chloe for her? Remember *that*, you humongous idiot?"

"Wait a minute," I say, holding up my hands, both of which she smacks at. "You're really coked up and you need a tranquilizer and you need to get your facts straight—"

"Are you saying this didn't happen, Victor?" she shouts, grabbing at me.

Holding her back, I look intently into her face and offer, "I'm not saying it didn't happen, Alison." I breathe in. "I'm just saying that I wasn't conscious when this occurred and I guess I'm saying that you weren't conscious either."

"Are you telling me we didn't have this conversation?" she screams. "Are you telling me I hallucinated it?"

I stare at her. "Well, in a nutshell, *yeah.*"

Someone starts knocking on the bathroom door, which provokes Alison into some kind of massive freak-out. I grab her by the shoulders and turn her around to face me.

"Baby, I was doing my MTV 'House of Style' interview"—I check the watch I'm not wearing—"ninety minutes ago, so—"

"Victor, it was *you!*" she shouts, pushing me away from her. "You were standing there outside my place telling me that—"

"You're *wasted!*" I cry out. "I'm leaving and yeah, baby—it *is* all over. I'm outta here and of this I'm certain!"

"If you think Damien's ever going to let you open a fucking *door* let alone a club after he finds out you're fucking his little girlfriend you're more pitifully deluded than I ever thought possible."

"That"—I stop, look back at her questioningly—"doesn't really mean anything to me."

I swing the door open, Alison standing motionless behind me. A whole group of people squeeze past me and though they probably despise Alison they decide to surround her and take notes while she sobs, her face a wreck.

"You are not a player," is the last thing Alison ever screams at me.

I slam the door shut.

We'll slide down the surface of things . . .

Lauren stands with Jason London and Elle Macpherson exchanging recipe tips for smart drinks even though someone shockingly famous's penis exploded when his smart drink was mixed with "the wrong elements" and everyone goes "oooh" but Lauren's not really listening because she's watching Damien schmoozing a group that includes Demi Moore, Veronica Webb and Paulina Porizkova, and when Elle kisses me on the cheek and compliments my stubble Lauren abruptly looks away from Damien and just stares at me blankly—a replicant—and I wipe my nose and move toward her, suddenly in a very huggy mood.

"Have you heard?" she asks, lighting a cigarette.

"That I'm in dire need of a crisis-management team? Yes."

"Giorgio Armani couldn't make it because he's in rehearsals for 'Saturday Night Live,' which he's hosting."

"Dig it," I murmur.

"What did Alison want to show you?" she asks. "The third claw growing out of her ass?"

I grab a martini from a passing waiter. "No."

"Oh damnit, Victor," she groans. "Just live up to it."

Chloe stands in the middle of the room chatting with Winona Ryder and Billy Norwich, and Baxter Priestly is perched nearby drinking a tiny white-wine spritzer and people squeezing past us block the view from where

Chloe and Damien stand of my hand clutching Lauren's while Lauren keeps staring at Damien, who's touching the black fabric of Veronica Webb's dress and saying things like "Love the dress but it's a tad Dracula-y, baby," and the girls laugh and Veronica grabs his hand playfully and Lauren's hand squeezes mine tightly.

"I really wouldn't call that flirting, baby," I tell her. "Don't get ruffled."

Lauren's nodding slowly as Damien, swigging a martini, shouts out, "Why don't you titillate me literally, *baby*," and the girls explode with laughter, fawning over him, and the entire room is humming around us and the lights of cameras are flashing behind every corner.

"I know you have a keen sense of the way people behave," Lauren says. "It's okay, Victor." She tosses back what's left of her jumbo-sized drink.

"Do you want to talk about it?"

"About what?" she asks. "Your Bravery-in-the-Face-of-Doom nomination?"

"I'd be thrilled if you moved on to soda pop, baby."

"Do you love Chloe?" she asks.

All I can say is, "You look very Uma-ish tonight."

In the interim Damien moves over to us and Lauren lets my hand drop from hers and while I light a cigarette Alison spots Damien and excuses herself from Heather Locklear and Eddie Veder and prowls over, hyperventilating, and hooks her arm through Damien's before he can say anything to Lauren, refusing to look at me, and then she plays with his hair and in a panic Damien pushes her hand away and in the background the "cute" magician performs card tricks for James Iha, Teri Hatcher, Liv Tyler, Kelly Slater and someone dressed disconcertingly like Willie Wonka and I'm trying to be cool but my fists are totally clenched and the back of my neck and my forehead are soaked with sweat.

"Well," Damien says hollowly. "Well, well . . . well."

"Loved you in *Bitch Troop*, darling," Alison gushes at Lauren.

"Oh shit," Damien mutters under his breath.

"Nice dress," Lauren says, staring at Alison.

"What?" Alison asks, shocked.

Lauren looks directly at Alison and, enunciating very clearly, nodding appreciatively, says, "I said *nice dress*."

Damien holds Alison back as JD and Beau walk up to Damien and they're with some white-blond surfer wearing nylon snowboarding pants and a faux-fur motorcycle jacket.

"Hey Alison, Lauren," I say. "This is JD and Beau. They're the stars of *Bill and Ted's Homosexual Adventure*."

"It's, um, time for dinner," JD says tentatively, trying not to notice Alison vibrating with rage, emitting low rumbling sounds. She finally looks over at Damien's falsely placid face and sneers, dropping her cigarette into his glass. Damien makes a strangled noise, then averts his eyes from the martini.

"Um, great," Damien says. "Dinnertime. Fantastic. Here, Beau." Damien hands Beau his martini glass. While we all watch, Beau stares at it and then very carefully places the glass on a nearby table.

"Yeah, great," I say, overly enthusiastic, unable to stop staring at the cigarette floating in the martini. "Hey, who's this?" I ask, shaking the surfer's limp hand.

"This is Plez," someone says.

"Hey Plez," Damien says, glancing quickly at Alison. "How ya doin'?"

"Plez is a snowboarder," JD says.

"And he won the world half-pipe championship," Beau adds.

"*And* he's a messenger at UPS," JD adds.

"Cha cha cha," I say.

Conversation stops. No one moves.

"Cha . . . cha . . . cha," I say again.

"So-o-o, dude—what are you doing in Manhattan?" Damien asks Plez, glancing quickly at Lauren.

"He just returned from Spain, where he was shooting a video for Glam Hooker," Beau says, patting Plez on the head.

Plez is shrugging amiably, eyes half-closed, reeking of marijuana, nodding out.

"How brill." I'm nodding too.

"Total brill," JD says.

"Not to mention fagulous," Beau gushes.

"Totally brill *and* totally fagulous," JD adds.

Chloe appears and her hand's freezing as it clasps mine and looking at the floor I'm thinking my god someone will have to do a lot of vacuuming and Lauren offers Baxter a tight smile and the gravity of the situation starts to become apparent to most of us as Bridget Fonda and Gerlinda Kostiff pass by.

"Let's, er, eat." Damien claps his hands, knocking himself out of some kind of reverie, startling all of us out of our own respective silences. Alison looks so drunk and is staring at Lauren with so much hatred that the urge to sneak away is almost overwhelming.

"The way you said that was so, um . . . debonair," I tell Damien.

"Well, I just think we should sit down before the nonessential personnel arrive at eleven," he says, shoving Alison away from the rest of us, at the same time holding tightly on to one arm.

A cue for everyone to move up the stairs to the second floor for dinner.

"A sense of frenzy in the air?" JD whispers to me.

"There's a mass branding at Club Lure in about two hours," I hiss at him. "It's Pork Night and your name's on the list."

"Oh Victor," JD says. "Be aware if you dare."

We'll slide down the surface of things . . .

How it got to be eleven so suddenly is confusing to us all, not that it really means anything, and conversation revolves around how Mark Vanderloo "accidentally" ate an onion-and-felt sandwich the other night while viewing the Rob Lowe sex tapes, which Mark found "disappointing"; the best clubs in New Zealand; the injuries someone sustained at a Metallica concert in Pismo Beach; how Hurley Thompson disappeared from a movie set in Phoenix (I have to bite my tongue); what sumo wrestlers actually *do*; a gruesome movie Jonathan just finished shooting, based on a starfish one of the producers found behind a fence in Nepal; a threesome someone fell into with Paul Schrader and Bruce Wagner; spinning lettuce; the proper pronunciation of "ooh la la." At our table Lauren's on one side of me, Chloe's on the other along with Baxter Priestly, Johnathon Schaech, Carolyn Murphy, Brandon Lee, Chandra North, Shalom Harlow, John Leguizamo, Kirsty Hume, Mark Vanderloo, JFK Jr., Brad Pitt, Gwyneth Paltrow, Patsy Kensit, Noel Gallagher, Alicia Silverstone and someone who I'm fairly sure is Beck or looks like Beck and it seems like everyone's wearing very expensive pantsuits. Earlier in the day I was upset that Chloe and I weren't seated at Damien's table (because there were things I *had* to say to David Geffen and an apology I *had* to make to Calvin) but right now, watching Alison slumped against Damien while trying to light a joint the size of a very long roll of film, everyone very buzzed, people knocking into each other as table-hopping on a very massive scale resumes while cappuccino's served, everything sliding in and out of focus, it's okay.

I'm trying to light a cigarette someone's spilled San Pellegrino on and Lauren's talking to a kneeling Woody Harrelson about hemp production and so I tap in to Chloe, interrupting what I'm sure is a stunning conversation with Baxter, and she turns reluctantly to me, finishing another Cosmopolitan, her face taut with misery, and then she simply asks, "What is it?"

"Um, baby, what's the story with Damien and Lauren?" I inquire gingerly.

"I am so bored with you, Victor, that I don't even know how to answer that," she says. "What are you talking about?"

"How long have you known about Damien and your so-called best friend Lauren?" I ask again, lowering my voice, glancing over at Lauren and Woody.

"Why is my so-called boyfriend asking someone he actually thinks supposedly cares?" she sighs, looking away.

"Honey," I whisper patiently, "they're having an affair."

"Who told you this?" she asks, recoiling. "Where did you read this? Oh god, I'm so tired."

"What are you so tired of?" I ask patiently.

She looks down glassy-eyed at the scoops of sorbet melting into a puddle on her plate.

"You're a big help," I sigh.

"Why do you even care? What do you want me to say? You wanna fuck her? You wanna fuck *him*? You—"

"Shhh. Hey baby, why would you think *that*?"

"You're whining, Victor." She waves a hand in front of my face tiredly, dismissing me.

"Alison and Damien are engaged—did you know *that*?" I ask.

"I'm not interested in the lives of other people, Victor," Chloe says. "Not now. Not tonight. Not when *we're* in serious trouble."

"I think you definitely need a toke off that major joint Alison's smoking."

"Why?" She snaps out of something. "Why, Victor? Why do you think I need to do drugs?"

"Because I have a feeling we're on the verge of having that conversation again about how lost and fat you were at fourteen."

"Why did you ask me last night not to wear this dress?" she asks, suddenly alert, arms crossed.

Pause. "Because . . . you'd resemble . . . Pocahontas, but really, baby, you look smashing and—" I'm just glancing around, smiling gently over at Beck, fidgeting with a Marlboro, searching for Chap Stick, smiling gently over at Beck again.

"No, no, no." She's shaking her head. "Because you don't care about things like that. You don't care about things that don't have anything to do with you."

"*You* have something to do with me."

"Only in an increasingly superficial way," she says. "Only because we're in this movie together."

"You think you know everything, Chloe."

"I know a fuck of a lot more than you do, Victor," she says. "Everyone knows a fuck of a lot more than you do and *it's not cute*."

"So you *don't* have any lip balm?" I ask carefully, glancing around to see if anyone heard her.

Silence, then, "How did you know Alison was going to wear that dress?" she suddenly asks. "I've been thinking about that all night. How did you know Alison was going to be wearing the same dress? And you *did* know, didn't you?"

"Baby," I say, semi-exasperated. "The way you look at things is so hard—"

"No, no, Victor," she says, sitting up. "It's very simple. It's actually very, very simple."

"Baby, you're very, very cool."

"I am so tired of looking at that empty expanse that's supposed to be your face—"

"Alfonse." I raise my hand at a passing busboy, making a pouring motion. "Mineral water for the table. *Con* gas?"

"And *why* does Damien keep asking me why I'm not wearing a *hat*?" she asks. "Is everyone demented or something?"

Chloe zones out on her reflection in a mirror situated across the room while Brad Pitt and Gwyneth Paltrow celebrate her choice of fingernail polish and gradually we drift away from one another and those who aren't doing drugs light up cigars so I grab one too and somewhere above us, gazing down, the ghosts of River Phoenix and Kurt Cobain and my mother are totally, utterly bored.

"Is Lauren dating Baxter?" I ask innocently, giving Chloe one last try for an answer, and I'm leaning in, nodding goodbye to Brad and Gwyneth.

"'Is Lauren dating Baxter?'" she mimics. "I need another Cosmopolitan and then I'm getting the hell out of here." She turns her attention to Baxter, completely ignoring me, and I'm totally startled so I do a few cool moves with the cigar and turn to Lauren, who seems to be paying attention to my plight.

"She looks displeased," Lauren says, glancing over at Chloe.

"My fault." I shrug. "Forget about it."

"Everyone here is just . . . so . . . dead."

"Alicia Silverstone doesn't look so dead. Noel Gallagher doesn't look so dead. JFK Jr. doesn't look so dead—"

"JFK Jr. never showed up, Victor."

"Would you like some more dessert?"

"I suppose it's all relative," she sighs, then starts drawing on a large cocktail napkin with purple Hard Candy nail polish.

"Are you dating Baxter Priestly?" I finally ask.

She looks up from the napkin briefly, smiles a private smile, continues drawing with the nail polish. "Rumor has it that *you* are," she murmurs.

"Rumor has it that Naomi Campbell's shortlisted for the Nobel Prize but really, what are the odds?" I ask, annoyed.

Lauren's looking at Alison, considering her, while Alison pitches forward in her chair, drunkenly grabbing onto Calvin Klein for support, everyone knocking back shots of Patrón tequila, a small gold bottle sitting half-empty in the middle of Damien's plate.

"She's like a tarantula," Lauren whispers.

Alfonse starts pouring San Pellegrino into extra glasses scattered around our table. "Could you please bring her another Diet Dr Pepper?" I ask him, pointing at Lauren.

"Why?" Lauren asks, overhearing me.

"Because everything needs to be redefined right now," I say. "Because things need to be redefined for me. People need to sober up, that's why, and—"

Something crawls up my neck and I whirl around to slap it away but it's just one of Robert Isabell's floral arrangements going limp. Lauren looks at me like I'm insane and I pretend to study the point where Mark Vanderloo's eyebrows don't meet. Someone says "Pass the chips," someone else says "Those aren't chips." I finally turn back to Lauren, who's still writing on the cocktail napkin, concentrating, her eyes slits. I notice the letters W, Q, J, maybe an R. *We'll slide down the surface of things.* Damien slowly disengages himself from his table and starts moving toward me, cigar in hand.

"Lauren—" I start.

"You're high," she says somewhat menacingly.

"I was high. I'm not high anymore. I am no longer high." I pause. "You said that somewhat menacingly."

I pause, testing the situation. "But do you have any coke?" and then, "Are you, like, carrying?"

She shakes her head then reaches down into my lap and still smiling sweetly squeezes my balls then picks up the napkin, kisses me on the cheek, whispers "I'm still in love with you" and glides away, floating past Damien, who tries to reach out for her but she's gliding away, floating past him, the expression on her face saying *don't touch.*

Damien just stands there, mutters something, closes and opens his eyes, then takes Lauren's seat next to mine as Lauren walks over to Timothy Hutton and gently turns to him in an exceedingly intimate way, and Damien's puffing on his cigar, staring at the two of them, and I'm waving smoke away, slouching in my seat, my cigar unlit.

Damien's saying things like "Have you ever felt like crawling under a table and living there for a week?"

"I've spent most of this night gasping," I'm conceding. "And I'm exhausted."

"I think this place is actually great," Damien says, gesturing at the room. "I just wish it wasn't such an awful night."

My eyes are still watering from the squeeze Lauren gave me but through the tears I notice she's not terribly far from the seat Damien vacated next to Alison's, and my heart speeds up, something tightens in my stomach, my armpits start tingling and Lauren's swaying her hips exaggeratedly and Alison's totally wired, sucking on a joint, greedily chatting away with Ian

Schrager and Kelly Klein, then Damien looks away from me and watches too as Lauren says something that causes Tim Hutton to raise his eyebrows and cough while Uma's talking to David Geffen. Her eyes gleaming, Lauren brings the cocktail napkin to her lips, kissing it, *wetting* it, and I'm holding my breath watching everything and Alison whispers something to Kelly Klein and Lauren leans away from Tim and with the hand holding the cocktail napkin pats Alison on the back and the napkin sticks and Damien makes a strangled noise.

On the napkin is one word in giant garish purple letters: CUNT.

Alison glances up briefly. She pushes Lauren's hand away.

Next to me, Chloe's watching too and she lets out a little whimper.

Damien lurches from the table.

Lauren's laughing gaily, walking away from Tim Hutton in mid-sentence. And then he notices the napkin on Alison's back.

Before Damien can get to Alison she's already reaching behind her neck and she feels the napkin and pulls it off and slowly brings it in front of her face and her eyes go wide and she lets out a giant mama of a scream.

She spots Lauren making her way out of the dining room and hurls a glass at her, which misses Lauren and explodes against the wall.

Alison leaps up from her chair and races toward Lauren but Lauren's out the door, heading up the stairs to the private VIP lounge that hasn't opened yet.

Damien gets to Alison and while he wrestles with her she starts sobbing hysterically and the napkin falls out of Alison's hand and somebody takes it for a souvenir and then I'm standing and about to run after Lauren when Chloe grabs my arm.

"Where are you going?" she asks.

"I'm going to try to, um, deal with this," I say, gesturing helplessly at the door Lauren just breezed through.

"Victor—"

"What, baby?"

"Victor—" she says again.

"Honey, I'll be back in twenty"—I check my wrist but there's no watch and then I look back at her—"in like ten minutes."

"Victor—"

"Honey, she needs some *air*—"

"In the VIP lounge?" Chloe asks. "In the VIP lounge, Victor? She needs some air in *the VIP lounge*?"

"I'll be right back."

"Victor—"

"What?" I say, loosening my arm from her grasp.

"Victor—"

"Honey, we're having a fly time," I say, pulling away. "Talk to Baxter. Spin some damage control. That's what I'm gonna do."

"I don't care," she says, letting go. "I don't care if you come back," Chloe says. "I don't care anymore," she says. "Do you understand?"

Dazed, I can only nod my head and rush out of the room.

"Victor—"

We'll slide down the surface of things . . .

I find Lauren in the private VIP room on the top floor where earlier today I interviewed prospective DJs but now it's empty except for the bartender setting up behind a stainless-steel slab. Holly just points over to a banquette, where Lauren's feet are sticking out from beneath a tablecloth, one high heel on, one high heel hanging off a totally delectable foot, and a just-opened bottle of Stoli Cristall is standing on the table and when a hand reaches up the bottle disappears, then reappears noticeably less full. The high heel falls off.

I wave my hand, dismissing Holly, and he shrugs and slouches out and I close the doors behind him as mellow music plays somewhere around us, maybe the Cranberries singing "Linger," and I'm passing the antique pool table in the center of the room, running my hands along the soft green felt, moving over to the booth where Lauren's splayed out. Except for candles and the very dim, very hip lighting and the chilly hues coming from the steel bar it's almost pitch black in the lounge, but then one of the spotlights outside on the street beams through the windows, scanning the room before disappearing again, only to beam back moments later, again bathing every-thing around us in a harsh, metallic glow.

"My psychiatrist wears a tiara," Lauren says from beneath the patterned tablecloth. "Her name is Dr. Egan and she wears a giant diamond tiara."

I'm silent for a minute before I can say, "That's . . . so depressing, baby."

Lauren struggles up out of the booth and, standing unsteadily, grabs the edge of the table for support, shakes her head to clear it and then dances slowly, gracelessly with herself across the raw concrete floor over to the pool table and I reach out and touch the strand of pearls I suddenly notice draped around her neck, trying to move with her.

"What are you doing, Victor?" she asks, dreamily. "Dancing? Is that dancing?"

"Squirming. It's called squirming, baby."

"Oh, don't squirm, lovebutton," she pouts.

"I think there's quite a bit to squirm about tonight," I say tiredly. "In fact, I think lovebutton's squirming is totally justified."

"Oh god, Victor," she groans, still swaying to the music. "You were such a cute, sweet, normal guy when I first met you." A long pause. "You were so sweet."

After a minute without moving, I clear my throat. "Um, baby, I don't think I was ever any of those things." A realization. "Except for, um, cute, of course."

She stops dancing, considers this, then admits, "That's probably the first honest thing you've probably ever said."

And then I ask, "Did you mean what you said down there?" Pause, darkness again. "I mean about us." Pause. "And all that," I add.

I hand her the bottle of vodka. She takes it, starts to drink, stops, puts it on the pool table. The rays from the spotlight cross her face, illuminating it for seconds, her eyes closed, tearing, her head slightly turned; a hand is brought up to her mouth, and it's curled.

"What?" I carefully move the icy bottle of vodka off the pool table so it won't leave a damp ring on the felt. "Is this all too bummerish?"

She nods slowly and then moves her face next to mine and the sounds of horns from limos in gridlock and the relentless roar of the massive crowd outside is carried up in waves to where we're stumbling around clutching each other and I'm muttering "Dump Damien, baby" into her ear as she pushes me away when she feels how hard I am.

"It's not that simple," she says, her back to me.

"Hey babe, I get it," I say casually. "Lust never sleeps, right?"

"No, Victor." She clears her throat, walks slowly around the pool table. I follow her. "It's not that. It's just not that simple."

"You have . . . star quality, baby," I'm saying, grasping, sending out a vibe.

She suddenly rushes up to me and holds on, shivering.

"Don't you think everything happens for a reason?" she's asking, breathing hard, moving against me. "Don't you think everything happens for a reason, Victor?" And then, "Victor, I'm so scared. I'm so scared for you."

"The time to hesitate is through," I whisper into her hair, pushing against her, easing her slowly against the pool table. "Okay, baby?" I'm whispering while kissing her mouth, my hands reaching down below her waist, and she's whispering back "Don't" and I'm reaching underneath her dress, unable to stop myself, not caring who sees us, who walks in through the door, immediately getting lost in the moment, my fingers grazing her panties, one finger slipping inside, touching first the hair there and then a crease and beyond that an entrance that I can actually feel dampen as my finger runs over it gently at first and then more insistently until another slips inside and Lauren's pressing herself against me, her mouth locked onto mine, but I push her back because I want to see the expression her face is making and now she's sitting on the pool table with both legs spread and raised up, her hands on the back of my neck grasping me closer, her mouth on my mouth again, making desperate noises that I'm making too but suddenly she pulls back, looking past me, and when I turn around, visible in the darkness of the VIP room is a silhouette of a man standing backlit against the windows that look over Union Square.

Lauren quickly disengages herself from me.

"Damien?" I ask.

The silhouette starts moving closer.

"Hey Damien?" I'm whispering, backing away.

As the silhouette moves closer it raises a hand, holding what looks like a rolled-up newspaper.

"Damien?" I'm whispering over and over.

The spotlight beam moves across the room, scanning it again, slowly catching everything in its glare, and as it passes over the silhouette's face, illuminating it, my mouth opens in confusion and then Hurley Thompson rushes at me, shouting, "*You fucker!*"

His fist slams against the side of my face before I can raise my arm up and in the background Lauren's crying out for me and after I manage to raise up my arms to block his blows Hurley changes position and starts lifting me up when each thrust of his fists reach my stomach and chest and then I'm falling, gasping for help, and Hurley's leaning down, pausing before he slaps my head with the rolled-up newspaper, hissing into my ear, "I know what you did, you fuck, I know what you said, you dumb fuck," and then he steps on my face and when he's gone I finally lift my head and through totally blurry vision I can make out Lauren standing by the exit and she flicks a switch and the room explodes with light and I'm shielding my eyes, calling out for her, but she doesn't answer.

Pages of the newspaper are scattered around me—it's tomorrow's *News* and on the page I'm looking down at, the blood drooling from my mouth staining the paper, is Buddy Seagull's column, the headline reading HUR-LEY THOMPSON FLEES SC3 AMID RUMORS OF DRUGS AND ABUSE, and there's a photo of Hurley and Sherry Gibson in "happier times" and on the bottom of the page in the boxed section called "What's Going On Here?" is a photo whose graininess suggests it was taken with a telephoto lens and it's of someone who's supposed to be me kissing Lauren Hynde on the mouth, our eyes closed, a caption in bold letters reading IT BOY VICTOR WARD SMOOCHING ACTRESS HYNDE AT GALA PREMIERE—DOES CHLOE KNOW?, and blood dripping from my face keeps swirling all over the paper and I stagger up and when I look in the mirror above the bar I try to smooth things out but after touching my mouth and trying to slick my hair back I end up wiping blood all over my forehead and after trying to get it off with a napkin I'm running downstairs.

We'll slide down the surface of things . . .

Everyone who was at the dinner has vacated the second floor and the space is now filled with other people. While I'm craning my neck, looking for someone familiar, JD appears and takes me aside.

"Just let go," I say uselessly.

"Hold on. What happened to your head?" JD asks calmly, handing me a napkin. "Why is there blood on your tux?"

"Nothing. I slipped," I mutter, looking down. "That's not blood—it's an AIDS ribbon."

JD flinches. "Victor, we all know Hurley Thompson just pulverized you, so you don't need to—"

"Where's Chloe?" I keep craning my neck, looking out across the room. "Where's Chloe, JD?"

JD breathes in. "That is, however, a problem."

"JD—don't fuck with me!" I'm shouting.

"All I saw was Hurley Thompson dropping a newspaper into Chloe's lap. He leaned into her while he placed his hand in an ice bucket and whispered into her ear until her face—which was staring down at the paper Hurley Thompson dropped into her lap—fell, um, apart."

I'm just staring at JD wide-eyed, wondering at what point in the last ten seconds my hands started gripping his shoulders.

"And?" I'm panting, my entire body goes clammy.

"And she ran out and Hurley lit a cigar, very pleased with himself, and then Baxter Priestly ran after her."

I'm so alarmed by this that I must look really bashed-up, because JD looks into my face and whispers, "Jesus, Victor."

"Everything's still sketchy, JD," I'm saying while clutching the side of my stomach Hurley did the most damage to.

"No," he says. "It's all clear to us." He pauses. "It's only sketchy to you."

"JD, Cindy Crawford always says—"

"Who gives a shit what Cindy Crawford says right now?" JD yells. "What are you talking about?"

I stare at him for a long time, confused, before I push him away and then I turn and race down the staircase, people rotating around me everywhere, cameras flashing, causing me to keep tripping into people who keep propping me up, until I'm finally on the first level, where there's so much cigar and pot and cigarette smoke the air's not breathable and I'm shoving people out of the way, constantly adjusting my focus, music booming out way too loud, minor chords crashing down around me, the Steadicam operator unable to keep up.

Bursting out the door, I'm confronted by a crowd so enormous that everyone in it is hidden and when I appear everything grows calm and then, slowly at first, they start shouting my name and seconds later they're screaming to be allowed in and I dive into the throng, pushing through it, constantly turning around, saying "Hello" and "Excuse me" and "You look great" and "It's cool, baby," and once I'm through the maze of bodies I spot the two of them down the block: Baxter trailing after Chloe, trying to subdue her, and she keeps breaking away, rocking the cars parked along the curb, hysterical, setting off their alarms each time she falls against one, and I'm taking in air in great gulps, panic-stricken but laughing too.

I try to run past Baxter to get to Chloe but he whirls around when he hears me approaching and grabs my jacket, wrestling me against the wall of a building, shouting into my face while I'm helplessly staring at Chloe, "*Get* out of here, Victor, just leave her the fuck alone," and Baxter's smiling as he's shouting this, traffic pulsing behind him, and when Chloe turns to glare at me, Baxter—who's stronger than I ever could have imagined— seems secretly pleased. Over his shoulder Chloe's face is ravaged, tears keep pouring from her eyes.

"Baby," I'm shouting. "That wasn't me—"

"Victor," Baxter shouts, warning me. "Let it go."

"It's a hoax," I'm shouting.

Chloe just stares at me until I go limp and finally Baxter relaxes too and a cab behind Chloe slows down and Baxter quickly breaks into a jog and when he reaches Chloe he takes her arm and eases her into the waiting cab but she looks at me before she falls into it, softening, slipping away, deflated, unreachable, and then she's gone and a smirking Baxter nods at me, casually amused. Then total silence.

Girls hanging out the window of a passing limousine making catcalls knock my legs back into motion and I run toward the club where security guards stand behind the barricades barking orders into walkie-talkies and I'm panting as I climb through the crowd and then I'm pulled by the doormen back onto the stairs leading up to the entrance, cries of grief billowing up behind me, steam from the klieg lights rising up into the sky and filling the space above the crowd, and I'm moving through the metal detectors again and running up one flight of stairs and then another, heading up to Damien's office, when suddenly I slam into a column on the third floor.

Damien's escorting Lauren to a private staircase that will lead them down a back exit onto the street and Lauren looks like she's breathing too hard—she actually seems thinner—as Damien talks rapidly into her ear even though her face is so twisted up it doesn't seem like she can comprehend anything Damien's saying as he closes the door behind them.

I rush downstairs to the first floor again, alarmingly fast, struggling through the crowd, too many people passing by, indistinct faces, just profiles, people handing me flowers, people on cellular phones, everyone moving together in a drunken mass, and I'm pushing through the darkness totally awake and people just keep dimly rolling past, constantly moving on to someplace else.

Outside again I push through the crowd avoiding anyone who calls my name and Lauren and Damien seem miles away as they vanish into a limousine and I shout "Wait" and I'm staring too long at the car as it disappears into the mist surrounding Union Square and I keep staring until some tiny thing in me collapses and my head starts clearing.

Everything looks washed out and it's cold and the night suddenly stops accelerating: the sky is locked in place, fuzzy and unmoving, and I'm stumbling down the block, then stopping to search my jacket for a cigarette, when I hear someone call my name and I look across the street at a limousine and Alison standing beside it, her face expressionless, and at her feet, on leashes, are Mr. and Mrs. Chow. When they see me their heads snap up and they start leaping, straining at their leashes excitedly, teeth bared, yapping, and I'm just standing there dumbly, touching my swollen lip, a bruised cheek.

Smiling, Alison drops the leashes.

6 Florent: a narrow, bleak 24-hour diner in the meat-packing district and I'm feeling grimy, slumped at a table near the front, finishing the coke I picked up at a bar in the East Village sometime in the middle of the night where I lost my tie, and a copy of the *News* is spread out in front of me, open to the Buddy Seagull column I've been studying for hours, uselessly since it reveals nothing, and behind me something's being filmed, a camera crew's setting up lights. I had gone by my place at around 4 but someone suspiciously well coiffed—a handsome guy, twenty-five, maybe twenty-six—was hanging out in front of the building, smoking a cigarette like he'd been waiting there a very long time, and another guy—someone in the cast I hadn't met yet—sat in a black Jeep talking into a cell phone, so I split. Bailey brings me another decaf frappuccino and it's freezing in Florent and I keep blowing confetti off my table but whenever I'm not paying attention it reappears and I glare over at the set designer and continuity girl who stare back and restaurant music's playing and each minute seems like an hour.

"How's it hanging, Victor?" Bailey's asking.

"Hey baby, what's the story?" I mutter tiredly.

"You doing okay?" he asks. "You look busted up."

I ponder this before asking, "Have you ever been chased by a chow, man?"

"What's a chow man?"

"A chow, a chow-chow. It's like a big fluffy dog," I try to explain. "They're mean as shit and they were used to guard palaces in like China and shit."

"Have I ever been chased by a chow?" Bailey asks, confused. "Like the last time I was . . . trying to . . . break into a palace?" His face is all scrunched up.

Pause. "I just want some muesli and juice right now, 'kay?"

"You look busted up, man."

"I'm thinking . . . Miami," I croak, squinting up at him.

"Great! Sunshine, deco, seashells, Bacardi, crashing waves"—Bailey makes surfing motions with his arms—"fashion shoots, and Victor making a new splash. Right on, man."

I'm watching the early-morning traffic cruise by on 14th Street and then I clear my throat. "Er . . . maybe Detroit."

"I'm telling you, baby," he says. "The world is a jungle. Wherever you go it's still the same."

"I just want some muesli and juice right now, okay, man?"

"You need to utilize your potential, man."

"There's a snag in your advice, man," I point out.

"Yeah?"

"You're—a—waiter."

I finish reading an article about new mascaras (Shattered and Roach are the season's most popular) and hip lipsticks (Frostbite, Asphyxia, Bruise) and glam nail polish (Plaque, Mildew) and I'm thinking, genuinely, Wow, progress, and some girl behind me with a floppy beach hat on and a bandeau bra top and saucer eyes is listening to a guy wearing a suit made of sixteenth-century armor saying "um um um" while snapping his fingers until he remembers—"Ewan McGregor!"—and then they both fall silent and the director leans in to me and warns, "You're not looking worried enough," which is my cue to leave Florent.

Outside, more light, some of it artificial, opens up the city, and the sidewalks on 14th Street are empty, devoid of extras, and above the sounds of faraway jackhammers I can hear someone singing "The Sunny Side of the Street" softly to himself and when I feel someone touch my shoulder I turn around but no one's there. A dog races by going haywire. I call out to it. It stops, looks at me, runs on. "Disarm" by the Smashing Pumpkins starts playing on the sound track and the music overlaps a shot of the club I was going to open in TriBeCa and I walk into that frame, not noticing the black limousine parked across the street, four buildings down, that the cameraman pans to.

5

A door slams shut behind me, two pairs of hands grab my shoulders and I'm shoved into a chair, and under the fuzzy haze of a black light, silhouettes and shadows come into focus: Damien's goons (Duke but not Digby, who was recast after we shot yesterday's breakfast) and Juan, the afternoon doorman at Alison's building on the Upper East Side, and as the lights get brighter Damien appears and he's smoking a Partagas Perfecto cigar and wearing skintight jeans, a vest with bold optical patterns, a shirt with starburst designs, a long Armani overcoat, motorcycle boots, and his hands—grabbing my sore face, squeezing it—are like ice and kind of soothing until he pushes my head back trying to snap my neck, but one of the goons—maybe Duke—pulls him away and Damien's making noises that sound like chanting and one of the mirror balls that used to hang above the dance floor lies shattered in a corner, confetti scattered around it in tall piles.

"That was a particularly hellish greeting," I say, trying to maintain my composure once Damien lets go.

Damien's not listening. He keeps pacing the room, making the chanting noises, and the room is so freezing that the air coming out of his mouth steams and then he walks back to where I'm sitting, towering over me even though he's not that tall, and looks into my face again, cigar smoke making my eyes water. He studies my blank expression before shaking his head disgustedly and backing away to pace the room without knowing which direction to take.

The goons and Juan just stare vacantly at me, occasionally averting their eyes but mostly not, waiting for some kind of signal from Damien, and I tense up, bracing myself, thinking, just don't touch the face, just anywhere but the face.

"Did anybody read the *Post* this morning?" Damien's asking the room. "The headline? Something about Satan escaping from hell?"

A few nods, some appreciative murmuring. I close my eyes.

"I'm looking at this place, Victor," Damien says. "And do you want to know what I'm thinking?"

Involuntarily I shake my head, realize something, then nod.

"I'm thinking, Jesus, the zeitgeist's in limbo."

I don't say anything. Damien spits on me, then grabs my face, smearing his saliva all over my nose, my cheeks, reopening a wound on my mouth where Hurley hit me.

"How do you feel, Victor?" he's asking. "How do you feel this morning?"

"I feel very . . . funny," I say, guessing, pulling back. "I feel very . . . unhip?"

"You look the part," Damien sneers, livid, ready to pounce, the veins in his neck and forehead bulging, grasping my face so tightly that when I yell out the sounds coming from my mouth are muffled and my vision blurs over and he abruptly lets go, pacing again.

"Haven't you ever come to a point in your life where you've said to yourself: Hey, this isn't right?"

I don't say anything, just continue sucking in air.

"I guess it's beside the point to tell you you're fired."

I nod, don't say anything, have no idea what kind of expression is on my face.

"I mean, what do you think you are?" he asks, baffled. "A reliable sales tool? Let's just put it this way, Victor: I'm not too thrilled by your value system."

I nod mutely, not denying anything.

"There's good in this business, Victor, and there's bad," Damien says, breathing hard. "And it's my impression that you can't discern between the two."

Suddenly something in me cracks. "Hey," I shout, looking up at him. "Spare me."

Damien seems pleased by this outburst and starts circling the chair, raising the cigar to his mouth, taking rapid light puffs, its tip glowing off then on then off.

"Sometimes even the desert gets chilly, Victor," he intones pretentiously.

"Please continue, O Wise One," I groan, rolling my eyes. "Fucking spare me, man."

He smacks me across the head, then he does it again, and when he does it a third time I wonder if that third slap was in the script, and finally Duke pulls Damien back.

"I may park wherever I feel like it, Victor," he growls, "but I also pay the fucking tickets."

Damien breaks free from Duke and grabs my cheek at the place Hurley's fist struck and twists it upward between two fingers until I'm shouting out for him to stop, reaching up to pull his hand away, but when he lets go I just fall back, limp, rubbing my face.

"I'm just like . . ." I'm trying to catch my breath. "I'm just like . . . trying to fit this into . . . perspective," I choke, slipping helplessly into tears.

Damien slaps my face again. "Hey, look at me."

"Man, you're shooting from the hip." I'm panting, delirious. "I admire that, man." I take in air, gasping. "I go to jail, right? I go directly to jail?"

He sighs, studying me, rubs a hand over his face. "You act very hard to be cool, Victor, but really you're very normal." Pause. "You're a loser." He shrugs. "You're an easy target with a disadvantage."

I try to stand up but Damien pushes me back down into the chair.

"Did you fuck her?" he suddenly asks.

I can't say anything since I don't know who he's talking about.

"Did you fuck her?" he asks again, quietly.

"I'll, um, take the Fifth," I mumble.

"You'll take *what*, you sonofabitch?" he roars, the two goons rushing over, holding him back from beating the shit out of me.

"The photograph's a lie," I'm shouting back. "The photo was faked. It looks real but it's not. That's not me. It must have been altered—"

Damien reaches into the Armani overcoat and throws a handful of photographs at my head. I duck. They scatter around me, one hitting my lap, faceup, the rest falling to the floor, different photos of Lauren and me making out. In a few shots our tongues are visible, entwined and glistening.

"What are . . . these?" I'm asking.

"Keep them. Souvenirs."

"What *are* these?" I'm asking.

"The originals, fuckhead," Damien says. "I've had them checked out. They weren't altered, fuckhead."

Damien crosses the room, gradually calming himself down, closes and locks a briefcase, then checks his watch.

"I suppose you've figured out that you're not opening this dump?" Damien's asking. "The silent partners have already been consulted on this minor decision. We've taken care of Burl, and JD's been fired too. He'll actually never work anywhere in Manhattan again because of his unfortunate association with you."

"Damien, hey," I say softly. "Come on, man, JD didn't do anything."

"He has AIDS," Damien says, slipping on a pair of black leather gloves. "He's not going to be around much longer anyway."

I just stare at Damien, who notices.

"It's a blood disease," he says. "It's some kind of virus. I'm sure you've heard of it."

"Oh, yeah," I say uncertainly.

"Baxter Priestly's with me now," Damien says, getting ready to make an exit. "It somehow seems . . ." He searches for the right word, cocks his head, comes up with "appropriate."

Juan shrugs at me as he follows Damien and the goons out of the club and I pick up one of the photographs of Lauren and me and turn it over as if there might be some kind of explanation for its existence on the back but it's blank and I'm drained, my head spinning, swearing "fuck fuck fuck" as I move over to a dusty sink behind what would have been the bar and I'm waiting for the director to shout "Cut" but the only sounds I'm hearing are Damien's limo screeching out of TriBeCa, my feet crunching what's left of the mirror ball, sleigh bells not in the shooting script, a buzzing fly circling my head which I'm too tired to wave away.

4

I'm standing at a pay phone on Houston Street, three blocks from Lauren's apartment. Extras walk by, looking stiff and poorly directed. A limousine cruises toward Broadway. I'm crunching on a Mentos.

"Hey pussycat, it's me," I say. "I need to see you."

"That's not possible," she says, and then less surely, "Who is this?"

"I'm coming over."

"I won't be here."

"Why not?"

"I'm going to Miami with Damien." She adds, "In about an hour. I'm packing."

"What happened to Alison?" I ask. "What happened to his *fiancée*?" I spit out. "Huh, Lauren?"

"Damien dumped Alison and she's put a contract out on his head," she says casually. "If you can believe that, which I actually can."

While I'm processing this information the cameraman keeps circling the pay phone, distracting me into forgetting my lines, so I decide to improvise and surprisingly the director allows it.

"What about . . . what about when you get back, baby?" I ask hesitantly.

"I'm going on location," she says, very matter-of-fact. "To Burbank."

"For what?" I'm asking, covering my eyes with my hand.

"I'm playing the squealing genie in Disney's new live-action feature

Aladdin Meets Roger Rabbit, which is being directed by—oh, what's his name?—oh yeah, Cookie Pizarro." She pauses. "CAA thinks it's my big break."

I'm stuck. "Give Cookie my, um, best," and then I sigh. "I really want to come over."

"You can't, honey," she says sweetly.

"You're impossible," I say through clenched teeth. "Then why don't you come meet *me?*"

"Where are you?"

"In a big deluxe suite at the SoHo Grand."

"Well, that sounds like neutral ground, but no."

"Lauren—what about last night?"

"My opinion?"

A very long pause that I'm about to break when I remember my line, but she speaks first.

"My opinion is: I guess you shouldn't expect too much from people. My opinion is: You're busted and you did it to yourself."

"I've been . . . I've been under . . . a lot of pressure, baby," I'm saying, trying not to break down. "I . . . stumbled."

"No, Victor," she says curtly. "You fell."

"You sound pretty casual, huh, baby?"

"That's what people sound like when they don't care anymore, Victor," she says. "I'm surprised it doesn't sound more familiar to you."

Pause. "There's nothing, um, very encouraging about that answer, baby."

"You sound like your tongue's pierced," she says tiredly.

"And you exude glamour and, um, radiance . . . even over the phone," I mumble, feeding another quarter into the slot.

"See, Victor, the problem is you've *got* to know things," she says. "But you don't."

"That picture wasn't us," I say, suddenly alert. "I don't know how, Lauren, but that wasn't—"

"Are you sure?" she asks, cutting me off.

"Oh come on," I yell, my voice getting higher. "What's the story, Lauren? I mean, Jesus, this is like a nightmare and you're taking it so—"

"I don't know, Victor, but I'm sure you'll wake up and figure it all out," she says. "I wouldn't necessarily bet on it but I think you'll figure it all out. In the end."

"Jesus, you sound like you don't want to ruin the surprise for me."

"Victor," she's sighing, "I have to go."

"It's not me, Lauren," I stress again. "That might be you. But that's *not* me."

"Well, it *looks* like you, Victor. The paper *says* it's you—"

"Lauren," I shout, panicking. "What in the hell's happening? Where in the fuck did that photo come from?"

"Victor," she continues calmly. "We cannot see each other anymore. We cannot talk to each other anymore. This relationship is terminated."

"You're saying this like you've just completed some kind of fucking assignment," I cry out.

"*You're* projecting," she says sternly.

"I urge you, baby, one last time to reconsider," I say, breaking down. "I want to be with you," I finally say.

"Trust me, Victor," she says. "You don't."

"Baby, he gets his shirts tailored—"

"Frankly I couldn't care less," she says. "Those are things *you* care about. Those are the things that make *you* decide a person's worth."

After a long pause I say, "I guess you heard about Mica."

"What about Mica?" she asks, sounding totally uninterested.

"She was, um, murdered, baby," I point out, wiping my nose.

"I don't think that was a murder," Lauren says carefully.

After another long pause I ask, "What was it?"

Finally, solemnly, she says, "It was a statement," giving it more meaning than I'm capable of understanding.

"Spare me, Lauren," I whisper helplessly.

She hangs up.

The camera stops rolling and the makeup girl drops a couple glycerin tears onto my face and the camera starts rolling again and just like in rehearsals I hang the phone up in such a way that it drops out of my hand, swinging by its cord, and then carefully, gently, I lift it up, staring at it. We don't bother reshooting and it's on to the next setup.

3

Chloe actually lets the doorman buzz me up after the director tells Ashton to give me the rundown so that I'm prepared for the following scene, which is basically that when Chloe skipped the shows she was supposed to do today it caused some kind of horrible ruckus and since "Hard Copy," "Inside Edition," "A Current Affair," "Entertainment Tonight" and "Nightline" have been calling all morning Chloe is heading to Canyon Ranch for two weeks with Baxter Priestly and in the elevator the director, getting fed up with me, hisses "Look anguished" and I try to but I'm just vaguely unhappy and when I glance uncertainly at the camera it rises up as the elevator doors open and follows me into the darkness of the hallway that leads to Chloe's loft.

Inside the apartment it's freezing, even with all the lights burning; the windows are covered with huge sheets of ice, and frost layers the kitchen cabinets and the giant glass coffee table, the floor slippery in places. The phone keeps ringing, competing with the TV in Chloe's bedroom, and as I walk in to turn it down a promo for this afternoon's "Patty Winters Show" appears, the host cradling a severely deformed four-year-old while Bette Midler sings "From a Distance" on the sound track, and then it's back to a soap opera, where a character says to another character, "That wasn't nice," and I move slowly over to the bathroom but Chloe isn't in there. The tub is full of suds and there are two empty containers of Ben & Jerry's Chubby Hubby ice cream sitting by the sink, next to the retainer Chloe uses to bleach her teeth, which sits beside a large hand mirror that with a twinge of panic I'm about to inspect, but then Chloe walks into the bedroom and I whirl around and the phone keeps ringing.

She's on a cellular, listening to someone, and looking remarkably composed, she glances over at me as she walks toward the bed, on top of which sits the set of Gucci luggage Tom Ford sent for her birthday, and she says something into the phone I can't hear, then clicks off, and I reconsider opening my arms and saying "Ta-da!" but instead ask "Who was that?" and then, when there isn't an answer, "That's not your phone."

"It's Baxter's," she says. "He gave it to me." Pause. "Since I can't answer my own."

"Baby," I start. "Are you okay?" I'm thinking about the hand mirror in the bathroom behind me, wondering if there was anything on it. "You're not back into . . ." I let my voice drift off.

It takes longer than I want for her to realize what I'm referring to and she says "No, Victor" but she flinches when she says this so I'm not too relieved.

The phone keeps ringing and Chloe keeps lifting sweaters out of her armoire and placing them in the suitcases on the bed and she's moving slowly, deliberately, nodding to herself, every move seemingly mapped out, only slightly distracted by my presence, but then she sighs and stops moving. She looks over at where I'm shivering, slumped in a giant white chair. In a mirror across the room I can make out my reflection and my face isn't as bruised as I feared. Chloe's asking "Why?" and the phone keeps ringing, a reminder.

"Why . . . what?"

"Just *why*, Victor."

"Baby," I say, holding my hands up, about to offer an explanation. "You're a, um, great source of . . . inspiration to, um, me."

"I want some kind of answer from you," she says calmly. "Don't free-associate. Just tell me why."

I take this in. "I can dig that, baby."

"If there was just some speck of feeling in you, Victor," she sighs, padding over to the closet.

"Oh please, baby—"

"Why, Victor?" she asks again.

"Baby, I—"

"I'm not going to cry. I cried all night," she says. "I'm not going to cry while you're here so just be straight with me."

"Baby, I need . . . I need . . ." I sigh, then start again. "Baby, see, this thing—"

"You never really answer a question directly if you can help it, do you?"

"Um . . ." I look up at her, confused. "What was the question?"

She's carefully placing T-shirts and panties on one side of the largest suitcase. She wraps the cord of a hair dryer around its handle, then places it in a smaller bag. "It's taken me a long time to like myself, Victor," she says, gliding by me. "I'm not going to let you change that."

"But you don't like yourself," I mutter wearily, shaking my head. "Not really," and then, "Baby, please stop moving around."

Baxter's cell phone rings. She picks it up off the bed and listens to whoever's calling, studying me until she finally turns away and says, "Yeah, okay. . . . I'll be ready. . . . I just need to meet with someone. . . . Okay, thanks. . . . Hugh Grant and Elizabeth Hurley? . . . Okay, great. . . . No, I'll be fine. . . . Yeah, he's here right now. . . . No, no, no—it's okay, *don't*. I'm fine, really. . . . I'll see you then."

She clicks off, moves directly into the bathroom and closes the door. The toilet flushes twice and then she walks back into the bedroom. I want to ask her who was on the phone so she'll have to say his name but I already know who it was and in the end I don't really want to hear her say his name.

"So can you tell me why, Victor?" she asks. "Why did all this happen?"

"Because, baby . . ." I swallow. "This is hard. . . . Come on, baby. . . . This is . . . all I know? . . . It's all . . . I am?" I say, hoping it's the right way of explaining.

"Everything you know is wrong," she says. "Everything you know is *wrong*."

"Oh man," I sigh.

"Just look at your life, Victor. You're going nowhere. You know girls named Vagina—"

"Hey, her name was *Yanni*, baby. It just *means* vagina."

"How many thousands of nightclub booths can you hang out in?" she's asking. "You just sit around Bowery Bar or Pravda or Indochine complaining about how much it sucks." She pauses, waiting. "And you do this four times a week?"

"I'm . . . pretty much exhausted, baby."

"No, you're sick," she says, staring deeply into the luggage, contemplating the arrangement of clothes, hands on hips. "You're soul sick, Victor."

"Baby, it's just"—I raise my head to look at her, confused—"some bad coke, but whatever." I sigh, giving up. "It's irrelevant."

"Everything is irrelevant with you."

"I'm . . . baffled. Why is everyone dissing me?"

"You spend your life trying to impress people you're impressed with, that's why."

"Why should I try to impress people who *don't* impress me, baby?"

"Because the people you want to impress aren't worth it?"

After taking this in, I clear my throat. "My . . . emotions at the moment are a little, um, mixed up," I whimper.

"You cater to people who don't really give a damn."

"Oh come on, baby," I exclaim. "They just pretend not to give a damn—"

She cuts me off with a look of total disbelief. "Do you actually listen to yourself?"

I shrug, miserably.

"I know it's difficult for you to adjust to reality, but isn't it time?" She zips one bag up, contemplates another.

"Baby, baby, this has been like the most difficult week, I think, of my life and"—I breathe in—"this has been so scary, so—"

"Oh, this tiny little world of yours," she says, waving me away.

"No, no, really, I'm sick of it, I'm sick of it all too, baby," I say, panting, sitting up in the giant white chair. "I'm sick of being friendly with like people who either hate me or or or are planning to kill me or—"

"Did you actually think you'd get away with this?" she asks, cutting me off.

I sigh, then pause for the appropriate amount of time before asking, "Why not?"

She stares at me, expressionless.

"People get away with more," I mutter.

"That's because everyone's smarter than you," she says. "That's because everything you know is wrong and everyone is smarter than you."

"Baby, that picture . . . I don't know what it was but that didn't happen, that never happened—"

"What never happened?" she asks, suddenly interested.

"What that photo showed," I say.

"You didn't have sex with or attempt to have sex with or kiss Lauren Hynde?" she asks. "Is that what you're saying?"

I consider this, reword what she asked me, then blurt out, "I'm saying that—"

She moves away from me. "Maybe you come to life when I'm not around—who knows?"

I'm gesturing with my hands, trying to make some kind of point, attempting to form even a sentence. "Didn't you like, um, didn't you *talk* to Lauren? Didn't she explain?" I ask hopefully.

"No," she says. "I like Lauren. I just never want to see her again." Chloe checks her watch, mumbles an inaudible curse.

I lift myself up from the chair and move toward the bathroom where Chloe's placing jars filled with creams and oils and powders into another Gucci bag. I notice that the hand mirror I saw by the sink isn't there anymore. A razor blade and a small transparent straw sit by a bottle of perfume and I am not imagining this.

"What?" she asks suddenly, turning around. "Why are you still here?"

"Because . . ." I smile sadly. "You're . . . my ideal mate?"

"A mirror's your ideal mate."

"Maybe . . . ," I start, haltingly. "Maybe if you didn't expect so much from me you might not be so . . . disappointed," I finally admit, and then, watching her reflection in the mirror, "Don't cry."

"I'm not crying," she says, surprised. "I'm yawning."

And back down in the lobby, on my way outside, dazed, shuffling across the marble floor, I bump into Tristan, an ex-model who deals drugs, chatting with Ashton, and Tristan's magnetic in a gorgeous kind of way and though I'm totally absent right now I'm able to instinctively shake his hand, make the prerequisite small talk, avoid the obvious (Buddy Seagull's column, the stains on my shirt, the bruise above my eyebrow), trade compliments about our hair, recommend one or two cool foreign movies, a new band from Nevada ("a really happening state," Tristan assures me), and then we move on.

Outside, on the steps leading down to the sidewalk, I turn around, and through the lobby doors I see Tristan getting into the elevator and I want to ask him who he's going to see and then maybe buy a couple of grams but instead I start panicking because I make a connection and Tristan spots me staring at him and he gives a little wave just as the elevator doors close and a horrible vision breaks open in front of me of Chloe in an ambulance, another detox center in the desert somewhere, another series of failed suicide attempts followed up with a successful one and I cry out and try to run back into the lobby but crew members are struggling to hold me back and

I'm crying out "No but *why* but *why* this wasn't in the script" until I collapse and a technician props me up on the steps where I'm still freaking out and shouting "But you don't understand you don't understand" and suddenly the director kneels beside me and gently tells the two crew members to let go, that it's okay, *shhh*.

I'm shaking so hard the director has to hold my face in his hands, steadying it, before he can talk to me.

Basically summing things up, he asks, "Do you really want to go back up there?"

I'm shaking so hard I can't answer him.

"Do you really want to go back up there?" he asks again. "Is this something your character would do?"

I'm inhaling and exhaling so hard I can't catch my breath and slowly people start moving away from me.

After what seems like hours I finally stand up when the urge to go back up to the apartment recedes (not all that unexpectedly, really) and over the sounds of construction and traffic I'm still hearing sleigh bells and someone from wardrobe is brushing off my jacket as I head down the steps leading to the sidewalk and the black sedan waiting for me at the curb which will take me back to my apartment where my viewpoint of this project will be, if not exactly clarified, then at least placed in some kind of perspective.

2 Outside my apartment building the *Details* reporter is playing hopscotch, wearing a citrus-colored catsuit, a white leather jacket, platform sneakers, braids held in place by plastic barrettes, and she's dialing a number on a cell phone, her fingernails half-covered with chipped brown polish. I trudge by her without saying a word, gingerly stepping over the remains of my crushed and mangled Vespa, which lies crumpled by the trash lining the curb, a cigarette dangling from my lips, my sunglasses on.

"Hey, we were supposed to meet this morning," she says, clicking off the cell phone.

I don't say anything, just busy myself looking for my keys.

"They canceled the piece on you anyway," she says.

"And you came to tell me in person?" I find the keys. "How intimidating."

"Don't you care?" she asks.

I sigh, take my sunglasses off. "What did you think of me?"

She cocks her head "meaningfully," studies the sidewalk, squinting, then looks back up at my face.

"I thought you were well-nigh inscrutable," she says, mimicking a British accent.

"Well, *I* thought *you* were a hodgepodge of banality," I say, mimicking a British accent too.

I open the door and step inside. She shrugs, skips away.

An eviction notice is pinned to my door and when I pull it off I glance over at the director and roll my eyes, groaning "Oh *puhleeeze*." The instant I walk into my apartment the phone starts ringing and I flop down on my beanbag chair, exhausted, and pick it up, yawning. "It's Victor—whass up?"

"This is Palakon calling," a voice says crisply.

"Palakon, I really can't talk now, so—"

"There's a manila envelope on your kitchen table," Palakon says, cutting me off. "Open it."

I stare into the kitchen from where I'm slouching and spot the envelope on the table.

"Okay," I say, "I'm opening the vanilla envelope, dude."

"No, Mr. Johnson," Palakon says, annoyed. "Please get up and go to the kitchen."

"Whoa," I say, impressed.

"I want you to take that envelope with you when you go to London to find Jamie Fields," Palakon says. "You have a reservation in a first-class cabin on the *QE2*. It leaves New York at four o'clock this afternoon. Your tickets are in that manila envelope on your kitchen table, along with—"

"Wait a minute, wait a minute," I say. "Hold on."

"Yes?" Palakon asks politely.

I pause for a long time, mulling things over before blurting out, "You could've at least put me on the fucking Concorde."

"You have a reservation in a *first-class* cabin on the *QE2*," Palakon says again, undeterred. "It leaves New York at four o'clock this afternoon. A car will be by to pick you up at one-thirty. Your tickets are in the manila envelope along with ten thousand dollars in cash for, er, expenses—"

"Need receipts?"

"That won't be necessary, Mr. Johnson."

"Cool."

"I will contact you on the ship. And don't forget to take the manila envelope with you. It's crucial."

"Why?" I ask.

"Because everything you need is in it."

"It's a nice manila envelope," I say finally.

"Thank you."

"How did you know I'd be able to go today, Palakon?"

"I read the *News*," he says. "I figured it out."

"Palakon—"

"Oh yes," Palakon says, before hanging up. "Take the hat with you too."

I pause before asking, "What hat?"

"You know which one."

He hangs up.

1   "You have potential," Jamie said.

We were lounging in a Camden flashback in the commons, splitting a Molson, our sunglasses on, our eyes glazed over, a peeled orange sitting untouched between us on a table, and we'd already read our horoscopes and I was wearing a T-shirt that read IF YOU'RE NOT WASTED THE DAY IS and waiting for my laundry to dry and she was alternating between playing with a pencil and smelling a Thai orchid a secret admirer had sent her and heavy-metal pop—Whitesnake or Glass Tiger—was playing from somewhere we couldn't figure out and it was driving us nuts and her dealer wasn't coming up until next Tuesday so we were fairly unresponsive toward certain events and in the sky things were getting dark.

We were lounging in the commons and we'd been talking about how shallow everyone was, ticking off the affairs we'd had with all these shallow people, and then Jamie saw someone she hated or she'd fucked (they usually existed in the same realm) and she leaned in and kissed me even before I could say "What's the story?" The guy, Mitchell, passed by. It wasn't enough that she and I had been screwing each other for the last two weeks or so; she needed people to know that we had.

"Man, did I get torqued last night," I yawned, stretching.

"Totally excellent," she said.

"Get a haircut," I muttered to someone with a ponytail shuffling by, and

Jamie eyed a maintenance worker trimming a rosebush and licked her lips naughtily.

She had long fingernails always painted with white polish and liked starting sentences with the words "Contrary to popular opinion . . ." She hated baseball caps on men but would wear one if she thought her hair looked bad or if she was too hungover to wash it. Her other pet peeves about men ranged along the predictable lines of: fake rap talk, urine or semen stains on jockey shorts (a type of underwear she abhorred), razor stubble, giving hickeys, carrying books around ("Camden isn't Yale for god's sake," she'd moan). Condoms didn't necessarily mean anything to her but she knew every guy on campus who had herpes (through some kind of deal with a lesbian nurse in Health Services who was in love with her), so it was all moot. Shakespeare "irritated" her.

I would tell her "I'm not looking for a serious relationship" and she would stare back at me like I was insane, as if I wasn't capable of one in the first place. I would tell her "Your roommate's really pretty," before moving on to long monologues about ex-girlfriends, every cheerleader I ever fucked, a cousin I fingerbanged at a party in Virginia Beach, or I'd brag about how much money my family had and I always inflated the amount because sometimes this was the only way to get her attention, even though she knew who my dad was, having seen him on CNN. She forgave me for a lot of flaws because I was "simply too good-looking."

At first she was so inexpressive and indifferent that I wanted to know more about her. I envied that blankness — it was the opposite of helplessness or damage or craving or suffering or shame. But she was never really happy and already, in a matter of days, she had reached a stage in our relationship when she no longer really cared about me or any thoughts or ideas I might have had. I'd try and fuck her into some kind of conciousness, desperate to make her come, and I'd fuck her so hard that she'd be drenched with sweat and red-faced and yelling out, the two of us on the mattress on the floor next to piles of books she'd stolen from the library and a couple of porno magazines I bought that we both whacked off over and her accountant was always calling or her therapist was always calling or her cousin lost in Ibiza was always calling and we'd have sad conversations about how much she hated her mother and wished she was dead like my mother was but I listened "intently" and took it easy on Jamie since I knew her first boyfriend died in a car accident coming back from cheating on her at a ski lodge in Brattleboro. "But he was so weird I really don't even want to talk about it," she'd finally say after an hour, after seventy minutes, sometimes eighty.

A limousine rolled up next to one of the dorms and a group of freshmen were sunning themselves beneath a darkening sky on a mattress pulled out from Booth House, which bordered the commons. A keg was being tapped and people drifted toward it and the wind tossing leaves around the lawn made Jamie and me look at how leafless the trees were. MTV was on the large-screen television set that hung above the fireplace and a VJ introduced a video but the sound was off and then there was static and people were really just hanging out, waiting for lunch, for another class to begin. Someone sat down next to us and started taping our conversation and someone else was explaining to someone behind me how a camcorder worked. Jamie was gazing at the giant NO PHOTOGRAPHY poster pinned on an unnecessary column in the middle of the room and I had just noticed a naked mannequin lying on its side that someone had discarded on the stairs leading up to the dining halls.

"Do you have any cash?" I asked her.

"Don't overdo it, baby," she warned, lowering her sunglasses, scanning the room.

I took my sunglasses off and checked my reflection in the lenses.

She snapped her fingers at me. "Hey, why don't you just start chewing with your mouth open. Why don't you just start licking your fingers after meals."

"I don't intend to take you anywhere nice," I told her.

"Nice butt," she murmured, ogling a Brazilian guy she hadn't fucked yet but would a week later as he passed by, bouncing a soccer ball on his knee as he crossed the length of the room while eating a bagel, his jeans perfectly ripped, wearing a tank top with a gym logo on it.

I agreed, teasingly.

"You fag," she yawned, taking the last swallow of Molson.

"He wears socks with sandals," I pointed out. "He still wears his high-school graduation ring."

"You, too, are in dire need of a maturity alert, my friend," she said.

"I don't wear Members Only jackets."

"Contrary to popular opinion this is not enough to not make you evil," she said.

"Evil?" I faux-gasped. "Black light posters are *in*. Bongos are *in*."

"Pervert," she said gleefully. "You have potential."

Sean Bateman, whom she had fucked, joined us, offered a distracted smile, nodding even though no one had said anything that required a nod. He wondered aloud if any of us had pot, mentioned something about Rupert getting arrested in Albany late last night or early this morning. Sean pulled a beer out of the jacket he had just taken off and handed it to Jamie, who opened it with her teeth. I noticed how nice Bateman's forearms were and someone was sadly strumming Led Zeppelin—I think it was "Thank You"—on a guitar and any light that had been streaming through the window we were all sitting next to disappeared and Sean whispered in my ear, "All the boys think she's a spy. . . ."

I nodded and managed to smile.

Jamie was eyeing me carefully.

"What?" I asked, confused.

"You're easy to unfold," she said to me in front of Sean.

"What's the story, baby?" I was asking, worried, blank-faced.

"You have potential," Jamie said, grinning. "You definitely have potential."

O   The camera slowly pans around my apartment, Smashing Pumpkins' "Stumbleine" pours out over the sound track: a vintage industrial fan, an empty fish tank, dried flowers, a candelabra, a bicycle, a kitchen custom-made from several kinds of stone, a glass-door refrigerator, a food processor unwashed and stained with the grain and pulp from a health shake, a set of martini glasses. In the bathroom there's a poster of Diana Rigg in "The Avengers" and candles from Agnès b. and in the bedroom there's a down comforter lying on a futon that was handcarved in a Japanese forest and the original poster for *La Dolce Vita* that Chloe gave me for a birthday hangs over it and in the closet in that bedroom is a black Paul Smith suit, a black turtleneck, jeans and white shirts, vests, an open-weave pullover sweater, a pair of brightly colored Hush Puppies, black desert boots. On my desk: free drink tickets, a Cohiba cigar still in its container, a Clash CD—*Sandinista!*—unopened, a check to Save the Rainforest returned because of insufficient funds, last year's Social Register, a Baggie of psilocybin mushrooms, a half-empty Snapple, a roll of Mentos, an ad ripped from a magazine of Tyson promoting a new lip balm and the dragon tattoo etched on his bicep has a Chinese inscription on it that translated means "don't trust anyone" and an old fax machine and falling out of the fax machine at this moment is a slip of fax paper that I pick up and read.

On it:

nie Marais, Christopher Lambert, Tommy Lee, Lauren Hutton, Claire Danes, Patty Hearst, Richard Grieco, Pino Luongo, Steffi

Graf, Michael J. Fox, Billy Crudup, Marc Jacobs, Marc Audibet,
the Butthole Surfers, George Clinton, Henry Rollins, Nike, Kim
Deal, Beavis and Butt-head, Anita Hill, Jeff Koons, Nicole
Kidman, Howard Stern, Jim Shaw, Mark Romanek, Stussy, Whit
Stillman, Isabella Rossellini, Christian Francis Roth, Vanessa
Williams, Larry Clark, Rob Morrow, Robin Wright, Jennifer
Connelly, RuPaul, Chelsea Clinton, Penelope Spheeris, Glenn
Close, Mandie Erickson, Mark Kostabi, René Russo, Yasmen,
Robert Rodriguez, Dr. Dre, Craig Kallman, Rosie Perez,
Campion Platt, Jane Pratt, Natasha Richardson, Scott Wolf,
Yohji Yamamoto, L7, Donna Tartt, Spike Jonze, Sara Gilbert,
Sam Bayer, Margaret Cho, Steve Albini, Kevin Smith, Jim
Rome, Rick Rubin, Gary Panter, Mark Morris, Betsey Johnson,
Angela Janklow, Shannen Doherty, Molly Ringwald, O. J.
Simpson, Michael DeLuca, Laura Dern, Rene Chun, the Brady
Bunch, Toni Braxton, Shabba Ranks, the Miller Sisters, Jim
Carrey, Robin Givens, Bruno Beuilacqua di Santangelo,
Huckleberry Finn, Bill Murr

I'm about to reread it for a fourth time, wiping tears off my face, when I
hear someone outside the front door and a key slipped into the lock,
unlocking the door, and the door opens and someone playing the building's
superintendent—"a young gorgeous guy"—peers in and spots me, wasted
on the beanbag chair beneath a giant framed poster of the Replacements'
Pleased to Meet Me LP, and the actor seems bewildered and finally he apol-
ogizes for missing his cue.

"I thought I heard voices, man," he says. "I thought I heard voices."

2

16 Everything surrounding the ship is gray or dark blue and nothing is particularly hip, and once or maybe twice a day this thin strip of white appears at the horizon line but it's so far in the distance you can't be sure whether it's land or more sky. It's impossible to believe that any kind of life sustains itself beneath this flat, slate-gray sky or in an ocean so calm and vast, that anything breathing could exist in such limbo, and any movement that occurs below the surface is so faint it's like some kind of small accident, a tiny indifferent moment, a minor incident that shouldn't have happened, and in the sky there's never any trace of sun—the air seems vaguely transparent and disposable, with the texture of Kleenex—yet it's always bright in a dull way, the wind usually constant as we drift through it, weightless, and below us the trail the ship leaves behind is a Jacuzzi blue that fades within minutes into the same boring gray sheet that blankets everything else surrounding the ship. One day a normal-looking rainbow appears and you vaguely notice it, thinking about the enormous sums of money the Kiss reunion tour made over the summer, or maybe a whale swims along the starboard side, waving its fin, showing off. It's easy to feel safe, for people to look at you and think some-one's going somewhere. Surrounded by so much boring space, five days is a long time to stay unimpressed.

15 I boarded the *QE2* still wearing the Comme des Garçons tux and I was so stoned by the time the driver Palakon had sent dropped me off at the passenger terminal on West 50th Street that how I actually got on the ship is a blur of images so imprecise you couldn't really even classify them as a montage: red, white and blue balloons floating in midair, crowds of photographers that I assumed were paparazzi but weren't, a porter assuring me that my luggage—faded Gucci bags hurriedly and badly packed—would be in my cabin when ("and if," he added) I got there, a live band playing "The Lambeth Walk." In my haze I vaguely realized that "things" had already been taken care of, since I moved through the whole embarkation process— security, passport, receiving a *QE2* VIP Gold Card—swiftly and with no hassles. But I was still so wasted that I barely made it up the gangway, and then only with the help of a couple of production assistants dressed as extras, one on either side of me, and a triple espresso from Starbucks, force-fed, as the band began playing a jaunty version of "Anything Goes."

In my cabin I opened a complimentary split of Perrier-Jouët and downed two crumbled Xanax with it and then slumped into an overstuffed armchair. My eyes were sore and glazed and only by squinting could I take in my surroundings: a telephone, a minifridge, an okay bed, an unopenable porthole blurred opaque by the salt air, baskets of fresh fruit and flowers that I glumly stared at. Impassively, I noticed a television and turned it on with a remote control it took me fifteen minutes to find, the prop sitting (inconspicuously, I thought) on top of the TV. I tried to focus and read a "Welcome Aboard" letter but started hyperventilating when I saw an invitation requesting my presence for cocktails with the ship's "cruise director." My maid, a cute little English thing, a tiny Courteney Cox maybe, introduced herself, and eyeing the bright new oversized orange felt Versace overcoat I'd unpacked and thrown across the bed, she smiled proudly and said, "I see you've already gotten acquainted with your life jacket," and I just mumbled whatever I was supposed to mumble at that point, which was, I think, "Just respect yourself, baby," then glared at her until she left and I relaxed back into my stupor.

As we started moving down the Hudson River I wrapped my head in a fluffy towel, started to sob inauthentically and then used one of the gift-box lotions I found when I hobbled into the bathroom to jerk off with but I was too wasted even to get half hard or to conjure up a fantasy about Lauren Hynde or Chloe Byrnes or, for that matter, Gwen Stefani. On the TV screen was a live feed of the horizon from the prow of the ship and now sky-scrapers were passing by and then we were under the Verrazano Bridge and then the sky was darkening and another world was taking over as it always does in times like these and then I was dreaming of things that I couldn't really remember later: I was making various Bart Simpson noises, Heather Locklear was a stewardess, I kissed and made up with Chris O'Donnell, the sound track was remixed Toad the Wet Sprocket and the special effects were cool and the filmmakers had hired a topnotch editor so the sequence really zipped and then there was a final shot—the camera moving closer and closer into the black hat Lauren Hynde gave me until the image was dis-torted by the hat's tiny red rose.

14 The first couple days "at sea" I was in a stupor, still recovering. Was it Saturday? Was it Tuesday? Was I dis-appointed either way? I compensated by sleeping all the time until alarms blared late one morning and I woke up, panicking, the reality that the *Details* piece was never going to run hitting hard, and I vaguely remembered something about a lifeboat drill—a reminder I barely noticed had been slipped under my door the night before when I came back from a crummy dinner in the Queen's Grill. Exhausted, I found the life jacket locked in some kind of coffin in my bathroom, grabbed my sun-glasses and ran-walked, hungover, along dozens of empty corridors and down two flights of stairs trying to follow the directions on a badly Xeroxed map until I found a deck filled with old people who were huddled in masses and staring rudely, annoyed by my tardiness as I muttered "Oh, give me a break" and muttered and muttered. "It's backwards, son," I was told by an officer, who struggled, fumbling, to untie the life jacket I had sloppily put on. While I stood there, the officer said, "Don't worry"—patting me on the shoulder as I flinched a dozen times—"you probably won't need it." I offered him a Mentos, told him he was a dead ringer for Kurt Loder, which he wasn't.

I wandered around on what was left of my Xanax and made an appointment for a massage that I actually kept. I did a little rehearsing, nailed a couple of scenes down, but they had already been shot, someone had already commented favorably on the dailies, so that whole enterprise could be construed as kind of a waste. The elderly and Japanese were everywhere, surrounded me at miserable dinners I ate alone in the Queen's Grill while staring at an issue of last month's *Interview* magazine because there were new photos by Jurgin Teller of Daniela Pestova contemplating a plate of spring rolls and a Corrine Day photo essay on martini glasses and the entire issue was filled with bruises and scars and underarm hair and beautiful, shiftless-looking guys lounging improbably in front of empty 7-Elevens at dusk somewhere in the "heartland" and all I could think about, holding back tears and wincing, was: that should have been me.

Jurassic Park was the only movie playing in the ship's Dolby-equipped auditorium so I ended up in the casino a lot, uselessly gambling away the money Palakon had left me, dropping a thousand dollars' worth of chips at the 21 table in what seemed like a matter of minutes. In the Queen's Lounge old couples sat on long couches everywhere, trying to complete massive jigsaw puzzles that they were getting absolutely nowhere with, and I was always getting lost and I couldn't find anything anywhere. I'd finally locate one of the ship's many bars and sit down, knock back a Mai Tai or four and smoke a pack of cigarettes until the strength to resume looking for my cabin wandered back to me. At one of these bars I was so bored I even flirted with a young German guy who in hushed tones kept inviting me to accompany him the next day to the gym—"da voorkoot stashoon"—and I politely declined by telling him that I had just recovered from a humongous heart attack. His response: "*Ja?*"

The next time I saw the German guy I was floating near the rim of the huge whirlpool bath in the spa and after that I sluggishly moved to the thalassotherapy pool and when I saw him saunter over, wearing a silver thong a little too confidently, I bolted toward a private inhalation booth, where I daydreamed about what I was going to do with the $300,000 F. Fred Palakon had offered me to find Jamie Fields. I came up with so many things that I almost passed out and had to be revived with a facial and an aromatherapy session administered by someone who looked like the Crypt-Keeper, as a Muzak version of "Hooked on a Feeling" was piped through the spa's sound system.

Occasionally the crew converged and the camera would follow me at a discreet distance, shots mainly of Victor on the upper-deck starboard railing, trying to light cigarettes, some rolled with marijuana, sunglasses on, wearing an oversized Armani leather jacket. I was told to look sad, as if I missed Lauren Hynde, as if I regretted my treatment of Chloe, as if my world were falling apart. I was encouraged to try and find Lauren in Miami, where she was staying with Damien, and I was given the name of a famous hotel, but I feigned seasickness and those scenes were scrapped since they really weren't in character anyway.

The Dave Matthews Band's "Crash into Me" played over the montage, not that the lyrics had anything to do with the images the song was played over but it was "haunting," it was "moody," it was "summing things up," it gave the footage an "emotional resonance" that I guess we were incapable of capturing ourselves. At first my feelings were basically so what? But then I suggested other music: "Hurt" by Nine Inch Nails, but I was told that the rights were sky-high and that the song was "too ominous" for this sequence; Nada Surf's "Popular" had "too many minor chords," it didn't fit the "mood of the piece," it was—again—"too ominous." When I told them I seriously did not think things could get any more fucking ominous than they already were, I was told, "Things get very much more ominous, Victor," and then I was left alone.

"I'm . . . a party person," I muttered to no one.

Innumerable old people passed by, limped through miles of corridors, slowly lifted themselves up dozens of broad staircases, the lost wandered the decks pretending they weren't, the ship sailed on.

13

The second night of the voyage I had another boring dinner in the Queen's Grill. The sommelier I'd befriended by ordering a $200 bottle of semi-decent red wine asked if I wanted to join the Mashioki family at the captain's table instead of sitting alone and I told Bernard that I simply couldn't, hinting at an indiscretion I'd committed with the Mashiokis' eldest daughter, a fat, dour teenager who was always wandering near the ship's kennels wearing an UP WITH LIFE T-shirt, visiting her "cat." The sommelier nodded gravely, brought me another small tin of Beluga, recommended the foie gras, went back to the business of his life while I slipped into my noncommittal dining mode. Afterwards, I dropped another grand of Palakon's at the 21 table and found the cinematographer, Felix, at the Captain's Bar, hunched over a giant snifter of brandy and chain-smoking Gauloises. I sidled up next to him and we had the obligatory "ominous" conversation.

"What's the story?" I asked, after ordering a split of champagne, maybe my tenth on that particular evening. "You're the guy shooting this, right?"

"You could say that," Felix said in a thick, not-quite-traceable accent.

"I just did," I pointed out. "How's it going? I just want your professional opinion."

"It is going better than the last one I did," Felix muttered.

"Which one was that?"

"A picture called *Shh! The Octopus*." He paused. "It was the third part of a soon to be completed quartet funded by Ted Turner that began with *Beware! The Octopus*, which was followed by *Watch Out! The Octopus*. The fourth part is called, tentatively, *Get the Hell Away from That Octopus*." Felix sighed again, distracted, and stared into his snifter. "The third one had a good cast. A very bitter Kristin Scott Thomas, an equally bitter Alan Alda, and Al Sharpton had signed on to play Whitney Houston's extremely bitter father—the bitter harpoonist." Felix paused. "David Hasselhoff is the first victim of the octopus." Pause. "Isn't it ironic, huh?"

A long pause occurred while I tried to process this information. Confused, I broke it hesitantly. "So-o-o . . . the octopus's name was . . . Shh?"

Felix glared at me, then finally sighed, waved to the bartender for another, even though he hadn't finished the brandy sitting in front of him.

"How am I doing?" I asked expectantly.

"Oh, you'll do," he sighed and then paused before phrasing carefully: "You have a . . . kind of . . . nonspecific . . . fabulosity—oh my god . . ." He groaned as his head dropped onto the bar.

I was looking around, not paying attention to all the faux-angst emanating from the cinematographer. "This isn't exactly what you'd call Babesville, huh?"

"It's about time you gave up your foolish dreams, Victor," Felix said sternly, lifting his head. "Your world's a little limited."

"Why's that, bro?"

"Haven't you read the rest of the script?" he asked. "Don't you know what's going to happen to you?"

"Oh man, this movie's so over." A semi-restlessness was settling in and I wanted to take off. "I'm improvising, man. I'm just coasting, babe."

"Just be prepared," Felix said. "You need to be prepared." He gulped down the rest of his brandy and watched intently as the bartender set the new snifter in front of him. "You *need* to pay attention."

"This really isn't happening," I yawned. "I'm taking my champagne elsewhere."

"Victor," Felix said. "Things get mildly . . . er, hazardous."

"What are you saying, Felix?" I sighed, sliding off the barstool. "Just make sure I'm lit well and don't play any colossal tricks on me."

"I'm worried that the project is . . . ill-conceived," he said, swallowing. "The writers seem to be making it up as it goes along, which normally I'm used to. But here . . ."

"I'm taking my champagne elsewhere," I sighed, tossing him a $100 chip from the casino.

"I think things will be getting out of hand," he said faintly before I wandered away.

In bed I finally had the sense to just smoke a large joint while listening on my Walkman to a bootleg Nirvana tape that Jerry Harrington had loaned me, and the live feed of the ship heading straight into darkness on the TV was the only light in the cabin as a dead guy sang me to sleep, dreams intervening, peaking with a voice shouting out, then fading, *hello? hello? hello?*

12

Just another sunny day and semi-balmy but with a constant headwind and I'm at the pool deck holding a towel, wandering around, amiably spacey with rock-star stubble, wearing a tight Gap tank top, sunglasses lowered at the girl with the total Juliette-Binoche-if-Juliette-Binoche-were-blond-and-from-Darien-Connecticut look lying on a chaise longue in a row of twenty: tall, statuesque, killer abs, a little too muscular maybe but the hardness offset by large, soft-looking breasts straining against a white gauzy half-shirt, the prerequisite curvy legs outlined beneath leopard-print Capri pants. On the table next to her, copies of *Vogue*, *Details*, a W Chloe and I are in, *Vanity Fair* and *Harper's Bazaar* are kept from flying overboard by a small pitcher of iced tea placed on top of them and I'm instinctively moving into frame, hitting my mark. The girl suddenly rummages through an enormous Chanel tote bag—and then—a mascara wand falls from her hand which I gracefully stoop down to pick up—a rehearsed gesture I'm pretty good at.

"Thank you," she says demurely, a familiar voice. She retrieves a pack of Silk Cuts from the Chanel tote and with absolutely no difficulty lights one. A cue to motion toward the empty chaise next to her.

"Please, go ahead," she says a little too loudly because of the Walkman she's wearing. I notice the case of the new Tricky cassette sticking out of the Chanel tote and mentally brush up on the last Tricky CD, reviews of certain Tricky concerts I've read, any Tricky details from my own past I'm about to use on the girl with the total Juliette Binoche look.

Even though it's too cold to take off the tank top—and not like it's doing a good job of hiding anything—I slip out of it without removing my sunglasses, lay the towel down and ease myself on top of it, flexing my abs to get her attention. She's reading a book with the words MARTIN AMIS in giant black letters on the cover and I'm hoping she's not a member of Amnesty International. A waiter appears and I order a light beer and a large bottle of mineral water, which he brings quickly. I tip him, he's gone.

When the girl takes the Walkman off I remember a line, make a move.

"Hey, didn't we meet at that barbecue Kevyn Aucoin threw in New York?"

She takes off her sunglasses, stubs the cigarette in an ashtray, smiles without squinting and says, "I don't think so."

"Well, what's the story?" I ask. "How do I know you? You look disturbingly familiar." I lean on my side, staring admiringly. "Though it could be because you're the only person on this boat born the same decade I was."

But some element keeps distracting us. There is a couple—handsome and maybe in their mid-forties, dressed in fashionable beachwear that proves they're in pretty good shape—standing by the railing. The man camcords the woman clowning around in a semi-forced way against the backdrop of the ocean moving slowly behind them and occasionally they glance over at where I'm lounging, the woman with a harsh, almost severe expression that morphs instantly into a garish smile whenever she catches me looking at her. The man is basically a blank and I'm totally not interested.

"Are those your parents?" I ask, nodding toward the couple.

"No, my parents are in the States," the girl says, glancing over as the couple now shuffles out of her line of vision when they notice her paying attention. "Actually, though, I do know Kevyn Aucoin. I just haven't been invited to one of his soirees."

"They're quite fun as soirees go," I tell her, perking up. "The whole gang is usually there. Cindy, Linda, Kate, the Sandras—Bullock, Bernhard and Gallin. Oh, and I met Sheryl Crow there too."

"I take it you're also a bold-faced name, no?" she asks.

"Just quasi-famous," I shrug.

The girl offers what doesn't seem like a fake smile.

"So maybe we've run into each other at various VIP fashion events?" I suggest. "Brushed by each other in the front room at Doppelganger's or Jet Lounge? Shared cocktails at a private screening where we weren't aware of each other's presence, hmm?" I'm arching my eyebrows faux-lasciviously but she's not amused.

"You're not a photographer, are you?" she asks suspiciously, her face tightening.

"Hey, no, baby, relax." I stall, then lift her iced tea and pick up W, flipping it open to the Star Spotting section, a photo of Chloe and me at a premiere at Radio City Music Hall. I hand it to the girl over the table. She glances at the page, then looks at me, then back at the photo.

"You're . . . Christian Slater?" she asks, confused.

"No, no, the one below that."

"Oh, I see."

I start feeling my face and then ask worriedly, "Is my head really that big?"

She focuses in on the right photo: Chloe in a practiced daze, me staring intently into the paparazzi's lens.

"Yes, that looks like you," she says. "And that's Chloe Byrnes, right?"

"I date her," I say, then, "I mean, I used to date her."

"Well, I dated Peter Morton," she says, handing back the magazine. "Peter Morton and I used to get photographed together too."

"So you're saying we're in the same boat?" I ask.

"Well, actually we *are*," she says, gesturing around, rolling her eyes and groaning inwardly at the line she has to deliver.

"Well, yeah, yes," I faux-chuckle. "That we, um, are."

"Marina," she says. "Marina Cannon."

"Hey, Victor Ward." I pause, letting the name resonate, then offer my hand and she takes it lightly. "And you're off to . . ." I leave an opening for the name of a place.

"Paris," she says. "Actually, Cherbourg and then Paris."

"Why Paris?" I ask. Then, quite suavely, "Though of course, why not?"

"Oh . . ." She pauses, looks at all that boring black water. "Let's just say certain individuals weren't sticking to the plan and leave it at that."

I immediately sense boyfriend troubles and pounce gingerly. "What's his name?" I ask softly.

"Gavin," she says, a bit perturbed but still smiling.

I make a face, mock-shiver. "Ooh, I don't trust anyone named Gavin." I make another face, grimacing, holding the expression until she notices, then ask casually, "Where's Gavin now?"

"Gavin plans to run with the bulls in Pamplona," she says dryly.

"He's a basketball player?" I ask, wilting. "I thought the Bulls were in Chicago."

She just stares at me, a flicker of panic creasing her features. Suddenly the gay German youth bounds down the stairs onto the pool deck, wearing a Garth Brooks tour T-shirt and giant black Nikes. He spots me and starts bounding over. I immediately feign sleep. Soon I feel a shadow cross my face and linger, followed by the sounds of footsteps bounding away. When I feel enough time has passed I open my eyes. Countless Japanese splash around in the pool. The noon whistle goes off. Elderly report: they're everywhere.

"Someone just . . . inspected you," Marina says.

"Just a fan. A hanger-on," I shrug. "It's tough but I'm used to it. So what do you do?"

"I model," she says simply. "Part time."

I sit up, swing my legs across the chaise, then realize the move is a little too urgent and reach for the light beer instead.

"But just a little bit," she adds, noticing. "Just here and there."

"Baby, that is *so* cool," I'm saying. "I knew you were a model. I knew you were recognizable."

"Well, I'm not Chloe Byrnes but I do okay."

"Yeah, Chloe . . . ," I say "wistfully."

"Oh, I'm sorry," Marina says and then—when I fail to say anything else—adds, "Anyway, I'm off to visit friends and do, oh, touristy things."

"Hey, roam if you want to. That's my motto, baby."

"So why are you sailing?" she asks. "Afraid to fly?"

"I saw *The Poseidon Adventure* twenty times as a small, frightened child," I explain. "My favorite line in movies is 'My God—it's a giant wall of water, heading *straight for us.*'"

A long pause on Marina's part that I'm responsible for, and then, "That's . . . your answer?"

"I'm going to London, babe," I say quickly. "I'm looking for a friend." I realize something, my eyes gliding over her body, and add, "But I'm in no hurry."

"So why do you have to find this friend?"

"Off the record? It's a long story."

"We're not going anywhere."

"Well, I was about to host this MTV show—"

"Oh really?" she asks, repositioning herself on the chaise. "About what?"

Without stalling: "Well, it was just going to be about me. My life, y'know, what I do during an average day."

"I . . . see," she says, somewhat contemplatively.

"And the whole modeling grind was getting me down and being quasi-famous was just getting too overwhelming so"—I breathe in for emphasis—"I decided to chuck it all and I thought, man, Europe's not that far away. But I didn't really want to participate in that whole Prague scene. I didn't want to sit in a moldy café with my PowerBook and *deal* with chicks from RISD. I just wanted to write some poetry and, y'know, make some videos . . . get away from that whole cyberspace scene. Just chill out . . . Get back to my roots. Gotta get back, back to my roots." I sip the light beer confidently. "Come back down to earth and get back to my roots."

"Your family's from Europe?" she asks.

"Er, well, I'm not sure, but I'm, I mean, I've *heard* I had a few roots there"—I pause—"Europe." I pause again. "Baby, I'm just really searching for some honesty."

She says nothing.

"Um, y'know, it's hard right now, it's so damn hard," I sigh. "I'm just beginning to adjust to *not* fending off autograph hunters and I'm not used to it yet. I need to detox from that whole celeb thing. But I'm just not used to it yet. Can't you tell how jittery I am? I think I just twitched." I pause, sip the light beer thoughtfully. "Do you know who I am now?" I open the W up again and show her the picture of Chloe and me at the premiere at Radio City, my thumb subtly blocking out Chloe's face.

"I'm not really sure I know who you are," she says. "But you look more familiar now."

"I was on the cover of *YouthQuake* magazine last month," I say. "Does that help?"

"So you're an actor too?" she asks.

"Yes. I know how to laugh, applaud, cry out in amazement, all on cue. Aren't you impressed?"

"I sense a supporting-actor Oscar in your future," she says, smiling.

"Thank you," I say, then faux-blanch. "*Supporting?*"

I notice the couple conferring with the director, who's looking schleppier by the minute, and then I notice Marina watching them too and the man turns his head away from us, freezing up when he notices us looking at him, and he nods at the director, who I don't think is noticing anything, and the three of them are huddled together as if forming a plan.

"So who is this person you're trying to find?" Marina asks.

"A girl I went to school with," I murmur.

"Where did you go to school?"

"Undergraduate? Camden College."

"And where did you get your master's?"

I pause. "Actually . . . I haven't gotten it yet."

"Well, she must be very important to you."

"Well, she's, um . . . yeah." I squint up into the sky, which looks weird, nonexistent. "I think it's like in her best interest if I, um, show up."

"Camden," Marina murmurs. "I think I know a couple of people who went to Camden." She concentrates for a moment. "Katrina Svenson?"

"Sure, yeah, right," I say, nodding. "Very good, um, Hacky Sack player."

"Paul Denton?"

"Oh yeah, Paulie, Paulie, Paulie."

"Sean Bateman?"

"Good buddy of mine."

"He's actually a fairly lousy individual."

"Baby, I am *so* glad *you* said that because, baby, I am *so* with you on that one."

I notice that the director has moved somewhere else and that the couple in fashionable beachwear has started heading toward our general vicinity. When I look over at Marina she's gathering up her magazines and Walkman and placing them in the Chanel tote, her skin flawless, the scent of flowers rising off her, playing let's-get-happy with my nostrils.

"Hey, what's the story?" I ask. "Where are you going?"

"I hate to dash off like this," she says apologetically, standing up. "But I'm feeling a little exposed." She grabs her towel.

"Um, well, how about—" I start.

"It was nice to meet you, Victor," she interrupts, concentrating on getting her things together. "I hope you have a pleasant voyage."

"Um, wait a minute," I say, standing up also. "What are you doing for dinner?"

"Call me. I'm in room 402. Deck 3." She starts walking away, offering a slight wave without turning around, and then she's gone.

I'm suddenly so cold I pull the Gap tank top back on and, leaving the towel on the chaise, decide to follow Marina, ask her to dinner again, reestablish our groovy rapport, inquire as to whether I freaked her out, if I wasn't behaving gentlemanly enough, if I came on too hard, if she knows Chloe maybe, which causes me to panic about my reputation, but the couple hurry over before I can rush away and they're older than they looked from far away and I busy myself with the towel and start folding it uselessly, my back to them, hoping they're not going to ask me to camcord a tiresome message for friends back home with the two of them framed against the dully sparkling miniwhitecaps stretching out to the horizon.

"Are you Victor Johnson?" the man behind me asks with an English accent. "Or is it Victor Ward?"

I drop the towel on the chaise and turn to face him, whipping off my sunglasses, smiling wide, and—tingling—admit, "Yeah."

"I don't think you'll remember us," the man starts, "but I'm Stephen Wallace and this is my wife, Lorrie." I take his hand and shake it and while I'm shaking Lorrie's hand Stephen says, "We're friends of your father's."

I let go of Lorrie's hand as the tingling immediately evaporates and then I place my sunglasses back on and pick up the towel. "Oh? Really?" is all I say, breathing in.

"Yes, we knew your parents when they were living in Washington," Stephen says. "In Georgetown."

"Oh wow," I'm saying unenthusiastically. "Am I like on 'Totally Hidden Video' or something?"

The Wallaces laugh "good-naturedly" and I'm reminded of a nonexistent appointment I need to keep.

"The last time we saw you, you must have been . . ." Stephen stops, looks at Lorrie for help. "What? Nine? Ten?"

"Oh, it was earlier than that," the woman says, tilting her head, consulting the sky.

"What year did your father move back to Washington from New York?" Stephen asks.

"It was the year Mom died," I say, running my hand through my hair, eyeing the waiter removing Marina's half-empty pitcher of iced tea and my beer bottle—a prop I almost reach for just to have something to hold on to.

"Right, right," the man murmurs, shaking his head sorrowfully.

The woman offers a generous, sympathetic smile.

"Don't worry," I say. "I don't dwell on what happened, so it's okay."

"Was that after you were at . . . ?" Stephen stops again, stuck. "Where did you go to school?"

"You went to Camden, right?" the woman asks, guessing.

"Yeah, it was actually during Camden when it happened," I say. "But she'd been sick a long time." I stare at them hard, making them grasp that it really doesn't matter now. What does is: I've forgotten Marina's last name, what deck she's on, her room number.

"Well, the last time we saw you you were practically a baby," the man says, chuckling, shifting modes. "You wouldn't remember. It was at a fundraiser at your parents' place in Georgetown."

I bring a hand to my forehead. "Dimly, yeah, dimly I remember."

"We just saw your father a month ago in Washington," Lorrie offers.

"Far out," I'm saying.

"He was at a dinner in a new restaurant on Prospect Street with Sam Nunn, Glen Luchford, Jerome Bunnouvrier and Katharine Graham, as well as two of the forensic experts on the defense team of the O. J. Simpson trial."

"God," I groan. "I wish I'd been there. It sounds like a blast. I've gotta split."

"And how's your sister?" Lorrie asks.

"Oh, she's cool. She's in Washington too," I'm guessing. "But I've gotta split."

"And where are you off to?" Stephen asks.

"Right now? Back to my cabin," I say.

"No, I meant in Europe," he says.

Lorrie keeps smiling at me, staring warmly, sending definite horny vibes my way.

"Well, I think Paris," I say. "Actually Cherbourg, then, um, Paris."

The woman immediately glances over at her husband when I say this but ultimately it's awkwardly done and the director has to retake this simple reaction shot four more times before proceeding to the rest of the scene. "Action" is called again and in the background extras resume their positions: old people milling around, the Japanese splashing all over the pool.

"Really?" Stephen asks. "What takes you to Paris?"

"Um, I'm going to . . . photograph Jim Morrison's grave for . . . *Us* magazine and . . . that's, um, for one, yeah. . . ." Pausing for emphasis, I then add, "And I'm also going to visit the Eiffel Tower, which everyone I know says is a 'must-see,' so-o-o . . ." I pause again. "And the Gothic Eurobeat scene is really big just now, so I might check that out."

The Wallaces stare at me blankly. Finally Lorrie clears her throat. "Where are you staying in Paris?" she asks.

I remember hotels Chloe and I stayed at and, avoiding the obvious, choose "La Villa Hotel."

"Oh yes, on Rue Jacob, just off Boulevard Saint-Germain," Lorrie says.

"That's the one," I say, pointing cheerfully at her. "I've gotta split."

"And was that your traveling companion?" Stephen asks, gesturing at the empty chaise Marina was lounging on.

Unsure of how to answer, I ultimately go with, "Oh no, not really. I'm on my own."

"I thought perhaps you two were together," Stephen adds, smiling.

"Well, who knows," I laugh, striking a pose, breaking it up by shifting my weight impatiently from one leg to the other and back again.

"She seems like a lovely girl," Lorrie says approvingly.

"She's a model," I point out, nodding.

"Of course," Stephen says. "And from what I hear so are you."

"And so I am," I say awkwardly. "I've gotta split."

"You know, Victor," Lorrie begins, "this is terrible but we did see you about three months ago in London at the opening of the Hempel Hotel but you were besieged by so many people that it made contact, well, a little difficult," she says apologetically.

"Well, that's just great, Lorrie," I say. "But I wasn't in London three months ago."

The two of them glance at each other again and though personally I think the look they exchange is a little overdone, the director, surprisingly, does not and the scene continues uninterrupted.

"Are you sure?" Stephen asks. "We're fairly certain it was you."

"Nope, not me," I say. "But it happens all the time. Listen—"

"We read that interview with you in—oh, what's the name of that magazine?" Stephen looks to Lorrie again.

"*YouthQuake?*" Lorrie guesses.

"Yes, yes, *YouthQuake*," Stephen says. "You were on the cover."

"Yeah?" I ask, brightening a little. "What did you think of it?"

"Oh, it was excellent," Stephen says. "Excellent."

"Yes," Lorrie adds. "We thoroughly enjoyed it."

"Yeah, I thought it turned out pretty good too," I say. "Dad wasn't too happy about it, though."

"Oh, but you've got to be yourself," Stephen says. "I'm sure your father understands that."

"Not really."

"Victor," Lorrie says, "we would love it if you joined us for dinner tonight."

"Yes, I think your father would be furious if he knew we were sailing together and we didn't have dinner at least one night," Stephen says.

"Or anytime you're in London," Lorrie adds.

"Yeah, yeah," I say. "But I don't think I'm *going* to London. I think I'm going to Paris first. I mean, Cherbourg, *then* Paris."

When I say this, Lorrie glances at Stephen again as if I've just made some kind of observation that displeases her.

"I've gotta split," I say again.

"Please join us tonight, Victor," the man reiterates, as if this really wasn't an invitation but a kind of friendly demand.

"Listen, I don't mean to like semi-blow you guys off but I'm really really tired," I say. They seem so worried by this excuse that I have to add, "I'll try, I really will, but I've given up on socializing and I'm really quite out of it."

"Please," Stephen says. "We're in the Princess Grill and our reservation's at eight."

"We insist, Victor," Lorrie says. "You must join us."

"I feel wanted, guys," I'm saying, walking away hurriedly. "That's great. I'll try. Nice to meet you, cheerio and all that."

I slip away and race around trying to find Marina, concentrating on all the practical places she might be. Nixing the Computer Learning Center, I hit various art galleries, the library, the bookshop, the Royal Shopping Promenade, elevators, the labyrinth of corridors, even the children's playroom. With a map in hand, I find then scope out the gym on deck 7: lines for the Lifecycles, the rowing machines, the treadmills, the aerobic room, jammed with elderly Japanese flopping around to lousy British synth-pop, with a male instructor with hideous teeth who waves me over to join in and I nearly barf. Drowsy, I go back to my cabin and lie down, vacantly noticing new pages of the script, faxed from somewhere, lying on a pillow along with the ship's daily paper, immigration formalities, invitations to parties. During this the entire sky is a low white cloud and the ship sails beneath it indifferently.

11

F. Fred Palakon calls after I've finished the room service dinner I ordered and *Schindler's List* is playing on the small television set situated above the bed, a movie I had no interest in seeing when it came out but now, since Friday, have watched three times since it takes up an enormous amount of hours. My notes thus far? One, the Germans were *not* very cool; two, Ralph Fiennes is *so* fat; and three, I need more pot. The connection when Palakon calls seems unusually crisp and clear, as if he's calling from somewhere on the ship, but since no one else has called I can't be sure.

"Well, finally," I mutter.

"How have you been, Victor?" he asks. "I hope you're well taken care of."

"I just finished dining sumptuously in my cabin."

Pause. "What did you have?"

Pause. "An . . . acceptable turbot."

Pause. "It sounds . . . delicious," Palakon says uncertainly.

"Hey, Palakon—why am I *not* in a penthouse?" I'm asking, suddenly sitting up. "Why do I *not* have a butler? Where's my Jacuzzi, man?"

"Gentlemen do not talk about money," Palakon says. "Especially when they're not paying."

"Whoa," I say, and then, "Who's a gentleman?"

"I'm trying to imagine that *you* are, dear Victor."

"What are you, Palakon? You talk like some kind of pampered weenie."

"Is that a cheap attempt to play upon my emotions, Mr. Ward?"

"This traveling-by-sea business is bor-ing," I say. "There's no one famous or young on this damn boat. There are sixteen hundred people on this damn boat and they're all *ancient*. Everyone has Alzheimer's, everyone's blind, everyone's hobbling around on crutches."

"Surely you're exaggerating."

"I'm really really tired of old people, Palakon," I say. "I'm just so tired."

"I'll call Cunard and tell them to set up a piercing parlor, a tattoo emporium, a cyberspace roller rink," Palakon says wearily. "Something that has that kind of grungy honesty you young people respond to so well."

"I'll still be so tired, Palakon."

"Then get some sleep," Palakon says hollowly. "Isn't that what people do who are tired?"

"I'm tired of muttering 'Where am I' whenever I find myself in the wrong corridor or some wrong deck that's like miles away from the deck I wanted to be on." I pause, then add, "Surrounded by old people!"

"I'm sure there is no shortage of you-are-here maps to help you out, Victor," he says, losing patience. "Ask one of the old people for directions."

"But the old people are blind!"

"Blind people often have an excellent sense of direction," Palakon practically shouts. "*They'll* tell you where you are."

"Yeah, but where *am* I, Palakon?"

"By my estimate somewhere in the middle of the Atlantic Ocean," Palakon sighs, giving up. "My god, must everything be explained to you?"

Mortified, I suddenly blurt out, "Yeah!"

"Mr. Ward, I'm just checking in," Palakon says, seemingly disinterested in my problems. "I'll call you once more before you arrive in Southampton."

"Hey, Palakon, about that," I start.

"Yes, Mr. Ward?"

"How about if I take a little side trip to France before going to London?" I ask.

A long pause before Palakon asks, "Why?"

"I met a girl," I say.

Another pause. "And so?"

"I—met—a—girl," I repeat.

"Yes, but I am not understanding you."

"Like, I'm gonna *go* with this *girl* to Paris, *duh*," I say loudly. "Why else do you think I'd be going there? To take part in a *fromage*-eating contest? Christ, Palakon, get your shit together."

"Victor," Palakon starts, "that's not a particularly good idea. Turning back—which is essentially what you'd be doing—is unthinkable at this point."

"*Hello?*" I say, sitting up. "Could you please *repeat* that? *Hello?*"

"Just go on about your business," Palakon sighs. "Just follow the script."

"Palakon, I want to go to Paris with this girl," I warn.

"That would be a grim alternative," Palakon warns back, gravely. "That would be self-destructive."

"But I think that's in my nature," I explain. "I think that's what my character's all about."

"Maybe this trip will change your character."

"I'm not so sure."

"I'll call you before you reach Southampton, Victor."

"Palakon, wait—"

He clicks off.

10

Around 12 I dress casually and rouse myself from the cabin, heading ostensibly to the midnight buffet being served in the Mauretania Room but really to any bar where I can very quickly down four vodka-and-cranberries and find Marina. Prowling along the upper starboard deck as if on a catwalk—it's cold out and dark—I'm spying into windows at all the joyless mingling taking place at the midnight buffet. I spot the gay German holding a plate piled high with smoked salmon and even though he's heading toward a table just a foot or two away from where I'm standing, I doubt he can see beyond his own reflection in the window, but then he begins to squint past his image and his face lights up so I whirl around and run straight into the Wallaces strolling along the deck. She's wearing what looks like a strapless Armani gown, Stephen's tuxedo jacket draped over her shoulders, protection from the midnight chill.

"Victor," Lorrie cries out. "Over here."

I bring a hand to my forehead to block out the nonexistent light that's blinding me. "Yes? Hello?"

"Victor," they both cry out in unison, just yards away. "Over *here!*"

I start limping as if in pain. "Jovially," I hold out a hand, but then I gasp, grimacing and reaching down to massage my ankle.

"Victor, we wondered where you were for dinner," Lorrie says. "Are you all right?"

"Yes, you were sorely missed," Stephen adds. "Is something wrong with your leg?"

"Well, I fell asleep," I start. "I was also, um, expecting a . . . phone call, but I . . . fell asleep."

Pause. "Did you get your call?" Lorrie asks semi-worriedly.

"Oh yes," I say. "So now everything's fine."

"But what happened to your leg?"

"Well, when I was reaching over for the phone . . . it, well, I accidentally fell *off* the chair I'd been sitting, er, *sleeping* in and then, well, while reaching for the phone . . . it actually fell and struck my"—a really long pause—"*knee*."

Another really long pause. No one says anything.

"So then I tried to stand up—all this while speaking into the phone—and then I actually tripped over the chair . . . by the TV . . ." I stop to let them interrupt.

Finally Stephen says, "That must have been quite a scene."

Picturing how ridiculous this scenario seems, I delicately reexplain: "Actually I handled it all quite suavely."

Lorrie and Stephen both nod, assuring me they're certain that I did. The following is just basic exposition—these lines fall easily and rapidly into place—because I can see, in the distance, Marina, her back to me, standing at the railing, gazing out over the black ocean.

"Tomorrow night, Victor?" Lorrie suggests, shivering.

"Please, Victor," Stephen demands. "I insist you have dinner with us tomorrow night."

"Jeez, you guys are persistent. Okay, okay, tomorrow night," I say, staring at Marina. "Oh wait—I'm having dinner with someone else tomorrow night. How about next week?"

"But we'll be off the boat next week."

"We will? Thank god."

"Please, bring your guest," Lorrie says.

"It's okay if I bring someone?" I ask.

"Oh good—a quartet," Stephen says, rubbing his paws together.

"Actually she's an American."

"Pardon?" Stephen leans in, smiling.

"She's an American."

"Why . . . yes, of course she is," Stephen says, confused. Lorrie tries not to stare incredulously at me and fails.

"And please," Stephen adds, "when you're in London you must stop by as well."

"But I'm definitely going to Paris," I murmur, staring off at the girl by the railing. "I'm definitely not going to England."

The Wallaces take this in stride, seem finally to accept this info, and exit by saying "Tomorrow night, then," like it's some kind of big deal they conjured up. But they seem sated and don't linger and I'm not even bothering to limp away from them. Instead I glide slowly over the deck to where

Marina's standing, wearing white slacks and a white cashmere sweater, and because of how these clothes fit on her she's semi-virginal, semi-naughty, and my steps become more timid and I almost slink back, stunned by how beautiful she looks right now and she's eating an ice cream cone and it's pink and white and the decks are generally well-lit but Marina's standing in a darkened spot, a place where it seems vaguely windier. Tapping her shoulder, I offer an inquiring look.

"Where did you get that?" I ask, pointing at the ice cream cone.

"Oh, hi," she says, glancing casually at me. "A nice elderly man—I believe his name was Mr. Yoshomoto—made it for me, though I don't think I asked him to."

"Ah." I nod and then gesture. "What are you looking at out there?"

"Oh, I know," she says. "It's all black."

"And it's cold," I say, mock-shivering.

"It's not so bad," she says. "I've been colder."

"I tried to find you earlier but I forgot your last name."

"Really?" she asks. "Why did you want to find me?"

"There was a jig-dancing contest I wanted us to enter," I say. "Hornpipes, the works."

"It's Gibson," she says, smiling.

"Let's reintroduce ourselves," I suggest, backing away. "Hi—I'm Victor Ward."

"Hello," she says, playing along. "I'm Marina Gibson."

"I hope I'm not bothering you."

"No, no, I'm glad you came by," she says. "You're a . . . nice distraction."

"From?"

She pauses. "From thinking about certain things."

Inwardly I'm sighing. "So where's Gavin now?"

She laughs, surprised. "Ah, I see you've memorized your lines." She wipes her lips with a paper napkin, then leans over and tosses what's left of the ice cream cone into a nearby trash bin. "Gavin's in Fiji with a certain baroness."

"Oh, a *certain* baroness?"

"Gavin's parents own something like—oh, I don't know—Coca-Cola or something but he never really has any money."

Something catches in me. "Does that matter to you?"

"No," she says. "Not at all."

"Don't look back," I'm saying. "You can never look back."

"I'm fairly good at severing all contacts with the past."

"I think that's a more or less attractive quality."

While leaning against the railing Marina just simply starts talking: the drastic hair changes, the career that semi–took off because of them, the shaky flights to Miami, getting old, how she likes to be shot with the light coming from the left to offset the tilt of a nose broken in a Rollerblading accident three years ago, a club in East Berlin called Orpheus where she met Luca Fedrizzi, the weekends they spent at Armani's house in Brioni, the meaninglessness of time zones, her basic indifference, a few key figures, what the point is. Some of the details are small (the way she would unroll the windows in her mother's Jaguar when racing back from parties in Connecticut so she could smoke, the horrifying bitchery between agents, books she never read, the grams of coke carried in compacts, the crying jags during shoots that would ruin two hours of carefully applied makeup), but the way she tells them makes her world seem larger. Of course during the modeling phase she was always strung out and brittle and so many friends died, lawsuits were started then abandoned, there were fights with Albert Watson, the ill-fated affair with Peter Morton, how everything fizzled out, her mother's alcoholism and the brother who died of cardiac arrhythmia linked to the ingestion of herbal Ecstasy tablets, and all of this leading up to the designer who fell in love with her—platonically—and subsequently died of AIDS, leaving Marina a substantial sum of money so she could quit modeling. We both admit we know someone who signed a suicide note with a smiley face.

At first I'm able to look as if I'm concentrating intensely on what she's saying and in fact some of it's registering, but really I've heard it all before; then, while talking, she moves closer and there's a quickening and I'm relieved. Silently focusing in on her, I realize that I've been activated. I stare into her face for over an hour, asking the appropriate questions, guiding her to certain areas, mimic responses that I'm supposed to have, offer sympathetic nods when they're required, sometimes there's a sadness in my eyes that's half-real, half-not. The only sound, besides her voice, is the sea moving below us, faraway waves lapping against the hull of the ship. I notice idly that there's no moon.

She sums things up bitterly by saying, "The life of a model—traveling, meeting a lot of superficial people—it's all just so—"

I don't let her finish that sentence, because my face is so close to hers—she's tall, we're the same height—that I have to lean in and kiss her lips lightly and she pulls back and she's not surprised and I kiss her lips lightly again and they taste like strawberries from the ice cream and cold.

"Don't. Please, Victor," she murmurs. "I can't."

"You're so beautiful," I whisper. "You're so beautiful."

"Victor, not . . . now."

I pull back and stretch, pretending nothing happened, but finally I can't help saying "I want to come to Paris with you" and she pretends not to hear me, folding her arms as she leans against the railing with a sad, placid expression that just makes her face seem dreamier.

"Hey, let's go dancing," I suggest, then check the watch I'm not wearing and casually pretend I was just inspecting a nonexistent freckle on my wrist. "We can go to the Yacht Club disco. I'm a good dancer."

"I don't think you'd like the Yacht Club," she says. "Unless you'd like to dance to the disco version of 'Don't Cry for Me, Argentina' for hours on end. There's a DJ named Jamtastica too."

"Well, what about a drink? It's not that late." I check the nonexistent watch again. "I've gotta stop doing that."

"It actually *is* getting late," she says. "I should get to sleep."

"You want to come by my room? For a drink?" I ask, following her as she walks away from the railing. "I have an unopened fruit basket in my room that we can share. I'll be on my best behavior."

"That's very sweet, Victor," she says. "But I'm tired."

"I want to come to Paris," I say suddenly.

Marina stops walking and turns to me. "Why?"

"Can I?" I ask. "I mean, we don't have to stay at the same place but can I like travel with you?"

"What about London?"

"London can wait."

"You're being impulsive," she says apprehensively, resuming walking.

"It's one of my many really really great qualities."

"Listen, let's just . . ." She sighs. "Let's just see how things go."

"Things are going fine," I say. "Things can only get better. Look, I'm embarrassed to admit this, but I've just spent the last hour gazing at you and and and now I want to come to Paris."

"What do you want me to say to that?"

"Just say yeah, cool, hip. Just say, 'Yes, Victor, you can come to Paris with me,'" I tell her and then, mock-seriously: "You know, I don't need an invitation, baby—I can just simply follow you."

"So you'd be, um, like *stalking* me through Paris?"

"Just say, 'Victor, you may come with me—I give you my permission,' and then I'll bow and kiss your feet and—"

"But I don't know if I can say that yet."

"I'm saving you the embarrassment of admitting what you really want to express."

"You have no idea what I want to express."

"But I know all about you now."

"But I don't know anything about *you*."

"Hey." I stop walking, spread my arms out wide. "This is all you need to know."

She stares, smiling. I stare back until I have to look away.

"Will you at least join me for dinner tomorrow night?" I ask "bashfully."

"That would be . . ." She stops, considering something.

"Um, babe? I'm waiting."

"That would be . . ." She pauses again, looking out past me at all that blackness.

I start chewing a nail, then check my pockets for Kleenex, a cigarette, Mentos, any prop to keep me occupied.

"That would be . . . nice."

I let out a great sigh of relief and hold my hand over my heart as if I've just recovered from an enormous blow. We aren't miked anymore when we say good night and the crew's been waved away and there's another kiss and in that kiss I can't help but sense some kind of pattern being revealed, and then departure.

9

While I'm getting dressed to meet Marina at the Queen's Grill Lounge at 7:30 before dinner with the Wallaces, the captain makes an announcement over the intercom, something about a distress signal emanating from a shipping vessel that the QE2 will be intercepting around 9 in order to pick up a diabetic crewman who ran out of insulin, and walking to the lounge I'm passing dozens of worried old people asking if this unscheduled stop is going to delay the arrival time at Southampton and the exceedingly patient ship directors, harried but sincere, assure them it will not and I'm wondering what if it fucking does? *You're old*. If I was a ship director my answer would've been, "It doesn't matter, you'll be *dead* before we dock this boat."

Tonight my hair's slicked back, I used a tiny splash of cologne, I'm wearing the Comme des Garçons tuxedo—freshly pressed—and I'm feeling semi-retro. When I called Marina this morning and suggested maybe lunch she said she planned to spend the day pampering herself out of her funk—facial, massage, yoga, aromatherapy, palm reading—and since I already felt linked to her I didn't have to be told to spend the day basically keeping to myself, bumming around, goofing off in the gym, replaying imaginary conversations with her while on the StairMaster, rehearsing the words I'd use during sex.

I order a martini, positioning myself on a plush antique couch by the bar where a steward lights my cigarette and 7:30 turns into 8:00 rather suddenly and I've ordered another martini and smoked two more Marlboro Lights, staring at the extras. It's a formal night on the ship and men are wearing tuxedos (I actually don't spot a single decent one) and cheesy sequined gowns hang off old women, everyone passing by on their way to various dining rooms, chattering incessantly about absolutely nothing.

From the bar phone I dial Marina's cabin but there's no answer.

At 8:15 the crew finally says it's time for the next setup, that the Wallaces are waiting. I stub out a half-smoked cigarette, cursing, and before I can finish the rest of the second martini the director takes it "gently but firmly" away, suggesting I've had "enough," that perhaps I should "pace" myself, that maybe this will "aid my performance." I grab the martini back from the director, finish it and, smacking my lips together, say loudly, "I—don't—think—so." I toss the Gold VIP Card prop at him and mutter, "Sign for it, doofus."

8 The Queen's Grill is jammed but the Wallaces are at a table for four up front by the entrance. As I make my way down the steps leading to the table, Stephen stands up, dressed in a tuxedo, waving me over as if this were some sort of grand occasion, Lorrie sitting primly next to him wearing the same strapless Armani gown from last night. There are huge flower arrangements everywhere in the Queen's Grill to navigate around and dozens of waiters carrying trays of champagne glasses brush past me. I gently bump into a maître d' at the table next to ours as he prepares crêpes for a group of Japanese women, who smile admiringly at the handsome young gaijin as he shakes Stephen Wallace's beefy hand.

"Ah, Victor—hello," Stephen says as a waiter pulls a chair out for me. "Where's your guest?"

"I'm not sure, man," I say, about to lift my wrist to check my nonexistent watch. "She said she'd meet me in the lounge for a drink and never showed." I pause glumly. "She knows where we're eating, but man, I'm bummed."

"Well, we do hope she comes," Stephen says. "In the meantime—champagne?"

"Definitely," I say, reaching for a glass.

"That's, um, mine," Lorrie says tentatively.

"Oops, sorry," I say as a waiter pours from a bottle of Dom Pérignon into a flute sitting by my napkin.

"So Victor, what is it you've been doing?" Stephen asks.

"You know, Stephen old chum," I start vaguely, pondering this while chugging down the bubbly, "I'm really not quite sure what I've been doing."

Dismayed, they both laugh.

"What do you two do?" I finally ask, catching my breath.

"Well, I work in an advertising agency in London—" Stephen starts.

"Oh really? That's nice," I interrupt. "But I actually meant on this boat, but whatever. Continue. Can I get another glass of champagne?"

"I open restaurants," Lorrie offers, a little too greedily, while a waiter fills my empty flute. "We were just in Manhattan scouting locations in TriBeCa. It would be my first in the States."

"Oh really?" I say again, groaning inwardly. "That's super. What kind of restaurants?" I finish the new glass of champagne and point to the flute again after the waiter finishes topping off Stephen's and Lorrie's glasses. Hesitantly, he fills mine again. Stephen then nods at the waiter, a gesture to bring another bottle.

"The last one I opened was in Holland Park," Lorrie says. "Which I would love to have you visit when you're in London."

"But see, I'm not—going—to—be—in—London, baby," I say, straining, leaning toward Lorrie for emphasis, but when I realize how rude that sounds, I add, "Though that's a very, um, cool offer."

"Lorrie's a splendid cook," Stephen adds.

"Oh really?" I say again, grinding my heels into the floor. "What's your specialty, babe?"

"It's a variation on classic Californian cuisine, you might say." Lorrie tilts her head thoughtfully.

When it becomes apparent that I'm supposed to say something, I ask, staring, "You mean compared to just . . . *Californian* cuisine?" and then, measuring each word carefully, totally not interested in an answer, "or . . . *post*–Californian cuisine?"

"There's definitely a Pacific Rim influence as well," Stephen adds. "I mean, we know it sounds awfully trendy, but there *is* a world of difference."

Stuck, I ask, "Between?"

"Between . . . Californian cuisine and, well, *post*–Californian cuisine," Stephen says, a little too patiently.

"And Pacific Rim as well," Lorrie adds.

There's a long pause.

"Does anybody have the time?" I ask.

Stephen checks his watch. "Eight-forty."

There's another long pause.

"So it's like the whole baby-vegetable-guava-pasta-blue-corn-scallops-in-wasabi-fajitas situation, huh?" I ask, glazing over.

"Well, that's in the ballpark," Lorrie says hesitantly.

I have nothing more to say and just when I'm about to look over at the director and shout out "Line!" I'm startled by the sound of a champagne bottle being uncorked, followed by Stephen asking, "So you're still going to Paris, Victor?"

"I think I was always going to Paris, Stephen old chap," I say.

"What's really taking you to Paris, Victor?" Stephen asks, his eyes narrowing. "Do you have friends there?"

"Actually I'll let you in on a little secret," I say.

"Yes?" they both say, leaning in.

"I *was* supposed to go to London," I admit, then smile sheepishly and whisper, "I got sidetracked."

"Well, I hope not for too long," Stephen says. "You must stop by London on your way back to the States."

"We'll see how things turn out in Paris, Stephen old chap," I say confidently, downing another glass of champagne.

Since my back is to the entrance of the Queen's Grill I don't see Marina come in but heads start turning and even though Stephen and Lorrie have never met Marina, their drone is interrupted by her arrival, and instinctively, on cue, I turn around. Marina looks stunning, effortlessly inhabiting the role that will create a star; Makeup and Costume have done an unbelievable job and her hair is pulled back so tightly and in such an elegant way that I'm practically squirming in my chair and then I'm holding out a hand, guiding her to the table. Delicately she accepts it, as if I were helping her cross a threshold she was wary about but since I'm on the other side—hey, it's okay. Introductions are made as she's seated.

"I'm so sorry I'm late," Marina says genuinely.

"Oh, that's okay," I say. "We were having a very, very interesting and lively conversation about . . ." Stuck, I have to look over at the Wallaces.

"Californian cuisine," Stephen reminds me.

"Oh yeah."

"Champagne?" Stephen asks Marina a little too eagerly.

"Thank you," Marina says as Stephen pours, and then, trying to insinuate herself immediately into the conversation, asks, "Are we supposed to be stopping soon?"

"In about fifteen minutes," Stephen says, placing the champagne back in its bucket. I lift out the bottle and pour myself another glass.

"Doesn't anybody find this odd?" Marina asks, letting the maître d' drape a napkin across her lap.

"I think the law of the sea requires vessels to help each other in times of distress," Stephen says. "I don't think the QE2 is exempt."

"It's really not that much of an inconvenience," Lorrie says, slowly looking Marina over.

"I don't know how they'll find that boat in all this fog," Marina says.

"Really—there's fog?" I ask, having assumed that I had been staring at a giant gray wall but actually it's a huge window that overlooks the starboard deck. "Whoa," I mutter.

"Well, radar is quite sophisticated these—" Stephen starts.

"Excuse me," Lorrie says, staring intently at Marina, "but do we know each other?"

Marina studies Lorrie. "I'm not—"

"I mean, have we met?" Lorrie asks. "You look remarkably familiar."

"She's a model," I interject. "Thass why."

"No, no, it's not that," Lorrie says, then, gently prodding, "Are you from New York? Could we have met there?"

"I don't believe we have," Marina says, then smiles and tightly adds, "But who knows?" She lifts her champagne flute, brings it to her lips but doesn't sip.

"But I'm sure we have," Lorrie murmurs, gazing. "Positive, in fact."

"Really?" Marina asks with a subtle kind of panic.

"Yes, I'm sure we've met," Lorrie insists.

"Where, darling?" Stephen asks.

"That's what I can't place," Lorrie murmurs.

"Are you in the States often?" Marina asks.

But our waiter arrives and Stephen suggests we order dinner now, before the boat makes its stop, which I'm all in favor of so this night can proceed elsewhere. Marina demurs, saying she really isn't that hungry. Stephen says something along the lines of "Well, my dear, you can't order off the children's menu," and that's our cue to "laugh heartily." First course: caviar. Second course: the girls opt for lobster medallions instead of foie gras. Third course: duck. Stephen orders two bottles of wine from the sommelier, who seems impressed by the selections.

"So how do you all know each other?" Marina asks.

"Actually we know Victor's father," Stephen says.

"Yes, I've never met these people before in my life."

"Oh really?" Marina asks, turning to me. "Who's your father?"

"I really don't want to get into that right now," I say. "I'm on vacation and I'd like to keep it that way."

"Were you in Berlin recently?" Lorrie suddenly asks Marina.

"No." Marina smiles but freezes up slightly before answering again. "No."

"I think it was Berlin, but your hair's different," Lorrie murmurs, implying something. "Yes, it was in Berlin."

"Darling, please," Stephen says. "Let's move on."

"I haven't been to Berlin in years," Marina says, frowning.

Lorrie's squinting at her. "This is driving me mad, but I know we've met."

"She's a model," I say, tugging at a waiter for more champagne. "That's *why*, baby."

The sommelier has opened both bottles of wine and after Stephen tastes each the sommelier decants them into carafes and the four of us concentrate on that. Gold-rimmed plates are placed in front of us as a tin of Beluga is wheeled toward the table. While the maître d' arranges the caviar on our respective plates and I'm babbling on about the new design—not the *old* design but the *new* design—of *Raygun* magazine, a photographer who has been combing the room interrupts us by asking if we'd like our picture taken.

"Great idea," I say too loudly, clapping my hands together.

"No, no," the Wallaces insist, shaking their heads.

"Perhaps after dinner," Lorrie says.

"Oh come on," I say, turning to Marina. "It'll be like a souvenir."

"Victor, no," Marina says. "Not right now."

"Yes, Victor," Stephen says. "Perhaps later."

The photographer crouches at the table, waiting for a decision.

"Well, damnit," I say. "Come on, guys. Oh, just take it," I tell the photographer. "Just do it."

"Victor, *please*," the Wallaces say in unison.

"I'm not feeling very photogenic right now," Marina adds improbably.

"Well, *I'm* camera-ready, babies," I exclaim. "Go for it, dude."

Just as the flash goes off I try to lean into Marina, who backs slightly away toward the maitre d', who has stepped aside, waiting patiently to continue serving the caviar.

The Wallaces glare at me sternly while I give the photographer my name and cabin number and ask for four copies. As he walks away, the captain announces over the intercom that the *QE2* will be stopping in a matter of minutes and to please stay seated, that there's really no need to get up since the fog will probably obliterate the view and we'll be moving again shortly. But most of the hoi polloi in the Queen's Grill ignore the captain's suggestion and drift from their tables to the starboard side, including—thankfully—the Wallaces, though it just seems like an excuse to confer with the director. The maître d' finishes serving the caviar and moves away. I'm pouring myself a glass of white wine from one of the carafes when Marina touches my shoulder.

"Victor," she says.

"I think they're mad at me," I say. "I don't think they liked having their picture taken. The fucking English, y'know? Jesus Christ. I mean, I know that you and I are used to it, but—"

"Victor," she says again.

"I know, I know, I'm sorry," I say. "But baby, you look *gorgeous*."

"Victor, you're drunk," she says.

"And you're gorgeous—"

"Victor, I have to talk to you."

"And I have to talk to *you*, baby." I grab her hand beneath the table.

"No, I'm serious," she says, pulling away.

"And so am I," I say, leaning toward her.

"Victor, stop it," she says. "You have *got* to sober up."

"Baby, you're—"

"I have to leave," she says, glancing over at the Wallaces. "Call me when you're through with dinner."

"No-no-no-no," I say, immediately sobering up. "No way, baby. You've *got* to stay. Don't leave me with—"

"I'm leaving and you're calling me in my cabin when you're through with dinner," Marina explains patiently.

"Why can't I come with you?" I ask. "What's the story? What's wrong?"

"I have to leave," she says, starting to get up.

"I'm coming too," I say, holding on to her arm. "I'll pretend I'm sick."

"No, that's not possible," she says. "Let *go*."

"Baby, come on—"

"It's imperative that you call me immediately after dinner," she says, pulling away from the table. "Do you know what 'imperative' means?"

"That I"—I squint up at her—"that I . . . have to call you after dinner?"

"Okay," she says, semi-relieved.

"Baby, what's happening?"

"There's no time to go into it now."

The Wallaces start heading back along with most of the other passengers, murmurs of disappointment floating around the dining room about what— that they didn't catch a glimpse of a diabetic seaman? I am so lost.

"Baby," I start. "I'm not comprehending this—"

"Tell them good night for me," Marina says, walking quickly out of the restaurant.

I watch as she disappears down a corridor, then notice a nearby waiter who takes in the expression on my face and shrugs sadly, sympathizing with me.

"Too bloody foggy," Stephen says, pulling Lorrie's chair out.

"Where did your friend go?" Lorrie asks, sitting down.

"I don't know," I sigh. "She's freaking out about something."

"I hope we didn't upset her," Lorrie says.

"Darling, eat your caviar," Stephen says.

Later the Wallaces insist I join them at a karaoke party in Club Lido but I'm drunk and the details surrounding me are swimming out of focus in front of my eyes and before I bolt for my cabin the camera moves in on dessert: a gold-rimmed plate, raspberries, blueberries, two scoops of vanilla mousse bordering a chocolate bonsai tree.

7

Back in my room pretty much totally sloshed I dial Marina Gibson's cabin but there's no answer. When I ask the operator to make sure she's ringing the right room, she pitches a snotty reply and I hang up on her and then scrounge around the minibar for a split of champagne, drinking it out of the bottle, foam cascading out of the head all over my hands which I wipe off on my complimentary *QE2* bathrobe. I look for a copy of the script, can't find it, give up, tumble around the room, light cigarettes, the view from the prow of the ship on the TV screen almost totally obscured by fog. The phone rings.

"Victor?" Marina sounds as if she's been crying.

"Hey baby," I say soothingly. "Did like Gavin call? What's the story? You sound bummed."

"We have to talk."

"Great," I say, sitting up. "How about my room?"

"No."

"Okay, okay," I say, then, guessing, "How about . . . your room?"

"I don't think it's safe," she whispers.

I pause, considering this. "Marina," I say softly. "I have condoms."

She hangs up.

I immediately dial her room back.

She picks up midway through the first ring.

"Hey baby, it's me," I say.

"This isn't going to work," she mutters to herself, sounding vaguely panicked.

"What do you mean?" I'm asking. "Do . . . *you* have condoms?"

"That *isn't* what I'm talking about!" she shouts.

"Whoa, baby," I start, holding the phone away, then bringing it back to my ear. "*What* isn't?"

"Victor, something's happening that needs to be explained to you."

"Listen, I'm sorry I'm rushing things," I apologize. "I'll read the rest of the script, we'll get to know each other, whatever."

"You're in fucking danger, Victor," she cries.

"Now don't go psycho on me, baby—"

"Victor, did anyone give you something to bring with you to London?" she asks breathlessly.

"What do you mean, baby?" I'm checking my hair in the mirror above the dressing table.

"Did anyone tell you to bring something—a package, an envelope, anything—to London?" she asks again, straining to calm down.

"Like what?"

"I don't know," she moans. "A gift or something. Something to bring someone."

"Oh yeah, right," I say, as if it's slowly dawning on me.

"What? What was it?" she asks in a rush.

I pause before giggling. "Just my beautiful self, baby."

"Damnit, Victor," Marina shouts. "Are you sure? Think carefully."

"At this point I don't think I can."

"Victor, *please*, you've got to sober up."

"I'm coming over to your room," I tell her. "You sound stressed. You need a massage. Let me administer my famous stress-reducing—"

"Just meet me in Club Lido—*now*."

"Baby, why not your room?" I whine, disappointed.

"Because it isn't safe," she says. "Because we have to meet where there are other people around."

"Hey baby—"

She hangs up. I'm supposed to look at the phone and shrug, which I do.

6

Cold water splashed on my face doesn't really hasten my sobriety so I just try not to lurch my way to Club Lido, which is actually close enough to my cabin that I'm able to get there without any passing out or major tripping going down. And Club Lido isn't crowded since the karaoke party the Wallaces mentioned has moved on to Mr. Kusoboshi's cabin, the bartender tells me when I take a seat and restrain myself from ordering a martini, sipping a light beer instead, occasionally staring out the large window that looks over the fog-shrouded deck and a small, shallow pool where steam rising from the lit water mixes in with all that fog. A crew member, exasperated, points out someone standing by the railing, the fog sometimes swirling around but mostly just a heavy wall of vaguely transparent granite sitting there, the figure lost within. I sloppily sign a bill for the beer then head outside.

On deck it's quiet, the sounds of the dry-ice machines churning out huge enveloping clouds of fog the only real noise, and the boat seems to be moving more slowly than usual. Marina's back is to me and she's wearing a very cool oversized hooded Prada wool jacket and when I touch her shoulder she automatically stiffens, still looking away, and I'm shivering and damp and she seems even taller and I try to bend down to check if she's wearing heels but oddly enough she has Nikes on her feet, which also look larger, though since I don't really remember ever seeing her feet what the hell am I talking about?

"Marina?" I'm asking. "Marina—is that you?"

There's a pause, then the hood nods.

"Hey, are you okay?" I squint, uselessly waving bad-smelling fake fog away. "What's the story? Did Gavin call you? What happened?"

"You can't go to Paris with me," she whispers, her voice raspy, as if she's been crying. "You have to go to London."

"Hey baby, why the change of heart?" I say, gripping her shoulder. "Hey, look at me."

The hood shakes its head.

"Victor," she says, pulling away, her back still to me. "You're drunk."

"How can you tell if you won't look at me?" I plead.

"I can smell it," the voice coughs.

"Hey baby, get closer," I murmur, leaning in. "I wanna come to Paris with you."

"Victor, you're drunk," the voice protests, moving away.

"I need a better excuse," I say. "You could at least—*ahem*—do me the honor of a more intelligent excuse." This is followed by an enormous belch, which I follow with an apology. I keep trying to get her to face me but she keeps pulling away, tightening the hooded jacket around her.

"Just *go*," she coughs, then mumbles something else.

"I'm not going anywhere," I say.

"Victor, please—"

"You wanted to talk to me," I point out. "I'm here. I'm ready. I'm in a fairly responsive mood."

"I just wanted to tell you that you can't come to Paris—"

"Hey baby, please look at me," I tell her. "Let's go into the bar and I'll order some coffee, a nice cappuccino, huh?"

Reaching around, she grabs my hand without turning to face me and whispers something about my room.

"What? What did you say, baby?" I whisper back, leaning into her, suddenly woozy with the prospect of sex, all the champagne, the smells coming off the Prada overcoat.

"Let's go to your room." She breathes in, her voice husky and thick.

"Baby," I start. "That is such a good—"

Still holding my hand, she turns and walks away, cutting a path through the fog along the deck, and it's hard to keep up with the long, wide strides she's taking and I'm mumbling "Baby, baby, slow down" but I just let her pull me along, rushing toward my cabin.

Once at my door, giggling and out of breath, I pull a key out of my pocket and drop it—laughing "You're taxing my mind-eye coordination, baby"—and I reach down, fumbling for the key, but she grabs it first and I try to grab her hand but when I finally stand up straight, gasping, she has already pushed the door open and is walking into the room, dragging me along and switching off all the lights, her back still to me. I fall onto the bed, reaching out for her leg as she walks by.

"I'll just be a minute," she says from the bathroom before closing the door.

Grunting, I sit up and slip my shoes off, hearing them drop by the side of the bed, and then reach over to turn some of the lights back on but I can't reach them and quickly realize I'm just too tired and too drunk to really do anything right now.

"Hey baby?" I call out. "Can we keep the lights on?" I fall back onto the bed. "Honey?"

The bathroom door opens and Marina briefly stands in the entrance, the hood now draped over her shoulders, but even by squinting I can't make out her features since she's backlit in the doorway, just a dark shape moving toward me, the door slowly closing partway behind her, and it's so freezing in the cabin that my breath steams in the half-light coming from the bathroom and she drops down onto the floor, her hair covering her face, and she proceeds to yank down my tuxedo pants along with the Calvin Klein boxerjockeys and tosses them in the corner and with both hands on my thighs spreads my legs open, moving in between them until her head is at my waist, and my dick—amazingly—is rock hard and she starts rolling her tongue around the head while sucking on it at the same time, her hand gripping the base and then, keeping the head in her mouth, she starts sliding her hand up and down the shaft.

"I want to kiss you," I groan, hooking my hands underneath her arms, trying to pull her on top of me, but her arms are bound up in the bulky jacket, which I finally manage to move down a little, revealing muscular pale shoulders and what looks like a tattoo, partly covered by the strap of a white tank top, on the right shoulder blade. Reaching out, I try to touch the tattoo. "Come on," I groan, "take your clothes off," but she keeps pushing me back, my cock moving in and out of her mouth, her hair hanging down, brushing across my hips, her tongue expertly sliding up the shaft, and then I'm angling myself so I can push the entire dick back into her mouth and with both hands holding my hips she starts swallowing it over and over and I'm making soft moaning noises, pulling my shirt up, not wanting to come on it, and I start jacking myself off while she eats my balls, a finger pressing against my asshole that I keep brushing away but she slips it in and I start coming and afterwards, panting, things spinning away from me, through a blurry lens I notice her moving around the room opening drawers and I'm murmuring "Why are you wearing a wig?" before I pass out, which I don't want to do because there are so many things I need to show her.

5 The noon whistle is what stops the dreaming. In the middle of the night I was wrapped in blankets after I passed out but no one removed the tuxedo shirt and bow tie. Unable to stay motionless in the tightly curled fetal position I'm in—due to a great deal of pain—I reach for the phone but in mid-reach realize I've missed brunch and there's no possibility I could keep anything down anyway so I nix room service. In desperate need of water, I stumble up, stagger to the bathroom in pain, squealing "Spare me, spare me," and drink greedily from the sink, which tastes awful, and then I stare at my reflection in the mirror, utterly confused: my face looks completely dehydrated and splotchy, the hair on my head is sticking up at weird angles in a totally ungroovy '80s kind of way and below that the sparse hair on my stomach is matted with dried semen. After a shower the day seems halfway salvageable and much less grim. I get dressed, take three Advil, flush my eyes with Visine, then fall into a violent heap on the bed.

I call Marina's room but there's no answer.

4 I find Marina's room and knock on the door but there's no answer and, predictably, it's locked. I knock again, place my ear against the door: silence. While lingering in the corridor, out of it, still hazy, wondering what I should do after I apologize for being drunk, I notice maids five doors down cleaning rooms, moving slowly this way. I take a walk along the starboard deck but end up pacing just one small stretch of it, sunglasses on, mumbling to myself, the wind off the Atlantic causing me to weave around, until I move back to Marina's hall. Her door is open now and a maid is given her cue to enter, leaving in the open doorway a giant canvas hamper piled high with laundry.

I knock, peering in, clearing my throat, causing the maid to look up while she's stripping the bed. Without smiling and with some sort of bossy Scottish accent, she asks, "May I help you?"

"Hello," I say, trying to be genial and totally failing. "I'm just looking for the girl whose room this is."

"Yes?" the maid asks, waiting, holding the bundle of sheets.

"I, um, left something here," I say, moving into the cabin, noticing an unopened fruit basket, knocked over, on the dressing table, the phone Marina used to call me on the floor in the corner next to the bed instead of the nightstand, as if whoever was last talking on it was huddled down on the floor, hiding behind the bed.

"Sir—" the maid begins impatiently.

"It's okay, it's okay," I'm saying. "She's my girlfriend."

"Sir, you should come back later," the maid says.

"No, no, it's okay," I'm saying, realizing that the room seems totally unlived in. I move past the maid to the closet and open it.

"Sir, you should wait until—"

I hold up a hand. "I said it's okay," I murmur.

The closet is completely empty: no clothes, no luggage, not even any hangers. I close the closet door and move past the maid over to the dressing table and start opening drawers. All of those are empty too.

"Sir, I'm asking you to leave," the maid says, looking me over unfavorably. "If you don't leave I'm going to have to call Security."

Ignoring her, I notice that the wall safe is open and a Prada handbag—nylon with the trademark metal triangle—is halfway hidden inside. As I move toward the safe, behind me the maid walks out of the cabin.

Slowly I unclasp the purse, opening it. I reach in and it's basically empty, except for an envelope.

Queasy, suddenly breathing hard, the hangover washing back over me intensely, I pull a series of Polaroids out of the envelope.

There are eight photographs of me. Two were taken backstage at what looks like a Wallflowers concert: a poster for the band in the background; a sweaty Jakob Dylan holding a red plastic cup behind me, a towel draped over his shoulders. Two were taken during a magazine shoot: hands in the frame with a makeup brush touching up my face, my eyes closed serenely, Brigitte Lancome setting up a camera off to the side. The other four: me standing next to a pool wearing shorts and a vest with no shirt, mattresses on the ground everywhere, and in two of the Polaroids it's bright out and a giant orange sun beats down through smog, and behind a long glass partition near a teenage Japanese waitress wearing a sarong, Los Angeles is spread out behind me. The other two Polaroids were taken at dusk and Rande Gerber has his arm around my shoulder while someone lights tiki torches in the frame next to us. This is a place I recognize from various magazines as the Sky Bar at the recently opened Mondrian Hotel. But my nose is different—wider, slightly flatter—and my eyes are set too close together; the chin is dimpled, more defined; my hair has never been cut so that it parts easily to one side.

I've never been to a Wallflowers concert

Or had my photo taken by Brigitte Lancome.

I've never been to the Sky Bar in Los Angeles.

I drop the photographs back in the Prada handbag, because I don't want to touch them anymore.

The bathroom reeks of bleach and disinfectant and the floor is wet and gleaming even though the maid hasn't started cleaning in here yet; a bath mat is still crumpled by the tub and towels lie damp, oddly stained, in the corner. There are no toiletries anywhere, no bottles of shampoo, no bars of soap lining the tub's edge. Then someone positions me by the tub so that I'm crouching next to it and I'm urged to move my hand to the drain and after feeling around in it my fingers come away stained slightly pink and when I move a finger farther into the drain I feel something soft and when I pull my hand away again—involuntarily, alarmed at what I'm touching, something soft—the pinkness is darker, redder.

Behind the toilet there's more blood—not a lot, just enough to make an impression—and when I run my fingers through it they come away streaked with pink as if the blood has been watered down or someone had tried to clean it up in a hurry and failed.

Just off to the side of the toilet, embedded in the wall, are two small white objects. I pull one of them out of the wall, applying pressure at a certain angle in order to extract it, and after inspecting the thing in my hand I turn to the crew. There's an empty silence, people are fixating on the bathroom's cold light.

"I may be out of it," I start quietly, breathing hard, "but this is a fucking tooth. . . ." And then I'm talking loudly, as if I'm accusing them of something, holding it out to them, my arm outstretched, offering it. "This is a fucking *tooth*," I'm repeating, shaking hard. "This is a fucking tooth," I say again, and then I'm told to race out of the room.

3 The crew directs me to Security but because there's not really such an office on board, this scene is shot near the library at a table meant to simulate an office. For "texture": an unplugged computer terminal, four blank spiral notebooks, an empty Diet Coke can, a month-old issue of *People*. A young British actor—who had small parts in *Trainspotting* and Jane Austen's *Emma*, and who seems lost even before I start talking—sits behind the makeshift desk, playing a clerk, pale and nervous and fairly cute as far as English actors playing clerks go.

"Hi, I'm Victor Ward, I'm in first class, cabin 101," I start.

"Yes?" The clerk tilts his head, tries to smile, almost succeeds.

"And I'm looking for a Marina Gibson—"

"Looking for?" he interrupts.

"Yes, I'm looking for a Marina Gibson, who's in cabin 402."

"Have you looked in cabin 402?" he interrupts.

"Yes, and she wasn't in cabin 402, and neither, it seems"—I take a deep breath and then, all in a rush—"was anyone else and I need to find her so I guess what I'm saying is that I'd like her, um, paged."

There's a pause that isn't in the script.

"Why do you need to page her, sir?" the clerk asks.

"Well," I say, stuck, "I . . . think she's lost." Suddenly I start shaking and have to grip the sides of the desk the actor's sitting at in order to control it. "I think she's lost," I say again.

"You *think* a passenger . . . is lost?" he asks slowly, moving slightly away from me.

"What I mean"—I breathe in—"is that I think maybe she moved to another cabin maybe."

"That's highly doubtful, sir," the clerk says, shaking his head.

"Well, I mean, she's supposed to have met me for lunch and she never showed up." My eyes are closed and I'm trying not to panic. "And I'd like her paged—"

"I'm sorry, sir, but we don't page people because they've missed a meal, sir," I hear the actor say.

"Could you please just confirm for me that she's in that room? Okay? Could you please just do that?" I ask, teeth clenched.

"I can confirm that, sir, but I cannot give out a passenger's room number."

"I'm not asking you to *give out* a room number," I say impatiently. "I'm not asking for a passenger's room number. I know her goddamn room number. Just confirm she's in room 402."

"Marina . . . ?"

"Marina Gibson," I stress. "Like Mel. Like *Mel* Gibson. Only the first name is *Marina*."

The clerk has pulled open one of the spiral notebooks, which supposedly contains a computerized listing of all the passengers on this particular crossing. Then he wheels over to the monitor, taps a few keys, pretends to appear authoritative, consults one graph and then another, lapses into a series of sighs.

"What room did you say, sir?"

"Cabin 402," I say, bracing myself.

The clerk makes a face, cross-checks something in the spiral notebook, then looks vacantly back up at me.

"That room isn't inhabited on this crossing," he says simply.

A long pause before I'm able to ask, "What do you mean? What do you mean, 'not inhabited'? I called that room last night. Someone answered. I talked to someone in that room. What do you mean, 'not inhabited'?"

"What I mean, sir, is that this particular room is not inhabited," the clerk says. "What I'm saying, sir, is that nobody is staying in that room."

"But . . ." I start shaking my head. "No, no, that's not right."

"Mr. Ward?" the clerk begins. "I'm sure she'll show up."

"How do *you* know?" I ask, blanching. "Where in the hell could she be?"

"Maybe she's in the women's spa," the clerk suggests, shrugging.

"Yeah, yeah, right," I'm muttering. "The women's spa." Pause. "Wait — there's a women's spa?"

"I'm sure there's a perfectly reasonable explanation for all this, Mr. Ward — "

"Hey, wait, don't say things like that," I say, shuddering, holding my hands up. "Whenever somebody says something like that, something is definitely fucked up."

"Mr. Ward, please — "

"I think she's in trouble," I say, leaning in. "Did you hear me? I said I think she's in trouble."

"But Mr. Ward, I don't even have a Marina Gibson on the passenger list," the clerk says. "There's no Marina Gibson registered for this crossing."

The clerk looks up at me as if he can't possibly comprehend the expression on my face.

I wait in the hall in a small chair, watching everyone who enters and exits the women's spa until it closes.

2   F. Fred Palakon calls at 7:00. I've been in my room since the women's spa closed at 5, mulling over the prospect of roaming the entire ship to look for whoever it was who called herself Marina Gibson, ultimately discarding that prospect because the photo from last night's dinner was slid under my door in a manila envelope stamped with the QE2 imprimatur. The photo didn't come out too well, the main reason being that the Wallaces aren't in it.

The couple sitting at the table in the Queen's Grill are people I've never seen before, who don't even vaguely resemble the Wallaces. The man glowering at me is much older than Stephen; and the woman, confused, looking down at her plate, is much dowdier and plainer than Lorrie.

Marina has turned her head away so her face is just a blur.

I'm the only one smiling and relaxed, which amazes me since the only things that look even remotely familiar are the small mound of caviar on my plate and the carafes of the wine Stephen ordered and the Japanese women, in shadows, at the next table.

The original and the three copies I requested are spread out on a desk I'm chain-smoking at, and it's so cold in the room I'm half-frozen, wearing two J. Crew sweaters under the giant Versace overcoat, and the remains of today's hangover linger, insistent, like some kind of reminder. I'm vaguely aware that tomorrow the QE2 docks in Southampton.

"So you're not going to Paris?" Palakon asks. "So you'll be in London after all?"

A long stretch of silence that I'm responsible for causes Palakon to snap, "Hello? *Hello?*"

"Yes," I say hollowly. "How did you figure that . . . out?"

"I just sensed a change of heart," Palakon says.

"How did you manage that?"

"Let's just say I know these precocious moments of yours usually come to an end," I hear him say. "Let's just say I concentrate intensely on you and what you have to say and do." A pause. "I'm also viewing everything from a different angle."

"I'm a lover, not a fighter, Palakon," I sigh.

"We've located Jamie Fields," Palakon says.

Briefly, I glance up. "So my job's over, right?"

"No," Palakon says. "Just made easier."

"What are you doing right now, Palakon?" I'm asking. "Some lackey's giving you a pedicure while you're eating a giant box of mints? That's what *I'm* picturing."

"Jamie Fields is in London," Palakon says. "You'll find her the day after tomorrow on the set of the movie she's shooting. All the information you need will be waiting for you at the hotel. A driver will pick you up—"

"A limo?" I ask, interrupting.

A pause, then Palakon gently says, "Yes, Mr. Ward, a limo—"

"Thank you."

"—will pick you up in Southampton and drive you into London, where I will contact you."

I keep moving all four copies of the photograph around, repositioning them while Palakon drones on. I light another cigarette before stubbing out the last one.

"Do you understand, Mr. Ward?"

"Yes, I understand, Mr. Palakon," I answer in a monotone.

Pause. "You sound on edge, Mr. Ward."

"I'm just trying to ascertain something."

"Is that it, or are you just trying to strike a pose?"

"Listen, Palakon, I've gotta go—"

"Where are you off to, Mr. Ward?"

"There's a gnome-making class that's starting in ten minutes and I wanna get a head start."

"I'll talk to you when you arrive in London, Mr. Ward."

"I've already marked it down in my datebook."

"I'm relieved to hear it, Mr. Ward."

1 I find Felix the cinematographer at the piano bar, hunched over an array of snifters half-filled with brandy as he stares miserably at his own reflection in the mirrors situated above the racks of alcohol, relentlessly smoking Gauloises. The pianist—who I'm just noticing much to my horror is also the male aerobics instructor with the hideous teeth—plays a mournful version of "Anything Goes." I take the stool next to Felix and slap the photograph next to his arm. Felix doesn't flinch. Felix hasn't shaved in what looks like days.

"Felix," I say, trying to contain myself. "Look at this photo."

"I don't want to look at any photos," Felix says miserably in his halting, untraceable accent.

"Felix, please, it's important," I say. "I think."

"I'm not supposed to look at the photo, Victor."

"Fuck it—just look at the fucking photo, Felix," I spit out, panicking.

Felix turns to me, muttering "Grouchy, grouchy," then glances tiredly at the picture. "Yeah? So? People having caviar, people not looking so happy." He shrugs. "It happens."

"Felix, I did *not* have caviar with *these* people," I'm saying. "Yet this photograph ex-ex-exists," I sputter.

"What do you mean?" Felix sighs. "Oh god, I'm so tired."

"But this is the wrong photo," I squeal giddily. "That's *not* the couple I had dinner with last night. These people are *not* the Wallaces. Do you understand, Felix? I—don't—know—these—people."

"But that's the picture, Victor," Felix says. "That's you."

"Yes, that's me," I say. "But who are these people, Felix?" For emphasis I'm running my hand over the photograph. "I mean, what is this? What the hell's going on?"

"Deluded youth," he sighs.

"Where, Felix? *Where?*" I ask, whirling around. "I don't see anyone under sixty on this goddamn boat."

Felix motions to the bartender for another.

"Felix," I say, breathing in. "I think I'm scared."

"You should be, but why?"

"A lot of reasons," I whisper.

"A certain amount of hardship is to be expected in this life."

"I know, I know, I need to accept the bad if I want to accept the good—oh god, Felix, just shut the fuck up and look at the fucking photo."

Felix's interest rises slightly as he holds the photo closer to his face and the atmosphere surrounding the bar is smoky and vague and the piano player continues with the mournful rendition of "Anything Goes" while various extras playing soused nannies, croupiers and beverage personnel listen, rapt, and I focus on the silence surrounding the music and try to get the bartender's attention.

"It's been altered," Felix says, clearing his throat.

"How do you know?"

"You should be able to see this girl's face." He points at Marina.

"Yeah, but I think she turned away when the flash went off."

"No," Felix says. "She didn't."

"How can you tell?"

"The position of her neck—see, here?" Felix runs a finger along Marina's throat. "The position of her neck suggests she was looking at the camera. Someone else has been—oh, how do you say?—superimposed over this girl." Felix pauses, then his eyes move to the Wallaces. "I assume the same thing happened with this couple," he says, squinting at the photo. "A rather crude job, actually." Felix sighs, placing the photo back on the bar. "But hell, who knows? Maybe you were really drunk and feeling rather friendly so you joined another table."

I'm shaking my head. "I'd *never* sit with those people," I'm saying. "Look at that woman's *hair*." I order an Absolut-and-cranberry from the bartender—with *lime*, I stress—and when he brings it I drink it quickly, but it totally fails to relax me.

"Maybe I just need to get laid," I sigh.

Felix starts giggling. "You will." He keeps giggling. "Oh, you will."

"Spare me the giggling, Felix."

"Haven't you read the new draft?" he's asking.

"I think the script keeps changing, Felix," I say. "I don't think this is what I signed on for."

"You're really not accustomed to disappointment, are you, Victor?"

"I think something bad happened to that girl," I'm saying meekly. "To . . . Marina."

"You think errors are being made?" Felix asks, taking a long swallow of brandy, moving one snifter aside for another. "I think people can know too much."

"I just . . . I just . . . think there's been some kind of—oh man—like emergency and . . ." My voice trails off. I stare over at the piano player, at the extras sitting at tables, on couches, nodding thoughtfully to the music. "And . . . I just think no one's responding—oh man."

"You need, I think, to find a more fruitful and harmonious way to live."

"I'm on the cover of *YouthQuake* magazine," I exclaim. "What in god's name are you talking about?"

"Perhaps the two are unrelated."

"Tell me I'm not being wrongheaded and foolish," I plead. "Tell me this isn't an 'extraneous matter,' Felix. I mean, I'm a fairly easygoing person."

"I know, I know," Felix says sympathetically, inhaling on a cigarette. "It's intolerable, eh?"

Finally I ask, "What about Palakon? How is he involved in this?"

"Who is Palakon?" Felix asks.

"Palakon," I sigh. "The guy who got me on this fucking boat."

Felix stays quiet, then stubs the cigarette out. "I don't know anyone named Palakon."

While signaling the bartender for another drink, I mutter, annoyed, "What?"

"Palakon's not in the script, Victor," Felix says carefully.

Pause. "Whoa—wait a minute, wait a minute." I hold up a hand. "Hello? *You* are driving blind, baby."

"No, no, I don't think so," Felix says. "And please don't call me 'baby,' Victor."

"Hold on, Felix," I say. "I'm talking about the guy I met at Fashion Café. That kind-of-euro twit who got me on this floating nursing home in the first place. *Palakon?*"

This doesn't register with Felix. I stare, dumbfounded.

"I met him after I was chased," I try to explain. "I met him at Fashion Café after I was chased by the black Jeep? F. Fred Palakon?"

Felix turns to me, looking more worried than bemused, and finally says, "We didn't shoot a chase scene, Victor." A long pause. "We didn't shoot anything in Fashion Café."

While staring back at the photo, I feel something in me collapse.

"There's no Palakon in the shooting script," Felix murmurs, also staring at the photo. "I've never heard of him."

While I'm breathing erratically, another drink is placed in front of me, but my stomach sours up and I push the drink toward Felix.

"I think this is the logical cutting-off point," Felix says, slipping away.

O On deck the air felt damp, the sky got unusually dark, almost black, clouds were bulging, distorted, a monster behind them, then thunderclaps, which merited some attention and made everyone feel vaguely apprehensive, and past that darkness, below that sky, land was waiting. On deck I lit a cigarette, the camera circling me, newly supplied Xanax eliminating nausea and distracting tics, and I kept my Walkman on, the Dave Matthews Band's "Crash into Me" buzzing in my ears through the headphones, spilling over onto the sound track. I sat on a bench, sunglasses on, blinking frantically, gripping a new magazine Gail Love started called A New Magazine until I couldn't sit still anymore. Images of Marina plunging into the black water, sinking leagues to the calm, sandy bottom, swallowed up without a trace, jumped playfully around the back of my mind, teasing me, or maybe she was leaping off the ship because there were worse things waiting. The hat Lauren Hynde gave me in New York and that Palakon told me to bring was missing, was confirmed "disappeared" after I tore my cabin apart looking for it, and though this shouldn't be a problem, I somehow knew that it was. I was told by the director that what I didn't know was what mattered most.

On deck I was aware of my feet moving listlessly past a cotton-candy kiosk opened for "the kids." On deck the Wallaces drifted by, intent on not dealing with me, and I was unable to interpret the signals their false smiles gave off and my heart continued pounding uneasily but really I was drawn out and apathetic and even that feeling seemed forced and I didn't fight it and there was nothing I could do. For courage I just kept telling myself that I was a model, that CAA represented me, that I'm really good in bed, that I had good genes, that Victor *ruled*; but on deck I started to semi-seriously doubt this. On deck the gay German youth passed by, ignoring me, but he never really fit into the story and my scenes with him were discarded and it didn't fuck up continuity. On deck members of the film crew were dismantling fog machines, placing them in crates.

Europe moved toward me, the ocean flowing darkly around us, clouds were dispersing, specks of light in the sky were growing wider until daylight reappeared. On deck I was gripping the railing, adding up the hours I had lost, depth and perspective blurring then getting sharper and someone was whistling "The Sunny Side of the Street" as he passed behind me but when I turned around, predictably, no one was there. Looking down at my feet, staring blankly, I noticed, next to my shoe, a stray piece of confetti, then I noticed another.

3

14 A street in Notting Hill.

In a row: a new Gap, a Starbucks, a McDonald's.

A couple walks out of the Crunch fitness center, carrying Prada gym bags, appearing vaguely energized, Pulp's "Disco 2000" blaring out of the gym behind them as they pass a line of BMWs parked tightly along the curb on this street in Notting Hill.

A group of teenagers, thin-hipped, floppy-haired, wearing T-shirts with ironic slogans on them, hang out in front of the Gap comparing purchases, someone's holding an Irvine Welsh paperback, they pass around a cigarette and in the overall void comment unfavorably about a motorbike roaring down the street and the motorbike slows down for a stoplight, then brakes.

Someone who looks like Bono walks a black Lab, snapping back its leash as the dog lunges for a piece of stray garbage it wants to devour—an Arch Deluxe wrapper.

A businessman strides by the Bono look-alike, frowning while he studies the front page of the *Evening Standard*, a pipe gripped firmly in his mouth, and the Bono look-alike walks past a fairly mod nanny wheeling a designer baby carriage and then the nanny passes two art students sharing a bag of brightly colored candy and staring at the mannequins in a store window.

A Japanese tourist videotapes posters, girls strolling out of Starbucks, the black Lab being walked by the Bono look-alike, the mod nanny, who has stopped wheeling the designer baby carriage since, apparently, the baby needs inspecting. The guy on the motorbike still sits at the light, waiting.

Pulp turns into an ominous Oasis track and everyone seems to be wearing Nikes and people aren't moving casually enough—they look coordinated, almost programmed, and umbrellas are opened because the sky above the street in Notting Hill is a chilly Dior gray, promising impending rain, or so people are told.

Over a significant period of time the following occurs:

Jamie Fields emerges on the street in Notting Hill, running out of an alley, desperately waving her arms, yelling garbled warnings at people, an anguished expression ruining (or adding to?) the beauty of her face, which is covered with brown streaks of grime.

A cab moving slowly down the street in Notting Hill almost slams into Jamie Fields and she throws herself, screaming, against it, and the driver, appropriately petrified, rolls up his window and speeds away, swerving past the guy on the motorbike, and the black Lab begins barking wildly and the two art students turn away from the mannequins and the fairly mod nanny starts wheeling the carriage in the opposite direction and the nanny bumps into the businessman, knocking the pipe from his mouth, and he turns around, miffed, mouthing *What the hell?* And then buildings start exploding.

First the Crunch gym, seconds later the Gap and immediately after that the Starbucks evaporate and then, finally, the McDonald's. Each of the four separate explosions generates a giant cumulus cloud of roaring flames and smoke that rises up into the gray sky and since the carefully planted bombs have caused the buildings to burst apart outward onto the walkways bodies either disappear into the flames or fly across the street as if on strings, their flight interrupted by their smashing into parked BMWs, and umbrellas knocked out of hands are lifted up by the explosions, some on fire, swinging across the gray sky before landing gently on piles of rubble.

Alarms are going off in every direction and the sky is lit up orange, colored by two small subsequent explosions, the ground continually vibrating, hidden people yelling out commands. Then, at last, silence, but only for maybe fifteen seconds, before people start screaming.

The group of teenagers: incinerated. The businessman: blown in half by the Starbucks explosion.

There is no sign of the Japanese tourist except for the camcorder, which is in pristine condition.

The guy on the motorbike waiting at the stoplight: a charred skeleton hopelessly tangled in the wreckage of the motorbike, which he has now melded into.

The fairly mod nanny is dead and the designer baby carriage she was wheeling looks like it was smashed flat by some kind of giant hand.

The black Lab has survived but the Bono look-alike isn't around. His hand—blown off at the wrist—still clutches the leash, and the dog, covered in ash and gore, freaked out, dashes madly toward a camera its trainer is standing behind.

And on the street in Notting Hill, a dazed Jamie Fields falls slowly to her knees while gazing up at the gray sky and bows her head guiltily, convulsing in horror and pain as a strange wind blows smoke away, revealing more rubble, more body parts, bathroom products from the Gap, hundreds of blackened plastic Starbucks cups, melted Crunch gym membership cards, even fitness equipment—StairMasters, rowing machines, a stationary bike, all smoldering.

The initial damage behind Jamie Fields seems terrible but after a certain amount of time has passed the street really doesn't look destroyed—just sort of vaguely wrecked. Only two BMWs have toppled over—corpses hanging out of the shattered windshields—and where mangled bodies lie, the gore surrounding them looks inauthentic, as if someone had dumped barrels containing smashed tomatoes across sidewalks, splattered this mixture on top of body parts and mannequins still standing behind decimated storefront windows—the blood and flesh of the art students—and it just seems too red. But later I will find out that this particular color looks more real than I could ever have imagined standing on the street in Notting Hill.

If you're looking at Jamie Fields right now, you'll notice that she's laughing as if relieved, even though she's surrounded by disconnected heads and arms and legs, but these body parts are made of foam and soon crew members are picking them up effortlessly. A director has already yelled "Cut" and someone is wrapping a blanket around Jamie and whispering something soothing in her ear, but Jamie seems okay and as she bows the sound of applause takes over, rising up to dominate the scene that played itself out on the street in Notting Hill on this Wednesday morning.

It's windier after the explosions and extras are letting makeup assistants wipe fake blood off their faces and a helicopter flies noisily over the scene and an actor who looks like Robert Carlyle shakes the director's hand and dollies are dismantled and stuntmen congratulate one another while removing earplugs and I'm following Jamie Fields to her trailer, where an assistant hands her a cell phone and Jamie sits down on the steps leading up into the trailer and lights a cigarette.

My immediate impressions: paler than I remember, still dazzling cheekbones that seem even higher, eyes so blue they look like she's wearing fake contacts, hair still blond but shorter now and slicked back, body more defined, chic beige slacks stretching over legs that seem more muscular, breasts beneath a simple velour top definitely implants.

A girl from Makeup wipes strategically placed smudges off Jamie's face, forehead and chin with a large wet cotton ball and Jamie, trying to talk into the cell phone, waves the girl away and growls "Later" as if she really means it. Trying to smile, the girl slinks away, devastated.

I position myself on the sidelines, leaning sexily against a trailer parked across from Jamie's so she'll have no problem immediately spotting me when she looks up: me grinning, my arms crossed, coolly disheveled in casual Prada, confident but not cocky. When Jamie actually does look up, irritably waving away another makeup girl, my presence—just feet away—doesn't register. I take off the Armani sunglasses and, simulating movement, pull out a roll of Mentos.

"Been there, done that," Jamie whispers tiredly into the cell phone, and then, "Yeah, seeing *is* believing," which is followed by "We shouldn't be talking on a cell phone," and finally she mutters "Barbados," and by now I'm standing over her.

Jamie glances up and without any warning to the person on the other end angrily snaps the cell phone shut and stands so quickly that she almost falls off the stairs leading into the compact white trailer with her name on the door, the expression on her face suggesting: Uh-oh, major freak-out approaching, duck.

"Hey baby," I offer gently, holding my arms out, head tilted, grinning boyishly. "Like, what's the story?"

"What the hell are you doing here?" she growls.

"Uh, hey baby—"

"Jesus Christ—what are you doing here?" She's glancing around, panicked. "Is this a fucking joke?"

"Hey, cool it, baby," I'm saying, moving closer, which causes her to move up the stairs backward, grabbing onto the railing in order not to trip. "It's cool, it's cool," I'm saying.

"No, it's *not* cool," she snaps. "Jesus, you've got to get the hell out of here—*now*."

"Wait a minute, baby—"

"You're supposed to be in New York," she hisses, cutting me off. "What are you doing here?"

I reach out to calm her down. "Baby, listen, if you—"

She slaps my hands away and backs up onto another stair. "Get away from me," and then, "What the hell were you doing at Annabel's last night?"

"Baby, hey, wait—"

"Stop it," she says, glancing fearfully behind me, causing me to turn around too, then I'm looking back at her. "I mean it—*leave*. I can't be seen here with you."

"Hey, let's discuss this in your trailer," I'm suggesting gently. "Let's talk in the trailer." Pause. "Would you like a Mentos?"

Incredulous, she pushes my hand away again. "Get the fuck off this set or I'll call Bobby, okay?"

"Bobby?" I'm asking. "Hey baby—"

"You're supposed to be in fucking New York—now goddamnit get the hell out of here."

I hold my hands up to show her I'm not hiding anything and back away. "Hey, it's cool," I murmur, "it's cool, I'm cool."

Jamie whirls around and before disappearing into the trailer turns back to shoot me an icy glare. The trailer door slams shut. Inside, someone fiddles with a lock. Then silence.

The smell of burning rubber is suddenly everywhere, causing a major coughing fit that I ease out of with the help of a couple of Mentos, then I bum a Silk Cut from another cute makeup girl, who looks like Gina Gershon, and then I'm lingering next to other people who might not have noticed me at first, until I move down Westbourne Grove, then down Chepstow Road, then I stop in at a really cool shop called Oguri and after that I spot Elvis Costello at the corner of Colville Road exiting a neo-Deco, turquoise-tiled public rest room.

13 Feeling really injured, trying to formulate a new game plan in order to halt vacuous wandering, I proceed to various newsstands in desperate need of a *New York Post* or a *New York News* to check out what course my life is taking back in Manhattan, but I can't find any foreign papers anywhere, just typical British rags with headlines blaring LIAM: MAN BEHIND THE MYTH or A DAY IN THE LIFE OF BIJOU PHILLIPS (an article I may or may not appear in, depending on what day) or CHAMPAGNE SALES SOAR AS SWINGING LONDON LEARNS TO PARTY. I stop by a Tower Records after downing a so-so iced decaf grande latte at one of the dozens of Starbucks lining the London streets and buy tapes for my Walkman (Fiona Apple, Thomas Ribiero, Tiger, Sparklehorse, Kenickie, the sound track of *Mandela*) and then walk outside into the stream of Rollerbladers gliding by in search of parks.

Rugby players and the whole rugby-player look are definitely in, along with frilly chiffons, neo-hippie patchworks and shaved heads; because of Liam and Noel Gallagher, I notice beards are more in vogue than they were last time I was here, which causes me to keep touching my face vacantly, feeling naked and vulnerable and so lost I almost step on two Pekingese puppies a bald neo-hippie rugby player with a beard is walking when I collide with him on Bond Street. I think about calling Tamara, a society girl I had a fling with last time she was in the States, but instead debate the best way of putting a positive spin on the Jamie Fields situation if F. Fred Palakon ever calls. Thunderstorms start rumpling my hair and I dash into the Paul Smith store on Bond Street, where I purchase a smart-looking navy-gray raincoat. Everything But the Girl's "Missing" plays over everything, occasionally interrupted by feel-good house music, along with doses of Beck's "Where It's At" and so on and so on.

I'm also being followed by a guy wearing wraparound black sunglasses who looks like he should be in a soap opera—handsome, with a too-chiseled chin and thick swept-up black hair—and resembles maybe a mod-dish Christian Bale, suspiciously blasé in a long black Prada overcoat, seemingly up to no good and vaguely plasticine.

Regrets: I never should have turned down that Scotch ad.

Mental note: eyeliner on men seems fairly cool this season.

At Masako I'm slumped in a velvet booth in back picking at sushi that tastes like ham, and the Christian Bale guy sits at a table for four up front in the deserted restaurant, grinning distantly, a camcorder sitting on an empty chair next to him, and doom music piped in through the stereo system fails to cheer anybody up.

When I walk up to him holding a San Pellegrino bottle, he pays his check and takes a final sip of cold sake, smiling arrogantly at me.

"You want my autograph? Is that it?" I'm asking and then my voice gets babyish. "Stop following me. Just leave me the fuck alone, okay?" A pause, during which he gets up and I back away. "Or else I'll pour this San Pelle-grino all over your head—got it?"

He just answers silently with a so-what? expression.

I watch as he glides confidently outside to where a boxy blue Jeep Commando waits at the curb in front of Masako, its windows tinted black, blocking out the face of the driver. Outside, I take note of various Tex-Mex restaurants, the postapocalyptic mood, my pseudoreality, then head back to the Four Seasons, where all I really want to do is take my shirt off.

12 Outside the Four Seasons obligatory paparazzi share cigarettes, glance idly at me as I stand there pretending to ruffle through my pockets for my room key while they wait for the occasional Town Car or limousine to roll up and dispense any-one snapworthy, which today does not include me. Inside: Ralph Fiennes is shaking hands with a twenty-year-old movie producer who I'm *sure* some-one I know has boned and Gabriel Byrne is simultaneously talking on a cell phone, being interviewed by *People* magazine and sipping a large cup of tea. In other words: it's all happening, it's all familiar. The only void: no message from Palakon, which doesn't relieve me in the way I imagined it would. I push the door to my suite open, turn on MTV—and with a ping, Everything But the Girl floats through the room, which right now is totally arctic. Shivering uncontrollably I push a bunch of Japanese fashion magazines scattered across the bed into a pile and then I'm flopping down, pulling the covers over me, dialing the kitchen for a protein shake and to see what time the hotel's gym closes.

Movement across the room causes me to whirl around.

Jamie Fields: legs slung over a floral-patterned swivel chair, wearing an ultrafashionable Prada camisole top, shimmery black disco pants, black stiletto shoes, black Armani sunglasses, and her face is masklike, but after my initial shock I'm projecting something vaguely apologetic onto it and she confirms this by removing the sunglasses, stoplight-red Hard Candy polish on her nails.

Jamie notices how distracting they are. "I know—it's ugly," she sighs, lighting a cigarette. "It's for the movie."

"Which one?" I'm asking.

She shrugs, exhaling. "Both?"

"How did you get in here?" I ask.

"I'm well acquainted with certain key staff members at the Four Seasons," she says casually. "They know me. They let me do whatever I want. It's a perk. Let's leave it at that."

I pause before asking, "Are you going to start flailing around again?"

"No. I'm sorry about all of that."

Another pause. "What happened back there?"

"Oh, I just thought you were someone else," she mutters. "Forget about it. Anywa-a-a-ay . . ."

"You thought *I* was someone else?" I ask. "Baby, that hurts."

"I know." Jamie reaches into a Gucci leather clutch envelope and pulls out a small gift-wrapped box. "So I thought this might ease your pain."

I reach out and hesitantly take the box. "What is it?"

"Cigars. Montecristos," she says, standing up, stretching. "I mean, I'm assuming you're still as trendy as you used to be." She takes a drag off the cigarette, makes a face, stubs it out in an ashtray. "I really don't think times have changed *that* much." She starts moving around the suite, not impressed but not unimpressed, just bizarrely neutral, fingering the curtains, studying various knickknacks of mine taking up space on a desk.

The phone suddenly rings. When I pick it up no one's there. I slowly place the phone back down.

"That keeps happening," I mutter.

Jamie continues to move around the room, runs her hands beneath desk-tops, inspects a lamp, then another, opens an armoire, gazes at the space behind the TV—Beck on a donkey, a Spice Girl swinging a lasso—then she lifts a remote control and seems on the verge of taking it apart when I interrupt.

"Baby, why don't you sit down?" I ask.

"I've been lunging around all day." She stretches again, resumes a more casual pose. "I can't stay still."

"Um, baby?" I begin awkwardly. "How did you find me?"

"Hey—" She looks back at me. "How did *you* find *me*?"

Pause. "You go first."

"I had my assistant call all the places I thought you'd be staying at." She sighs, continues. "The Connaught, the Stafford, Claridge's, the Dorchester, the Berkeley, the Halcyon, then—boom—the Four Seasons."

A long pause, during which I just stare at her, dumbfounded.

"What?" she asks. "What is it?"

"How about the fucking Hempel? Why didn't you check the fucking Hempel? Jesus, baby."

A smile creeps up but she stops it when she realizes something and this causes her to groan, flopping back into the swivel chair.

"Don't make me put my sunglasses back on, Victor," she warns.

The phone rings again. I sigh, reach over to the nightstand, pick the phone up, listen. Silence, a series of beeps unevenly spaced, two clicks, a patch of far-off static, another beep, then silence. I look back at Jamie in the swivel chair, playing thoughtfully with her sunglasses, legs dangling over an armrest, before I slowly place the phone back down.

"I asked for Victor Johnson's room but then I remembered—or read somewhere—that you changed your name. To Victor Ward." She pauses, smiles playfully. "Why?"

"Various committees assumed it was a smart PR move to jump-start my career." I shrug. "It made me semi-famous."

"A misconception made you semi-famous," she corrects.

"I've traveled quite well on that misconception."

"It was a suit that got you the gig."

"It was also an inordinate amount of sheer cool."

"Why do I have the feeling your father made you change the name?" She smiles playfully again. "Huh? Did Daddy make a request?"

"I don't talk about my father—"

"Oh god, *whatever.*" She stands up again, then flops down in the chair again, sighs a number of times. "Listen, I'm just here to tell you I'm sorry about freaking out and, y'know, have a good time in London and all that and, um, I'll see you in another eight years."

"So are you gonna freak out again?" I ask, playing it cool, moving across the bed so that I'm closer to her.

"I'm feeling, um, reformed."

"Oh, that's good."

Pause. "That depends on your definition of good," she says.

"What's the story, baby?" I sigh mock-wearily. "What are you doing? Where are you going?"

"Today was the last day of the shoot," she says. "We finished the interiors last week in Pinewood." Pause. "So I'm basically free, free, free."

"Well, then I'm glad I caught you."

"Caught me?" she asks, stiffening, vaguely annoyed. "Why are you glad you *caught me*, Victor?"

Suddenly her cell phone rings. She pulls it out of a Lulu Guinness handbag I hadn't noticed before and answers it. While staring directly at me, she says, "Yes? . . . It's fine. . . . Right. . . . No, I'm at the Four Seasons. . . . Is that the buzzword for the day? . . . Let's see a show of hands. . . . Yes. . . . Sounds delicious. . . . Right. . . . Later." She clicks off, stares blankly at me.

"Who was that?" I ask, shivering, my breath steaming.

"No one you know," she murmurs, and then, barely audible, "yet."

I'm lying on my side now, running my hands slinkily across the floral print of the comforter, drawing attention to my hands because of the way they're moving, and my shirt's become untucked in a not-too-suggestive way and when I look down "sheepishly," then back up with a seductive smile, Jamie is glaring at me with a noxious expression. When I revert to not being so studly, she relaxes, stretches, groans.

"I've *got* to get something to eat," she says.

"Baby, are you famished?"

"Beyond famished."

"Hey, I saw that movie." I grin, faux-mischievously. "What about room service?" I suggest, my voice deepening.

She stands there, contemplating something, glances back at the TV, then her eyes carefully scan the ceiling. Finally she murmurs, "Let's get out of here."

"Where to?"

"Let's go out for dinner."

"Now? It's only five," I point out. "Is anything open yet?"

"I know a place," she murmurs. Something on the ceiling, in the corner, dominates Jamie's attention and she moves toward it, reaching up, then— realizing something—stops herself. She turns around, tries to smile, but apparently she can't help it: the room seems to worry her in some way.

"Baby, it's just a set," I'm saying. "Forget about it."

11

Though the restaurant doesn't serve until 6 Jamie gets us into Le Caprice at 5:30 with a cryptic phone call she makes in the cab on the way to Arlington Square.

"I was supposed to have dinner with Amanda Harlech but I think this will be much more, er, interesting," she says, tucking the cell phone back into her handbag.

"That's me," I say. "A blast from the past."

While sitting across the table from her in Le Caprice I'm aware that Jamie Fields is so beautiful that she's starting to blow away whatever residual memories of Lauren Hynde I might have held on to and after knocking back a martini and some white wine we order crab-and-corn chowder and a plate of chargrilled squid and the two of us start relaxing into the moment, only briefly interrupted on Jamie's part by a few giant yawns and a slightly deadened look behind those very cool blue eyes. I order another martini, momentarily thinking, This is gonna be so easy.

"Where did you go after shooting today?" I ask.

"I had a Himalayan rejuvenation treatment at Aveda in Harvey Nichols," she says. "I needed it. I deserved it."

"Cool, hip."

"So what are you doing in London, Victor?" she asks. "How did you find me?"

"Baby," I'm saying, "it was purely accidental."

"Uh-huh," she says somewhat dubiously. "What were you doing on the set this morning?"

"I was just browsing, doing some shopping in Nothing Hill, minding my own business and—"

"It's Notting Hill, Victor," Jamie says, motioning to a waiter for more bread. "*Notting* Hill. Continue."

I stare at her, sending out vibes; some hurtle back at me, others land softly, sticking.

She's waving a hand in front of my face. "Hello? Victor?"

"Oh yeah," I say, blinking. "Um, could you repeat the question?"

"How—did—you—find—me?" she asks tensely.

"I just stumbled onto . . . things, y'know?" I squint, making an airy motion with my hands, hoping it clarifies.

"That sounds like you but I'm not buying it."

"Okay, okay," I say, grinning sexily at her, leaning in, seeing how far I can push this mode. "Someone at a party—"

"Victor," she interrupts, "you're a very good-looking guy. You don't need to push it with me, okay? I get it."

The sexy grin fades and I sit back and take a sip of the martini, then carefully wipe my lips with a napkin.

"Proceed," she says, arms crossed, staring.

"Someone at a party I was at mentioned, um, something," I say, distracted, shrugging everything off. "Maybe it was at the Groucho Club. I think it was someone who went to Camden with us—"

"You *think*?"

"Baby, I was so loaded—"

"Oh shit, Victor, *who* was it?"

"Wait—I'm sorry, I think it was someone I bumped into at Brown's—"

"*Who*, for god's sake?"

I lean in, grinning sexily and purring, "I see I have your full attention now."

"Victor," she says, squirming. "I want to know."

"Baby," I say, "let me tell you something."

"Yeah?" she asks expectantly.

"I never reveal my sources," I whisper to her in the empty restaurant and then lean back, satisfied.

She relaxes and, to prove she's okay with this, takes a final spoonful of chowder and licks the spoon thoughtfully. Now it's her turn to lean in. "We have ways of making you talk," she whispers back.

Playfully, I lean in again and say with a husky voice, "Oh, I bet you do."

But Jamie doesn't smile at this—just suddenly seems preoccupied with something else, which may or may not concern me. Withdrawn and pensive, she sighs and fixes her eyes on a point behind my back. I turn around and glance at a row of David Bailey photographs lining the wall.

"Hey baby," I start, "you seem tired all of a sudden. Are you like really beat?"

"If you had to deliver lines like 'Once Farris gets hold of the scepter it's over for your planet' all day, you'd be soul-sick too," she says tiredly. "Japanese investors—what's left to say?"

"Hey, but I *am* soul-sick," I exclaim, trying to cheer her up. "A girlfriend once told me so," I say mock-proudly.

"Who are you seeing now?" she asks listlessly.

"I'm off relationships for now. 'Be more sensitive, be more macho.' Jesus, forget it." Pause. "I'm chasing hookers instead."

"Speaking of which—what ever happened to Chloe Byrnes?" she asks. "Or did she OD yet?" Jamie shrugs, then reconsiders. "I suppose I would've heard about that."

"No, she's cool," I say, figuring out how to play the current situation, landing on: "We're on hiatus. Like on vacation."

"What? That's code for she dumped your ass?"

"No," I start patiently. "It means every . . . relationship has its, like, um—oh yeah—ups and downs."

"I take it this is a down?"

"You could say so."

"Thank you."

"You're welcome," I say glumly.

"I heard she had a run-in with heroin," Jamie says lightly.

"I can't confirm that rumor," I say.

"Because it isn't true?" Jamie pulls out a pack of cigarettes.

"Hey baby—"

"It's okay," she says patiently. "You can smoke in restaurants in London."

"That's not what I'm hey-babying about."

"So just give me the lowdown. Chloe's not dead: have I got that much right?" she asks.

"No, she's not dead, Jamie," I say, mildly pissed off.

"Well, rumor has it, Victor . . . ," Jamie says, shaking her head faux-sadly, lighting the cigarette.

"I don't give a shit about what gossip you've heard."

"Oh, stop right there, please." Jamie sits back, exhaling smoke, arms crossed, marveling at me. "Is this the same Victor Johnson I knew way back when, or have you suddenly got your act together?"

"I'm just saying Chloe—"

"Oh, I don't really want to hear about your relationship with Chloe Byrnes." She cuts me off irritably, nodding at a waiter to remove a bowl. "I can just imagine. Weekends in South Beach, lunches with Andie MacDowell, discussions revolving around 'Will Chloe get into fashion heaven or not,' debating the color yellow, you keep finding syringes in Chloe's Prada handbag—"

"Hey," I snap. "It was a *nasal* habit."

"Ooh." Jamie's eyes light up. "Is that *on* the record?"

"Oh shit, I don't give a crap what people think," I mutter, pushing myself away from the table. "Like I really care what people think, Jamie."

A pause. "*I* think you're adapting well," she says, smiling.

"Yeah, *I'm* a genius, baby."

"So why is the genius in London and not back in New York?" Jamie asks herself. "Let me guess: he's doing research on that screenplay he always wanted to write."

"Hey, I'm a genius, baby," I tell her. "I know you might find that hard to believe, but there it is."

"How snazzy," she says, then fatigue overtakes her and she whimpers, "Oh no, I'm having flashbacks—the eighties are coming back to me and an anxiety attack is imminent." She holds herself, shivering.

"That's a good thing, baby," I say, urging, "Float into it."

"No, Victor," she says, shaking her head. "Contrary to popular opinion, that is most definitely *not* a good thing."

"Hey baby, why not?"

"Because it brings back our college years and I, for one, have no desire to relive them."

"Oh come on, baby—you had fun at Camden. Admit it," I say. "And don't look at me like I'm insane."

"Fun?" she asks, appalled. "Don't you remember Rupert Guest? Hanging out with *him* was fun?"

"He was a drug dealer, baby," I say. "He wasn't even enrolled."

"He wasn't?" she asks, confused, then, remembering something both private and horrific, groans, "*Oh god.*"

"I remember Roxanne Forest, however," I say, teasing her. "And some *really* good times with that Swedish chick—Katrina Svenson."

"Oh gross," she sighs, then she quickly recovers and decides to play along. "Do you remember David Van Pelt? Mitchell Allen? Those were *my* good times."

A considerable pause. "In that case—not friends of mine, baby."

I recognize the current expression on Jamie's face—time to taunt—and then she throws me a name, but I'm staring at the black floor beneath us, trying to remember David Van Pelt or Mitchell Allen, momentarily zoning out, and I don't hear the name Jamie just mentioned. I ask her to repeat it.

"Lauren Hynde?" Jamie says, in a certain tone of voice. "Do you remember her?"

"Um, no, not really," I say casually, reacting to her tone.

"You must remember Lauren, Victor." She says this sighing, looking away. "Lauren Hynde?"

"It doesn't ring a bell," I say blankly. "Why? Should it?"

"You left me for her."

After a long silence, trying to remember the particular sequence of events during any given term, I end up saying, "No."

"Oh Jesus, this might've been a mistake." Jamie's moving around in her chair, uncomfortably, as if she's trying to unstick herself from the seat.

"No, I remember her," I say, looking directly at Jamie. "But I also remember that I'd taken a term off and when I came back in December you weren't around—"

"I also had taken the term off, Victor," she counters.

"Baby, the point is . . ." Defeated, knowing there never was a point, that there never would be anything that could wrap this up neatly, I just ask quietly, "Are you still pissed?"

"Oh yeah, it destroyed me," she says, rolling her eyes. "I had to move to Europe to get over the genius."

"Have you really lived here *that* long?" I'm asking, mystified. "That's . . . impossible."

"I live in New York, dodo," she says. "I work in New York."

"Why don't we ever see each other?"

"I think the combination of your self-absorption and my fear of just about everyone in Manhattan conspires against us."

"Oh baby, you're so tough," I'm telling her. "Nobody scares you."

"Do you know Alison Poole?" she asks.

"Um." I cough lightly and then mutter, "I'll pass on that one."

"That's not what I heard—"

"Hey, when's the last time you saw me?" I ask, cutting her off. "Because the Klonopin I'm on affects long-term memory."

"Well," she starts, "I saw photos of you at the shows in WWD last week."

"You mean the Todd Oldham show?" I'm asking. "Do you still have that issue?"

"No, you were at the Calvin Klein show," she says.

"Oh yeah," I say vacantly. "Yeah, that's right."

"I guess I became aware of you—*and* that I wasn't going to be able to escape you—when I saw a Gap ad you did a couple years ago," she says. "It was a pretty decent black-and-white photo of just your head and it said something like 'Even Victor Ward Wears Khakis' or whatever. It gave off the impression that you wore those khakis rather proudly, Victor. I was damn impressed."

"Did we—" I start, then shake my head. "Forget it."

"What? Did we end up hating each other? Did we end up the way we thought we always knew we would? Did *I* end up wearing khakis because of that fucking ad?"

"No, did we . . . ever do a fashion shoot for *GQ* together?"

A long pause. She stares disconcertingly at my near-empty martini glass. "How many of those have you had?" Another pause. "Boy—I think you need to get off the Klonopin, guy."

"Forget it. I knew it was a crazy question, forget it," I say, trying to smile, shaking my head. "So who's been sleeping in *your* bed?"

"I'm enjoying the art of being semi-single," she sighs.

"I'm seeing your face in a new light," I say, resting my chin in the palm of my hand, staring straight at her. "And you're lying."

"About what?" she asks hesitantly.

"About being single."

"How would you know?"

"Because girls who look like you are never single," I say faux-confidently. "Plus I know you, Jamie. You like guys too much."

She just stares at me, mouth open, and then starts laughing hysterically and doesn't stop cracking up until I ask, "Did you have cheekbones like that back at Camden?"

She takes a couple of deep breaths, reaches over to finish my martini and, flushed, panting, asks, "Victor, what do you expect me to say to that?"

"You dropped a bomb on me, baby," I murmur, staring at her.

Startled, pretending not to be, she asks, "I did what?"

"You dropped a bomb on me," I say. "You, like, affected me."

"When did this happen?"

"When we first met."

"And?"

"And now I'm in the same state."

"Well, get over it," she says. "Get over yourself as well."

"You're thinking something, though," I say, refusing to break eye contact, not even blinking.

"Yes, I am," she says finally, smiling.

"What are you thinking, Jamie?"

After a pause and looking directly back at me, she says, "I'm thinking you're a potentially interesting person who I might want to get reacquainted with."

"You've always been one of the fifty most inspiring women in the world to me."

"Would you like to get reacquainted, Victor?" she asks, daring me, lowering her eyes, then raising them back up, widening them.

Suddenly the way she says this and the look on her face—total sex—flusters me, and with my face burning, I try to complete a sentence but only "I, um, don't know . . ." comes out. I end up staring down at the table.

"Don't be shocked," she says. "I'm not saying let's fuck. I'm just saying maybe we can get . . . reacquainted."

"Hey, nothing shocks me anymore, baby."

"That's good," she says after a while, studying me. "That's very good, Victor."

After the table has been cleared and we've split a dessert, she asks, "What are you thinking about?"

After a long pause, debating which way to go, I say, "I'm thinking, Does she still do drugs?"

"And?" she asks teasingly.

"And . . . does she have any on her right now?"

Smiling, getting into the spirit, Jamie says, "No." A slight pause. "But I know where you can get some."

"Waiter?" I lift my hand. "Check, please?"

After he brings it, Jamie realizes something.

"You're actually paying?" she asks. "Oh my god."

"Hey baby, I'm flush," I say. "I'm on a roll. I'm happening."

Watching me slap down the appropriate amount of cash, including a giant tip, Jamie murmurs, "Maybe things really have changed."

10

As the Chemical Brothers' "Setting Sun" blasts out on cue we're back in Notting Hill at some industrial billionaire's warehouse—one of the more elaborate sets so far, which is really a massive series of warehouses within one enormous building—and it's a party for Gary Hume, though in actuality it's in honor of Patsy and Liam and getting in is hard if you're not like us but Jamie's whisked through a silver archway right behind Kate Moss and Stella Tennant by guards wearing headsets, and the feel of what's going on outside the warehouse is "just another giant media event" with the prerequisite camera vans parked in front, barricades, fans reaching out, fame, people's names on the back of jackets, kids looking at us thinking that's what we want to look like, thinking that's who we want to be. When I ask Jamie about the identity of the industrial billionaire she tells me he funds certain wars and is also a "friendly" alcoholic and then we bump into Patsy Palmer and Martine McCutcheson and we all end up telling Nellie Hooper how much we adore the new Massive remix as Damon Albarn kisses Jamie on both cheeks.

Inside: most of the vast empty spaces in the warehouse look like restaurant kitchens with giant windows steamed over and it's freezing because of all the mammoth ice sculptures on display and bands are playing on different floors (the Jon Spencer Blues Explosion's in the basement) and everyone's doing Gucci poses while drinking Tsingtao beer but it's also a kind of Gap-T-shirt-and-Prada-penny-loafers night, no pitfalls, camcorders everywhere, Carmen Electra in a purple Alaïa dress dancing with one of the ice sculptures, and sometimes the party's in black-and-white and sometimes it's in glaring color like in the new Quicksilver ads and the mood is all basically very antistyle and we're shivering like we're lodged in an iceberg somewhere that's floating off the coast of Norway or a place equally cold.

Music is melodic trip-hop on the level where Jamie and I have staked out a small lime-green couch below a massive steel staircase, white flowers surrounding us everywhere, a giant digital clock face glows in the dark, projected yards above us on the ceiling, and we're doing mellow coke Jamie scored effortlessly and because she stole a Waring blender from one of the kitchens we're drinking bright-orange slushy tequila punches and sometime during all of this Jamie changed into black Jil Sander, and unimportant paparazzi try to snap some shots but Jamie's weary and I'm looking a little too wired to be camera-ready so I push them away, snarling, "Hey, she needs her privacy. Jesus—we're just *people*," and someone else floats by, taking up their interest, and I watch, a little disappointed, as the paparazzi follow, leaving us behind. Shadows are being taken aside and whispered to. We light each other's cigarettes.

"Thank you, Victor," Jamie says, exhaling. "You didn't need to be that, um, firm, but I'm glad you're feeling so . . . protective."

"Everyone's so thin and gorgeous, baby," I'm gushing, the cocaine flowing through me. "And their teeth are, like, *white*. It's not exactly how I remember London, baby."

"Well, since most of the people here are Americans I wouldn't worry about your memory."

"This is the coolest party," I'm gushing.

"I thought you'd be impressed," she sighs.

"What do you think of this place?" I ask, moving closer to her on the lime-green couch.

"Well," she says, looking around, "I think it looks a little too much like a new Philippe Starck hotel."

"*Too* much?" I'm asking, confused. "I think it's multi-useful, but baby, I don't want to talk about interior design, baby."

"Well, what *do* you want to talk about?" she says. "Besides yourself."

"No, baby, I wanna talk about *you*." Pause. "Well, you *and* me." Another pause. "But let's start with you. Can I have the coke?"

She slips the vial into my hand. "Let me guess—you want to be one of those guys whose ex-girlfriends never get over them, right?"

I turn to the wall, do a few quick blasts and offer my nose for inspection. She nods her head, meaning it's fine, then I slip the vial back to her while she waves over to some guy in a gray three-button Prada suit who's talking to Oliver Payton. The guy in the suit waves back somewhat semi-pretentiously, I feel. They are both holding pythons.

"Who's that?" I'm asking.

"Someone who did the legs in that new Tommy Hilfiger ad," Jamie says.

"This is the coolest party, baby," I'm gushing.

"You're feeling great *and* looking even better, right?"

I'm nodding. "The better you look, the more you see."

"I'm seeing Emily Lloyd maintaining remarkable poise while eating a giant grilled shrimp," Jamie yawns, opening the vial, turning away. "I'm so exhausted."

"Hey look, there's Lulu Guinness—she made your bag," I'm saying, totally wired. "Hey, and there's Jared Leto—he's supposed to play me in the movie they're making of my life."

Jamie flinches and turns back to me, wiping her nose and taking a large gulp of tequila punch. "You need someone to teach you important life lessons, Victor."

"Yeah, yeah, baby, exactly," I'm saying. "But I think *you're* just having a hard time dealing with my hypermasculine vibe."

"Don't be a wuss, baby," she warns.

"Hey, if you didn't come to party, don't bother knocking on my door." I scoot closer to her, our thighs touching.

"Yeah, that's me." She lights a cigarette, smiling. "Little Miss Trouble."

"What happened to us at Camden, baby?" I'm asking. "Because for the life of me I cannot remember."

"Well, I think what happened was that first we established that you were an idiot," she says casually, exhaling.

"Uh-huh, uh-huh, but I think I have major credibility now—"

"You also had gigantic intimacy problems that I doubt you've overcome."

"Oh spare me, spare me." I'm giggling. "Come on, baby." Leaning into her, I open my arms wide. "What could have possibly been wrong with *me*?"

"Besides not knowing your place?" she asks. "And that you liked to fuck complete strangers?"

"Hey, I thought *you* were the slutty one, baby," I say. "I also think that *I've*, er, evolved."

"*I* dumped *you*, Victor," she says, reminding me, but it's not harsh because she's leaning in, smiling.

"But it's not like you broke my heart," I whisper because we're close enough.

"That's because you didn't have one," she whispers back, leaning closer. "But hey, I don't necessarily find that . . . unsexy."

Looking into her face, I realize that she's more willing than I first thought and since I'm not in the mood yet I lean back, away from her, playing it cool, looking over the crowd, guzzling the punch. She pauses, reflects on something and sits up a little, sips her punch too, lets me leave a hand not holding my cigarette on her thigh.

"Rumor has it you fled the States, baby," I'm saying. "Why?"

"Rumor?" she asks, knocking my hand away by crossing her legs. "Who told you that?" Pause. "There are *rumors* about me?"

"Hey baby, you're a star." I'm shrugging. "You're in the press."

"You didn't even know I lived in New York, Victor," she says, frowning. "Jesus—what *are* you talking about? *What* press?"

"So . . . you did *not* flee the States?" I ask tentatively. "So-o-o you're *not*, like, hiding out here?"

"*Flee* the States? *Hiding* out here?" she asks. "For fuck's sake, Victor—get your shit together. Does it look like I'm hiding out?"

"Well, um, baby, I heard things—"

"I came here to make a lousy sci-fi movie," she says. "Who were you talking to? Who told you this garbage?"

"Hey baby, I heard things." I shrug. "I heard something about boyfriend troubles. I'm very well connected, you know."

She just stares at me and then, after the appropriate amount of time passes, shakes her head and mutters, "Oh my god."

"So when are you coming back?" I'm asking.

"To where?" she asks. "To where *you're* going? I don't think so."

"To the States, baby—"

"The *States*? Who in the fuck calls it the *States*?"

"Yeah, the States, baby." I'm shrugging. "You wanna join me?"

A long pause that's followed by "Why are you so concerned whether I come back or not?"

"I'm not, baby, I'm not," I say, paying attention to her again, moving closer again. "I just want to know when and if you're leaving and if, uh, you need a lift."

"I don't know, Victor," she says, not moving away. "I don't know what I'm doing. In fact I don't even know what I'm doing at this party with you."

"Hey, I don't believe that," I say. "Come on, baby."

"Why don't you believe that?"

"Because of the way you said it." I shrug, but this time I'm staring at her intently.

She studies me too, then shudders. "I have a terrible feeling you're gonna end up on a late-night talk show in a pink tuxedo in about three years."

"Hey," I whisper huskily, "I'm built to last, baby." It's the cue for a kiss. "Baby—come to where the flavor is."

The lights flicker, then dim, the chorus to U2's "Staring at the Sun" bursts out and she tilts her neck so her mouth is more easily available to mine, confetti starts drifting down around us, and Raquel Welch in *One Million Years B.C.* suddenly starts running around, projected on an entire wall above our heads, and as our lips touch there's an insistency on her part that I'm reacting to but Tara Palmer-Tomkinson and the hat designer Philip Treacey stop by and that's when Jamie and I disengage and as we're all chatting Jamie asks Tara where the closest rest room is and as they all leave together Jamie winks at me and I not only experience a Camden flashback but also realize that I'm going to get laid *and* make $300,000. Note to self: why bother modeling anymore? New plan: remember all the girls I dated who might need locating. I start mentally composing a list, wondering if Palakon would be even mildly interested.

I'm staring at a group of Japanese guys hunched over a small TV set smoking cigars and drinking bourbon while watching a tape of "Friends" and after one of them notices me he can't stop staring and, flattered, I pretend not to notice and, unsure of whether Jamie took the vial of cocaine with her, I start rifling through the Mark Cross suede tote bag she's carrying in this scene as the Smashing Pumpkins' "1979" starts playing at an earsplitting level, people crying out in protest until it's turned down and replaced by the melodic trip-hop at low volume.

Inside the tote bag Jamie might have slipped the vial into: a Gucci snakeskin wallet, a miniature Mont Blanc fountain pen, an Asprey address book, Calvin Klein sunglasses, a Nokia 9000 cell phone, a Nars lip gloss, a Calvin Klein atomizer and a Sony ICD-50 portable digital recorder that I stare at questioningly until I'm cued to press Play and when I do, I hear my voice echoing hollowly in the empty space at Le Caprice.

"I um, don't know . . ."

"Don't be shocked. I'm not saying let's fuck. I'm just saying maybe we can get . . . reacquainted."

"Hey, nothing shocks me anymore, baby."

"That's good. . . . That's very good, Victor."

A voice above me, someone hanging over the banister wearing a Gucci tux, someone way too exquisitely handsome and my age, a guy who might or might not be Bentley Harrolds, the model, totally drunk, his tumbler filled to the brim with clear liquid dangling precariously from a hand attached to a sagging wrist:

"Oh, what a circus," he groans. "Oh, what a show."

I immediately turn off the recorder and drop it back into Jamie's tote bag, then look up at Bentley, flashing a sexy grin that causes Bentley's eyes to widen and then he's leering at me, blood rushing to his head turning his face crimson, and still hanging over the banister, he slurs, "You certainly don't make a mundane first impression."

"And you're Bentley Harrolds," I say and then, gesturing toward the glass, "Hey bud, what are you drinking?"

"Er . . ." Bentley looks at his hand and then back at me, his eyes crossed with concentration. "I'm sipping chilled Bacardi," and then, still staring down at me: "You're full-frontal gorgeous."

"So I've been told," I say, and then, "How gorgeous?"

Bentley's moving down the staircase and now he's standing over me, swaying back and forth, flushed.

"You look like Brad Pitt," Bentley says. "After he's just wrestled a large . . . furry . . . *bear*." Pause. "And that gets me hot."

"Just give me a minute to calm down."

"What were you doing going through Jamie Fields' tote bag, by the way?" Bentley asks, trying to sit, but I'm scooting all over the couch, making it virtually impossible. He gives up, sighs, tries to focus.

"Um, I suppose you don't want to hear about my strenuous workout in the Four Seasons gym this morning instead, huh?"

A long pause while Bentley considers this. "I . . . might"—he gulps—"faint."

"You wouldn't be the first."

The Japanese guy keeps swigging bourbon and glancing over at me, then nudges another Japanese guy, who waves him away and goes back to watching "Friends," chowing down on a carton of Häagen-Dazs Chocolate Midnight Cookies. With a grunt, Bentley squeezes down next to me on the lime-green couch and—concentrating on my arms, chest and legs—finally has to admit something.

"I'm capable of being thrilled by you, Victor."

"Ah, I thought you recognized me."

"Oh, you're recognizable, all right," Bentley guffaws.

"Well, that's me."

Bentley pauses, considers something. "Can I ask you something, Victor?"

"Shoot."

Bentley shakes his head side to side slowly and in a low voice warns, "Oh, you shouldn't suggest that."

"I meant"—I clear my throat—"go ahead."

Bentley clears his throat lightly, then asks, totally serious, "Are you still dating Stephen Dorff?"

Jamie suddenly flops down between us as I'm coughing up the tequila punch, taking in air. "There's a croquet game on the sixth floor and accessories on five," she says, kissing Bentley on the cheek.

"Hello, darling," Bentley says, kissing her back.

"Why are you choking?" Jamie asks me. "Why is he choking?" she asks Bentley, and then, "Oh Bentley, what *did* you do?"

"Moi?" Bentley whines. "Oh, just asked a personal question that got exactly the kind of response that satisfied me immensely."

"I didn't answer any question," I croak, wiping my mouth.

"Well, give Bentley an answer now, baby," Bentley says.

Playing along—but also panicked—I shrug. "Maybe it's true."

Bentley takes this in calmly, then, totally deadpan, his eyes closed with pain and longing, asks, "Would you move in with me, please?"

"How disco, baby," I say, recovering. "But I'm, um"—I glance over at Jamie, who seems like she could care less—"involved."

Another long pause on Bentley's part, during which he tosses back what's left of the chilled rum and gathers his thoughts. "Well, then," he asks, "can I . . . watch?"

"Er, no."

"He was looking through your purse, Jamie," Bentley says, immediately sober, pointing a finger at me.

"Hey, I was looking for the coke," I say.

"Jesus, Victor," she says, reaching into a jacket pocket. "*Here*. You don't need to go through my things." But the annoyance lasts only a millisecond because she's waving back at Iris Palmer and Honor Fraser, while Bentley bows his head, raising his empty glass.

"Iris looks fabulous," Jamie murmurs.

"How do you and Mr. Ward know each other, Jamie?" Bentley asks, leaning over. "And I'll leave him alone—I promise. It's just that I was flirting with Harry Nuttall *all* evening and then I had my sights set on Robbie but it's all just been intolerably *arid*—" And then, squinting into the crowd, "Oh my god, who invited Zandra Rhodes?"

"We went to Camden College together, Bentley," Jamie says. "However, I graduated." She turns to me. "Did you?"

"Oh, that's right," Bentley says. "Bobby told me that."

"Who's Bobby, baby?" I'm asking, trying to get her attention.

Bentley suddenly pretends to be looking around, "busying himself," his eyes widening exaggeratedly, and over his shoulder the Japanese guy keeps staring in such a strange way that it's starting to cause me major discomfort and maybe Jamie notices this too because she leans in, blocking the view, and kisses me softly on the lips and maybe that's an answer to the Bobby inquiry. While I'm staring into Jamie's face—her expression saying basically "hey, it's okay"—Bentley dramatically clears his throat and Jamie pulls back, almost shamefully. Again I'm left staring at the Japanese guy.

"So Victor," Bentley says, staring at me with all the subtlety of a raven, "what do you think of London?"

"Phony Beatlemania has bitten the dust, I see."

"How tongue-in-chic."

"Hey Joaquin, hey man," I call out, waving Joaquin Phoenix over, and he's dressed in a brown Prada suit and has his hair swept back and he shakes my hand and, recognizing Jamie, kisses her on the cheek and nods briefly at Bentley.

"Hey, how's this party, man?" I'm asking. "Wild, huh?"

"It's very . . . unstuffy," Joaquin says, giving the party behind him a cursory look. "I kind of like it. Better than last night, huh?"

"Yeah man," I'm saying. "So what are you doing in town, man?"

Joaquin flinches, pretends he didn't hear me. "What?"

"What are you doing in town, man?" I ask, staring up into his face.

"Uh, Victor, man," Joaquin says. "I told you last night I'm shooting that John Hughes movie in Hampstead."

"Oh," I say. "Yeah, yeah, that's right."

"Did you two see each other last night?" Bentley asks, suddenly paying close attention, emphasis on all the wrong places.

"We were at Annabel's," Joaquin sighs, scratching at a sideburn. "It was a party for Jarvis Cocker that Catrina Skepper threw." He takes a sip from a bottle of Tsingtao.

"Man, I guess I'm just like, um, really . . . jet-lagged," I say, forcing a casual grin. "Yeah, that was such a fun party."

"It was okay." Joaquin shrugs.

He doesn't stay long because Iris Palmer and Bella Freud whisk him away and Bentley lights another cigarette for Jamie, who's just staring on a continuous basis in a very hard, weird way at me, as if she's trying to figure something out. I play along by cocking my head, looking confused, grinning dumbly, fooling around with my own cigarette that Bentley insists on trying to light, shrugging my shoulders guy-like.

"I think Joaquin's harelip is *fabulous*," Bentley intones dramatically.

"Why did you tell him you were at Annabel's last night?" Jamie asks me.

"Because, baby, I was," I say. "Yeah, Jarvis and I hung out and then Joaquin and I, er, hung out some more and . . . it was just like clowns to the left of us, jokers to the right, y'know, baby?"

Jamie nods, inhales on the cigarette, then says, "But you weren't there, Victor."

"Hey, how do you know, baby?" I'm asking.

"Because I was there, Victor," she says.

A long pause and then, feigning outrage, I ask, "And you didn't say *hello*? Jesus, baby."

"I didn't say hello, Victor, because you were not there," Jamie says. "I would've remembered if you had been there, Victor."

"Well, Joaquin says he saw me there—so hey." I lift my arms up, shrugging, hoping this gesture will do for an answer. "Maybe you didn't see me."

Bentley's pulling white roses out of chrome vases, smelling them, fastening one to his lapel, squinting out at the rest of the room, at the extras sweeping past. Jamie keeps staring at me. I'm nodding my head to the music, trying to get a grip.

"What are you doing in London, Victor?" Jamie asks.

"Having a fly time, bay-bee," I say, leaning up into her face, kissing her again on the lips, this time harder, a tongue slipping through. Jamie kisses back but suddenly it's broken because of shadows standing over us and someone saying, "Kula Shaker's performing on the sixth floor."

Above us is this impossibly gorgeous couple, smiling wryly at Jamie as if she'd just done something wrong, and the girl is wearing a white Yohji Yamamoto sheer slip dress and I vaguely recognize her as Tammy, this model from Kentucky, and she's holding hands with Bruce Rhinebeck, also model handsome and wearing a shiny Gucci fitted suit with a Dolce & Gabbana leather jacket over it and he automatically hands Jamie the joint they're sharing.

"And word is flashing about that the DJ on the roof is Laurent Garnier," Bruce says. "Sounds crunchy, huh?"

"Hey guys," Jamie says, and then, an afterthought, "Oh, this is Victor Ward."

"Ah, terrific," Bruce says, not ungentlemanly. "Another expatriate."

"Nice eyebrows, bud," I tell Bruce.

"Thanks," he says. "They're mine."

"We're bored and need to split," Tammy says.

"Can we go to Speed tonight?" Bentley asks. "LTJ Bukem is spinning. Or we can stay here because I think I'm having the time of my life."

"I've had the most terrible day," Tammy says. "I just want to go home and collapse."

"What are you drinking?" Jamie asks, taking the glass out of Tammy's hand. "Can I have a sip?"

"It's rum, tonic and lime juice," Tammy says. "We overheard somewhere that it's the new drink of the decade."

"Drink of the decade?" Bentley groans. "Oh, how horribly disgusting. What horribly disgusting person so named that measly little cocktail?"

"Actually it was Stella McCartney," Tammy says.

"Oh, she's wonderful," Bentley says, sitting up. "I love Stella—ooh, let me have a sip." He smacks his lips after tasting the drink. "Oh my god—I think Stella's right. This little baby *is* the new drink of the decade. Jamie—alert the media. Somebody—nab a publicist."

"I spent most of the day at the Elite Premier offices." Tammy yawns, leaning into Bruce. "Then lunch in Chelsea."

"Oh, where?" Bentley asks, studying a white rose.

"Aubergine," Tammy sighs. "I spent what could have been two hours in Vent and then I had drinks at the Sugar Club before coming here. Oh Jesus, what a day."

"I had that Craig McDean photo shoot," Bruce says, taking the joint back from Jamie. "Then I watched representation for the Spice Girls sign a gargantuan record deal and had an early dinner at Oxo Tower with Nick Knight, Rachel Whitehead and Danny Boyle."

"You're a man of substance." Jamie smiles.

"I'm a preeminent tastemaker." Bruce smiles back.

"You're sheer genius, baby," Tammy tells Jamie.

"And you're the fall's most revealing fashion trend," Bentley tells Tammy.

"A-list all the way," Bruce says, squeezing Tammy's hand.

"What is this?" I'm asking. "Night of the Perpetually Chic?"

"It looks like everybody's going somewhere, but they're not, really," Tammy says, looking around.

"Let's face it, the impression I get is: boom—this is over," Bruce says, finishing the roach.

Since the tape of "Friends" is being rerun, the Japanese guy has engaged two of his buddies to start looking at me and he's gesturing wildly and I'm trying to recall the ads I did that appeared in Japan but can't come up with any and Bruce is noticing my discomfort so he glances back at the Japanese guys and then Tammy and Jamie follow suit and I notice an almost imperceptible nod on Tammy's part that makes Bruce suggest, "Maybe, guys, it's time we escape."

Jamie leans into me and whispers, "Why don't you come with us?"

"Where are you guys going?" I ask as she helps me stand.

Tammy and Bruce lift Bentley up off the lime-green couch and Bentley sloshes around and they steady him and then guide his weaving body down a staircase.

"We're going back to our house."

"What's our house?"

"A place we all inhabit," she says. "Does that simplify matters for you?"

"Why don't you come back to the Four Seasons with me?"

"*You* may do whatever you want, Victor." Jamie leans in and kisses me so hard I back into a giant vase of white roses, my head pressed into them, petals brushing over my cheeks, my scalp, my neck.

"I'm just glad you're here," she purrs before guiding me downstairs to Bruce's Jaguar. "And safe," she adds quietly.

"All this persuasion," I moan.

9

Bruce races recklessly in a skillful way through London streets, Tammy in the front seat next to him lighting another joint, both of them occasionally eyeing us distantly in the rearview mirror, and even with the air-conditioning blasting the windows are steamed over and I'm between Bentley and Jamie and she's clinging to me in the darkness of the backseat and that Robert Miles song "One and One" is blasting out of the speakers and I'm hungrily kissing her lips, craving her in a way I never did at Camden, while also contending with Bentley, who keeps reaching over, brushing confetti off the Versace jacket I'm wearing, and every time I push him away he makes doomed noises and Jamie keeps stroking my dick, which is stiff and raging against my thigh, and I have to keep repositioning myself and finally my hand wraps around hers, guiding it, applying more pressure, and when I'm too lost in Jamie, that's when Bentley's hand sneaks in and grabs something in my pocket and rubbing it he starts making gratified noises and then, when he realizes it's just a roll of Mentos, there's another doomed noise.

As Bruce makes a sweeping U-turn, changing direction because of streets blocked off due to bomb threats in Trafalgar Square, Primal Scream's "Rocks Off" blasts out and the Jaguar speeds up, careening around a corner, noise from the song pouring over us, and the windows are rolled down, wind rushing in, and every time Jamie touches me I'm seeing blue and leaping around with desire and then she kicks off her shoes and swings her legs up over my thighs so her feet lie across Bentley's lap and I'm leaning down, lights from the city flashing around us.

"You're so beautiful," she's whispering to me as my head drops down to hers, my face burning.

One or two more traffic delays provoke cursing. Bentley quarrels briefly with Bruce until he finds a still of Matthew McConaughey romping in a stream that someone left in the backseat and Bentley ends up staring at it, occupied, and finally Bruce maneuvers the Jaguar into a driveway where a small gate slides open and when we pass through it a blinding light shoots out from points on the roof of the black house we've driven up to and then that light slowly fades as Bruce pulls out some kind of remote device and touches a few buttons and once it's dark everything vanishes except for the clouds in the open sky above us.

8 Inside the black house there's a doorway that I follow Jamie through and Bentley and Bruce and Tammy scatter, dispersing upstairs to bedrooms, and Jamie and I are in a dark place, and she's lighting candles and offering me a drink that smells like Sambuca and we both pop a Xanax to come off the coke before heading toward a hot bath in a room that smells of freshly painted walls where more candles are lit and Jamie tears off the Jil Sander suit and helps me undress, and she finally pulls my Calvin Klein boxer-jockeys off while I'm on the bathroom floor, delirious and giggling, my legs up in the air, Jamie standing over me, candlelight throwing her elongated shadow over the walls and ceiling, and my hand's reaching for her ass and then we're in the water.

After the bath she pushes me onto a sprawling bed and I'm drugged out and turned on and a Tori Amos CD plays softly in the background and then I'm lying on my side, marveling at her, my hand running along the sparse hair on her cunt, fingers slipping in and out, strumming along it, while I let her suck on my tongue.

"Listen," she keeps whispering, breaking away.

"What, baby?" I whisper back. "What is it?"

She doesn't want to fuck so she starts giving me head and I swing her around and start eating her pussy which is hot and tight and I'm taking it slow, licking with long strokes of my tongue, sometimes all the way up to her asshole spread above me, and then driving the tongue in deeper and faster, sometimes stiffening it, making my tongue rigid and fucking her with it, then taking as much of her pussy into my mouth as I can, sucking on the whole thing, and then I flick the tip of my tongue over her clit and that's when she sits up on my face, humping it while I reach up, massaging her nipples as she comes touching her clit with her middle finger, my mouth slobbering all over her hand, and she's making weeping sounds and when I come she tries to steady my hips with her chest because they're thrusting up involuntarily and with her hand pumping my cock I shoot all over her, ejaculating endlessly and so hard I have to bury my face and mouth back into her pussy to muffle the shouts my orgasm forces me to make and then I drop back, wetness from her vagina smeared all over my chin, lips, nose, and then it's silent except for my breathing. The CD that was playing has stopped, a few candles have burned out, I'm spinning.

In the darkness I hear her ask, "You came?"

"Yeah," I pant, laughing.

"Okay," she says, the bed making rustling noises as she gets off it, carefully holding up an arm as if she's afraid of dropping something.

"Hey baby—"

"Good night, Victor."

Jamie walks toward the door, swings it open, light from the hallway causes me to squint, shielding my eyes, and when she closes the door blackness blossoms out of control and still spinning I'm also moving upward toward something, a place where there's someone waiting to meet me, voices calling out *follow, follow*.

I'm waking up because of the sun streaming through the skylight and chic steel beams onto the bed where I'm staring at the geometric patterns etched on those chic steel beams. I tentatively sit up, bracing myself, but I've apparently slept off what should have been a major hangover. I check out the surroundings: a room done in ash gray and totally minimalist, a large steel vase filled with white tulips, lots of gorgeous chrome ashtrays scattered everywhere, a steel nightstand where a tiny black phone sits on a copy of next month's *Vanity Fair* with Tom Cruise on the cover, a Jennifer Bartlett painting hanging over the bed. I open a steel blind and peer out at what looks like a reasonably fashionable London street, though I'm not quite sure where. There are no clocks in the room so I have no idea what time it is but the way the clouds are racing past the sun above the skylight suggests it's not morning.

I call the Four Seasons asking for messages but there aren't any and a flicker of panic I think I can control starts spreading and I wash it off in the shower adjacent to the bedroom, the stall made up of pale-green and dark-gray tiles, and the bathtub Jamie and I used last night is drained, melted candles on its rim, Kiehl's products neatly lined up next to stainless-steel sinks. I dry off and take a Ralph Lauren bathrobe hanging from a hook and drape it over me before opening the door very slowly because I'm unsure of what's behind it.

6

I'm standing on what looks like the second floor of a three-story town house and everything is stark and functional and so open you can't really hide anywhere. I'm moving down a hallway—passing bedrooms, a study, two bathrooms, rows of empty shelves—heading toward a staircase that will take me to the first floor, and the color scheme incorporates aqua and apple and cream but ash dominates—the color of chairs and couches and comforters and desks and vases and the carpets lining the bleached oak floors—and then moving down the stairs, gripping the cold steel railing, I step into a huge open space divided in two by a series of tall steel columns and the floors are suddenly terrazzo and the windows are just cubes of opaque glass. There's a dining area where Frank Gehry chairs surround a giant Budeiri granite table below diffused lighting. There's a salmon-hued kitchen where shelves hang by steel rods and the vintage refrigerator contains yogurt, various cheeses, a tin of unopened caviar, Evian, half a round of focaccia; and in a cupboard, Captain Crunch, bottles of wine. The whole place seems transitory and it's freezing and I'm shivering uncontrollably and there's a profusion of cell phones piled on a fancy pink table and I'm thinking this is all too 1991.

The sound of Counting Crows on a stereo coming from the giant space in the middle of the house is what I'm moving toward and as I turn a steel column what comes into view is a massive pistachio-colored sofa and a big-screen TV with the volume off—Beavis and Butt-head sitting rigid—along with an unplugged pinball machine standing next to a long bar made of distressed granite where two backgammon boards sit and I'm coming up behind a guy wearing a USA Polo Sport sweatshirt and baggy gray shorts hiked up a little too high and he's leaning over a computer where diagrams of airplanes keep flashing across the blue screen and on that desk is an Hermès rucksack with a copy of a book by Guy Debord hanging out of it along with various manila envelopes someone's doodled drawings of caterpillars all over. The guy turns around.

"I am freezing," he shouts. "I am *fucking freezing.*"

Startled, I just nod and murmur, "Yeah . . . it's cold, man."

He's about six foot one with thick black hair cut very short and swept back, his impossibly natural-looking tan covering an underlying pink hue, and when I see those cheekbones I'm immediately thinking: Hey, that's Bobby Hughes. Dark-green eyes flash over at me and a bleachy white smile lifts up a chiseled jawline.

"Please allow me to introduce myself," he says, holding out a hand attached to a muscular forearm, bicep bulging involuntarily. "I'm Bobby."

"Hey man," I say, taking it. "I'm Victor."

"Sorry if I'm a little sweaty." He grins. "I was just down in the gym. But sweet Jesus it's cold in here. And I have no idea where the goddamn thermostat is."

"Oh?" I say, stuck, then try to nod. "I mean . . . *oh.*" Pause. "There's a gym . . . here?"

"Yeah"—he gestures with his head—"in the basement."

"Oh yeah?" I say, forcing myself to be more casual. "That's so cool . . . man."

"They're all at the store," he says, turning back to the computer, lifting a Diet Coke to his lips. "You're lucky you're here—Bruce is cooking tonight." He turns back around. "Hey, you want some breakfast? I think there's a bag of croissants in the kitchen somewhere and if Bentley didn't drink it, maybe some OJ left."

Pause. "Oh, that's okay, that's okay. I'm cool." I'm nodding vacantly.

"You want a Bloody Mary?" He grins. "Or maybe some Visine? Your eyes look a little red, my friend."

"No, no . . ." A pause, a shy smile, an inward breath, then exhaling, barely. "It's okay. It's cool."

"You sure, guy?" he asks.

"Um, yeah, uh-huh."

Expelled his first term from Yale for "unruly behavior," Bobby Hughes started modeling convincingly enough for Cerutti at eighteen to skyrocket from that gig into an overnight sensation. This was followed by becoming Armani's favorite model and then various million-dollar deals, sums unheard of for a man at that time. There was the famous Hugo Boss ad where Bobby was flipping off the camera, the tag line "Does Anybody Really Notice?" below him in red neon letters, and then the historic Calvin Klein commercial of just Bobby in his underwear looking vacant and coughing while a girl's voice-over whispered, "It will co-opt your ego," and when GQ still ran models on the cover, Bobby's face was there endlessly, dead-eyed and poised. He was the boytoy in two Madonna videos, the "sad lost guy" in a Belinda Carlisle clip and shirtless in countless others because he had a set of breathtaking abdominals before anyone was really paying attention to the torso, and he was probably the major force in starting that craze. During his career he walked thousands of runways, garnering the nickname "The Showstopper." He was on the cover of the Smiths' last album, *Unfortunately*. He had a fan club in Japan. He had great press, which always pushed the notion that beneath the drifting surfer-dude image Bobby Hughes was "alert" and had a "multifaceted personality." He was the highest-paid male model for a moment during the 1980s because he simply had the best features, the most sought-after look, the perfect body. His calendar sold millions.

He gave his last interview to *Esquire* during the winter of 1989, which was where he said, not at all defensively, "I know exactly what I'm going to do and where I'm going," and then he more or less just vacated the New York fashion scene—all this before my life in the city really began, before I was known as Victor Ward, before I met Chloe, before my world began to take shape and started to expand—and then the occasional grainy photograph of him would show up in certain European fashion magazines (Bobby Hughes attending an embassy party in Milan, Bobby Hughes standing in the rain on Wardour Street dressed in Paul Smith green, Bobby Hughes playing volleyball on the beach in Cannes or in the lobby at the Cap d'Antibes at dawn wearing a tuxedo and holding a cigarette, Bobby Hughes asleep in the bulkhead seats on the Concorde), and because he had stopped giving interviews there were always tabloid rumors about his engagement to Tiffani-Amber Thiessen or how he "almost" broke up Liz Hurley and Hugh Grant or how he *did* break up Emma Thompson and Kenneth Branagh. He supposedly had firsthand knowledge of certain S&M bars in Santa Monica. He supposedly was going to star in the sequel to *American Gigolo*. He supposedly had squandered the fortune he'd accumulated on failed restaurants, on horses and cocaine, on a yacht he named *Animal Boy*. He supposedly was heading back to modeling at an age that was considered "iffy" at best. But he never did.

And now he's here in the flesh—four years older than me, just a foot away, tapping keys on a computer terminal, sipping Diet Coke, wearing white athletic socks—and since I'm not really used to being around guys who are so much better-looking than Victor Ward, it's all kind of nerve-racking and I'm listening more intently to him than to any man I've ever met because the unavoidable fact is: he's too good-looking to resist. He can't help but lure.

"Um, I'm kind of lost," I start, hesitantly. "Where . . . exactly am I?"

"Oh." He looks up, stares straight at me, blinks once or twice, then decides something. "You're in Hampstead."

"Oh yeah?" I say, relieved. "My friend Joaquin Phoenix—you know, River's brother?"

Bobby nods, staring intently.

"Well, he's shooting the new John Hughes movie in, um, Hampstead," I say, suddenly feeling ridiculous in this robe. "I think," I add, a little stressed.

"Oh, that's cool," Bobby says, turning back to the computer.

"Yeah, we saw him at the party last night."

"Hey, how was that party?" he asks. "I'm sorry I missed it."

"The party was, well . . ." Nervously, I try to explain. "Let's see, who was there? Well, it was in Notting Hill—"

"Of course," he says derisively, which almost puts me at ease.

"Oh gosh, I know, man, I know." Stuck, just staring at him as he glances back at the computer screen, I tighten the robe around me.

"It was for the painter Gary Hume, right?" he asks, coaxing.

"Oh yeah," I say. "But everyone knew it was really for Patsy and Liam."

"Right, right," he says, tapping three keys and rapidly calling onto the screen more airplane diagrams. "Who was there? What luminaries showed up?"

"Well, um, Kate Moss and Stella Tennant and Iris Palmer and I think Jared Leto and Carmen Electra and, um, Damon Albarn and . . . we drank orange punch and . . . I got pretty wasted . . . and there were lots of . . . ice sculptures."

"Yeah?"

"Where were you, man?" I ask, finally easing into a more comfortable vibe.

"I was in Paris."

"Modeling?"

"Business," he says simply.

"But not modeling?"

"No, that's all over," he says, checking something in a notebook that lies open next to the computer. "I completed that part of my life."

"Oh yeah man," I say, nodding. "I know what you mean."

"Really?" He grins, looking over his shoulder. "Do you?"

"Yeah." I shrug. "I'm thinking of calling it quits too."

"So what are you doing in London, then, Victor?" Bobby asks.

"Off the record?"

"Modeling?" He grins again.

"Oh spare me, man, *spare me*," I laugh. "No way—I mean, I really want to get out of that, branch out."

"It's a very rough life, right?"

"Man, it's so hard."

"Potentially devastating."

"I'm just kicking back and taking a breather."

"I think that's a smart move."

"Yeah?"

"It can ruin people. I've seen people destroyed."

"Me too, man. I am so with you."

"I have no stomach for it," he says. "I have absolutely no stomach for it."

"But . . . you have, like, a great stomach, man," I say, confused.

"What?" Bobby looks down at himself, realizes where I'm coming from and starts smiling, his confused expression turning sweet. "Oh, right. Thanks. Hmm."

"So when did you get in?" I ask, beginning the bonding process.

"This morning," he yawns, stretching. "How about you?"

"A couple days ago," I tell him.

"You came in from New York?"

"Yeah man."

"What's New York like these days?" he asks, concentrating on the screen again. "I'm rarely there. And what I read about I'm not sure I can handle. Maybe I'm just all grown up or something."

"Oh, y'know, it's all kind of, um, bogus, man," I say. "Young people are such idiots, you know what I'm saying?"

"People applauding madly as supermodels gyrate down runways? No thanks, man."

"Oh man, I am so with you."

"What do you do there?"

"The usual. Modeling. I helped open a club last week." I pause. "I'm up for a part in *Flatliners II*."

"God, it's freezing," he shouts again, hugging himself. "Are you cold too?"

"I'm a little chilly," I concede.

He pads out of the room and from somewhere in the house he yells, "Where is the fucking heater in this place?" and then he calls out, "Should we start a fire?"

CDs scattered on top of one of the giant speakers include Peter Gabriel, John Hiatt, someone named Freedy Johnston, the last Replacements album. Outside, through glass doors, a small terrace is surrounded by a garden filled with white tulips, and tiny birds congregate on a steel fountain, and as the wind picks up and shadows start crossing the lawn they decide something's wrong and fly away in unison.

"So who lives here?" I ask as Bobby pads back into the room. "I mean, I know it's a set, but it's pretty nice."

"Well, sometimes I rent it from someone," he says as he heads toward the computer and studies the screen. "And right now I'm sharing it with Tammy and Bruce, who I think you've met."

"Yeah, they're cool."

"And Bentley Harrolds, who's an old friend of mine, and Jamie Fields, whom"—a pause, without looking up at me—"I take it you know from college."

"Yeah, yeah." I'm nodding. "Right. She's cool too."

"Yeah," Bobby says wearily, flicking off the screen, sighing. "We're all pretty damn cool."

I consider going somewhere, debate, then decide to press ahead.

"Bobby?"

"Yeah?" He's looking over at me again.

"I just want to, um, let you know that—this is going to sound *really* corny—but you were"—I take a deep breath—"a really, like, a really, like an inspiration to a lot of us and you were like a major influence and I just want to let you know that." I pause, look away, distressed, my eyes watering. "Did I just sound totally weird?"

Silence, then, "No. No, you didn't, Victor." He's staring at me warmly. "It's good. I like it. Thank you."

Relief washes over me, my throat tightens, and with difficulty, my voice totally strained, I manage, "No problem, man."

Voices outside in the yard. A gate opens, then closes. Four gorgeous people dressed in black, wearing sunglasses and carrying chic grocery bags, move through the darkening garden and toward the house. Bobby and I watch them from behind the glass doors.

"Ah, the troops return," Bobby says.

I wave at Jamie as the group walks toward the expanse of window I'm standing behind, but no one waves back. Bentley scowls, flicking away a cigarette. Bruce, holding two bags piled high with groceries, playfully nudges Tammy off the stone path. Jamie strides forward, staring straight ahead impassively, chewing gum.

"Why can't they see me?" I'm asking.

"That's one-way glass," Bobby says.

"Oh," I say. "That's . . . cool."

The four of them stagger through a back entrance and into the kitchen, a series of small electronic beeps sounding as someone closes the door. Turning, Bobby and I watch as they drop grocery bags on a large steel counter. We move closer, hitting our marks. Jamie is the first to see us and she whips off her sunglasses, smiling.

"So you're awake," Jamie says, walking toward us.

I smile at her and as she heads toward me I start expecting a kiss and I close my eyes, bouncing lightly up and down on the soles of my feet. A small rush of lust starts gaining momentum and then gets out of control, shoots out all over the place. But Jamie passes by and I open my eyes and turn around.

She and Bobby are embracing and he's kissing her hungrily, making noises. It takes too long for Jamie to notice me standing there staring, and as she pulls back a little Bobby hangs on and won't let go.

"You guys meet?" is all Jamie can ask after taking in the expression on my face.

"Yeah." I nod.

"Hey, let go," Jamie squeals, pushing Bobby off her. "Let go, let go."

But Bobby doesn't—he just keeps leaning in, kissing her face, her neck. I just stand there watching, hot, suddenly clearheaded.

"I think it's cocktail hour," Bentley says, pouting.

Tammy walks by where I'm standing. "We ran into Buffy. She just got back from climbing Everest. There were two deaths. She lost her cell phone."

I have no idea who this is directed at, so I just slowly nod my head.

"Hey, I'm ravenous," Bobby says, still holding Jamie in his arms, but she's not struggling anymore. "When are we eating?" he calls out. "*What* are we eating?" Then he whispers something into Jamie's ear and she giggles and then slaps his arms, grabbing at them with both hands where his biceps bulge.

"I'm making bruschetta," Bruce calls out from the kitchen. "Porcini risotto, prosciutto and figs, arugula and fennel salad."

"Hurry," Bobby bellows, nuzzling Jamie's face, squeezing her tighter. "Hurry, Bruce. I'm *starving*."

"Victor, what are you wearing under that robe?" Bentley asks, staring at me, holding a bottle of Stoli. "Wait—don't tell me. I don't think I can han-dle it." Walking back into the kitchen, he calls out, "I have your underwear, by the way."

"I'm taking a bath," Tammy says, batting her gray eyes at me. "You look remarkably put-together considering last night's carousing." She pouts, pushes her lips out. "It *is* five o'clock, though."

"Good genes." I shrug.

"Nice robe," she says, drifting upstairs.

"Hey, it's freezing in here," Bobby says, finally letting go of Jamie.

"Then get dressed," she says bitterly, walking away. "And get over yourself as well."

"Hey!" Bobby says, mock-stunned, his mouth opening, his jaw dropping in a parody of shock. He lunges toward her and Jamie squeals, delighted, and dashes into the kitchen and I'm seeing everything clearly, noticing that I've been standing in the same place for the last several minutes. Bentley calls out, "Be careful, Bobby—Jamie's got a gun."

And then Jamie's walking up to me, out of breath. Behind her Bobby's tearing through groceries, conferring with Bruce. Bentley asks one of them to taste a fresh batch of martinis.

"Where are my clothes?" I ask her.

"In the closet," she sighs. "In the bedroom."

"You guys make a really great couple," I tell her.

"Are all the doors locked?" Bobby's calling out.

Jamie mouths *I'm sorry* to me and turns away.

Bobby's moving around, slaps Jamie's ass as he walks past making sure everything's secure.

"Hey?" he asks somebody. "Did you forget to turn the alarms on again?"

5   As the sun goes down the crew gets shots of a flawless dusk sky before it turns black while the house inside brightens and the six of us—Bentley and Tammy and Bruce and Jamie and Bobby and myself—are slouching in the Frank Gehry chairs that surround the granite table in the dining area and I'm hanging back shyly as two handheld cameras circle us, creating a montage. Then plates and wine bottles are being passed around and despite the Bobby-Hughes-as-stumbling-block-to-$300,000-factor I start feeling peaceful and accepting and in the mood for anything and the constant attention these new friends are pushing my way makes me start ignoring certain things, especially the way Jamie's eyes widen as they move back and forth between me and Bobby, sometimes cheerfully, other times not. I'm fielding questions about Chloe—the table genuinely impressed I was her boyfriend—and the *YouthQuake* cover and the band I quit and my workout routine and various muscle supplements and no one asks "Who are you?" or "Where are you from?" or "What do you want?"—questions that aren't pertinent because they all seem to know. Bentley even mentions press he read about last week's club opening that made it into London papers and he promises to show me the clippings later, no innuendo attached.

Winking, private glances, general sassiness toward Felix and the director, but no smirking since we're all basically advertising ourselves and in the end we're all linked because we "get it." And I'm trying very hard to stay unimpressed as the conversation revolves around the peaks and valleys of everyone's respective press, where we were during the 1980s, what this will all look like on a movie screen. Groaning compliments to Bruce about the risotto segue into talk about that bombing of a hotel in Paris on Boulevard Saint-Germain two days ago while U2's *Achtung Baby* plays softly in the background and we ask each other if anyone we knew in L.A. was injured during the recent rash of earthquakes. It's warmer in the house now.

And for long stretches of time it feels like I'm back in New York, maybe at Da Silvano at a great table, somewhere in front, a photographer waiting outside in the cold on Sixth Avenue until decaf espressos are finished and the last round of Sambuca is ordered, Chloe tiredly picking up the check and maybe Bobby's there too. Right now, tonight, Bobby's quieter than the others but he seems happening and fairly content and every time I make sure to fill his wineglass with an excellent Barbaresco he keeps thanking me with a nod and a relaxed smile, his eyes lingering on mine, only sometimes distracted by the lights and cameras and various assistants swirling around us. Party invitations for tonight are discussed then dismissed and people opt for home because everyone's tired. Bruce lights a cigar. Tammy and Jamie prepare massive joints. Everyone's drifting away as I start clearing the table.

In the kitchen Bobby taps me on the shoulder.

"Hey Victor," he asks. "Can you do me a favor?"

"Sure, man," I say, wiping my hands on the most expensive dish towel I've ever held. "Anything."

"I was supposed to meet a friend who's going to stay here this weekend," Bobby begins.

"Yeah?"

"I'm supposed to pick him up around ten," Bobby says, moving closer, glancing at his watch. "But I'm totally beat."

"Man, you look great but"—I cock my head while searching his face for flaws—"maybe a little tired."

"If I called a car for you, could you go to Pylos—"

"Pylos? Hey, cool."

"—and pick him up for me?" Bobby's standing so close I can feel his breath. "I hate asking you but they're all fairly wasted." He gestures with his head at Tammy and Bruce and Bentley and Jamie, rolling around halfway behind the steel columns in front of the giant TV set, arguing over which video to watch. "I noticed you didn't really drink tonight," Bobby says. "So I'm assuming that maybe you wouldn't mind going."

"Well, I'm a *little* shaky from last night but—"

"Yeah, last night," Bobby murmurs, momentarily far away.

"So where's this club?" I ask quickly, redirecting him.

"The driver knows where it is," Bobby says. "He'll wait outside Pylos with the car. Just let the doorman know that you're my guest and Sam will be in the VIP room."

"Why don't you just put me on the guest list?"

"Victor, this place is so fashionable you can't get in even if you're *on* the guest list."

"How will I know who Sam is?" I ask hesitantly.

"He's Asian and small and his name is Sam Ho. Believe me, you'll know him when you see him," Bobby explains. "He's a little, uh, theatrical."

"Okay, guy." I shrug, genuinely confused. "Who is he?" And then, "Are you guys planning to party later?"

"No, no—he doesn't deal drugs," Bobby says. "Haven't you heard of Sam Ho?" Bobby asks. "He's a superfamous Asian model."

"Uh-huh, cool." I'm nodding.

"Hey, don't worry," he says. "It's not an improbable meeting. It's in the script."

"Oh, I know, I know," I say, trying to assure him.

"Here." Bobby hands me an envelope that I didn't notice he was holding. "Give this to Sam. He'll know what it means. And then I'll see you guys back here."

"Cool, cool."

"I hate like hell to do this, man, but I'm just wiped out."

"Hey Bobby," I say, "stop beating yourself up. I'll go. I've been wanting to go to Pylos since it opened—what? Four weeks ago, right?"

"It's sort of on again, off again."

Bobby walks me outside into the misty night, where a black limousine waits at the curb and Felix has already set up the next shot.

Bobby looks into my eyes. "I really appreciate this, Victor."

"No, man, I'm honored."

"Can we do that again?" the director asks. "Victor—put an emphasis on *I'm*. Okay, go ahead—we're still rolling."

Bobby looks into my eyes. "I really appreciate this, Victor," he says with even more feeling.

"No, man, *I'm* honored."

"You rule, man."

"No, man, *you* rule."

"Uh-uh. *You* rule, Victor."

"I can't believe that Bobby Hughes is telling me *I* rule," I gasp, pausing to take in a breath. "No, *you* rule."

Bobby hugs me and when he's about to step away I keep hugging, unable to stop.

The driver moves in to open the passenger door and I recognize him as the guy who picked me up in Southampton (a scene that will be cut). He has red hair and seems cool.

"Hey Victor," Bobby calls before I get into the limo.

"Yeah, man?" I ask, turning around.

"Do you speak French?" he asks, just a shadow standing in the darkness outside the house.

It takes me thirty seconds to form the words "Un . . . petit peu."

"Good," he says, disappearing. "Neither do any of us, really."

And then the evening leads to its logical conclusion.

4 In the limo heading toward Charing Cross Road Everything But the Girl's "Wrong" plays while I'm studying the small white envelope Bobby gave me to hand over to Sam Ho and there's the raised outline of a key folded inside a note but because I respect Bobby I don't even consider opening it and then it's 11 p.m. and the limo turns into a rainy alley where a sign reads DANCETERIA followed by a wobbly arrow that directs us to the back door of Pylos. Figures under umbrellas flock around a rope and behind that rope the proverbial "big guy"—this one wearing a Casely Hayford Chinese shirt, a Marie Antoinette wig and a black jacket with the words HELL BENT stitched over the heart in red— yells into a megaphone "Nobody else is coming in!" but then he spots me as I'm jumping out of the limo and as I approach an empty space that opens up for me the bouncer leans in and I say "I'm a guest of Bobby Hughes."

The guy nods and lifts the rope while whispering something into a walkie-talkie and I'm whisked up the steps, and just inside the door a young-model type with the dress code down pat ('70s Vivienne Westwood and a fake-fur coat) and obviously immediately infatuated leads me to the VIP room through various corridors and walkways blinking with infrared lights, fashion students trancing out on flickering patterns splattered across the walls, and lower in the club it's suddenly more humid and we're passing groups of teenagers united over computer screens and dealers peddling tabs of Ecstasy, and then the floor drops away and we're on a steel catwalk and beneath us a giant dance floor teems with a monster crowd and we pass a DJ booth with four turntables and some legendary DJ spinning seamless ambient drum and bass—rhythmic and booming—along with his apprentice, who's this widely praised Jamaican kid, and their set is being played live on various pirate radio stations throughout England tonight and all the gold-electric light strobing out of control everywhere causes the rooms we keep moving through to spin around and I'm about to lose my balance just as my guide ushers me past two hulking goons and into the VIP room and when I try to make conversation with her—"Quite a popular venue, huh?"—she just turns away, muttering "I'm booked."

Behind the curtains it's a mock–airport lounge but with discoey white lights and burgundy velvet booths, a giant poster stretches across a black wall with the word BREED in purple spectral lettering and dozens of UK record-company executives in Mad Max gear hang out with tattooed models from Holland and managing directors from Polygram share bananas and sip psybertronic drinks with magazine editors and half of a progressive British hip-hop act wearing schoolgirl uniforms is dancing with modeling agency bookers along with ghosts, extras, insiders, various people from the world at large. Paparazzi hunt for celebs. It's freezing in the VIP room and everyone's breath steams.

I order a Tasmanian beer from the bug-eyed bartender wearing a velour tuxedo who unashamedly tries to sell me a joint laced with Special K as he lights my cigarette, wild fluorescent patterns spiraling across the mirrored wall behind him while Shirley Bassey sings the "Goldfinger" theme and an endless reel of Gap ads flashes on various video monitors.

In the mirrored wall I immediately spot the Christian Bale–looking guy who followed me into Masako yesterday standing next to me and I whirl around and start talking to him and he's annoyed and pulling away but the director takes me aside and hisses, "Sam Ho's an *Asian*, you nitwit."

"Hey man, I know, I know," I say, holding my hands up. "It's cool. It's cool."

"Then who is *that*?" the director asks, nodding over at the Christian Bale guy.

"I thought he was in the movie," I say. "I thought you guys casted him."

"I've never seen him before in my life," the director snaps.

"He's a buddy of, um, mine," I say, waving over at him. The Christian Bale guy looks at me like I'm insane and turns back to his beer.

"Over *there*," the director says. "Sam Ho's over *there*."

A fairly beautiful Asian kid about my age, slight with blond hair and black roots, wearing sunglasses, sweaty and humming to himself, leans against the bar waiting for the bartender, repeatedly wiping his nose with the hand that's waving cash. He's wearing a tie-dyed T-shirt, inside-out Levi's 501s, a Puffer jacket and Caterpillar boots. Sighing to myself, thinking, Oh dear, I make my way over to where Sam Ho's standing and the first time I glance at him he notices and smiles to himself but then the bartender glides by, ignoring him, causing Sam to start dancing up and down in a frustrated jig. Sam lowers the sunglasses and glares at me as if it's my fault. I look away but not before noticing the word SLAVE tattooed on the back of his hand.

"Oh, stop being so elusive," he groans theatrically, in a heavy accent.

"Hey, are you Sam Ho?" I ask. "Like, the model?"

"You're cute but I think also brain-fried," he says without looking at me.

"Far out," I say, undeterred. "Isn't this place great?"

"I could quite happily live here," Sam says, bored. "And it's not even rave night."

"It's changing the definition of what a hip night out means, huh?"

"Stop holding out on me, baby," Sam shouts at the bartender as he races by again, juggling three bottles of Absolut Citron.

"So what's the story?" I'm asking. "When's Fetish Evening?"

"*Every* evening is Fetish Evening in clubland, darling," Sam groans, and then, glancing sideways at me, asks, "Am I being sought after?" He checks out my wrist. "Nice arm veins."

"Thanks. They're mine," I say. "Listen, if you *are* Sam Ho, I have a message for you from someone."

"Oh?" Sam's interest perks up. "Are you a little errand boy?"

"Dirty deeds and they're done dirt cheap."

"Oh, and you quote AC/DC lyrics too," Sam says faux-sweetly. "Who wants to give me a message?"

"Bobby Hughes," I say flatly.

Suddenly Sam Ho is in my face, standing so close I have to back away, almost tipping over. "Hey!" I warn.

"What?" Sam's asking, grabbing me. "Where? Where is he? Is he here?"

"Hey, watch the *shirt*!" I cry out, removing his hand from the collar, gently pushing him away. "No, I'm here instead."

"Oh, sorry," Sam says, backing off a little. "You're very, very cute—whoever you are—but you are *no* Bobby Hughes." A pause, then Sam seems crestfallen and panicked. "You two aren't a duo—are you?"

"Hey, watch it, Sam," I snap. "I've got a very strong reputation and *no*."

"Where is he?" Sam demands. "Where's Bobby?"

"Here," I say, handing him the envelope. "I'm just here to give you this and—"

Sam's not listening to me. He tears the envelope open greedily and pulls out the key and squints while reading the note and then he starts shivering

uncontrollably and hugging himself, a beatific smile softening the angles of
his face, making him seem less queeny, slightly more serene, not so jumpy.
In seconds he's matured.

"Oh—my—God," Sam's saying, lost, holding the note against his chest.
"Oh my god—he's *essential*."

"That's a fan talking," I point out.

"Can I buy you a drink?" Sam asks. "Let me guess—a yuppie beer with a
lime stuffed in it?"

"The name's Victor," I point out. "Victor Ward."

"Victor, you're the spitting image of a boy I always wanted to fuck in high
school but never had the nerve to approach." To calm himself down he
lights a Marlboro and exhales dramatically.

"I find that hard to believe, Sam," I sigh. "So, like, spare me, okay?"

"Are you staying with Bobby?" he asks suspiciously.

"Yeah," I say, shrugging. "He's a friend."

"No—he's a god, *you're* the friend," Sam corrects. "Are you in the house
on Charlotte Road?"

"Er, no, we're in Hampstead."

"Hampstead?" Sam looks back at the note. "But it says here you're on
Charlotte Road."

"I only stay in hotels," I tell him. "So I'm really not sure where we are." I
pause, stub out my cigarette. "It's just a set anyway."

"Okay." Sam breathes in. "Do you have a car, and please say yes because
I don't want to have to hijack a cab."

"Actually," I say, "I have a car and driver out back."

"Oh, this is excellent," Sam says. "But we have to elude someone."

"Who?" I ask, glancing around the VIP room.

"Those guys," Sam says, nodding his head. "Don't look, don't look.
They're under that gold arch—over there. They just love to play games
with me."

What looks like two bodyguards dressed in identical Armani overcoats
stand close together not even conferring with each other beneath a blue
light that accentuates the size of already enormous heads and they're being
cruised by various fashion victims but their arms are crossed and they don't
seem distracted. Their focus is on Sam, at the bar, leaning in to me.

"Who are they?"

"My father's idea," Sam says. "He's not happy about certain elements of
my life."

"He has you followed?" I'm asking, stunned. "Jesus, and I thought my
dad was a major fussbudget."

"I'm going to tell them I need to use the rest room and then"—he raps
his fingers against my chest—"ooh, nice pecs—that I'm going home with

you." He stuffs the envelope into his pocket. "They're usually too scared to enter the men's room with me—for the *obvious* reasons." Sam checks his watch and takes a deep breath. "I will tell them—before I disappear into the night—that I'm coming back after a much-needed piss to take *you* home with *me*, my little freak. Got it?"

"I—I guess that's, um, cool," I say, making a face.

"What color is the car?"

"It's a black limo," I say, trying not to look over at the bodyguards. "A guy with red hair is driving."

"Fabulous," Sam gushes. "I will see you out there. And remember— *hurry*. They look bulky but they can *move*."

"Are you sure this is all right?"

"I'm twenty-six," Sam says. "I can do what I want. Let's *boogie*."

"Um."

"Be careful on your way out," Sam says. "One of them usually carries a bottle of hydrochloric acid and is basically very stern." Sam pauses. "They used to work at the Israeli embassy."

"Is that a club?"

Sam Ho stops smiling and relaxes and touches the side of my face tenderly. "You're so mainstream," he murmurs.

I'm in the middle of telling him, "Hey, I'm just a very *quiet* clubgoer— but I'm very tuned in," when he runs over to the bodyguards, points at me and says something that causes Bodyguard #1 to seriously blanch and then they both nod reluctantly as Sam scampers out of the room and Bodyguard #2 nods at #1 and follows Sam while Bodyguard #1 turns his attention to me, staring, and I turn away looking like I'm figuring out what I should be doing, hopelessly play with a Marlboro.

I glance over at the Christian Bale guy, who's still standing just a foot away at the bar, and leaning in, I ask, "Are we in the same movie?" He just starts scowling.

On cue, a girl sitting in one of the burgundy velvet booths yells her approval when Iggy Pop's "Lust for Life" blasts out and she jumps up onto a platform, tearing off a Stussy dress and an Adidas T-shirt and in only her bra and Doc Martens starts thrashing around, twisting, doing what looks like the breaststroke, and at the precise moment Bodyguard #1 glances over at her a production assistant I didn't notice before cues me by whispering, "*Now*. Go, now!" and I casually pogo out of the VIP room while all the extras cheer.

3 In the alley outside Pylos I jump over the rope and tumble into a crowd of hip-hop enthusiasts waiting in the rain to gain entrance and once I've pushed through them I spin around to see if either of the bodyguards has followed me but I think I lost them when I pretended to duck into a DJ booth. Sam's already in the limo, sticking his head out the window, calling "Hey! Hey!" as I sprint over to the car and yell "Hurry!" to the driver. The limo skids out of the alley and into Charing Cross Road, horns echoing behind us, and Sam has broken into the minibar, popping open a split of champagne, drinking straight from the bottle and finishing it in less than a minute while I just stare tiredly and then he starts shouting at the driver, "Go faster go faster, *go faster!*" and keeps trying to hold my hand. In his calmer moments Sam shows me his crystals, demands LSD, hands me a pamphlet about brain-wave harmonizers, sings along to "Lust for Life" as it bursts from speakers in the back of the limo and he's drinking deeply from a bottle of Absolut and shouting "I'm a pillhead!" while sticking his head out the sunroof as the limo races through the drizzle back to the house.

"I'm seeing Bobby, I'm seeing Bobby," he singsongs, blitzed out, bouncing up and down on the seat.

I light a cigarette, trying to perfect my scowling. "Can you *please* mellow out?"

The limousine stops in front of the darkened house and then, once the gate opens, slowly pulls into the driveway. The roof lights immediately flash on, blinding us even through the limousine's tinted windows, then slowly fade.

Sam Ho opens the door and jumps out drunkenly, shambling toward the darkness of the house. At an upstairs window a silhouette appears, peering from behind a blind, and then the light goes out. "Hey Sam," I call, swinging my legs out of the limo. "There's an alarm system—be careful." But he's gone. Above us the sky has cleared and there's really nothing up there except for half a moon.

The driver waits for me to step from the limo and I'm suddenly surprised by how tired I am. I get out of the car and stretch, and then, just standing there, avoiding the house and what's going on within it, light a cigarette.

"Were we followed?" I ask the driver.

"No." He shakes his head curtly.

"Are you sure?" I ask.

"The second unit took care of it," he says.

"Hmm." I take a drag off the cigarette, flick it away.

"Is there anything else I can do for you?" he asks.

I consider the offer. "No. No, I don't think so."

"Well then, good night." The driver closes the door I just stepped out of and walks around the car, back to the driver's side.

"Hey," I call out.

He glances up.

"Do you know a guy named Fred Palakon?"

The driver stares at me until he loses interest and looks elsewhere.

"Right," I say tensely. "O-kay."

I open a gate and then it closes automatically behind me and then I'm walking through the darkened garden while REM's "How the West Was Won" plays and above me, in the house, the lights in some of the windows don't reveal anything. The back door that leads into the kitchen is half-open and after I've walked in and closed it there's that series of electronic beeps. I move uncertainly through the space—nobody's downstairs, there's no sign of the crew, everything's spotless. I pull an Evian out of the fridge. A video— the end of *Die Hard 2*—silently plays on the giant TV, credits roll, then the tape starts rewinding itself. I brush confetti off the giant pistachio-colored sofa and lie down, waiting for someone to appear, occasionally glancing toward the stairs leading up to the bedrooms, listening intently, but hear only the whirring of the tape being rewound and the REM song fading. I vaguely imagine Jamie and Bobby together, maybe even with Sam Ho, in bed, and there's a pang; but after that, nothing.

A script lies on the coffee table and absently I pick it up, open it to a random page, an odd scene, descriptions of Bobby calming someone down, feeding me a Xanax, I'm weeping, people are getting dressed for another party, a line of dialogue ("what if you became something you were not") and my eyes are closing. "Fall asleep," is what I imagine the director would whisper.

2 Wakened suddenly out of a brief dreamless nap by someone calling "Action" softly (though when I open my eyes and look around the living room there's no one here), I get off the couch, noticing vacantly that the script I fell asleep reading has disappeared. I pick up the Evian bottle, take a long, deep swallow and carry it with me as I move uncertainly through the house, past spaces where someone has turned off various lights while I was sleeping. In the kitchen I'm staring into the refrigerator for what seems like days, unsure of what to do, when there's a strange noise below me—a rapid thumping sound, followed by maybe a muffled wail, and at the same instant the lights in the kitchen dim once, then twice. I look up, quietly say "Hello" to myself. Then it happens again.

Because of the way the set is lit, a door I never noticed in a hallway adjacent to the kitchen practically glows now. A framed Calvin Klein poster covers the top half: Bobby Hughes on a beach, shirtless, white Speedos, impossibly brown and hard, not seeing a near-naked Cindy Crawford standing next to him because he's looking directly into the camera, at you. Drawn to it, I run my hand along the glass it's encased in and the door slowly swings open onto a staircase dotted with confetti and my breath immediately starts steaming because of how freezing it suddenly is and then I'm moving down the stairs, gripping the icy railing, heading toward the bottom. Another thump, the strange faraway wailings, the lights dimming again.

Belowground I'm moving down a plain, undecorated hallway, one arm extended, fingers trailing along the cold brick wall that lines this corridor, humming to myself—*hush hush, keep it down now, voices carry*—and I'm heading toward a door with another Calvin Klein poster on it, another beach scene, another shot of Bobby proudly baring his abdominals, another beautiful girl ignored behind him, and in a matter of seconds I'm standing in front of it, straining to assemble the vague noises I'm hearing on a sound track where the volume's too low. There's a handle, something I'm supposed to turn, and piles of confetti are scattered all over the concrete floor.

Vacantly, in this instant, I'm thinking of my mother and the George Michael concert I attended just days after she died, the azaleas on the block we lived on in Georgetown, a party where no one was crying, the hat Lauren Hynde gave me in New York, the tiny red rose on that hat. A final sip of Evian and I turn the handle, shrugging, the lights dimming once again.

"It's what you don't know that matters most," the director said.

Movement behind me. I turn around as the door opens.

Jamie's walking toward me quickly, dressed in sweats, her hair pulled back, wearing yellow rubber gloves that run all the way up to her elbows.

I smile at her.

"*Victor*," she shouts. "No—*don't*—"

The door swings open.

I turn, confused, looking into the room.

Jamie yells something garbled behind me.

Fitness equipment has been pushed aside into the corners of what looks like a soundproofed room and a mannequin made from wax covered in either oil or Vaseline, slathered with it, lies twisted on its back in some kind of horrible position on a steel examination table, naked, both legs spread open and chained to stirrups, its scrotum and anus completely exposed, both arms locked back behind its head, which is held up by a rope connected to a hook in the ceiling.

Somebody wearing a black ski mask is sitting in a swivel chair next to the examination table, screaming at the mannequin in what sounds like Japanese.

Bruce sits nearby, staring intently at a metal box, his hands poised over the two levers that protrude from either side.

Bentley Harrolds camcords the proceedings—the camera aimed solely at the mannequin.

I'm smiling, confused, weirded out at how focused Bentley seems and shocked at how gruesome and inauthentic the waxwork looks.

The figure in the black ski mask keeps shouting in Japanese, then signals to Bruce.

Bruce nods grimly and moves his hand to a lever, pressing it, causing lights to flicker, and in a flash my eyes move from the wires connected to the box over to where they have actually been inserted into gashes and cuts on what I'm just realizing are the mannequin's nipples, fingers, testicles, ears.

The mannequin springs grotesquely to life in the freezing room, screeching, arching its body up, again and again, lifting itself off the examination table, tendons in its neck straining, and purple foam starts pouring out of its anus, which also has a wire, larger, thicker, inserted into it. Bunched around the wheels on the table legs are white towels spotted heavily with blood, some of it black. What looks like an intestine is slowly emerging, of its own accord, from another, wider slit across the mannequin's belly.

There is, I'm noticing, no camera crew around.

I drop the Evian bottle, startled, causing Bentley to glance over at where I'm standing.

Behind me, Jamie screams, *"Get him out of here!"*

Sam Ho is making noises I have never heard another person make before, and in between these arias of pain he's screaming, "I'm sorry I'm sorry I'm sorry," and the figure in the swivel chair rolls out of view of the camcorder and takes off the ski mask.

Sweaty and exhausted, Bobby Hughes mutters—I'm not sure to whom—the words "Kill him" and then, to Bentley, "Keep rolling."

Bruce stands and with a small sharp knife swiftly slices off Sam Ho's penis. He dies screaming for his mother, blood shooting out of him like a fountain until there's none left.

Somebody cuts the lights.

I'm trying to leave the room but Bobby blocks my exit and my eyes are closed and I'm chanting "please man please man please man," hyperventilating, breaking out into sobs. Someone who might be Jamie is attempting to hug me.

1

"Victor," Bobby's saying. "Victor, come on . . . come on, man, it's cool. Stand up—that's it."

We're in one of the ash-gray bedrooms upstairs. I'm on the floor hugging Bobby's legs, convulsing, unable to stop myself from moaning. Bobby keeps feeding me Xanax and for short stretches of time the shuddering subsides. But then I'm in the bathroom—Bobby waiting patiently outside—vomiting until I'm just gagging up spit, retching. When I'm through I lie there in a fetal position, my face pressed against the tiles, breathing erratically, hoping he'll leave me alone. But then he's kneeling beside me, whispering my name, trying to prop me up, and I keep clutching him, weeping. He places another pill in my mouth and leads me back into the bedroom, where he forces me to sit on the bed while he leans over me. Sometime during all this my shirt came off, and I keep clawing at my chest, grabbing myself so hard that patches of skin are reddened, on the verge of bruising.

"Shhh," he says. "It's okay, Victor, it's okay."

"It's not okay," I blurt out, sobbing. "It's not okay, Bobby."

"No, it *is*, Victor," Bobby says. "It's cool. You're gonna be cool, okay?"

"Okay," I'm sniffling. "Okay okay man."

"Good, that's good," Bobby says. "Just keep breathing in like that. Just relax."

"Okay man, okay man."

"Now listen to me," Bobby says. "There are some things that you need to know." He's handing me a tissue, which I can't help tearing apart the second my fingers touch it.

"I just want to go home," I'm whimpering, shutting my eyes tight. "I just want to go home, man."

"But you can't," Bobby says soothingly. "You can't go home, Victor." Pause. "That isn't going to happen."

"Why not?" I ask, like a child. "Please, man—"

"Because—"

"I swear to God I won't tell anyone, Bobby," I say, finally able to look at him, wiping my eyes with the tattered Kleenex, shuddering again. "I swear to God I won't say anything."

"No, you won't," Bobby says patiently, his tone changing slightly. "I know that. I already know that, Victor."

"Okay I'll go, okay I'll go," I say, blowing my nose, sobbing again.

"Victor," Bobby begins softly. "You were—hey, look at me."

I immediately look at him.

"Okay, that's better. Now listen to me." Bobby breathes in. "You were the last person Sam Ho was seen alive with."

He pauses.

"Do you understand what I'm saying?" he asks.

I'm trying to nod.

"You were the last person seen with Sam Ho—okay?"

"Yeah, yeah."

"And when his body is discovered, traces of your semen will be found in him, okay?" Bobby's saying, nodding slowly, his eyes radiating patience, as if he were talking to a little kid.

"What? *What?*" I can feel my face crumpling again and suddenly I'm crying, pushing him away. "That didn't happen, that didn't happen, man, that can't—"

"Think back to what happened the other night, Victor," Bobby says, holding me tight, resting his head on my shoulder.

"What happened? What happened, man?" I say, suddenly hugging him, smelling his neck.

"You were in bed with Jamie, remember?" he says softly. "That will be the last time that ever happens." Pause. He hugs tighter. "Do you hear me, Victor?"

"But nothing happened, man," I sob into his ear, shivering. "I swear nothing happened, man—"

A flash. My loud orgasm, its intensity, how I came all over my hands, my stomach, onto Jamie, how she wiped me off with her own hands, her careful exit, the angle she held her arm up as she left the room, the way I shielded my eyes from the light in the hallway, how I spun into sleep.

"Did you hear me, Victor?" Bobby asks, pulling gently away. "Do you understand now?" Pause. "Okay? Do you understand that nothing will ever happen between you and Jamie again?"

"I'll leave, man, it's okay, man, I'll leave, I won't tell anyone—"

"No, Victor, shhh, listen to me," Bobby says. "You can't go."

"Why not, man, just let me go, man—"

"Victor, you can't go anywhere—"

"I want to go, man—"

"Victor, if you attempt to leave we will release photos and a videotape of you having sex with the ambassador's son—"

"Man, I didn't—"

"If you go anywhere they will be sent directly to—"

"Please help me, man—"

"Victor, that's what I'm trying to do."

"What . . . ambassador's son?" I ask, choking. "What in the fuck are you talking about, Bobby?"

"Sam Ho," Bobby says carefully, "is the Korean ambassador's son."

"But—but how . . . I didn't . . . I didn't do anything with him."

"There are a lot of things you're going to have to reconcile, Victor," Bobby says. "Do you understand?"

I nod dumbly.

"You shouldn't be shocked by any of this, Victor," Bobby says. "This is expected. This was in the script. You shouldn't be surprised by any of this."

"But . . ." I open my mouth but my head falls forward and I start crying, silently. "But . . . I am, man."

"We need you, Victor," Bobby's saying, stroking my shoulder. "There are so many people who are afraid to move forward, Victor, who are afraid to try things." He pauses, continues stroking. "Everybody's afraid of changing, Victor." Pause. "But we don't think you are."

"But I'm a—" I gasp involuntarily, trying to ward off tiny waves of black panic from morphing into nausea. "But I'm a . . . really very together person, Bobby."

Bobby feeds me another small white pill. I swallow gratefully.

"We like you, Victor," he says softly. "We like you because you don't have an agenda." Pause. "We like you because you don't have any answers."

I gag reflexively, wipe my mouth, shudder again.

Outside it's almost dusk again and night sounds are registering and tonight there are parties we have to attend and in rooms throughout the second floor the rest of the houseguests are taking showers, getting dressed, memorizing lines. Today there were massages and Tammy and Jamie had their hair done at a salon that's so chic it doesn't even have a name or a phone number. Today there was a shopping expedition at Wild Oats in Notting Hill, which produced a crate of Evian water and Moroccon takeout that still sits in the salmon-hued kitchen. Today the Velvet Underground played throughout the house and on the computer in the living room various files were erased and mounds of information on disk were being terminated. Today the gym was washed and sterilized and towels and clothing were shredded and burned. Today Bentley Harrolds went to the Four Seasons along with Jamie Fields and they checked me out, retrieved my belongings, tipped various porters, made no arrangements with the front desk concerning how anyone might find me. Today travel plans were finalized and right now luggage is being packed since we are leaving for Paris tomorrow. Somewhere in all this a body was discarded and a videotape of its torture was sent to the appropriate address. Today the film crew left a message with the address of a house in Holland Park and instructions to meet them there no later than 9:00 tonight.

Clothes—a simple black Armani suit, a white Comme des Garçons shirt, a red Prada vest—lie across an ash-gray divan in the corner of the room. Bobby Hughes is wearing slippers and pouring mint tea from a black ceramic pot that he sets back down on a chrome table. Now he's choosing which Versace tie I should wear tonight from a rack hanging in a walk-in closet.

When we hug again, he whispers insistently into my ear.

"What if one day, Victor"—Bobby breathes in, holding me tighter— "what if one day you became whatever you're not?"

O First we sipped Stolis at Quo Vadis in Soho for some European MTV benefit, then we arrived at the party in Holland Park in two Jaguar XK8s, both of them red and gleaming, parked at conspicuous angles in front of the house. People definitely noticed and started whispering to each other as the six of us walked in together and at that precise moment Serge Gainsbourg's "Je T'Aime" started playing continuously for the rest of the evening. There was no discernible center at the party, its hosts were invisible, guests had to come up with strained explanations as to why they were there and some had completely forgotten who had invited them, no one really knew. Emporio Armani underwear models moved through a crowd consisting of Tim Roth, Seal, members of Supergrass, Pippa Brooks, Fairuza Balk, Paul Weller, Tyson, someone passing around large trays of osso buco. Outside there was a garden filled with roses and below tall hedges children dressed in Tommy Hilfiger safari shirts were drinking candy-colored punch made with grenadine and playing a game with an empty bottle of Stolichnaya, kicking it along the expanse of plush green lawn, and beyond them, just night. Smells floating around inside the house included tarragon, tobacco flowers, bergamot, oak moss. "Possibly," I muttered to someone.

I was slouching in a black leather armchair while Bobby, in a suit he found on Savile Row, kept feeding me Xanax, whispering the sentence "You'd better get used to it" each time he departed. I kept petting a ceramic cat that was perched next to the armchair I was frozen in, occasionally noticing an oversized book lying on the floor with the words *Designing with Tiles* on its cover. There was an aquarium filled with cumbersome black fish that struck me as essential. And everyone had just gotten back from L.A. and people were heading to Reykjavík for the weekend and some people seemed concerned about the fate of the ozone layer while others definitely did not. In a bathroom I tranced out on a bar of monogrammed soap that sat in a black dish while I stood on a shaggy wool carpet, unable to urinate. And then I was biting off what was left of my fingernails while Sophie Dahl introduced me to Bruce and Tammy before they drifted off to dance beneath the hedges and there were giant banana fronds situated everywhere and I just kept wincing but Sophie didn't notice.

Almost always in my line of vision, Jamie Fields somehow managed to completely avoid me that night. She was either laughing over a private joke with Amber Valletta or shaking her head slightly whenever a tray of hors d'oeuvres—almojabanas specially flown in from a restaurant in San Juan—was offered and she was saying "I do" to just about anything that was asked of her. Bentley stared as an awkward but well-bred teenage boy drinking pinot noir from a medium-sized jug developed a crush on me in a matter of seconds and I just smiled wanly at him as he brushed stray bits of confetti off the Armani jacket I was wearing and said "cool" as if it had twelve os in it. It wasn't until much later that I noticed the film crew was there too, including Felix the cinematographer, though none of them seemed fazed, and then a small patch of fog started parting and I realized that maybe none of them knew about Sam Ho and what happened to him, the freakish way he died, how his hand twitched miserably, the tattoo of the word SLAVE blurring because of how hard his body vibrated. Bobby, looking airbrushed, handed me a napkin and asked me to stop drooling.

"Mingle," Bobby whispered. "Mingle."

Someone handed me another glass of champagne and someone else lit a cigarette that had been dangling from my lips for the past half hour and what I found myself thinking less and less was "But maybe I'm right and they're wrong" because I was yielding, yielding.

38 The film crew follows Tammy into the dining area, where she has a tense breakfast with Bruce. She sips lukewarm hot chocolate, pretending to read *Le Monde*, and Bruce hostilely butters a piece of almond bread until he breaks the silence by telling Tammy he knows horrible things about her past, keeps mentioning a stint in Saudi Arabia without elaborating. Bruce's hair is wet and his narrow face is flushed pink from a recent shower and he's wearing a pistachio-colored Paul Smith T-shirt and later he will be attending a prestigious rooftop luncheon somewhere in the 16th arrondissement that Versace is throwing to which only good-looking people have been invited and Bruce has decided to wear a black body shirt and gray Prada shoes to the rooftop luncheon and he's really going only because of a canceled booking last month.

"So you'll be appreciated," Tammy says, lighting a thin cigarette.

"You don't appreciate me."

"Don't be absurd," she mutters.

"I know who you're seeing this afternoon."

"What else are you doing today?" she asks tonelessly.

"I'll go to the Versace luncheon. I'll have a club sandwich. I'll nod when it's appropriate." Pause. "I'll stick to the script."

The camera keeps circling the table they're sitting at and nothing's registering on Tammy's face and Bruce's hand shakes slightly as he lifts an Hermès coffee cup and then without sipping any café au lait puts it back on its saucer and closes his green eyes, lacking the energy to argue. The actor playing Bruce had a promising career as a basketball player at Duke and then followed Danny Ferry to Italy where Bruce immediately got modeling jobs and in Milan he met Bobby who was dating Tammy Devol at the time and things just flew from there. A vase—a prop—filled with oversized white tulips sits nonsensically between them.

"Don't be jealous," Tammy whispers.

A cell phone sitting on the table starts ringing and neither one of them moves to pick it up but it might be Bobby so Bruce finally answers. It's actually Lisa-Marie Presley, looking for Bentley—whom she calls "Big

Sistah"—but Bentley's sleeping because he got in at dawn accompanied by an NYU film student he picked up at La Luna last night because the NYU film student had a tinted-blond chevron that accentuated already enormous lips and a penchant for nonbloodletting bondage that Bentley couldn't resist.

"Don't be jealous," Tammy says once more, before leaving.

"Just stick to the script," Bruce warns her.

As Tammy casually picks up a Vuitton box sitting on a chrome table in the hallway, the opening piano strains from ABBA's "S.O.S." begin playing and the song continues over the rest of Tammy's day, even though on the Walkman she wears throughout the city is a tape Bruce made for her—songs by the Rolling Stones, Bettie Serveert, DJ Shadow, Prince, Luscious Jackson, Robert Miles, an Elvis Costello song that used to mean something to both of them.

A Mercedes picks Tammy up and a Russian driver named Wyatt takes her to Chanel in Rue Cambon where she breaks down in an office, crying silently at first and then gasping until Gianfranco arrives and gets a sense that maybe something is "off" and scurries away after calling for an assistant to calm Tammy down. Tammy's freaked, barely gets through the fittings, and then she meets the son of the French premier at a flea market in Clignancourt and soon they're sitting in a McDonald's, both wearing sunglasses, and he's three years younger than Tammy, sometimes lives in a palace, hates the nouveau riche, fucks only Americans (including his nanny, when he was ten). Tammy "ran into" him on Avenue Montaigne outside Dior four months ago. She dropped something. He helped pick it up. His car was waiting. It was getting dark.

The French premier's son has just returned from Jamaica and Tammy halfheartedly compliments him on his tan and then immediately inquires about his cocaine problem. Has it resolved itself? Does he care? He just smiles evasively, which he realizes too late is the wrong move because she gets moody. So he orders a Big Mac and Tammy picks at a small bag of fries and his flat is being painted so he's staying at the Presidential Suite at the Bristol and it's freezing in the McDonald's, their breath steaming whenever they talk. She studies her fingertips, wondering if cocaine is bad for your hair. He mumbles something and tries to hold her hand. He touches her face, tells her how sensitive she is. But it's all hopeless, everything's a label, he's late for a haircut. "I'm wary," she finally admits. He actually—Tammy doesn't know this—feels broken. They make vague plans about meeting again.

She walks away from the McDonald's, and outside where the film crew's waiting it's warm and raining lightly and the Eiffel Tower is only a shadow in a giant wall of mist that's slowly breaking up and Tammy concentrates on the cobbled streets, a locust tree, a policeman strolling by with a black German shepherd on a leash, then she finally gets back into the Mercedes the Russian named Wyatt is driving. There's a lunch at Chez Georges that she's just going to have to skip—she's too upset, things keep spiraling away from her, another Klonopin doesn't help—and she calls Joan Buck to explain. She dismisses the car, takes the Vuitton box and loses the film crew in the Versace boutique on Rue du Faubourg Saint-Honoré. No one knows where Tammy is for the next thirty-five minutes.

She hands the Vuitton box to a strikingly handsome Lebanese man slouching behind the wheel of a black BMW parked tightly against a curb somewhere in the 2nd arrondissement, actually not far from Chez Georges so she changes her mind and decides to show up for the lunch where the film crew is waiting and the director and Felix the cinematographer keep apologizing for losing her and she dismisses them by shrugging vacantly, muttering "I got lost" and greeting people sweetly. She's told good news by her agent: Tammy has the next cover for British *Vogue*. Everyone's wearing sunglasses. A discussion about "Seinfeld" and ceiling fans commences. Tammy declines a glass of champagne, then reconsiders.

The sky is starting to clear and clouds are dissolving and the temperature rises ten degrees in fifteen minutes so the students eating lunch in the open courtyard at the Institute of Political Studies start sunning themselves as the BMW the Lebanese is driving rolls to a stop on the Boulevard Raspail, where a different film crew is waiting on neighboring rooftops prepared to record the following events with telephoto lenses.

Below them everyone's sighing with pleasure and students are drinking beer and lying shirtless across benches and reading magazines and sharing sandwiches while plans to skip classes start formulating and someone with a camcorder roams the courtyard, finally focusing in on a twenty-year-old guy who's sitting on a blanket weeping silently while reading a note from his girlfriend who has just left him and she's written that they will never get back together again and he's rocking back and forth telling himself it's okay, it's okay, and the camcorder angles away and focuses in on a girl giving another girl a back rub. A German television crew interviews students on the upcoming elections. Joints are shared. Rollerbladers whiz by.

The instructions the Lebanese received were simple: just remove the top of the Vuitton box before leaving the car, but since Bobby Hughes lied about when the bomb will go off—he simply told the driver to park the car and leave it on Boulevard Raspail in front of the institute—the driver will die in the blast. The Lebanese, who was involved in the planning of an attack in January on CIA headquarters in Langley, is eating M&M's and thinking about a girl named Siggi he met last month in Iceland. A student named Brigid walks by the BMW and notices the Lebanese leaning over the passenger seat and she even registers the panic on his face as he lifts something up in the seconds before the car explodes.

A simple flash of light, a loud sound, the BMW bursts apart.

The extent of the destruction is a blur and its aftermath somehow feels beside the point. The point is the bomb itself, its placement, its activation—that's the statement. Not Brigid blown apart beyond recognition or the force of the blast flinging thirty students closest to the car forty, fifty feet into the air or the five students killed instantly, two of them by flying shrapnel that sailed across the courtyard and was embedded in their chests, and not the other section of car, which flies by, lopping off an arm, and not the three students immediately blinded. It's not the legs blown off, the skulls crushed, the people bleeding to death in minutes. The uprooted asphalt, the blackened trees, the benches splattered with gore, some of it burned—all of this matters just as much. It's really about the will to accomplish this destruction and not about the outcome, because that's just decoration.

A stunned silence and then—among the conscious covered with blood, not always their own—the screaming starts.

Fifty-one injured. Four people will never walk again. Three others are severely brain-damaged. Along with the driver of the BMW, thirteen are dead, including an older man who dies, blocks away, of a heart attack at the time of the blast. (A week later a teacher's assistant from Lyons will die from head injuries, raising the number of dead to fourteen.) By the time the flashing blue lights of ambulances start arriving at the darkening scene, the film crew has packed up and disappeared and will show up later in the week at another designated spot. Without staring through the lens of the cameras, everything at that distance looks tiny and inconsequential and vaguely unreal to them. You can tell who is dead and who is not only by the way the bodies look when they're picked up.

And later that night at a very cool, sexy dinner in an upstairs room at the Hôtel Crillon, past a door flanked by dark-haired, handsome guards, Tammy mingles with Amber Valletta, Oscar de la Renta, Gianfranco Ferré, Brad Renfro, Christian Louboutin, Danielle Steel, the Princess of Wales, Bernard Arnault and various Russians and *Vogue* editors and everyone is into very serious slouching and some people just got back from Marrakech—a few less jaded because of that trip—and others pay their respects to Tammy as she huddles in a corner gossiping with Shalom Harlow about how all the girls are dating so many inappropriate people (nobodies, gangsters, fishermen, *boys*, members of the House of Lords, Jamaicans with whom they have no rapport) and Tammy's fanning herself with an invitation to a party at Queen that a boy who looks just like Christian Bale offered her but she's going to bypass it in favor of one in the 16th arrondissement that Naomi's throwing and then sashimi's served and more cigarettes are

bummed then lit and Tammy leans into John Galliano and whispers
"You're so nuts, baby" and she's drinking too much red wine and switches to
Coke and more than one lesbian vaguely comes on to her and someone
wearing a kimono asks how Bruce Rhinebeck is and Tammy, gazing at a figure prancing by in the darkness, answers "Wait" dreamily because she's realizing it's really just another difficult evening.

37

A giant set—high-tech and industrial with hints of Art
Deco and Mission—appropriating an apartment in
either the 8th or the 16th arrondissement is where
Jamie Fields, Bobby Hughes, Bentley Harrolds, Tammy Devol, Bruce
Rhinebeck and myself live during autumn in Paris. We're inhabiting a
5,000-square-foot triplex that has been paid for with Iraqi money washed
through Hungary. To get into the house you have to deactivate an alarm
and walk through a courtyard. Inside, a swirling circular staircase joins all
three floors and the color scheme is muted olive green and light brown and
soft pink, and in the basement there's a gym, its walls lined with Clemente
drawings. An expansive open kitchen designed by Biber contains cabinets
made from Makassar ebony and dyed tulipwood and there's a Miele oven
and two dishwashers and a glass-door refrigerator and a Sub-Zero freezer
and custom-made wine and spice racks and an industrial restaurant sprayer
installed in a stainless-steel alcove with teak-lined drying racks holding
gilded polka-dotted china. A giant mural by Frank Moore looms above the
kitchen table, which a silk Fortuny shade hangs over.

Serge Mouille chandeliers are suspended over sparkling green-and-
white terrazzo floors and rugs designed by Christine Van Der Hurd. Everywhere there are glass walls and giant white citronella candles and glass-box
towers filled with CDs and white glass fireplaces and Dialogica chairs covered in Giant Textiles chenille and padded leather doors and stereo systems
and Ruhlman armchairs in front of TV sets hooked up to a digital satellite
system that picks up five hundred channels around the world, and book-
cases filled with bowl arrangements line the walls everywhere and piles of
cellular phones lie in heaps on various tables. And in the bedrooms there
are blackout curtains designed by Mary Bright and rugs by Maurice Velle

Keep and Hans Wegner's lounges and ottomans in Spinneybeck leather and divans covered in a Larson chenille and dwarf fruit trees often sit next to them and the walls in all the bedrooms are leather upholstered. The beds were made in Scandinavia and the sheets and towels are by Calvin Klein.

A complicated video-monitoring system runs throughout the apartment (and the outside cameras are equipped with built-in illuminators) along with a vast alarm system. Codes are memorized and, since the sequence is changed weekly, rememorized. The two BMWs parked in the garage have been equipped with global-positioning tracking systems, as well as untraceable license plates, bulletproof windshields, run-flat tires, blinding halogen lights in front and back, ramming bumpers. The apartment is swept twice a week—phone lines, outlets, PowerBooks, lampshades, toilets, everything electrical. Behind locked doors are rooms and behind those rooms are other locked doors and in those rooms dozens of pieces of luggage—mostly Vuitton and Gucci—are lined up waiting to be used. In other hidden rooms there are heavy-duty sewing machines, strips of explosives, hand grenades, M-16 rifles, machine guns, a filing cabinet containing battery chargers, detonators, Semtex, electric blasting caps. A closet contains dozens of designer suits lined with Kevlar, which is thick enough to stop bullets from high-powered rifles or flying bomb fragments.

All the phones in the house analyze callers' voices for subaudible microtremors that occur when a speaker is stressed or lying, giving the listener constant LED readings. All the phones in the house are installed with analyzers that send electrical pulses down the line and, bouncing them back, provide an affirmative reading for the listener if the call is being traced. All the phones in the house have a digital binary code scrambler that converts voices to numbers and allows the person on the other end of the line to decode it but keeps third parties from hearing anything but static.

Suddenly, that first week in Paris, Bobby threw an elaborate cocktail party in honor of Joel Silver, who ended up bragging to Richard Donner, who had just flown in from Sacramento, about his new three-million-dollar trailer and someone else was flying his dogs over on the Concorde and then Serena Altschul showed up and gave us the inside scoop on the Bush tour and a soon-to-be-slain rap star and Hamish Bowles arrived with Bobby Short and then—boom boom boom, one after the other—Crown Princess Katherine of Yugoslavia, Prince Pavlos of Greece, Princess Sumaya of Jordan and Skeet Ulrich, who was wearing a Prada suit and a shirt with spread collars and seemed happy at first to see me even if the last time we bumped into each other I ended up running away from him down a darkened street in SoHo. Skeet worriedly noticed the way I eyed a dropped Mentos lying on the terrazzo floor. I bent down and, after brushing it off, popped the Mentos into my mouth and started chewing rapidly.

"You just need to, um, put a positive spin on things," Skeet told me hesitantly.

"I'm saying hello to oblivion," I told Skeet, chewing rapidly.

He paused, shrugged, nodded glumly and immediately walked away.

Aurore Ducas passed by and so did Yves Saint-Laurent and Taki. An Iraqi ambassador spent the entire party standing close to Bobby, who kept making hand motions my way, urging me to mingle. I spent the early part of the evening chatting nervously to Diane Von Furstenberg and Barry Diller and trying to move closer to Jamie, who sometimes was ignoring me and sometimes laughing hysterically while petting a basset hound someone had dragged in, and bartenders poured champagne into thin crystal flutes while staring blankly past us. And predictably the party got hipper as it kept gliding further along and people started dancing to Republica and Kate Moss and Naomi Campbell arrived with The Artist Formerly Known As Prince and Tom Ford showed up with Dominique Browning and I had a heavy conversation with Michael Douglas about high-end safaris while I held a plate of lobster looking fairly benign and "I'm Your Boogie Man" by KC and the Sunshine Band blasted out, which was Jamie's cue to start dancing and my cue to just stare wonderingly at her. Baptiste Pitou did the flower arrangements. The word PARTY kept flashing above us in bright, multicolored lettering.

Bruce left the party the moment the French premier's son showed up and Tammy locked herself in an upstairs bathroom with a bottle of champagne and fell into a fairly hysterical state and someone—this zonked-out NYU film student who'd spent a few nights in the apartment and was lighting everybody's cigarettes—gave me his phone number, signing the back of an old issue of Le Monde with an important pen he borrowed from a certain luminary. A new David Barton gym was opening somewhere in Pigalle and a baffled Princess Sumaya of Jordan gasped "Ooh—how perfect." The director and Felix, along with most of the film crew, were thrilled by the direction the party was taking. I ended up slumped over on a bench in the courtyard and drunkenly said "Bonjour, dude" to Peter Jennings as he left and my foot had fallen asleep so I limped back into the party and tried to dance with Jamie but Bobby wouldn't let me.

36

The shows we attended today: Gaultier, Comme des Garçons and—after a stop at the new Frank Malliot place located somewhere beneath the Champs Élysées—Galliano (a giant white curtain, uncharacteristic modern lighting, "Stupid Girl" by Garbage blaring, models bowing, we needed alibis), and then inevitably Les Bains for a dinner in honor of Dries von Noten and male bouncers pull us in and I'm wearing Prada and mellowing out on immense dosages of Xanax and it's a big hyped-up bash and I'm saying "Hey baby" in strained variations to Candelas Sastre and Peter Beard and Eleanore de Rohan-Chabot and Emmanuel de Brantes and Greg Hansen and a dentist I visited briefly in Santa Fe when Chloe was on location there and Ines Rivero and there are way too many photographers and store buyers and PR types and all the girls are carrying straw bags and wearing dresses the colors of crayons and the club is decked out with immense flower arrangements made up of gardenias and roses. I keep overhearing the word "insects" and when I light a cigarette I'm just noticing the thousand francs clutched in my hand that for some reason Jamie gave me during the Galliano show while I sat next to her trembling violently. This morning over breakfast Bobby said nothing about where he was heading off to today but since so many scenes are being shot without me I just frantically memorize my lines and show up according to the production schedule, staying inconspicuous, staying out of sight.

I walk over to where the film crew waits and I hit my mark, lighting Jamie's cigarette. She's wearing a tight sequined pantsuit by Valentino and carefully applied winged eyeliner. Eric Clapton starts playing over the sound system, which is my cue.

"Eric Clapton sucks."

"Oh yeah?" she asks. "That's just great."

I grab a glass of champagne off a tray a waiter gliding by is holding and we're both out in the open standing next to each other on the dance floor, looking at everything else but us.

"I want you," I say, wanly smiling, nodding to Claudia Schiffer as she passes by. "I want you very badly."

"That's not in the script, Victor," she warns, smiling wanly too. "That's not going to play."

"Jamie, please," I say. "We can talk. Bobby's not here yet."

"Just knock those date-rape fantasies out of that pretty little head of yours," she says, exhaling.

"Baby," I say genuinely. "I don't want to hurt you."

"You're about to hurt both of us if you keep this up."

"Keep what up?" I ask.

She turns even farther away. I move closer.

"Hey Jamie—" I reach out to touch her shoulder. "What's the story?"

"You don't even know where you are, Victor," she says grimly, but still smiling, even managing little waves at people who wave first. "You have no idea where you are."

"Show me."

"I can't afford to do that, Victor."

"You don't love him," I say. "I can tell. You don't love Bobby. It's a job, right? It's part of the plan, right? You're just acting, right?"

She says nothing.

Bobby parts a green velvet curtain and walks in wearing a dazzling Valentino tuxedo with a Prada backpack strapped over his shoulders that he didn't check and he surveys the room while lighting a cigarette, briefly blinded by paparazzi, and he just came from a party at Anahi and his hair looks wet and he starts moving toward us, grinning tightly as he strides across the dance floor.

"I think you're afraid of him," I say. "But you don't love him."

"Let's just get through this week, okay?" she says, tensing up.

"Tell me you love him—say it," I whisper. "Tell me you even like him."

The camera suddenly stops circling, holding us both in the frame tightly while we stare helplessly as Bobby comes nearer.

"Be quiet," she says, nodding at someone passing by in the shadows.

"I'll say something to him," I whisper. "I don't care."

"Let's lower the volume, Victor," she warns, smiling widely.

"I hope that's a humorous reference to something I didn't hear you say, Victor," Bobby says, leaning in and kissing Jamie on the mouth.

"Mmm," Jamie purrs, tasting her lips. "Margarita?"

"What are you talking about, Bobby?" I deliver the line in such a way that it's impossible to tell whether I'm feigning innocence or acting hard but Bobby's distracted by something across the room and in a suave way doesn't seem to care.

"I'm starving," Jamie says.

"What?" Bobby murmurs, craning his neck.

"I said I'm starving," she repeats anxiously.

Vaguely panicked, I swallow another Xanax and focus on an MTV crew interviewing Nicole Kidman, who has a bindi on her forehead.

"Rhinebeck is in a rotten mood," Bobby says, staring over at Bruce slouched stony-faced in a booth on the outer limits of the party with Tammy beside him, gorgeous and shell-shocked, wearing sunglasses, both of them surrounded by a smattering of young Londoners.

"I think he'll be okay," Jamie says. "It'll be over soon."

"Yeah, but Tammy's getting damaged and that could screw things up," Bobby says. "Excuse me."

Bobby walks over to the booth, shaking hands with everyone who's impressed by his presence, and when he leans in, Bruce barely registers him and then Bentley strolls over with Marc Jacobs and finally Tammy looks up at Bentley as he shows her the watch he's wearing and she smiles briefly at Marc but the moment the entire booth bursts into cackling her face becomes a mask.

"Talk to him," I'm telling Jamie. "Tell him it's over between you two. Tell him it'll be okay."

"It'll be okay?" she asks. "You dummy," she mutters.

"I'm just trying to articulate how I'm really feeling."

"Your primary responsibility, Victor, at this juncture, is to just—"

"Shut up," I say softly.

"Get over me."

"You started this."

"*This* is just the tip of the iceberg," Jamie says, and then she can't help it—her face relaxes and glancing over at me her eyes acknowledge mine and she whispers quickly, "Please, Victor, just act low-key and we'll talk later."

"When?" I whisper back.

Bobby returns with Bentley and Marc Jacobs and Marc and Bentley just got back from checking out Marc's headquarters at the Pont Neuf and Marc's very nervous because one of the new hot designers is a teenage drag queen who gets his inspiration from a Chihuahua named Hector.

"I was trapped in a conversation with a Belgian iconoclast and Mr. Jacobs here saved me," Bentley says, waving a fly away.

Marc bows and then kisses Jamie on the cheek, nonchalantly nods my way and says, "Hey, Victor."

"Jesus, it's freezing in here," Bentley says, his breath steaming, and then, eyeing me, adds, "You're looking tired, Victor. Gorgeous but tired."

"I'm cool, I'm cool," I say evenly. "Everything's cool."

"Here—you forgot this." Bobby hands Bentley the Prada backpack while Marc charms Jamie by making goofy faces behind Bentley's back, causing even Bobby to crack half a smile.

"Why didn't you check it for me?" Bentley whines. "Jesus, Bobby."

"I didn't know I was going to stay." Bobby shrugs, staring at me.

After I'm seated at a table with Donatella Versace, Mark Vanderloo, Katrine Boorman, Azzedine Alaïa, Franca Sozzani and the Belgian iconoclast and we've all laughed at other people's expense and smoked dozens of cigarettes and waiters have cleared away plates of food that were barely looked at let alone touched and all of us have whispered secret things to the person on our left, Jamie walks by the table with a joint and asks for a light from Donatella, who's sitting next to me, and Jamie—while pretending to talk to Donatella, who's talking to Franca—tells me that Bobby is leaving for Beirut tomorrow and then he's traveling on to Baghdad and Dublin, where he's meeting with a member of a Virginia paramilitary group, and he'll be back in five days. I'm listening intently as she says this and she's encouraging me to laugh gaily and she relays this information in such a way that if you were across the room—as Bobby is now—you would assume she was telling Donatella how terrific Victor looks or contemplating aloud how fabulous her life turned out and Jamie takes just one hit off the joint before leaving it for the rest of the table to smoke and my foot has fallen asleep, and limping away, trying to follow her, I bump into slow-moving silhouettes and shadows and I notice Bentley making a dashing exit with the Prada backpack and then the rock group Autour de Lucie starts tuning up, about to perform their first song, a cover of the Who's "Substitute."

35

ABBA's "Voulez-Vous" blasts out over the sound track and in front of Les Bains a white Range Rover waits and in the front passenger seat the director from another film crew is going over tonight's sequence while in back various assistants staring intently ahead communicate on wireless headphones with the second unit, which has already set up at the designated site. With the Prada backpack slung over his shoulder Bentley hops into the Range Rover as it pulls away, followed by a black Citroën, toward the Boulevard Saint-Germain. Café Flore has been canvassed all week and a detailed description of its layout yielded the best table to leave the Prada backpack at.

Bentley studies the following scene on two pieces of fax paper, memorizes his lines.

The cab drops Bentley off a block away from Café Flore and he walks quickly, purposefully, over to that outside table just off the sidewalk where Brad, the actor playing the NYU film student Bentley picked up at La Luna last week, is sitting with two friends—Seattle waif boys who attended Camden with Brad—and they're all stylishly chewing gum and smoking Marlboros, slouching in their seats with perfect hair, and an empty Starbucks cup sits in the middle of the table and by Brad's feet is a Gap bag filled with newly bought T-shirts. "Ooh, let's play dress-up," Brad says when he sees Bentley maneuvering toward the table in his Versace tuxedo.

Café Flore is packed, shimmering, every table filled. Bentley notices this with a grim satisfaction but Bentley feels lost. He's still haunted by the movie *Grease* and obsessed with legs that he always felt were too skinny though no one else did and it never hampered his modeling career and he's still not over a boy he met at a Styx concert in 1979 in a stadium somewhere in the Midwest, outside a town he has not been back to since he left it at eighteen, and that boy's name was Cal, who pretended to be straight even though he initially fell for Bentley's looks but Cal knew Bentley was emotionally crippled and the fact that Bentley didn't believe in heaven didn't make him more endearing so Cal drifted off and inevitably became head of programming at HBO for a year or two. Bentley sits down, already miked, in a crimson-and-forest-green chair and lights a cigarette. Next to them Japanese tourists study maps, occasionally snap photos. This is the establishing shot.

"Hey Bentley," Brad says. "This is Eric and Dean. They went to Camden and are both aspiring models. We've been comparing diets."

"So that's why I thought you all looked so cool," Bentley says, the Camden reference causing him to flash on Victor and what's in store for him.

"Laurent Garnier is spinning tonight at Rex," Brad says hopefully.

"Maybe, maybe," Bentley says, nodding, exhaling smoke, and then, looking over at the tattoo circling Dean's wrist, "Nice."

"Do you have it?" Brad asks, referring to the Ecstasy Bentley was supposed to bring to Café Flore.

"I'm going to have to go to Basil's flat," Bentley says offhandedly, smiling at Dean again.

"Oh man," Brad groans, disappointed. "That'll take forever."

"Patience—hey, you're only twenty-three, what's the rush?" Bentley asks, patting Brad's thigh, giving it a tight squeeze, which relaxes Brad, causes him to look down, blush slightly. "It'll take me twenty minutes at most," Bentley promises, bending the cigarette into an ashtray. He stands up.

"How do I know you'll come back?" Brad asks, looking up at him.

"I'll leave this," Bentley says, hefting the Prada bag into Brad's lap. "Just hold on to it."

"Will you please hurry?" Brad says, grinning. "We're in dire need of stimulants."

"You look just like Jon Bon Jovi," Bentley tells him.

"So I've been told." Brad smiles proudly.

"That's what makes you so cool."

"Where's that ABBA coming from?" Dean asks, twisting around in his chair.

"I'll be back," Bentley says, brushing dots of confetti off Brad's shoulder. "I'll be back." The Arnold Schwarzenegger impersonation doesn't work a second time and Bentley, who actually doesn't think Brad is half bad, silently cringes.

"What's that?" Bentley asks, having noticed the crude drawing of what looks like a leaf and a number Brad is doodling on a napkin.

"A design for a tattoo I want to get."

"Why the number four?" Bentley asks, squinting.

"It's my favorite number."

"I think it's nice you have one."

"And see?" Brad asks. "That's a leaf."

But it's time for Bentley to go, there are cues, signals given across the boulevard, emanating from various cars and vans, strategically parked, cameras whirring.

"You're gorgeous, baby," Brad says, kissing Bentley lightly on the mouth.

"Don't lose that," Bentley says, pointing at the Prada bag.

"I'll hold on to it, don't worry, just get the stuff," Brad says impatiently, urging Bentley to go, tightly clutching the Prada bag.

Bentley walks away, disappearing into the crowd wandering the sidewalk tonight. "He has the coolest apartment" is the last thing Bentley ever hears Brad say.

After walking a block Bentley cuts across Boulevard Saint-Germain and hops into the black Citroën waiting at the curb, and as he smiles a shadow crosses his face.

A telephoto lens slowly moves in on the Prada backpack sitting on Brad's lap.

The force of the first explosion propels Brad into the air. A leg is blown off from the thigh down and a ten-inch hole is ripped open in his abdomen and his mangled body ends up lying in the curb on Boulevard Saint-Germain, splashing around in its own blood, writhing into its death throes. The second bomb in the Prada backpack is now activated.

Dean and Eric, both spattered with Brad's flesh and bleeding profusely from their own wounds, manage to stumble over to where Brad has been thrown, screaming blindly for help, and then, seconds later, the other blast occurs.

This bomb is much stronger than the first and the damage it causes is more widespread, creating a crater thirty feet wide in front of Café Flore.

Two passing taxis are knocked over, simultaneously bursting into flame.

What's left of Brad's corpse is hurled through a giant Calvin Klein poster on a scaffolding across the street, splattering it with blood, viscera, bone.

Eric is blown through the window of the Emporio Armani boutique across the street.

Dean's body is spun onto a spiked railing that separates the sidewalk from the boulevard and hangs there, jackknifed.

Shrapnel spreads out in all directions, hitting a middle-aged woman sitting inside the café, spraying into her neck, face and chest, killing her within moments.

A Japanese woman who had been sitting next to Brad's table stumbles, dazed, out of the smoke, both arms blown off at the elbow, before collapsing into the debris on the sidewalk.

A young Armenian lies half on the street, half on the sidewalk, his head blown apart, his moped still between his legs.

A severed arm dangles from the edge of the white overhang and large clumps of flesh are splattered across the Café Flore sign.

From behind the cameras on rooftops and inside various vans so much of it is the usual: bleeding people running out of thick black smoke, the screams of the wounded and dying, a man crawling along the boulevard vomiting blood, gasping for air, charred bodies hanging out of cars that happened to pass by Café Flore in the instant the bombs went off, shopping bags standing in blood outside the entrance. The shock, the sirens, a hundred wounded—it's all so familiar. The director is relying on a top-notch editor to put the footage together and he tells the crew it's time to move on. As the Range Rover drives quickly past the scene, crossing in front of the black Citroën, Bentley briefly notices a woman lying on the sidewalk screaming, her thigh torn open, and while lighting a cigarette he tells the director, "Take me back to Les Bains, s'il vous plaît," where he listens to Jean Tripplehorn blab away about the cheese puffs at Taillevent for an hour and Bentley tells her he disapproves of interracial relationships.

34

People leaving. Bobby this morning, Tammy to Jacques Levy's for the weekend, Bruce to check out the floor plans of the terminals at Orly airport, Bentley on vacation, "perhaps Greece, perhaps not," which leaves me escorting Jamie to the Carita salon on Rue du Faubourg Saint-Honoré, where Jamie has—in no particular order—her hair colored, a massage, aromatherapy and anti-stress treatments, an energy-balanced magnetic manipulation session, and then she's guided by a New Age adviser (eighteen, gorgeous) to a "beach of calm" complete with the sounds of prerecorded shellfish cavorting somewhere on a large, craggy rock. I'm waiting with the bodyguards and the bodyguards are waiting because of Brazilian millionaires, an empress or two, the Princess of Monaco, Judith Godreche, and we're all sipping a 1992 Château de Bellet and I'm on Xanax while the film crew shoots me flipping glumly through a photography book about '60s movie magazines until the boom operator knocks one of the bodyguards in the head and the director gets bored and the crew moves on to an early dinner and the next setup.

At the Opéra Garnier feelings are mixed about the Japanese libretto but we're really there for the paparazzi waiting at the bottom of the stairs while Jamie and I are standing at the top of the stairs. And Christiana Brandolini is there and Sao Schlumberger loses a contact lens and Irene Amic hisses "You're stepping on my hem" but when she turns and sees my face, panicked and caught in the glow of a chandelier, she relents and smiles, whispering something about how beautiful I am, and then Candy Spelling's waving to Jamie, and Amira Casar and Astrid Kohl tell me about a party a week ago at Les Bains that I wasn't invited to.

I spot the Christian Bale look-alike I first saw on Bond Street in London, now wearing a tuxedo and nodding slowly when he notices me staring over at him transfixed. Jamie and I decide to leave during the first intermission.

A black Citroën takes us to the Buddha Bar and after we sit at a table, shaken, saying nothing, just staring hopelessly at each other, Jamie reaches into her Prada bag and calls Hôtel Costes and since she knows Jean Louis and Gilbert a room is waiting by the time we arrive at 239 Rue Saint-Honoré. The first assistant director glances at a call sheet and tells both of us to be on the main set by 9:00 tomorrow. It's midnight and Jamie rushes into the lobby, hugging herself in a Helmut Lang ponyskin coat, and then it's my turn to follow her.

The door to our room closes behind me and Jamie and I fall on the bed while I'm kissing her mouth and her arms are wrapped around my shoulders and after I'm naked I'm shaking so hard that she has to pull back. Then someone knocks on the door.

Jamie stands up, also naked, pulls on the Helmut Lang overcoat, lazily strides over to the door. She opens it without asking who it is.

A film crew I haven't seen before enters the room. A large Panavision camera is wheeled in, lights are positioned. The first AD tells me where to lie on the bed while Jamie confers with the director and the script supervisor. The propmaster opens a bottle of champagne, pours two glasses. A joint—not a prop—is introduced into the scene and then Jamie's lying next to me and I'm lighting the joint. Someone rumples the blankets on the bed and the director calls "Playback" and Jane Birkin starts sighing "Je T'Aime" on a CD and the film crew is just a shadow behind the lights and it's so cold in the room steam keeps pouring out of our mouths.

Jamie lies on her back and dreamily inhales on the joint I hand her, holding smoke in until she slowly breathes it out—a cue for her to start speaking in a halting, deliberate tone, her voice breathy and lost, her eyes half-closed.

"Bobby . . . strolled . . . into Superstudio Industria. . . . It was a shoot that had gone late . . . was it for an Anne Klein campaign? . . . I can't remember. . . . People were making a hundred thousand dollars a day and it seemed worth it . . . and it was maybe ten-thirty or eleven and . . . in December 1990 . . . four years ago? . . . five? . . . and there had been a power failure of some kind . . . this blackout . . . and candles were being lit but you still couldn't see anything and it was freezing. . . . It had gotten so cold . . . in just a matter of minutes. . . . I had goose bumps all over my body at Industria that night . . . and there was this shape moving in the darkness . . . a figure . . . tall . . . kept getting closer to where I was standing alone . . . and then it started . . . circling me . . . a mass . . . this shape . . . and it was whistling a song . . . which sounded familiar. . . . 'On the Sunny Side of the Street,' it kept singing . . . and then I noticed the camera crew . . . following him at a discreet distance . . . but they had no lights . . . and they were still filming this . . . this shape, this thing . . . and when he lit a cigarette . . . in that instant I saw his face and recognized him immediately. . . . He took me to the VIP room at that Club Xerox . . . and somewhere in the background was the film crew . . . and somewhere beyond that the Who was playing. . . .

"I can't tell you exactly . . . what I was motivated by. . . . I can't really go into detail. . . . It had been an unhappy period in my life. . . . I hated my body . . . the way I looked. . . . I was taking pills, I was seeing shrinks, I went to the gym because I knew no one would like me otherwise. . . . I even thought about plastic surgery. . . . I was twenty-three. . . . My mother and father had just gone through a terrible divorce and my mother was having . . . some kind of nervous breakdown . . . and my dreams at night were just hours of black space . . . sometimes interrupted by bones and that song Bobby was whistling that night at Industria. . . . I had just completed a failed relationship with a famous photographer and had a brief affair with a boy from an Aerosmith video. . . . There were things I wanted. . . . I wanted to be on the cover of more magazines . . . I wanted to be beautiful . . . I wanted to be rich, I wanted to be famous. . . . I had been photographed by Lindbergh and Elgort and Demarchelier and . . . shows, I had done so many shows . . . but I was still mid-level. . . . My grief seemed endless. . . . I wanted something else . . . and then there was what Bobby wanted . . . and in our meeting I . . . evolved. . . . Bobby came in and saw how limited my world was . . . and he motivated me. . . . I never felt I was pretty enough and he made me . . . feel attractive. . . . He indulged me and I, in turn, became cheerful. . . . He told me that physically I was perfect . . . and I decided then that I would follow him . . . anywhere . . . so I spent a spring with him in Los Angeles and he introduced me to his friend . . . 'the genius,' a man named Mr. Leisure . . . and Steven Meisel got involved and my career started taking off. . . . But you've got to know, Victor, that . . . I was not aware of what Bobby did . . . I hadn't been told of his plans. . . . All I really knew was he wasn't a morning person . . . and neither was I . . . and at an opening at MOCA . . . something called 'The History of the Polka Dot' . . . when—"

"I went to that."

"—we were standing in a corner . . . he was so soft-spoken . . . and started telling me things . . . and midway through . . . I had to ask him to stop. . . ."

Jamie starts to cry silently. I relight the joint and hand it to her. Without sitting up she takes it, inhales, coughs a little.

"How did he recruit people? . . . It was only models . . . and famous models. . . . He wasn't interested in anyone else. . . . He would use the fact that as a model all you do all day is stand around and do what other people tell you to do. . . . He preyed on that . . . and we listened . . . and it was an analogy that made sense . . . in the end . . . when he asked . . . things of us . . . and it wasn't hard to recruit people . . . everyone wanted to be around us . . . everyone wanted to be movie stars . . . and in the end, basically, everyone was a sociopath . . . and all the girls' hair was chignoned . . . and the Who was always playing somewhere. . . .

"I remember very little about the beginning of that period. . . . After I had been inducted . . . there were so many long gray stretches . . . dieting . . . going to the gym, which was an obsession of Bobby's . . . absences . . . giant spaces . . . so many things I blocked out. . . . It was such an aimless existence. . . . Everything we did was up-to-the-minute . . . the restaurants we ate in . . . the hotels we stayed at . . . the people we hung out with. . . . In New York we joked about never staying at an address that wasn't a 10021 zip code . . . chartered 737s flew us to weddings . . . waiters never rushed us . . . we were allowed to smoke cigarettes anywhere we wanted . . . people didn't want to like us because we were young and rich and beautiful . . . and no one—I mean *no one*, Victor—was happy about my success . . . but that was—according to Bobby—'human nature' . . . but still, no one—and this is very important, Victor—*no one* was skeptical of us. . . .

"And we traveled . . . Palm Beach . . . Aspen . . . Nigeria . . . Christmases in St. Bart's . . . a week at Armani's home in Pantelleria . . . and Bobby made sure I started really getting work, and then it was Cindy Crawford and Paulina Porizkova and . . . and Claudia Schiffer . . . and Yasmeen Ghauri . . . Karen Mulder and Chloe Byrnes and Tammy Devol and Naomi and Linda and Elaine and . . . and Jamie Fields . . . and you had to know the codes to understand how things worked in this world . . . it was almost like sign language . . . and people learned how to behave in my presence . . . and girls were treating me differently now that I was dating Bobby Hughes . . . and then the dark patterns started appearing . . . and when I told Bobby 'No one's being themselves, everyone's so phony,' Bobby said 'Shhh' and then whispered 'That *is* being themselves.' . . .

"Bobby would try and educate me . . . make me understand . . . what he was doing . . . where he was going with this whole thing . . . and he told me 'Baby, George Washington was a terrorist' and I'd look into that face and see those eyes . . . those lips . . . and things would just start unraveling and I became educated. . . . He would tell me that you show the world things and in showing the world you teach it what you want. . . . He would give me E. M. Forster novels and I never understood them and for some reason . . . Bobby was relieved by this. . . . He told me things like 'We are just reflections of our time' and he never really got more precise than that. . . . I would ask him questions like 'What does fin de siècle mean?' and he would talk for an hour about the inherent evil . . . in rap music . . . and the Who was always playing in the background somewhere. . . .

"I knew Bobby wasn't faithful. . . . He was sleeping with big models . . . famous socialites in good shape . . . the occasional guy or . . . underage girl—girls who attended Spence or Chapin or Sacred Heart—and if he got in trouble with their mothers he'd fuck them too. . . . He would weigh girls . . . you had to be a certain weight . . . and mostly but not all the time a certain height . . . in order to fuck Bobby Hughes. . . . If you got on that scale and passed, then he . . . fucked you. . . ."

My arms are falling asleep and I adjust my position, light another joint a crew member hands me.

"A lot of girls disappeared or . . . OD'd . . . or they 'had accidents,' and by this time I was breaking down on the Concorde when I would see the curvature of the earth and the clouds seemed hundreds of miles below us . . . and I'd freak out . . . even on large amounts of Xanax and at the height of my fame. . . . I was responsible for the increased suicide rate among . . . teenage girls and young women who realized they would never look like me. . . . I was told this in editorials . . . angry letters from overweight mothers . . . essays by women in NOW. . . . I was told I was destroying lives . . . but it didn't touch me because no one we knew was real . . . people just seemed . . . fake and . . . Bobby liked that I felt this way. . . . It 'helped,' he said . . . and anyway, in the end I was too famous for him to get rid of. . . ."

Her voice quavers, regains its composure, then falters again and she just starts murmuring strings of words, how she moved into films, her first movie, *Night of the Bottomless Pit*, the arrangement of fake passports, soldiers of fortune from Thailand, Bosnia, Utah, new social security numbers, heads struck with such force they broke open as easily as soft-boiled eggs, a form of torture where the victim has to swallow a rope. "In Bombay . . . ," and now she shudders, swallowing rapidly, eyes clamped shut, tears immediately pouring out of the slits. "In Bombay . . ." She refuses to follow through and then starts shrieking about a serial killer Bobby befriended in Berlin and I hop out of bed and tell the director "Hey, it's over" and while they pack up to leave Jamie writhes on the bed, sobbing hysterically, clawing at the sheets, sometimes shouting out names in Arabic.

33 Outside the building in the 8th or 16th under a hazy sheen of floating mist the film crew waits after the director and Felix the cinematographer have set up a simple establishing shot that will be of the six of us walking "gaily" to a black Citroën waiting at the curb that will take us to a party at Natacha. But this crew doesn't know that earlier this afternoon the film crew I was introduced to the other night at Hôtel Costes has been let into the house by Bobby and has spent the last three hours laying cable, setting up lights, filming sequences I'm not in, including a long unresolvable argument between Tammy and Bruce, a sex scene with Jamie and Bobby, another segment with Bruce, alone, playing a guitar, strumming the old Bread song "It Don't Matter to Me," and they now move quietly around the living room — electricians and a beautiful key grip and the black-bearded director — all conferring with a cinematographer who resembles Brad Pitt in *Johnny Suede* and upstairs in Bentley's room the first AD keeps parting the Mary Bright blackout curtains, peering out at the other film crew in the street, offering updates over the muffled sounds of another fight between Tammy and Bruce — this one not filmed — concerning the actor playing the French premier's son and predictably doors are slammed, voices are raised, doors are slammed again.

I'm wearing a Prada suit totally unaware of who helped me put it on and I'm positioned in one of the Dialogica chairs in the living room, playing with a lime-green tie someone chose for me. On the TV screen, with the sound off, reruns of "Cheers" followed by "Home Improvement" run endlessly on a tape someone stuck into the VCR. A PA hands me a book of notes that Bobby made, I'm told, especially for me. Continents are investigated, floor plans of the Ritz have been reproduced, an outline was printed from a computer of the TWA terminal at Charles de Gaulle, diagrams of the layout of Harry's Bar in Venice, handwriting experts preoccupied with verifying signatures are interviewed, entries from a diary someone named Keith kept concerning a trip he made to Oklahoma City, pages about plastic explosives, the best wiring, the correct timer, the right container, the best detonator.

I'm reading "Semtex is made in Czechoslavakia." I'm reading "Semtex is an odorless, colorless plastic explosive." I'm reading "Libya has tons of Semtex." I'm reading "It takes 6 oz. of Semtex to blow up an airliner." I'm reading a profile on a newly manufactured plastic explosive called Remform, which is made and distributed only "underground" in the U.S. and is still unavailable in Europe. I'm reading a list of Remform's "pros and cons." I'm reading the words Bobby has scrawled on the side of a page: *More useful than Semtex?* and then two words that I stare at until they move me to get up out of the Dialogica chair and walk purposefully into the kitchen to make myself a drink: ". . . tests pending . . ."

On this much Xanax it's remarkably easy to concentrate solely on the making of a Cosmopolitan. You think of nothing else while pouring cranberry juice, Cointreau and lemon citron into a shaker filled with ice that you yourself attacked with an ice pick and then you're rolling a lime and slicing it open, squeezing the juice into the shaker, and then you're pouring the cocktail through a strainer into a giant martini glass, and back in the living room Makeup fixes my hair and I can't help but keep imagining what Jamie and Bobby are doing in their bedroom and I'm glancing up at the ceiling and while sipping the Cosmopolitan I zone out on the Paul McCartney and Wings sticker on the front of the notebook Bobby made for me.

"Didn't we hang in Sérifos?" the hairdresser asks me.

"We didn't hang out in Sérifos," I say, and then, "Oh yeah."

I attempt to read an interview in *Le Figaro* that Jamie gave on Wednesday but I'm unable to follow it, realizing midway through that I'm unable to speak or read French. I barely notice the hand grenade leaning against an automatic rifle on the table my drink is sitting on. Why this Paul McCartney and Wings sticker is on my notebook is a question easier to concentrate on. Crew members debate whether the latest U2 record really cuts it, until the director calls out for silence.

Bobby glides in. I look up solemnly from whatever it is I'm doing. "You look nice," he says.

I soften, smile weakly.

"What are you drinking?" he asks.

I have to look at the color of the drink before answering, "A Cosmopolitan."

"Can I have a sip?"

"Sure." I hand him the martini glass.

Bobby takes a sip, brightens up and smiles. "Great Cosmo, dude."

A very long pause while I wait for him to hand the drink back. "I . . . appreciate the compliment."

"Listen, Victor," Bobby starts, kneeling down in front of me.

I tense up, cross my legs, the copy of *Le Figaro* slipping to the terrazzo floor.

"I appreciate you watching Jamie and—"

"Hey man, I—"

"—I just wanted to let you know that—"

"Hey man, I—"

"Hey, shhh, chill out." He breathes in, stares intently up at me. "Listen, if I chastise you at times, if I seem to"—he pauses effectively—"warn you a little too harshly about where your place is in all of this, it's just to keep you on your feet." He pauses again, holding direct eye contact. "I really trust you, Victor." Another pause. "Really."

A long pause, this one on my part. "What's going to happen, Bobby?" I ask.

"You'll be prepped," Bobby says. "You'll be told what you need to know. You'll be given just the right amount of infor—"

Upstairs someone slams a door and Tammy cries out and then it's silent. Someone stomps down a hallway, cursing. From inside Tammy's room Prodigy starts blasting out. Bobby flinches, then sighs. "*That*, however, is getting out of hand."

"What's the story?" I ask slowly.

"Tammy's conducting an affair that is important to us but shouldn't mean anything to Bruce." Bobby sighs, still on his haunches in front of me. "But it does. And that is proving to be a problem. Bruce needs to get over it. Quickly."

"What is"—I start, breathe in—"the problem?"

"The problem . . ." Bobby stares at me sternly. Finally a smile. "The problem really doesn't concern you. The problem will be resolved soon enough."

"Uh-huh, uh-huh," I'm saying, trying to sip the drink.

"Are you okay, Victor?" Bobby asks.

"As well as . . . can be"—I gulp—"expected."

"I actually think you're better than that," Bobby says, standing up.

"Meaning what?" I ask, genuinely interested.

"Meaning that I think you've adapted well."

A long pause before I'm able to whisper, "Thank you."

Bruce walks down the circular staircase wearing a black Prada suit and a bright-orange turtleneck, holding a guitar and a bottle of Volvic water. Ignoring both of us, he flops down in a corner of the room and starts strumming chords before settling again on the Bread song "It Don't Matter to Me," and the entire crew is silent, waiting. Bobby studies Bruce for a long time before turning back to me.

"Look," Bobby says. "I understand where you're coming from, Victor. We plant bombs. The government disappears suspects."

"Uh-huh."

"The CIA has more blood soaked into its hands than the PLO and the IRA combined." Bobby walks over to a window, peels back a dark, lacy curtain and stares out at the other crew milling about on the street, just silhouettes whispering into walkie-talkies, movement in the mist, more waiting. "The government *is* an enemy." Bobby turns to face me. "My god, *you* of all people should know *that*, Victor."

"But Bobby, I'm not . . . political," I blurt out vaguely.

"Everyone is, Victor," Bobby says, turning away again. "It's something you can't help."

My only response is to gulp down the rest of the Cosmopolitan.

"You need to get your worldview straightened out," Bobby's telling me. "You need to get your information about the world straightened out."

"We're killing civilians," I whisper.

"Twenty-five thousand homicides were committed in our country last year, Victor."

"But . . . I didn't commit any of them, Bobby."

Bobby smiles patiently, making his way back to where I'm sitting. I look up at him, hopefully.

"Is it so much better to be uninvolved, Victor?"

"Yes," I whisper. "I think it is."

"Everyone's involved," he whispers back. "That's something you need to know."

"I'm just, man, I'm just, man, I'm just—"

"Victor—"

"—man, having a hard time having to, like, justify this and . . ." I stare at him pleadingly.

"I don't think you have to justify anything, man."

"Bobby, I'm an . . . American, y'know?"

"Hey Victor," Bobby says, staring down at me. "So am I."

"Why me, Bobby?" I ask. "Why do you trust me?"

"Because you think the Gaza Strip is a particularly lascivious move an erotic dancer makes," Bobby says. "Because you think the PLO recorded the singles 'Don't Bring Me Down' and 'Evil Woman.'"

Silence until the phone rings. Bobby picks up. Bruce stops playing the guitar. It's the film crew from outside and they're ready. Bobby tells them we'll be right out. The film crew inside is already packing it in. The director, obviously satisfied, confers with Bobby, who keeps nodding while staring over at Bruce. On cue Tammy, Bentley and Jamie walk down the circular spiral staircase, and outside the film crew shoots us three times walking from the front door to the black Citroën, the six of us laughing, Bentley leading the way, Jamie and Bobby holding on to each other "playfully," Bruce and I flanking Tammy and she's clasping our hands, looking at each of us happily, because in the movie the crew outside is shooting I'm supposed to be in love with her. Jamie has to take a black Mercedes to Natacha because she's wearing a dress that cost $30,000.

And at Natacha MTV's filming a party upstairs where the girls are all wasted and beautiful and the guys are looking their hunkiest and everyone's wearing sunglasses and waiting for assistants to light their cigarettes and there's another party downstairs where Lucien Pellat-Finet is hanging out with the hat designer Christian Liagré and Andre Walker shows up on the arm of Claudia Schiffer who's wearing a feathered jumpsuit and has a red pageboy and Galliano's wearing a little black trilby hat and Christian Louboutin plays "Je T'Aime" on the piano with Stephanie Marais by his side singing the Jane Birkin part and we're receiving fans at the table we're slouched at, people flocking around us, whispering things, the prerequisite number of oohs and aahs, caviar sitting untouched on silver plates in front of us and it's all really youthquakey and the mood is light until Ralph and Ricky Lauren show up and tonight's theme is the unbearable lightness of being and everything is ubiquitous, the smell of shit rising up faintly from somewhere and floating all over the room.

"Victor," Bobby warns, after someone's handed me a packet of cocaine, reminding me of my assignment tomorrow. "And hey Bentley, pay attention."

Bentley's glassy-eyed from spending most of the day in a tanning bed and he's spacing out on good-looking teenage guys in muscle Ts. My foot has fallen asleep, the tingling moving slowly up my leg, my eyes glancing over at my name on tonight's invite. Photographers are taking pictures of our table. Tammy gazes away, her mouth caked with Urban Decay lipstick.

"He's madly in love with that busboy." Jamie smiles, lighting a cigarette.

We all turn our heads.

"I read an article about good-looking busboys in *Time* magazine." Bentley shrugs. "What can I say? I'm easily influenced."

"We're not going ahead with the Venice project," Bobby says loudly, over the din of the party.

"Harry's Bar?" Bruce asks, turning away from Tammy.

"No." Bobby shakes his head while waving to someone across the room.

Idly, without asking, I realize this means Harry's Bar will not be blown up.

In the darkness downstairs at Natacha an MTV camera crew interrupts Bobby's discussion of something called the "Band on the Run" project. A VJ begs Bobby and Jamie and Bentley to move closer together so the camera can get all three of them in the frame. Happily, they comply.

"It's about attitude as lifestyle," Jamie's saying.

"You're starting to sound like a Calvin Klein ad, baby, and I don't like it," Bobby growls.

Jamie waves playfully at the camera until Bobby's asked about his involvement with Amnesty International. I turn away, notice Dennis Rodman striding confidently around the room in a loincloth, a giant pair of wings and a diamond nose ring. When I turn back to the table the VJ is asking Bentley how he likes Paris.

"I love everything but the Americans," Bentley yawns, being vaguely entertaining. "Americans are notoriously inept at foreign languages. My idea of tedium? Listening to some nitwit from Wisconsin try and order a glass of ice at Deux Magots."

From behind me I hear the segment director say to someone, "We're not running that."

"You should let people proceed at their own pace, Bentley," Jamie says gently, leaning in, plucking an unlit cigarette from his hand. "Don't have a tizzy."

"What are you all wearing?" the VJ asks, lights and a camera swinging around to the rest of us. "Just go with it."

It's freezing in Natacha, everyone's breath is steaming and we're waving away flies, the floor littered with piles of confetti, and the smell of shit is even more pervasive after I do a couple of hits from the packet of coke that I reluctantly hand back to Bentley. Markus Schenkenberg, who thinks he's my friend but who is not, pulls a chair up next to mine, another photo op, another black snakeskin jacket to show off, another chance for him to tell me, "We're not infallible, Victuh."

"Is that on the record or off the record?"

Markus yawns as Beatrice Dalle catwalks by, then glances back over at me.

"He's a terrorist," I tell Markus, motioning to Bobby.

"No," Markus says, shaking his head. "He doesn't look like a terrorist. He's way too gorgeous."

"Reject the hype, girlfriend," I sigh, slouching deeper into my chair. "That guy's a terrorist."

"No," Markus says, shaking his head. "I know terrorists. That guy doesn't look like a terrorist."

"You're a daredevil," I yawn, giving him shark eye. "You're a total renegade."

"I'm a little out of control," Markus admits. "I'm thinking of jamming out right now."

"He's the villain," I sigh.

Someone from Camden is leaning into Jamie, a French guy named Bertrand who was Sean Bateman's roommate, whispering something in her ear, both of them staring at me. Jamie keeps nodding until Bertrand says something that causes her to stiffen up and stop nodding and she has to push Bertrand away, her face falling apart. Bertrand glares at me while folding back into the crowd. Mario Sorrenti and David Sims materialize, surrounding Markus. Bobby starts table-hopping with Shoshanna Lonstein, a former Talking Head, the magician David Blaine and Snoopy Jones. In tears, Tammy runs away from Bruce, who has China Chow perched on his knees, and a dealer Bentley sent over named the Grand Poobah whispers "Have you been experienced?" in my ear and arrangements are made.

32

A shot of Scotch tape being applied with rubber gloves to a white metal gas canister. This shot—with the camera slowly pulling back—is intercut with one of me taking a shower, slowly soaping my chest, my legs, the camera gliding gratuitously up over my ass, water cascading down the flexing muscles in my back. Another shot of the thick metal canister sitting on a Hans Wegner ottoman. A quick montage of my character dressing—slipping on Calvin Klein boxer-jockeys, a lime-green Prada turtleneck, a Yohji Yamamoto suit with a close-up of the label for the audience's gratification. A close-up of my face, a hand entering the frame to slip on a pair of black Ray-Bans (an instance of well-paid product placement). Another close-up: a Xanax tablet placed on my tongue, a bottle of Volvic water tilted toward my lips. A shot of the gas canister being packed into a Louis Vuitton tote bag.

An exterior shot of Hozan. A brief interior shot of me eating a late lunch and in this shot the Christian Bale guy walks past me but I don't notice because I'm concentrating on the patrolmen walking by carrying sub-machine guns, because I'm distracted by the arm that has fallen asleep. Shots of me moving down Rue de Fourey toward the Seine. A shot of me on Pont Marie crossing the Ile Saint-Louis with Notre Dame looming up above me, the sky gray and overcast. Then I'm crossing the Seine onto the Left Bank. A shot of me turning right on Boulevard Saint-Germain. A shot of me descending into a métro station. This shot lingers for several seconds on a crowd of straggling tourists.

A shot of me on a train, where I'm sitting down with the Louis Vuitton tote bag. Directions: Place the bag under your seat, casually open a copy of Le Monde, furrow your brow, pretend to read, look up at the handsome teenage boy flirting with you. A shot of Victor forcing a smile, looking down, a subtle refusal, a small movement of the head, a gesture that says I'm not interested. Another shot of the boy: a shrug on his part, half a grin. I'm repeating a song lyric under my breath—when Jupiter aligns with Mars when Jupiter aligns with Mars—and since I haven't been told what's in the Louis Vuitton tote bag it's easy to slip it under the seat. Later I will find out that the bomb was placed in a 35-pound gas canister along with bolts, shards of glass and assorted nails and that this is what I was carrying around in the tote bag I checked at Hozan during the lunch I had earlier this afternoon, the tote bag I carried effortlessly while strolling through the streets of Paris.

The blast will be blamed on an Algerian guerrilla or a Muslim fundamentalist or maybe the faction of an Islamic group or a splinter group of handsome Basque separatists, but all of this is dependent on the spin the head of France's counterespionage service gives the event. I don't control the detonator. An image from childhood: you're on a tennis court, you're raising a racket, Fleetwood Mac's *Rumours* plays on an eight-track somewhere and it's the beginning of summer and your mother is still alive but you know there are darker times ahead.

Fifteen minutes after I leave the train, just after 6 p.m., at the juncture of Boulevard du Montparnasse and Boulevard Saint-Michel, across the street from Closerie des Lilas, the bomb kills ten people immediately. Seven others die during the following three days, all of them from severe burns. One hundred and thirty are treated for injuries, twenty-eight of them in serious condition. Later a scene will be shot in which Bobby expresses his anger that the bomb didn't explode underground, where the damage would have been "far greater," instead of on the Pont Royal, which is partially in open air. It was, he stressed, supposed to go off at the Saint-Michel–Notre Dame station, along the Seine, just as the doors opened onto the platform opposite the cathedral.

Instead: a flash.

A shot of the windows on the train imploding from the force of the blast.

A shot of doors folding in half.

A shot of the train lurching forward, burning.

A shot of a scattering crowd.

Various shots of people blown apart, extras and stuntmen thrown out of the lightweight steel car and onto the tracks.

Shots of body parts—legs and arms and hands, most of them real—skidding across the platform. Shots of mutilated people lying in piles. Shots of faces blown off. Shots of shredded melting seats. Survivors stand around in the thick black smoke, coughing, bursting into tears, choking on the stench of gunpowder. A shot of the Christian Bale guy grabbing a fire extinguisher, pushing through the panicked crowd to reach the burned-out hulk of the subway car. Over the sound track Serge Gainsbourg's "Je T'Aime" starts playing.

A montage: hundreds of police officers arriving at the area beside the bridge that crosses the Seine and leads to Notre Dame. Victor walking by the Gap while someone in an oversized Tommy Hilfiger shirt Rollerblades by. Victor having a drink at a brasserie on Rue Saint-Antoine, playing with his Ray-Bans. The French premier flying to the scene in a helicopter, while

Tammy and the French premier's son—shot by the second unit—fritter away the day at Les Halles after being called away from the Louvre (a call Bruce made from a phone booth on Rue de Bassano, near the Arc de Triomphe) and they're wearing matching sunglasses and Tammy seems happy and she makes him smile even though he's hungover from a coke binge that went on so long he started vomiting blood. She hands him a dandelion. He blows on it, coughs from the exertion.

And then: shots of security checks carried out on roads, at borders, in various department stores. Shots of the damaged train being towed to a police laboratory. A montage of the sweeps through Muslim neighborhoods. A Koran—a prop left by the French film crew—along with computer disks disclosing plans to assassinate various officials, is found in a trash can near a housing project in Lyons and, because of a clue Bobby planted, an actor cast in the role of a young Algerian fugitive is shot to death outside a mosque.

31

Wearing an Armani suit lined with Kevlar, I usher Jamie past the metal barricades the police erected in front of the Ritz because certain Japanese diplomats are staying at the hotel this week and even with my invitation and Jamie's appearance in the show, "for precautions" we still need to produce our passports so they can be compared with our names on lists that are scanned at three separate checkpoints by the time we get backstage. Metal detectors supply totally inadequate protection, as Jamie slips through them effortlessly.

Backstage is freezing, camcorders surrounding everyone, personal trainers are French-inhaling sloppily wrapped joints and a very mean-streaky teenager who starred in Poltergeist 5: The Leg stands, debating, by a table lined with champagne bottles. I'm vaguely listening as Jamie talks with Linda Evangelista about how neither of them was cast in the latest blockbuster, about a sunrise in Asia, about Rupert Murdoch. Barely able to smile when Linda taps my shoulder and says, "Hey Vic, cheer up," I down another glass of champagne, concentrating on the models rushing around us, the smell of shit again rising up everywhere, my arm and one side of my neck falling asleep.

A runway has been set up over the downstairs swimming pool for a fashion show by a famous Japanese designer just out of rehab and the show opens with a video of the designer's boyfriend's last trip to Greenland, a voice-over blah-blahs about his communion with nature and then the sounds of cold, icy winds are whooshing behind us, melding into Yo La Tengo, and as all the lights become very white the models, led by Jamie, start strolling barefoot down the catwalk toward a giant gray screen and I'm watching her on a small video monitor backstage along with Frédéric Sanchez and Fred Bladou, who produced the music for the show, and to communicate my appreciation I'm tapping a foot. They don't notice.

At the party afterwards I'm posing for the paparazzi—as instructed—with Johnny Depp and then Elle Macpherson and then Desmond Richardson and Michelle Montagne and then I'm sandwiched between Stella Tennant and Ellen Von Unwerth, a strained goofy expression lining my features. I even give a brief interview to MTV Taipei but the smell of shit is causing my eyes to water, a black stench filling my nose, and I have to break away from the photo ops to down another glass of champagne, and when my vision returns to normal and I'm able to breathe calmly through my mouth I spot the actor playing the French premier's son.

He's lighting a cigar with a very long match, waving away a fly while chatting with Lyle Lovett and Meg Ryan, and without really even trying I find myself approaching him, suddenly aware of just how completely tired I am. One brief movement—I reach out and touch his shoulder, quickly withdrawing the hand.

He turns laughing, in the middle of a joke he's telling, the smile turning hard when he sees it's me.

"What do you want?" he asks.

"I need to talk to you," I say quietly, trying to smile.

"No you don't." He turns away, starts gesturing.

"Yeah man, I do," I say, touching his shoulder again. "I think it's important that we talk."

"Get out of here," he says impatiently. Having lost Lyle and Meg to their own conversation, he says something harsh in French.

"I think you're in danger," I say quietly. "I think if you keep seeing Tammy Devol you will be in danger. I think you're already in danger—"

"I think *you* are an idiot," he says. "And I think *you* are in danger if you don't leave here now."

"Please—" I reach out to touch him again.

"Hey," he exclaims, finally facing me.

"You've got to stay away from them—"

"What? Did Bruce send you?" He sneers. "How pathetic. Tell Bruce Rhinebeck to be a man and talk to me himself—"

"It's not Bruce," I'm saying, leaning into him. "It's all of them—"

"Get the fuck away from me," he says.

"I'm trying to help you—"

"Hey, did you hear me?" he spits. "Is anybody there?" He taps a finger rudely against my temple with such force that my eyes flutter and I have to lean up against a column for support.

"Just fuck off," he says. "Get the fuck out of here."

Suddenly Jamie grabs my arm and pulls me away from the actor, hissing into my ear "That was stupid, Victor" as we move through the crowd.

"Au revoir, dude," the actor calls out, mimicking the clichéd accent of a young American.

"That was so stupid," Jamie hisses again, keeps repeating it as she pulls me through the crowd, stopping three, four, eleven times to pose for photos.

Outside the Ritz the Christian Bale guy is at the base of the verdigrised column in the Place Vendôme but I don't say anything to Jamie, just nod sadly at him as he glares at us. I follow Jamie as we walk along the iron gate leading to the Cour Vendôme. A policeman says something to Jamie and she nods and we turn along the south edge of the plaza. She's cursing, unable to get to our car, and I'm trailing behind her, swallowing constantly, eyes tearing up, my chest sore and constricted. The Christian Bale guy is no longer at the base of the column. Finally Jamie leans into the window of a nondescript black BMW that brought us here and lets it go.

Bobby left this morning holding a boarding pass for a British Airways Paris-to-London shuttle. Our instructions: arrive at the Ritz, appear in fashion show, poison pool with LiDVl96# caplets, let our photos be taken, order drinks in the Ritz bar, wait twenty minutes, leave laughing. Gossip that Jamie Fields might be dating Victor Ward while Bobby Hughes is away might be—as per Bobby's notes—"an excellent distraction."

A montage of Jamie and Victor walking along Quai de la Tournelle, staring up at the turrets of Notre Dame, looking out at barge traffic on the Seine, Jamie trying to calm me down as I freak out, clawing at my face, hyperventilating, wailing "I'm gonna die, I'm gonna die," and she maneuvers us to a walled-off area somewhere on Boulevard Saint-Michel and we end up shooting my breakdown again, near Quai de Montebello, where I'm fed more Xanax. Then a cab takes us to Boulevard Saint-Germain and we're sitting at a sidewalk table at Les Deux Magots, where I concede, "I'm just wearing uncomfortable socks I bought at the Gap." I blow my nose, laughing miserably.

"It'll be okay," she says, handing me another Kleenex.

"Don't you want me, baby?" I'm asking.

Jamie nods. "Even though I think you tipped that cabdriver a hundred dollars?" Pause. "Sure."

"No wonder he whistled at me."

At the room we always share in Hôtel Costes our bed is already turned down and sprinkled lightly with confetti and I place a .25-caliber Walther automatic on the nightstand and while I'm fucking Jamie she positions herself so that it's easier for me to look at the videos flashing by on the TV screen, to which with both hands she keeps directing my attention, because even with her eyes closed, Jamie says, she can sense my yearning, can feel the need radiating out of my eyes, the unbearableness of it. She might have felt a spark, she might have wept. I might have said "I love you."

Afterwards, slouching in a chair across from the bed, naked, smoking a cigarette, I ask her, "What was Bertrand talking to you about?"

"Where?" she asks without pausing. "Who?"

"At Natacha the other night," I say, exhaling. "Bertrand. He said something to you. You pushed him away."

"I did?" she says, lighting a cigarette dreamily. "Nothing. Forget about it."

"Do you remember him from Camden?" I ask.

"I think so," she answers carefully. "Camden?"

"He was Sean Bateman's roommate—"

"Baby, please," she says, her breath steaming. "Yes. Bertrand from Camden. Yes. At Natacha. Okay."

After I put out the cigarette, washing another Xanax down with a glass of champagne, I ask, "Is Bertrand involved?"

"Is Bertrand involved?" she asks, repeating the question slowly, writhing on the bed, her long tan legs kicking at the sheets.

"Is Bertrand involved in the 'Band on the Run' project?" I ask.

"No," she says clearly. And then, "That's Bobby's game."

"Jamie, I—"

"Victor, why were you in London?" she asks, still staring away from me. "What were you doing there?" Then, after a long pause, closing her eyes, just the word "Please?"

Breathing in, answering without hesitation, I say, "I was sent to look for you."

A long pause, during which she stops kicking at the sheets. "By who, Victor?"

"By a man who said your parents were looking for you."

Jamie sits up, covering her breasts with a towel. "What did you say?" With a trembling hand she puts out the cigarette.

I breathe in. "A man named Palakon offered me money to come and find—"

"Why?" she asks, suddenly alert, gazing at me maybe for the first time since we entered the hotel room.

"So I could bring you back to the States," I sigh.

"This—" She stops, checks herself. "This was in the script? This Palakon was in the script?"

"I don't know anymore," I say. "I've lost touch with him."

"He . . . told you my *parents* were looking for me?" she asks, sitting up, panicking. "My parents? That's crazy, Victor. Oh god, Victor—"

"He offered me money to find you," I sigh.

"To find me?" she asks, clutching herself. "To find me? Why did you do it? What are you talking about?"

"I had to get out of town, I had to—"

"Victor, what happened?"

"I came on the *QE2*," I say. "He offered me money to sail across the ocean to find a girl I went to school with. I wasn't even going to come to London. I met a girl on the ship. I was going to Paris with her." I stop, not knowing where to go with this.

"What happened?" Jamie asks. "Why didn't you?"

"She . . . disappeared." I suddenly can't catch my breath and everything starts tumbling out of me: Marina's disappearance, our scenes together, the photos of the boy who looked like me I found in the Prada bag, at the Wallflowers concert, at the Sky Bar, at the Brigitte Lancome photo shoot, the teeth embedded in the bathroom wall, the trace of blood behind the toilet, her name missing on the passenger manifest, the altered photographs of the dinner with the Wallaces.

Jamie's not looking at me anymore. "What was the date?"

"The date of . . . what?"

Jamie clarifies. The night I met Marina in the fog. The night when we stumbled back to my room. The night when I was too drunk. The night the figure moved through my room opening drawers as I slowly passed out. I give her a date.

"What was her name, Victor?"

"What?" I'm suddenly lost, far away from Jamie.

"What was her name, Victor?" Jamie asks again.

"It was Marina," I sigh. "What does it matter, Jamie?"

"Was her name . . ." Something in Jamie's voice catches and she breathes in and finishes the sentence: "Marina Cannon?"

Thinking about it, hearing someone else say her name, clarifies something for me. "No. It wasn't Cannon."

"What was it?" she asks, fear vibes spreading out.

Which causes me to answer, enunciating clearly, "Her name was Marina Gibson."

Jamie suddenly holds out a hand and turns her head away, a gesture we haven't rehearsed. When I move unsurely toward the bed and gently pull her face to mine, an enormity in her expression causes me to reel back. Jamie scrambles out of bed and rushes into the bathroom, slamming the door. This is followed by the sounds of someone muffling screams with a towel. Empty spaces on the bed allow me to lie back and contemplate the ceiling, lights from a Bush video flashing across my face in the dark. Turning up the volume eliminates the noise coming from the bathroom.

30

Tammy and I sit on a bench outside the Louvre next to the glass pyramid at the main entrance where right now a line of Japanese students files by. From somewhere lounge music plays and we're both wearing sunglasses and Tammy has on Isaac Mizrahi and I'm dressed in Prada black and while waiting for the director we light cigarettes and guardedly mention a trendy restaurant, a place where we drank Midori margaritas together. I'm on a lot of Xanax and Tammy's hungover from the heroin she did last night and her hair's peroxided and when someone from the crew asks me a question as we're both handed steaming cups of cappuccino, I say, "I have no opinion on that."

And then, trying to lighten Tammy's mood, I tell her about the last time I did heroin, how I barely woke up the next morning, how when I drank a Coke and puked it up minutes later it was still carbonated, fizzing in the toilet water. She keeps muttering her lines, trying to remember hollow dialogue about our "relationship." We have already shot this scene four times this morning but Tammy's distracted and keeps forgetting what she's supposed to do or say, putting a mournful spin on what should be innocuous line readings because she's thinking about the French premier's son and not Bruce Rhinebeck, who we're supposed to be discussing in this scene. Plus the international crew speaks various languages so production meetings require interpreters, and the director keeps complaining that preproduction was rushed, that the script needs work. An acting coach has been hired and motivation is discussed, a sense-memory exercise is conducted, we practice breathing. Vacantly I notice that the fountains surrounding the pyramid aren't working today.

The director kneels next to us, leaning in, his breath steaming in the cold morning air. "This scene is supposed to be played very, um, tenderly," he explains, lowering his sunglasses. "You both like Bruce. You don't want to hurt his feelings. Bruce is your fiancé, Tammy. Bruce is your best friend, Victor." The director pauses gravely. "Yet your love, that overwhelming passion for each other, is just too strong. You can't keep it a secret from Bruce any longer. I *want* that urgency—okay, darlings?"

Tammy nods mutely, her hands clutched into fists. I tell the director, "I'll comply."

"I know," the director says. "That's good."

The director steps away, confers briefly with Felix the cinematographer. I turn to Tammy as someone says "Action." A boom mike hangs over our heads.

I have to smile and reach out to touch Tammy's hand. She has to smile back, which she accomplishes with some difficulty.

"It's cold," she says, shivering.

"Yes," I'm saying. "You need to stay warm."

"I suppose so," she says abstractly. "I'm sorry about last night."

"Where's Bruce?" I ask. "What's the story, baby?"

"Oh Victor, please don't," Tammy sighs. "He went to Athens. I don't ever want him to come between us again. I'll tell him everything when he gets back. Everything. I promise."

"He already suspects," I say. "It doesn't matter."

"If I could only turn back time," she says, but not at all wistfully.

"Can I believe the magic in your sighs?" I lean in for a kiss.

"You know you can." This is said too indifferently.

The director calls "Cut." He walks over and kneels down next to Tammy again. "Baby?" he asks. "Are we all right?"

Tammy's unable to even nod, just keeps scratching a point on her back that she can't quite reach.

"It's all about a light touch, baby," he's saying, lowering his sunglasses.

Tammy sniffs, says "I know" but she doesn't and she's shivering too hard for the scene to continue, so the director takes her aside and as they walk away from the crew Tammy keeps shaking her head, trying to pull away. Freezing, I light a cigarette, squint at the Seine, the smell of shit everywhere, the Louvre sitting behind us long and boring, then I imagine a Saab with a poodle in the passenger seat driving by. My foot has fallen asleep.

Tammy keeps looking back at me, making sure I'm aware of the schedule, but I'm already checking the face of the watch I was given last night by a member of the French film crew.

In digital numbers it reads 9:57.

Someone from the French film crew Rollerblades by, then slows down, making sure I notice him before he nods and glides off.

I stand up, flicking the cigarette away, and walk over to the director's chair and pick up a black Prada backpack sitting beneath it.

"I have to use the rest room," I tell a PA.

"Cool." He shrugs, inspecting a tattoo, a staff of musical notes, emblazoned on his bicep. "It's your life."

I take the bag and wait at the museum's entrance until the watch hits 10:00 exactly.

As instructed, I place the headphones of a Walkman over my ears, adjusting the volume while securing it to a clip attached to the belt I'm wearing.

I press Play.

The beginning of Ravel's "Bolero" starts booming through the headphones.

I'm stepping onto an escalator.

The black Prada backpack must be placed next to one of three pay phones in the carousel at the bottom of the Allée de Rivoli escalator.

From the opening strains of "Bolero" until its final crashing cymbals: 12 minutes and 38 seconds.

At 10:01 the bomb is officially activated.

I'm unfolding a map directing me where to go.

At the bottom of the escalator six of the French film crew, including its director, are waiting, grim-faced, all in black.

The director nods encouragingly from behind the Steadicam operator. The director wants this sequence done in one continuous shot. The director motions for me to remove the sunglasses that I forgot to take off while I was moving down the escalator.

Walking slowly through the Hall Napoléon, "Bolero" blaring, gathering momentum, I try not to walk sporadically, keeping a steady rhythm by counting the steps I'm taking, by focusing my eyes on the floor, by making a wish.

At 10:04 I spot the phones.

At 10:05 I place the Prada bag at my feet. I pretend to make a call at the phone that takes credit cards.

I check my watch at 10:06.

I move away from the phone bank, the film crew walking alongside me.

I'm supposed to stop and buy a Coke from a concession stand, which I do, taking a single sip before dumping it in a nearby trash bin.

I'm moving back into the hall, the film crew walking alongside me, the Steadicam operator moving in front of me.

10:08. "Bolero" grows more insistent, moving at a faster pitch.

But suddenly the crew is slowing down, causing me to slow down also. Glancing up, I notice their stunned faces.

The Steadicam operator stops moving, lifts his head away from the viewfinder.

Someone touches my arm.

I rip the Walkman off my head and whirl around, panicked.

It's a PA from the American film crew.

A young girl who looks like Heather Graham. The concerned expression on her face melds oddly into relief. She's panting, smiling uneasily now.

"You left this at the phone booth," she says.

She's holding out the Prada backpack.

I stare at the backpack.

"Victor?" she says, glancing first at the French crew and then back at me. "They're ready for you. I think Tammy's, um, recovered."

Total silence.

"Victor?" she asks. "Here." She hands me the Prada bag.

"Oh . . . yeah?" I take the bag from her.

I immediately hand the bag to a PA on the French crew.

Trembling, the PA takes the bag and hands it to the director.

The director looks at the Prada bag and then immediately hands it back to the PA, who winces.

"Who are these people?" the girls asks, grinning, waiting for an introduction.

"What?" I hear myself asking.

"What's going on?" she asks a little more insistently, still grinning.

The director snaps his fingers and is quickly handed a cell phone. He flicks open the mouthpiece, presses buttons and, turning away, whispers something urgently in French.

"Who?" I ask lamely. "What do you mean?"

10:09.

"That crew," she says, and then, leaning in, whispering, "The crew, like, behind you?"

"Them?" I turn around. "Oh, they just started following me around," I say. "I don't know who they are."

The French PA's breathing is actually audible, his eyes keep widening helplessly.

"Bolero" keeps rising.

An infinite number of possibilities appear.

I'm taking the slightest breaths.

The girl says, "Victor, come on, I think we should go." She touches my arm with a small hand.

I look over at the director. He nods curtly.

On the escalator, I turn around.

The French crew has already disappeared.

"Why did they take your bag, Victor?" the girl is asking. "Do you know them?"

"Hey baby," I say tiredly. "Hey, mellow out. Be quiet."

"But Victor, why did those people take your bag?" she asks.

"Bolero" ends.

The tape in the Walkman automatically clicks off.

I don't bother checking my watch.

At the pyramid Tammy stares at me quizzically, casually checking her watch, seemingly recovered.

"I got lost," I say, shrugging.

In the hazy distance, from where I'm slouching, the PA who looks like Heather Graham is already talking with the director and Felix, and both of them keep glancing over at me—suspicion, whispers, a general aura of cold worry—and confetti is scattered all around, some of it simply falling from somewhere above us, but I'm barely aware of anything. I could be in Malibu lying on a beach towel. It could be 1978 or 1983. The sky could be black with spaceships. I could be a lonely girl draping scarves over a dorm room lamp. All week I've been having dreams made up entirely of helicopter pull-away shots, revealing a giant metallic space, the word "beyond" floating above that space in white and gold letters. Someone from the crew hands me a tambourine.

29

Tonight everyone is packed into the first-floor Windsor Suite at the Ritz. Among the minglers: Kristen Mc-Menamy, Sting and Trudie Styler, Kate Moss, Jennifer Saunders, Bryan Ferry, Tina Turner, Donatella Versace, Jon Bon Jovi, Susie Bick, Nadja Auermann in a bubble-lace cocktail dress, Marie-Sophie Wilson in Inca pink, a handful of newly rich Russians, a famous producer just out of prison or rehab, does it matter? A large pug waddles throughout the room, desperately trying to avoid being stepped on. I have no idea what this party is about though it could be for the new fragrance Pandemonium. I feel pinned together, on the verge of collapse, my mouth dry from too much Xanax. We spent the day on a yacht, nodding sympathetically at one another. Oribe dropped in and did everyone's hair. Someone standing in the corner faints, I notice idly while lighting a cigarette. Disco classics blare.

Jamie's wearing—under protest—the bright-yellow leopard-silk crinoline Bobby insisted upon and she's talking to Shalom Harlow and Cecilia Chancellor, the three of them giggling tiredly, and in a black polo neck and hip-hugger pants, Cecilia's a little deaf right now because her boyfriend spent the day following her around lighting firecrackers.

When Jamie glances over at me it's with a look that reminds me: You. Are. Alone.

Someone with blond dreadlocks and a chin spike is behind me, demanding a beer.

Bertrand Ripleis joins Jamie, kisses Shalom, wraps an arm around Cecilia's waist, glares at me occasionally.

But I'm distracted by the fly that keeps hovering over a giant silver bowl piled high with Beluga, by the faint but noticeable smell of shit filling the room—"Do you smell that?" I keep asking people; "Oh yes," they keep replying knowingly—and by the guy lolling about in a white lab coat, by the diagrams of rockets and the files stamped with security classifications I saw scattered on a table in an upstairs bedroom in the house in the 8th or the 16th, and by the girl slouching next to me holding a parasol, moaning "How démodé" and then "So last season."

"It's all pretty dim," I concur, shivering.

"Oh, you're so ruthless," she sighs, twirling the parasol, dancing away, stranding me. I have been standing in the same position for so long that my leg has fallen asleep.

A trimmer Edgar Cameron—a minor, fleeting acquaintance from New York I haven't seen since last Christmas and whose girlfriend, Julia, is a reasonably fashionable vacuum I fucked after I first started dating Chloe—has nodded at me several times since he entered the party and now, since I'm standing alone, holding a glass of champagne, trying not to seem too bereft, I am a prime candidate for a visit. Julia told me that Edgar owns a hairless cat and is such a drunk that he once ate a squirrel he found in an alley off Mercer Street "on a dare." I used to kiss Julia like I really cared, like I was going to stick around.

"I owe you money, Victor," Edgar says apologetically, once he makes his way over. "I know, I know. I owe you—what? Oh let's just make it an even two hundred." He pauses worriedly. "Will you take francs?"

"Edgar, you don't owe me any money," I say softly, staring over at Jamie posing for a photographer.

"Victor, that's very cool of you but I would've picked up *my* part of the tab at Balthazar the other night if only I'd—"

"Edgar, what are you talking about?" I sigh, interrupting him.

"Last week?" Edgar says, vaguely waving to someone. "At Balthazar. In New York. When you picked up the check. You put it on your card."

Pause. "I wasn't at Balthazar last week, Edgar," I say carefully. "I haven't been in New York in . . ." My voice trails off, something tiny and hard in me starts unfolding.

But Edgar's laughing. "You seemed to be in a much better mood the other night. Paris bumming you out? Oh look, there's Mouna Al-Rashid."

"You could say that," I whisper. "Edgar . . . when did we have dinner?"

"Last Tuesday," Edgar says, not laughing anymore, his smile fading. "At Balthazar. A whole bunch of us. You put it on your card. Everyone gave you cash. . . ." Pause. Edgar stares at me as if I'd suddenly fallen asleep. "Except me. I offered to go to a cash machine but—"

"I wasn't there, Edgar," I say softly, my eyes watering. "That wasn't me."

"But we went dancing afterwards, Vic," Edgar says. "You were celebrating." He pantomimes someone having a good time. "B-list models all night, a booth at Cheetah, the works."

I wipe away a tear that spills out of one eye, trying to smile. "Oh man."

"Victor, I mean, I don't . . ." He tries to laugh. "I mean, I called you at your apartment the next day. I left a message. I offered to take you to lunch."

"I don't remember any of this, Edgar," I choke.

"Well, you seemed very upbeat," he says, trying to convince me. "You were talking about going back to school, to Columbia or NYU." Pause. "You weren't smashed, Victor. In fact I don't even think you were drinking." Another pause. "Are you . . . okay?" Again, a pause. "Do you have any pot?"

"Are *you* okay, Edgar?" I ask back. "Maybe *you* were really drunk, maybe—"

"Victor, my girlfriend, you know, Julia? Well—"

"No, not really."

"Well, she said she ran into you at the Gap the next day," Edgar says, frowning. "The one on Fifth Avenue? Downtown?" Pause. "She said you were buying sunscreen and looked, um, fairly cheerful."

"Wait—who else was with us?" I ask. "At Balthazar?"

"Well, it was me and Julia and—oh god, Victor, is this a joke?"

"Just tell me," I say, wiping another tear that races down my cheek. "Please?"

"Well, it was me and Julia and Rande Gerber, Mira Sorvino, someone from Demi Moore's production company, Ronnie Newhouse, someone from the Cardigans, and of course Damien and Lauren Hynde."

Very carefully I hand the champagne glass I'm holding to Edgar, who tentatively takes it from me, mystified.

"Victor, you were actually quite enchanting that night," Edgar says.

"Really. There's no need to cry. My god, you and Damien patched things up, the club's a resounding success and—"

"Edgar, please don't." Adrenaline rushing through me, I fumble around in my jacket pocket, find two Xanax, throw them in my mouth, toss my head back. I take the glass of champagne out of Edgar's hand and down it so quickly I start coughing.

"You and Damien were talking about opening another place," Edgar says. "In TriBeCa, I believe."

"Edgar," I say, leaning into him, breathing heavily. "I don't think that was me."

"Well, whoever it was, he was . . ." Edgar flinches, moves away slightly. "He was extremely, um, well-behaved and . . . I actually must be off. Later, Victor." He disappears into the nothingness of the party.

I'm hot even though steam keeps pouring from my mouth with every exhale and "Beyond"—the word that shows up in my dreams—keeps flashing over the party, buzzing electric near the ceiling. It seems that everyone in this room has been here for ten hours.

"It's not fun to scare people away, is it, Victor?" Felix, the cinematographer, suddenly appears, wearing a chartreuse jacket with little epaulets on the shoulders. His subsequent wink is some kind of cue. I'm trying to recover and failing.

"I suppose," I manage.

The director, whom I didn't notice, makes himself more apparent by standing in front of me and staring grimly.

"A stellar evening," he says.

"What?" I ask, and then, "Oh. I suppose."

"Is something wrong?" the director asks. "Is something troubling you, Victor?"

"No, um, I'm just overwhelmed."

"Well, you have a lot to live up to, right?"

"Yes, that's right." I'm nodding. "And I'm freaking out because of it."

"Victor," he starts.

"Yes?"

"Who have you been holding court with recently?" the director asks. "I mean, besides the people in the house."

"Oh . . . no one." I shrug. "Just . . . me."

"What was going on in the Louvre this morning?" Felix suddenly asks. "Dimity, the PA, mentioned you were being followed around by a camera crew."

"Dimity has no idea what she's talking about," I say, finding my voice. "Even though she is, in her own . . . way, quite, um, a wonderful"—I gulp—"person."

"We would also like to know what happened to the actor playing Sam Ho," the director says without warning. "Do you have any idea concerning his whereabouts?"

The name—Sam Ho—resonates dully, and briefly I'm transported back to the gym in the basement of that house in London, Jamie screaming, Bobby in a ski mask, Bruce holding a knife, the blood and wires, the flickering lights, the gutted mannequin, the party we went to the next night and the girl who ignored me there.

"I don't want to talk about . . . the past," I manage to say. "Let's concentrate on the pr-pr-present."

"You were the last one with the actor after you left Pylos," Felix says. "You were supposed to stay with the limo once you exited the club."

Pause. "Well . . . ," I start. "Have you talked to the . . . driver?"

"We've been unable to locate him as well," the director says. "What happened that night, Victor?"

"Victor, did Sam Ho come back to the house with you that night?" Felix asks. "This is very important, so think carefully."

"No, he did not," I say, straining, flushed.

"You're lying," the director snaps.

"I'm profoundly insulted by that remark."

"Oh Jesus," he sneers.

"Victor," Felix says calmly, though his attitude seems menacing. "What happened to Sam Ho that night? After the two of you left Pylos?"

"He . . . started coming on to me—"

"But where were you going?" the director asks, advancing closer. "Why didn't you stay outside the club? The crew was outside. They said they saw you run to the limousine. They said it took off screeching."

"Do you really think I'm going to make some kind of—I don't know—surprise announcement concerning where . . . I mean, Jesus . . ."

"Where did the two of you go?"

"I don't know," I say, crumpling. "We . . . went for a ride . . . at Sam's request . . . and we . . . were going for a ride . . . to another club, I think." I start squinting, pretending to think. "I don't really remember. . . . I think Bobby told me to bring him back to the house but—"

Felix and the director shoot glances at each other.

"Wait," the director says. "Bobby told you to bring Sam back?"

"Yeah," I say. Following Felix's gaze, I see Bobby across the room.

Bobby's looking fresh and relaxed and lights a cigarette Cameron Diaz is holding and he glances over at me and, when he sees who I'm talking to, does a very casual double take and excuses himself from the group he's standing with, people I can't even recognize because of how blurry my vision has rapidly become.

"But that wasn't in the script," Felix says. "That was most definitely not in the script."

"Why did Bobby want Sam Ho back at the house, Victor?" the director asks very quietly.

I shrug helplessly, notice the confetti dotting the sleeve of the black jacket I'm wearing.

Bobby's hand lands on that arm, and smiling widely for Felix and the director, he says, "I need to talk to our boy here—can I please have him?" But it's not really a question because it's shaped in the form of a demand.

"No," the director says. "You can't."

"Am I interrupting something?" Bobby asks boyishly, tightening his grip on my arm.

"Yes," the director says. "We were having a conversation about inconsistencies."

"Hey man, I'm not the script supervisor, dude," Bobby says. "Take it up with someone else."

Felix and the director don't say anything. It's almost as if they're obeying a silent vibe Bobby's sending out: I'm beautiful, I have a purpose, go back to your dream.

We brush past extras, Bobby's arm around my neck, and he's patting my shoulder, maneuvering me to where Jamie's waiting by the exit, laughing fakely at what someone she doesn't really know says, and then Bobby asks me, "What would you think if all these people were to die and this entire hotel came crashing down?" He's grinning, serious.

"Oh dude," I whisper, breaking up. "Oh man."

"Here—take this," Bobby says, slipping a tablet into my mouth, offering me his glass of champagne while caressing the back of my neck. "It's like a rainbow."

28

In the shower in the bathroom Jamie and Bobby share Bobby's admiring the tans we acquired on the yacht today, at the shocking whiteness where our boxer-briefs blocked out the sun, at the white imprints Jamie's bikini left behind, the paleness almost glowing in the semi-darkness of the bathroom, the water from the massive chrome head smashing down on us and both our cocks are sticking up at sharp angles and Bobby's pulling on his prick, stiff and thick, his balls hanging tightly beneath it, the muscles in his shoulders flexing as he strokes himself off and he's looking at me, our eyes meeting, and in a thick voice he grunts, "Look at your dick, man," and I look down at the cock I'm jerking off and past that, at my thickly muscled legs. . . .

In the shower Bobby lets me make out with Jamie and Bobby's head is between her legs and Jamie's knees buckle a couple of times and Bobby keeps propping her up with an arm and his face is pushed up into her cunt and she's arching her back, pushing herself onto his tongue, and one of his hands is gripping my cock, soaping it up, and then Bobby starts sucking it and it gets so hard I can feel the pulse in it and then it gets even harder, the shaft keeps thickening and Bobby pulls it out of his mouth and studies it, squeezing it, and then he flicks his tongue over the head and then he lifts it up by the tip and starts flicking his tongue in brief, precise movements over the place where the head meets the shaft as Jamie hungrily moans "do it do it" while fingering herself in the semi-darkness and then Bobby places the entire shaft into his mouth, taking as much of my cock as he comfortably can, sucking eagerly, wetly, while crouching down on his haunches, still stroking his own prick, and below it the curves of his thighs keep swelling as he repositions himself. I'm bending my neck back, letting the water stream down my chest, and when I look back down Bobby's looking up at me and grinning, his hair wet and pressed down on his forehead, his tongue extended, pink against his face. Then Bobby motions for me to turn around so that he can spread the cheeks of my ass and I can feel him extending his tongue up in it and then he removes his tongue and sticks his index finger halfway up my asshole and keeps fingerfucking me until he's pushed the entire finger as far as it can go, causing my cock to keep twitching uncontrollably. . . .

I drop to my knees and start licking Jamie's pussy, my fingers spreading her lips, and as her hands massage my hair I lean her against the shower wall—Bobby still behind me on his knees, his finger moving in and out of my asshole, another hand running over my hard, cubed abs—and I keep running my tongue from her clit to her asshole and placing one of her legs over my shoulder I suck her clit into my mouth as I fuck her with two then three fingers and then I move my tongue into her asshole, fucking it with my tongue while my fingers tug on her clit, and when I stand up Bobby's finger slips out of my hole and I turn Jamie around and squatting down behind her I spread her small, firm ass cheeks open and start pumping my tongue in and out of her asshole and then I slide my tongue deep inside her anus and keep it there while rubbing her clit until she comes. . . .

After we dry off we move into Jamie and Bobby's bedroom, next to the giant bed which has been stripped of its sheets, and all the lights in the room are on so we can see everything and Jamie's squeezing my cock, sucking on its head, and I'm watching Bobby walk over to a drawer and when he bends down his ass cheeks spread wide, briefly exposing his asshole as he picks up a bottle of lotion, and when he turns around his cock is sticking up in a full erection and he strides back to us as I'm watching Jamie put one finger inside her pussy and then pull it out and then she starts stroking her clit and then she brings that finger up to my mouth and I start sucking on it. She sticks her finger back into her vagina and when she pulls it out she offers it to me again and I take her hand, licking the saltiness from her finger, sucking on it, and then I pull her face to mine and while I kiss her my hands slide down to her ass, then up to her waist and then up to the heavy firmness of her tits, my palms passing lightly over her tiny nipples, causing them to harden, while she keeps trembling, moaning. Then I lay her on the bed and kneeling at the side of it I smell her cunt lips, inhaling deeply, beads of water still clinging to her pubic hair, and I'm breathing gently on her and with one finger I trace the outline of her labia, not parting them yet, just teasing, and then I slide one finger deep into her pussy, playing with her clit as I watch it deepen in color, and she's lying back on the bed, her eyes closed, and then I'm strumming my tongue along her clit and then I lift her hips up and I'm spreading her ass open until I can see the pink inside it. . . .

I move my mouth back up to her tits, sucking hard on the nipples while squeezing the breasts beneath them, and then I slide down again, my tongue traveling down the line bisecting her body, and Jamie raises then spreads her legs, her clit totally engorged now, but I barely touch it at first, deliberately avoiding it, causing Jamie to shift around continuously, trying to place herself against my tongue, whimpering, and when my tongue lightly laps at it her clit gets firmer, bigger, and my hands are squeezing the backs of her legs and then the insides of her thighs and I'm still fucking her with my tongue and when I lift her hips up again I start sucking on her asshole. Bobby's leaning in, staring intently as my tongue goes in and out of her anus while he strokes his prick off. "God, you're so wet," I'm whispering. "You're so fucking wet." I start pumping a finger into her vagina and Jamie's bucking her hips as I move my mouth up and suck the whole labia into my mouth and then I lick her clit again, causing Jamie to thrash out another orgasm. . . .

In front of me Jamie steps into Bobby's arms and he places a huge hand under her chin and tilts her face upward and he kisses her deeply, their pink tongues entwined, and Jamie's hand falls onto Bobby's cock and she squeezes it and then she eases Bobby down onto the bed next to where I'm lying, his head at my feet, his dick at my face, and Jamie drops to her knees beside the bed and starts licking the sides of Bobby's prick while she's staring at me and Bobby's moaning and he's tonguing my feet and Jamie raises then lowers her mouth, taking in as much of his cock as she can while Bobby's hips keep thrusting upward. She climbs onto the bed and raises herself over Bobby's dick then slowly lowers herself, her eyes riveted on mine as his cock slides into her pussy, and then she pulls it out until she's rubbing her slit over the head and then she falls onto it again and it slides into her effortlessly and then she stops, stays still, letting her cunt accustom itself, and then she starts riding Bobby's cock, rising up to its tip then lowering herself down hard onto his pelvis, Bobby groaning as he pumps into her, and suddenly all her muscles contract at once and she's trying not to come but she loses control and starts yelling "fuck me fuck me fuck" and somewhere across the room a beeper goes off, is ignored. . . .

I'm on my knees in front of Bobby and he's urging me to lift his penis up so I can smell his balls and then he pushes my head back and slides his cock all the way into my mouth and I'm gagging, choking for air, but Bobby keeps it there until my throat relaxes, his hands on either side of my head guiding me up and down on his penis, then pulling it way out but keeping the head in my mouth and then pushing his cock back into my throat until my upper lip is buried in his pubic hair and my nose is pressing against his hard, taut abdomen, his balls tight against my chin. When I look up, his head is thrown back, only the point of his chin visible above the thickly corded column of his neck. Bobby's abdominal muscles taper down from under his chest to the narrower ones at the base of his stomach and one of my hands is rubbing over them, my other hand on the place where his back fleshes out into the curves of his ass, and I'm swallowing hard, my lips slicked over with my own spit and Bobby's pre-come, and I run my tongue around the head, sucking up and down, going all the way to the base of it in a slow, steady motion, my nose buried in Bobby's sweaty pubic hair, and then he starts fucking my face harder. . . .

Bobby falls back on the bed and hoists me up, positioning me so he can start sucking my dick while I'm sucking his, and he's deep-throating me, his head going all the way down and all the way up each time, sucking hard on my cock as it emerges from his mouth coated with saliva and then swallowing it as he goes back down, our hips rotating slightly, in rhythm. Then Bobby rolls over and lies flat on his stomach, one knee cocked, his balls resting on the bed beneath the crack of his ass, and Jamie's spreading the cheeks of Bobby's ass apart and, panting, I lean down and kiss his asshole, immediately sticking my tongue in it, and Bobby's responding by raising his hips until he's on his knees and elbows and I start drilling his asshole with my tongue, feeling it expand slightly then contract and then expand again and then Jamie moves to the top of the bed and spreads her legs in front of his face, holding his head, and he tries to get at her pussy but she's sitting on it and he moves backward taking Jamie with him until she's lying on her back, raising and spreading her legs in front of Bobby's face, and he starts eating her pussy until he turns her over onto her hands and knees and starts eating her pussy from behind and he's emitting loud groaning noises that are muffled from between her legs and I start lubing Bobby's asshole with the lotion he brought to the bed. . . .

I'm sitting back on my heels and Jamie leans over and starts sucking my cock, spitting on it until it's slathered with saliva, and then I stand on my knees and push Jamie away, keeping Bobby's ass spread with the fingers of one hand and lubing my cock up with the other, and then I guide the head of my penis up against his asshole, grasping his hips, holding them steady, shoving gently forward until I can't help myself—I start fucking him really hard, my stomach slapping up against his ass while Jamie holds on to me, bringing me back each time I lunge forward. I let go of one hip and reach down and around to find Bobby's hand stroking his stiff dick, jerking it off, matching each stroke with my thrusts, and I close my hand around Bobby's and the rocking motion we're making causes my hand to automatically go back and forth and I start riding him harder, breathing so fast I think my heart's going to stop, totally flushed. "Easy, easy," I hear him moan. "Don't come yet. . . ."

Bobby grabs my cock and helps me guide it into Jamie's pussy and I slide my penis up into her while holding her thighs from beneath, reaching my arms around them, doubling her up, and then I grab both her tits and start sucking on them while I'm fucking her, her cunt sucking on my cock as she rocks from side to side, her pussy totally responding and sucking me in when I pull back, and then I'm slamming into her, grunting with each thrust, and her face is bright red and she's crying out, heaving against me, and then I pull out and turn her over, spreading her ass cheeks with the thumb and finger of one hand and while I'm sliding a finger in and out Bobby slathers my cock with more lube and, grasping Jamie's hips while rotating my own, I push my rock-hard cock slowly into Jamie's rectum, feeling it stretch out, not even waiting until she's loosened up to start fucking her ass really hard. Bobby leans down, watching my dick disappear then reappear, Jamie's asshole clinging to it, and then positions himself at the head of the bed and grasping the headboard for leverage he slides his hips forward, raising and spreading his legs so Jamie can eat out his asshole while he jerks off. Releasing a hip, I reach down and squeeze Jamie's breasts again, running my hand down her stomach until I find her clit, and with two fingers I start rubbing it, then fingerfucking her while she continues eating Bobby's ass out, sometimes sucking his dick. . . .

Jamie stands up on the bed and straddles Bobby at hip level. She lowers herself over his cock and grasps it with one hand and then feeds it up into her cunt until she's sitting down on it, leaning forward, flattening out on Bobby, her breasts pushed into his face, and Bobby holds them with both hands while sucking on her nipples. I'm crouching between Bobby's legs inside Jamie's and I spread her cheeks and start fingering her asshole, which is pushed out and distended from the pressure of having Bobby's large cock filling her. I sit back on my heels, my erection twitching, and when I spread Jamie's cheeks even wider she raises her hips, causing Bobby to slide out of her until only the head of his cock remains inserted between the lips of her cunt and then my cock slides effortlessly back up into Jamie's ass. Carefully Jamie settles back down on Bobby's cock while I bounce gently up and down, Bobby's cock going all the way in while my dick slides halfway out, and we can both feel Jamie's vaginal muscles contracting powerfully during her orgasm as she convulses between us. . . .

"Here, lift up," Bobby's saying as I raise my hips, and he quickly slides a towel under my ass and I'm touching the contours of his chest, tracing the line bisecting his body, and he's spreading my legs while leaning over and kissing me hard on the mouth, his lips thick and wet, and one finger, then two fingers, start moving in and out of my asshole and both of us are glistening with sweat and my head's in Jamie's lap and she's holding me, whispering things in my ear, leaning over and stroking my erection. "Yeah, show me that dick, Victor," Bobby says. "Keep stroking it, that's it. Spread your legs. Wider. Lift them up. Let me see your asshole." He lifts my legs up and pushes my knees back and I can feel him spreading my legs open, inspecting that area. "Yeah, you've got a nice pink butthole, man. I'm looking at it right now. You want me to fuck it, huh?" I'm bracing myself, gazing intently up at Bobby, who is expressionless, and I'm not sure how many fingers are in my ass right now and his hand starts moving in a circular motion, fingers moving deeper until I have to grab his wrist, whispering "Easy, man, easy" and with his other hand he keeps twisting my nipples until they're sore and burning and my head's lodged in Jamie's armpit and I have to strain my muscles to keep from coming too soon. . . .

"Wait," I groan, lifting my head up. "Do you have a condom?"

"What?" he asks. "Oh man, do you care?"

"It's okay." I lean back.

"You want me to fuck you?" he's asking.

"Yeah, it's okay."

"You want me to fuck you with this cock?" he's asking, hoisting my legs up over his shoulders.

"Yeah, fuck me."

Jamie watches carefully as Bobby slides his long, thick cock in and out of my asshole and then starts increasing the length and depth of his thrusts, pulling his prick almost all the way out and then slamming it in again, his cock pumping my prostate, and I'm looking up at him and shouting out and his abs are straining with each thrust and he tries to steady himself by holding on to my shoulders, the muscles in his arms bulging with the effort, and his eyebrows are furrowed and his face—usually impassive—now scowls briefly with pleasure. "Yeah, fuck him, fuck him harder," Jamie's chanting. Bobby keeps slipping his cock in and out of me, both of us groaning with relief, intensity rising, and then I'm yelling out, convulsing uncontrollably, both of us bucking wildly as I start ejaculating, shooting up onto my shoulders and then my chest as Bobby keeps fucking me, my anus contracting around his thrusting cock. "Yeah, that's it, that's it, man," Bobby groans, coming, collapsing on top of me. . . .

27

Afterwards, back in the shower by myself, water spraying over me, I'm delicately touching my asshole, which seems distended, tender, slick with lotion and Bobby's semen, the flesh feeling pierced. Stepping out of the shower, I dry off, avoiding my reflection in a giant mirror, afraid of what I might see in it. I scan the counter for a comb, deodorant, aspirin. I peer into a medicine cabinet but it's empty. I start opening drawers: a Breitling watch, two Cartier tank rings (one citrine, one amethyst), a pair of diamond-studded sunglasses, a bottle of cologne called Ambush, a container of Shiseido moisturizer. In another drawer: dozens of Chanel lipsticks, an issue of *Harper's Bazaar* with Tammy on the cover, a few dried roses and—in a clear plastic bag in the bottom drawer of the bathroom Jamie and Bobby share—a large black hat, folded over.

I hesitate before taking the bag out of the drawer, because something in me says not to. Instinct says not to.

I'm holding the bag up in front of my face, averting my eyes.

The sound of a fly whirring around my head causes me to look at the bag.

In the bag is the hat Lauren Hynde gave me in New York.

The hat Palakon told me to bring with me on the *QE2*.

Its entire inner flap has been removed.

A large, gaping hole exists where the small red rose was.

One side of the hat is dotted with pink and green confetti.

I can't even touch the bag anymore. I just keep swallowing involuntarily until I carefully place it back in the drawer and then I slowly close the drawer. But this is a dream, this is a movie—repeating that calms me down but in the back of my mind, faintly, darkly, is the sound of laughter and it's coming from a grave and it's whispery, blaming.

Naked, clutching a towel, I slowly move into the bedroom where Jamie and Bobby are sleeping deeply, gracefully, on a flat sheet soaked with our sweat even though it's so cold in this room

the room is a trap. The question about the hat will never be asked. The question about the hat is a big black mountain and the room is a trap. A photo of your expressionless face is on the cover of a magazine, a gun lies on top of an icy nightstand. It's winter in this room and this room is a trap

that my breath is steaming as I keep staring down at Jamie and Bobby sleeping on the bed.

On Bobby's shoulder is a tattoo, black and shapeless, I never noticed before.

A QE2 flashback, a montage with strobe lights.

The smell of the sea, an October afternoon, the Atlantic moving slowly below us, midnight, meeting Marina outside Club Lido, her voice raspy from crying, the fog machines, Marina backlit in front of a bathroom drawer, how shy she seemed at the railing, how purposefully she moved around my cabin, the hooded parka.

There was the hair hanging over Marina's face. And there was the hooded parka.

There was the tattoo, black and shapeless, on her right shoulder blade.

This tattoo did not exist the afternoon we first met.

You never saw Marina's face that night.

"You have to go to London," a voice whispered.

That night, you never touched her body.

You understand that something incomplete is being revealed.

An unscheduled stop mid-crossing.

Someone climbs aboard a ship.

A girl you didn't save was doomed.

It's all very clear but you have to keep guessing.

It's what you don't know that matters most. This is what the director told you.

I dress, then stagger outside.

When I look back up at the house he's standing in a bedroom window. He's looking down at me. He's holding a finger to his lips. He's saying "Shhh."

26

Because métro service doesn't begin until 5:30 I'm walking aimlessly through a dark early-morning fog, staggering for long stretches, until automatic timers turn the streetlights off and clubs are just closing and a figure, a specter, strolling by smiles venomously at me and in the fog the outlines of glass and concrete towers keep shifting shapes and without thinking about direction I find myself walking toward the Eiffel Tower, through the Parc du Champ de Maris and then across the Seine on the Pont d'Iéna and then past the Palais de Chaillot. A pigeon bursts out of the fog, leaving a swirling trail behind. Without warning, leaning against a black Citroën, in the fog, is the Christian Bale look-alike.

"Victor?" he asks, rock-faced, subdued. He's wearing a black cardigan, ankle boots, a Prada overcoat.

Silently I walk up to him, the streets littered with confetti, the fog locking in on us.

"Someone wants to see you," he says simply.

I just nod and without any prodding get into the back of the Citroën, lying flat across the seat, then curling up once the car starts moving, and I'm making noises in the backseat, sometimes weeping. He tells me not to crack up. He remarks delicately about an opening in my destiny. But I'm paying minimal attention, listening to him as closely as I would listen to a brick, a tree, a pile of sand. Finally, absurdly, I ask, "Do you know who I am?" On the radio: something emblematic of where I'm at in this moment, something like "Don't Fear the Reaper" or "I'm a Believer."

A hotel on Avenue Kléber.

Following the Christian Bale guy down a hallway lined with photos of mostly dead celebrities, I'm so drowsy I can barely keep up with him and the lights above us keep flickering chicly and at the far end we arrive at a door covered with a thin sheet of frost.

Inside the room all the lights are dimmed, and sitting at a desk, Sky-TV glowing soundlessly on a large-screen television behind him, legs primly crossed, smoking a cigarette, is F. Fred Palakon.

I appear seemingly nonplussed.

"Hello, Victor," Palakon says. "How *are* things?" he asks menacingly. "Remember me?"

The Christian Bale guy closes the door behind us, then locks it.

Palakon gestures toward the edge of the bed. After I sit down, facing him, he recrosses his legs, regarding me unfavorably. It's freezing in the hotel room and I rub my hands together to keep them warm.

"I got . . . lost," is all I say, shamefully.

"Well, not really," Palakon says. "Not what you'd technically call 'lost,' but I suppose there's some truth in your statement."

I'm staring at the carpet, at the patterns revealing themselves in the carpet, and I keep rubbing my hands together to keep them warm.

"I see you've taken up with quite a crowd," Palakon says. "I shouldn't be surprised. A hip, happening, gorgeous young thing like yourself, all alone in Paris." He says this with such harsh articulation that I have to flinch and look away. "I see you have a tan."

"Palakon, I—"

"Mr. Ward, please don't say anything," Palakon warns. "Not yet."

"Palakon, you never called me in England," I say in a rush. "What was I supposed to do?"

"That is because I was informed you never checked into the Four Seasons," Palakon says sharply. "How were we supposed to call you when we had no idea where you were?"

"But . . . that's not true," I say, sitting up. "Who told you that? I mean, what are you talking about, Palakon?"

"It means that there are no records of you ever staying at the Four Seasons," Palakon says. "It means that if someone tried to contact you at the Four Seasons we were simply told that neither a Mr. Victor Ward nor a Mr. Victor Johnson was staying there." An icy pause. "What happened to you, Victor?"

"But I checked in," I'm protesting. "The driver who picked me up in Southampton saw me check in."

"No, Victor," Palakon says. "The driver saw you *walk* in. He did not see you check in."

"This is wrong," I'm muttering.

"All attempts to get in touch with you at the Four Seasons proved fruitless," Palakon says, glaring. "When we finally tried to make actual *physical* contact, as in *searching* the hotel for you, we came up with nothing."

"Ask him," I say, pointing at the Christian Bale guy, standing behind me. "He's been following me ever since I got to London."

"Not really," Palakon says. "He lost you that night after you were at Pylos and didn't find you again until the other night, when he spotted you at the opera." Pause. "With Jamie Fields."

I don't say anything.

"But because of your actions let's just say his part has been beefed up considerably."

"Palakon," I start. "I don't care about the money anymore. I just want to get the hell out of here."

"That's very noble, Mr. Ward, but you were supposed to get Jamie Fields out of London and back to the States," Palakon says. "Not traipse off to Paris. So the money—as of now—is beside the point."

Looking down again, I mutter, "I traipsed, I traipsed, I admit it, I traipsed . . ."

"Why are you . . ." Palakon sighs, looks up at the ceiling, curved and stained, and then, thoroughly annoyed, back at me. "Why are you in Paris, Mr. Ward?"

I'm still muttering, "I traipsed, I traipsed . . ."

"Mr. Ward," Palakon snaps. "*Please.*"

"What else do you know?" I ask. "How did you find me?"

Palakon sighs again, puts his cigarette out, runs his hands over the jacket of a very natty suit.

"Since you had mentioned that you were going to follow that girl you met on the ship to Paris, we simply pursued a few theories."

"Who is 'we,' Palakon?" I ask hesitantly.

"Does the third person alarm you?"

"Who's . . . the third person?"

"Mr. Ward, what is the situation as of now?"

"The . . . situation is . . . the situation is . . ." Grasping, unable to figure it out, I just give up. "The situation is out of my control."

Palakon takes this in. "That's too bad." After a thoughtful pause, he asks, gently, "Can it be remedied?"

"What does that . . . mean?" I ask. "Remedied? I told you—it's out of my control."

Palakon runs a hand along the desk he's sitting at and then, after a long pause, asks, "Are you in any position to fix things?"

"I don't know." I'm vaguely aware of my feet and arms slowly falling asleep as I sit slumped on the edge of the bed. "I'm not sure."

"Well, let's start with does she trust you?" he asks. "Is she willing to leave? Is she coming back to the States?" Another pause. "Is she in love with you?"

"We've . . . been intimate," I say hollowly. "I'm not sure—"

"Congratulations," Palakon says. "So you've become a duo. How cute. How"—he tilts his head—"apropos."

"Palakon, I don't think you know what's going on." I swallow. "I don't think you're in the same movie," I say carefully.

"Just get Jamie Fields out of Paris," Palakon says. "Just get her back to

New York. I don't care how you do it. Promise her things, marry her, perform a kidnapping, whatever."

I'm exhaling steam. "She has . . . a boyfriend."

"That has never been an impediment for you before, Mr. Ward," Palakon says. "Who is it? Who's she seeing? Someone in that house? Not Bruce Rhinebeck. And it can't be Bentley Harrolds."

"It's Bobby Hughes," I say hollowly.

"Ah, of course," Palakon says. "I'd forgotten about him."

"How's that possible?" I ask, confused.

"Depending on what planet you live on, Victor, it's not so hard."

A long patch of silence.

"There's a small problem, Palakon."

"If it's small it's not a problem, Mr. Ward."

"Oh, I think this is," I say, my voice getting tiny.

"Just take Jamie Fields back to the United States," Palakon says. "That's all you need to do."

"There's a small problem," I repeat.

"My patience ran out the minute we met, Mr. Ward. What is it?"

"Well, you see," I say, leaning in for emphasis, smiling involuntarily, my heart tightening, whispering loudly, "They're all murderers."

Palakon sighs wearily. "Excuses, excuses. Oh Mr. Ward, you can do better than that. You're not *that* lazy."

In a calm and purposeful fashion I try to express everything that has been happening: how they memorize maps, passwords, warning signals, airline timetables, how they learn to strip, assemble and load an array of light machine guns—M16s, Brownings, Scorpions, RPGs. Kalashnikovs—to throw off tails, how one day they had to eliminate everything in our computer system that connected them to Libya. I tell Palakon about the detailed maps of various American and Israeli embassies scattered throughout the house, that at any given time three million dollars in cash is hidden in a closet downstairs next to the gym, that we know certain people only by code names, that intermediaries lunch frequently in the house and there are so many parties. I tell Palakon about how fake passports are arranged and how those passports are constantly being shredded and burned, how Bobby is always traveling to Belgrade or to Zagreb and visas are applied for in Vienna and there are anxious consultations and trips to villas in outlying suburbs. How I am constantly being introduced to just another young Palestinian with a "troubled past" or to someone who was partially blinded by an Israeli letter bomb, patriots who had strayed from the path, people offering pretexts for refusing to negotiate, beautiful men boasting of secret alliances.

I tell Palakon about the bombing of the Institute of Political Studies, the bombing at Café Flore, the bombing on the métro at Pont Royal. I tell Palakon about a car lined with 120 pounds of explosives that rolled down a hill in Lyons and smashed into a police station, killing eight people, four of them children, injuring fifty-six. I explain the attempted bombing of the Louvre, how Jamie Fields poisoned the pool at the Ritz, the whispered references to TWA flights leaving Charles de Gaulle, how new social security numbers were invented, aerial reconnaissance photos were taken, certain vanishings accomplished. I tell Palakon about a chaotic party, then about another chaotic party, while I'm gripping the comforter and it all seems so insubstantial that I'm reminded of a Basque separatist movement's motto one of the scriptwriters showed me one day in a red spiral notebook: "Action Unites. Words Divide."

Palakon studies me. He sighs, then keeps sighing for what seems like minutes.

"If I believe you, Mr. Ward—and I don't know if I'm there yet—what does this have to do with—"

"Hey, I didn't make this up," I shout. "I'm not that good an actor."

"I'm not saying you made it up, Victor," Palakon says, shrugging. "What I'm thinking, however, is that perhaps you have a more active imagination than I realized. Maybe you've seen too many movies, Mr. Ward."

Something suddenly flashes in front of me. A somber realization.

"The hat," I say. "They have the hat."

Palakon glances over at the Christian Bale guy.

Palakon looks back at me.

"What do you mean?" Palakon asks tentatively.

"They have the hat," I say. "The hat you told me to bring."

"Yes?" Palakon asks, drawing out the word. "What . . . exactly are you saying?"

"I found the hat that Lauren Hynde gave me," I say. "It was in their bathroom. It was in their bathroom—Jamie and Bobby's."

"I'm confused," Palakon says. "Did you give it to them?"

"No. I didn't."

"But . . ." Palakon shifts around uncomfortably in his chair until he is sitting erect, his back straight. A new, ominous mood fills the room. "What are you saying? How did they get it?"

"I don't know," I say. "It disappeared from my cabin on the QE2," I say. "I found it an hour ago in a bathroom drawer," I say.

Palakon stands up, starts pacing, scowling to himself. He's taking stances that say: this changes everything.

The Christian Bale guy is leaning over, his hands on his knees, taking deep breaths.

Everything suddenly seems displaced, subtle gradations erase borders, but it's more forceful than that.

"Palakon?" I ask, slowly. "Why was that hat so important?"

No answer.

"Why did Lauren Hynde give me that hat?" I ask. "Why is the hat so important, Palakon?"

"Who says it is?" Palakon asks, distracted, harassed, still pacing.

"Palakon," I sigh. "I may be a lot of things, but stupid is not one of them." Finally I'm so scared that I start breaking down. "I need help. You've got to get me out of here. I don't care about the money anymore. They'll kill me. I mean it, Palakon. They will kill me." Panicking, doubled over on the bed, I envision my corpse on a beach, someone's idea of a "flourish," and there's a breeze, it's midday, a figure disappears into a cove. "I shouldn't even be here—oh fucking god—I shouldn't even be here."

"You weren't followed," Palakon says. "Please Mr. Ward, calm down."

"I can't," I'm whining, still doubled over, clutching myself. "I can't, I cannot, I—"

"Mr. Ward, is there anyone who can help you?" Palakon asks. "Anyone you can put us in touch with?"

"No no no, there's no one—"

"What about family? What about your parents? Maybe something can be arranged. Something monetary. Do they know where you are?"

"No." I breathe in. "My mother's dead. My father—I can't, I can't bring my father into this."

Palakon suddenly stops pacing.

"Why not?" Palakon asks. "Maybe if you put us in touch with your father he could come over here and we could make an arrangement to somehow extract you from this mess—"

"But, Palakon, what mess? What do you mean, a mess? And I can't can't get my father involved." I'm shaking my head, weeping. "No, no, I can't, no—"

"Victor, why can't you get your father involved?"

"Palakon, you don't understand," I'm whispering.

"Mr. Ward, I'm trying to help you—"

"I can't I can't I—"

"Mr. Ward—" Palakon shouts.

"My father is a U.S. senator," I scream, glaring up at him. "My father is a fucking U.S. senator. That is why he can't get involved, Palakon," I scream. "Okay? Okay?"

Palakon swallows grimly, taking this in. Visibly alarmed, he closes his eyes, concentrating. Waves lap at the body on the beach and behind it hard brown surfers ride buoyantly over green swells below a burning sun high above the horizon and beyond them there's an island—boulders, woods, an old granite quarry, the smell of salt—and on that island another figure disappears into a cove and then it's night.

"Your father is Samuel Johnson?" Palakon asks.

"Yes," I hiss, still glaring at him. "Didn't you know this when you first contacted me?"

"No, we didn't," Palakon says quietly, humbled. "But now I"—he clears his throat—"see."

"No you don't," I'm saying mindlessly, moving my head back and forth like a child. "No you don't."

"Victor, you don't need to explain to me who your father is," Palakon says. "I think I understand." He pauses again. "And because of this I also understand why this makes the situation more . . . delicate."

I start giggling. "Delicate? The situation is delicate?" I stop giggling, gasp in a sob.

"Victor, we can help you, I think—"

"I'm trapped, I'm trapped, I'm trapped, and they'll kill me—"

"Mr. Ward," Palakon says, kneeling, leaning in to where I'm sitting on the edge of the bed. "Please, we will help you but—"

When I try to hug him he pushes me gently away.

"—you have got to act as if nothing has happened. You have got to pretend that you don't know anything. You've got to play along until I can figure something out."

"No, no, no—"

Palakon motions for the Christian Bale guy. I feel a pair of hands on my shoulders. Someone's whispering.

"I'm afraid, Palakon," I sob.

"Don't be, Mr. Ward," Palakon says. "We know where you are. In the meantime I have to figure some things out. We'll contact you—"

"You've got to be careful," I say. "Everything's bugged. Everything's wired. Everything's being filmed."

They're helping me stand up. I'm trying to cling to Palakon as they lead me to the door.

"You must calm down, Mr. Ward," Palakon says. "Now let Russell take you back and we'll contact you within a couple of days, possibly sooner. But you must remain calm. Things are different now and you must remain calm."

"Why can't I stay here?" I plead, struggling as I'm being led to the door. "Please let me stay here."

"I need to get a full view," Palakon says. "Right now it's just a partial view. And I need to get a full view."

"What's happening, Palakon?" I ask, finally motionless. "What's the story?"

"Just that something has gone terribly wrong."

In the backseat of the black Citroën everything is covered with confetti and it seems like hours before Russell drops me off on Boulevard Saint-Marcel and then I'm crossing through the Jardin des Plantes and then I'm at the Seine and above me the morning sky is white and I'm thinking, Stay indoors, go to sleep, don't get involved, view everything without expression, drink whiskey, pose, accept.

25

I'm standing at a pay phone on Rue du Faubourg Saint-Honoré, calling Felix at the Ritz. The phone in his room rings six times before he answers. I'm taking off my sunglasses then putting them on, again and again.

"Hello?" Felix asks tiredly.

"Felix, it's me," I say. "It's Victor."

"Yes?" Felix asks. "What is it? What do you want?"

"We have to talk." Across the street from where I'm standing someone's behaving oddly—weird hair, waving car fumes away with a newspaper, laughing uncontrollably. Across the street the sun is rising, then decides not to.

"Oh Victor, I am so tired of this," Felix says. "I am so tired of you."

"Felix, please, not now, please don't go into a rant now," I'm saying. "There are things you need to know," I'm saying. "I've figured some things out and I need to tell you these things."

"But I'm not interested in listening to you anymore," Felix says. "In fact, nobody is, Victor. And frankly I don't think there's anything *you* need to tell anyone, except of course if it's about your hair or your gym routine or who you plan to fuck next week."

(Bobby flies to Rome and then to Amman, Jordan, on Alitalia. A bag in the overhead compartment in first class contains spools of electric wire, needle-nosed pliers, silicon, large kitchen knives, aluminum foil, packets of Remform, hammers, a camcorder, a dozen files containing diagrams of military weapons, missiles, armored cars. On the plane Bobby reads an article in a fashionable magazine about the President's new haircut and what it means and Bobby memorizes lines he needs to deliver and flirts with a stewardess who mentions in passing that her favorite song is John Lennon's "Imagine." In a soothing voice Bobby compliments her career choice. She's asking him what it was like being on the Oprah Winfrey show. He's recalling a visit to room 25 at the Dreamland Motel. He's planning a catastrophe. He's contemplatively eating a brownie.)

"Felix, remember when you were asking me what happened to Sam Ho?" I'm saying. "Remember about the other film crew? The one Dimity saw me with at the Louvre yesterday?"

"Victor, please, just calm down," Felix says. "Get a grip. None of this matters anymore."

"Oh, yes it does, Felix, it does matter."

"No," he says. "It doesn't matter."

"Why not?" I'm asking. "Why doesn't it matter?"

"Because the movie's over," Felix says. "The production has been shut down. Everybody's leaving tonight."

"Felix—"

"You've been shockingly unprofessional, Victor."

(Jamie's in traffic circling the Arc de Triomphe, then she's turning down Avenue de Wagram, making a right onto Boulevard de Courcelles, heading for Avenue de Clichy to meet Bertrand Ripleis, and Jamie's thinking that this seems like the longest day of the year and she's thinking about a particular Christmas tree from her childhood, but it was never really the tree that impressed her, it was the ornaments adorning the tree, and then she's remembering how afraid of the ocean she was as a little girl—"too watery," she'd tell her parents—and then she's eighteen, in the Hamptons, a summer dawn, freshman year at Camden is a week away and she's staring out at the Atlantic, listening to a boy she met backstage at a Who concert at Nassau Coliseum snoring lightly behind her and two years later, in Cambridge, he'll commit suicide, pulled toward a force he could not evaluate, but now it was the end of August and she was thirsty and a giant gull circled above her and mourning didn't matter yet.)

"Please, please, Felix, we have to talk." I'm practically gasping and I keep turning around to see if anyone's watching me.

"But you aren't listening, you little fool," Felix snaps. "The movie is over. You don't need to explain anything to me because it doesn't matter anymore. It does not apply."

"But they killed Sam Ho that night, Felix, they killed him," I say in a rush. "And there's another movie being shot. One you don't know about. There's another crew here and Bruce Rhinebeck killed Sam Ho—"

"Victor," Felix interrupts softly. "Bruce Rhinebeck came over this morning and talked to us—the director, the writer, myself—and he explained the, um, situation." A pause. "Actually he explained *your* situation."

"What situation? *My* situation? I don't have a situation."

Felix groans. "Forget it, Victor. We're leaving tonight. Back to New York. It's over, Victor. Goodbye."

"Don't trust him, Felix," I shout. "He's lying. Whatever Bruce told you, it's a lie."

"Victor," Felix says tiredly.

I suddenly notice that Felix's accent has disappeared.

(Bruce replaces the cardboard frame in a piece of Gucci luggage with sheets of dark plastic that disguise the explosives, which are made up of narrow gray odorless strips. Embedded in the strips: gold-plated nickel wire. Bruce has lined up fifty-five pounds of plastic explosives end to end, then attached them to a detonator. The detonator is powered by AAA batteries. Occasionally Bruce glances at an instruction manual. Bentley stands behind him, arms crossed, staring silently at Bruce, at the back of his head, at how beautiful Bruce is, thinking, If only . . . , and when Bruce turns around Bentley plays it cool, just nods, shrugs, stifles a yawn.)

"I suppose I can tell you since obviously you don't like Bruce, even though *I* think he's quite charming and should have been the star of this production," Felix drones haughtily. "You know why Bruce should have been the star of this production, Victor? Because Bruce Rhinebeck has star quality, Victor, that's why."

"I know, I know, Felix," I'm saying. "He should've been the star, he should've been the star."

"According to Bruce he has really tried to help you, Victor."

"Help me with what?" I shout.

"He says you are under extreme emotional pressure, possibly due to a major drug habit," Felix sighs. "He also says you tend to hallucinate frequently and that nothing coming out of your mouth is to be believed."

"Jesus fucking Christ, Felix," I shout. "These people are murderers, you asshole. They're fucking terrorists." Realizing how loud this comes out, I whirl around to see if anyone's behind me, then lower my voice and whisper, "They're fucking terrorists."

"He also said he thinks that you're quite possibly an insane individual and also—however improbable the director and I thought this sounded—rather dangerous." Felix adds, "He also said that you'd tell us they were terrorists. So."

"He builds bombs, Felix," I whisper harshly into the phone. "Oh fuck that—*he's* insane, Felix. That's all a lie."

"I'm terminating this phone call, Victor," Felix says.

"I'm coming over, Felix."

"If you do I'll call the police."

"Please, Felix," I'm moaning. "For god's sake."

Felix doesn't say anything.

"Felix?" I moan. "Felix, are you there?"

Felix keeps pausing.

"Felix?" I'm crying silently, wiping my face.

And then Felix says, "Well, perhaps you could be useful."

(In the Jardin du Luxembourg he's hungover again—another cocaine binge, another sleepless dawn, another sky made up of gray tile—but Tammy kisses the French premier's son, fortifying him, and in a flea market at Porte de Vanves, both her hands on his chest, he's hooking her in with his right arm and he's wearing slippers. "Soul mates?" he asks. Tammy smells like lemons and has a secret, something she wants to show him back at the house in the 8th or the 16th. "I have enemies there," he says, buying her a rose. "Don't worry, Bruce is gone," she says. But he wants to talk about a trip to southern California he's taking in November. "S'il vous plaît?" Tammy whines, eyes sparkling, and back at the house Tammy closes the door behind him, locking it as instructed, and Bentley's making drinks in the kitchen and hands the French premier's son a martini glass filled to the brim with a cloudy gimlet and as he sips it he senses something behind him and then—as planned—Bruce Rhinebeck rushes into the room shouting, holding up a claw hammer, and Tammy turns away and closes her eyes, clamping her hands over her ears as the French premier's son starts screaming and the noise being made in that room is the worst ever and Bentley wordlessly pours the pitcher of drugged alcohol into the sink and wipes the counter with an orange sponge.)

I start weeping with relief. "I can be useful," I say. "I can be, I can be really useful—"

"Bruce left a bag here. He forgot it."

"What?" I'm pressing the phone closer to my ear, wiping my nose with the sleeve of my jacket. "What, man?"

"He left a Gucci tote bag behind," Felix says. "I suppose you could come by and pick it up. That is, if you can be bothered, Victor—"

"Felix, wait—you've got to get rid of that bag," I say, suddenly nauseous with adrenaline. "Don't get near that bag."

"I'll leave it with the concierge," Felix says, annoyed. "I have no intention of seeing you."

"Felix," I shout. "Don't get near that bag. Get everyone out of the hotel—"

"And do not try contacting us," Felix says over me. "We've shut down the production office in New York."

"Felix, get out of the hotel—"

"Nice working with you," Felix says. "But not really."

"Felix," I'm screaming.

(On the opposite side of Place Vendôme, twenty technicians are at various lookout points and the director is studying a video playback monitor of the footage shot earlier today of Bruce Rhinebeck leaving the hotel, a toothpick in his teeth, Bruce posing for paparazzi, Bruce laughing mildly, Bruce hopping into a limousine with bulletproof windows. By now the French film crew has been outfitted with ear protection for when the demolition team begins detonating the bombs.)

I start racing toward the Ritz.

(In a pale-pink room, Felix hangs up the phone. The suite Felix occupies is in fairly close proximity to the center of the hotel, which ensures that the explosion will cause as much structural damage as possible.

The Gucci tote bag sits on the bed.

It's so cold in the room that Felix's breath steams.

A fly lands on his hand.

Felix unzips the tote bag.

He stares into it, quizzically.

It's filled with red and black confetti.

He brushes the confetti away.

Something reveals itself.

"No," Felix says.

The bomb swallows Felix up, vaporizing him instantly. He literally disappears. There's nothing left.)

24

A thundering sound.

Immediately, in the 1st arrondissement, all electricity goes dead.

The blast shatters the Ritz from the center—almost front to back—weakening its structure as the pulse spreads to both sides of the hotel.

The windows flex, then shatter, imploding.

A gigantic wall of concrete and glass rushes toward the tourists in the Place Vendôme.

A ball of fire boils toward them.

A huge mass of black smoke, multilayered, irregular, rises up over Paris.

The shock wave lifts the Ritz up, unhinging nearly all the support beams.

The building starts sliding into the Place Vendôme, its collapse accompanied by a whooshing roar.

Then another deafening roar.

Chunks of debris keep falling, walls keep cracking apart, and there's so much dust the Place Vendôme looks as if a sandstorm has struck.

The explosion is followed by the customary "stunned silence."

The sound of glass continuing to shatter is an introduction to the screaming.

Boulders of concrete litter the streets surrounding the Ritz and you have to climb over them to get into the Place Vendôme, where people are running around covered in blood and screaming into cell phones, the sky above them overcast with smoke. The entire face of the hotel has been blown off, rubber roofing is flapping in the wind and several cars, mostly BMWs, are burning. Two limousines lie overturned and the smell of burned tar is everywhere, the streets and sidewalks entirely scorched.

The body of a Japanese man dangles from the third story, caught between floors, drenched with blood, a huge shard of glass embedded in his neck, and another body hangs tangled in a mass of steel girders, its face frozen in anguish, and I'm limping past piles of rubble with arms sticking out of them and past Louis XV furniture, a candelabra ten feet high, antique chests, and people keep staggering past me, some of them naked, tripping over plaster and insulation, and I pass a girl whose face is cut in half, the lower part of her body torn away, and the leg lying nearby is completely embedded with screws and nails, and another woman, blackened and writhing, one hand blown off, is screaming, dying, and a Japanese woman in the bloody tatters of a Chanel suit collapses in front of me, both her jugular vein and her carotid artery sliced open by flying glass, causing every breath she takes to gurgle blood.

Staggering toward a giant slab of concrete angled directly in front of the hotel, I see four men try to pull a woman out from beneath it and her leg comes off—detaches effortlessly—from what's left of her body, which is surrounded by unrecognizable chunks of flesh from which bones protrude. A man whose nose was slashed off by a shard of glass and a sobbing teenage girl lie next to each other in a widening pool of blood, her eyes burned out of their sockets, and the closer you move to what's left of the main entrance, the number of arms and legs scattered everywhere doubles and the skin sandblasted from bodies sits everywhere in giant, papery clumps, along with the occasional dead-body dummy.

I'm passing faces lashed with dark-red cuts, piles of designer clothes, air-conditioning ducts, beams, a playpen and then a baby that looks as if it has been dipped in blood, which slumps, mangled, on a pile of rubble. Nearby a small child lies bleeding continuously from his mouth, part of his brain hanging out the side of his head. Dead bellmen lay scattered among magazines and Louis Vuitton luggage and heads blown off bodies, even one of a chisel-faced boyfriend of a model I knew back in New York, many of them BBR (what Bruce Rhinebeck calls Burned Beyond Recognition). In a daze, wandering past me: Polly Mellon, Claudia Schiffer, Jon Bon Jovi, Mary Wells Laurence, Steven Friedman, Bob Collacello, Marisa Berenson, Boy George, Mariah Carey.

Paths are made through the concrete boulders blocking Place Vendôme, and the paparazzi arrive first, followed by CNN reporters and then local television crews, and then, finally, ambulances carrying rescue teams followed by blue-black trucks carrying antiterrorist police wearing flak jackets over paratrooper jumpsuits, gripping automatic weapons, and they start wrapping victims in blankets and hundreds of pigeons lie dead, some of the injured birds haphazardly trying to fly, low to the ground above the debris, and later the feet of children in a makeshift morgue are being tagged and parents are being ushered out of that morgue howling and bodies will have to be identified by birthmarks, dental records, scars, tattoos, jewelry, and at a nearby hospital are posted the names of the dead and injured, along with their condition, and soon the rescue workers outside the Ritz are no longer in rescue mode.

23

I sit in a revival theater on Boulevard des Italiens. I collapse on a bench in the Place du Parvis. At one point during the day I'm shuffling through Pigalle. At another point I just keep crossing then recrossing the Seine. I wander through Aux Trois Quartiers on Boulevard de la Madeleine until the glimpse I catch of myself in a mirror at a Clinique counter moves me to rush back to the house in the 8th or the 16th.

Inside the house Bentley sits at a computer in the living room, wearing a Gap tank top and headphones from a Walkman. He's studying an image that keeps flashing itself at different angles across the screen. My throat is aching from all the smoke I inhaled and when I pass a mirror my reflected face is streaked with grime, hair stiff and gray with dust, my eyes yellow. I move slowly up behind Bentley without his noticing.

On the computer screen: the actor who played Sam Ho lies naked on his back in a nondescript wood-paneled bedroom, his legs lifted and spread apart by an average-looking guy, maybe my age or slightly older, also naked, and in profile he's thrusting between Sam's legs, fucking him. Bentley keeps tapping keys, scanning the image, zooming in and out. Within a matter of minutes the average-looking guy fucking Sam Ho is given a more defined musculature, larger pectorals, what's visible of his cock shaft is thickened, the pubic hair lightened. The nondescript bedroom is transformed into the bedroom I stayed at in the house in Hampstead: chic steel beams, the Jennifer Bartlett painting hanging over the bed, the vase filled with giant white tulips, the chrome ashtrays. Sam Ho's eyes, caught red in the flash, are corrected.

I bring a hand up to my forehead, touching it. This movement causes Bentley to swivel around in his chair, removing the headphones.

"What happened to you?" he asks innocently, but he can't keep up the facade and starts grinning.

"What are you doing?" I ask, numb, hollowed out.

"I'm glad you're back," Bentley says. "Bobby wants me to show you something."

"What are you doing?" I ask again.

"This is a new program," Bentley says. "Kai's Photo Soap for Windows 95. Take a peek."

Pause. "What does it . . . do?" I swallow.

"It helps make pictures better," Bentley says in a baby's voice.

"How . . . does it do that?" I ask, shivering.

The sex-scene photo is scanned again and Bentley concentrates on tapping more keys, occasionally referring to pages torn from a booklet and spread out on the table next to the computer. In five minutes my head—in profile—is grafted seamlessly onto the shoulders of the average-looking guy fucking Sam Ho. Bentley zooms out of the image, satisfied.

"A big hard *disk*"—Bentley glances over at me—"is mandatory. As well as a certain amount of patience."

At first I'm saying, "That's cool, that's . . . cool," because Bentley keeps grinning, but a hot wave of nausea rises, subsides, silencing me.

Another key is tapped. The photograph disappears. The screen stays blank. Another two keys are tapped and then a file number is tapped and then a command is tapped.

What now appears is a series of photographs that fill the screen in rapid succession.

Sam Ho and Victor Ward in dozens of positions, straining and naked, a pornographic montage.

Bentley leans back, satisfied, hands behind his head, a movie pose even though no camera is around to capture it.

"Would you like to see another file?" Bentley asks, but it's really not a question because he's already tapping keys.

"Let's see," he muses. "Which one?"

A flash. A command is tapped. A list appears, each entry with a date and file number.

"VICTOR" CK Show
"VICTOR" Telluride w/S Ulrich
"VICTOR" Dogstar concert w/K Reeves
VICTOR Union Square w/L Hynde
"VICTOR" Miami, Ocean Drive
"VICTOR" Miami, lobby, Delano
VICTOR QE2 series
"VICTOR" Sam Ho series
VICTOR Pylos w/S Ho
"VICTOR" Sky Bar w/Rande Gerber
"VICTOR" GQ Shoot w/J Fields, M Bergin
"VICTOR" Café Flore w/Brad, Eric, Dean
"VICTOR" Institute of Political Studies
"VICTOR" New York, Balthazar
"VICTOR" New York, Wallflowers
"VICTOR" Annabel's w/J Phoenix
"VICTOR" 8oth and Park w/A Poole
"VICTOR" Hell's Kitchen w/Mica, NYC

As Bentley continuously scrolls down the screen it becomes apparent that this list goes on for pages and pages.

Bentley starts tapping keys, landing on new photos. He enhances colors, adjusts tones, sharpens or softens images. Lips are digitally thickened, freckles are removed, an ax is placed in someone's outstretched hand, a BMW becomes a Jaguar which becomes a Mercedes which becomes a broom which becomes a frog which becomes a mop which becomes a poster of Jenny McCarthy, license plates are altered, more blood is spattered around a crime-scene photo, an uncircumcised penis is suddenly circumcised. Tapping keys, scanning images, Bentley adds motion blur (a shot of "Victor" jogging along the Seine), he's adding lens flair (in a remote desert in eastern Iran I'm shaking hands with Arabs and wearing sunglasses and pouting, gasoline trucks lined up behind me), he's adding graininess, he's erasing people, he's inventing a new world, seamlessly.

"You can move planets with this," Bentley says. "You can shape lives. The photograph is only the beginning."

After a long time passes, I say in a low voice, staring silently at the computer, "I don't want to hurt your feelings, but . . . I think you suck."

"Were you there or were you not?" Bentley asks. "It all depends on who you ask, and even that really doesn't matter anymore."

"Don't . . ." But I forget what I was going to say.

"There's something else you need to see," Bentley says. "But you should take a shower first. Where have you been? You look like shit. Let me guess. Bar Vendôme?"

In the shower, breathing erratically, I'm flashing over the two files in the giant list containing my name with the most recent dates.

"VICTOR" Washington DC w/Samuel Johnson (father)
"VICTOR" Washington DC w/Sally Johnson (sister)

22

After the shower, I'm led downstairs at gunpoint (which Bobby thought was excessive, needless, but not Bruce Rhinebeck) to a room hidden within a room in what I assume is some kind of basement in the house in the 8th or the 16th. This is where the French premier's son, chained to a chair, is slowly being poisoned. He's naked, gleaming with sweat, confetti floats on a puddle of blood congealing on the floor beneath him. His chest is almost completely blackened, both nipples are missing, and because of the poison Bruce keeps administering he's having trouble breathing. Four teeth have been removed and wires are stretching his face apart, some strung through broken lips, causing him to look as if he's grinning at me. Another wire is inserted into a wound on his stomach, attaching itself to his liver, lashing it with electricity. He keeps fainting, is revived, faints again. He's fed more poison, then morphine, as Bentley videotapes.

It smells sweet in the room underground and I'm trying to avert my eyes from a torture saw that sits on top of a Louis Vuitton trunk but there's really nowhere else to focus and music piped into the room comes from one of two radio stations (NOVA or NRJ). Bruce keeps yelling questions at the actor, in French, from a list of 320, all of them printed out in a thick stack of computer paper, many of them repeated in specific patterns, while Bobby stares levelly from a chair out of camera range, his mouth downturned. The French premier's son is shown photographs, glares wildly at them. He has no idea how to respond.

"Ask him 278 through 291 again," Bobby mutters at one point. "At first in the same sequence. Then repeat them in C sequence." He directs Bruce to relax the mouth wires, to administer another dose of morphine.

I'm slouching vacantly against a wall and my leg has fallen asleep because of how long I've been stuck in this particular position. Sweat pours down the sides of Bentley's face as he's camcording and Bobby's concerned about camera angles but Bentley assures him Bruce's head isn't in the frame. The French premier's son, momentarily lucid, starts shouting out obscenities. Bobby's frustration is palpable. Bruce takes a break, wiping his forehead with a Calvin Klein towel, sips a warm, flat Beck's. Bobby lights a cigarette, motions for Bruce to remove another tooth. Bobby keeps folding his arms, frowning, staring up at the ceiling. "Go back to section four, ask it in B sequence." Again, nothing happens. The actor doesn't know anything. He memorized a different script. He's not delivering the performance that Bobby wants. He was miscast. He was wrong for this part. It's all over. Bobby instructs Bruce to pour acid on the actor's hands. Pain floods his face as he gazes at me, crying uselessly, and then his leg is sawed off.

21

The actor playing the French premier's son realizes it doesn't matter anymore how life should be—he's past that point now in the underground room in the house in the 8th or the 16th. He was on the Italian Riviera now, driving a Mercedes convertible, he was at a casino in Monte Carlo, he was in Aspen on a sunny patio dotted with snow, and a girl who had just won the silver medal in the Model Olympics is on her tiptoes, kissing him jealously. He was outside a club in New York called Spy and fleeing into a misty night. He was meeting famous black comedians and stumbling out of limousines. He was on a Ferris wheel, talking into a cell phone, a stupefied date next to him, eavesdropping. He was in his pajamas watching his mother sip a martini, and through a window lightning was flickering and he had just finished printing his initials on a picture of a polar bear he'd drawn for her. He was kicking a soccer ball across a vast green field. He was experiencing his father's hard stare. He lived in a palace. Blackness, its hue, curves toward him, luminous and dancing. It was all so arbitrary: promises, pain, desire, glory, acceptance. There was the sound of camera shutters clicking, there was something collapsing toward him, a hooded figure, and as it fell onto him it looked up and he saw the head of a monster with the face of a fly.

20

We're at a dinner party in an apartment on Rue Paul Valéry between Avenue Foch and Avenue Victor Hugo and it's all rather subdued since a small percentage of the invited guests were blown up in the Ritz yesterday. For comfort people went shopping, which is understandable even if they bought things a little too enthusiastically. Tonight it's just wildflowers and white lilies, just W's Paris bureau chief, Donna Karan, Aerin Lauder, Inès de la Fressange and Christian Louboutin, who thinks I snubbed him and maybe I did but maybe I'm past the point of caring. Just Annette Bening and Michael Stipe in a tomato-red wig. Just Tammy on heroin, serene and glassy-eyed, her lips swollen from collagen injections, beeswax balm spread over her mouth, gliding through the party, stopping to listen to Kate Winslet, to Jean Reno, to Polly Walker, to Jacques Grange. Just the smell of shit, floating, its fumes spreading everywhere. Just another conversation with a chic sadist obsessed with origami. Just another armless man waving a stump and whispering excitedly, "Natasha's coming!" Just people tan and back from the Ariel Sands Beach Club in Bermuda, some of them looking reskinned. Just me, making connections based on fear, experiencing vertigo, drinking a Woo-Woo.

.   .   .

Jamie walks over to me after Bobby's cell phone rings and he exits the room, puffing suavely on a cigar gripped in the hand holding the phone, the other hand held up to his ear to block the din of the party.

"He's certainly in hair heaven," Jamie says, pointing out Dominique Sirop. Jamie's looking svelte in a teensy skirt and a pair of $1,500 shoes, nibbling an Italian cookie. "You're looking good tonight."

"The better you look," I murmur, "the more you see."

"I'll remember that."

"No you won't. But for now I'll believe you."

"I'm serious." She waves a fly away from her face. "You're looking very spiffy. You have the knack."

"What do you want?" I ask, recoiling from her presence.

Behind her Bobby walks quickly back into the room. He grimly holds hands with our hostess, she starts nodding sympathetically at whatever lie he's spinning and she's already a little upset that people in the lobby are dancing but she's being brave and then Bobby spots Jamie and starts moving through the crowd toward us though there are a lot of people to greet and say goodbye to.

"That's a loaded question," Jamie says glacially.

"Do you know how many people died at the Ritz yesterday?" I ask.

"I didn't keep track," she says, and then, "Don't be so corny."

"That was Bertrand," Bobby says to no one in particular. "I've gotta split."

"You look freaked," Jamie says slowly. "What happened?"

"I'll tell you later, back at the house," he says, taking her champagne glass, drinking half.

"Why are you leaving, Bobby?" Jamie asks carefully. "Where are you going?"

"I guess my social life is much busier than yours," Bobby says, brushing her off.

"You brute." She grins. "You savage."

"Just stay for the dinner," Bobby says, checking his watch. "Then come back to the house. I'll be there by eleven."

Bobby kisses Jamie hard on the mouth and tries to act casual but something's wrong and he can barely control his panic. I try not to stare. He notices.

"Stop gawking," he says irritably. "I'll be back at the house by eleven. Maybe sooner."

On his way out Bobby stops behind Tammy who's swaying from side to side, listening rapturously to a drug dealer called the Kaiser, and Bobby motions from across the room to Jamie, mouthing, *Watch her.* Jamie nods.

"Is Bobby gone?" Jamie's asking.

"You're in fine form tonight," I spit out, glaring. "Do you know how many people died at the Ritz yesterday?"

"Victor, please," she says genuinely while trying to smile, in case anyone's watching. But the French film crew is surrounding a cluster of mourners laughing in the corner of the cavernous living room. Blenders are whirring at a bar, there's a fire raging in the fireplace, cell phones keep being answered.

"They killed the French premier's son yesterday too," I say calmly, for emphasis. "They cut off his leg. I watched him die. How can you wear that dress?" I ask, my face twisted with loathing.

"Is Bobby gone?" she asks again. "Just tell me if he's left yet."

"Yes," I say disgustedly. "He left."

Visibly, she relaxes. "I have to tell you something, Victor," she says, gazing over my shoulder, then glancing sideways.

"What?" I ask. "You're all grown up now?"

"No, not that," she says patiently. "You and I—we can't see each other anymore."

"Oh really?" I'm glancing around the room. "Why not?"

"It's too dangerous."

"Is it?" I ask, smirking. "What a cliché."

"I'm serious."

"I don't want to talk to you anymore."

"I think this whole thing has gotten out of hand," Jamie says.

I start giggling uncontrollably until a sudden spasm of fear causes my eyes to water, my face to contort. "That's . . . all?" I cough, wiping my eyes, sniffling. "Just . . . out of hand?" My voice sounds high and girlish.

"Victor—"

"You are not playing by the rules," I say, my chest tightening. "You are not following the script."

"There *are* no rules, Victor," she says. "What rules? That's all nonsense."

·   ·   ·

She pauses. "It's too dangerous," she says again.

"I'm feeling a lack of progress," I'm saying. "I think we're all living in a box."

"I assume you understand more about Bobby now," she says. "It's easier, isn't it? It's easier to gauge the fear factor now, isn't it?"

A long pause. "I suppose," I say, without looking at her.

"But you'll still be in my . . . periphery."

"I suppose," I say again. "How reassuring."

"You also need to stay away from Bertrand Ripleis."

"Why?" I'm barely listening.

"He hates you."

"I wondered why he was always snarling at me."

"I'm serious," she says, almost pleadingly. "He still holds a grudge," she says, trying to smile as she waves to someone. "From Camden."

"About what?" I ask, irritation and fear laced together.

"He was in love with Lauren Hynde," she says. "He thinks you treated her shittily." A pause. "This is on the record." Another pause. "Be careful."

"Is this a joke or like some kind of French thing?"

"Just stay away from him," she warns. "Don't provoke."

"How do you know this?"

"We're . . . incommunicado." She shrugs.

A pause. "What's the safety factor?" I ask.

"As long as you stay away from him?"

I nod.

A tear, one tiny drop, slips down her cheek, changes its mind and evaporates, while she tries to smile.

"So-so," she whispers.

Finally I say, "I'm leaving."

"Victor," Jamie says, touching my arm before I turn away.

"What?" I groan. "I'm leaving. I'm tired."

"Victor, wait," she says.

I stand there.

"In the computer," she says, breathing in. "In the computer. At the house. There's a file." She pauses, nods at a guest. "The file is called 'Wings.'" Pause. As she turns away, she says, "You need to see it."

"Why do I need to see it?" I ask. "I don't care anymore."

"Victor," she starts. "I . . . think I . . . knew that girl you met on the

QE2. . . ." Jamie swallows, doesn't know where to look, tries to compose herself, barely succeeds. "The girl who disappeared from the QE2 . . ."

I just stare at her blankly.

When Jamie grasps my reaction—its hatefulness—she just nods to herself, muttering, "Forget it, forget it."

"I'm leaving." I'm walking away as it starts raining confetti.

Because of how the apartment is lit, extras have to be careful not to trip over electric cables or the dolly tracks that line the center of the living room, and in the lobby the first AD from the French film crew hands me tomorrow's call sheet and Russell—the Christian Bale guy—is wearing little round sunglasses, smoking a joint, comparing shoe sizes with Dermot Mulroney, but then I realize that they're both on separate cell phones and not talking to each other and Russell pretends to recognize me and "drunkenly" shouts, "Hey, Victor!"

I pretend to smile. I reach out to shake his hand.

"Hey, come on, dude," he says, brushing the hand away. "We haven't seen each other in months." He hugs me tightly, dropping something in my jacket pocket. "How's the party?" he asks, stepping back, offering me the joint. I shake my head.

"Oh, it's great, it's cool," I'm saying, chewing my lips. "It's very cool." I start walking away. "Bye-bye."

"Great," Russell says, slapping my back, returning to his conversation on the cell phone as Dermot Mulroney opens a bottle of champagne gripped between his knees.

In the cab heading back to the house in the 8th or the 16th I find a card Russell slipped in my pocket. A time. Tomorrow. An address. A corner I should stop at. Directions to that corner. Suggestions on how to behave. All of this in tiny print that I'm squinting at in the back of the cab until I'm nauseous. I lean my head against the window. The cab swerves around a minor traffic accident, passing patrolmen carrying submachine guns patiently strolling the streets. My back aches. Impatiently I start wiping makeup applied earlier off my face with a cocktail napkin.

·   ·   ·

At the house, after paying the cab fare.

I press the code to deactivate the alarm. The door clicks open.

I tumble through the courtyard.

The living room is empty—just the furniture pushed aside earlier this afternoon by the French film crew.

Without taking off my overcoat I move over to the computer. It's already on. I tap a key. I enter a command.

I type in WINGS.

A pause. The screen flashes.

WINGS ASSGN# 3764 appears.

Letters start appearing. A graph starts unfolding.

NOV 15

BAND ON THE RUN

Beneath that: 1985

And then: 511

I scroll down to another page. A map appears on the screen: a highway, a route. It leads to Charles de Gaulle airport. Below this the Trans World Airlines logo appears.

TWA.

Nothing else.

I start tapping keys so I can print out the file. Two pages.

Nothing happens. I'm breathing heavily, flushed with adrenaline. Then I hear four beeps in quick succession.

Someone is entering the courtyard.

I realize the printer's not switched on. When I switch it on, it makes a soft noise, then starts humming.

I press another key: a flash.

Voices from outside. Bobby, Bentley.

Page 1 of the WINGS file slowly prints out.

Keys are being entered into the various locks on the front door.

Page 2 of the WINGS file follows page 1, slightly overlapping it.

In the foyer, the door opens: footsteps, voices.

I pull the two pages out of the printer, shoving them inside my jacket, then flick off the computer and the printer. I lunge toward a chair.

But I'm realizing that the computer was on when I came in.

I fall toward the computer, flicking it back on, and lunge again toward the chair.

.   .   .

Bobby and Bentley walk into the living room, followed by members of the French film crew, including the director and the cameraman.

My head rests on my knees and I'm breathing hard.

A voice—I'm not sure which one—asks, "What are you doing here?"

I don't say anything. It's winter in here.

"Victor?" Bobby's asking, carefully. "What are you doing here?"

"I felt sick," I say, gasping, looking up, squinting. "I don't feel well." A pause. "I ran out of Xanax."

Bentley glances at Bobby and, while walking by me, mumbles disinterestedly. "Tough shit."

Bobby looks over at the director, who's studying me as if making a decision. The director finally nods at Bobby: a cue.

Bobby shrugs, flops onto a couch, unknots his tie, then takes off his jacket. The shoulder of his white Comme des Garçons shirt is lightly flecked with blood. Bobby sighs.

Bentley reappears and hands Bobby a drink.

"What happened?" I ask, needing to hear myself. "Why did you leave the party?"

"There was an accident," Bobby says. "Something . . . occurred."

He sips his drink.

"What?" I ask.

"Bruce Rhinebeck is dead," Bobby says, looking past me, taking another sip of his drink with a steady hand.

Bobby doesn't wait for me to ask how this happened but I wasn't going to ask anything anyway.

"He was defusing a bomb in an apartment on Quai de Béthune." Bobby sighs, doesn't elaborate. "For what it's worth."

I stay where I'm sitting for as long as I can without going totally insane, but then the director motions for me to stand, which I do, wobbling.

"I'm . . . going to bed," I say and then, pointing with my finger, add, "upstairs."

Bobby says nothing, just glances at me indifferently.

"I'm . . . exhausted." I start walking away. "I'm fading."

"Victor?" Bobby asks suddenly.

"Yeah?" I stop, casually turn around, relax my face.

"What's that?" Bobby asks.

I'm suddenly aware that my body is covered with damp sweat and my stomach keeps unspooling reams of acid. "What?" I ask.

"Sticking out of that pocket?" He points at my jacket.

I look down innocently. "What's what?"

Bobby gets off the couch and walks over so quickly he almost collides into me. He rips the piece of paper that's bothering him out of my jacket.

He inspects it, turning it over, and then stares back at me.

He holds the page out, his mouth turned downward, sweat sprinkled across his temples, the bridge of his nose, the skin under his eyes. He grins horribly: a rictus.

I take the page from him, my hand moist and trembling.

"What is it?" I ask.

"Go to bed," he says, turning away.

I look down at the page.

It's the call sheet for tomorrow that the first AD handed out as I left the party on Rue Paul Valéry.

"I'm sorry about Bruce," I say hesitantly, because I don't mean it.

Upstairs. I'm freezing in bed, my door locked. I devour Xanax but still can't sleep. I start masturbating a dozen times but always stop when I realize that it's getting me nowhere. I try to block out the screaming from downstairs with my Walkman but someone from the French film crew has slipped in a ninety-minute cassette composed entirely of David Bowie singing "Heroes" over and over in an endless loop, another crime with its own logic. I start counting the deaths I haven't taken part in: postage stamps with toxin in the glue, the pages of books lined with chemicals that once touched can kill within hours, the Armani suits saturated with so much poison that the victim who wears it can absorb it through the skin by the end of a day.

At 11:00 Tammy finally twirls into the room, holding a bunch of white lilies, her arms dotted with sores, most of them concentrated in a patch in the crook of her elbow. Jamie trails behind her. I've read the scene and know how it's supposed to play. When Jamie is told of Bruce's death she simply says "Good" (but Jamie knew what was going to happen to Bruce Rhinebeck, she knew in London, she knew when we arrived in Paris, she knew the first afternoon she played tennis with Bruce, she knew from the beginning).

When Tammy is told she gazes at Bobby vapidly, puzzled. On cue Jamie takes the lilies out of Tammy's hand as it relaxes, losing its grip. "Liar," Tammy whispers and then she whispers "Liar" again and after she's able to process Bobby's weak smile, the French crew standing behind him, the camera filming her reaction, she feels like she's dropping and in a rush she starts screaming, wailing interminably, and she's not even wondering anymore why Bobby walked into her life and she's told to go to sleep, she's told to forget Bruce Rhinebeck immediately, she's told that he murdered the French premier's son, she's told that she should be grateful that she's unharmed, while Bentley (I swear to god) starts making a salad.

19 Preoccupation with the fallout from Bruce's death
reverberates mildly throughout the house in the 8th or
.the 16th and because of this there are no errands to
complete and everyone seems sufficiently distracted for me to slip away.
Endless conversations concern title changes, budget reductions, the leasing
of an eighty-foot-tall tower crane, roving release dates, a volatile producer in
L.A. seething over a rewrite. Before leaving I shoot a scene with Tammy
concerning our characters' reactions toward Bruce's death (motorcycle
accident, a truck carrying watermelons, Athens, a curve misjudged) but
since she's not even capable of forming sentences let alone mimicking
movements I shoot my lines standing in a hallway while a PA feeds me
Tammy's lines far more convincingly than Tammy ever did (cutaways to
Tammy will presumably be inserted at a later date). For the scene to end, a
wig is placed on another PA's head and the giant Panaflex dollies in on my
"saddened yet hopeful" face while we hug.

Jamie is either pretending to ignore me or just doesn't register my
presence while she's sitting at the computer in the living room—vacantly
scanning diagrams, decoding E-mails—as I try to walk casually past her.

Outside, the sky is gray, overcast.

An apartment building on Quai de Béthune.

I'm turning the corner at Pont de Sully.

A black Citroën sits parked at the curb on Rue Saint-Louis-en-l'Isle and
seeing the car causes me to walk faster toward it.

Russell drives us to an apartment building on Avenue Verdier in the
Montrouge section of the city.

I'm carrying a .25-caliber Walther automatic.

I'm carrying the WINGS file printouts, folded in the pocket of my black
leather Prada jacket.

I swallow a Xanax the wrong way then chew a Mentos to get the taste off
my tongue.

Russell and I run up three flights of stairs.

On the fourth floor is an apartment devoid of furniture except for six
white folding chairs. The walls are painted crimson and black, and

cardboard storage boxes sit stacked on top of one another in towering columns. A small TV set is hooked up to a VCR that rests on top of a crate. Darkness is occasionally broken by lamps situated throughout the apartment. It's so cold that the floor is slippery with ice.

F. Fred Palakon sits in one of the white folding chairs next to two of his associates—introduced to me as David Crater and Laurence Delta—and everyone's in a black suit, everyone just slightly older than me. Cigarettes are lit, files are opened, Starbucks coffee is offered, passed around, sipped.

Facing them, I sit in one of the white folding chairs, just now noticing in a shadowy corner the Japanese man sitting in a white folding chair next to a window draped with crushed-velvet curtains. He's definitely older than the other men—flabbier, more listless—but his age is indeterminate. He slouches back into the shadows, his eyes fixed on me.

Russell keeps pacing, talking quietly into a cell phone. Finally he clicks off and leans in to Palakon, whispering something displeasing.

"Are you certain?" Palakon asks.

Russell closes his eyes, sighs while nodding.

"Okay," Palakon says. "We don't have much time, then."

Russell brushes past, taking his stance at the door behind me, and I turn around to make sure he's not leaving.

"Thank you for coming, Mr. Ward," Palakon says. "You followed directions splendidly."

"You're . . . welcome."

"This needs to be brief," Palakon says. "We don't have much time here today. I simply wanted to introduce my associates"—Palakon nods at Delta and Crater—"and have a preliminary meeting. We just need you to verify some things. Look at a few photographs, that's all."

"Wait. So, like, the problem, like, hasn't been solved?" I ask, my voice squeaking.

"Well, no, not yet. . . ." Palakon falters. "David and Laurence have been briefed on what you told me two days ago and we're going to figure out a way to extract you from this . . ." Palakon can't find a word. I'm waiting. "This . . . situation," he says.

"Cool, cool," I'm saying nervously, crossing my legs, then changing my mind. "Just some facts? Cool. Some photos? Okay. That's cool. I can do that."

A pause.

"Um, Mr. Ward?" Palakon asks gingerly.

"Uh, yeah?"

"Could you please"—Palakon clears his throat—"remove your sunglasses."

A longer pause, followed by a realization. "Oh. Sorry."

"Mr. Ward," Palakon starts, "how long have you been living in that house?"

"I . . . don't know," I say, trying to remember. "Since we came to Paris?"

"When was that?" Palakon asks. "Exactly."

"Maybe two weeks . . ." Pause. "Maybe . . . it could be four?"

Crater and Delta glance at each other.

"I guess, maybe . . . I don't really know . . . I'm just not sure. . . . I'm not good with dates."

I try to smile, which just causes the men in the room to flinch, obviously unimpressed with the performance so far.

"I'm sorry . . . ," I mutter. "I'm sorry. . . ."

Somewhere a fly buzzes loudly. I try to relax but it's not happening.

"We want you to verify who lives in the house with you," Palakon says.

"It's a . . . set," I'm saying. "It's a set."

Palakon, Delta, Crater—they all stare at me blankly.

"Yes. Okay." I keep crossing then recrossing my legs, shivering. "Yes. The house. Yes."

Palakon reads from a page in his folder. "Jamie Fields, Bobby Hughes, Tammy Devol, Bentley Harrolds, Bruce Rhinebeck—"

I cut him off. "Bruce Rhinebeck is dead."

A professional silence. Crater looks over at Delta, and Delta, without returning eye contact and staring straight ahead, just nods.

Palakon finally asks, "You can verify this?"

"Yes, yes," I mutter. "He's dead."

Palakon turns a page over, makes a note with his pen, then asks, "Is Bertrand Ripleis also staying with you?"

"Bertrand?" I ask. "No, he's not staying in the house. No."

"Are you sure of this?" Palakon asks.

"Yes, yes," I'm saying. "I'm sure. I went to Camden with him, so I know who he is. I'd know if he was staying in the house." I'm realizing at the instant I say this that I probably would not know, that it would be easy not to know if Bertrand Ripleis was living in the house in the 8th or the 16th with us, because of how vast it is and how it keeps changing and how it seems new rooms are being built every day.

Palakon leans in and hands me a photograph.

"Is this Bertrand Ripleis?" he asks.

It could be an Armani ad shot by Herb Ritts—a desert landscape, Bertrand's handsome face scowling seductively, jaw clenched and lips casually pursed, small sunglasses giving off a skull effect. But he's exiting a van, he doesn't realize this picture is being shot from a vantage point far away, he's holding a Skorpion machine pistol, he's wearing a Tommy Hilfiger T-shirt.

"Yeah, that's him," I say blankly, handing Palakon back the photo. "But he doesn't live in the house."

"Does anyone in the house have contact with Bertrand Ripleis?" Crater asks.

"Yes," I say. "I think they all do."

"Do you, Mr. Ward?" Palakon asks.

"Yes . . . I said I think they all do."

"No," Palakon says. "Do *you* have contact with Bertrand?"

"Oh," I say. "No, no. I don't."

Scribbling, a long silence, more scribbling.

I glance over at the Japanese man, staring at me, motionless.

Palakon leans in and hands over another photo, startling me.

It's a head shot of Sam Ho, with Asian script running along the bottom of the photograph.

"Do you recognize this person?" Palakon asks.

"Yeah, that's Sam Ho," I say, starting to cry. My head drops forward and I'm looking at my feet, convulsing, gasping out sobs.

Papers are shuffled, extraneous sound caused by embarrassment.

I take in a deep breath and try to pull myself together, but after I say "Bruce Rhinebeck and Bobby Hughes tortured and killed him in London a month ago" I start crying again. At least a minute passes before the crying subsides. I swallow, clearing my throat. Russell leans over, offers a Kleenex. I blow my nose, mumble, "I'm sorry."

"Believe me, Mr. Ward, we don't like to see you this distraught," Palakon says. "Are you okay? Can you continue?"

"Yeah, yeah, I'm fine," I say, clearing my throat again, wiping my face.

Palakon leans in and hands me another photo.

Sam Ho is standing on a wide expanse of sand, what looks like South Beach stretching out behind him, and he's with Mariah Carey and Dave Grohl and they're listening intently to something k.d. lang is telling them. In the background people set up lights, hold plates of food, seem posed, talk guardedly into cell phones.

"Yeah, yeah, that's him too," I say, blowing my nose again.

Crater, Delta and Palakon all share contemplative glances, then fix their attention back on me.

I'm staring over at the Japanese man when Palakon says, "This picture of Sam Ho was taken in Miami." He pauses.

"Yeah?" I ask.

"Last week," Palakon says.

Trying not to appear surprised, I quickly recover from the words "last week" and say, coolly, "Well, then, that's not him. That's not Sam Ho."

Delta looks back at the Japanese man.

Crater leans in to Palakon and with his pen points out something in the folder Palakon has resting on his lap.

Palakon nods irritably.

I start freaking out, writhing in my chair.

"They can alter photos," I'm saying. "I saw Bentley Harrolds do it yesterday. They're constantly altering—"

"Mr. Ward, these photographs have been thoroughly checked out by a very competent lab and they have not been altered in any way."

"How do you know?" I'm calling out.

"We have the negatives," Palakon says tightly.

Pause. "Can the negatives be altered?" I ask.

"The negatives were not altered, Mr. Ward."

"But then . . . who the hell is that guy?" I ask, writhing in the chair, gripping my hands together, forcing them apart.

"Hey, wait a minute," I'm saying, holding my hands up. "Guys, guys, wait a minute."

"Yes, Mr. Ward?" Palakon asks.

"Is this . . . is this for real?" I'm scanning the room, looking for signs of a camera, lights, some hidden evidence that a film crew was here earlier or is right now maybe in the apartment next door, shooting me through holes strategically cut into the crimson and black walls.

"What do you mean, Mr. Ward?" Palakon asks. "'Real'?"

"I mean, is this like a movie?" I'm asking, shifting around in my chair. "Is this being filmed?"

"No, Mr. Ward," Palakon says politely. "This is not *like* a movie and you are not being filmed."

Crater and Delta are staring at me, uncomprehending.

The Japanese man leans forward but not long enough to let me see his face clearly.

"But . . . I . . ." I'm looking down at the photo of Sam Ho. "I . . . don't . . ." I start breathing hard, and since the air is so cold and thick in this room it burns my lungs. "They . . . listen, they . . . I think they double people. I mean, I don't know how, but I think they have . . . doubles. That's not Sam Ho . . . that's someone else. . . . I mean, I think they have doubles, Palakon."

"Palakon," Crater says. The tone in his voice suggests a warning.

Palakon stares at me, mystified.

I'm fumbling in my pocket for another Xanax and I keep trying to reposition myself to keep my arms and legs from falling asleep. I let Russell light a cigarette someone's handed me but it tastes bad and I'm not capable of holding it and when I drop it on the floor it lands hissing in a puddle of melting ice.

Delta reaches down for his Starbucks cup.

Another photo is handed to me.

Marina Gibson. A simple color head shot, unevenly reproduced on an 8 × 10.

"That's the girl I met on the *QE2*," I say. "Where is she? What happened to her? When was this taken?" And then, less excited, "Is she . . . okay?"

Palakon pauses briefly before saying, "We think she's dead."

My voice is cracking when I ask, "How? How do you know this?"

"Mr. Johnson," Crater says, leaning in. "We think this woman was sent to warn you."

"Wait," I say, unable to hold the photo any longer. "Sent to warn me? Warn me about *what*? Wait a minute. Jesus, wait—"

"That's what we're trying to piece together, Mr. Johnson," Delta says.

Palakon has leaned toward the VCR and presses Play on the console. Camcorder footage, surprisingly professional. It's the *QE2*. For an instant, the actress playing Lorrie Wallace leans against a railing, demurely, her head tilted, and she's alternating staring at the ocean with smiling at the person behind the camera, who quickly pans over to where Marina lies on a chaise longue, wearing leopard-print Capri pants, a white gauzy half-shirt, giant black tortoiseshell sunglasses that cover almost half her face.

"That's her," I say. "That's the girl I met on the *QE2*. How did you get this tape? That's the girl I was going to go to Paris with."

Palakon pauses, pretending to consult his file, and finally, hopelessly, again says, "We think she's dead."

"As I was saying, Mr. Johnson," Crater says, leaning toward me a little too aggressively, "we think that Marina Cannon was sent to warn—"

"No, wait, guys, wait," I'm saying. "It was Gibson. Her name was Gibson."

"No, it was Cannon," Delta says. "Her name was Marina Cannon."

"Wait, wait, guys," I'm saying. "Sent to warn me by who? About what?"

"That's what we're trying to piece together," Palakon says, overly patient.

"We think that whoever sent her didn't want you making contact with Jamie Fields, and by extension Bobby Hughes, once you arrived in London," Crater says. "We think she was provided as a distraction. As an alternative."

"Provided?" I'm asking. "*Provided*? What in the fuck does that mean?"

"Mr. Ward—" Palakon starts.

"Jamie told me she knows her," I say suddenly. "That she knew her. Why would Marina want me to stay away from Jamie if they knew each other?"

"Did Jamie Fields say *how* she knew her? Or in what context she knew her?" Palakon asks. "Did Jamie Fields let you know what their connection was?"

"No . . . ," I'm murmuring. "No . . ."

"Didn't you ask?" Crater and Delta exclaim at the same time.

"No," I say, dazed, murmuring. "No . . . I'm sorry . . . no . . ."

From behind me Russell says, "Palakon."

"Yes, yes," Palakon says.

On the TV screen the camera keeps panning across the length of the deck and, whenever Marina glances at it, always back to Lorrie Wallace. But once it stays for several moments on Marina, who gazes at it almost as if the camera were daring her.

"Where did you get this?" I'm asking.

"It's not an original," Delta says. "It's a copy."

"That's an answer?" I ask, jaw clenched.

"It doesn't matter how we got it," Delta snaps.

"The Wallaces took that," I say, staring at the screen. "Turn it off."

"The Wallaces?" I hear someone ask.

"Yeah." I'm nodding. "The Wallaces. They were this couple from England. This English couple. I forget what they do. What they told me. I think she opens restaurants. Whatever. Turn it off, just turn it off."

"How did you meet them?" Palakon asks, pressing a button, causing the TV to flash black.

"I don't know. They were just on the ship. They introduced themselves to me. We had dinner." I'm moaning, rubbing my hands over my face. "They said they knew my father—"

Some kind of connection is automatically made and resonates among the three men sitting across from me.

"Oh shit," Delta says.

Immediately Crater mutters, "Jesus, Jesus, Jesus."

Palakon keeps nodding involuntarily, his mouth opening slightly so he can take in more air.

Delta furiously writes down something on the folder resting in his lap.

"Jesus, Jesus, Jesus," Crater keeps muttering.

The Japanese man lights a cigarette, his face illuminated briefly by the match. Something's wrong. He's scowling.

"Palakon?" Russell calls out behind me.

Palakon looks up, knocked out of his concentration.

I turn around.

Russell taps his watch. Palakon nods irritably.

"Did Marina Cannon ask you anything?" Delta asks hurriedly, leaning in.

"Oh shit," I mutter. "I don't know. Like what?"

"Did she ask you if—" Crater starts.

I suddenly remember and, interrupting Crater, I murmur, "She wanted to know if anyone gave me anything to bring with me to England."

her departure from the Queen's Grill, the desperate phone call she made later that night, and I was drunk and grinning at myself in a mirror in my cabin, giggling, and there was blood in her bathroom and who else except Bobby Hughes knew she was on that ship and you were heading toward another country and there was a tattoo, black and shapeless, on her shoulder

I'm wiping sweat off my forehead and the room starts slanting, then it catches itself.

"Such as?" Palakon asks.

I'm grasping at something, and finally realize what it is.

"I think she meant"—I look up at Palakon—"the hat."

Everyone starts writing something. They wait for me to continue, to elaborate, but since I can't, Palakon coaxes me by asking, "But the hat disappeared from the QE2, right?"

I nod slowly. "But maybe . . . I'm thinking . . . maybe she took it and . . . and gave it . . . to someone."

"No," Delta mutters. "Our sources say she didn't."

"Your *sources*?" I'm asking. "Who in the fuck are your sources?"

"Mr. Ward," Palakon starts. "This will all be explained to you at a later date, so please—"

"What was in the hat?" I'm asking, cutting him off. "Why did you tell me to bring that hat? Why was it torn apart when I found it? What was in the hat, Palakon?"

"Mr. Ward, Victor, I promise you that at our next meeting I'll explain," Palakon says. "But we simply don't have time now—"

"What do you mean?" I'm asking, panicking. "You have more important things to do? I mean, holy shit, Palakon. I have no idea what's going on and—"

"We have other photos to show you," Palakon interrupts, handing three glossy 8 × 10s to me.

Two people dressed in tropical clothing on a foamy shore. Yards and yards of wet sand. The sea rests behind them. White sunlight, purple at the edges, hangs above the couple. Because of their hair you can tell it's windy. He's sipping a drink from a coconut shell. She's smelling a purple lei hanging from her neck. In another photo she's (improbably) petting a swan. Bobby Hughes stands behind her, smiling (also improbably) in a kind way. In the last photo Bobby Hughes is kneeling behind the girl, helping her pick a tulip.

The girl in all three photos is Lauren Hynde.

I start weeping again.

"That's . . . Lauren Hynde."

A long pause, and then I hear someone ask, "When did you last have contact with Lauren Hynde, Victor?"

I keep weeping, unable to hold it together.

"Victor?" Palakon asks.

"What is she doing with him?" I sob.

"Victor met her while they were students at Camden, I believe," Palakon says softly to his colleagues, an explanation that doesn't accomplish anything, but I nod silently to myself, unable to look up.

"And after that?" someone asks. "When did you last have contact with Lauren Hynde?"

Still weeping, I manage, "I met her last month . . . in Manhattan . . . at a Tower Records."

Russell's cell phone rings, jarring all of us.

"Okay," I hear him say.

After clicking off he implores Palakon to start moving.

"We've got to go," Russell says. "It's time."

"Mr. Johnson, we'll be in touch," Delta says.

I'm reaching into my jacket pocket while wiping my face.

"Yes, this was . . . illuminating," Crater says, not at all sincerely.

"Here." Ignoring Crater, I hand Palakon the printout of the WINGS file. "This is something I found in the computer in the house. I don't know what it means."

Palakon takes it from me. "Thank you, Victor," he says genuinely, slipping it into his folder without even looking at it. "Victor, I want you to calm down. We will be in touch. It might even be tomorrow—"

"But since I last saw you, Palakon, they blew up a fucking hotel," I shout. "They killed the French premier's son."

"Mr. Ward," Palakon says gently, "other factions have already taken blame for the bombing at the Ritz."

"What other factions?" I'm shouting. "They did it. Bruce Rhinebeck left a bomb at the fucking Ritz. There are no other factions. They *are* the faction."

"Mr. Ward, we really—"

"I just don't feel you're concerned about my welfare, Palakon," I say, choking.

"Mr. Ward, that's simply not true," Palakon says, standing, which causes me to stand as well.

"Why did you send me to find her?" I'm shouting. "Why did you send me to find Jamie Fields?" I'm about to grab Palakon but Russell pulls me back.

"Mr. Ward, please," Palakon says. "You must go. We'll be in touch."

I fall into Russell, who keeps propping me up.

"I don't care anymore, Palakon. I don't care."

"I think you do, Mr. Ward."

"Why is that?" I ask, bewildered, staring at him. "Why do you think that?"

"Because if you didn't care, you wouldn't be here."

I take this in.

"Hey, Palakon," I say, stunned. "I didn't say I wasn't scared shitless."

18 Russell races down the stairs in the building on Avenue Verdier two steps at a time and I'm tumbling behind him, for support grabbing on to a marble banister that's so encased with ice it burns my hand, and outside on the street I hold that hand up, panting, telling Russell to slow down.

"We can't," Russell says. "We have to go. Now."

"Why?" I'm asking uselessly, bent over. "Why?"

I brace myself to be pulled along toward the black Citroën but Russell suddenly stops moving and he's breathing in, composing himself.

Disoriented, I stand up straight. Russell casually nudges me.

I'm looking over at him, confused. He's pretending to smile at someone.

Jamie Fields is walking uncertainly toward us, clutching a small white paper bag—no makeup, sweatpants, hair pulled back with a scrunchie, Gucci sunglasses.

Behind her the French film crew is piling equipment into a blue van that's double-parked on Avenue Verdier.

"What are you doing here?" she asks, lowering her sunglasses.

"Hey," I'm saying, gesturing mindlessly.

"What's going on?" she asks, a little mystified. "Victor?"

"Oh yeah, y'know, just hanging," I'm saying vacantly, semi-stunned. "I'm just . . . hanging, um, baby."

Pause. "What?" she asks, laughing, as if she hasn't heard me. "Hanging?" She pauses. "Are you okay?"

"Yeah, baby, I'm fine, I'm cool," I'm saying, gesturing mindlessly. "It looks like rain, huh, baby?"

"You're white," she says. "You look like you've been . . . crying." She reaches out a hand to touch my face. Instinctively I pull away.

"No, no, no," I'm saying. "No, I haven't been crying. I'm cool. I was just yawning. Things are cool."

"Oh," she says, followed by a long pause.

"Whoa," I add to it.

"What are you doing here?" she asks.

"Well, baby, I'm here with"—I glance at Russell—"my friend and we're . . ." I land on, "Well, *I'm* taking French lessons from him."

She just stares at me. Silence.

"You know, baby, I can't speak a word of it. So." I shrug.

She's still staring at me. More silence.

"Not—one—word," I say stiffly.

"Right," she says, but now she's staring at Russell. "You look totally familiar. Have we met?"

"I don't think so," Russell says. "But maybe."

"I'm Jamie Fields," she says, holding out a hand.

"I'm Christian Bale," Russell says, taking it.

"Oh right," she says. "Yeah, I thought I recognized you. You're the actor."

"Yeah, yeah." He's nodding boyishly. "I recognized you too."

"Hey, looks like we're all famous, huh?" I chuckle dreadfully. "How about that, huh?"

"I really liked you in *Newsies* and *Swing Kids*," Jamie says, not at all facetiously.

"Thanks, thanks." Russell keeps nodding.

"And also *Hooked*," Jamie says. "You were great in *Hooked*."

"Oh thanks," Russell says, blushing, smiling on cue. "That's so nice. That's so cool."

"Yeah, *Hooked*," Jamie murmurs, staring thoughtfully into Russell's face.

A long pause follows. I concentrate on the film crew lifting a camera into the back of the van. The director nods at me. I don't nod back. From inside the van ABBA's "Knowing Me, Knowing You" keeps playing, a reminder of something. I'm squinting, trying to remember. The director starts moving toward us.

"So what are you doing in Paris?" Jamie asks Russell.

"Oh, just hanging," Russell says confidently.

"And . . . teaching French?" Jamie laughs, confused.

"Oh it's just a favor," I'm saying, laughing with her. "He's owing me a favor."

Behind us, walking out of the front entrance of the apartment building on Avenue Verdier, are Palakon, Delta, Crater—all in overcoats and sunglasses—without the Japanese man. They maneuver past us, walking purposefully down the block, conferring with one another. Jamie barely notices them since she's preoccupied with staring at Russell. But the director stops walking toward me and stares at Palakon as he passes by, and something in the director's face tightens and he worriedly glances back at me and then once more at Palakon.

"It's a favor," Russell says, putting on Diesel sunglasses. "I'm between roles. So it's cool."

"He's between roles," I'm saying. "He's waiting for a good part. One worthy of his skills."

"Listen, I gotta split," Russell says. "I'll talk to you later, man. Nice meeting you, Jamie."

"Yeah," Jamie says tentatively. "You too, Christian."

"Peace," he says, moving off. "Victor, I'll be in touch. Au revoir."

"Yeah man," I say shakily. "Bonjour, dude," I'm saying. "Oui, monsieur."

Jamie stands in front of me, arms folded. The crew waits, slouching by the van, its engine running. I'm focusing on slowing down my heartbeat. The director starts walking toward us again. My vision keeps blurring over, getting wavy. It starts drizzling.

"What are you doing here?" I ask, trying not to whimper.

"I'm picking up a prescription for Tammy," she says.

"Uh-huh. Because she's, like, very sick, right?"

"Yeah, she's very upset," Jamie says coolly.

"Well, right, because she should be."

I'm wetting my lips, panic coursing through the muscles in my legs, my arms, my face—all tingling. Jamie keeps staring, appraising me. A longer pause. The director is jogging up the street, grimly advancing toward us, toward me.

"So let me get this straight," Jamie starts.

"Uh-huh."

"You're taking French lessons."

"Uh-huh."

"From Christian Bale?"

"No, we're having an affair," I blurt out. "I didn't want to bring him to the house."

"I don't necessarily find that unbelievable."

"No, no, it's French lessons," I'm saying. "Merci beaucoup, bon soir, je comprends, oui, mademoiselle, bonjour, mademoiselle—"

"All right, all right," she mutters, giving up.

The director is getting closer.

"Send them away," I whisper. "Please, just send them away, send them the fuck away," I say, putting my sunglasses on.

Jamie sighs and walks over to the director. He's on a cell phone and he snaps the mouthpiece closed as she approaches. He listens to her, adjusting a red bandanna knotted around his neck. I'm crying silently to myself and as Jamie walks back to me I start shivering. I rub a hand across my forehead, a headache's building.

"Are you okay?" she asks.

I try to speak but can't. I'm only vaguely aware that it's starting to rain.

In a cab heading back to the house she asks me, "So where did you take your French lessons?"

I can't say anything.

"How did you and Christian Bale meet?" she asks.

The cab lurches forward in traffic, its windows streaked with rain. The air inside the cab is heavy with invisible things. I'm slouching in the back of the cab. My foot has fallen asleep.

"What is this?" she asks. "Are you doing your big deaf routine?"

"What's in the bag?" I ask, nodding at the white shape in Jamie's lap.

"Tammy's prescription," she says.

"For what? Methadone?"

"Halcion."

"I hope you got her a lot," I say, and then, "Can I have some?"

"No," Jamie says. "What were you really doing with that guy?"

I blurt out, "How did you know Marina Gibson?"

"Oh god," she groans. "Are we back to that?"

"Jamie," I warn, then relent. "Please."

"I don't know," she says irritably. "I knew her in New York. Modeling. Whatever. Nightlife."

I start giggling. "You're lying."

"Oh shit."

I ask softly, "Could this have all been prevented?"

Finally she answers flatly, "That's speculative."

"Who else is involved with this?" I ask.

She sighs. "It's all very small." Pause. "The larger the group, the greater the danger of detection. You know."

"I'm sure that works well on paper."

"Did you look at the file?" she asks.

"Yes," I murmur.

"Good," she says, relaxing, and then, "I think Christian Bale's cool." She checks her fingernails. "In a fairly obvious way."

I turn to look at her. "What does that mean?"

"Christian Bale wasn't in *Hooked*, Victor," Jamie says. "He wasn't in that movie."

I stall, then move into, "Maybe he was just being . . . polite."

"Don't bother," she mutters.

And outside the house in the 8th or the 16th patches of sunlight start streaming through the dissolving clouds and Jamie and I open the gate and move together silently through the courtyard. Inside, with Bruce Rhinebeck gone the house seems less heavy, better, emptier, even with the second unit setting up. Bobby sits at the computer while talking on a cell phone, smoking a cigarette, tapping ashes into a Diet Coke can, stacks of spiral notebooks piled high on the desk in front of him, lounge music playing in the background. A pool table has been delivered, another BMW is ready to be picked up, new wallpaper has been ordered, there's a party somewhere tonight. "It's all confirmed," Bobby says simply. Inside the house it's twenty degrees. Inside the house, shit, its fragrance, churns everywhere, muddy and billowing. Inside the house there's a lot of "intense activity" and everything's quickly being lit.

I'm just trying not to cry again while standing behind Bobby. On the computer screen: designs for a device, a breakdown of the components that make up the plastic explosive Remform, prospective targets. Jamie's in the kitchen, carefully reading Tammy's prescription while pulling a bottle of Evian out of the refrigerator.

"How's she doing?" Jamie asks Bobby.

"If it's any consolation?" he asks back. "Better."

Jamie walks past me blindly and moves slowly up the spiral staircase, maneuvering around crew members, thinking maybe she should feel more for me than she really does but my fear doesn't move her, it's isolated, it's not hip, it doesn't sing.

I'm touching Bobby's shoulders because I need to.

He stretches away from me, mutters "Don't" and then, "That's not a possibility anymore."

A long silence, during which I try to learn something.

"You look thin," Bobby says. "When's the last time you worked out? You're looking too skinny. Slightly whitish too."

"I just need some sleep, man."

"That's not an explanation," Bobby says. "You need a motivational workshop."

"I don't think so," I say, my voice cracking.

But Bobby might as well be submerged in a pool. We might as well be having a conversation underneath a waterfall. He doesn't even need to be in this room. He's just a voice. I might as well be talking on the phone with someone. I could be viewing this through a telescope. I might as well be dreaming this. Something hits me: *but isn't that the point?*

Bobby walks silently into the kitchen.

"Things are, um, falling apart," I'm saying. "And no one's acting like they are."

"What's falling apart?" Bobby says, walking back up to me. "I think things are right on schedule."

Pause.

"What . . . schedule?" I'm asking. "What . . . things?" Pause. "Bobby?"

"What things?"

"Yeah . . . what things?"

"Just things." Bobby shrugs. "Just things. Things about to happen."

Pause.

"And . . . then?"

"And then?"

"Yeah . . . and then?"

"And then?"

I'm nodding, tears spilling down my face.

"And then? Boom," he says serenely, lightly slapping my face, his hand the temperature of an icicle.

On cue from upstairs: Jamie starts screaming.

Even within the artfully lit shadows of the bathroom Tammy Devol and Bruce Rhinebeck shared, you can easily make out the bathtub overflowing with dark-red water, Tammy's floating face, its shade a light blue, her eyes open and yellowish. Our attention is also supposed to be drawn to the broken Amstel Light bottle that sits on the tub's edge and the groovy patterns her blood made on the tiled walls as it shot out of her veins. Tammy's slashed wrists have been cut to the bone—but even that wasn't "enough," because somehow she managed to slice her throat open very deeply

(but you know it's too deep, you know she couldn't have done this, though you can't say anything because you know that scenes are filmed without you and you know that a different script exists in which you are not a character and you know it's too deep)

and because it smells so much like what I imagined a room covered in blood would smell like and Jamie's screaming so loudly, it's hard to start piecing things together, make the appropriate connections, hit that mark, and I can't stop gasping.

It's the things you don't know that matter most.

Two propmen, both wearing dust masks, swiftly force themselves past us and lift Tammy nude from the tub, her wrists and neck looking like they burst open outward, and a large purple dildo slides out of her cunt, splashing back into the bloody bathwater. My eyes are homing in on her navel ring.

Jamie has backed out of the bathroom and into Bentley's arms. She struggles, hugs him, pulls away again. She holds a hand to her mouth. Her face is red, like it's burning.

In a corner of the bedroom Bobby is talking to the director, both of them motionless except for an occasional nod.

Jamie tries to get away from Bentley and shambles madly toward Tammy's bedroom but she's blocked because another propman, also wearing a dust mask, is hauling a mattress soaked with blood down the hallway, to be burned in the courtyard.

Jamie stares at the stained mattress in horror—at its truth—and Bentley holds on to her as she flings herself at Tammy's bed, Bentley falling with her, and screaming, she lunges for the script on Tammy's nightstand and hurls it at Bobby and the director. She struggles with a pillow, absurdly. Her screaming intensifies, is a variation on the earlier screaming.

Bobby glances over at Jamie, distracted. He watches passively, trying to listen to something the director is telling him while Jamie scratches at her face, makes gurgling noises, pleads with anyone who will listen.

I can't form a sentence, all reflexes zapped. I'm feebly reaching out a hand to steady myself, cameras swinging around us, capturing reactions.

Bobby slaps Jamie across the face while Bentley continues holding on to her.

"No one cares," Bobby's saying. "I thought we agreed on that."

Jamie makes noises no one can translate.

"I thought we agreed on that," Bobby's saying. "You understand me? No one cares." He slaps her across the face, harder. This time it gets her attention. She stares at him. "This reaction of yours is useless. It carries no meaning with anyone here and it's useless. We agreed that no one would care."

Jamie nods mutely and just as it seems she's going to relax into the moment, she suddenly freaks out. Bentley is panting with exertion, trying to wrestle her down, but he's laughing because he's so stressed out, and someone from the crew keeps rationalizing, frivolously, "No one could have saved her." I'm trying to move the other way, gracefully aiming for the door. I'm trying to wake up momentarily by turning away from this scene, by becoming transparent, but also realizing that the Halcion prescription Jamie picked up was meant not for Tammy but only for herself.

17

Midnight and I'm drinking Absolut from a plastic cup, overdressed in a black Prada suit with Gucci boots and eating Xanax, a cigarette burning between my fingers. A party at a massive new Virgin megastore that maybe Tommy Hilfiger has something to do with sponsoring; there's a stage, there's supposed to be bands, there's an Amnesty International banner, there's supposed to be the ubiquitous benefit concert (though right now the Bangles' "Hazy Shade of Winter" is blasting over the sound system), there's loads of negativity. There's the lead singer from the Verve, there are two members from Blur wearing vintage sneakers, there's Andre Agassi and William Hurt and three Spice Girls and people milling around holding guitars, there are the first black people I've seen since I've been in France, there're a lot of major dudes from Hollywood (or not enough, depending on who you ask), there are trays of ostrich on tiny crackers, opossum on bamboo skewers, shrimp heads tied up in vines, huge plates of tentacles draped over clumps of parsley, but I really can't keep anything down and I'm looking for a leather sofa to fall into because I can't tell if people are really as disinterested as they appear or just extremely bored. Whatever—it's infectious. People keep swatting away flies when they aren't busy whispering or lurking. I'm just saying "Hi." I'm just following directions. It's really an alarming party and everyone is a monster. It's also a mirror.

And then a giant intake of breath. Uncertain of what I'm seeing.

On the edge of the crowd, beyond the crowd, perfectly lit, cameras flashing around her, surrounded by playboys, her hair sleek and dark gold, is a girl.

Chloe.

Everything rushes back and it knocks me forward, stunned, and I start pushing through the crowd dumbly, adrenaline washing through me, my breath exhaling so hard I'm making noises and Elle Macpherson glimpses me and tries reaching over to say "Hi" but when she sees how freaked out I look—face twisted, gasping—something dawns on her and she decides to ignore me.

At the precise moment Elle turns away I see Bertrand Riple is across the record store, his eyes focused as if on a target, grimly advancing toward Chloe.

Frantic, I start making swimming motions, butterfly strokes, to facilitate my way through the crowd, knocking into people, but it's so packed in the Virgin megastore that it's like moving upward and sideways across a slope and Chloe seems miles away.

It's shocking how fast Bertrand Ripleis is moving toward her and he's practicing smiles, rehearsing an intro, a way to kiss her.

"No, no, no," I'm muttering, pushing forward, the party roaring around me.

Bertrand suddenly gets stuck, first by a waiter holding a tray of hors d'oeuvres, who Bertrand angrily knocks away, and then by an unusually insistent Isabelle Adjani, straining to keep up his side of the conversation. When he glances over, sees how much ground I've covered, he pushes her aside and starts cutting across to Chloe laterally.

And then I'm reaching out, my hand falling on Chloe's shoulder, and before even looking at her—because there's so much anxiety coursing through me—I glance over in time to see Bertrand suddenly stop, staring at me blank-faced until he retreats.

"Chloe," I say, my voice hoarse.

She turns around, ready to smile at whoever just said her name, but when she sees it's me she seems confused and she doesn't say anything.

People are swarming around us and I start crying, wrapping my arms around her, and in a haze I realize she's hugging me back.

"I thought you were in New York," she's saying.

"Oh baby, no, no," I'm saying. "I'm here. I've been here. Why did you think that?"

"Victor?" she asks, pulling back. "Are you okay?"

"Yeah, baby, I'm cool," I say, still crying, trying not to.

Upstairs, at Chloe's request a PR person maneuvers us to a bench in the VIP section, which looks out over the rest of the party. Chloe's chewing Nicorette, carefully blotting her lipstick, and gold and taupe brow color has been applied to the outer corners of her eyes and I keep grabbing her hand, clutching it, and sometimes she squeezes back.

"How are you?" she asks.

"Oh great, great." Pause. "Not so great." Another pause. "I think I need some help, baby." I try to smile.

"It's not drugs . . . is it?" she asks. "We're not being bad . . . are we?"

"No, no, no, not that, I just—" I smile tightly, reach out again to rub her hand. "I just missed you so much and I'm just so glad you're here and I'm just so sorry for everything," I say in a rush, breaking down again.

"Hey, shhh, what's bringing this on?" she asks.

I can't talk. My head slips from my hands and I'm just sobbing, tears pouring out.

"Victor? Is everything okay?" she asks softly. "What's going on?"

I take in a giant breath, then sob again.

"Victor, what's wrong?" I hear her ask. "Do you need any money? Is that it?"

I keep shaking my head, unable to speak.

"Are you in trouble?" she asks. "Victor?"

"No, no, baby, no," I say, wiping my face.

"Victor, you're scaring me."

"It's just, it's just, this is my worst suit," I say, trying to laugh. "Wardrobe dressed me. The director insisted. But it's just not fitting right."

"You look nice," she says, relaxing a little. "You look tired but you look nice." She pauses, then adds sweetly, "I've missed you."

"Oh baby . . ."

"I know I shouldn't but I do."

"Hey, hey . . ."

"I left about a dozen messages on your machine in New York last week," she says. "I guess you never got them."

"No." I clear my throat, keep sniffling. "No, I guess I didn't."

"Victor—"

"So are you seeing anyone?" I ask, hope cracking my voice apart. "Did you come here with anyone?"

"Please. No unpleasant questions. Okay?"

"Hey, come on, Chloe, just let me know."

"Victor, Jesus," she says, pulling back. "We already talked about that. I'm not seeing anyone."

"What happened to Baxter?" I ask, coughing.

"Baxter Priestly?" she asks. "Victor—"

"Yeah, Baxter." I wipe my face with my hand, then wipe my hand on my pants, still sniffling.

"Nothing. Why?" Chloe pauses, chewing tensely. "Victor, I'm suddenly really, really worried about you."

"I thought he was in the same movie," I blurt out. "I thought his part got bigger."

"He's been written out," she says. "Not like that should mean anything to you."

"Baby, listen, I'm just so happy to see you."

"You're shaking," she says. "You're really shaking."

"I'm just . . . so cold," I say. "What are you doing here?"

"Well, the shows," she says, staring at me strangely.

"Yeah, yeah." I reach for her hand again. "What else?"

"I'm also narrating a documentary on the history of the negligee."

"That's so cool, baby."

"Some might say," she concedes. "And yourself? What are you doing in Paris?"

"I'm just, um, moving on to the next project, y'know?" I say.

"That's . . . constructive."

"Yeah. Go figure," I say. "I don't have a master plan yet."

At the entrance of the VIP section, at the top of the steel staircase, Bobby is conferring with Bertrand, who is jabbing his finger at where Chloe and I are sitting while he angrily leans into Bobby and Bobby just nods "understandingly" and makes a calming motion with his hand, which Bertrand pushes away disgustedly. Bobby sighs visibly and as he starts making his way over to us, he's joined by Bentley.

With maximum effort I light a cigarette. Exhaling, I make a face and hand the cigarette to Chloe.

"No, I'm not smoking anymore," she says, smiling, taking the cigarette from me and dropping it into a nearby beer bottle. "I shouldn't even be chewing this stuff," she says, making a face.

Bobby and Bentley get closer, casually determined.

"We can't talk here," I'm saying. "I can't talk here."

"It's really loud," she says, nodding.

"Listen." I breathe in. "Where are you staying?"

"At Costes," she says. "Where are *you* staying?"

"I'm just, um, just staying with some people."

"Who?"

"Bobby Hughes," I say because I can't get away with a lie.

"Oh really?" she says. "I didn't know you knew him."

"And Jamie Fields. I went to Camden with her. But they're a couple. Bobby and Jamie are a couple."

"You don't need to explain, Victor."

"No, no, no, it's not like that," I keep insisting. "They're together. I'm just staying at their place."

A careful pause. "But didn't you use to date her?" Chloe asks.

"Yeah, yeah, but she's with Bobby Hughes now," I say.

"What's he like?" Chloe asks, and then, "Victor, you've got to calm down, you're freaking me out."

"I'm not seeing Jamie Fields," I say. "I have no interest whatsoever in Jamie Fields anymore."

"Victor, you don't need to explain," Chloe says. "I said it's okay."

"I know, I know." My eyes are wet and blinking.

"So what's the address?" she asks. "Where you are?"

I'm too afraid to give it out so I just tell her the name of a street in the 8th.

"Posh," she says, and then, uneasily, "People live there?"

"So I'll call you, okay?"

Suddenly Chloe looks up at someone behind me and, smiling widely, jumps off the bench and shouts, "Oh my god—Bentley!"

"Chloe baby," Bentley cries out, swingerish, as he grabs her in a giant hug.

She's squealing happily, spinning around, Bobby silently waiting on the sidelines, listening patiently to their requisite small talk. I force myself to acknowledge Bobby's presence as he continues to stare at Chloe, his eyes black and waxy, but then Chloe's smiling at him and suddenly cameras are flashing all around us and as the four of us stand together, pretending we're not posing casually for the paparazzi, Bobby lifts Chloe's hand up.

"How gallant," Chloe whispers mock-seriously as Bobby kisses her hand and when he lifts that hand to kiss it the urge to knock his face away almost destroys me and I fall back on the bench, defeated.

Bobby's saying, "We're sorry we have to take him away from you." He gestures vaguely at me.

This moves me to say, "I think I'm being accosted."

"It's okay," Chloe says. "I have a show tomorrow morning."

"Let's leave, Victor," Bentley says. "Come on, guy."

"Leave for what?" I ask, refusing to get up from the bench. "It's midnight."

"No it's not," Bobby says, checking his watch.

"Leave for what?" I ask again.

"We have a dinner party we're late for," Bobby explains to Chloe. "Plus a really shitty band's about to play. It's a good opportunity to split."

"Baby." Bentley's kissing Chloe again. "We are definitely partying while you're here. That is a promise."

"It's great to see you again, Bentley," Chloe says, and then to Bobby, "And it's nice to finally meet you."

Bobby blushes on cue. "And you," is all he says but it's so loaded with references that I start shaking uncontrollably.

"Let's go," Bentley's saying to me. "Get up."

"Maybe you should just leave without me," I tell him. "It's too late to eat."

"I have a remarkable metabolism," Bobby says. "It'll be okay."

"Chloe," I say. "Do you want to have a drink with me?"

"Victor," Bobby says, hurt.

Chloe gauges Bobby's reaction. "Listen, I have to unpack. I'm jet-lagged," Chloe says. "We have a press conference tomorrow morning. I have a photo shoot with Gilles Bensimon at twelve, so ... not tonight, sorry."

"Let's cancel," I tell Bobby.

"That's impossible," Bobby says crisply. "I'm starving."

"Victor, it's really okay," Chloe says. "I have to go anyway. I'm totally jet-lagged. I came straight here from the airport."

"Can I see you tomorrow?" I ask.

A pause. For some reason she glances over at Bobby. "Sure," Chloe says. "Call me."

"Okay." I glance nervously at Bobby. "I will."

Chloe reaches over and wipes a smudge of lipstick off my cheek. She kisses me, she disappears.

The three of us look on as the party swallows her up.

"Come on, Victor," Bobby says.

"No," I say, not getting up from the bench.

"Ooh, he's being a little skittish," Bentley says.

Bobby tugs "playfully" at my sleeve.

"Come on. It's time to revel."

I slowly raise myself but it's really Bobby lifting up my entire weight with just one arm, pulling me off the bench. It's slippery walking down the staircase because the record store is encased in ice, and gold confetti streams down over us hideously, flies swarming everywhere.

16

Outside the Virgin megastore a limousine is waiting, an immense carnival surrounds us, bouncers fend off people way too hopeful of getting in. Tormented, I throw up twice beside the limo while Bobby lights a cigar.

"Time to depart, Victor," Bentley says grimly. "Get your ass up."

"And do what?" I croak. "Stick it in your face?"

"Promises, promises," Bentley sighs, mock-wearily. "Just get the fuck up. That's a boy."

"You're just making noise," I say, standing up.

On the sidewalk Bertrand stares at me and I'm staring back hatefully and then I break away from Bentley and Bobby and rush toward him, my fist raised high above my head, but Bobby ends up holding me back. Bertrand just smiles smugly, within inches of my reach. Slouching away, Bertrand curses in French, something I can't understand.

15

In the limousine moving back to the house I'm sitting between Bentley and Bobby.

"Chloe Byrnes," Bobby's saying. "How . . . intriguing."

My head is resting on my knees and I'm swallowing back dry heaves, breathing deeply.

"I like Chloe Byrnes," Bobby says. "She's not afraid to embrace her sensuality," he murmurs. "Amazing body." Pause. "Quite . . . distracting." He laughs darkly.

"If you ever touch her, Bobby, I swear to god I will fucking kill you, I swear to god," I say, enunciating each word.

"Ooh, how confrontational," Bentley giggles.

"Shut up, you faggot," I mutter.

"That's the pot calling the kettle black," Bentley says. "Or so I hear."

Bobby starts giggling too. "Boys, boys."

"Did you hear me, Bobby?" I ask.

Bobby keeps giggling and then, in a very tight voice, squeezing my thigh, says, "You have neither the clout nor the experience to make a threat like that, Victor."

14

In my bedroom at the house in the 8th or the 16th, sleeplessness is interrupted by the occasional unbearable dream—chased by raptors down hotel corridors, the word "beyond" appearing repeatedly, something wet keeps flying across the upper corner of the frame, making slapping noises, I'm always brushing my hair, trying to find the most accurate way possible to create a part, and I'm canceling dream appointments, keeping things loose, tumbling down steep flights of stairs that are too narrow to navigate and I'm always over water and everyone I run across has a face resembling mine. Waking up, I realize: you're just someone waiting casually in the dark for a rustling outside your door and there's a shadow in the hall.

I open the door. The director from the French film crew is waiting. He seems nervous. He's holding a videotape, expectantly. He's wearing an expensive parka.

Without being invited in, he slips past me, closes the door. Then he locks it.

"What do you want?" I ask, moving back to the bed.

"I know we haven't talked much during the shoot, Victor," he starts apologetically, without the accent I expected.

"I have nothing to say to you," I mutter.

"And I understand," he says. "In fact I think I understand why even more now."

"That's okay because I don't care, I have my own problems," I say, and then, yawning, "What time is it?"

"It's light out," he offers.

I reach over to the nightstand and swallow two Xanax. I tip a bottle of Evian to my mouth. I stare at the director hatefully.

"What's that?" I ask, motioning to the tape in his hand. "Dailies?"

"Not exactly," he says.

I realize something. "Does Bobby know you're here?"

He looks away apprehensively.

"I think you should leave," I'm saying. "If Bobby doesn't know you're here I think you should leave."

"Victor," the director says. "I've debated showing you this." He pauses briefly. He decides something and shuffles toward a large-screen TV that's ensconced in a white-oak armoire across from the bed I'm shivering in. "But in light of what's about to happen, I think it's probably imperative that you view this."

"Hey, hey, wait," I'm saying. "No, please, don't—"

"I really think you should see this, Victor."

"Why?" I'm pleading, afraid. "Why?"

"This isn't for you," he says. "This is for someone else's benefit."

He blows confetti off the tape before slipping it into the VCR below the TV. "We think that Bobby Hughes is getting out of hand."

I'm wrapping myself in a comforter, freezing, steam pouring from my mouth because of how cold it is in the house.

"I think things need to be reduced for you," the director says. "In order for you to . . . see things clearly." He pauses, checks something on the VCR's console. "Otherwise we'll be shooting this all year."

"I don't think I have the energy to watch this."

"It's short," the director says. "You still have some semblance of an attention span left. I checked."

"But I might get confused," I say, pleading. "I might get thrown off—"

"Thrown off *what*?" the director snaps. "You're not even *on* anything to get thrown off *of*."

He presses Play on the console. I motion for him to sit next to me on the bed because I'm getting so tense I need to hold his hand even though he's wearing leather gloves, and he lets me.

Blackness on the screen blooms into random footage of Bobby.

Bobby on Boulevard du Montparnasse. Bobby sitting in La Coupole. Bobby heading down the Champs Élysées. Bobby taking notes while waiting for the Vivienne Westwood show to begin, sitting in a giant room in the basement of the Louvre. Bobby crossing Rue de Rivoli. Bobby crossing Quai des Celestins. He's turning down Rue de l'Hôtel-de-Ville. He enters the métro station at Pont Marie. He's on a train, grabbing an overhead handrail as the train slowly enters the Sully-Morland station. A shot of Bobby on an Air Inter flight from Paris to Marseilles, reading a copy of *Le Figaro*. Bobby's picking up a rental car at the Provence airport.

"What are these? Highlights?" I'm asking, relaxing a little.

"Shh. Just watch," the director says.

"Bobby doesn't know you're showing me this," I ask again. "Does he?"

Bobby gets off a plane that just landed at Le Bourget airport.

Bobby walks along the Place des Voyages and into a restaurant called Benoît.

Bobby in the tunnel on the Place de l'Alma, near its east end, crouching by the concrete divider that separates the eastbound and westbound lanes.

Suddenly a scene I don't remember shooting. Café Flore. It's only me in the shot and I'm tan, wearing white, my hair slicked back, and I'm looking for a waitress.

"This cappuccino sucks, dude," I'm muttering. "Where's the froth?" A boom mike is visible above my head.

A voice—Bobby's—says, "We're not here for the cappuccino, Victor."

"Maybe you're not, baby, but I want some froth."

A shot of a line of schoolgirls singing as they walk along Rue Saint-Honoré.

Then static.

And then a close-up: airplane tickets to Tel Aviv.

Bobby's outside Dschungel, a club in Berlin, calling a girl a slut. A famous American football player is idling behind him.

Bobby in front of a Jewish synagogue in Istanbul.

Bobby wearing a skullcap. Bobby praying in Hebrew.

Bobby at the Saudi embassy in Bangkok.

Bobby drifting out of a bungalow in Tripoli, walking past a discarded radio antenna, an expensive Nikon camera swinging around his neck. A group of men follow him, wearing head scarves, holding Samsonite briefcases.

Someone singing a love song in Arabic plays over the sound track.

Bobby hops into a battered Mercedes 450SEL. A Toyota bus with bulletproof windows trails the Mercedes as it heads into a dark, vast desert.

The camera pans to a bulldozer scooping out a giant pit.

More static.

And then a black Citroën heads down Route Nationale through southern Normandy outside a farm village called Male.

The handheld camera shakes as it follows Bobby walking through what looks like a Ralph Lauren advertisement—an intensely green landscape, a gray overcast sky—and Bobby's so well-groomed it's astonishing; he's wearing a black wool blazer, a black cashmere turtleneck, Gucci boots, his hair's impeccable, he's holding a large bottle of Evian water. He's following a path.

Two golden retrievers bound into the frame, greeting Bobby as he nears what looks like a converted barn. He's passing under a proscenium. He's passing a catering truck. The barn is made of limestone and chicly shaped logs. As he approaches the front door Bobby turns his head toward the camera and grins, saying something the viewer can't hear while pointing at an antique bird feeder that hangs next to the front door of the converted barn.

Bobby knocks on that door. He leans down to pet the dogs. The dogs are photogenic, relaxed. Suddenly both their heads snap up and, bounding out of frame, they immediately run to whoever's behind the camera.

The door opens. A figure, mostly obscure in the shadowy doorway, shakes Bobby's hand. The figure notices the camera, gestures toward it, annoyed. The figure motions Bobby inside.

And then F. Fred Palakon, his face clearly visible, looks outside before closing the door.

The director leans over, letting go of my hand, and rewinds the tape to the moment F. Fred Palakon's face emerges from the shadows of the converted barn.

Once again F. Fred Palakon shakes Bobby's hand.

Once again F. Fred Palakon gestures toward the camera.

The director presses Pause on the VCR's console, freezing on Palakon's face the instant Palakon notices the camera, and right now Palakon's staring into the bedroom I'm occupying in the house in either the 8th or the 16th.

"I know this isn't exactly reassuring," the director says.

I'm cowering on the other side of the bed, delusional, backed up against the wall, floundering.

"Just consider what it means," he says. "Reflect."

I start crying. "I'm gonna die, I'm gonna die, they're gonna kill me—"

"Victor—"

"No, no, no," I'm groaning, thrashing around on the bed.

"At any rate," the director says, ejecting the tape from the VCR, "this is not a fantasy."

I lie on the bed, finally motionless, my hands over my face.

"What is it, then?" I groan mindlessly. "Punishment?"

"No." Before slipping out, the director says, "It's an instruction."

13

An hour later I'm vaguely aware of brushing my teeth in the shower. I barely dry myself off—the towel keeps dropping from my hands. I get dressed. Numb, giggling to myself in the darkness of my bedroom, I accidentally start forming a plan.

12 Walking slowly down the circular staircase into the living room, fear grafted onto my face, I can't stop shaking. A cameraman is gloomily sipping a cup of watery coffee while leaning against the big Panaflex camera that takes up so much space in the foyer and the director's sitting in the director's chair, staring at a video console, preparing a scene I will not be appearing in. The crew mills around. Someone actually says to someone else, "It scarcely matters." There's a lot of shrugging and slinking off.

I'm promising myself that this will be the last time I see any of these people.

Bentley has spent all morning being prepped for a segment on MTV's "House of Style—Dubai!" and right now he's facing a mirror in the corner of the living room as a stylist blow-dries his hair and Bentley, shouting over the noise, explains to an interviewer, "It's the classic bistro look in what's basically a modern kitchen." The interviewer wants to touch on eyeball fashion, what country has the sexiest soldiers, and then, "Ooh, can I have a pretzel?" I'm trying to block a tear with my finger. My heart feels sore, on the verge of bursting. I manage a wave, a small acknowledgment, to Bentley. The interviewer whispers something to Bentley while gawking at me and Bentley mutters "I already did" and they scream hysterically while giving each other high fives.

Jamie's lying on a couch, a pink face mask over her eyes, recovering from the abortion she had yesterday afternoon, hungover from the Planet Hollywood opening she had to attend last night, and she's talking sullenly into a cell phone. A book, an astrological forecast for Aquarians, lies on her chest and she looks like someone dropped her, picked her up, then laid her across the couch. She's pressing a flower into her face, fingers stained from newspaper ink. She holds up a hand warily as I pass and mouths *Shhh—it's my manager* and someone with a handheld camera crouches low, capturing Jamie's blank face on super-8.

Bobby sits at the computer wearing Helmut Lang jeans and a Helmut Lang moleskin jacket, a rusted-green Comme des Garçons sweater underneath. On the computer screen are the words BRINK OF DESTRUCTION and automatically I'm thinking, Who's Brink? and I've never heard of that band, and Bobby, in one of his "barely tolerant" moods, asks me, "Where are you going?"

"To see Chloe," I say, stiffly walking past him to the kitchen. I force myself to peer into the refrigerator, struggling to be casual, a very hard moment. Outside, lightning flickers and then, on cue, thunder sounds.

Bobby's considering what I just said.

"Are you trying to rescue her?" he muses. "Or are you trying to rescue yourself?" He pauses. "That's not really a solution," he says, and then, less sweetly, "Is it?"

"I'm just going to make sure everything's okay with her."

"I think that's another movie," Bobby says. "And I think you're confused."

"So you have a problem?" I ask, walking back into the living room.

"No," he says. "I just don't think that's all you're going to do." He shrugs. "It's just a . . . quandary."

"Do I really need to make arrangements with you in order to visit my ex-girlfriend?" I ask. "It's pretty fucking simple—"

"Hey, don't talk that way to me." He scowls.

"—to grasp, Bobby. I'm going to see Chloe. Bye-bye."

Bobby's expression subtly changes, becoming bored, almost trusting.

"Don't act so wounded," he finally says, flashing a warning look. "You're not very good at it."

It seems impossible that I will ever get out of this house. Under my breath I'm telling myself, *It's just another scene, it's just another phase*, like it's a lyric from a song that means something.

"Do you think I'm lying?" I ask.

"No, no," Bobby says. "I just think there's a hole in your truth."

"Well, what do you want to hear?" I ask, daring him.

He ponders this, then simply turns back to the computer screen. "I think I've decided to listen to something else."

"What does that mean?" I ask.

"You want it translated?" he mutters. "Sober up. Learn your ABCs."

"I'm just trying to have a so-called normal conversation," I say.

"I don't think you're being particularly successful," he says.

"I'm not going to be put off by your negativity," I'm saying, teeth clenched. "Later, dude."

The director glances up at me and nods, once.

"Okay, we need some spontaneous sound bites," the interviewer from "House of Style" says.

I'm walking by Bentley as he shows off a stack of 1960s movie magazines, a book of photographs featuring dismembered dolls, a new tattoo in the shape of a demon laced across his bicep.

"We'll miss you," Bentley says, batting his eyes at me.

Outside, it's raining lightly. A bearded man worriedly walks a dog. A girl glides by holding a dozen sunflowers. I break down again, tears spilling out of my eyes. I hail a cab. Inside the cab, I'm trying not to shriek. A moment of doubt rises, but I blame it on the rain and then I tell the driver, "The American embassy."

11 I'm sufficiently calm to minimize crying, to curb the hyperventilating. But I'm also on so much Xanax that the following is merely a dark blur and the only thing keeping this scene from being totally black is the mid-level panic that still beats through me, acting as a dull light.

I'm just assuming we're on Avenue Gabriel as the taxi stops in front of what I'm just assuming is the American embassy. I give the driver whatever bills I have left in my wallet—250, maybe 300 francs. I don't care, I tell myself as I stumble from the cab.

I'm vaguely aware of walking up steps past a sentry box into the building. I'm glancing sideways at members of the Police Urbaine, at a machine gun, at a security camera, at a guard who responds only slightly with bland suspicion when I move by, serenely smiling.

In the lobby I'm allowed to walk through a metal detector without incident. I'm allowed to step up to a plexiglass window.

I tell the woman sitting behind the plexiglass window that I need to speak to an official. "Un officiale . . . ?"

In English, she asks if I have an appointment with anyone.

"No," I say.

She asks me my name.

I tell her, "Victor Johnson."

She asks me what this concerns.

I tell her, "A bomb." I tell her, "It concerns a bomb."

She picks up a phone, utters words into it I can't hear. She continues to explain something that I'm too numb to decipher.

Two policemen carrying machine guns suddenly move into my line of vision, guarding me, not saying a word, standing at attention, waiting.

A young man, familiar-looking and nondescript, vaguely European, vaguely not, wearing a gray Prada suit with a stylish green tie, moves quickly down a corridor to where I'm standing.

The young man asks, "How can I help you, Mr. Johnson?"

"We need to talk elsewhere," I'm saying.

"What is this about?" he asks carefully.

"I know the people who planted the bomb at the Ritz," I say. "I know where they live. I know their names. I know who they are."

The official just stares at me, unsure of how to respond. "You do?"

"Yes," I say solemnly. "I do."

"And?" he asks, waiting.

"They blew up the Institute of Political Studies," I say. "They're also responsible for the bombing at Café Flore." Breaking down, I tell him, "They're responsible for the bomb that went off in the métro last week." Confidence collapses and I start crying.

The official seems to take this in stride. He makes a decision.

"If you would please wait here," he says to me.

He leans and says something in French to the two guards, who because of this command nod, relax a little, even as they move in closer.

"No," I'm saying. "I don't want to wait here."

"Please, let me get someone in Security to talk with you," the official says politely.

"Let me please come with you," I'm saying. "They might have followed me—"

"Just calm down, Mr. Ward—I'll be right back," he says, walking away.

A third guard has joined the other two and I'm in the middle of a triangle, surrounded, and then something black explodes in my stomach.

"Hey," I'm saying. "How did you know my name was Ward?" And then I start shouting, "How did you know my name? I didn't give you that name. How did you know my name was Ward?"

But he's just a silhouette in the corridor, and then even his shadow disappears.

The guards move in closer and I'm sighing urgently to get across to them how distressed I am, fear speeding out of control, the smell of shit suffocating me, and I'm making gestures that don't mean anything to them, there's no reaction on the guards' impassive faces, nothing. Movement, people, sounds start curving toward me and new silhouettes are gliding down a hallway in my direction. Two more guards, the young official, another figure. And I'm breathing louder as the shadows get closer, progressing toward me, and I'm wiping my hands over my face, glancing behind the plexiglass window, but the woman's not there anymore, and then I hear a voice.

"Mr. Ward?" it asks.

Slowly, dumbly, I turn around.

F. Fred Palakon stands in front of me, dramatically backlit from the light at the end of the hallway.

I try to run.

10

An interrogation room. It's freezing. There's a ventilator in the ceiling and confetti's everywhere, pasted onto the walls, the floor, the chairs we're sitting on, scattered in piles across the table Palakon and David Crater and Laurence Delta and Russell and the Japanese man from the apartment on Avenue Verdier are all sitting behind. There's also an inspector lieutenant of the First Section of the Paris Prefecture of Police taking notes and someone who came in from Lyons for Interpol. This man is so familiar-looking it becomes distracting. Smoke has been produced for added atmosphere.

"You never wanted me to find Jamie Fields," I'm saying, unable to contain myself. "This was never about her, Palakon."

Palakon sighs. "Mr. Ward, the fact remains—"

"Palakon," I'm warning, my heart speeding up. "I swear to god, unless you tell me what this is all about I'm not saying another fucking word."

"Mr. Ward, please—"

"No, Palakon—fuck you." I stand up, kicking the chair away.

"Mr. Ward, please sit down."

"Not until you tell me what the fuck's going on, Palakon."

"We're here to help you, Mr. Ward," Palakon says gently.

"Oh fucking stop it," I spit out. "Just tell me what the fuck's happening. Jesus Christ, you have fucking offices in the fucking *embassy*? What— you're all having brunch together?"

Palakon glances at Crater, then at Delta, at the Japanese man, who scowls impatiently and gives Palakon a hesitant nod.

Calmly, deliberately, Palakon asks, "Well, Victor, what would you like to know?"

"Who do you work for?" I ask.

Palakon considers this, doesn't know where to go.

"Oh shit, Palakon."

I glance over at the inspector from Interpol, who seems to just be taking up space, barely paying attention to the proceedings. But those cheekbones, that jawline—I've seen them before and I'm trying to place where I met him.

"I'm just figuring out the best way to explain—"

"Fuck the best way," I shout. "Just fucking say it. Who do you work for?"

"I'm an independent contractor, Mr. Ward—"

I cut him off. "I'm not saying anything else until you tell me who you work for."

A long pause, during which Delta sighs heavily, then nods at Palakon.

"Who in the fuck do you work for?" I ask. "Because Jamie Fields has nothing to do with any of this, right?"

"Not . . . exactly." Palakon tilts his head.

"Goddamnit, Palakon, I'm so fucking sick of your bullshit," I scream.

"Mr. Ward—"

"They killed Tammy Devol," I'm screaming. "They fucking raped her and cut her throat open. Bobby Hughes ordered it done."

Everyone just stares at me blankly from across the table like I've lost it or as if losing it isn't understandable.

"Mr. Ward—" Palakon starts, his patience dropping.

"Fuck you, Palakon!" I'm screaming. "Who in the fuck do you work for?" I'm at the table now, gripping its edges, glaring into Palakon's face. "Fucking tell me who you work for," I'm screaming at maximum volume, my face twisted into a grimace.

Palakon draws in a breath and stares icily at me.

He says, simply, "I work for your father."

Palakon pauses, looks away, sighing, then back at me.

"I work for your father, Mr. Ward."

This is uttered so matter-of-factly, delivered so deadpan, that its existence opens a door and if you looked through that door you would see me moving above a winter road then descending rapidly and no one's there to catch me and I'm hitting pavement. What this implies simply is that truth equals chaos and that this is a regression. A physical sensation causes me to ignore everything in this room—to turn away from Russell running his hand through his hair, turn away from the Japanese man lighting another cigarette, turn away from the fly buzzing around my head. These men are perpetrators and the table they're sitting behind suddenly seems vaster and they're making plans, they're jotting memoranda, they're casting motives, they're plotting itineraries. Something invisible is forming itself in the cold air in the interrogation room and it's directed at me, wheeling forward. But the familiarity of the inspector from Interpol interrupts everything, makes me remember an earlier scene, and something emerges, obliterates the fuzz.

"What do you mean?" I ask quietly.

"I was hired by your father," Palakon says. "He came to me."

I slowly move away from the table, my hand on my mouth, and I'm sitting back down in the chair I'd kicked away.

"Mr. Ward," the Japanese man starts, with a thick accent. "Your father is leaving the U.S. Senate quite soon. Is this correct?"

I stare blankly at him. "I . . . don't know."

The Japanese man continues. "Your father will be making a bid for the—"

"Wait," I say, cutting him off. "What does this have to do with anything?"

"Victor," Palakon starts, "your father—"

The Japanese man interrupts. "Mr. Palakon, please. May I speak?"

Palakon nods uncertainly.

"We have not been formally introduced," the Japanese man says.

"Who are you?" I ask.

He hesitates. "And for reasons owing to our mutual personal safety, Mr. Johnson, we will not be."

"Oh shit," I'm muttering, clenching up. "Oh shit oh shit—"

"Mr. Johnson, your father is leaving the United States Senate." The Japanese man pauses. "He is interested in moving on, shall we say?" The Japanese man gestures with his hands, tries to smile kindly but is incapable. "To a higher place. He is planning to announce his bid for a higher office, for—"

"Oh shit oh shit oh shit." My moaning cuts him off, distracting the Japanese man.

"Mr. Ward," Crater starts, "when your father came to us, he was concerned about certain . . . well, proclivities you had toward—"

"What he's trying to say, Victor," Palakon interrupts, "is that you're not exactly an unknown quantity."

"I'm not a what?" I'm asking.

"In certain circles, in certain media circles, people know who you are." Delta this time. "You're a target."

Palakon and Crater nod subtly.

"There were certain aspects of your life that your father felt were affecting"—Delta pauses—"certain . . . possibilities from forming."

"Listen, Victor," Crater says impatiently. "Your dad basically wanted you to take a vacation."

"Why did he want that?" I ask slowly, in a very restrained voice.

"He felt that some of your . . . antics, let's say . . ." Palakon has trouble completing this sentence. He checks a file resting on the table, as the room seems to grow smaller. "Well, they were distracting." Palakon pauses. "They were . . . unnecessary. There was the possibility of bad publicity," he delicately adds.

"There was a concern that things might not fall into place properly," the Japanese man says. "There were worries that things might not work out in New Hampshire since you—"

"We don't need to go there quite yet," Palakon says, cutting him off.

"Yes, of course," the Japanese man says. "You're quite right."

"Victor, your father didn't want you harmed in any way," Palakon says. "He simply wanted you to, well, take a break for a little while. He wanted you . . . preoccupied. He didn't want you in the States." Palakon pauses. "So he came to us. Things were discussed. Arrangements were made."

Silence, empty and graceless. I'm just staring at them, unable to take all this in because of certain details my mind cannot accept, and that lack of acceptance keeps spreading and I'm looking at this through a window and it's being boarded up and it's night and no one has said or is going to say who they really are.

We'll slide down the surface of things.

It's what you don't know that matters most.

The room slopes, then rights itself.

Outside, thunder.

You are beyond uneasiness. You force yourself to look at them. You stop yourself from falling over. You try to care. But you can't. Even if you wanted to, you can't. And now, in this room, it occurs to you that they know this too. *Confusion and hopelessness don't necessarily cause a person to act.* Someone from my first publicist's office told me this a long time ago. Only now does it resurface. Only now does it mean anything to me.

"Why did you use Jamie Fields as an excuse?" I hear myself ask.

"We delved into your past," Palakon says. "Interviews were done. There were discussions. Choices were made."

"We did not know, however, about Jamie Fields' connection with Bobby Hughes," Delta says, scratching the cleft in his chin.

"That was a mistake," Palakon concedes lamely.

"We assumed she was in Europe shooting a movie," Delta says. "That's all."

"Oh shit, that's a lie," I moan. "That is a fucking out-and-out lie. You knew more than that. Jesus Christ."

"Mr. Ward—" Palakon starts.

"You asked me to bring that hat with me and give it to Jamie Fields."

"Yes," Palakon says. "This is true. But we still had no idea she was involved with Bobby Hughes. We didn't even know of Bobby Hughes' existence until . . . it was too late."

"So does Bobby Hughes know who you are?" I ask, flashing on the videotape the director showed me.

"Yes," Palakon says. "Not personally. But we're fairly certain he knows of us."

"Do they know you sent me? That you're the reason I'm here?" I'm asking, trying to piece things together.

"It appears that way," Palakon says. "We don't think Jamie Fields told him."

"When did they find out?"

"It could have been as early as when you and I first met," Palakon says. "We're not sure."

"And what do they want?"

Palakon breathes in. "They want us to fail," Palakon says. "Obviously they are trying their best to ensure that this happens."

"Fail what?" I'm asking. "Who's *they*?" I'm asking.

"Well, who they are *exactly* is impossible to answer," Palakon says. "Actually there are many answers. But they obviously have decided to use you—your presence—to their advantage."

"Mr. Ward," Delta says, "we learned at a late date that Jamie Fields has connections with a faction that works in opposition to the faction Bobby Hughes belongs to. Once we found this out we discussed the possibilities of how this could affect the outcome of the situation, of your situation. We decided that any problems arising from that connection—in relation to harming you—were remote. And if you were placed in any danger we would step in and remove you from the situation."

Crater speaks. "Jamie Fields, at that point, had no immediate contact with Bobby Hughes. At that juncture we thought you were safe."

"Jamie Fields works for a counterintelligence organization that has infiltrated Mr. Hughes' organization," Palakon says. "At the time you were sent, we had no idea this was happening. We didn't know until you disappeared from London what the situation was." He pauses. "Until it was too late."

"But they met a long time ago," I mutter. "Jamie told me she'd met Bobby years ago, that they were hanging out for years."

"They had met, this was confirmed," Palakon allows, nodding. "But Bobby Hughes meets a lot of people. Not all of them tend to work for him. Not all of them end up being recruited."

Pause. "What about the hat you asked me to bring?" I ask.

Palakon sighs. "The hat I asked you to bring was intended for the group that Jamie Fields works for." A long pause suggests that this is an answer.

"So . . . Jamie Fields doesn't work for Bobby Hughes?" I ask.

"No, she doesn't, Mr. Ward," Palakon says. "Jamie Fields works for the United States government."

"What was . . . in the hat?" I ask tentatively.

All around: heavy sighs, a smattering of flinches, men repositioning themselves. Palakon glances over at Crater, who nods, resigned. I'm on the verge of placing where I first met the Interpol inspector but Russell distracts me by lighting a cigarette. There's no relief in knowing Jamie doesn't work for Bobby, because I don't believe it.

"In the seams of the hat," Palakon starts, "was a prototype for a new form of plastic explosive."

I turn ice cold, chills wash over my body in one enormous wave and veins freeze up, start tingling. I'm writhing in my chair, unable to sit still.

"We were uncertain of how detectable it was," Palakon says. "We needed a carrier. We needed someone no one would suspect. Someone who could transfer this sample to Europe."

"But once you boarded the QE2, Victor, you had obviously been spotted," Crater says. "Something got leaked. We're not sure how."

"I'm not . . . really clear on this," I manage to say.

"I agreed to get you out of the country for your father and I did," Palakon says. "I also agreed to something else." He pauses. "I owed . . . a favor. To another party." Another pause. "I agreed to bring this other party the prototype for Remform. But the two things—you heading to Europe and the delivery of the plastique—were not related. Your father knew nothing of that. This was my mistake and I take full responsibility. But things were urgent and moving fast and I needed to find a carrier immediately. You were available."

"What exactly is Remform?" I'm asking.

"It's a plastic explosive that escapes detection from, well, just about anything," Palakon says. "Metal detectors, x-ray machines, trace detectors, electron-capture vapor detectors, tagging, trained dogs." Palakon shrugs. "It's highly efficient."

"Who was the Remform . . . for?" I ask.

"It doesn't matter. It's not something you need to know, Victor, but it definitely was not intended for Bobby Hughes. In fact, quite the opposite. It slipped into the wrong hands." Palakon pauses gravely. "I thought you would be protected. You weren't. I'm sorry. The Remform was stolen—we now realize—during your voyage on the QE2. And we did not—I swear to you, Victor—understand the situation until we met last week at the hotel."

"We didn't realize any of this until Palakon made contact with you last week," Delta confirms.

"I didn't realize where the Remform was located until you told me," Palakon says.

"Why don't you guys just tell Jamie what's going on?" I ask.

"That would be far too dangerous for her," Palakon says. "If we attempted any kind of contact and she was found out, an enormous amount of time and effort would have been wasted. We cannot risk that."

"Does my father know any of this?" I ask.

"No."

I'm stuck, can't form a sentence.

"The fact remains that Bobby Hughes has the Remform and obviously has plans to manufacture and use it," Palakon says. "That was not supposed to happen. That was definitely not supposed to happen."

"But . . . ," I start.

"Yes?"

The room waits.

"But you know Bobby Hughes," I say.

"Pardon?" Palakon asks. "I know of him."

"No, Palakon," I say. "You know him."

"Mr. Ward, what are you talking about?"

"Palakon," I shout. "I saw you in a videotape shaking Bobby Hughes' hand, you fucking bastard, I saw you shake that asshole's hand. Don't tell me you don't know him."

Palakon flinches. "Mr. Ward, I'm not sure what you're talking about. But I have never met Bobby Hughes face-to-face."

"You're lying, you're fucking lying," I shout. "Why are you lying, Palakon? I saw a videotape. You were shaking his hand." I'm out of the chair again, stomping toward him.

Palakon swallows grimly, then launches into, "Mr. Ward, as you well know, they are quite sophisticated at altering photographs and videotapes." Palakon stops, starts again. "What you probably saw was just a movie. A special effect. Just a strip of film that was digitally altered. Why they showed this to you I don't know. But I have never met Bobby Hughes before—"

"Blah blah blah," I'm screaming. "What a load of shit. No way, man." There's so much adrenaline rushing through me that I'm shaking violently.

"Mr. Ward, I think you have been a victim of this as well," Palakon adds.

"So you're telling me we can't believe anything we're shown anymore?" I'm asking. "That *everything* is altered? That everything's a lie? That everyone will believe this?"

"That's a fact," Palakon says.

"So what's true, then?" I cry out.

"Nothing, Victor," Palakon says. "There are different truths."

"Then what happens to us?"

"We change." He shrugs. "We adapt."

"To what? Better? Worse?"

"I'm not sure those terms are applicable anymore."

"Why not?" I shout. "Why aren't they?"

"Because no one cares about 'better.' No one cares about 'worse,'" Palakon says. "Not anymore. It's different now."

Someone clears his throat as tears pour down my face.

"Mr. Ward, please, you've helped us enormously," Crater says.

"How?" I sob.

"Because of that printout you gave to Palakon, we believe that Bobby Hughes is using the Remform in a bombing this week," Crater explains. "A bombing that we now have the power to stop."

I mumble something, looking away.

"We think this has to do with a bombing scheduled for Friday," Palakon says matter-of-factly. "That date is November 15. We think '1985' is actually a misprint. We think the 8 is actually an 0."

"Why?"

"We think 1985 is actually 1905," Crater says. "In military parlance that's 7:05 p.m."

"Yeah?" I mutter. "So?"

"There's a TWA flight leaving Charles de Gaulle this Friday, November 15, at 7:05," Palakon says.

"So what?" I'm asking. "Aren't there a lot of flights leaving on that date, near that time?"

"Its flight number is 511," Palakon says.

9

I'm told to stay calm.

I'm told they will contact me tomorrow.

I'm told to return to the house in the 8th or the 16th and pretend nothing has happened.

I'm told that I can be placed, eventually, in a witness protection program. (I'm told this after I have collapsed on the floor, sobbing hysterically.)

I'm told again to stay calm.

On the verge of trust, I realize that the inspector from Interpol is the actor who played the clerk at the security office on the QE2.

I'm told, "We'll be in touch, Mr. Ward."

I'm told, "You'll be watched."

"I know," I say hollowly.

Since I have no more Xanax left and it's starting to rain I head over to Hôtel Costes, where I wait in the café pretending to be pensive, drinking tea, smoking Camel Lights out of a pack someone left discarded at the table next to mine, until Chloe walks in with a famous ballerina, a well-known former junkie just out of rehab and the Aphex twins, and they all start chatting pleasantly with Griffin Dunne, who's standing at the front desk, and then everyone but Chloe walks away and in a trance I move forward while she checks her messages and I grab her, embracing her fearfully while glancing around the hushed lobby and then I'm kissing her lips, entering her life again, and we're both crying. The concierge turns his head away.

I start relaxing but a film crew has followed Chloe into the lobby and a camera starts panning around us and we're asked to "do that" once more. Someone yells "Action." Someone yells "Cut." I stop crying and we do it again.

8 Afternoon and outside silvery clouds glide through the sky as a soft rain keeps drifting over a steel-gray Paris. There were two shows today—one at the Conciergerie, one in the gardens of the Musée Rodin—and she was being paid a zillion francs, naysayers abounded, the catwalks seemed longer, the paparazzi were both more and less frantic, girls were wearing bones, bird skulls, human teeth, bloody smocks, they held fluorescent water pistols, there was serious buzz, there was zero buzz, it was the epitome of hype, it was wildly trivial.

From room service we order a pot of coffee that she doesn't drink, a bottle of red wine of which she has only half a glass, a pack of cigarettes but she's not smoking. An hour passes, then another. Flowers sent by various designers fill the suite, are of colors and shapes conspicuous enough so that we can easily concentrate on them when we're not talking to each other. A pigeon sits nestled on the ledge outside the window, humming. At first we keep saying "What does it matter?" to each other, ad-libbing like we have secrets we don't care about revealing, but then we have to stick to the script and I'm sucking on her pussy causing her to climax repeatedly and we arrange ourselves into a position where I'm lying on my side, my cock slowly pumping in and out of her mouth, arching my back with each movement, her hands on my ass, and I don't relax until I come twice, my face pressed against her vagina, and later she's crying, she can't trust me, it's all impossible and I'm pacing the suite looking for another box of tissues to hand her and she keeps getting up and washing her face and then we attempt to have sex again. Her head leans against a pillow. "Tell me," she's saying. "Possibly," she's saying. "It's not beyond you," she's saying. We're watching MTV with the sound off and then she tells me I need to shave and I tell her that I want to grow a beard and then, while forcing a smile, that I need a disguise and she thinks I'm serious and when she says "No, don't" something gets mended, hope rises up in me and I can envision a future.

After trying to sleep but kept awake by remembering how I got here I reposition myself on the bed next to Chloe, trying to hold her face in my hands.

"I thought it would solve everything if I . . . just left," I tell her. "I was just . . . directionless, y'know, baby?"

She smiles unhappily.

"I had to get my priorities straightened out," I'm whispering. "I needed to clear my head."

"Because?"

A sigh. "Because where I was going . . ." I stop, my throat tightens.

"Yeah?" she whispers. "Because where you were going . . . ," she coaxes.

I breathe in and then I'm reduced.

"There was no one there," I whisper back.

"You needed to clear your head?"

"Yeah."

"So you came to Paris?"

"Yeah."

"Victor, there are parks in New York," she says. "You could have gone to a library. You could have taken a walk." Casually she reveals more than she intended. I wake up a little.

"The impression I got before I left was that you and Baxter—"

"No," she says, cutting me off.

But that's all she says.

"You could be lying to me, right?" I ask shakily.

"Why would I bother?" She reaches toward the nightstand for a copy of the script.

"It's okay, though," I'm saying. "It's okay."

"Victor," she sighs.

"I was so afraid for you, Chloe."

"Why?"

"I thought you'd gotten back on drugs," I say. "I thought I saw something

in your bathroom, back in New York . . . and then I saw that guy Tristan—
that dealer?—in your lobby and oh Jesus . . . I just lost it."

"Victor—"

"No, really, that morning, baby, after the opening—"

"It was just that night, Victor," she says, stroking the side of my face.
"Really."

"Baby, I freaked—"

"No, no, shhh," she says. "It was just some dope I got for the weekend. It
was just for that weekend. I bought it. I did a little of it. I threw the rest
away."

"Put that down—please, baby," I tell her, motioning at the script she's
holding, curled in her other hand.

Later.

"There were so many relatively simple things you couldn't do, Victor,"
she says. "I always felt like you were playing jokes on me. Even though I
knew you weren't. It just felt that way. I always felt like a guest in your life.
Like I was someone on a list."

"Oh baby . . ."

"You were so nice to me, Victor, when we first met," she says. "And then
you changed." She pauses. "You started treating me like shit."

I'm crying, my face pressed into a pillow, and when I lift my head up I
tell her, "But baby, I'm very together now."

"No, you're freaking me out now," she says. "What are you talking about?
You're a mess."

"I'm just . . . I'm just so afraid," I sob. "I'm afraid of losing you again . . .
and I want to make you understand that . . . I want to fix things. . . ."

Her sadness creases the features of her face, making it look as if she's concentrating on something.

"We can't go back," she says. "Really, Victor."

"I don't want to go back," I'm saying.

"A smart suit," she sighs. "Being buff. A cool haircut. Worrying about
whether people think you're famous enough or cool enough or in good
enough shape or . . . or whatever." She sighs, gives up, stares at the ceiling.
"These are not signs of wisdom, Victor," she says. "This is the bad planet."

"Yeah," I say. "Yeah, baby . . . I think I was paying too much attention to
the way things looked, right? I know, baby, I know."

"It happens." She shrugs. "You have the standard regrets."

I start crying again. Chloe's asking "Why?" She touches my arm. She's
asking "Why?" again.

"But I can't find anything else . . . to put in its place," I say, choking.

"Baby—"

"Why didn't you just dump me?" I sob.

"Because I'd fallen in love with you," she says.

My eyes are closed and I can hear her turning pages and Chloe breathes in as she delivers the following line ("warmly w/affection"): "Because I still am in love with you."

I pull away, wiping my face blindly.

"There are so many things I want to tell you."

"You can," she says. "I'll listen. You can."

My eyes fill up with tears again and this time I want her to see them.

"Victor," she says. "Oh baby. Don't cry or you're gonna make me cry."

"Baby," I start. "Things aren't the way . . . you might think they are. . . ."

"Shhh, it's okay," she says.

"But it's not," I say. "It's so not okay, it's not."

"Victor, come on—"

"But I plan to stick around a little while," I say in a rush before bursting into tears again.

I'm closing my eyes and she stirs lightly on the bed, turning pages in the script, and she keeps pausing, deciding whether to say something or not, and I'm saying, clearing my throat, my nose hopelessly stuffed, "Don't, baby, don't, just put it away," and Chloe sighs and I hear her drop the script onto the floor next to the bed we're lying on and then she's holding my face in her hands and I'm opening my eyes.

"Victor," she says.

"What?" I'm asking. "What is it, baby?"

"Victor?"

"Yeah?"

Finally she says, "I'm pregnant."

A problem. Things get sketchy. We skipped a stage. I missed a lesson, we moved backward, we disappeared into a valley, a place where it's always January, where the air is thin and I'm pulling a Coca-Cola out of a bucket of ice. The words "I'm pregnant" sounded harsh to me but in an obscure way. I'm in the center of the room, flattened out by this information and what it demands from me. I keep trying to form a sentence, make a promise, not wander away. She's asking are you coming in? I'm telling myself you always took more than you gave, Victor. I keep trying to postpone the next moment but she's staring at me attentively, almost impatient.

"And yes, it's yours," she says.

Because of how startled I am, all I can ask is, "Can you, like, afford to do this now?" My voice sounds falsetto.

"It's not like I've been underpaid," she says, gesturing around the suite. "It's not like I can't retire. That's not an issue."

"What is?" I ask, swallowing.

"Where you're going to be," she says quietly. "What role you're going to take in this."

"How do you . . . know it's mine?" I ask.

She sighs. "Because the only person I've been with since we broke up"— she laughs derisively—"is you."

"What do you mean?" I ask. "What about Baxter?"

"I never slept with Baxter Priestly, Victor," she shouts.

"Okay, okay," I'm saying.

"Oh Jesus, Victor," she says, turning away.

"Hey baby, what is it?"

"Four weeks ago? Remember? That day you came over?"

"What?" I'm asking, thinking, four weeks ago? "Yeah?"

Silence.

"That day you called me out of the blue?" she asks. "It was a Sunday and you called me, Victor. I'd just gotten back from Canyon Ranch. I met you at Jerry's? Remember? In SoHo? We sat in a booth in the back? You talked about going to NYU?" She pauses, staring at me wide-eyed. "Then we went back to my place. . . ." She looks away. She softly says, "We had sex, then you left, whatever." She pauses again. "You were having dinner that night with Viggo Mortensen and Jude Law and one of the producers of *Flatliners II* and Sean MacPherson was in town with Gina and I didn't really want to go and you didn't invite me—and then you never called. . . . That week I read that you had dinner at Diablo's—maybe it was a Buddy Seagull column—and you and Damien had patched things up and then I ran into Edgar Cameron who said he had had dinner with you at Balthazar and you guys had all gone to Cheetah afterwards and . . . you just never called me again and . . . oh forget it, Victor—it's all in the past, right? I mean, isn't it?"

Four weeks ago I was on a ship in the middle of an ocean.

Four weeks ago on that ship there was blood pooled behind a toilet in the cabin of a doomed girl.

Four weeks ago I was in London at a party in Notting Hill.

Four weeks ago I was meeting Bobby Hughes. Jamie Fields hugged me while I stood screaming in a basement corridor.

Four weeks ago I was not in New York City.

Four weeks ago an impostor arrived in Chloe's apartment.

Four weeks ago on that Sunday he undressed her.

I'm saying nothing. Reams of acid start unspooling in my stomach and I'm vibrating with panic.

"Baby," I'm saying.

"Yeah?"

I start getting dressed. "I've gotta go."

"What?" she asks, sitting up.

"I've gotta get my stuff," I say in a controlled voice. "I'm moving out of the house. I'm coming back here."

"Victor," she starts, then reconsiders. "I don't know."

"I don't care," I say. "But I'm staying with you."

She smiles sadly, holds out a hand. "Really?"

"Yeah," I say. "Really. I'm totally, totally sure of it."

"Okay." She's nodding. "Okay."

I fall on the bed, wrapping my arms around her. I kiss her on the lips, stroking the side of her face.

"I'll be back in an hour," I say.

"Okay," she says. "Do you want me to come with you?"

"No, no," I'm saying. "Just wait here. I'll be right back."

At the door, something shifts in me and I turn around.

"Unless . . . you want to come with me?" I ask.

"How long will you be?" She's holding the script again, flipping through it.

"An hour. Probably less. Maybe forty minutes."

"Actually," she says, "I think I'm supposed to stay here."

"Why?"

"I think I'm supposed to shoot a scene."

"What am I supposed to do?" I ask.

"I think"—Chloe squints at the script and then, looking up—"you're supposed to go."

"And then?" I ask.

"And then?" Chloe says, smiling.

"Yeah."

"You're supposed to come back."

7 There's no need to punch in the code to deactivate the alarm system in the house in the 8th or the 16th. The door leading into the courtyard just swings open.

Walking quickly through the courtyard, I grab my keys out of the Prada jacket I'm wearing but I don't need them because that door's open too.

Outside, it's late afternoon but not dark yet and the wind's screaming is occasionally broken up by distant thunderclaps.

Inside, things feel wrong.

In the entranceway I lift a phone receiver, placing it next to my ear. The line is dead. I move toward the living room.

"Hello?" I'm calling out. "Hello? . . . It's me. . . . It's Victor. . . ."

I'm overly aware of how silent and dark it is in the house. I reach for a light switch. Nothing happens.

The house smells like shit, reeks of it—damp and wet and fetid—and I have to start breathing through my mouth. I pause in a doorway, bracing myself for a surprise, but the living room is totally empty.

"Bobby?" I call out. "Are you here? Where are you," and then, under my breath, "you fuck."

I'm just noticing that cell phones are scattered everywhere, across tables, under chairs, in piles on the floor, dozens of them smashed open, their antennas snapped off. Some of their transmission bars are lit but I can't get an outside line on any of them and then I

you are the sort of person who doesn't see well in the dark

turn into the darkness of the kitchen. I open the refrigerator door and then the freezer and light from inside illuminates a section of the black, empty kitchen. I grab a bottle that lies on its side in the freezer and take a swig from a half-empty gallon of Stoli, barely tasting it. Outside, the wind is a hollow roaring sound.

In a drawer adjacent to the sink I find a flashlight and just as I turn toward another drawer something zooms past me. I whirl around.

A reflection in the gilt-edged mirror that hangs over the stove: my grave expression. Then I'm laughing nervously and I bring a hand to my forehead, leaving it there until I'm calm enough to find the .25-caliber Walther I hid last week in another drawer.

With the beam from the flashlight I'm noticing that the microwave's door is open and inside it's splattered with a dried brown mixture of twigs, branches, stones, leaves. And then I notice the cave drawings.

They're scrawled everywhere. Giant white spaces heavily decorated with stick figures of buffalos, crudely drawn horses, dragons, what looks like a serpent.

"Just be cool just be cool just be cool," I'm telling myself.

Suddenly, over the speaker system that runs throughout the house, a CD clicks on and covering the sound of wind roaring outside: water rushing, various whooshing noises, Paul Weller's guitar, Oasis, Liam Gallagher echoing out, singing the first verse from "Champagne Supernova," and it blasts through the darkness of the house.

"This is so fucked, this is so fucked," I'm muttering, on the edge of panic but not in it yet and the yellow fan of light washing across the walls keeps shaking as I move farther into the house and

where were you while we were getting hi-i-i-igh?

the house smells so much like shit I keep gagging. One hand is holding the flashlight and I clamp the other, holding the gun, over my nose and mouth.

in the champagne supernova in the skyyyyyy

I bend down, pick up another cell phone. I pull up the antenna, flipping the phone open. No transmission bars.

I aim the flashlight down a hallway and then I shine its beam up into the circular staircase and I'm squinting, trying to make out the dim star shapes that seem to have appeared everywhere.

But then I see that those star shapes are actually pentagrams and they're drawn with red paint everywhere on the walls, on the ceiling, on the stairs leading to the second floor.

Something turns in the darkness behind me.

I whirl around.

Nothing.

I run up the stairs. Every five steps, I stop and look over my shoulder, waving the beam of the flashlight into the darkness floating below me.

in a champagne supernova, in a champagne supernova in the sk-k-yyyyyyyyy

I hesitate at the top of the staircase and then I'm drifting unsteadily along one side of the hallway and I'm feeling along the wall for light switches.

I turn hesitantly around another corner and—except for the pentagrams and the cell phones scattered everywhere—the set is immaculate, un-touched, everything in its place.

I make it to the room I've been staying in, my shadow moving across its door as I walk toward it. My hand freezes, then I reach tentatively for the doorknob, thinking, Don't open it don't open it don't

After I open it I pocket the gun and shift the flashlight into my other hand. I reach out for a light switch but can't feel one.

I shine the flashlight across the room.

I open a drawer—it's empty. I open another drawer—also empty. All my clothes are gone. The passport I'd hidden, wedged beneath my mattress, isn't there.

In the bathroom—all my toiletries are gone.

A giant red pentagram is slashed across the mirror.

where were you while we were getting h-i-i-i-i-i-ighhhh

I move toward the closet, my heart pounding.

All my clothes have been removed.

And in their place, posted all over the walls of the small walk-in closet, are Polaroid shots of me and Sam Ho, naked, sweaty, delirious, having sex.

A larger photo rests in the middle of this collage.

I'm driving a butcher knife deep into Sam Ho's chest and I'm lost and grinning, my eyes red, caught in the flash, my expression addressing the camera, asking *do you like this? are you pleased?*

I pull away from the closet, slamming the door shut. On the door another giant pentagram, this one black and dripping, announces itself.

I shift the light over to another wall blighted with pentagrams and then focus the light on a series of letters spread high above me, floating against a huge expanse of pristine white wall over my bed, and I'm squinting, trying to focus, and I slowly fan the beam across the letters until I'm saying the words out loud.

D iSA Pp EAR
HEre

The words cause me to sag against the wall and I'm gripping the gun so tightly I can barely feel it and the Oasis song is revolving into its climax and its endless soloing and as I stumble out of the room my shadow looms against another massive red pentagram.

The CD clicks off.

Silence.

And then my shoes are making noises moving down the hallway and they echo in the silence and suddenly lightning throws my silhouette against a wall and the wind outside keeps howling. I'm freezing. I pass another pentagram.

Within the silence of the house I suddenly hear one distinct sound.

Moaning.

Coming from down the hallway.

Keeping the gun held in an outstretched hand, I start moving down that hall, toward where the moaning is coming from.

Bentley's room.

Another pentagram looms over me. Outside, the wind keeps gusting and then there's a peal of thunder. A vague fear keeps growing but never really defines itself—it's just inevitable—and nearing panic, I bring a hand to my lips to keep my mouth from twitching and then I'm stepping forward, moving into the room.

I lower the flashlight's beam, running it across the terrazzo floor.

"Oh my god," I whisper to myself.

A dark shape in the middle of the room, until I wave my flashlight over it. Bentley.

He's splayed out across the floor, his mouth gagged with a black hand-kerchief, taped over, and his arms are outstretched, pulled above his head, each one tied separately to bedposts, rope and chain intricately entwined and wrapped around each wrist. His legs are spread and more rope and chain is tied around his ankles and connected to the legs of a white-oak armoire.

He's signaling me with his eyes.

Attached to each thigh and bicep is some kind of device connected to its own timer—red digital numbers glowing in the dark and counting down.

Moving toward him, slipping on patches of ice, I notice another device strapped to his chest as I drop to my haunches and place the flashlight and the gun on the floor. Crouching beside Bentley, I pull the gag out of his mouth. He immediately starts panting.

"Help me, Victor, help me, Victor," he squeals, his voice cracking on my name, and he starts sobbing with relief, but my own voice is thick with panic as I tell him, "Calm down, it's okay, it's okay."

My legs start cramping up as I try to unlock the device connected above his right knee and Bentley starts babbling, "What did you tell him what did you tell him what did you tell him Victor oh god what did you tell Bobby?"

"I didn't tell him anything," I murmur, shining the flashlight over the device, trying to figure out the easiest way of removing it.

But I'm afraid to touch it.

"Who did this?" I'm asking.

"Bruce Rhinebeck," he screams.

"But Bruce is dead," I scream back. "Bruce died in that explosion—"

"Hurry, Victor, just hurry," Bentley moans in a voice that doesn't sound like him. "I don't want to die I don't want to die," he says, teeth clenched, and then he starts making shrill little screams.

"Shhh . . . ," I murmur. Wind is now throwing rain against the win-dows. I keep peering at the device on his leg, having no idea how to remove it, and I'm taking deep breaths that turn into short fast breaths, my mouth wide open.

"Okay," I say, simply gripping the device and tugging up on it, but it's strapped too tightly to his leg.

Suddenly—a sound.

A clicking noise.

It's coming from the device strapped to Bentley's right arm.

Bentley stiffens.

Silence.

Then another sound—*tch tch tch tch*.

Bentley makes eye contact with me, looking briefly as if I'd offended him in some way, but then his eyes come hideously alive and he starts opening and closing his fingers in anticipation.

Silence.

Bentley begins to weep.

Another clicking noise, followed by a whirring sound.

"Don't let me die," he's crying. "Please I don't want to die I don't want to die oh god no—"

Bentley suddenly realizes what's going to happen and starts snarling in anticipation.

There's a loud *whoompf* as the device goes off, the noise of its activation muffled by flesh.

A thick, ripping sound. A mist of blood.

Bentley's body jumps.

The arm skids along the floor, the hand still clenching and unclenching itself.

And then he starts screaming, deafeningly.

Blood pours out of the stump at his shoulder like water gushing from a hose and it just keeps splashing out, fanning across the terrazzo floor and under the bed.

Bentley's mouth opens in a frozen scream and he starts gasping.

I'm grimacing, shouting out, "No no no no."

It's a special effect, I'm telling myself. It's makeup. Bentley is just a prop, something spasming wildly beneath me, his head whipping furiously from side to side, his eyes snapped open with pain, his voice just gurgling sounds now.

The sharp smell of gunpowder wraps around us.

I'm trying not to faint and I pull the gun up and, crouching down, hold it against the rope attached to his other arm.

"Shoot it," he gasps. "Shoot it."

I push it into the coil of rope and chain and pull the trigger.

Nothing.

Bentley's whining, pulling against his restraints.

I pull the trigger again.

Nothing.

The gun isn't loaded.

In the flashlight's glare the color of Bentley's face is gray verging on white as blood keeps draining out of him, and his mouth keeps opening, making wheezing sounds.

Forcing my hands to steady themselves I start uselessly tearing at the ropes and chain, trying to unknot them, and outside the wind keeps rising up, howling.

Another terrible moment.

Another clicking noise. This one at his left leg.

Silence.

tch tch tch tch

Then the whirring sound.

Bentley understands what is happening and starts shrieking even before the device goes off and I'm urinating in my pants and I whirl away, screaming with him, as the device makes its *whoompf* sound.

A horrible crunching noise.

The device shreds his leg at the knee and when I turn around I see his leg slide across the floor and watch it knock into a wall with a hard thud, splattering it with blood, and I'm crying out in revulsion.

Bentley starts going in and out of shock.

I close my eyes.

The device on the other leg goes off.

"Shoot me!" he's screaming, eyes bulging, swollen with pain, blood gushing out of him.

Desperately I try to unknot the rope wrapped around the device on his chest, my heartbeat thumping wildly in my ears.

"Shoot me!" he keeps screaming.

The timer makes its characteristic noises.

I uselessly hold the Walther against his head and keep pulling the trigger and it keeps snapping hollowly.

The other arm is blown off and blood splatters across the wall above the bed, splashing over another pentagram. Bentley's tongue is jutting out of his mouth and as he starts going into his death throes he bites it off.

The device on his chest makes a whirring noise.

It opens him up.

His chest isn't there anymore.

Intestines spiral up out of him. A giant splat of blood hits the ceiling and it smells like meat in this room—it's sweet and rank and horrible—and since it's so cold, steam pours out of his wounds, gusts of it rising over the blood and chunks of flesh scattered across the floor and my legs are stiff from crouching so long and I stagger away and outside the wind keeps moaning.

I'm backing into the hallway and there are dripping sounds as flesh slides down walls and bright lines of it are streaked across Bentley's twitching face, his mouth hanging open, and he's lying on a shiny mat of blood and clumps of flesh that covers the entire floor and I'm walking out of the room, one hand gripping the flashlight, the other hand smearing blood on anything I touch, wherever I have to steady myself.

6 I race to a bathroom, panting, keeping my head down, eyes on the floor even as I'm turning corners, and in the bathroom mirror it looks like someone has painted my face red and the front of my shirt is matted thick with blood and flesh and I'm pulling my clothes off screaming and then I fall into the shower and I'm hitting my chest and pulling my hair, my eyes squeezed shut, tilting forward, falling against a tiled wall, my hands held out in front of me.

I find clothes in Bobby's room and dizzily just pull them on, dressing quickly, keeping my eyes on the bedroom door. Numb and singing softly to myself while crying, I quickly tie the laces on a pair of Sperry deck shoes I slipped on.

As I stagger through the upstairs hallway I run past Bentley's room because I can't bear to see what's in it and I'm sobbing but then I suddenly stop when I realize there's a new odor filling the house, overpowering the aroma of shit that hung in it before.

On my way out I place the smell.

It's popcorn.

5 The light outside the house has totally faded and the wind keeps screaming high above the courtyard I'm weaving through, a light rain slapping at my face, and the wind is blowing confetti into piles high against the walls like snowdrifts made up of gold and green and purple paper and there are bicycles I never noticed before lying on their sides, their upended wheels spinning in the wind. And in a corner a vague shape is slumped over and when I freeze, noticing it, the courtyard suddenly becomes quiet, which is my cue to slowly move closer.

Above Jamie's head, another sloppy pentagram and in streaky red letters the words

DiSAp p Ear
HERe

An empty Absolut bottle rests by her side and she's sitting propped up, stunned, barely lucid, and when I feel her cheek it's hot, her face puffy. I crouch down. Her eyes are closed and when she opens them she recognizes me but shows no particular interest and we just stare at each other uncertainly, both with dead eyes. She's wearing a white Gucci pantsuit, the collar lightly spattered with blood, but I can't see any wounds because someone has wrapped her in plastic.

"Jamie . . . are you okay?" I ask hollowly. "Should I get help?"

A shaky sigh. She says something I can barely hear.

"What?" I'm asking. "I can't hear you."

"You're . . . supposed to be . . . at the . . . hotel," she sighs.

"Let me get help—"

"Don't get help," she whispers and then she gestures vaguely to something behind me. I turn, squinting. It's the mattress Tammy Devol was murdered on, half-burned, lying in a blackened clump and dotted with white and silver confetti, in the middle of the courtyard.

"I'll call an ambulance," I'm saying.

"No . . . don't, Victor," she says, her voice muffled.

"I want to help you," I say, straining to sound hopeful.

She grabs my wrists, her face drawn and tense, her eyes half-closed. "Don't. I don't want . . . any . . . help."

"What happened?" I'm asking.

"Totally . . . fucked . . . up," she whispers, smiling.

She starts shrugging, losing interest in me.

"Hey Jamie, talk to me—what happened, what happened here?"

"I . . . watched . . . that scene . . . of you at the embassy," she whispers. "They . . . lied to you, Victor." She keeps shuddering and I'm smoothing confetti out of her hair.

"About what?" I'm asking. "What did they lie about?" My voice is hoarse from screaming and her voice is low, the voice of a ghost, of someone lost in sleep, and from somewhere behind us there's a faint crashing sound in the wind.

"Palakon works against the Japanese," she says in a painful rush. "But he also works . . . for them."

She starts giggling, high, a little girl.

"What Japanese?" I'm asking.

"Everything's . . . connected . . . to the Japanese," she says. "Everything is bought with Japanese . . . money from . . . Japanese banks and they . . . supply everything, Victor." Dreamily she starts a list, offers it entirely without tone.

"Plastique . . . blasting caps . . . digital timers . . ."

"Why Japanese, Jamie?" I ask soothingly, stroking her face.

"Because . . . they want your . . . father elected."

Pause. "They want him elected to . . . what?"

"Palakon is . . . also working . . . against your father," she whispers. "Did you hear me . . . Victor?" She tries to laugh. "Your father hired him . . . but he works against him . . . too."

Wind screams suddenly through the courtyard.

"He's also working for . . . the people who don't"—something slices through her, she shifts—"want your father elected."

"Palakon told me my father hired him, Jamie," I say.

"But Palakon has . . . no affinity . . . ," she says in a wavery voice. "I watched . . . the tape of that scene . . . at the embassy . . . and he lied. He knew about my connection . . . with Bobby . . . before he sent you. He lied about that."

"Jamie, why did Palakon send me?"

"Your father wanted you . . . out of the country," she says. "Palakon did that . . . but the people who don't want your father elected . . . also were in touch with . . . Palakon and . . . they had something else in mind." She sighs. "A proposal . . ."

"Like what?" I'm asking loudly, over the wind.

"A scenario . . ." Her eyes are drifting, half-closed, but she still manages a shrug.

"What scenario, Jamie?"

She's trying to remember something. "What if you . . . Victor . . . got hooked up with a . . . certain organization . . . and what if this information . . . was leaked? How much could Palakon be paid . . . to take care of that as well? . . . Either way Palakon couldn't lose. He set it all up."

I wipe away a tear that rolls halfway down her face and the gusting wind causes confetti to swirl wildly everywhere around us.

"How?" I'm asking.

"He offered . . . Palakon offered you to . . . Bobby. They made a . . . deal."

"What deal? Why?"

"Palakon"—she swallows thickly—"had promised Bobby . . . a new face. Bobby wanted a man . . . so Palakon sent you. It fit perfectly. Your father wanted you gone . . . and Bobby needed a new face. Palakon put the two together." She coughs, swallows again. "At first Bobby was mad . . . when he found out it was you. . . . Bobby knew who you were . . . who your father was. He didn't like it."

"I thought Bobby liked using people who were famous," I say. "I thought celebrities had an instant cover."

"Your father . . ." Jamie's shaking her head slowly. "It was too much . . . it made Bobby suspicious. He didn't like it and that's when . . . Bobby was convinced Palakon was working for someone . . . else."

Silence.

"What happened, Jamie?" I ask slowly.

"Bobby realized he could . . . use you to his advantage."

"His advantage? How, Jamie?" Panic starts rising.

"Bobby contacted your—"

"No, no, no," I'm saying, grabbing her shoulders.

"Bobby and your father—"

"No, Jamie, no." I'm closing my eyes.

"Your father and Bobby talked, Victor."

"No . . . no . . ."

Everything's slipping behind me, floating away.

"The Japanese . . . were angry at Bobby when he . . . made a deal with . . . your dad." Jamie breathes in. "They just wanted you gone . . . out of the country . . . but now they had to protect you."

"Why?"

"Because if Bobby . . . went to the press with . . . stuff about you . . . and the things you did with us . . . it would destroy your father's chances." Jamie leans her head back and something passes through her, causing her forehead to crease. "The Japanese . . . want your father . . . to win."

Another gust drowns out a sentence. I lean in closer but she's turning away. I place my ear to her mouth.

"Palakon didn't know . . . what was in the hat, Victor," she says. "That was another lie."

"Then why did he tell me to bring it?" I ask.

"Bobby knew what was in the hat. . . . Bobby told him . . . to tell you to bring it," she says. "Bobby needed someone to bring the . . . Remform over here."

Her voice suddenly turns gentle, curious almost. "Palakon didn't know what was in it . . . until later . . . and then he found out and . . . and . . ." She trails off. Her eyes open, then close. "The Remform . . . was supposed to come . . . to me."

"Jamie, hey, look at me," I whisper loudly. "How did you get into this? Why did Palakon send me to find you?"

"He knew I was . . . involved with Bobby. Palakon always knew that, Victor . . . okay? Palakon thought it would work to his advantage . . . that you and I knew each other at . . . Camden."

She's drifting.

"Jamie, hey, *Jamie.*" With my hands I gently maneuver her face closer to mine. "Who was Marina Cannon?"

Her face crumples slightly. "She was on the ship . . . to warn you, Victor. . . . You were supposed to go with her."

"What happened, Jamie?"

"Bobby sent people . . . from New York to watch you . . . to make sure you would not go to Paris." She starts crying softly.

"Are you talking about the Wallaces?" I'm asking. "That English couple?"

"I don't know . . . I don't know their names. They got back to us and—"

"The ship stopped, Jamie."

"—Palakon also wanted you to go to London."

"It stopped, Jamie. The ship stopped. They said there was a distress signal."

"I know . . . I know . . ."

"The fucking ship *stopped*, Jamie," I'm shouting. "In the middle of the ocean it stopped."

"Bobby didn't want you to go to Paris. He didn't want you to come to London either . . . but he definitely didn't want you to go to Paris." She smiles secretly to herself.

"Was it Bobby? Was Bobby on the ship that night?"

"Victor—"

"I saw the tattoo," I shout. "What happened to Marina?"

"I don't know," she mumbles. "I found out after you told me . . . that night in the hotel . . . and I confronted Bobby. He wouldn't say . . . he just wanted the Remform."

"What else did he want?" I ask.

"He wanted you . . . dead."

I close my eyes, don't open them for a long time.

"I don't know . . . ," she says. "Bobby thought . . . bringing you in was a bad idea . . . but then he realized he could . . . frame you."

"For Sam Ho's murder?"

She just nods. "And once . . . that happened . . . other ideas emerged."

"What other ideas?"

"Oh Victor . . . ," she sighs. "Victor . . . it's all been a setup. Even in New York . . . that girl who died . . . that DJ . . ."

"Mica?" I ask.

"Whoever . . . you went to meet at Fashion Café . . . for a new DJ. Do you remember?"

I nod dumbly even though she's not looking.

"She was killed the night before . . . I saw a report."

"Oh Jesus oh Jesus."

"It was all a setup."

"Whose side are you on, Jamie?" I'm asking.

She smiles and when she smiles her upper lip splits open but there's no blood.

"Who do you work for?"

"It . . . hardly matters . . . now."

"Who did you work for?" I scream, shaking her.

"I was working against . . . Bobby," she mutters. "To do that, Victor . . . I had to work for him."

I pull back, panting.

"I worked for the group . . . Marina worked for . . . and I worked for the group Bobby worked for . . . and I worked for Palakon . . . just like you do—"

"I don't work for Palakon."

"Yes . . . you do." She swallows again with great difficulty. "You have . . . ever since you met him." She starts shivering.

"Jamie, how's Lauren Hynde involved in all this?" I'm asking. "Look at me—how's Lauren Hynde involved? She gave me the hat. I've seen pictures of her with Bobby."

Jamie starts laughing, delirious.

"You remember Lauren Hynde from Camden, right?" I say. "She knows Bobby. She gave me the hat." I pull Jamie closer to my face. "They set me up with her, didn't they?"

"That wasn't . . . Lauren Hynde, Victor." Jamie sighs.

"It *was* Lauren Hynde," I say. "It was, Jamie."

"You didn't pay . . . attention." She sighs again. "That girl was not Lauren—"

"Jamie, I know that girl," I say. "She's Chloe's best friend. What are you saying?"

"That was someone else." Jamie keeps sighing.

"No, no, no . . ." I'm shaking my head adamantly.

"Lauren Hynde died in . . . December 1985 . . . in a car accident . . . outside Camden, New Hampshire."

She leans into me, lowering her voice, almost as if she's afraid someone is listening, and I'm thinking, She's just a shell, and something huge and shapeless is flying over us in the darkness, hanging above the courtyard, and a voice says, You all are.

"I've gotta talk to Bobby," I gasp. "Where's Bobby?"

"No, Victor, don't—"

"Where did he go, Jamie? Tell me."

"He went to—" She gasps, rolls her head back. "He was on his way to . . ." She trails off.

"Where is he?" I scream, shaking her.

"He . . . went to Hôtel Costes," she gasps. "To see . . . Chloe."

I stand up and start moaning, the wind stinging my face, and Jamie's saying "Wait, wait, don't" and holding on to my arm, gripping it, but I yank it away.

"Victor . . ."

"I'm leaving." Panic bursts through me, spreading. "What do you want, Jamie?"

She says something I can't hear.

Hurriedly I lean in.

"What is it?"

She mumbles something.

"I can't hear you, Jamie," I whisper.

Her last words as she drifts off: "I'm . . . not . . . Jamie Fields," is all she says.

And on cue a giant eruption of flies swarm into the courtyard in one massive black cloud.

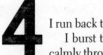

I run back to the hotel.

I burst through the entrance doors and force myself to walk calmly through the lobby and into an elevator.

Once I reach Chloe's floor I race down the hallway.

I start pounding on her door.

"Chloe? Chloe—are you okay?" I'm calling out, my voice high and girlish. "Open up. Chloe? It's me."

The door opens and Chloe stands there, smiling, wearing a white robe.

"You changed," she says, glancing at Bobby's clothes. "Where's your stuff?"

I push past her and shamble into the room, running through the suite, panicked, not knowing what I'd do if I found him here.

"Who was here?" I'm asking, flinging open the bathroom door.

"Victor, calm down," Chloe says.

"Where is he?" I'm asking, opening a closet door, slamming it shut. "Who was here?"

"Bobby Hughes came over," she says, shivering, sitting down on a high-back chair in front of a desk where she was writing something in a large spiral notebook. She crosses her legs and stares at me sternly.

"What did he want?" I ask, calming down.

"He just wanted to talk." She shrugs. "He wanted to know where you were—"

"What did he say?"

"Victor—"

"Just answer me, goddamnit. What did he say?"

"He wanted to talk," she says, shocked. "He wanted to have some champagne. He brought some by. He said it was to patch things up with you—whatever that means. I said no thank you, of course, and—"

"Did you really?"

A long pause. "I just had half a glass." She sighs. "He wanted me to save it for you. It's over there in the ice bucket."

"And"—I breathe in—"what else?" Relief washes over me so hard that tears blur my vision.

"Nothing. It was fine. He was celebrating—what, I don't know." She pauses, signifying something. "He was sorry he missed you—"

"Yeah, I bet," I mutter.

"Victor, he's . . ." She sighs, then decides to go with it. "He's worried about you."

"I don't care," I say.

"I said he's worried about you," she exclaims.

"Where is he?"

"He had to go," she says, clutching herself, shivering again.

"Where?"

"I don't know, Victor," she says. "There was a party somewhere. There was another party somewhere."

"What party? Where?" I ask. "It's very important, Chloe."

"I don't know where he went," she says. "Listen, we had some champagne, we chatted briefly and then he went off to a party. What's wrong with you? Why are you so frightened?"

Silence.

"Who was he with, baby?" I ask.

"He was with a friend," she says. "Someone who looked like Bruce Rhinebeck but I don't think it was Bruce."

A long pause. I'm just standing in the middle of the suite, my arms at my sides. "Bruce Rhinebeck?"

"Yeah, it was weird. He kind of looked like Bruce. But something was off about the guy. The hair was different or something." She grimaces, rubs her stomach. "The guy said his name was Bruce but he didn't give a last name, so who knows, right?"

I'm just standing there.

"This isn't happening," I murmur.

Bruce Rhinebeck is dead.

"What's not happening?" she asks, annoyed.

Bruce Rhinebeck was defusing a bomb in an apartment on Quai de Béthune, and Bruce Rhinebeck is dead.

"That wasn't Bruce Rhinebeck, baby."

"Well, it looked like Bruce Rhinebeck," Chloe says. This sounds too harsh and she moves into a gentler mode. "That's all I'm saying, okay? Victor, just calm down." She grimaces again.

I start pulling luggage out of the closet.

She turns around. "What are you doing?"

"We're getting out of here," I say, throwing the Gucci luggage on the bed. "Now."

"Out of where, Victor?" Chloe asks impatiently, shifting around in the chair.

"Out of Paris," I say. "We're going back to New York."

"Victor, I have shows tomor—"

"I don't care," I shout. "We're getting the hell out of here."

"Victor, I'm worried about you too," she says. "Sit down for a minute. I want to talk."

"No, no—I don't want to talk," I'm saying. "I just want to get out of here."

"Stop it," she says, doubling over. "Just sit down."

"Chloe—"

"I have to use the bathroom," she says. "But don't pack anything. I want to talk to you."

"What's wrong?" I ask.

"I don't feel well," she mutters.

"Did you eat anything?" I ask, suddenly concerned.

"No, I just had that champagne."

I glance over at the ice bucket, at the bottle of Cristal lodged in it, the empty champagne flute sitting on the desk.

She gets up from the desk. I watch her.

She brushes past me.

I'm staring at the glass and then I'm moving toward it.

Looking down into the glass, I notice granules of some kind.

And then I'm looking down at something else.

On the chair where Chloe was sitting is a huge bloodstain.

I'm staring at it.

And then I'm saying, "Chloe?"

She turns around and says, "Yeah?"

And I don't want her to see how scared I suddenly am but then she sees where my gaze is directed.

She starts breathing harshly. She looks down at herself.

The entire bottom half of her robe is soaked dark red with blood.

"Chloe . . . ," I say again.

She staggers over to the bathroom door and grabs the edge of it to balance herself and blood starts running down her legs in thin rivulets and when she lifts up the robe we both can see her underwear soaked with blood and she pulls it off, panicking, and suddenly a huge gush of blood expels itself from beneath the robe, splashing all over the bathroom floor.

She gasps, a thick noise comes out of her throat and she doubles over, grabbing her stomach, then she screams. Looking surprised and still clutching her stomach, she vomits while staggering backward, collapsing onto the bathroom floor. There are strands of tissue hanging out of her.

"Chloe," I scream.

She starts scrambling across the bathroom floor, leaving a trail, a drag mark of dark red blood.

I'm crawling with her in the bathroom and she's making harsh panting sounds, sliding across the tiles toward the bathtub.

Another spray of blood comes out of her, along with a horrible ripping sound. She raises up a hand, screaming, and I'm holding on to her and I can feel the screams buzzing through her, followed by another squelching, ripping noise.

In the bathroom I grab the phone and push zero.

"Help us," I'm screaming. "Someone's dying up here. I'm in Chloe Byrnes' room and you've got to send an ambulance. She's bleeding to death—oh fucking god she's bleeding to death—"

Silence and then a voice asks, "Mr. Ward?"

It's the director's voice.

"Mr. Ward?" it asks again.

"No! No! No!"

"We'll be right up, Mr. Ward."

The line goes dead.

Bursting into tears, I hurl the phone away from me.

I run out of the bathroom but on the phone by the bed there's no dial tone.

Chloe's calling my name.

From where I'm standing the entire bathroom floor seems washed with blood, as if something within her had liquefied.

Blood keeps fanning out from between her legs and some of it looks sandy, granular. A thick ring of flesh slides across the floor as Chloe cries out in pain and she keeps crying as I hold her and then she bursts into a series of hysterical, exhausted sobs and I'm telling her everything will be okay, tears pouring from my eyes. Another long crooked rope of flesh falls out of her.

"Victor! Victor!" she screams madly, her skin yellowing, her screams turning liquid, her mouth opening and closing.

I press a towel against her vagina, trying to stem the bleeding, but the towel is drenched in a matter of seconds. She keeps making harsh panting sounds, then defecates loudly, arching her back, another piece of flesh lurching out of her, followed by another rush of blood that splashes onto the floor.

There is warm blood all over my hands and I'm yelling out, "Baby please it's okay baby please it's okay baby—"

Another explosion of blood pours from between her legs, sickeningly hot, her eyes bulging, another giant intake of breath, and I can actually hear the horrible sounds coming from inside her body. Another harsh, startling yell.

"Make it stop oh god make it stop," she screams, begging me, and I'm sobbing, hysterical too.

Another chunk of flesh, white and milky, spews out. After the next flash of pain cuts through her she can't even form words anymore. She's finally relaxing, trying to smile at me, but she's grimacing, her teeth stained with blood, the entire inside of her mouth coated violet, and she's whispering things, one hand tightly clasping mine while the other pounds spastically against the tiled floor, and the bathroom reeks powerfully of her blood, and as I'm holding Chloe, her eyes fix on mine and I'm sobbing, "I'm sorry baby I'm so sorry baby," and there is surprise in those eyes as she realizes how imminent her death actually is and I'm lapsing in and out of focus, disappearing, and she starts making animal noises and she's sagging in my arms and then her eyes roll back and she dies and her face turns white very quickly and slackens and the world retires from me and I quit everything as water the color of lavender keeps streaming out of her.

I shut my eyes and clap my hands over my ears as the film crew rushes into the room.

3

We're on a motorway. In a large van. We're heading toward the airport. The driver is the best boy from the French film crew. I'm catatonic, lying on the floor of the van surrounded by camera equipment, the legs of my pants sticky with Chloe's blood, and sometimes what's outside the windows of the van is just blackness, and other times it's a desert, maybe somewhere outside L.A., and other times it's a matte screen, sometimes electric blue, sometimes blinding white. Sometimes the van stops, then revs up and starts accelerating. Sometimes technicians are shouting orders into walkie-talkies.

The director sits in the front passenger seat, going over call sheets. On the dashboard is an Uzi submachine gun.

There's one interlude that plays itself out very quickly on the ride to the airport.

It starts with a warning call from the driver, who is glancing anxiously into the rearview mirror.

A black truck is following us on the motorway.

The first AD and the gaffer crouch down by the rear windows, both of them holding Uzis.

They take aim.

The black truck revs up and starts pounding down on us.

The air inside the van suddenly feels radioactive.

The van shudders violently as it's hit by bullets.

Tiny rapid flashes of light exit the barrels of the Uzis the first AD and the gaffer are aiming at the black truck, which keeps racing defiantly toward us.

I try to balance myself as the van lurches forward.

The black truck's windshield shatters, crumples.

The truck veers to the right and collides with several cars.

The black truck quietly careens off the motorway and overturns.

The van guns its engine, racing away.

Two seconds later a large fireball appears behind us.

I'm lying on the floor, panting, until the property master and a PA lift me up so that I'm facing the director.

Outside, it's a desert again and I'm moaning.

The van swerves into another lane.

The director pulls a pistol from inside his jacket.

I just stare at it.

The only thing that wakes me is the director saying, "We know where Bobby Hughes is."

And then I'm lunging for the gun, grabbing it, checking to see if it's loaded, but the PA pulls me back and I'm told to calm down and the director takes the gun from my hands.

"Bobby Hughes is trying to kill you," the director is saying.

The property master is securing a knife sheath around my calf. A large silver blade with a black handle is slipped into it. The Prada slacks I'm wearing are pulled down over the sheath.

The director is telling me they would like to see Bobby Hughes dead. I'm being asked if this is a "possibility."

I'm nodding mindlessly. I keep moaning with anticipation.

And then we can smell the jet-fuel fumes everywhere and the driver brakes the van to a hard stop, tires screeching, jerking us all forward.

"He needs to be stopped, Victor," the director says.

After the gun is slipped into my jacket I'm sliding out of the van and the crew is following me, cameras rolling, and we're racing into the airport. Over the sound track: the noise of planes taking off.

2 The crew direct me to a men's room on the first concourse and I'm running toward the door, slamming against it with my shoulder, and the door flies open and I stumble inside. The men's room has already been lit, but not for the scene Bobby was expecting.

Bobby's standing at a sink, inspecting his face in a mirror.

I'm screaming as I run toward him at full sprint, my fist raised, the gun in it.

Bobby turns, sees me, sees the crew following me, and his face seizes with shock and he screams, enraged, "You fucks!" and raising his voice even higher, yells again. *"You total fucks!"*

He pulls out a gun that I knock out of his hand and it slides across the tiled floor under a sink, and Bobby's ducking instinctively as I throw myself forward into him, grabbing at his face, screaming.

He reaches out and pulls my head back and slams into me so hard I'm lifted off the ground and thrown against a tiled wall and then I'm sliding to the floor, coughing.

Bobby staggers back, then reaches out and grabs the lower part of my face.

I suddenly raise an arm, slamming my hand into his mouth, and he reels backward, turning a corner, skidding.

I lurch forward and slam him into a wall. I push the gun into his face, screaming, *"I'm going to kill you!"*

He swipes at the gun.

I pull the trigger—a bullet opens up a giant hole in the tiled wall behind him. I fire again—four, five, six times, until the gun is empty and the wall is blown apart.

Bobby stops cowering, looks up, first at the empty gun I'm holding and then at my face.

"Fuck you!" he screams, rocketing forward.

He grabs my collar, then clumsily attempts to get me into a headlock. I shove the hand that's holding the gun under his chin, pushing him away. He moves his head back, my hand slipping off. I try again, this time with the other hand and harder, and my fist connects with his chin. When Bobby lets go he tears my shirt open and he lunges forward again, grabbing my shoulders and bringing my face up to his.

"You . . . are . . . dead," he says, his voice low and hoarse.

It's like we're dancing, colliding with each other before we crash into a wall, almost knocking over the cameraman.

We keep hugging each other until Bobby maneuvers around and smashes my face against a wall-length mirror, once, twice, my head impacting against it until the mirror cracks and I fall to my knees, something warm spreading across my face.

Bobby staggers away, looking for his gun.

I lurch up, blinking blood out of my eyes.

A gaffer tosses me a clip to reload with.

I catch it and then slam Bobby back against a stall door. I duck as his fist comes flying toward me, Bobby leaping on me like we're in a mosh pit, his face completely tensed up, and he's slapping at me madly, out of control.

He slams my head against a urinal and then grabs my scalp and shoves my head down as he brings his knee up into it, my forehead connecting, my neck snapping violently.

Bobby pulls me back and starts dragging me across the tiled floor to where his gun rests, now next to the trash can.

"Get it—get his gun," I'm screaming at the crew as Bobby keeps hauling me across the floor.

Desperately, I grab for a stall door handle, hanging on to it.

Bobby grunts, reaches down and grabs the waistband of the Prada slacks I'm wearing and pulls me up until I'm standing with him and then both of us are tumbling backward.

I land on top of him, then roll over, get on one knee and stand up, then run into a stall, slamming and locking the door so I can slip the new clip into the gun but Bobby tears the door off its hinges and throws me out, hurling me against a sink, my hand trying to block the force of impact, and then I'm smashing into the mirror above the sink, shattering it, the clip slipping from my gun.

I shove away from him but Bobby's scratching at my face now and I'm lashing out blindly. Again we both fall, sprawling, the gun knocked out of my hand, skidding along the icy floor, and when I spot Bobby's gun under the sink I reach out but his boot is suddenly on my hand, crushing it, and a giant bolt of pain causes me to become more alert.

Then another boot is on my head, grinding into my temple, and I flip over and grab Bobby's foot, twisting until he loses his balance and slips, falling on his back.

Staggering to my feet, I regain my footing and reach for his gun.

I point the barrel where he's lying on the floor but Bobby kicks out a leg, knocking the gun from my hand.

He lunges up and knocks me back, slamming into my side, and I'm not prepared for the ferocity of Bobby's fist connecting with the side of my head and there's a cracking sound and as he lurches toward me he grabs my throat with both hands, pushing me to the floor.

He's straddling me, shutting off my windpipe, and I'm making choking sounds, both of Bobby's hands clamping my throat even tighter.

And he's grinning, his teeth stained red with blood.

I shove one hand under his chin, trying to push him off.

With one hand crushing my neck, he easily reaches over and grabs his gun.

I'm kicking out, unable to move, my hands pounding the tiled floor.

Bobby holds the gun at chest level, riding me, the barrel tilted toward my face.

I try to scream, lashing my head back and forth.

He pulls the trigger.

I close my eyes.

Nothing.

He pulls it again.

Nothing. For a second we're both still.

And then I spring up yelling and I hit Bobby hard, knocking him backward.

He goes sprawling, blood jetting from his nostrils.

I'm sitting on the floor, looking around madly for my gun and the new clip.

I spot them under the sink, a few feet away.

I start crawling toward them.

Standing, turning in a circle, Bobby reaches into his jacket for a new clip and quickly reloads.

I reach under the sink and slip in the clip, tensing up, closing my eyes.

Bobby fires. A bullet splinters another mirror above me.

He fires again, missing, the bullet thudding into the wall behind me. Tile explodes next to my face as he keeps firing.

I roll over onto my side, aiming at him.

"No!" he cries, falling to the floor, crouching down.

I pull the trigger, screaming while firing.

Nothing.

Bobby's gun is jammed, not firing, and I realize, too late, that somehow the safety on mine got switched on.

He's running at me.

Fumbling, I drop the gun and, still on my back, pull my pant leg up.

Bobby tosses his gun away and shouts out, scrambling toward where I'm lying on the floor.

I pull the knife up out of its sheath.

Bobby sees the knife before he falls on me, and tries to turn away.

I bury the blade in his shoulder to the hilt.

He screams, rolling over.

I yank the knife out, weeping, and when I plunge it into his throat Bobby's expression turns surprised and his face tightens up.

Bobby pushes himself away, making hissing noises, a thick stream of blood squirting out of the wound in his throat, which gets bigger, gaping, as he staggers back.

His knees buckle and he keeps trying to close the wound with his hands, but he can't breathe.

I start inching toward a gun, my hand reaching out until it lands on the smooth, cold metal.

Wincing, I struggle into a sitting position.

The crew keeps filming, moving in as Bobby bleeds to death.

Swooning with pain, I stagger up and aim the gun at his head.

"Ith too laye," he gasps, blood pumping out of his throat in arcs as he manages to grin. "Ith too laye."

I check the safety.

And when I fire at close range it knocks me back, hard.

I stagger toward the exit. I look back and where Bobby's head was there is now just a slanted pile of bone and brain and tissue.

The director is helping me into the production office that has been set up in a first-class lounge, because he wants to show me something on the video console. The crew is high-fiving one another, preparing to clean up.

I wince when the director grabs my arm.

"Don't worry, nothing's broken," the director says, excited. "You're just badly bruised."

1 I'm sitting on a couch by a bank of windows while the crew's doctor wraps my fingers with bandages, applies alcohol to disinfect various wounds, and I'm whispering "Everyone's dead" to myself and a video monitor has been wheeled over to where I'm sitting and the director takes a seat next to me.

"Everyone's dead," I say again, in a monotone. "I think Jamie Fields is dead."

"Don't rush to conclusions." The director brushes me off, peering at another console.

"She was wrapped in plastic and dying," I murmur.

"But her death wasn't in vain," the director says.

"Oh?" I'm asking.

"She tipped you off," the director explains. "She saved lives. She saved an airliner."

As if to remind me, the director hands me the printout I took from the computer in the house in the 8th or the 16th.

WINGS. NOV 15. BAND ON THE RUN. 1985. 511.

"Victor," the director says. "Watch this. It's rough and certain elements have to be edited out, but just watch."

He pulls the console closer and black-and-white video images, hastily shot with handheld cameras, flash across the monitor, but I'm zoning out on the month I grew a goatee after reading an article about them in *Young Guy* magazine, the afternoon I debated for hours the best angle a new designer beret should be tilted on my head, the various bodies I rejected because the girl didn't have any tits, she wasn't "toned" enough, she wasn't "hard" enough, was "too old" or not "famous" enough, how I waved hi to a model who kept calling my name from across First Avenue and all the CDs you bought because movie stars in VIP rooms late at night told you that the bands were cool. "You were never taught what shame means, Victor," said a girl I didn't think was hot enough to lay but who I otherwise thought was pretty nice. "Like I care," I told her before I walked into a Gap. I'm vaguely aware that my entire body has fallen asleep.

On the video monitor, soldiers storm a plane.

"Who are . . . they?" I ask, vaguely gesturing.

"French commandos along with the occasional CIA agent," the director says blithely.

"Oh," I say in a soft voice.

Delta and Crater find what they think is a bomb in the first-class cabin and begin to dismantle it.

but it's not really a bomb, it's a decoy, the agents are on the wrong plane, there's a bomb on a plane but not this one, what they found isn't really a bomb because this is the movie and those are actors and the real bomb is on a different plane

The extras playing passengers are streaming out of the plane and they're congratulating the commandos and shaking hands with Delta and Crater, and paparazzi have arrived at the gate, snapping photos of these men who saved the plane. And when I notice Bertrand Ripleis playing one of the commandos in the background of a shot I start breathing harder.

"No," I'm saying, realizing something. "No, no, this is wrong."

"What?" the director asks, distracted. "What do you mean? What's wrong?"

Bertrand Ripleis is smiling, looking straight into the camera, almost as if he knows I'm watching this. He's anticipating my surprise and the moans that start emanating from within me.

I know who you are and I know what you're doing

"The bomb isn't on that plane," I'm saying.

I glance down at the WINGS printout, crumpled in my hands.

BAND ON THE RUN

1985

511

"It's a song . . . ," I'm saying.

"What do you mean?" the director asks.

"It's a song," I'm saying. "It's not a flight."

"What's a song?"

"The song," I'm saying. "It's a song called '1985.'"

"It's a song?" the director asks. He doesn't understand.

"It's on a Wings album," I'm saying. "It's on the *Band on the Run* album."

"And?" the director asks, confused.

"It's not a flight number," I'm saying.

"What isn't?"

"Five-one-one," I say.

"Five-one-one isn't the flight number?" the director asks. "But this is it." The director gestures toward the video screen. "That's flight five-one-one."

"No," I'm saying. "It's how long the song is." I take in a deep breath, exhaling shakily. "That song is five minutes and eleven seconds long. It's not a flight number."

And in another sky, another plane is reaching cruising altitude.

O Night over France, and a giant shadow, a monstrous backdrop, is forming itself in the sky as the 747 approaches 17,000 feet, climbing to cruising altitude. The camera moves in on an airmail parcel bearing a Georgetown address, in which a Toshiba cassette player has been packed. The device will be activated as the opening piano notes to the song "1985" by Paul McCartney and Wings (*Band on the Run*; Apple Records; 1973) start playing. The bomb will detonate on the final crashing cymbal of the song—five minutes and eleven seconds after it began. A relatively simple microchip timer and strips of Remform equaling twenty ounces are in the Toshiba cassette player, and the parcel has been placed near the skin of the plane, where it will break through the fuselage, weakening the frame, causing the plane to break apart with greater ease. The plane is traveling at 350 miles an hour and is now at an altitude of 14,500 feet.

A giant crunching sound interrupts the pilot's conversation over the cockpit recording.

A violent noise, a distinct crashing sound, is followed by massive creaking, which rapidly starts repeating itself.

Smoke immediately starts pouring into the main cabin.

The front end of the 747—including the cockpit and part of the first-class cabin—breaks away, plunging toward earth as the rest of the plane hurtles forward, propelled by the still intact engines. A complete row near the explosion—the people strapped in those seats screaming—is sucked out of the aircraft.

This goes on for thirty seconds, until the plane starts breaking apart, a huge section of ceiling ripping away to reveal a wide vista of black sky.

And with its engines still running, the plane keeps flying but then drops three thousand feet.

The noise the air makes is like a siren.

Bottles of liquor, utensils, food from the kitchen—all fly backward into the business-class and coach cabins.

And the dying comes in waves.

People are rammed backward, bent in half, pulled up out of their seats, teeth are knocked out of heads, people are blinded, their bodies thrown through the air into the ceiling and then hurled into the back of the plane, smashing into other screaming passengers, as shards of aluminum keep breaking off the fuselage, spinning into the packed plane and shearing off limbs, and blood's whirling everywhere, people getting soaked with it, spitting it out of their mouths, trying to blink it out of their eyes, and then a huge chunk of metal flies into the cabin and scalps an entire row of passengers, shearing off the tops of their skulls, as another shard flies into the face of a young woman, halving her head but not killing her yet.

The problem is that so many people are not ready to die, and they start vomiting with panic and fear as the plane drops another thousand feet.

Something else within the plane breaks.

In the next moment, another roar as the plane starts breaking up more rapidly and the dying comes in waves.

Someone is spun around frantically before being sucked out of the hull of the craft, twirling into the air, his body hitting the frame and tearing in two, but he's still able to reach out his hands for help as he's sucked screaming from the plane. Another young man keeps shouting "Mom Mom Mom" until part of the fuselage flies backward, pinning him to his seat and ripping him in half, but he just goes into shock and doesn't die until the plane smashes haphazardly into the forest below and the dying comes in waves.

In the business section everyone is soaked with blood, someone's head is completely encased with intestines that flew out of what's left of the woman sitting two rows in front of him and people are screaming and crying uncontrollably, wailing with grief.

The dying are lashed with jet fuel as it starts spraying into the cabin.

One row is sprayed with the blood and viscera of the passengers in the row before them, who have been sliced in two.

Another row is decapitated by a huge sheet of flying aluminum, and blood keeps whirling throughout the cabin everywhere, mixing in with the jet fuel.

The fuel unleashes something, forces the passengers to comprehend a simple fact: that they have to let people go—mothers and sons, parents and children, brothers and sisters, husbands and wives—and that dying is inevitable in what could be a matter of seconds. They realize there is no hope. But understanding this horrible death just stretches the seconds out longer as they try to prepare for it—people still alive being flung around the aircraft falling to earth, screaming and vomiting and crying involuntarily, bodies contorted while they brace themselves, heads bowed down.

"Why me?" someone wonders uselessly.

A leg is caught in a tangle of metal and wires and it waves wildly in the air as the plane continues to drop.

Of the three Camden graduates aboard the 747—Amanda Taylor ('86), Stephanie Meyers ('87) and Susan Goldman ('86)—Amanda is killed first when she's struck by a beam that crashes through the ceiling of the plane, her son reaching out to her as he's lifted out of his seat into the air, his arms outstretched as his head mercifully smashes against an overhead bin in the craft, killing him instantly.

Susan Goldman, who has cervical cancer, is partly thankful as she braces herself but changes her mind as she's sprayed with burning jet fuel.

The plane ignites and a huge wave of people die by inhaling flames, their mouths and throats and lungs charred black.

For some, a minute of falling while still conscious.

Onto a forest situated just seventy miles outside Paris.

The soft sounds of bodies imploding, torn apart on impact.

A massive section of the fuselage lands and because of an emergency backup system, all the lights in the plane continue flickering as a hail of glowing ash rains down.

A long pause.

The bodies lie clustered in clumps. Some—but very few—of the passengers have no marks on them, even though all their bones have been broken. Some passengers have been crushed to half or a third or even a quarter of their normal size. One man has been so compressed he resembles some kind of human bag, a shape with a vague head attached to it, the face pushed in and stark white. Other passengers have been mutilated by shrapnel, some so mangled that men and women become indistinguishable, all of them naked, their clothes blown off on the downward fall, some of them flash-burned.

And the smell of rot is everywhere—coming off dismembered feet and arms and legs and torsos propped upright, off piles of intestines and crushed skulls, and the heads that are intact have screams etched across their faces.

And the trees that don't burn will have to be felled to extract airplane pieces and to recover the body parts that ornament them, yellow strings of fatty tissue draped over branches, a macabre tinsel. Stephanie Meyers is still strapped in her seat, which hangs from one of those trees, her eyeballs burned out of their sockets. And since a cargo of party confetti and gold glitter—two tons of it—were being transported to America, millions of tiny dots of purple and green and pink and orange paper cascade over the carnage.

This is what makes up the forest now: thousands of steel rivets, the unbroken door of the plane, a row of cabin windows, huge sheets of insulation, life jackets, giant clumps of wiring, rows of empty seat cushions—belts still fastened—shredded and covered with blood and matted with viscera, and some of the seat backs have passengers' impressions burned into them. Dogs and cats lie crushed in their kennels.

For some reason the majority of passengers on this flight were under thirty, and the debris reflects this: cell phones and laptops and Ray-Ban sunglasses and baseball caps and pairs of Rollerblades tied together and camcorders and mangled guitars and hundreds of CDs and fashion magazines (including the *YouthQuake* with Victor Ward on the cover) and entire wardrobes of Calvin Klein and Armani and Ralph Lauren hang from burning trees and there's a teddy bear soaked with blood and a Bible and various Nintendo games along with rolls of toilet paper and shoulder bags and engagement rings and pens and belts whipped off waists and Prada purses still clasped and boxes of Calvin Klein boxer-briefs and so many clothes from the Gap contaminated with blood and other body fluids and everything reeks of aviation fuel.

The only things that suggest living: a wind billows across the wreckage, the moon rises into an expanse of sky so dark it's almost abstract, confetti and glitter continue raining down. Aviation fuel starts burning the trees in the forest, the word CANCELED appears on a big black arrival board at JFK airport in New York, and the next morning, as the sun rises gently over cleanup crews, church bells start ringing and psychics start calling in with tips and then the gossip begins.

5

9 I'm walking through Washington Square Park, carrying a Kenneth Cole leather portfolio that holds my lawbooks and a bottle of Evian water. I'm dressed casually, in Tommy Hilfiger jeans, a camel-hair sweater, a wool overcoat from Burberrys. I'm stepping out of the way of Rollerbladers and avoiding clusters of Japanese NYU film students shooting movies. From a nearby boom box Jamaican trip-hop plays, from another boom box the Eagles' "New Kid in Town," and I'm smiling to myself. My beeper keeps going off. Chris Cuomo keeps calling, as does Alison Poole, whom I rather like and plan to see later this evening. On University, I run into my newly appointed guru and spiritual adviser, Deepak.

Deepak is wearing a Donna Karan suit and Diesel sunglasses, smoking a cigar. "Partagas Perfecto," he purrs in a distinct Indian accent. I purr back "Hoo-ha" admiringly. We exchange opinions about a trendy new restaurant (oh, there are so many) and the upcoming photo shoot I'm doing for *George* magazine, how someone's AIDS has gone into remission, how someone's liver disease has been cured, the exorcism of a haunted town house in Gramercy Park, the evil spirits that were flushed out by the goodwill of angels.

"That's so brill, man," I'm saying. "That's so genius."

"You see that bench?" Deepak says.

"Yes," I say.

"You think it's a bench," Deepak says. "But it isn't."

I smile patiently.

"It's also you," Deepak says. "You, Victor, are also that bench."

Deepak bows slightly.

"I know I've changed," I tell Deepak. "I'm a different person now."

Deepak bows slightly again.

"I am that bench," I hear myself say.

"You see that pigeon?" Deepak asks.

"Baby, I've gotta run," I interrupt. "I'll catch you later."

"Don't fear the reaper, Victor," Deepak says, walking away.

I'm nodding mindlessly, a vacant grin pasted on my face, until I turn around and mutter to myself, "I *am* the fucking reaper, Deepak," and a pretty girl smiles at me from underneath an awning and it's Wednesday and late afternoon and getting dark.

8

After a private workout with Reed, my personal trainer, I take a shower in the Philippe Starck locker room and as I'm standing in front of a mirror, a white Ralph Lauren towel wrapped around my waist, I notice Reed standing behind me, wearing a black Helmut Lang leather jacket. I'm swigging from an Evian bottle. I'm rubbing Clinique turnaround lotion into my face. I just brushed past a model named Mark Vanderloo, who recited a mininarrative about his life that was of no interest to me. A lounge version of "Wichita Lineman" is piped through the gym's sound system and I'm grooving out on it in my own way.

"What's up?" I ask Reed.

"Buddy?" Reed says, his voice thick.

"Yeah?" I turn around.

"Give Reed a hug."

A pause in which to consider things. To wipe my hands on the towel wrapped around my waist.

"Why . . . man?"

"Because you've really come a long way, man," Reed says, his voice filled with emotion. "It's weird but I'm really choked up by all you've accomplished."

"Hey Reed, I couldn't have done it without you, man," I'm saying. "You deserve a bonus. You really got me into shape."

"And your attitude is impeccable," Reed adds.

"No more drinking binges, I've cut down on partying, law school's great, I'm in a long-term relationship." I slip on a Brooks Brothers T-shirt. "I've stopped seriously deluding myself and I'm rereading Dostoyevsky. I owe it all to you, man."

Reed's eyes water.

"And you stopped smoking," Reed says.

"Yep."

"And your body fat's down to seven percent."

"Oh man."

"You're the kind of guy, Victor, that makes this job worthwhile." Reed chokes back a sob. "I mean that."

"I know, man." I rest a hand on his shoulder.

As Reed walks me out onto Fifth Avenue he asks, "How's that apple diet working out?"

"Great," I say, waving down a cab. "My girlfriend says my seminal fluid tastes sweeter."

"That's cool, man," Reed says.

I hop into a cab.

Before the door closes, Reed leans in and, offering his hand after a pause, says, "I'm sorry about Chloe, man."

7

After some impassioned clothing removal I'm sucking lightly on Alison's breasts and I keep looking up at her, making eye contact, rolling my tongue across her nipples and holding on to her breasts, applying slight pressure but not squeezing them, and she keeps sighing, content. Afterwards Alison admits she never faked an orgasm for my benefit. We're lying on her bed, the two dogs—Mr. and Mrs. Chow—snuggled deeply in the folds of a neon-pink comforter at our feet, and I'm running my hands through their fur. Alison's talking about Aerosmith as a Joni Mitchell CD plays throughout the room at low volume.

"Steven Tyler recently admitted that his first wet dream was about Jane Fonda." Alison sighs, sucks in on a joint I didn't hear her light. "How old does that make him?"

I keep stroking Mr. Chow, scratching his ears, both his eyes shut tight with pleasure.

"I want a dog," I murmur. "I want a pet."

"You used to hate these dogs," Alison says. "What do you mean, a pet? The only pet you ever owned was the Armani eagle."

"Yeah, but I changed my mind."

"I think that's good," Alison says genuinely.

A long pause. The dogs reposition themselves, pressing in close to me.

"I hear you're seeing Damien tomorrow," Alison says.

I stiffen up a little. "Do you care?"

"What are you seeing him about?" she asks.

"I'm telling him"—I sigh, relax—"I'm telling him that I can't open this club with him. Law school's just too . . . time-consuming."

I take the joint from Alison. Inhale, exhale.

"Do you care?" I ask. "I mean, about Damien?"

"No," she says. "I've totally forgiven Damien. And though I really can't stand Lauren Hynde, compared to most of the other wenches that cling to guys in this town she's semi-acceptable."

"Is this on the record?" I grin.

"Did you know she's a member of WANAH?" Alison asks. "That new feminist group?"

"What's WANAH?"

"It's an acronym for We Are Not A Hole," she sighs. "We also share the same acupuncturist." Alison pauses. "Some things are unavoidable."

"I suppose so." I'm sighing too.

"And she's also a member of PETA," Alison says, "so I can't totally hate her. Even if she was—even if she *is*—fucking what was once my fiancé."

"What's PETA?" I ask, interested.

"People for the Ethical Treatment of Animals." Alison slaps me playfully. "You should know that, Victor."

"Why should I know that?" I ask. "Ethical treatment of . . . *animals*?"

"It's very simple, Victor," she says. "We want a world where animals are treated as well as humans are."

I just stare at her. "And . . . you don't think that's . . . happening?"

"Not when animals are being killed as indiscriminately as they are now. No."

"I see."

"There's a meeting on Friday at Asia de Cuba," Alison says. "Oliver Stone, Bill Maher, Alec Baldwin and Kim Basinger, Grace Slick, Noah Wyle, Mary Tyler Moore. Alicia Silverstone's reading a speech that Ellen DeGeneres wrote." Alison pauses. "Moby's the DJ."

"Everyone will be wearing camouflage pants, right?" I ask. "And plastic shoes? And talking about how great fake meat tastes?"

"Oh, what's that supposed to mean?" she snaps, rolling her eyes, distinctly less mellow.

"It doesn't mean anything."

"If you heard about leg-hold traps, the torture of baby minks, the maiming of certain rabbits—not to even mention medical experiments done on totally innocent raccoons and lynxes—my god, Victor, you'd wake up."

"Uh-huh," I say. "Oh baby," I mutter.

"It's animal abuse and you're just lying there."

"Honey, they save chickens."

"They have no voice, Victor."

"Baby, they're chickens."

"You try seeing the world through the eyes of an abused animal," she says.

"Baby, I was a model for many years," I say. "I did. I have."

"Oh, don't be so flippant," she moans.

"Alison," I say, sitting up a little. "They also want to protect fruits and vegetables, okay?"

"What's wrong with that?" she asks. "It's eco-friendly."

"Baby, peaches don't have mothers."

"They have skin, Victor, and they have flesh."

"I just think you're reality-challenged."

"Who isn't?" She waves me away. "Animals need as much love and respect and care as we give people."

I consider this. I think about all the things I've seen and done, and I consider this.

"I think they're better off without that, baby," I say. "In fact I think they're doing okay."

I'm hard again and I roll on top of her.

Later, afterwards, Alison asks me something.

"Did Europe change you, Victor?"

"Why?" I ask sleepily.

"Because you seem different," she says softly. "Did it?"

"I guess," I say after a long pause.

"How?" she asks.

"I'm less . . ." I stop. "I'm less . . . I don't know."

"What happened over there, Victor?"

Carefully, I ask her, "What do you mean?"

She whispers back, "What happened over there?"

I'm silent, contemplating an answer, petting the chows. One licks my hand.

"What happened to Chloe over there, Victor?" Alison whispers.

6 At Industria for the *George* magazine photo shoot I can't fathom why the press is making such a big deal about this. Simple before-and-after shots. Before: I'm holding a Bass Ale, wearing Prada, a goatee pasted on my face, a grungy expression, eyes slits. After: I'm carrying a stack of lawbooks and wearing a Brooks Brothers seersucker suit, a bottle of Diet Coke in my left hand, Oliver Peoples wireframes. THE TRANSFORMATION OF VICTOR WARD (UH, WE MEAN JOHNSON) is the headline on the cover for the January issue. The photo shoot was supposed to be outside St. Albans in Washington, D.C.—a school I had sampled briefly before being expelled—but Dad nixed it. He has that kind of clout. The Dalai Lama shows up at Industria, and I'm shaking hands with Chris Rock, and one of Harrison Ford's sons—an intern at *George*—is milling about, along with various people who resigned from the Clinton administration, and MTV's covering the shoot for "The Week in Rock" and a VJ's asking me questions about the Impersonators' new huge contract with DreamWorks and how I feel about not being in the band anymore and I give a cute sound bite by saying, "Law school's easier than being in that band," and it's all very *Eyes of Laura Mars* but it's also faux-subdued because everyone's very respectful of what happened to Chloe.

John F. Kennedy, Jr., who's really just another gorgeous goon, is shaking my hand and he's saying things like "I'm a big fan of your dad's" and I'm saying "Yeah?" and though I'm basically calm and amused, there's one awkward moment when someone who went to Camden accosts me and I simply can't place him. But I'm vague enough that he can't become suspicious and then he simply slouches away, giving up.

"Hey!" An assistant with a cell phone rushes over to where I'm standing. "Someone wants to talk to you."

"Yeah?" I ask.

"Chelsea Clinton wants to say hi," the assistant pants.

I take the phone from the assistant. Over static I hear Chelsea ask, "Is it really you?"

"Yeah." I'm grinning "sheepishly." I'm blushing, "red-faced."

A Eureka moment handled suavely.

I find it a little difficult to relax once the photo session starts.

The photographer says, "Hey, don't worry—it's hard to be yourself."

I start smiling secretly, thinking secret things.

"That's it!" the photographer shouts.

Flashes of light keep going off as I stand perfectly still.

On my way out I'm handed an invitation by a nervous groupie to a party for PETA tomorrow night that the Gap is sponsoring at a new restaurant in Morgan's Hotel.

"I don't know if I can make it," I tell a supermodel who's standing nearby.

"You're the outgoing type," the supermodel says. I read recently that she just broke up with her boyfriend, an ex-model who runs a new and very fashionable club called Ecch! She smiles flirtatiously as I start heading out.

"Yeah?" I ask, flirting back. "How do you know?"

"I can tell." She shrugs, then invites me to a strip-poker game at someone named Mr. Leisure's house.

5 On the phone with Dad.

"When will you be down here?" he asks.

"In two days," I say. "I'll call."

"Yes. Okay."

"Has the money been transferred?" I ask.

"Yes. It has."

Pause. "Are you okay?" I ask.

Pause. "Yes, yes. I'm just . . . distracted."

"Don't be. You need to focus," I say.

"Yes, yes. Of course."

"Someone will let you know when I'm there."

A long pause.

"Hello?" I ask.

"I—I don't know," he says, breathing in.

"You're unraveling," I warn. "Don't," I warn.

"We really don't need to see each other while you're here," he says. "I mean, do we?"

"No. Not really," I say. "Only if you want." Pause. "Are there any parties you want to show me off at?"

"Hey—" he snaps.

"Watch it," I warn.

It takes him forty-three seconds to compose himself.

"I'm glad you'll be here," he finally says.

Pause. I let it resonate. "Are you?"

"Yes."

"I'm glad I'll be there too."

"Really?" He breathes in, trembling.

"Anything to help the cause," I say.

"Are you being sarcastic?"

"No." Pause. "You figure it out." I sigh. "Do you even really care?" Pause. "If there's anything you need . . ." He trails off.

"Don't you trust me?" I ask.

It takes a long time for him to say, "I think I do."

I'm smiling to myself. "I'll be in touch."

"Goodbye."

"Goodbye."

4 I meet Damien for drinks at the Independent, not far from the club he and I are supposed to open a month from now in TriBeCa. Damien's smoking a cigar and nursing a Stoli Kafya, which personally I find disgusting. He's wearing a Gucci tie. I want to make this quick. Bittersweet folk rock plays in the background.

"Did you see this?" Damien asks as I swing up onto a stool.

"What?" I ask.

He slides a copy of today's New York Post across the bar, open to "Page Six." Gossip about the women Victor Johnson has been involved with since Chloe Byrnes' unfortunate death in a Paris hotel room. Peta Wilson. A Spice Girl. Alyssa Milano. Garcelle Beauvais. Carmen Electra. Another Spice Girl.

"For mature audiences only, right?" Damien says, nudging me, arching his eyebrows up.

There's a little hug between the two of us, not much else.

I relax, order a Coke, which causes Damien to shake his head and mutter "Oh, man" too aggressively.

"I guess you know why I'm here," I say.

"Victor, Victor, Victor," Damien sighs, shaking his head.

I pause, confused. "So . . . you *do* know?"

"I forgive you entirely," he says, acting casual. "Come on, you know that."

"I just want out, man," I say. "I'm older. I've got school."

"How *is* law school?" Damien asks. "I mean, this isn't a rumor, right? You're really doing this?"

"Yeah." I laugh. "I am." I sip my Coke. "It's a lot of work but . . ."

He studies me. "Yeah? But?"

"But I'm adapting," I finally answer.

"That's great," Damien says.

"Is it?" I ask seriously. "I mean, really. Is it?"

"Victor," Damien starts, grasping my forearm.

"Yeah, man?" I gulp, but I'm really not afraid of him.

"I am constantly thinking about human happiness," he admits.

"Whoa."

"Yeah," he says, tenderly sipping his vodka. "Whoa."

"Is everything going to be cool?" I ask. "I'm really not leaving you in a lurch?"

Damien shrugs. "It'll be cool. Japanese investors. Things will work out."

I smile, showing my appreciation. But I'm still very cool about the situation, so I move on to other topics. "How's Lauren?" I ask.

"Ooh—ouch," Damien says.

"No, no, man," I say. "I'm just asking."

Damien hits me lightly on the shoulder. "I know, man. I'm just goofing off. I'm just playing around."

"That's good," I say. "I can deal."

"She's great," he says. "She's very cool."

Damien stops smiling, motions to the bartender for another drink. "How's Alison?"

"She's fine," I say evenly. "She's really into PETA. This People for the Ethical Treatment of . . . oh shit, whatever."

"How unpredictable she is," Damien says. "How, er, slippery," he adds. "I guess people really do change, huh?"

After a careful pause, I venture, "What do you mean?"

"Well, you've become quite the clean-cut, athletic go-getter."

"Not really," I say. "You're just looking at the surface."

"There's something else?" he asks. "Just kidding," he adds desultorily.

"There's no swimsuit competition, dude," I warn.

"And I just got a bikini wax?" He lifts his arms, sarcastic.

Finally.

"No hard feelings?" I ask genuinely.

"No feelings at all, man."

I stare at Damien with admiration.

"I'm going to the Fuji Rock Festival," Damien says when I start listening again. "I'll be back next week."

"Will you call me?"

"What do you think?"

I don't bother answering.

"Hey, who's this Mr. Leisure everyone's talking about?" Damien asks.

3

Bill, an agent from CAA, calls to let me know that I have "won" the role of Ohman in the movie *Flatliners II*. I'm in a new apartment, wearing a conservative Prada suit, on my way out to make an appearance at a party that I have no desire to attend, and I lock onto a certain tone of jadedness that Bill seems to feed off of.

"Tell me what else is going on, Bill," I say. "While I'm brushing my hair."

"I'm trying to develop interest in a script about a Jewish boy who makes a valiant attempt to celebrate his bar mitzvah under an oppressive Nazi regime."

"Your thoughts on the script?" I sigh.

"My thoughts? No third act. My thoughts? Too much farting."

Silence while I continue slicking my hair back.

"So Victor," Bill starts slyly. "What do you think?"

"About what?"

"*Flatliners II*," he screams, and then, after catching his breath, adds in a very small voice, "I'm sorry."

"Far out," I'm saying. "Baby, that's so cool," I'm saying.

"This whole new look, Victor, is really paying off."

"People tell me it's exceedingly hip," I concede.

"You must have really studied all those old Madonna videos."

"In order."

"I think you are controlling the zeitgeist," Bill says. "I think you are in the driver's seat."

"People *have* commented that I'm near the wheel, Bill."

"People are paying attention, that's why," Bill says. "People love repentance."

A small pause as I study myself in a mirror.

"Is that what I'm doing, Bill?" I ask. "Repenting?"

"You're pulling a Bowie," Bill says. "And certain people are responding. It's called reinventing yourself. It's a word. It's in the dictionary."

"What are you trying to say to me, Bill?"

"I am fielding offers for Victor Johnson," Bill says. "And I am proud to be fielding offers for Victor Johnson."

A pause. "Bill . . . I don't think . . ." I stop, figure out a way to break the news. "I'm not . . . That's not me."

"What do you mean? Who am I talking to?" Bill asks in a rush, and then, in a low, whispery voice, he asks, "This isn't Dagby, is it?" I can almost hear him shuddering over the line.

"Dagby?" I ask. "No, this isn't Dagby. Bill, listen, I'm going to school now and—"

"But that's just a publicity stunt, I assume," Bill yawns. "Hmm?"

Pause. "Uh, no, Bill. It's not a publicity stunt."

"Stop, in the name of love, before you break my heart," Bill says. "Just give me a high-pitched warning scream when you read lines like that to me again."

"It's not a line, Bill," I say. "I'm in law school now and I don't want to do the movie."

"You've been offered the role of an astronaut who helps save the world in *Space Cadets*—which is going to be directed by Mr. Will Smith, thank you very much. You will have four Hasbro action-figure dolls coming out by next Christmas and I will make sure that they are totally intact, genitalia-wise." Bill veers into an endless spasm of coughing and then he croaks, "If you know what I mean."

"That sounds a little too commercial for me right now."

"What are you saying? That *Space Cadets* doesn't rock your world?" I hear Bill tapping his headset. "Hello? Who am I speaking to?" Pause. "This isn't Dagby, is it?"

"What else could I do?" I'm sighing, checking my face for blemishes, but I'm blemish-free tonight.

"Oh, you could play someone nicknamed 'The Traitor' who gets his ass beaten in a parking lot in an indie movie called *The Sellout* that is being directed by a recently rehabbed Italian known only as 'Vivvy,' and your per diem would be twenty Burger King vouchers and there would *not* be a wrap party." Bill pauses to let this sink in. "It's your decision. It's Victor Johnson's decision."

"I'll let you know," I say. "I have a party to go to. I've gotta split."

"Listen, stop playing hard to get."

"I'm not."

"Not to be crass, but the dead-girlfriend thing—an inspired touch, by the way—is going to fade in approximately a week." Bill pauses. "You have to strike now."

I laugh good-naturedly. "Bill, I'll call you later."

He laughs too. "No, stay on the line with me."

"Bill, I gotta go." I can't stop giggling. "My visage is wanted elsewhere."

2   A party for the blind that Bacardi rum is sponsoring some-where in midtown that my newly acquired publicists at Rogers and Cowan demanded I show up at. Among the VIPs: Bono, Kal Ruttenstein, Kevin Bacon, Demi Moore, Fiona Apple, Courtney Love, Claire Danes, Ed Burns, Jennifer Aniston and Tate Donovan, Shaquille O'Neal and a surprisingly swishy Tiger Woods. Some seem to know me, some don't. I'm having a Coke with someone named Ben Affleck while Jamiroquai plays over the sound system in the cavernous club we're all lost in and Gabé Doppelt just has to introduce me to Bjork and I have to pose with Giorgio Armani and he's hugging me as if we go a long way back and he's wearing a navy-blue crew-neck T-shirt, a navy cashmere sweater, navy corduroy jeans and a giant Jaeger–Le Coultre Reverso wristwatch. And there are so many apologies about Chloe, almost as if it was her fault that she died on me (my information is "massive hemorrhaging due to the in gestion of fatal quantities of mifepristone—also known as RU 486"). Mark Wahlberg, fire-eaters and a lot of blabbing about generational malaise, and everything smells like caviar.

Just so much gibberish and so chicly presented. Typical conversations revolve around serial killers and rehab stints and the amount of "very dry" pussy going around as opposed to just "dry" and the spectacularly self-destructive behavior of an idiotic model. I'm so uncomfortable I resort to sound bites such as: "I'm basically a law-abiding citizen." The phrase "back to school"—employed every time a reporter's microphone is pushed into my face—becomes an overwhelming drag and I have to excuse myself, asking directions to the nearest rest room.

In the men's room two fags in the stall next to mine are comparing notes on how to live in a plotless universe and I'm just on my cell phone checking messages, taking a breather. Finally they leave and it becomes quiet, almost hushed, in the rest room and I can listen to messages without holding a hand against my ear.

I'm muttering to myself—Damien again, Alison, my publicist, certain cast members from a TV show I've never seen—but then I have to stop because I realize that the men's room isn't empty.

Someone's in here and he's whistling.

Clicking the cell phone off, I cock my head because it's a tune that seems familiar.

I peer carefully over the stall door but can't see anyone.

The whistling echoes, and then a voice that's deep and masculine but also ghostly and from another world sings, haltingly, "on the . . . sunny side of the street. . . ."

I yank open the stall door, my cell phone dropping onto the tiles.

I walk over to the row of sinks beneath a wall-length mirror so I can survey the entire bathroom.

There's no one in here.

The bathroom is empty.

I wash my hands and check every stall and then I leave, merging back into the party.

1 Back at the new apartment Dad bought me on the Upper East Side. The walls in the living room are blue and Nile green and the curtains draped over the windows looking out onto 72nd Street are hand-painted silk taffeta. There are antique coffee tables. There are beveled French mirrors in the foyer. There are Noguchi lamps and scruffed-up armchairs situated in pleasant positions. Paisley pillows line a couch. There is a ceiling fan. There are paintings by Donald Baechler. I actually have a library.

Modern touches in the kitchen: a slate-and-marble mosaic floor, a black-and-white photographic mural of a desert landscape, a prop plane flying over it. Metal furniture from a doctor's office. The dining room windows have frosted glass. Custom-made chairs circle a table that was purchased at Christie's at auction.

I walk into the bedroom to check my messages, since a flashing light indicates five more people have called since I left the club twenty minutes ago. In the bedroom, a Chippendale mirror that Dad sent hangs over a mahogany sleigh bed made in Virginia in the nineteenth century, or so they say.

I'm thinking of buying a Dalmatian.

Gus Frerotte's in town. Cameron Diaz called. And then Matt Dillon. And then Cameron Diaz called again. And then Matt Dillon called again.

I flip on the TV in the bedroom. Videos, the usual. I switch over to the Weather Channel.

I stretch, groaning, my arms held high above my head.

I decide to run a bath.

I carefully hang up the Prada jacket. I'm thinking, That's the last time you're wearing that.

In the bathroom I lean over the white porcelain tub and turn the faucets, making sure the water is hot. I add some Kiehl's bath salts, mixing them around with my hand.

I'm thinking of buying a Dalmatian.

I keep stretching.

Something on the floor of the bathroom catches my eye.

I lean down.

It's a tiny circle, made of paper. I press my index finger on it.

I bring my hand up to my face.

It's a piece of confetti.

I stare at it for a long time.

A small black wave.

It starts curling toward me.

Casually, I start whistling as I move slowly back into the bedroom.

When I'm in the bedroom I notice that confetti—pink and white and gray—has been dumped all over the bed.

Staring into the Chippendale mirror over the bed, I brace myself before glimpsing the shadow behind an eighteenth-century tapestry screen that stands in the corner.

The shadow moves slightly.

It's waiting. It has that kind of stance.

I move over to the bed.

Still whistling casually, I lean toward the nightstand and, laughing to myself, pretending to struggle with the laces on the shoes I'm kicking off, I reach into a drawer and pull out a .25-caliber Walther with a silencer attached.

I start padding back toward the bathroom.

I'm counting to myself.

Five, four, three—

I immediately change direction and move straight up to the screen, the gun raised.

Gauging head level, I pull the trigger. Twice.

A muffled grunt. A wet sound—blood spraying against a wall.

A figure dressed in black, half his face destroyed, falls forward, toppling over the screen, a small gun clenched in the gloved fist of his right hand.

I'm about to bend over and pull the gun out of his hand when movement behind my back causes me to whirl around.

Silently leaping toward me over the bed, now above me, an oversized knife in an outstretched hand, is another figure clad in black.

Instantly I take aim, crouching.

The first bullet whizzes past him, punching into the Chippendale mirror, shattering it.

As he falls onto me, the second bullet catches him in the face, its impact throwing him backward.

He lies on the carpet, kicking. I stagger up and quickly fire two bullets into his chest. He immediately goes still.

"Shit, shit, shit," I'm cursing, fumbling for a cell phone, dialing a number I only half remember.

After three tries, a transmission signal.

I punch in the code, breathing hard.

"Come on, come on."

Another signal. Another code.

And then I dial another number.

"It's DAN," I say into the mouthpiece.

I wait.

"Yes." I listen. "Yes."

I give the location. I say the words "Code 50."

I hang up. I turn off the bathwater and quickly pack an overnight bag.

I leave before the cleaners arrive.

I spend the night at the Carlyle Hotel.

O I meet Eva for dinner the next night at a supertrendy new Japanese restaurant just above SoHo, in the newly glam area of Houston Street, and Eva's sipping green tea at a booth in the packed main room, waiting patiently, an advance copy of the *New York Observer* (with a particularly favorable article about my father that's really about the new Victor Johnson and all the things he's learned) folded on the table next to where she's resting her wrists. I'm shown to our booth a little too enthusiastically by the maître d', who holds my hand, offers condolences, tells me I look ultracool. I take it in stride and thank him as I slide in next to Eva. Eva and I just smile at each other. I remember to kiss her. I remember to go through the motions, since everyone's looking at us, since that's the point of the booth, since that's the point of this appearance.

I order a premium cold sake and tell Eva that I got the part in *Flatliners II*. Eva says she's very happy for me.

"So where's your boyfriend tonight?" I ask, smiling.

"A certain guy is out of town," Eva says evasively.

"Where is he?" I ask, teasing her.

"He's actually at the Fuji Rock Festival," she says, rolling her eyes, sipping the green tea.

"I know someone who went to that."

"Maybe they went together."

"Who knows?"

"Yes," she says, opening a menu. "Who knows?"

"The point is: you don't know."

"Yes, that is the point."

"You look beautiful."

She doesn't say anything.

"Did you hear me?" I ask.

"Nice suit," she says without looking up.

"Are we making shoptalk?"

"You're getting quite the press these days," Eva says, tapping the copy of the *Observer*. "Wherever you seem to go there's a paparazzi alert."

"It's not all sunglasses and autographs, baby."

"What does that mean?"

"Aren't these people ridiculous?" I ask, vaguely gesturing.

"Oh, I don't know," she says. "The simplicity is almost soothing. It's like being back in high school."

"Why is it like that?"

"Because you realize that hanging out with dumb people makes you feel much smarter," she says. "At least that's how I viewed high school."

"Where were you while we were getting high?" I murmur to myself, concentrating on avoiding eye contact with anyone in the room.

"Pardon?"

"My mind is definitely expanding," I say, clearing my throat.

"Without us this is all just trash," she agrees.

I'm reaching for the edamame.

"Speaking of," Eva starts. "How's Alison Poole?"

"I have a feeling I'm breaking her heart."

"I have a feeling you're good at breaking hearts," Eva says.

"She keeps asking questions about Chloe Byrnes," I murmur.

Eva doesn't say anything. Soon she's sipping a Stolichnaya Limonnaya vodka and I'm picking at a plate of hijiki.

"What did you do today?" I ask before realizing I'm not particularly interested, even though I'm squeezing Eva's thigh beneath the table.

"I had a photo shoot. I had lunch with Salt-n-Pepa. I avoided certain people. I contacted the people I didn't avoid." Eva breathes in. "My life right now is actually simpler than I thought it was going to be." She sighs, but not unhappily. "If there are some things I'm not used to yet, it's still sweet."

"I dig it," I say. "I hear where you're coming from, baby," I say, mimicking a robot.

Eva giggles, says my name, lets me squeeze her thigh harder.

But then I'm looking away and things get difficult. I down another cup of sake.

"You seem distracted," Eva says.

"Something happened last night," I murmur.

"What?"

I tell her, whispering.

"We need to be careful," Eva says.

Suddenly a couple is loomin over us and I hear someone exclaim, "Victor? Hey man, what's up."

Breathing in, I look up with a practiced smile.

"Oh, hi," I say, reaching out a hand.

A fairly hip couple, our age. The guy—who I don't recognize—grabs my hand and shakes it with a firm grip that says "please remember me because you're so cool," and the girl he's with is bouncing up and down in the crush of the restaurant and she offers a little wave and Eva nods, offers a little wave back.

"Hey Corrine," the guy says, "this is Victor Ward—oh, sorry"—the guy catches himself—"I mean Victor *Johnson*. Victor, this is Corrine."

"Hey, nice to meet you," I say, taking Corrine's hand.

"And this is Lauren Hynde," the guy says, gesturing toward Eva, who keeps smiling, sitting perfectly still.

"Hi, Lauren, I think we met already," Corrine says. "At that Kevyn Aucoin benefit? At the Chelsea Piers? Alexander McQueen introduced us. You were being interviewed by MTV. It was a screening of that movie?"

"Oh, right, right, of course," Eva says. "Yeah. Right. Corrine."

"Hey, Lauren," the guy says, a little too shyly.

"Hi, Maxwell," Eva says with an undercurrent of sexiness.

"How do you guys know each other?" I ask, looking first at Maxwell and then at Eva.

"Lauren and I met at a press junket," Maxwell explains. "It was in L.A. at the Four Seasons."

Eva and Maxwell share a private moment. I'm silently retching.

"Popular spot?" Maxwell asks me.

I pause before asking, "Is that a true-or-false?"

"Man, you're all over the place," he says, lingering.

"Just fifteen minutes."

"More like an hour." Maxwell laughs.

"We're so sorry about Chloe," Corrine interrupts.

I nod gravely.

"Are you guys going to that party at Life?" she asks.

"Oh yeah, sure, we'll be there," I say vaguely.

Corrine and Maxwell wait at the table while Eva and I stare at them vacantly until they finally realize we're not going to ask them to join us and then they say goodbye and Maxwell shakes my hand again and they disappear into the throng at the bar and the people waiting there look at Corrine and Maxwell differently now because they stopped at our table, because they gave the illusion that they knew us.

"God, I don't recognize anybody," I say.

"You have to check those photo books that were given to you," Eva says. "You need to memorize the faces."

"I suppose."

"I'll test you," Eva says. "We'll do it together."

"I'd like that," I say.

"And how is Victor Ward?" Eva asks, smiling.

"He's helping define the decade, baby," I say sarcastically.

"Significance is rewarded in retrospect," Eva warns.

"I think this *is* the retrospect, baby."

We both collapse into major giggling. But then I'm silent, feeling glum, unable to relate. The restaurant is impossibly crowded and things are not as clear as I need them to be. The people who have been waving at our table and making *I'll call you* motions saw how Corrine and Maxwell broke the ice and soon they will be all over us. I down another cup of sake.

"Oh, don't look so sad," Eva says. "You're a star."

"Is it cold in here?" I ask.

"Hey, what's wrong? You look sad."

"Is it cold in here?" I ask again, waving away a fly.

"When are you going to Washington?" she finally asks.

"Soon."

6

O Jamie told me, "You're the only sign in the horoscope that's not a living thing."

"What do you mean?" I muttered.

"You're a Libra," she said. "You're just a set of scales."

I was thinking, This is just a fling, right? I was thinking, I want to fuck you again.

"But I thought I was a Capricorn," I sighed.

We were lying on a field bordered by red and yellow trees and I had my hand thrown up to block my eyes from the sun slanting through the branches, its heat striking my face, and it was September and summer was over and we were lying on the commons lawn and from an open window we could hear someone vomiting in a room on the second floor of Booth House and Pink Floyd—"Us and Them"—was playing from somewhere else and I had taken off my shirt and Jamie had haphazardly rubbed Bain de Soleil all over my back and chest and I was thinking about all the girls I had fucked over the summer, grouping them into pairs, placing them in categories, surprised by the similarities I was finding. My legs had fallen asleep and a girl passing by told me she liked that story I read in a creative writing workshop. I nodded, ignored her, she moved on. I was fingering a condom that was lodged in my pocket. I was making a decision.

"I don't take that class," I told Jamie.

"No future, no future, no future—for you," Jamie half-sang.

And now, in a hotel room in Milan, I remember that I started to cry on the field that day because Jamie told me certain things, whispered them in my ear so matter-of-factly it suggested she really didn't care who heard: how she wanted to bomb the campus to "kingdom fuck," how she was the one responsible for her ex-boyfriend's death, how someone really needed to slit Lauren Hynde's throat wide open, and she kept admitting these things so casually. Finally Jamie was interrupted by Sean Bateman stumbling over, holding a six-pack of Rolling Rock, and he lay down next to us and kept cracking his knuckles and we all started taking pills and I was lying between Sean and Jamie as they exchanged a glance that meant something secret.

Sean whispered into my ear at one point, "All the boys think she's a spy."

"You have potential," Jamie whispered into my other ear.

Crows, ravens, these flying shadows, were circling above us and above that a small plane flew across the sky, its exhaust fumes forming the Nike logo, and when I finally sat up I stared across the commons and in the distance, the End of the World spread out behind them, was a film crew. It seemed that they were uncertain as to where they were supposed to be heading but when Jamie waved them over they aimed their cameras at where we were lying.

1 The next day production assistants from the French film crew feed me heroin as they fly me into Milan on a private jet someone named Mr. Leisure has supplied, which is piloted by two Japanese men. The plane lands at Linate airport and the PAs check me into the Principe di Savoia on a quiet Friday afternoon in the off-season. I stay locked in a suite, guarded by a twenty-three-year-old Italian named Davide, an Uzi strapped across his chest. The film crew is reportedly staying in the Brera section of town but no one provides me with a phone number or an address and only the director makes contact, every three days or so. One night Davide moves me to the Hotel Diana and the following morning I'm moved back to the Principe di Savoia. I'm told that the crew is now filming exteriors outside La Posta Vecchia. I'm told that they will be leaving Milan within the week. I'm told to relax, to stay beautiful.

2 I call my sister in Washington, D.C.
The first time, her machine picks up.
I don't leave a message.
The second time I call, she answers, but it's the middle of the night there. "Sally?" I whisper.

"Hello?"

"Sally?" I whisper. "It's me. It's Victor."

"Victor?" she asks, groaning. "What time is it?"

I don't know what to say so I hang up.

Later, when I call again, it's morning in Georgetown.

"Hello?" she answers.

"Sally, it's me again," I say.

"Why are you whispering?" she asks, annoyed. "Where are you?"

Hearing her voice, I start crying.

"Victor?" she asks.

"I'm in Milan," I whisper between sobs.

"You're where?" she asks.

"I'm in Italy."

Silence.

"Victor?" she starts.

"Yeah?" I say, wiping my face.

"Is this a joke?"

"No. I'm in Milan. . . . I need your help."

She barely pauses before her voice changes and she's asking, "Whoever this is, I've gotta go."

"No no no no—wait, Sally—"

"Victor, I'm seeing you for lunch at one, okay?" Sally says. "What in the hell are you doing?"

"Sally," I whisper.

"Whoever this is, don't call back."

"Wait, Sally—"

She hangs up.

3 Davide is from Legnano, an industrial suburb northwest of Milan, and he has black and golden hair and he keeps eating peppermint candies from a green paper bag as he sits in a little gold chair in the suite at the Principe di Savoia. He tells me he used to be a champagne delivery boy, that he has ties to the Mafia, that his girlfriend is the Italian Winona Ryder. He flares his nostrils and offers penetrating looks. He smokes Newport Lights and sometimes wears a scarf and sometimes doesn't. Sometimes he lets slip that his real name is Marco. Today he's wearing a cashmere turtleneck in avocado green. Today he's playing with a Ping-Pong ball. His lips are so thick it looks as if he were born making out. He plays a computer game, occasionally looking over at the music videos flashing by on MTV-Italia. I gaze at him restlessly from my bed as he keeps posing in place. He makes spit bubbles. Rain outside thrashes against the window and Davide sighs. The ceiling: a blue dome.

4 Another day. Outside, rain pours down continuously, the wrong kind of weather. I'm eating an omelette that Davide ordered up but it has no taste. Davide tells me that his favorite TV newscaster is Simone Ventura and that he met her once at L'Isola. In the suite next to ours a Saudi prince is behaving badly with a beautiful married woman. The director from the French film crew calls. It has been a week since we last spoke.

"Where's Palakon?" I automatically ask.

"Ah," the director sighs. "There's that name again, Victor."

"Where is he?" I'm gasping.

"We've been through this a hundred times," the director says. "There is no Palakon. I've never heard that name."

"That's just too heavy for me to accept at this point."

"Well, lighten up," the director says. "I don't know what else to tell you."

"I want to go back," I'm weeping. "I want to go home."

"There's always that possibility, Victor," the director says. "Don't discount it."

"Why aren't you paying attention to me anymore?" I ask. "You haven't called in a week."

"Plans are forming," is all the director says.

"You haven't called me in a week," I shout. "What am I doing here?"

"How . . . shall I put this?" the director ponders.

"You're thinking the project is unrealized," I spit out, panicking. "Don't you? That's what you think. But it isn't."

"How shall I put this?" the director says again.

"Tactfully?" I whisper.

"Tactfully?"

"Yes."

"Your role is over, Victor," he says. "Don't be shocked," he says.

"Should I read this . . . as a warning?"

"No." He considers something. "Just a long period of adjustment."

"You mean . . . that I could be here until when? August? Next year?"

"Someone is going to extract you from this sooner or later," the director says. "I'm just not sure exactly when." He pauses. "Davide will watch over you and someone will be in touch shortly."

"What about you?" I wail. "Why can't *you* do anything? Call Palakon."

"Victor," the director says patiently, "I'm at a loss. I'm moving on to another project."

"You can't, you can't," I'm shouting. "You can't leave me here."

"Because I'm moving on, someone else will be brought in to oversee what your, um, future role might be."

"This isn't happening," I murmur.

I start crying again.

Davide looks up from his computer game. He offers a moment of attention, a random smile.

"In the meantime . . ." The director trails off.

Before hanging up, the director says he will try to speed things along by putting me in contact with a war criminal "who might know what to do" with me, and then the director's gone and I never speak to him again.

5 Occasionally I'm allowed out for a walk. Davide always makes a series of calls. We always take the service elevator down. Davide is always armed inconspicuously. On the walk he closely scrutinizes every stranger that passes by. Since it's the off-season and there's no one in town, I'm allowed to browse through the Prada men's boutique on Via Montenapoleone. We have a drink at Café L'Atlantique on Viale Umbria. Later we share a plate of sushi at Terrazza on Via Palestro. I have so many little theories. I'm still piecing together clues—there's only a blueprint, there's only an outline—and sometimes they come together, but only when I'm drinking from a cold, syrupy bottle of Sambuca. Davide has one big theory that explains everything. "I like the really cool way you express yourself, Davide," I say. Looking down, I add, "I'm sorry." He mentions something about Leonardo and *The Last Supper* and how cute the waitress is.

And in the late afternoon there's a polluted sky above Milan and it gets dark rather rapidly and then Davide and I are wandering through the fog floating around us and while walking along the Via Sottocorno I notice a limousine idling by the curb and models with orange hair and frostbite-blue lipstick are moving toward a bank of lighted windows and I break away from Davide and run into Da Giacomo and I glimpse Stefano Gabbana and Tom Ford, who glances over at me and nods casually before Davide pulls me out of the restaurant. This outburst means it's time to go back to the hotel.

6 Back in the room shaped like a beehive Davide tosses me a *Playboy* before he takes a shower. December's Playmate and her favorite things: military insignia, weapon designs, visiting the Pentagon's national command center. But I'm watching MTV and a segment about the Impersonators—the huge DreamWorks contract, an interview with the band, the new single "Nothing Happened" off their soon-to-be-released CD *In the Presence of Nothing*. I slowly move to a mirror and in it my face looks ghostly, transparent, a vacant stare reminds me of something, my hair is turning white. I can hear Davide taking a shower, jets of water splashing against tile, Davide whistling a pop hit from four years ago. When Davide opens the bathroom I'm huddling on the bed, wilted, half-asleep, sucking on a lozenge.

"You are still alive," Davide says, but as he reads the line I can swear he places a subtle emphasis on the pronoun.

Davide's naked, carelessly drying himself off in front of me. Huge biceps, coarse hair tufting out from his armpits, the cheeks of his ass are like melons, the muscles in his stomach push out his belly button. He notices me watching and smiles emphatically. I tell myself he's here to ward off danger.

Once dressed, Davide is in a gray mood and barely tolerant of any despair emanating from where I'm writhing on the bed, and I'm crying endlessly and staring at him. He stares back, puzzled, low key. He starts watching a soft-core porn film, Japanese girls having sex on a foam-rubber mattress.

His cell phone rings.

Davide answers it, dulled out, eyes empty.

He speaks quickly in Italian. Then he listens. Then he speaks quickly again before clicking off.

"Someone's coming," Davide says. "To see us."

I'm humming *listen to the wind blow, watch the sun rise.*

7

A knock on the door.

Davide opens it.

A beautiful young girl enters the room. Davide and the girl embrace and chat amiably in Italian while I stare, dazed, from the bed. The girl is holding an envelope and in the envelope is a videocassette. Without being introduced, she hands it to me.

I stare at it dumbly, then Davide impatiently yanks it out of my hand and slips it into the VCR beneath the television set.

Davide and the girl move over to another room in the suite as the tape starts playing.

8 It's an episode of "60 Minutes" but without the sound.

Dan Rather introduces a segment. Behind him a mock-up of a magazine story. My father's face. And below that, half in shadow, is my face.

Azaleas. At the home of Pamela Digby Churchill Hayward Harriman. A dinner party for Samuel Johnson. A fund-raiser for his presidential bid. The guests: Ruth Hotte and Ed Huling and Deborah Gore Dean and Barbara Raskin and Deborah Tannen and Donna Shalala and Hillary Clinton and Muffy Jeepson Stout. There's Ben Bradlee and Bill Seidman and Malcolm Endicott Peabody. There's Clayton Fritcheys and Brice Clagett and Ed Burling and Sam Nunn. There's Marisa Tomei and Kara Kennedy and Warren Christopher and Katharine Graham and Esther Coopersmith.

And Dad's standing with a woman in her mid-forties wearing a Bill Blass cocktail dress. I glimpse her only briefly.

Now Dan Rather's interviewing my father in his office.

Dad has obviously had a face-lift and his upper-lip-to-nose area has been shortened, droopy lids have been lifted and his teeth are bleached. He's laughing, relaxed.

Then a series of photos flash by. Dad with Mort Zuckerman. Dad with Shelby Bryan. Dad with Strom Thurmond. Dad with Andrea Mitchell.

Suddenly: file footage. An interview with my mother from the mid-1980s. A clip of my father and mother at the White House, standing with Ronald and Nancy Reagan.

Dan Rather interviewing my father again.

A montage: Brooks Brothers, Ann Taylor, Tommy Hilfiger.

And then I'm walking along Dupont Circle being interviewed by Dan Rather.

This is suddenly intercut with footage that the "Entertainment Tonight" crew shot last fall of me working out with Reed at his gym.

Various shots from my portfolio: Versace, CK One, an outtake from Madonna's *Sex*. Paparazzi shots of me leaving a nightclub called Crush. A shot of me leaving the Jockey Club.

I'm being interviewed by Dan Rather downstairs at Red Sage.

I'm laughing, relaxed, wearing wire-rimmed glasses. I'm dressed preppily in a Brooks Brothers suit. I'm nodding at everything that is being asked of me.

Dan Rather shows me a photo from a *Vogue* layout where I'm wearing Calvin Klein boxer-briefs and painting Christy Turlington's toenails. Dan Rather is gesturing, making comments about my physical attractiveness.

I keep nodding my head as if ashamed.

And then: a photo of Chloe Byrnes, followed by various magazine covers.

A shot of Hôtel Costes in Paris.

A montage of her funeral in New York.

I'm sitting in the front row, crying, Alison Poole and Baxter Priestly both offering comfort.

Interviews with Fred Thompson and then Grover Norquist and then Peter Mandelson.

Shots of me walking through Washington Square Park.

Dad again. He's walking out of the Palm with that woman in her mid-forties, dark hair, pretty but also plain enough not to be intimidating. They're holding hands.

Outside the Bombay Club she's there again, kissing him lightly on the cheek.

I recognize this woman.

This woman is Lorrie Wallace.

The Englishwoman who ran into me on the QE2.

The woman married to Stephen Wallace.

The woman who wanted me to go to England.

The woman who recognized Marina.

I lunge for the TV, trying to turn up the volume while Lorrie Wallace is being interviewed. But there's no sound, just static.

Finally Dad and Lorrie Wallace at Carol Laxalt's annual Christmas party. Dad's standing by a poinsettia. He's shaking John Warner's hand.

And in the background, sipping punch from a tiny glass cup, is F. Fred Palakon, a giant Christmas tree twinkling behind him.

I hold a hand over my mouth to stop the screaming.

9

I'm calling my sister again.

It rings three, four, five times.

She picks up.

"Sally?" I'm breathing hard, my voice tight.

"Who is this?" she asks suspiciously.

"It's me," I gasp. "It's Victor."

"Uh-huh," she says dubiously. "I'd really prefer it—whoever this is—if you would stop calling."

"Sally, it's really me, please—" I gasp.

"It's for you," I hear her say.

The sound of the phone being passed to someone else.

"Hello?" a voice asks.

I don't say anything, just listen intently.

"Hello?" the voice asks again. "This is Victor Johnson," the voice says. "Who is this?"

Silence.

"It'd be really cool if you stopped bothering my sister," the voice says. "Okay?"

Silence.

"Goodbye," the voice says.

A click.

I'm disconnected.

10 Davide wants some privacy. He hands me a sweater, suggesting I go for another walk. The girl is smoking a cigarette, sitting naked on a plush tan couch. She glances over at me, waiting. Numb, I comply.

At the door, standing in the hallway, I ask Davide, "How do you know I'll come back?"

"I trust you," he says, smiling, urging me out.

"Why?" I ask.

"Because," he says, gesturing, still smiling, "you have no place to go."

The way he says this is so charming I just nod and actually thank him. "Thank you," I say to Davide.

Behind him the girl walks toward the bed. She stops, twisting her muscular body, and whispers something urgently in Italian to Davide.

Davide closes the door. I hear him lock it.

11 I take the service elevator down to the lobby and outside it's night and the streets are wet and water drips down the facades of the buildings I pass but it's not raining. A taxi cruises by. I step out of the way of fast-skating Rollerbladers. And I'm still feeling filmed. How many warnings had I ignored?

12 Back at the hotel, an hour later. I take the service eleva-
tor up to my floor. I move slowly down the empty hall-
way. At my room, I pull out a key, knocking first.
There's no answer.
The key slips into the lock.
I push the door open.

Davide lies naked in a pile in the bathroom. No specific visible wound,
but his skin is broken in so many places I can't tell what happened to him.
The floor beneath Davide is washed over with blood, dotted with smashed
hotel china. Dramatic lightning from outside. There's no sign of the girl.
Blaming myself, I walk downstairs to the bar.

13 In a nearby room in the Principe di Savoia a propmaster
is loading a 9mm mini-Uzi.

14

Sinead O'Connor was singing "The Last Day of Our Acquaintance" and it was either 11:00 or 1:00 or maybe it was 3:15 and we were all lying around Gianni's pool in the big house on Ocean Drive and there were about twenty of us and everyone was talking into a cell phone and doing dope and I had just met Chloe earlier that week. She was lying on a chaise longue, burning under the sun, and her lips were puffy from collagen injections and my skull was on fire from a hangover caused by a dozen mango daiquiris and I was carefully eyeing the forty-carat diamond she was wearing, and the lemonade I was drinking stung my mouth and everyone was saying "So what?" and there had been a cockroach sighting earlier and people were basically becoming unglued. There were boys everywhere—slim, full-lipped, big-bulged, sucking in their cheeks—and there were also a couple of rock stars and a teenage gay guy from Palestine bragging about a really cool stone-throwing he'd attended in Hebron. All of this under a calm gumball-blue sky.

And Sinead O'Connor was singing "The Last Day of Our Acquaintance" and a girl lying across from me was positioned in such a way that I could see her anus and she would reach under her bikini bottom and scratch it, then bring her fingers to her face and lightly smell them. On a huge Bang & Olufsen TV that had been wheeled out, an episode of "The X-Files" was playing where someone's dog had been eaten by a sea serpent and for some reason everyone was reading a book called *The Amityville Horror* and tired from last night's premiere for a new movie called *Autopsy 18*—the guy hunched over the Ouija board, the girl just back from Madonna's baby shower, the kid playing with a cobra he'd bought with a stolen credit card. A big murder trial was going on that week in which the defense team convinced me that the victim—a seven-year-old girl fatally beaten by her drunken father—was actually guilty of her own death. Mermaids had been spotted during a swim before dawn.

"Could you kill somebody?" I heard a voice ask.

A moment passed before another voice answered, "Yeah, I guess so."

"Oh, so what?" someone else moaned.

Someone walked by with a panting wolf on a leash.

And Sinead O'Connor was singing "The Last Day of Our Acquaintance" and I had spent part of the morning trimming my pubic hair and everyone was checking various gossip columns to see if they had made it but they were basically one-shots and it was never going to happen for any of them and there was a Rauschenberg in the bathroom and a Picasso in the pantry and the guy I had slept with the night before—a boy who looked like Paul Newman at twenty—started talking about a friend who had been murdered in Maui last week and then everyone around the pool joined in and I couldn't follow the conversation. A tiny rift with a drug dealer? An irate exporter/importer? A run-in with a cannibal? Who knew? Was his death bad? He had been lowered into a barrel of hungry insects. A poll was taken. On a scale of 1 to 10—being lowered into a barrel of hungry insects? Opinions were offered. I thought I was going to faint. This conversation was the only indication that anyone here knew anybody else. I lit a cigarette I bummed from River Phoenix. I was just becoming famous and my whole relationship to the world was about to change.

And Sinead O'Connor was singing "The Last Day of Our Acquaintance" and someone tossed Pergola the keys to one of the Mercedes parked in the garage and it was just too hot out and a jet flew overhead and I jealously studied Bruce Rhinebeck's face smirking at me from the cover of a magazine and the guy I'd slept with the night before whispered to me "You're a piece of shit" and there was my "stunned disbelief" and me saying "So what?" and I was so tan my nipples had changed color and I looked down at my muscled body admiringly but a fly was dozing on my thigh and when I brushed it away it came back, hovering. A Brazilian boy asked me how I got my abs that cubed and I was so flattered I had to concentrate very seriously in order to answer him.

An injured bat had crawled out from beneath a chaise longue and it was chirping and flapping its wings uselessly and a few of the teenage boys stood around it silently. The bat rolled over, upended, and when one of the boys kicked it, the bat screamed. Someone struck it with a branch, and a puff of dust flew off its skin. Light was flickering across the water in the vast pool and I was watching everything through binoculars. A servant brought me a piece of birthday cake and a can of Hawaiian Punch as I had requested. The bat was wriggling on the ground next to a discarded cell phone. Its spine was broken and it tried to bite anyone who got near it. The boys continued torturing it. Someone brought out a fork.

There was no system to any of this. At that point Chloe Byrnes wasn't a real person to me and on that afternoon in the house on Ocean Drive a few decisions had to be made, the priority being: I would never dream of leaving any of this. At first I was confused by what passed for love in this world: people were discarded because they were too old or too fat or too poor or they had too much hair or not enough, they were wrinkled, they had no muscles, no definition, no *tone*, they weren't hip, they weren't remotely famous. This was how you chose lovers. This was what decided friends. And I had to accept this if I wanted to get anywhere. When I looked over at Chloe, she shrugged. I observed the shrug. She mouthed the words *Take . . . a . . . hike. . . .* On the verge of tears—because I was dealing with the fact that we lived in a world where beauty was considered an accomplishment—I turned away and made a promise to myself: to be harder, to not care, to be cool. The future started mapping itself out and I focused on it. In that moment I felt as if I was disappearing from poolside in the villa on Ocean Drive and I was floating above the palm trees, growing smaller in the wide blank sky until I no longer existed and relief swept over me with such force I sighed.

One of the teenage boys was ready to pounce on me, and the boy splashing in the pool, I realized faintly, could have been drowning and no one would have noticed. I avoided thinking about that and concentrated on the patterns in a bathing suit that Marky Mark was wearing. I might not even remember this afternoon, I was thinking. I was thinking that a part of me might destroy it. A cold voice inside my head begged me to. But I was being introduced to too many cool people and I was becoming famous and at that point I had no way of understanding one thing: if I didn't erase this afternoon from my memory and just walk out that door and leave Chloe Byrnes behind, sections of this afternoon would come back to me in nightmares. This was what the cold voice assured me. This was what it promised. Someone was praying over the half-smashed bat but the gesture seemed far away and unimportant. People started dancing around the praying boy.

"You want to know how this all ends?" Chloe asked, eyes closed.

I nodded.

"Buy the rights," she whispered.

I turned away so she couldn't see the expression on my face.

And as the final crashing verse of "The Last Day of Our Acquaintance" boomed out, I faded away and my image overlapped and dissolved into an image of myself years later sitting in a hotel bar in Milan where I was staring at a mural.

15

I'm drinking a glass of water in the empty hotel bar at the Principe di Savoia and staring at the mural behind the bar and in the mural there is a giant mountain, a vast field spread out below it where villagers are celebrating in a field of long grass that blankets the mountain dotted with tall white flowers, and in the sky above the mountain it's morning and the sun is spreading itself across the mural's frame, burning over the small cliffs and the low-hanging clouds that encircle the mountain's peak, and a bridge strung across a pass through the mountain will take you to any point beyond that you need to arrive at, because behind that mountain is a highway and along that highway are billboards with answers on them—who, what, where, when, why—and I'm falling forward but also moving up toward the mountain, my shadow looming against its jagged peaks, and I'm surging forward, ascending, sailing through dark clouds, rising up, a fiery wind propelling me, and soon it's night and stars hang in the sky above the mountain, revolving as they burn.

The stars are real.

The future is that mountain.

picador.com

blog
videos
interviews
extracts